GEORGE ELIOT, BORN MARY ANN EVANS, was one of the most distinguished English novelists of the nineteenth century. Author of such timeless classics as *The Mill on the Floss, Adam Bede,* and *Middlemarch,* she brought to letters a stunning combination of qualities hard to find in any other writer: a deeply ethical feeling for humanity, wide-ranging sympathy, sharp humor, and the profound intellectual accomplishments of an extraordinarily probing mind.

SILAS
MARNER

❖

GEORGE ELIOT

Afterword by G. Robert Stange

WSP

WASHINGTON SQUARE PRESS, INC. • NEW YORK

SILAS MARNER

A *Washington Square Press* edition
1st printing......................November, 1948
21st printing....................December, 1967

A new edition of a distinguished
literary work now made available in
an inexpensive, well-designed format

L

Published by
Washington Square Press, Inc., 630 Fifth Avenue, New York, N.Y.

WASHINGTON SQUARE PRESS editions are distributed in the
U.S. by Simon & Schuster, Inc., 630 Fifth Avenue, New
York, N.Y. 10020 and in Canada by Simon & Schuster
of Canada, Ltd., Richmond Hill, Ontario, Canada.

SILAS MARNER

PART ONE

Part One

CHAPTER I

IN THE DAYS when the spinning-wheels hummed busily in the farmhouses—and even great ladies, clothed in silk and thread-lace, had their toy spinning-wheels of polished oak—there might be seen in districts far away among the lanes, or deep in the bosom of the hills, certain pallid undersized men, who, by the side of the brawny country-folk, looked like the remnants of a disinherited race. The shepherd's dog barked fiercely when one of these alien-looking men appeared on the upland, dark against the early winter sunset; for what dog likes a figure bent under a heavy bag? —and these pale men rarely stirred abroad without that mysterious burden.

The shepherd himself, though he had good reason to believe that the bag held nothing but flaxen thread, or else the long rolls of strong linen spun from that thread, was not quite sure that his trade of weaving, indispensable though it was, could be carried on entirely without the help of the Evil One.

In that far-off time superstition clung easily around every person or thing that was at all unwonted, or even intermittent and occasions merely, like the visits of the pedler or the knife-grinder. No one knew where wandering men had their homes or their origin; and how was a man to be explained unless you at least knew somebody who knew his father and mother?

To the peasants of old times, the world outside their own direct experience was a region of vagueness and mystery: to their untravelled thought a state of wandering was a conception as dim as the winter life of the swallows that came back with the spring; and even a settler, if he came from distant parts, hardly ever ceased to be viewed with a remnant of distrust, which would have prevented any surprise if a long course of inoffensive conduct on his part had ended in the commission of a crime; especially if he had any reputation for knowledge, or showed any skill in handicraft.

All cleverness, whether in the rapid use of that difficult instrument the tongue, or in some other art unfamiliar to villagers, was in itself suspicious: honest folk, born and bred in a visible manner, were mostly not over-wise or clever—at least, not beyond such a matter as knowing the signs of the weather; and the process by which rapidity and dexterity of any kind were acquired was so wholly hidden, that they partook of the nature of conjuring.

In this way it came to pass that those scattered linen-weavers—emigrants from the town into the country—were to the last regarded as aliens by their rustic neighbors, and usually contracted the eccentric habits which belong to a state of loneliness.

In the early years of this century, such a linen-weaver, named Silas Marner, worked at his vocation in a stone cottage that stood among the nutty hedgerows near the village of Raveloe, and not far from the edge of a deserted stone-pit. The questionable sound of Silas's loom, so unlike the natural cheerful trotting of the winnowing-machine, or the simpler rhythm of the flail, had a half-fearful fascination for the Raveloe boys, who would often leave off their nutting or birds'-nesting to peep in at the window of the stone cottage, counterbalancing a certain awe at the mysterious action of the loom, by a pleasant sense of scornful superiority, drawn from the mockery of its alternating noises, along with the bent tread-mill attitude of the weaver.

But sometimes it happened that Marner, pausing to adjust an irregularity in his thread, became aware of the small scoundrels, and, though chary of his time, he liked their intrusion so ill that he would descend from his loom, and, opening the door, would fix on them a gaze that was always enough to make them take to their legs in terror. For how was it possible to believe that those large brown protuberant eyes in Silas Marner's pale face really saw nothing very distinctly that was not close to them, and not rather that their dreadful stare could dart cramp, or rickets, or a wry mouth at any boy who happened to be in the rear? They had, perhaps, heard their fathers and mothers hint that Silas Marner could cure folks' rheumatism if he had a mind, and add, still more darkly, that if you could only speak the devil fair enough, he might save you the cost of the doctor.

Such strange, lingering echoes of the old demon-worship might perhaps even now be caught by the diligent listener among the gray-haired peasantry; for the rude mind with difficulty associates the ideas of power and benignity. A shadowy conception of power that by much persuasion can be induced to refrain from inflicting harm, is the shape most easily taken by the sense of the Invisible in the minds of men who have always been pressed close by primitive wants, and to whom a life of hard toil has never been illuminated by any enthusiastic religious faith. To them pain and mishap present a far wider range of possibilities than gladness and enjoyment: their imagination is almost barren of the images that feed desire and hope, but is all overgrown by recollections that are a perpetual pasture to fear.

"Is there anything you can fancy that you would like to eat?" I once said to an old laboring man, who was in his last illness, and who had refused all the food his wife had offered him. "No," he answered, "I've never been used to nothing but common victual, and I can't eat that." Experience had bred no fancies in him that could raise the phantasm of appetite.

And Raveloe was a village where many of the old echoes lingered, undrowned by new voices. Not that it was one of those barren parishes lying on the out-skirts of civilization—inhabited by meagre sheep and thinly-scattered shepherds: on the contrary, it lay in the rich central plain of what we are pleased to call Merry England, and held farms which, speaking from a spiritual point of view, paid highly-desirable tithes. But it was nestled in a snug, well-wooded hollow, quite an hour's journey on horseback from any turnpike, where it was never reached by the vibrations of the coach-horn, or of public opinion.

It was an important-looking village, with a fine old church and large churchyard in the heart of it, and two or three large brick-and-stone homesteads, with well-walled orchards and ornamental weathercocks, standing close upon the road, and lifting more impos-ing fronts than the rectory, which peeped from among the trees on the other side of the churchyard—a village which showed at once the summits of its social life and told the practised eye that there was no great park and manor-house in the vicinity, but that there were several chiefs in Raveloe who could farm badly quite at their ease, drawing enough money from their bad farming, in those war times, to live in a rollicking fashion, and keep a jolly Christmas, Whitsun, and Easter-tide.

It was fifteen years since Silas Marner had first come to Raveloe; he was then simply a pallid young man, with prominent, short-sighted brown eyes, whose appearance would have had nothing strange for people of average culture and experience, but for the villagers near whom he had come to settle it had mysterious peculiarities which corresponded with the exceptional nature of his occupation, and his advent from an unknown region called "North'ard." So had his way of life—he invited no comer to step across his doorsill, and he never strolled into the village to drink a pint at the Rainbow, or to gossip at the wheelwright's: he sought no man or woman, save for the purposes of his calling, or in order to supply himself with necessaries; and it was soon clear to the Raveloe lasses that he would never urge one of them to accept him against her will—quite as if he had heard them declare that they would never marry a dead man come to life again.

This view of Marner's personality was not without another ground than his pale face and unexampled eyes; for Jem Rodney, the mole-catcher, averred that one evening as he was returning homeward he saw Silas Marner leaning against a stile with a heavy bag on his back, instead of resting the bag on the stile as a man in his senses would have done; and that, on coming up to him, he saw that Marner's eyes were set like a dead man's, and he spoke to him, and shook him, and his limbs were stiff, and his hands clutched the bag as if they'd been made of iron; but just as he had made up his mind that the weaver was dead, he came all right again, like, as you might say, in the winking of an eye, and said "Good-night," and walked off.

All this Jem swore he had seen, more by token that it was the very day he had been mole-catching on Squire Cass's land, down by the old saw-pit. Some said

Marner must have been in a "fit," a word which seemed to explain things otherwise incredible; but the argumentative Mr. Macey, clerk of the parish, shook his head, and asked if anybody was ever known to go off in a fit and not fall down. A fit was a stroke, wasn't it? and it was in the nature of a stroke to partly take away the use of a man's limbs and throw him on the parish, if he'd got no children to look to. No, no; it was no stroke that would let a man stand on his legs, like a horse between the shafts, and then walk off as soon as you can say "Gee!"

But there might be such a thing as a man's soul being loose from his body, and going out and in, like a bird out of its nest and back; and that was how folks got over-wise, for they went to school in this shell-less state to those who could teach them more than their neighbors could learn with their five senses and the parson. And where did Master Marner get his knowledge of herbs from—and charms, too, if he liked to give them away? Jem Rodney's story was no more than what might have been expected by anybody who had seen how Marner had cured Sally Oates, and made her sleep like a baby, when her heart had been beating enough to burst her body, for two months and more, while she had been under the doctor's care. He might cure more folks if he would; but he was worth speaking fair, if it was only to keep him from doing you a mischief.

It was partly to this vague fear that Marner was indebted for protecting him from the persecution that his singularities might have drawn upon him, but still more to the fact that, the old linen-weaver in the neighboring parish of Tarley being dead, his handicraft made him a highly welcome settler to the richer housewives of the district, and even to the more provident cottagers, who had their little stock of yarn at the year's end. Their sense of his usefulness would have counteracted any repugnance or suspicion which was not confirmed by a deficiency in the quality or the tale of the cloth he wove for them. And the years had rolled on without producing any change in the impressions of the neighbors concerning Marner, except the change from novelty to habit.

At the end of fifteen years the Raveloe men said just the same things about Silas Marner as at the beginning; they did not say them quite so often, but they believed them much more strongly when they did say them. There was only one important addition which the years had brought: it was, that Master Marner had laid by a fine sight of money somewhere, and that he could buy up "bigger men" than himself.

But while opinion concerning him had remained nearly stationary, and his daily habits had presented scarcely any visible change, Marner's inward life had been a history and a metamorphosis, as that of every fervid nature must be when it has fled, or been condemned to solitude. His life, before he came to Raveloe, had been filled with the movement, the mental activity, and the close fellowship, which, in that day as in this, marked the life of an artisan early incorporated in a narrow religious sect, where the poorest layman has a chance of distinguishing himself by gifts of speech, and has, at the very least, the weight of a silent voter in the government of his community.

Marner was highly thought of in that little hidden world, known to itself as the church, assembling in Lantern Yard; he was believed to be a young man of exemplary life and ardent faith; and a peculiar interest had been centred in him ever since he had fallen, at a prayer-meeting, into a mysterious rigidity and suspen-

sion of consciousness, which, lasting for an hour or
more, had been mistaken for death. To have sought a
medical explanation for this phenomenon would have
been held by Silas himself, as well as by his minister
and fellow-members, a wilful self-exclusion from the
spiritual significance that might lie therein.

Silas was evidently a brother selected for peculiar
discipline; and though the effort to interpret this discipline was discouraged by the absence, on his part,
of any spiritual vision during his outward trance, yet
it was believed by himself and others that its effect was
seen in an accession of light and fervor. A less truthful
man than he might have been tempted into the subse-
quent creation of a vision in the form of resurgent
memory; a less sane man might have believed in such
a creation; but Silas was both sane and honest, though,
as with many honest fervent men, culture had not defined any channels for his sense of mystery, and so it
spread itself over the proper pathway of inquiry and
knowledge.

He had inherited from his mother some acquaintance with medical herbs and their preparation—a
little store of wisdom which she had imparted to him
as a solemn bequest—but of late years he had had doubts
about the lawfulness of applying this knowledge, believing that herbs could have no efficacy without
prayer, and that prayer might suffice without herbs;
so that his inherited delight to wander through the
fields in search of foxglove and dandelion and colts-
foot, began to wear to him the character of a temptation.

Among the members of his church there was one
young man, a little older than himself, with whom he
had long lived in such close friendship that it was the
custom of their Lantern Yard brethren to call them

David and Jonathan. The real name of the friend was William Dane, and he, too, was regarded as a shining instance of youthful piety, though somewhat given to over-severity towards weaker brethren, and to be so dazzled by his own light as to hold himself wiser than his teachers. But whatever blemishes others might discern in William, to his friend's mind he was faultless; for Marner had one of those impressible, self-doubting natures which, at an inexperienced age, admire imperativeness and lean on contradiction.

The expression of trusting simplicity in Marner's face, heightened by that absence of special observation, that defenceless deer-like gaze which belongs to large prominent eyes, was strongly contrasted by the self-complacent suppression of inward triumph that lurked in the narrow slanting eyes and compressed lips of William Dane.

One of the most frequent topics of conversation between the two friends was Assurance of salvation: Silas confessed that he could never arrive at anything higher than hope mingled with fear, and listened with wonder when William declared that he had possessed unshaken assurance ever since, in the period of his conversion, he had dreamed that he saw the words "calling and election sure" standing by themselves on a white page in the open Bible. Such colloquies have occupied many a pair of pale-faced weavers, whose unnurtured souls have been like young winged things, fluttering forsaken in the twilight.

It had seemed to the unsuspecting Silas that the friendship had suffered no chill even from his formation of another attachment of a closer kind. For some months he had been engaged to a young servant-woman, waiting only for a little increase to their mutual savings in order to their marriage; and it was a great delight to him that Sarah did not object to William's occasional presence in their Sunday interviews. It was at this point in their history that Silas's cataleptic fit occurred during the prayer-meeting; and amidst the various queries and expressions of interest addressed to him by his fellow-members, William's suggestion alone jarred with the general sympathy towards a brother thus singled out for special dealings. He observed that to him, this trance looked more like a visitation of Satan than a proof of divine favor, and exhorted his friend to see that he hid no accursed thing within his soul.

Silas, feeling bound to accept rebuke and admonition as a brotherly office, felt no resentment, but only pain, at his friend's doubts concerning him; and to this was soon added some anxiety at the perception that Sarah's manner towards him began to exhibit a strange fluctuation between an effort at an increased manifestation of regard and involuntary signs of shrinking and dislike. He asked her if she wished to break off their engagement; but she denied this: their engagement was known to the church, and had been recognized in the prayer-meetings; it could not be broken off without strict investigation, and Sarah could render no reason that would be sanctioned by the feeling of the community.

At this time the senior deacon was taken dangerously ill, and, being a childless widower, he was tended night and day by some of the younger brethren or sisters. Silas frequently took his turn in the night-watching with William, the one relieving the other at two in the morning. The old man, contrary to expectation, seemed to be on the way to recovery, when one night Silas, sitting up by his bedside, observed that his usual audible breathing had ceased. The candle was burning low, and he had to lift it to see the patient's face distinctly. Examination convinced him that the deacon was dead—had been dead some time, for the limbs were rigid.

Silas asked himself if he had been asleep, and looked at the clock: it was already four in the morning. How was it that William had not come? In much anxiety he went to seek for help, and soon there were several friends assembled in the house, the minister among them, while Silas went away to his work, wishing he could have met William to know the reason of his non-appearance. But at six o'clock, as he was thinking of going to seek his friend, William came, and with him the minister.

They came to summon him to Lantern Yard, to meet the church members there; and to his inquiry concerning the cause of the summons the only reply was, "You will hear." Nothing further was said until Silas was seated in the vestry, in front of the minister, with the eyes of those who to him represented God's people fixed solemnly upon him. Then the minister, taking out a pocket-knife, showed it to Silas, and asked him if he knew where he had left that knife? Silas said he did not know that he had left it anywhere out of his own pocket—but he was trembling at this strange interrogation. He was then exhorted not to hide his sin, but to confess and repent. The knife had been found in the bureau by the departed deacon's bedside—found in the place where the little bag of church money had lain, which the minister himself had seen the day before. Some hand had removed that bag; and whose hand could it be, if not that of the man to whom the knife belonged?

For some time Silas was mute with astonishment: then he said. "God will clear me: I know nothing about the knife being there, or the money being gone. Search me and my dwelling; you will find nothing but three pound five of my own savings, which William Dane knows I have had these six months."

At this William groaned, but the minister said, "The proof is heavy against you, brother Marner. The money was taken in the night last past, and no man was with our departed brother but you, for William Dane declares to us that he was hindered by sudden sickness from going to take his place as usual, and you yourself said that he had not come; and, moreover, you neglected the dead body."

"I must have slept," said Silas. Then after a pause, he added, "Or I must have had another visitation like that which you have all seen me under, so that the thief must have come and gone while I was not in the body, but out of the body. But, I say again, search me and my dwelling, for I have been nowhere else."

The search was made, and it ended—in William Dane's finding the well-known bag, empty, tucked behind the chest of drawers in Silas's chamber! On this William exhorted his friend to confess, and not to hide his sin any longer. Silas turned a look of keen reproach on him, and said, "William, for nine years that we have gone in and out together, have you ever known me to tell a lie? But God will clear me."

"Brother," said William, "how do I know what you may have done in the secret chambers of your heart, to give Satan an advantage over you?"

Silas was still looking at his friend. Suddenly a deep flush came over his face, and he was about to speak impetuously, when he seemed checked again by some inward shock, that sent the flush back and made him tremble. But at last he spoke feebly, looking at William.

"I remember now—the knife wasn't in my pocket."

William said, "I know nothing of what you mean."

The other persons present, however, began to inquire where Silas meant to say that the knife was, but he would give no further explanation; he only said, "I am sore stricken; I can say nothing. God will clear me."

On their return to the vestry there was further deliberation. Any resort to legal measures for ascertaining the culprit was contrary to the principles of the church in Lantern Yard, according to which prosecution was forbidden to Christians, even had the case held less scandal to the community. But the members were bound to take other measures for finding out the truth, and they resolved on praying and drawing lots. This resolution can be a ground of surprise only to those who are unacquainted with that obscure religious life which has gone on in the alleys of our towns. Silas knelt with his brethren, relying on his own innocence being certified by immediate divine interference, but feeling that there was sorrow and mourning behind for him even then—that his trust in man had been cruelly bruised.

The lots declared that Silas Marner was guilty. He was solemnly suspended from church-membership, and called upon to render up the stolen money; only on confession, as the sign of repentance, could he be received once more within the folds of the church. Marner listened in silence. At last, when everyone rose to depart, he went towards William Dane and said, in a voice shaken by agitation:

"The last time I remember using my knife, was when I took it out to cut a strap for you. I don't remember putting it in my pocket again. *You* stole the money, and you have woven a plot to lay the sin at my door. But you may prosper, for all that; there is no just God that governs the earth righteously, but a God of lies, that bears witness against the innocent."

There was a general shudder at this blasphemy.

William said meekly, "I leave our brethren to judge whether this is the voice of Satan or not. I can do nothing but pray for you, Silas."

Poor Marner went out with that despair in his soul— that shaken trust in God and man, which is little short of madness to a loving nature. In the bitterness of his wounded spirit, he said to himself, "*She* will cast me off, too." And he reflected that, if she did not believe the testimony against him, her whole faith must be upset as his was. To people accustomed to reason about the forms in which their religious feeling has incorporated itself, it is difficult to enter into that simple, untaught state of mind in which the form and the feeling have never been severed by an act of reflection. We are apt to think it inevitable that a man in Marner's position should have begun to question the validity of an appeal to the divine judgment by drawing lots; but to him this would have been an effort of independent thought such as he had never known; and he must have made the effort at a moment when all his energies were turned into the anguish of disappointed faith. If there is an angel who records the sorrows of men as well as their sins, he knows how many and deep are the sorrows that spring from false ideas for which no man is culpable.

Marner went home, and for a whole day sat alone, stunned by despair, without any impulse to go to Sarah and attempt to win her belief in his innocence. The second day he took refuge from benumbing unbelief, by getting into his loom and working away as usual; and before many hours were past, the minister and one of the deacons came to him with the message from Sarah, that she held her engagement to him at an end. Silas received the message mutely, and then turned away from the messengers to work at his loom again. In a little more than a month from that time, Sarah was married to William Dane; and not long afterwards it was known to the brethren in Lantern Yard that Silas Marner had departed from the town.

CHAPTER II

EVEN PEOPLE whose lives have been made various by learning, sometimes find it hard to keep a fast hold on their habitual views of life, on their faith in the Invisible, nay, on the sense that their past joys and sorrows are a real experience, when they are suddenly transported to a new land, where the beings around them know nothing of their history, and share none of their ideas—where their mother earth shows another lap, and human life has other forms than those on which their souls have been nourished. Minds that have been unhinged from their old faith and love, have perhaps sought this Lethean influence of exile, in which the past becomes dreamy because its symbols have all vanished, and the present, too, is dreamy because it is linked with no memories. But even *their* experience may hardly enable them thoroughly to imagine what was the effect on a simple weaver like Silas Marner, when he left his own country and people and came to settle in Raveloe.

Nothing could be more unlike his native town, set

within sight of the widespread hillsides, than this low, wooded region, where he felt hidden even from the heavens by the screening trees and hedgerows. There was nothing here, when he rose in the deep morning quiet and looked out on the dewy brambles and rank tufted grass, that seemed to have any relation with that life centring in Lantern Yard, which had once been to him the altar-place of high dispensations. The white-washed walls; the little pews where well-known figures entered with a subdued rustling, and where first one well-known voice and then another, pitched in a peculiar key of petition, uttered phrases at once occult and familiar, like the amulet worn on the heart; the pulpit where the minister delivered unquestioned doctrine, and swayed to and fro, and handled the book in a long-accustomed manner; the very pauses between the couplets of the hymn, as it was given out, and the recurrent swell of voices in song: these things had been the channel of divine influences to Marner—they were the fostering home of his religious emotions—they were Christianity and God's kingdom upon earth. A weaver who finds hard words in his hymn-book knows nothing of abstractions; as the little child knows nothing of parental love, but only knows one face and one lap towards which it stretches its arms for refuge and nurture.

And what could be more unlike that Lantern Yard world than the world in Raveloe?—orchards looking lazy with neglected plenty; the large church in the wide churchyard, which men gazed at lounging at their own doors in service-time; the purple-faced farmers jogging along the lanes or turning in at the Rainbow; homesteads, where men supped heavily and slept in the light of the evening hearth, and where women seemed to be laying up a stock of linen for the life to come. There were no lips in Raveloe from which a word could fall that would stir Silas Marner's benumbed faith to a sense of pain.

In the early ages of the world, we know, it was believed that each territory was inhabited and ruled by its own divinities, so that a man could cross the bordering heights and be out of the reach of his native gods, whose presence was confined to the streams and the groves and the hills among which he had lived from his birth. And poor Silas was vaguely conscious of something not unlike the feeling of primitive men, when they fled thus, in fear or in sullenness, from the face of an unpropitious deity. It seemed to him that the Power he had vainly trusted in among the streets and at the prayer-meetings, was very far away from this land in which he had taken refuge, where men lived in careless abundance, knowing and needing nothing of that trust, which, for him, had been turned to bitterness. The little light he possessed spread its beams so narrowly, that frustrated belief was a curtain broad enough to create for him the blackness of night.

His first movement after the shock had been to work in his loom; and he went on with this unremittingly, never asking himself why, now he was come to Raveloe, he worked far on into the night to finish the tale of Mrs. Osgood's table-linen sooner than she expected— without contemplating beforehand the money she would put into his hand for the work. He seemed to weave, like the spider, from pure impulse, without re- flection. Every man's work, pursued steadily, tends in this way to become an end in itself, and so to bridge over the loveless chasms of his life. Silas's hand satisfied itself with throwing the shuttle, and his eye with seeing the little squares in the cloth complete themselves under his effort. Then there were the calls of hunger;

and Silas, in his solitude, had to provide his own breakfast, dinner, and supper, to fetch his own water from the well, and put his own kettle on the fire; and all these immediate promptings helped, along with the weaving, to reduce his life to the unquestioning activity of a spinning insect. He hated the thought of the past; there was nothing that called out his love and fellowship toward the strangers he had come amongst; and the future was all dark, for there was no Unseen Love that cared for him. Thought was arrested by utter bewilderment, now its old narrow pathway was closed, and affection seemed to have died under the bruise that had fallen on its keenest nerves.

But at last Mrs. Osgood's table-linen was finished, and Silas was paid in gold. His earnings in his native town, where he worked for a wholesale dealer, had been after a lower rate; he had been paid weekly, and of his weekly earnings a large proportion had gone to objects of piety and charity. Now, for the first time in his life, he had five bright guineas put into his hand; no man expected a share of them, and he loved no man that he should offer him a share. But what were the guineas to him who saw no vista beyond countless days of weaving? It was needless for him to ask that, for it was pleasant to him to feel them in his palm, and look at their bright faces, which were all his own; it was another element of life, like the weaving and the satisfaction of hunger, subsisting quite aloof from the life of belief and love from which he had been cut off.

The weaver's hand had known the touch of hard-won money even before the palm had grown to its full breadth; for twenty years, mysterious money had stood to him as the symbol of earthly good, and the immediate object of toil. He had seemed to love it little in the years when every penny had its purpose for him; for he loved the *purpose* then. But now, when all purpose was gone, that habit of looking towards the money and grasping it with a sense of fulfilled effort made a loam that was deep enough for the seeds of desire; and as Silas walked homeward across the fields in the twilight, he drew out the money and thought it was brighter in the gathering gloom.

About this time an incident happened which seemed to open a possibility of some fellowship with his neighbors. One day, taking a pair of shoes to be mended, he saw the cobbler's wife seated by the fire, suffering from the terrible symptoms of heart-disease and dropsy, which he had witnessed as the precursors of his mother's death. He felt a rush of pity at the mingled sight and remembrance, and, recalling the relief his mother had found from a simple preparation of foxglove, he promised Sally Oates to bring her something that would ease her, since the doctor did her no good.

In this office of charity, Silas felt, for the first time since he had come to Raveloe, a sense of unity between his past and present life, which might have been the beginning of his rescue from the insect-like existence into which his nature had shrunk. But Sally Oates's disease had raised her into a personage of much interest and importance among the neighbors, and the fact of her having found relief from drinking Silas Marner's "stuff" became a matter of general discourse.

When Dr. Kimble gave physic, it was natural that it should have an effect; but when a weaver who came from nobody knew where, worked wonders with a bottle of brown waters, the occult character of the process was evident. Such a sort of thing had not been known since the Wise Woman at Tarley died; and she had charms as well as "stuff"; everybody went to her when their children had fits. Silas Marner must be a person of the same sort, for how did he know what would bring back Sally Oates's breath, if he didn't know a fine sight more than that? The Wise Woman had words that she muttered to herself, so that you couldn't hear what they were, and if she tied a bit of red thread round the child's toe the while, it would keep off the water in the head. There were women in Raveloe, at the present time, who had worn one of the Wise Woman's little bags round their necks, and, in consequence, had never had an idiot child, as Ann Coulter had. Silas Marner could very likely do as much, and more; and now it was all clear how he should have come from unknown parts, and be so "comical looking." But Sally Oates must mind and not tell the doctor, for he would be sure to set his face against Marner; he was always angry about the Wise Woman, and used to threaten those who went to her that they should have none of his help any more.

Silas now found himself and his cottage suddenly beset by mothers who wanted him to charm away the whooping-cough, or bring back the milk, and by men who wanted stuff against the rheumatics or the knots in the hands; and to secure themselves against a refusal, the applicants brought silver in their palms.

Silas might have driven a profitable trade in charms as well as in his small list of drugs; but money on this condition was no temptation to him; he had never known an impulse towards falsity, and he drove one after another away with growing irritation, for the news of him as a wise man had spread even to Tarley, and it was long before people ceased to take long walks for the sake of asking his aid. But the hope in his wisdom was at length changed into dread, for no one believed him when he said he knew no charms and could work no cures, and every man and woman who had an accident or a new attack after applying to him, set the misfortune down to Master Marner's ill-will and irritated glances. Thus it came to pass that his movement of pity towards Sally Oates, which had given him a transient sense of brotherhood, heightened the repulsion between him and his neighbors, and made his isolation more complete.

Gradually the guineas, the crowns, and the half-crowns, grew to a heap, and Marner drew less and less for his own wants, trying to solve the problem of keeping himself strong enough to work sixteen hours a day on as small an outlay as possible. Have not men, shut up in solitary imprisonment, found an interest in marking the moments only by straight strokes of a certain length on the wall, until the growth of the sum of straight strokes, arranged in triangles, has become a mastering purpose. Do we not wile away moments of inanity or fatigued waiting by repeating some trivial movement or sound, until the repetition has bred a want, which is incipient habit? That will help us to understand how the love of accumulating money grows an absorbing passion in men whose imaginations, even in the very beginning of their hoard, showed them no purpose beyond it.

Marner wanted the heaps of ten to grow into a square, and then into a larger square; and every added guinea, while it was itself a satisfaction, bred a new desire. In this strange world, made a hopeless riddle to him, he might, if he had had a less intense nature, have sat weaving, weaving—looking towards the end of his pattern, or towards the end of his web, till he forgot the riddle, and everything else but his immediate sensations; but the money had come to mark off his weaving into periods, and the money not only grew, but it remained with him.

He began to think it was conscious of him, as his loom was, and he would on no account have exchanged those coins, which had become his familiars, for other coins with unknown faces. He handled them, he counted them, till their form and color were like the satisfaction of a thirst to him; but it was only in the night, when his work was done, that he drew them out to enjoy their companionship. He had taken up some bricks in his floor underneath his loom, and here he had made a hole in which he set the iron pot that contained his guineas and silver coins, covering the bricks with sand whenever he replaced them.

Not that the idea of being robbed presented itself often or strongly to his mind: hoarding was common in country districts in those days; there were old laborers in the parish of Raveloe who were known to have their savings by them, probably inside their flock-beds; but their rustic neighbors, though not all of them as honest as their ancestors in the days of King Alfred, had not imaginations bold enough to lay a plan of burglary. How could they have spent the money in their own village without betraying themselves? They would be obliged to "run away"—a course as dark and dubious as a balloon journey.

So, year after year, Silas Marner had lived in this solitude, his guineas rising in the iron pot, and his life narrowing and hardening itself more and more into a mere pulsation of desire and satisfaction that had no relation to any other being. His life had reduced itself to the functions of weaving and hoarding, without any contemplation of an end toward which the functions tended.

The same sort of process has perhaps been undergone by wiser men, when they have been cut off from faith and love—only, instead of a loom and a heap of guineas, they have had some erudite research, some ingenious project, or some well-knit theory.

Strangely Marner's face and figure shrank and bent themselves into a constant mechanical relation to the objects of his life, so that he produced the same sort of impression as a handle or a crooked tube, which has no meaning standing apart. The prominent eyes that used to look trusting and dreamy, now looked as if they had been made to see only one kind of thing that was very small, like tiny grain, for which they hunted everywhere: and he was so withered and yellow, that, though he was not yet forty, the children always called him "Old Master Marner."

Yet even in this stage of withering a little incident happened, which showed that the sap of affection was not all gone. It was one of his daily tasks to fetch his water from a well a couple of fields off, and for this purpose, ever since he came to Raveloe, he had had a brown earthenware pot, which he held as his most precious utensil among the very few conveniences he had granted himself. It had been his companion for twelve years, always standing on the same spot, always lending its handle to him in the early morning, so that its form had an expression for him of willing helpfulness, and the impress of its handle on his palm gave a satisfaction mingled with that of having the fresh, clear water.

One day, as he was returning from the well, he stumbled against the step of the stile, and his brown pot, falling with force against the stones that overarched the ditch below him, was broken in three pieces. Silas picked up the pieces and carried them home with grief in his heart. The brown pot could never be of use to him any more, but he stuck the bits together and propped the ruin in its old place for a memorial.

This is the history of Silas Marner until the fifteenth year after he came to Raveloe. The livelong day he sat in his loom, his ear filled with its monotony, his eyes bent close down on the slow growth of sameness in the brownish web, his muscles moving with such even repetition that their pause seemed almost as much a constraint as the holding of his breath. But at night came his revelry: at night he closed his shutters, and made fast his doors, and drew forth his gold.

Long ago the heap of coins had become too large for the iron pot to hold them, and he had made for them two thick leather bags, which wasted no room in their resting-place, but lent themselves flexibly to every corner. How the guineas shone as they came pouring out of the dark leather mouths! The silver bore no large proportion in amount to the gold, because the long pieces of linen which formed his chief work were always partly paid for in gold, and out of the silver he supplied his own bodily wants, choosing always the shillings and sixpences to spend in this way.

He loved the guineas best, but he would not change the silver—the crowns and half-crowns that were his own earnings, begotten by his labor; he loved them all. He spread them out in heaps and bathed his hands in them; then he counted them and set them up in regular piles, and felt their rounded outline between his thumb and fingers, and thought fondly of the guineas that were only half earned by the work in his loom, as if they had been unborn children—thought of the guineas that were coming slowly through the coming years, through all his life, which spread far away before him, the end quite hidden by countless days of weaving.

No wonder his thoughts were still with his loom and his money when he made his journeys through the fields and the lanes to fetch and carry home his work, so that his steps never wandered to the hedge-banks and the lane-side in search of the once familiar herbs: these too belonged to the past, from which his life had shrunk away, like a rivulet that has sunk far down from the grassy fringe of its old breadth into a little shivering thread, that cuts a groove for itself in the barren sand.

But about the Christmas of that fifteenth year, a second great change came over Marner's life, and his history became blent in a singular manner with the life of his neighbors.

CHAPTER III

THE GREATEST MAN in Raveloe was Squire Cass, who lived in the large red house with the handsome flight of stone steps in front and the high stables behind it, nearly opposite the church. He was only one among several landed parishioners, but he alone was honored with the title of Squire; for though Mr. Osgood's family was also understood to be of timeless origin—the Raveloe imagination having never ventured back to that fearful blank when there were no Osgoods—still, he merely owned the farm he occupied; whereas Squire Cass had a tenant or two, who complained of the game to him quite as if he had been a lord.

It was still that glorious war-time which was felt to be a peculiar favor of Providence towards the landed interest, and the fall of prices had not yet come to carry the race of small squires and yeomen down that road to ruin for which extravagant habits and bad husbandry were plentifully anointing their wheels.

I am speaking now in relation to Raveloe and the parishes that resembled it; for our old-fashioned country life had many different aspects, as all life must have when it is spread over a various surface, and breathed on variously by multitudinous currents, from the winds of heaven to the thoughts of men, which are forever moving and crossing each other with incalculable results.

Raveloe lay low among the bushy trees and the rutted lanes, aloof from the currents of industrial energy and Puritan earnestness: the rich ate and drank freely, accepting gout and apoplexy as things that ran mysteriously in respectable families, and the poor thought that the rich were entirely in the right of it to lead a jolly life; besides, their feasting caused a multiplication of orts, which were the heirlooms of the poor.

Betty Jay scented the boiling of Squire Cass's hams, but her longing was arrested by the unctuous liquor in which they were boiled; and when the seasons brought round the great merry-makings, they were regarded on all hands as a fine thing for the poor. For the Raveloe feasts were like the rounds of beef and the barrels of ale—they were on a large scale, and lasted a good while, especially in the winter-time.

After ladies had packed up their best gowns and top-knots in bandboxes, and had incurred the risk of fording streams on pillions with the precious burden in rainy or snowy weather, when there was no knowing how high the water would rise, it was not to be supposed that they looked forward to a brief pleasure. On this ground it was always contrived in the dark seasons, when there was little work to be done, and the hours were long, that several neighbors should keep open house in succession.

So soon as Squire Cass's standing dishes diminished in plenty and freshness, his guests had nothing to do but to walk a little higher up the village to Mr. Osgood's, at the Orchards, and they found hams and chines uncut, pork-pies with the scent of the fire in them, spun butter in all its freshness—everything, in fact, that appetites at leisure could desire, in perhaps greater perfection, though not in greater abundance, than at Squire Cass's.

For the Squire's wife had died long ago, and the Red House was without that presence of the wife and mother which is the fountain of wholesome love and fear in parlor and kitchen; and this helped to account not only for there being more profusion than finished excellence in the holiday provisions, but also for the frequency with which the proud Squire condescended to preside in the parlor of the Rainbow rather than under the shadow of his own dark wainscot; perhaps, also, for the fact that his sons had turned out rather ill.

Raveloe was not a place where moral censure was severe, but it was thought a weakness in the Squire that he had kept all his sons at home in idleness; and though some license was to be allowed to young men whose fathers could afford it, people shook their heads at the courses of the second son, Dunstan, commonly called Dunsey Cass, whose taste for swapping and betting might turn out to be a sowing of something worse than wild oats.

To be sure, the neighbors said, it was no matter what became of Dunsey—a spiteful, jeering fellow, who seemed to enjoy his drink the more when other people went dry—always provided that his doings did not bring trouble on a family like Squire Cass's with a monument in the church, and tankards older than King George. But it would be a thousand pities if Mr. Godfrey, the eldest, a fine, open-faced, good-natured young man who was to come into the land some day, should take to going along the same road with his brother, as he had seemed to do of late. If he went on in that way, he would lose Miss Nancy Lammeter; for it was well known that she had looked very shyly on him ever since last Whitsuntide twelve-month, when there was so much talk about his being away from home days and days together. There was something wrong, more than common—that was quite clear; for Mr. Godfrey didn't look half so fresh-colored and open as he used to do.

At one time everybody was saying, What a hand-some couple he and Miss Nancy Lammeter would make! and if she could come to be mistress at the Red House, there would be a fine change, for the Lam-meters had been brought up in that way, that they never suffered a pinch of salt to be wasted, and yet everybody in their household had of the best, according to his place. Such a daughter-in-law would be a saving to the old Squire, if she never brought a penny to her fortune; for it was to be feared that, notwithstanding his incomings, there were more holes in his pocket than the one where he put his own hand in. But if Mr. Godfrey didn't turn over a new leaf, he might say "Good-bye" to Miss Nancy Lammeter.

It was the once hopeful Godfrey who was standing, with his hands in his side-pockets and his back to the fire, in the dark wainscoted parlor, one late November afternoon in that fifteenth year of Silas Marner's life at Raveloe. The fading gray light fell dimly on the walls decorated with guns, whips, and foxes' brushes, on coats and hats flung on the chairs, on tankards sending forth a scent of flat ale, and on a half-choked fire, with pipes propped up in the chimney-corners: signs of a domestic life destitute of any hallowing charm, with which the look of gloomy vexation on Godfrey's blond face was in sad accordance. He seemed to be waiting and listening for some one's approach, and presently the sound of a heavy step, with an accompanying whistle, was heard across the large, empty entrance-hall.

The door opened, and a thick-set, heavy-looking young man entered, with the flushed face and the gratuitously elated bearing which mark the first stage of intoxication. It was Dunsey, and at the sight of him Godfrey's face parted with some of its gloom to take on the more active expression of hatred. The handsome brown spaniel that lay on the hearth retreated under the chair in the chimney-corner.

"Well, Master Godfrey, what do you want with me?" said Dunsey in a mocking tone. "You're my elders and betters, you know; I was obliged to come when you sent for me."

"Why, this is what I want—and just shake yourself sober and listen, will you?" said Godfrey, savagely. He had himself been drinking more than was good for him, trying to turn his gloom into uncalculating anger. "I want to tell you, I must hand over that rent of Fowler's to the Squire, or else tell him I gave it to you; for he's threatening to distrain for it, and it'll all be out soon, whether I tell him or not. He said, just now, before he went out, he should send word to Cox to distrain, if Fowler didn't come and pay up his arrears this week. The Squire's short o' cash, and in no humor to stand any nonsense; and you know what he threatened, if ever he found you making away with his money again. So, see and get the money, and pretty quickly, will you?"

"Oh!" said Dunsey, sneeringly, coming nearer to his brother and looking in his face. "Suppose, now, you get the money yourself, and save me the trouble, eh? Since you was so kind as to hand it over to me, you'll not refuse me the kindness to pay it back to me: it was your brotherly love made you do it, you know."

Godfrey bit his lips and clenched his fist. "Don't come near me with that look, else I'll knock you down."

"Oh no, you won't," said Dunsey, turning away on his heel, however. "Because I'm such a good-natured brother, you know. I might get you turned out of house and home, and cut off with a shilling any day. I might tell the Squire how his handsome son was married to that nice young woman, Molly Farren, and was very unhappy because he couldn't live with his drunken wife, and I should slip into your place as comfortable as could be. But you see, I don't do it—I'm so easy and good-natured. You'll take any trouble for me. You'll get the hundred pounds for me—I know you will."

"How can I get the money?" said Godfrey, quivering. "I haven't a shilling to bless myself with. And it's a lie that you'd slip into my place: you'd get yourself turned out, too, that's all. For if you begin telling tales, I'll follow. Bob's my father's favorite, you know that very well. He'd only think himself well rid of you."

"Never mind," said Dunsey, nodding his head sideways as he looked out of the window. "It 'ud be very pleasant to me to go in your company—you're such a handsome brother, and we've always been so fond of quarrelling with one another, I shouldn't know what to do without you. But you'd like better for us both to stay at home together; I know you would. So you'll manage to get that little sum o' money, and I'll bid you good-bye, though I'm sorry to part."

Dunstan was moving off, but Godfrey rushed after him and seized him by the arm, saying with an oath:

"I tell you I have no money: I can get no money."

"Borrow of old Kimble."

"I tell you, he won't lend me any more, and I shan't ask him."

"Well, then, sell Wildfire."

"Yes, that's easy talking. I must have the money directly."

"Well, you've only got to ride him to the hunt to-morrow. There'll be Bryce and Keating there, for sure. You'll get more bids than one."

"I daresay, and get back home at eight o'clock, splashed up to the chin. I'm going to Mrs. Osgood's birthday dance."

"Oho!" said Dunsey, turning his head on one side, and trying to speak in a small, mincing treble. "And there's sweet Miss Nancy coming; and we shall dance with her, and promise never to be naughty again, and be taken into favor, and—"

"Hold your tongue about Miss Nancy, you fool," said Godfrey, turning red, "else I'll throttle you."

"What for?" said Dunsey, still in an artificial tone, but taking a whip from the table and beating the butt-end of it on his palm. "You've a very good chance. I'd advise you to creep up her sleeve again: it 'ud be saving time, if Mollie should happen to take a drop too much laudanum some day, and make a widower of you. Miss Nancy wouldn't mind being a second, if she didn't know it. And you've got a good-natured brother, who'll keep your secret well, because you'll be so very obliging to him."

"I'll tell you what it is," said Godfrey, quivering, and pale again, "my patience is pretty near at an end. If you'd a little more sharpness in you, you might know that you may urge a man a bit too far, and make one leap as easy as another. I don't know but what it is so now: I may as well tell the Squire everything myself—I should get you off my back, if I got nothing else. And, after all, he'll know sometime. She's been threatening to come herself and tell him. So, don't flatter yourself that your secrecy's worth any price you choose to ask. You drain me of money till I have nothing to pacify *her* with, and she'll do as she threatens some day. It's all one. I'll tell my father everything myself, and you may go to the devil."

Dunsey perceived that he had overshot his mark, and that there was a point at which even the hesitating Godfrey might be driven into decision. But he said, with an air of unconcern:

"As you please; but I'll have a draught of ale first." And ringing the bell, he threw himself across two chairs, and began to rap the window-seat with the handle of his whip.

Godfrey stood still, with his back to the fire, uneasily moving his fingers among the contents of his side-pockets, and looking at the floor. That big muscular frame of his held plenty of animal courage, but helped him to no decision when the dangers to be braved were such as could neither be knocked down nor throttled. His natural irresolution and moral cowardice were exaggerated by a position in which dreaded consequences seemed to press equally on all sides, and his irritation had no sooner provoked him to defy Dunstan and anticipate all possible betrayals, than the miseries he must bring on himself by such a step seemed more unendurable to him than the present evil. The results of confession were not contingent, they were certain; whereas betrayal was not certain. From the near vision of that certainty he fell back on suspense and vacillation with a sense of repose.

The disinherited son of a small squire, equally disinclined to dig and to beg, was almost as helpless as an uprooted tree, which, by the favor of earth and sky, has grown to a handsome bulk on the spot where it first shot upward. Perhaps it would have been possible to think of digging with some cheerfulness if Nancy Lammeter were to be won on those terms; but, since he must irrevocably lose *her* as well as the inheritance, and must break every tie but the one that degraded him and left him without motive for trying to recover his better self, he could imagine no future for himself on the other side of confession but that of " 'listing for a soldier"—the most desperate step, short of suicide, in the eyes of respectable families.

No! he would rather trust to casualties than to his own resolve—rather go on sitting at the feast, and sipping the wine he loved, though with the sword hanging over him and terror in his heart, than rush away into the cold darkness where there was no pleasure left. The utmost concession to Dunstan about the horse began to seem easy, compared with the fulfillment of his own threat. But his pride would not let him recommence the conversation otherwise than by continuing the quarrel. Dunstan was waiting for this, and took his ale in shorter draughts than usual.

"It's just like you," Godfrey burst out, in a bitter tone, "to talk about my selling Wildfire in that cool way—the last thing I've got to call my own, and the best bit of horse-flesh I ever had in my life. And if you'd got a spark of pride in you, you'd be ashamed to see the stables emptied, and everybody sneering about it. But it's my belief you'd sell yourself, if it was only for the pleasure of making somebody feel he'd got a bad bargain."

"Ay, ay," said Dunstan, very placably, "you do me justice, I see. You know I'm a jewel for 'ticing people into bargains. For which reason I advise you to let *me* sell Wildfire. I'd ride him to the hunt to-morrow for you, with pleasure. I shouldn't look so handsome as you in the saddle, but it's the horse they'll bid for, and not the rider."

"Yes, I daresay—trust my horse to you!"

"As you please," said Dunstan, rapping the window-seat again with an air of great unconcern. "It's *you* have got to pay Fowler's money; it's none of my business. You received the money from him when you went to Bramcote, and *you* told the Squire it wasn't paid. I'd nothing to do with that; you chose to be so obliging as to give it to me, that was all. If you don't want to pay the money, let it alone; it's all one to me. But I was willing to accommodate you by undertaking to sell the horse, seeing it's not convenient to you to go so far to-morrow."

Godfrey was silent for some moments. He would have liked to spring on Dunstan, wrench the whip from his hand, and flog him to within an inch of his life; and no bodily fear could have deterred him; but he was mastered by another sort of fear, which was fed by feelings stronger even than his resentment. When he spoke again it was in a half conciliatory tone.

"Well, you mean no nonsense about the horse, eh? You'll sell him all fair, and hand over the money? If you don't, you know, everything 'ull go to smash, for

I've got nothing else to trust to. And you'll have less pleasure in pulling the house over my head, when your own skull's to be broken too."

"Ay, ay," said Dunstan, rising; "all right. I thought you'd come round. I'm the fellow to bring old Bryce up to the scratch. I'll get you a hundred and twenty for him, if I get you a penny."

"But it'll perhaps rain cats and dogs to-morrow, as it did yesterday, and then you can't go," said Godfrey, hardly knowing whether he wished for that obstacle or not.

"Not *it*," said Dunstan. "I'm always lucky in my weather. It might rain if you wanted to go yourself. You never hold trumps you know—I always do. You've got the beauty, you see, and I've got the luck, so you must keep me for your crooked sixpence; you'll *ne*-ver get along without me."

"Confound you, hold your tongue!" said Godfrey, impetuously. "And take care to keep sober to-morrow, else you'll get pitched on your head coming home, and Wildfire might be the worse for it."

"Make your tender heart easy," said Dunstan, opening the door. "You never knew me to see double when I'd got a bargain to make; it 'ud spoil the fun. Besides, whenever I fall, I'm warranted to fall on my legs."

With that, Dunstan slammed the door behind him, and left Godfrey to that bitter rumination on his personal circumstances which was now unbroken from day to day save by the excitement of sporting, drinking, card-playing, or the rarer and less oblivious pleasure of seeing Miss Nancy Lammeter. The subtle and varied pains springing from the higher sensibility that accompanies higher culture, are perhaps less pitiable than that dreary absence of impersonal enjoyment and consolation which leaves ruder minds to the perpetual urgent companionship of their own griefs and discontents.

The lives of those rural forefathers, whom we are apt to think very prosaic figures—men whose only work was to ride round their land, getting heavier and heavier in their saddles, and who passed the rest of their days in the half-listless gratification of senses dulled by monotony—had a certain pathos in them nevertheless. Calamities came to *them* too, and their early errors carried hard consequences: perhaps the love of some sweet maiden, the image of purity, order, and calm, had opened their eyes to the vision of a life in which the days would not seem too long, even without rioting; but the maiden was lost, and the vision passed away, and then what was left to them, especially when they had become too heavy for the hunt, or for carrying a gun over the furrows, but to drink and get merry, or to drink and get angry, so that they might be independent of variety, and say over again with eager emphasis the things they had said already any time that twelvemonth.

Assuredly, among these flushed and dull-eyed men there were some whom—thanks to their native human kindness—even riot could never drive into brutality; men who, when their cheeks were fresh, had felt the keen point of sorrow or remorse, had been pierced by the reeds they leaned on, or had lightly put their limbs in fetters from which no struggle could loose them; and under these sad circumstances, common to us all, their thoughts could find no resting-place outside the ever trodden round of their own petty history.

That, at least, was the condition of Godfrey Cass in this six-and-twentieth year of his life. A movement of compunction, helped by those small, indefinable influences which every personal relation exerts on a pliant nature, had urged him into a secret marriage, which was a blight on his life.

It was an ugly story of low passion, delusion, and waking from delusion, which needs not to be dragged from the privacy of Godfrey's bitter memory. He had long known that the delusion was partly due to a trap laid for him by Dunstan, who saw in his brother's degrading marriage the means of gratifying at once his jealous hate and his cupidity. And if Godfrey could have felt himself simply a victim, the iron bit that destiny had put into his mouth would have chafed him less intolerably. If the curses he muttered half aloud when he was alone had had no other object than Dunstan's diabolical cunning, he might have shrunk less from the consequences of avowal. But he had something else to curse—his own vicious folly, which now seemed as mad and unaccountable to him as almost all our follies and vices do when their promptings have long passed away.

For four years he had thought of Nancy Lammeter, and wooed her with tacit, patient worship, as the woman who made him think of the future with joy: she would be his wife, and would make home lovely to him, as his father's home had never been; and it would be easy, when she was always near, to shake off those foolish habits that were no pleasures, but only a feverish way of annulling vacancy.

Godfrey's was an essentially domestic nature, bred up in a home where the hearth had no smiles, and where the daily habits were not chastened by the pretence of household order. His easy disposition made him fall in unresistingly with the family courses, but the need of some tender, permanent affection, the longing for some influence that would make the good he preferred easy to pursue, caused the neatness, purity, and liberal orderliness of the Lammeter household, sunned by the smile of Nancy, to seem like those fresh, bright hours of the morning when temptations go to sleep and leave the ear open to the voice of the good angel, inviting to industry, sobriety, and peace.

And yet the hope of this paradise had not been enough to save him from a course which shut him out of it forever. Instead of keeping fast hold of the strong silken rope by which Nancy would have drawn him safe to the green banks where it was easy to step firmly, he had let himself be dragged back into mud and slime, in which it was useless to struggle. He had made ties for himself which robbed him of all wholesome motive and were a constant exasperation.

Still, there was one position worse than the present: it was the position he would be in when the ugly secret was disclosed; and the desire that continually triumphed over every other was that of warding off the evil day, when he would have to bear the consequences of his father's violent resentment for the wound inflicted on his family pride—would have, perhaps, to turn his back on that hereditary ease and dignity which, after all, was a sort of reason for living, and would carry with him the certainty that he was banished forever from the sight and esteem of Nancy Lammeter.

The longer the interval, the more chance there was of deliverance from some, at least, of the hateful consequences to which he had sold himself; the more opportunities remained for him to snatch the strange gratification of seeing Nancy, and gathering some faint indications of her lingering regard. Towards this gratification he was impelled, fitfully, every now and then, after having passed weeks in which he had avoided her as the far-off, bright-winged prize that only made him spring forward and find his chain all the more galling.

One of those fits of yearning was on him now, and it would have been strong enough to have persuaded him to trust Wildfire to Dunstan rather than disappoint the yearning, even if he had not had another reason for his disinclination towards the morrow's hunt. That other reason was the fact that the morning's meet was near Batherley, the market-town where the unhappy woman lived, whose image became more odious to him every day; and to his thought the whole vicinage was haunted by her.

The yoke a man creates for himself by wrong-doing will breed hate in the kindliest nature; and the good-humored, affectionate-hearted Godfrey Cass was fast becoming a bitter man, visited by cruel wishes, that seemed to enter, and depart, and enter again, like demons who had found in him a ready-garnished home.

What was he to do this evening to pass the time? He might as well go to the Rainbow, and hear the talk about the cock-fighting: everybody was there, and what else was there to be done? Though, for his own part, he did not care a button for cock-fighting. Snuff, the brown-spaniel, who had placed herself in front of him, and had been watching him for some time, now jumped up in impatience for the expected caress. But Godfrey thrust her away without looking at her, and left the room, followed humbly by the unresenting Snuff—perhaps because she saw no other career open to her.

CHAPTER IV

DUNSTAN CASS, setting off in the raw morning, at the judiciously quiet pace of a man who is obliged to ride to cover on his hunter, had to take his way along the lane which, at its farther extremity, passed by the piece of unenclosed ground called the Stone-pit, where stood the cottage, once a stone-cutter's shed, now for fifteen years inhabited by Silas Marner. The spot looked very dreary at this season, with the moist trodden clay about it, and the red, muddy water high up in the deserted quarry. That was Dunstan's first thought as he approached it; the second was, that the old fool of a weaver, whose loom he heard rattling already, had a great deal of money hidden somewhere.

How was it that he, Dunstan Cass, who had often heard talk of Marner's miserliness, had never thought of suggesting to Godfrey that he should frighten or persuade the old fellow into lending the money on the excellent security of the young Squire's prospects? The resource occurred to him now as so easy and agreeable, especially as Marner's hoard was likely to be large enough to leave Godfrey a handsome surplus beyond his immediate needs, and enable him to accommodate his faithful brother, that he had almost turned the horse's head towards home again.

Godfrey would be ready enough to accept the suggestion: he would snatch eagerly at a plan that might save him from parting with Wildfire. But when Dunstan's meditation reached this point, the inclination to go on grew strong and prevailed. He didn't want to give Godfrey that pleasure: he preferred that Master Godfrey should be vexed. Moreover, Dunstan enjoyed the self-important consciousness of having a horse to sell, and the opportunity of driving a bargain, swaggering, and possibly taking somebody in. He might have all the satisfaction attendant on selling his brother's horse, and not the less have the further satisfaction of setting Godfrey to borrow Marner's money. So he rode on to cover.

Bryce and Keating were there, as Dunstan was quite sure they would be—he was such a lucky fellow.

"Heyday!" said Bryce, who had long had his eye on Wildfire, "you're on your brother's horse to-day: how's that?"

"Oh, I've swopped with him," said Dunstan, whose delight in lying, grandly independent of utility, was not to be diminished by the likelihood that his hearer would not believe him—"Wildfire's mine now."

"What! has he swopped with you for that big-boned hack of yours?" said Bryce, quite aware that he should get another lie in answer.

"Oh, there was a little account between us," said Dunsey, carelessly, "and Wildfire made it even. I accommodated him by taking the horse, though it was against my will, for I'd got an itch for a mare o' Jortin's—as rare a bit o' blood as ever you threw your leg across. But I shall keep Wildfire, now I've got him, though I'd a bid of a hundred and fifty for him the other day, from a man over at Flitton—he's buying for Lord Cromleck—a fellow with a cast in his eye, and a green waistcoat. But I mean to stick to Wildfire; I sha'n't get a better at a fence in a hurry. The mare's got more blood, but she's a bit too weak in the hind-quarters."

Bryce of course divined that Dunstan wanted to sell the horse, and Dunstan knew that he divined it (horse-dealing is only one of many human transactions carried on in this ingenious manner); and they both considered that the bargain was in its first stage, when Bryce replied, ironically:

"I wonder at that now; I wonder you mean to keep him; for I never heard of a man who didn't want to sell his horse getting a bid of half as much again as the horse was worth. You'll be lucky if you get a hundred."

Keating rode up now, and the transaction became more complicated. It ended in the purchase of the horse by Bryce for a hundred and twenty, to be paid on the delivery of Wildfire, safe and sound, at the Batherley stables. It did occur to Dunsey that it might be wise for him to give up the day's hunting, proceed at once to Batherley, and, having waited for Bryce's return, hire a horse to carry him home with the money in his pocket. But the inclination for a run, encouraged by confidence in his luck, and by a draught of brandy from his pocket-pistol at the conclusion of the bargain, was not easy to overcome, especially with a horse under him that would take the fences to the admiration of the field.

Dunstan, however, took one fence too many, and got his horse pierced with a hedge-stake. His own ill-favored person, which was quite unmarketable, escaped without injury; but poor Wildfire, unconscious of his price, turned on his flank and painfully panted his last.

It happened that Dunstan, a short time before, having had to get down to arrange his stirrup, had muttered a good many curses at this interruption, which had thrown him in the rear of the hunt near the moment of glory, and under this exasperation had taken the fences more blindly. He would soon have been up with the hounds again, when the fatal accident happened; and hence he was between eager riders in advance, not troubling themselves about what happened behind them, and far-off stragglers, who were as lucky as not to pass quite aloof from the line of road in which Wildfire had fallen.

Dunstan, whose nature it was to care more for immediate annoyances than for remote consequences, no sooner recovered his legs, and saw that it was all over with Wildfire, than he felt a satisfaction at the absence of witnesses to a position which no swaggering could make enviable. Reinforcing himself, after his shake, with a little brandy and much swearing, he walked as fast as he could to a coppice on his right hand, through which it occurred to him that he could make his way to Batherley without danger of encountering any member of the hunt.

His first intention was to hire a horse there and ride home forthwith, for to walk many miles without a gun in his hand and along an ordinary road, was as much out of the question to him as to other spirited young men of his kind. He did not much mind about taking the bad news to Godfrey, for he had to offer him at the same time the resource of Marner's money; and if Godfrey kicked, as he always did, at the notion of making a fresh debt from which he himself got the smallest share of advantage, why, he wouldn't kick long: Dunstan felt sure he could worry Godfrey into anything.

The idea of Marner's money kept growing in vividness, now the want of it had become immediate; the prospect of having to make his appearance with the muddy boots of a pedestrian at Batherley, and to encounter the grinning queries of stablemen, stood unpleasantly in the way of his impatience to be back at Raveloe and carry out his felicitous plan; and a casual visitation of his waistcoat pocket, as he was ruminating, awakened his memory to the fact that the two or three small coins his fore-finger encountered there, were of too pale a color to cover that small debt, without payment of which the stable-keeper had declared he would never do any more business with Dunsey Cass.

After all, according to the direction in which the run had brought him, he was not so very much farther from home than he was from Batherley; but Dunsey, not being remarkable for clearness of head, was only led to this conclusion by the gradual perception that there were other reasons for choosing the unprecedented course of walking home.

It was now nearly four o'clock, and a mist was gathering: the sooner he got into the road the better. He remembered having crossed the road and seen the finger-post only a little while before Wildfire broke down; so, unbuttoning his coat, twisting the lash of his hunting-whip compactly round the handle, and rapping the tops of his boots with a self-possessed air, as if to assure himself that he was not at all taken by surprise, he set off with the sense that he was undertaking a remarkable feat of bodily exertion, which somehow and at some time he should be able to dress up and magnify to the admiration of a select circle at the Rainbow.

When a young gentleman like Dunsey is reduced to so exceptional a mode of locomotion as walking, a whip in his hand is a desirable corrective to a too bewildering dreamy sense of unwontedness in his position; and Dunstan, as he went along through the gathering mist, was always rapping his whip somewhere. It was Godfrey's whip, which he had chosen to take without leave because it had a gold handle; of course no one could see, when Dunstan held it, that the name *Godfrey Cass* was cut in deep letters on that gold handle—they could only see that it was a very handsome whip. Dunsey was not without fear that he might meet some acquaintance in whose eyes he would cut a pitiable figure, for mist is no screen when people get close to each other; but when he at last found himself in the well-known Raveloe lanes without having met a soul, he silently remarked that that was part of his usual good luck. But now the mist, helped by the evening darkness, was more of a screen than he desired, for it hid the ruts into which his feet were liable to slip—hid everything, so that he had to guide his steps by dragging his whip along the low bushes in advance of the hedgerow. He must soon, he thought, be getting near the opening at the Stone-pits: he should find it out by the break in the hedgerow. He found it out, however, by another circumstance which he had not expected—namely, by certain gleams of light, which he presently guessed to proceed from Silas Marner's cottage.

That cottage and the money hidden within it had been in his mind continually during his walk, and he had been imagining ways of cajoling and tempting the weaver to part with the immediate possession of his money for the sake of receiving interest. Dunstan felt as if there must be a little frightening added to the cajolery, for his own arithmetical convictions were not clear enough to afford him any forcible demonstration as to the advantages of interest; and as for security, he regarded it vaguely as a means of cheating a man by making him believe that he would be paid. Altogether, the operation on the miser's mind was a task that Godfrey would be sure to hand over to his more daring and cunning brother: Dunstan had made up his mind to that; and by the time he saw the light gleaming through the chinks of Marner's shutters, the idea of a dialogue with the weaver had become so familiar to him, that it occurred to him as quite a natural thing to make the acquaintance forthwith.

There might be several conveniences attending this course: the weaver had possibly got a lantern, and Dunstan was tired of feeling his way. He was still nearly three-quarters of a mile from home, and the lane was becoming unpleasantly slippery, for the mist was passing into rain. He turned up the bank, not without some fear lest he might miss the right way, since he was not certain whether the light were in front or on the side of the cottage. But he felt the ground before him cautiously with his whip handle, and at last arrived safely at the door. He knocked loudly, rather enjoying the idea that the old fellow would be frightened at the sudden noise. He heard no movement in reply: all was silence in the cottage. Was the weaver gone to bed, then? If so, why had he left a light? That was a strange forgetfulness in a miser.

Dunstan knocked still more loudly, and without pausing for a reply pushed his fingers through the latch-hole, intending to shake the door and pull the latch-string up and down, not doubting that the door was fastened. But to his surprise, at this double motion the door opened, and he found himself in front of a bright fire which lit up every corner of the cottage— the bed, the loom, the three chairs, and the table—and showed him that Marner was not there.

Nothing at that moment could be much more inviting to Dunsey than the bright fire on the brick hearth: he walked in and seated himself by it at once.

There was something in front of the fire, too, that would have been inviting to a hungry man, if it had been in a different stage of cooking. It was a small bit of pork suspended from the kettle-hanger by a string passed through a large door-key, in a way known to primitive housekeepers unpossessed of jacks. But the pork had been hung at the farthest extremity of the hanger, apparently to prevent the roasting from proceeding too rapidly during the owner's absence. The old staring simpleton had hot meat for his supper, then? thought Dunstan. People had always said he lived on mouldy bread, on purpose to check his appetite. But where could he be at this time, and on such an evening, leaving his supper in this stage of preparation, and his door unfastened?

Dunstan's own recent difficulty in making his way suggested to him that the weaver had perhaps gone outside his cottage to fetch in fuel, or for some such brief purpose, and had slipped into the Stone-pit. That was an interesting idea to Dunstan, carrying consequences of entire novelty. If the weaver was dead, who had a right to his money? Who would know where his money was hidden? *Who would know that anybody had come to take it away?* He went no farther into the subtleties of evidence: the pressing question, "Where *is* the money?" now took such entire possession of him as to make him quite forget that the weaver's death was not a certainty. A dull mind, once arriving at an inference that flatters a desire, is rarely able to retain the impression that the notion from which the inference started was purely problematic. And Dunstan's mind was as dull as the mind of a possible felon usually is.

There were only three hiding-places where he had ever heard of cottagers' hoards being found: the thatch, the bed, and a hole in the floor. Marner's cottage had no thatch; and Dunstan's first act, after a train of thought made rapid by the stimulus of cupidity, was to go up to the bed; but while he did so, his eyes traveled eagerly over the floor, where the bricks, distinct in the firelight, were discernible under the sprinkling of sand. But not everywhere; for there was one spot, and one only, which was quite covered with sand, and sand showing the marks of fingers, which had apparently been careful to spread it over a given space. It was near the treddles of the loom.

In an instant Dunstan darted to that spot, swept away the sand with his whip, and, inserting the thin end of the hook between the bricks, found that they were loose. In haste he lifted up two bricks, and saw what he had no doubt was the object of his search: for what could there be but money in those two leathern bags? And, from their weight, they must be filled with guineas. Dunstan felt round the hole, to be certain that it held no more; then hastily replaced the bricks, and spread the sand over them.

Hardly more than five minutes had passed since he entered the cottage, but it seemed to Dunstan like a long while; and though he was without any distant recognition of the possibility that Marner might be alive, and might re-enter the cottage at any moment, he felt an undefinable dread laying hold on him, as he rose to his feet with the bags in his hand. He would hasten out into the darkness, and then consider what he should do with the bags. He closed the door behind him immediately, that he might shut in the stream of light; a few steps would be enough to carry him beyond betrayal by the gleams from the shutter-chinks and the latch-hole. The rain and darkness had got thicker, and he was glad of it; though it was awkward walking with both hands filled, so that it was as much as he could do to grasp his whip along with one of the bags. But when he had gone a yard or two, he might take his time. So he stepped forward into the darkness.

CHAPTER V

WHEN DUNSTAN CASS turned his back on the cottage, Silas Marner was not more than a hundred yards away from it, plodding along from the village with a sack thrown round his shoulders as an overcoat, and with a horn lantern in his hand. His legs were weary, but his mind was at ease, free from the presentiment of change.

The sense of security more frequently springs from habit than from conviction, and for this reason it often subsists after such a change in the conditions as might have been expected to suggest alarm. The lapse of time during which a given event has not happened, is, in this logic of habit, constantly alleged as a reason why the event should never happen, even when the lapse of time is precisely the added condition which makes the event imminent. A man will tell you that he has worked in a mine for forty years, unhurt by an accident, as a reason why he should apprehend no danger, though the roof is beginning to sink; and it is often observable, that the older a man gets, the more difficult it is to him to retain a believing conception of his own death.

This influence of habit was necessarily strong in a

man whose life was so monotonous as Marner's—who saw no new people and heard of no new events to keep alive in him the idea of the unexpected and the changeful; and it explains simply enough why his mind could be at ease, though he had left his house and his treasure more defenceless than usual.

Silas was thinking with double complacency of his supper: first, because it would be hot and savory; and secondly, because it would cost him nothing. For the little bit of pork was a present from that excellent housewife, Miss Priscilla Lammeter, to whom he had this day carried home a handsome piece of linen, and it was only on occasion of a present like this, that Silas indulged himself with roast meat. Supper was his favorite meal, because it came at his time of revelry, when his heart warmed over his gold; whenever he had roast meat, he always chose to have it for supper. But this evening, he had no sooner ingeniously knotted his string fast round his bit of pork, twisted the string according to rule over his door-key, passed it through the handle, and made it fast on the hanger, than he remembered that a piece of very fine twine was indispensable to his "setting up" a new piece of work in his loom early in the morning. It had slipped his memory, because, in coming from Mr. Lammeter's, he had not had to pass through the village; but to lose time by going on errands in the morning was out of the question.

It was a nasty fog to turn out into, but there were things Silas loved better than his own comfort; so, drawing his pork to the extremity of the hanger, and arming himself with his lantern and his old sack, he set out on what, in ordinary weather, would have been a twenty minutes' errand. He could not have locked his door without undoing his well-knotted string and retarding his supper; it was not worth his while to make that sacrifice. What thief would find his way to the Stone-pits on such a night as this? and why should he come on this particular night, when he had never come through all the fifteen years before? These questions were not distinctly present in Silas's mind; they merely serve to represent the vaguely-felt foundation of his freedom from anxiety.

He reached his door in much satisfaction that his errand was done: he opened it, and to his short-sighted eyes everything remained as he had left it, except that the fire sent out a welcome increase of heat. He trod about the floor while putting by his lantern and throwing aside his hat and sack, so as to merge the marks of Dunstan's feet on the sand in the marks of his own nailed boots. Then he moved his pork nearer to the fire, and sat down to the agreeable business of tending the meat and warming himself at the same time.

Anyone who had looked at him as the red light shone upon his pale face, strange, straining eyes, and meagre form, would perhaps have understood the mixture of contemptuous pity, dread and suspicion with which he was regarded by his neighbors in Raveloe. Yet few men could be more harmless than poor Marner. In his truthful, simple soul, not even the growing greed and worship of gold could beget any vice directly injurious to others. The light of his faith quite put out, and his affections made desolate, he had clung with all the force of his nature to his work and his money; and like all objects to which a man devotes himself, they had fashioned him into correspondence with themselves. His loom, as he wrought in it without ceasing, had in its turn wrought on him, and confirmed more and more the monotonous craving for its monotonous response. His gold, as he hung over it and saw it grow, gathered his power of loving together into a hard isolation like its own.

As soon as he was warm he began to think it would be a long while to wait till after supper before he drew out his guineas, and it would be pleasant to see them on the table before him as he ate his unwonted feast. For joy is the best of wine, and Silas's guineas were a golden wine of that sort.

He rose and placed his candle unsuspectingly on the floor near his loom, swept away the sand without noticing any change, and removed the bricks. The sight of the empty hole made his heart leap violently, but the belief that his gold was gone could not come at once—only terror, and the eager effort to put an end to the terror. He passed his trembling hand all about the hole, trying to think it possible that his eyes had deceived him; then he held the candle in the hole and examined it curiously, trembling more and more. At last he shook so violently that he let fall the candle, and lifted his hands to his head, trying to steady himself, that he might think. Had he put his gold somewhere else, by a sudden resolution last night, and then forgotten it?

A man falling into dark waters seeks a momentary footing even on sliding stones; and Silas, by acting as if he believed in false hopes, warded off the moment of despair. He searched in every corner, he turned his bed over, and shook it, and kneaded it; he looked in his brick oven where he laid his sticks. When there was no other place to be searched, he kneeled down again and felt once more all round the hole. There was no untried refuge left for a moment's shelter from the terrible truth.

Yes, there was a sort of refuge which always comes with the prostration of thought under an overpowering passion: it was that expectation of impossibilities, that belief in contradictory images, which is still distinct from madness, because it is capable of being dissipated by the external fact. Silas got up from his knees trembling, and looked round at the table: didn't the gold lie there after all? The table was bare. Then he turned and looked behind him—looked all round his dwelling, seeming to strain his brown eyes after some possible appearance of the bags where he had already sought them in vain. He could see every object in his cottage—and his gold was not there.

Again he put his trembling hands to his head, and gave a wild, ringing scream, the cry of desolation. For a few moments after, he stood motionless; but the cry had relieved him from the first maddening pressure of the truth. He turned, and tottered towards his loom, and got into the seat where he worked, instinctively seeking this as the strongest assurance of reality.

And now that all the false hopes had vanished, and the first shock of certainty was passed, the idea of a thief began to present itself, and he entertained it eagerly, because a thief might be caught and made to restore the gold. The thought brought some new strength with it, and he started from his loom to the door. As he opened it the rain beat in upon him, for it was falling more and more heavily.

There were no footsteps to be tracked on such a night—footsteps? When had the thief come? During Silas's absence in the daytime the door had been locked, and there had been no marks of any inroad on his return by daylight. And in the evening, too, he said to himself, everything was the same as when he had left it. The sand and bricks looked as if they had not been moved. *Was* it a thief who had taken the bags? or was it a cruel power that no hands could reach which had delighted in making him a second time desolate?

He shrank from this vaguer dread and fixed his mind with struggling effort on the robber with hands, who could be reached by hands. His thoughts glanced at all the neighbors who had made any remarks, or asked any questions which he might now regard as a ground of suspicion. There was Jem Rodney, a known poacher, and otherwise disreputable: he had often met Marner in his journeys across the fields, and had said something jestingly about the weaver's money; nay, he had once irritated Marner, by lingering at the fire when he called to light his pipe, instead of going about his business.

Jem Rodney was the man—there was ease in the thought. Jem could be found and made to restore the money: Marner did not want to punish him, but only to get back his gold which had gone from him, and left his soul like a forlorn traveler on an unknown desert. The robber must be laid hold of. Marner's ideas of legal authority were confused, but he felt that he must go and proclaim his loss; and the great people in the village—the clergyman, the constable, and Squire Cass—would make Jem Rodney, or somebody else, deliver up the stolen money. He rushed out in the rain, under the stimulus of this hope, forgetting to cover his head, not caring to fasten his door; for he felt as if he had nothing left to lose. He ran swiftly, till want of breath compelled him to slacken his pace as he was entering the village at the turning close to the Rainbow.

The Rainbow, in Marner's view, was a place of luxurious resort for stout and rich husbands, whose wives had superfluous stores of linen; it was the place

where he was likely to find the powers and dignities of
Raveloe, and where he could most speedily make his
loss public. He lifted the latch, and turned into the
bright bar or kitchen on the right hand, where the less
lofty customers of the house were in the habit of assembling, the parlor on the left being reserved for
the more select society in which Squire Cass frequently
enjoyed the double pleasure of conviviality and condescension. But the parlor was dark tonight, the chief
personages who ornamented its circle being all at Mrs.
Osgood's birthday dance, as Godfrey Cass was. And in
consequence of this, the party on the high-screened
seats in the kitchen was more numerous than usual;
several personages, who would otherwise have been
admitted into the parlor and enlarged the opportunity
of hectoring and condescension for their betters, being
content this evening to vary their enjoyment by taking
their spirits-and-water where they could themselves
hector and condescend in company that called for
beer.

CHAPTER VI

THE CONVERSATION, which was at a high pitch
of animation when Silas approached the door of
the Rainbow, had, as usual, been slow and intermittent
when the company first assembled. The pipes began to
be puffed in a silence which had an air of severity; the
more important customers, who drank spirits and sat
nearest the fire, staring at each other as if a bet were
depending on the first man who winked; while the

beer-drinkers, chiefly men in fustian jackets and smock-frocks, kept their eyelids down and rubbed their hands across their mouths, as if their draughts of beer were a funereal duty attended with embarrassing sadness.

At last, Mr. Snell, the landlord, a man of a neutral disposition, accustomed to stand aloof from human differences as those of beings who were all alike in need of liquor, broke silence, by saying in a doubtful tone to his cousin the butcher:

"Some folks 'ud say that was a fine beast you druv in yesterday, Bob?"

The butcher, a jolly, smiling, red-haired man, was not disposed to answer rashly. He gave a few puffs before he spat and replied, "And they wouldn't be fur wrong, John."

After this feeble, delusive thaw, the silence set in as severely as before.

"Was it a red Durham?" said the farrier, taking up the thread of discourse after the lapse of a few minutes.

The farrier looked at the landlord, and the landlord looked at the butcher, as the person who must take the responsibility of answering.

"Red it was," said the butcher, in his good-humored, husky treble—"and a Durham it was."

"Then you needn't tell *me* who you bought it of," said the farrier, looking round with some triumph; "I know who it is has got the red Durhams o' this country-side. And she'd a white star on her brow, I'll bet a penny?" The farrier leaned forward with his hands on his knees as he put this question, and his eyes twinkled knowingly.

"Well; yes—she might," said the butcher, slowly, considering that he was giving a decided affirmative. "I don't say contrairy."

"I know that very well," said the farrier, throwing

himself backward again, and speaking defiantly; "if *I* don't know Mr. Lammeter's cows, I should like to know who does—that's all. And as for the cow you've bought, bargain or no bargain, I've been at the drenching of her—contradick me who will."

The farrier looked fierce, and the mild butcher's conversational spirit was roused a little.

"I'm not for contradicking no man," he said, "I'm for peace and quietness. Some are for cutting long ribs—I'm for cutting 'em short myself; but *I* don't quarrel with 'em. All I say is, it's a lovely carkiss—and anybody as was reasonable, it 'ud bring tears into their eyes to look at it."

"Well, it's the cow as I drenched, whatever it is," pursued the farrier, angrily; "and it was Mr. Lammeter's cow, else you told a lie when you said it was a red Durham."

"I tell no lies," said the butcher, with the same mild huskiness as before, "and I contradick none—not if a man was to swear himself black: he's no meat o' mine, nor none o' my bargains. All I say is, it's a lovely carkiss. And what I say I'll stick to; but I'll quarrel wi' no man."

"No," said the farrier, with bitter sarcasm, looking at the company generally; "and p'rhaps you arn't pig-headed; and p'rhaps you didn't say the cow was a Red Durham; and p'rhaps you didn't say she'd got a star on her brow—stick to that, now you're at it."

"Come, come," said the landlord; "let the cow alone. The truth lies atween you: you're both right and both wrong, as I allays say. And as for the cow's being Mr. Lammeter's, I say nothing to that; but this I say, as the Rainbow's the Rainbow. And for the matter o' that, if the talk is to be o' the Lammeters, *you* know the most upo' that head, eh, Mr. Macey? You remember when first Mr. Lammeter's father come into these parts, and took the Warrens?"

Mr. Macey, tailor and parish-clerk, the latter of which functions rheumatism had of late obliged him to share with a small-featured young man who sat opposite him, held his white head on one side, and twirled his thumbs with an air of complacency, slightly seasoned with criticism. He smiled pityingly, in answer to the landlord's appeal, and said:

"Ay, ay; I know, I know; but I let other folks talk. I've laid by now, and gev up to the young uns. Ask them as have been to school at Tarley: they've learnt pernouncing; that's come up since my day."

"If you're pointing at me, Mr. Macey," said the deputy-clerk, with an air of anxious propriety, "I'm nowise a man to speak out of my place. As the psalm says—

'I know what's right, nor only so,
But also practise what I know.' "

"Well, then, I wish you'd keep hold o' the tune, when it's set for you; if you're for prac*tis*ing, I wish you'd prac*tise* that," said a large, jocose-looking man, an excellent wheelwright in his week-day capacity, but on Sundays leader of the choir. He winked, as he spoke, at two of the company, who were known officially as the "bassoon" and the "key-bugle," in the confidence that he was expressing the sense of the musical profession in Raveloe.

Mr. Tookey, the deputy-clerk, who shared the unpopularity common to deputies, turned very red, but replied, with careful moderation—"Mr. Winthrop, if you'll bring me any proof as I'm in the wrong, I'm not the man to say I won't alter. But there's people set up their own ears for a standard, and expect the whole choir to follow 'em. There may be two opinions, I hope."

"Ay, ay," said Mr. Macey, who felt very well satisfied with this attack on youthful presumption; "you're right there, Tookey: there's allays two 'pinions; there's the 'pinion a man has of himsen, and there's the 'pinion other folks have on him. There'd be two 'pinions about a cracked bell, if the bell could hear itself."

"Well, Mr. Macey," said poor Tookey, serious amidst the general laughter, "I undertook to partially fill up the office of parish-clerk by Mr. Crackenthorp's desire, whenever your infirmities should make you unfitting; and it's one of the rights thereof to sing in the choir—else why have you done the same yourself?"

"Ah! but the old gentleman and you are two folks," said Ben Winthrop. "The old gentleman's got a gift. Why, the Squire used to invite him to take a glass, only to hear him sing the 'Red Rovier'; didn't he, Mr. Macey? It's a nat'ral gift. There's my little lad Aaron, he's got a gift—he can sing a tune off straight, like a throstle. But as for you, Master Tookey, you'd better stick to your 'Amens': your voice is well enough when you keep it up in your nose. It's your inside as isn't right made for music: it's no better nor a hollow stalk."

This kind of unflinching frankness was the most piquant form of joke to the company at the Rainbow, and Ben Winthrop's insult was felt by everybody to have capped Mr. Macey's epigram.

"I see what it is plain enough," said Mr. Tookey, unable to keep cool any longer. "There's a consperacy to turn me out o' the choir, as I shouldn't share the Christmas money—that's where it is. But I shall speak to Mr. Crackenthorp; I'll not be put upon by no man.'

"Nay, nay, Tookey," said Ben Winthrop. "We'll

pay you your share to keep out of it—that's what we'll do. There's things folks 'ud pay to be rid on, besides varmin."

"Come, come," said the landlord, who felt that paying people for their absence was a principle dangerous to society; "a joke's a joke. We're all good friends here, I hope. We must give and take. You're both right and you're both wrong, as I say. I agree wi' Mr. Macey here, as there's two opinions; and if mine was asked, I should say they're both right. Tookey's right and Winthrop's right, and they've only got to split the difference and make themselves even."

The farrier was puffing his pipe rather fiercely, in some contempt at this trivial discussion. He had no ear for music himself, and never went to church, as being of the medical profession, and likely to be in requisition for delicate cows. But the butcher, having music in his soul, had listened with a divided desire for Tookey's defeat and for the preservation of the peace.

"To be sure," he said, following up the landlord's conciliatory view, "we're fond of our old clerk; it's nat'ral, and him used to be such a singer, and got a brother as is known for the first fiddler in this countryside. Eh, it's a pity but what Solomon lived in our village, and could give us a tune when we liked; eh, Mr. Macey? I'd keep him in liver and lights for nothing—that I would."

"Ay, ay," said Mr. Macey, in the height of complacency; "our family's been known for musicianers as far back as anybody can tell. But them things are dying out, as I tell Solomon every time he comes round; there's no voices like what there used to be, and there's nobody remembers what we remember, if it isn't the old crows."

"Ay, you remember when first Mr. Lammeter's

father come into these parts, don't you, Mr. Macey?" said the landlord.

"I should think I did," said the old man, who had now gone through that complimentary process necessary to bring him up to the point of narration; "and a fine old gentleman he was—as fine, and finer nor the Mr. Lammeter as now is. He came from a bit north'ard, so far as I could ever make out. But there's nobody rightly knows about those parts: only it couldn't be far north'ard, nor much different from this country, for he brought a fine breed o' sheep with him, so there must be pastures there, and everything reasonable. We heared tell as he'd sold his own land to come and take the Warrens, and that seemed odd for a man as had land of his own, to come and rent a farm in a strange place. But they said it was along of his wife's dying: though there's reasons in things as nobody knows on—that's pretty much what I've made out; yet some folks are so wise, they'll find you fifty reasons straight off, and all the while the real reason's winking at 'em in the corner, and they niver see't. Howsomever, it was soon seen as we'd got a new parish'ner as know'd the rights and customs o' things, and kep' a good house, and was well looked on by everybody. And the young man—that's the Mr. Lammeter as now is, for he'd niver a sister—soon begun to court Miss Osgood, that's the sister o' the Mr. Osgood as now is, and a fine, handsome lass she was—eh, you can't think—they pretend this young lass is like her, but that's the way wi' people as don't know what come before 'em. *I* should know, for I helped the old rector, Mr. Drumlow as was. I helped him marry 'em."

Here Mr. Macey paused; he always gave his narrative in instalments, expecting to be questioned according to precedent.

"Ay, and a partic'lar thing happened, didn't it, Mr. Macey, so as you were likely to remember that marriage?" said the landlord, in a congratulatory tone.

"I should think there did—a *very* partic'lar thing," said Mr. Macey, nodding sideways. "For Mr. Drumlow—poor old gentleman, I was fond on him, though he'd got a bit confused in his head, what wi' age and wi' taking a drop o' summat warm when the service come of a cold morning. And young Mr. Lammeter he'd have no way but he must be married in Janiwary, which, to be sure, 's a unreasonable time to be married in, for it isn't like a christening or a burying, as you can't help; and so Mr. Drumlow—poor old gentleman, I was fond on him—but when he come to put the questions, he put 'em by the rule o' contrairy, like, and he says, 'Wilt thou have this man to thy wedded wife?' says he, and then he says, 'Wilt thou have this woman to thy wedded husband?' says he. But the partic'larest thing of all is, as nobody took any notice on it but me, and they answered straight off 'yes,' like as if it had been me saying 'Amen,' i' the right place, without listening to what went before."

"But *you* knew what was going on well enough, didn't you, Mr. Macey? You were live enough, eh?" said the butcher.

"Lor bless you!" said Mr. Macey, pausing, and smiling in pity at the impotence of his hearer's imagination—"why, I was all of a tremble: it was as if I'd been a coat pulled by the two tails, like; for I couldn't stop the parson, I couldn't take upon me to do that; and yet I said to myself, I says, 'Suppose they shouldn't be fast married, 'cause the words are contrairy?' and my head went working like a mill, for I was allays uncommon for turning things over and seeing all round 'em; and I says to myself, 'Is 't the meanin' or the words as makes folks fast i' wedlock?' For the parson meant right, and the bride and bridegroom meant right. But then, when I come to think on it, meanin' goes but a little way i' most things, for you may mean to stick things together and your glue may be bad, and then where are you? And so I says to mysen, 'It isn't the meanin', it's the glue.' And I was worreted as if I'd got three bells to pull at once, when we went into the vestry, and they begun to sign their names. But where's the use o' talking?—you can't think what goes on in a 'cute man's inside."

"But you held in for all that, didn't you, Mr. Macey?" said the landlord.

"Ay, I held in tight till I was by mysen wi' Mr. Drumlow, and then I out wi' everything, but respectful, as I allays did. And he made light on it, and he says, 'Pooh, pooh, Macey, make yourself easy,' he says; 'it's neither the meaning nor the words—it's the regester does it—that's the glue.' So you see he settled it easy; for parsons and doctors know everything by heart, like, so as they aren't worreted wi' thinking what's the rights and wrongs o' things, as I'n been many and many's the time. And sure enough the wedding turned out all right, on'y poor Mrs. Lammeter—that's Miss Osgood as was—died afore the lasses was growed up; but for prosperity and everything respectable, there's no family more looked on."

Every one of Mr. Macey's audience had heard this story many times, but it was listened to as if it had been a favorite tune, and at certain points the puffing of the pipes was momentarily suspended, that the listeners might give their whole minds to the expected words. But there was more to come; and Mr. Snell, the landlord, duly put the leading question.

"Why, old Mr. Lammeter had a pretty fortin, didn't they say, when he come into these parts?"

"Well, yes," said Mr. Macey; "but I daresay it's as much as this Mr. Lammeter's done to keep it whole. For there was allays a talk as nobody could get rich on the Warrens: though he holds it cheap, for it's what they call Charity Land."

"Ay, and there's few folks know so well as you how it come to be Charity Land, eh, Mr. Macey?" said the butcher.

"How should they?" said the old clerk, with some contempt. "Why, my grandfather made the groom's livery for that Mr. Cliff as came and built the big stables at the Warrens. Why, they're stables four times as big as Squire Cass's, for he thought o' nothing but hosses and hunting, Cliff didn't—a Lunnon tailor, some folks said, as had gone mad wi' cheating. For he couldn't ride; lor bless you! they said he got no more grip o' the hoss than if his legs had been cross-sticks: my grandfather heared old Squire Cass say so many and many a time. But ride he would as if Old Harry had been a-driving him; and he'd a son, a lad o' sixteen; and nothing would his father have him do, but he must ride and ride—though the lad was frighted, they said. And it was a common saying as the father wanted to ride the tailor out o' the lad, and make a gentleman on him—not but what I'm a tailor myself, but in respect as God made me such, I'm proud on it, for 'Macey, tailor,' 's been wrote up over our door since afore the Queen's heads went out on the shillings. But Cliff, he was ashamed o' being called a tailor, and he was sore vexed as his riding was laughed at, and nobody o' the gentlefolks hereabout could abide him. Howsomever, the poor lad got sickly and died, and the father didn't live long after him, for he got queerer nor

ever, and they said he used to go out i' the dead
o' the night, wi' a lantern in his hand, to the stables,
and set a lot o' lights burning, for he got as he couldn't
sleep; and there he'd stand, cracking his whip and
looking at his hosses; and they said it was a mercy as
the stables didn't get burnt down wi' the poor dumb
creaturs in 'em. But at last he died raving, and they
found as he'd left all his property, Warrens and all, to
a Lunnon Charity, and that's how the Warrens come
to be Charity Land; though, as for the stables, Mr.
Lammeter never uses 'em—they're out o' all charicter—
lor bless you! if you was to set the doors a-banging in
'em, it 'ud sound like thunder half o'er the parish."

"Ay, but there's more going on in the stables than
what folks see by daylight, eh, Mr. Macey?" said the
landlord.

"Ay, ay; go that way of a dark night, that's all,"
said Mr. Macey, winking mysteriously, "and then make
believe, if you like, as you didn't see lights i' the stables,
nor hear the stamping o' the hosses, nor the cracking
o' the whips, and howling, too, if it's tow'rt daybreak.
'Cliff's Holiday' has been the name of it ever sin' I
were a boy; that's to say, some said it was the holiday
Old Harry gev him from roasting, like. That's what
my father told me, and he was a reasonable man,
though there's folks nowadays know what happened
afore they were born better nor they know their own
business."

"What do you say to that, eh, Dowlas?" said the
landlord, turning to the farrier, who was swelling with
impatience for his cue. "There's a nut for *you* to crack."

Mr. Dowlas was the negative spirit in the company,
and was proud of his position.

"Say? I say what a man *should* say as doesn't shut
his eyes to look at a finger-post. I say, as I'm ready to

wager any man ten pound, if he'll stand out wi' me any dry night in the pasture before the Warren stables, as we shall neither see lights nor hear noises, if it isn't the blowing of our own noses. That's what I say, and I've said it many a time; but there's nobody 'ull ventur a ten-pun' note on their ghos'es as they make so sure of."

"Why, Dowlas, that's easy betting, that is," said Ben Winthrop. "You might as well bet a man as he wouldn't catch the rhumatise if he stood up to's neck in the pool of a frosty night. It 'ud be fine fun for a man to win his bet as he'd catch the rhumatise. Folks as believe in Cliff's Holiday aren't agoing to ventur near it for a matter o' ten pound."

"If Master Dowlas wants to know the truth on it," said Mr. Macey, with a sarcastic smile, tapping his thumbs together, "he's no call to lay any bet—let him go and stan' by himself—there's nobody 'ull hinder him; and then he can let the parish'ners know if they're wrong."

"Thank you! I'm obliged to you," said the farrier, with a snort of scorn. "If folks are fools, it's no business o' mine. *I* don't want to make out the truth about ghos'es: I know it a'ready. But I'm not against a bet—everything fair and open. Let any man bet me ten pounds as I shall see Cliff's Holiday, and I'll go and stand by myself. I want no company. I'd as lief do it as I'd fill this pipe."

"Ah, but who's to watch you, Dowlas, and see you do it? That's no fair bet," said the butcher.

"No fair bet?" replied Mr. Dowlas, angrily. "I should like to hear any man stand up and say I want to bet unfair. Come now, Master Lundy, I should like to hear you say it."

"Very like you would," said the butcher. "But it's

no business o' mine. You're none o' my bargains, and I aren't a-going to try and 'bate your price. If anybody'll bid for you at your own vallying, let him. I'm for peace and quietness, I am."

"Yes, that's what every yapping cur is, when you hold a stick up at him," said the farrier. "But I'm afraid o' neither man nor ghost, and I'm ready to lay a fair bet. *I* aren't a turntail cur."

"Ay, but there's this in it, Dowlas," said the landlord, speaking in a tone of much candor and tolerance. "There's folks, i' my opinion, if they can't see ghos'es, not if they stood as plain as a pike-staff before 'em. And there's reason i' that. For there's my wife, now, can't smell, not if she'd the strongest o' cheese under her nose. I never see'd a ghost myself; but then I says to myself, 'Very like I haven't got the smell for 'em.' I mean, putting a ghost for a smell, or else contrairi-ways. And so, I'm for holding with both sides; for, as I say, the truth lies between 'em. And if Dowlas was to go and stand, and say he'd never seen a wink o' Cliff's Holiday all the night through, I'd back him; and if anybody said as Cliff's Holiday was certain sure for all that, I'd back *him*, too. For the smell's what I go by."

The landlord's analogical argument was not well received by the farrier—a man intensely opposed to compromise.

"Tut, tut," he said, setting down his glass with re-freshed irritation; "what's the smell got to do with it? Did ever a ghost give a man a black eye? That's what I should like to know. If ghos'es want me to believe in 'em, let 'em leave off shulking i' the dark and i' lone places—let 'em come where there's company and candles."

"As if ghos'es 'ud want to be believed in by any-body so ignirant!" said Mr. Macey, in deep disgust at the farrier's crass incompetence to apprehend the conditions of ghostly phenomena.

CHAPTER VII

YET THE NEXT MOMENT there seemed to be some evidence that ghosts had a more condescending disposition than Mr. Macey attributed to them; for the pale, thin figure of Silas Marner was suddenly seen standing in the warm light, uttering no word, but looking round at the company with his strange, unearthly eyes. The long pipes gave a simultaneous movement, like the antennæ of startled insects, and every man present, not excepting even the skeptical farrier, had an impression that he saw, not Silas Marner in the flesh, but an apparition; for the door by which Silas had entered was hidden by the high screened seats, and no one had noticed his approach.

Mr. Macey, sitting a long way off the ghost, might be supposed to have felt an argumentative triumph, which would tend to neutralize his share of the general alarm. Had he not always said that when Silas Marner was in that strange trance of his, his soul went loose from his body? Here was the demonstration: nevertheless, on the whole, he would have been as well contented without it.

For a few moments there was a dead silence, Marner's want of breath and agitation not allowing him to speak. The landlord, under the habitual sense that he was bound to keep his house open to all company, and confident in the protection of his unbroken neutrality, at last took on himself the task of adjuring the ghost.

"Master Marner," he said, in a conciliatory tone, "what's lacking to you? What's your business here?"

"Robbed!" said Silas, gaspingly. "I've been robbed! I want the constable—and the Justice—and Squire Cass—and Mr. Crackenthorp."

"Lay hold on him, Jem Rodney," said the landlord, the idea of a ghost subsiding; "he's off his head, I doubt. He's wet through."

Jem Rodney was the outermost man, and sat conveniently near Marner's standing-place; but he declined to give his services.

"Come and lay hold on him yourself, Mr. Snell, if you've a mind," said Jem, rather sullenly. "He's been robbed and murdered, too, for what I know," he added, in a muttering tone.

"Jem Rodney!" said Silas, turning and fixing his strange eyes on the suspected man.

"Ay, Master Marner, what do ye want wi' me?" said Jem, trembling a little, and seizing his drinking-can as a defensive weapon.

"If it was you stole my money," said Silas, clasping his hands entreatingly, and raising his voice to a cry, "give it me back—and I won't meddle with you. I won't set the constable on you. Give it me back, and I'll let you—I'll let you have a guinea."

"Me stole your money!" said Jem angrily. "I'll pitch this can at your eye if you talk o' *my* stealing your money."

"Come, come, Master Marner," said the landlord, now rising resolutely, and seizing Marner by the shoulder, "if you've got any information to lay, speak it out sensible, and show as you're in your right mind, if you expect anybody to listen to you. You're as wet as a drownded rat. Sit down and dry yourself, and speak straight forrard."

"Ah, to be sure, man," said the farrier, who began to feel that he had not been quite on a par with himself and the occasion. "Let's have no more staring and screaming, else we'll have you strapped for a madman. That's why I didn't speak first—thinks I, the man's run mad."

"Ay, ay, make him sit down," said several voices at once, well pleased that the reality of ghosts remained still an open question.

The landlord forced Marner to take off his coat, and then to sit down on a chair aloof from everyone else, in the centre of the circle and in the direct rays of the fire. The weaver, too feeble to have any distinct purpose beyond that of getting help to recover his money, submitted unresistingly. The transient fears of the company were now forgotten in their strong curiosity, and all faces were turned toward Silas, when the landlord, having seated himself again, said:

"Now then, Master Marner, what's this you've got to say—as you've been robbed? Speak out."

"He'd better not say again as it was me robbed him," cried Jem Rodney, hastily. "What could I ha' done with his money? I could as easy steal the parson's surplice, and wear it."

"Hold your tongue, Jem, and let's hear what he's got to say," said the landlord. "Now then, Marner."

Silas now told his story, under frequent questioning as the mysterious character of the robbery became evident.

This strangely novel situation of opening his trouble

to his Raveloe neighbors, of sitting in the warmth of a hearth not his own, and feeling the presence of faces and voices which were his nearest promise of help, had doubtless its influence on Marner, in spite of his passionate preoccupation with his loss. Our consciousness rarely registers the beginning of a growth within us any more than without us: there have been many circulations of the sap before we detect the smallest sign of the bud.

The slight suspicion with which his hearers at first listened to him, gradually melted away before the convincing simplicity of his distress: it was impossible for the neighbors to doubt that Marner was telling the truth, not because they were capable of arguing at once from the nature of his statements to the absence of any motive for making them falsely, but because, as Mr. Macey observed, "Folks as had the devil to back 'em were not likely to be so mushed" as poor Silas was. Rather, from the strange fact that the robber had left no traces, and had happened to know the knick of time, utterly incalculable by mortal agents, when Silas would go away from home without locking his door, the more probable conclusion seemed to be, that his disreputable intimacy in that quarter, if it ever existed, had been broken up, and that, in consequence, this ill turn had been done to Marner by somebody it was quite in vain to set the constable after. Why this preternatural felon should be obliged to wait till the door was left unlocked, was a question which did not present itself.

"It isn't Jem Rodney as has done this work, Master Marner," said the landlord. "You mustn't be a-casting your eye at poor Jem. There may be a bit of reckoning against Jem for the matter of a hare or so if anybody was bound to keep their eyes staring open, and niver to wink; but Jem's been -a-sitting here drinking his can, like the decentest man i' the parish, since before you left your house, Master Marner, by your own account."

"Ay, ay," said Mr. Macey; "let's have no accusing o' the innicent. That isn't the law. There must be folks to swear again' a man before he can be ta'en up. Let's have no accusing o' the innicent, Master Marner."

Memory was not so utterly torpid in Silas that it could not be awakened by these words. With a movement of compunction as new and strange to him as everything else within the last hour, he started from his chair and went close up to Jem, looking at him as if he wanted to assure himself of the expression in his face.

"I was wrong," he said—"yes, yes—I ought to have thought. There's nothing to witness against you, Jem. Only you'd been into my house oftener than anybody else, and so you came into my head. I don't accuse you—I won't accuse anybody—only," he added, lifting up his hands to his head, and turning away with bewildered misery, "I try—I try to think where my guineas can be."

"Ay, ay, they're gone where it's hot enough to melt 'em, I doubt," said Mr. Macey.

"Tchuh!" said the farrier. And then he asked, with a cross-examining air, "How much money might there be in the bags, Master Marner?"

"Two hundred and seventy-two pounds, twelve and sixpence, last night when I counted it," said Silas, seating himself again with a groan.

"Pooh! why they'd be none so heavy to carry. Some tramp's been in, that's all; and as for the no footmarks, and the bricks and the sand being all right—why, your eyes are pretty much like an insect's, Master Marner;

they're obliged to look so close, you can't see much at a time. It's my opinion as, if I'd been you, or you'd been me—for it comes to the same thing—you wouldn't have thought you'd found everything as you left it. But what I vote is, as two of the sensiblest o' the company should go with you to Master Kench, the constable's—he's ill i' bed, I know that much—and get him to appoint one of us his deppity; for that's the law, and I don't think anybody 'ull take upon him to contradick me there. It isn't much of a walk to Kench's; and then, if it's me as is deppity, I'll go back with you, Master Marner, and examine your premises; and if anybody's got any fault to find with that, I'll thank him to stand up and say it out like a man."

By this pregnant speech the farrier had re-established his self-complacency, and waited with confidence to hear himself named as one of the superlatively sensible men.

"Let us see how the night is, though," said the landlord, who also considered himself personally concerned in this proposition. "Why, it rains heavy still," he said returning from the door.

"Well, I'm not the man to be afraid of the rain," said the farrier. "For it'll look bad when Justice Malam hears as respectable men like us had a information laid before 'em and took no steps."

The landlord agreed with this view, and after taking the sense of the company, and duly rehearsing a small ceremony known in high ecclesiastical life as the *nolo episcopari*, he consented to take on himself the chill dignity of going to Kench's. But to the farrier's strong disgust, Mr. Macey now started an objection to his proposing himself as a deputy-constable; for that oracular old gentleman, claiming to know the law, stated, as a fact delivered to him by his father, that no doctor could be a constable.

"And you're a doctor, I reckon, though you're only a cow-doctor, for a fly's a fly, though it may be a hoss fly," concluded Mr. Macey, wondering a little at his own "cuteness."

There was a hot debate upon this, the farrier being of course indisposed to renounce the quality of doctor, but contending that a doctor could be a constable if he liked—the law meant, he needn't be one if he didn't like. Mr. Macey thought this was nonsense, since the law was not likely to be fonder of doctors than of other folks. Moreover, if it was in the nature of doctors more than of other men not to like being constables, how came Mr. Dowlas, to be so eager to act in that capacity?

"*I* don't want to act the constable," said the farrier, driven into a corner by this merciless reasoning; "and there's no man can say it of me, if he'd tell the truth. But if there's to be any jealousy and en*v*ying about going to Kench's in the rain, let them go as like it— you won't get me to go, I can tell you."

By the landlord's intervention, however, the dispute was accommodated. Mr. Dowlas consented to go as a second person disinclined to act officially; and so poor Silas, furnished with some old coverings, turned out with his two companions into the rain again, thinking of the long night hours before him, not as those do who long to rest, but as those who expect to "watch for the morning."

CHAPTER VIII

WHEN GODFREY CASS returned from Mrs. Osgood's party at midnight, he was not much surprised to learn that Dunsey had not come home. Perhaps he had not sold Wildfire, and was waiting for another chance—perhaps, on that foggy afternoon, he had preferred housing himself at the Red Lion at Batherley for the night, if the run had kept him in that neighborhood; for he was not likely to feel much concern about leaving his brother in suspense. Godfrey's mind was too full of Nancy Lammeter's looks and behavior, too full of the exasperation against himself and his lot, which the sight of her always produced in him, for him to give much thought to Wildfire, or to the probabilities of Dunstan's conduct.

The next morning the whole village was excited by the story of the robbery, and Godfrey, like every one else, was occupied in gathering and discussing news about it, and in visiting the Stone-pits. The rain had washed away all possibility of distinguishing footmarks, but a close investigation of the spot had disclosed, in the direction opposite to the village, a tinder-box with a flint and steel, half sunk in the mud. It was not Silas's tinder-box, for the only one he had ever had was still standing on his shelf; and the inference generally accepted was, that the tinder-box in the ditch was somehow connected with the robbery.

A small minority shook their heads, and intimated their opinion that it was not a robbery to have much light thrown on it by tinder-boxes, that Master Marner's tale had a queer look with it, and that such things had been known as a man's doing himself a mischief, and then setting the justice to look for the doer. But when questioned closely as to their grounds for this opinion, and what Master Marner had to gain by such false pretences, they only shook their heads as before, and observed that there was no knowing what some folks counted gain; moreover, that everybody had a right to their own opinions, grounds or no grounds, and that the weaver, as everybody knew, was partly crazy.

Mr. Macey, though he joined in the defence of Marner against all suspicions of deceit, also poohpoohed the tinder-box; indeed, repudiated it as a rather impious suggestion, tending to imply that everything must be done by human hands, and that there was no power which could make away with the guineas without moving the bricks. Nevertheless, he turned round rather sharply on Mr. Tookey, when the zealous deputy, feeling that this was a view of the case peculiarly suited to a parish-clerk, carried it still further, and doubted whether it was right to inquire into a robbery at all when the circumstances were so mysterious.

"As if," concluded Mr. Tookey—"as if there was nothing but what could be made out by justices and constables."

"Now, don't you be for over-shooting the mark, Tookey," said Mr. Macey, nodding his head aside, admonishingly. "That's what you're allays at; if I throw a stone and hit, you think there's summat better than hitting, and you try to throw a stone beyond. What I said was against the tinder-box: I said nothing against justices and constables, for they're o' King George's making, and it 'ud be ill-becoming a man in a parish office to fly out again' King George."

While these discussions were going on amongst the group outside the Rainbow, a higher consultation was being carried on within, under the presidency of Mr. Crackenthorp, the rector, assisted by Squire Cass and other substantial parishioners. It had just occurred to Mr. Snell, the landlord—he being, as he observed, a man accustomed to put two and two together—to connect with the tinder-box, which, as deputy-constable, he himself had had the honorable distinction of finding, certain recollections of a peddler who had called to drink at the house about a month before, and had actually stated that he carried a tinder-box about with him to light his pipe. Here, surely was a clue to be followed out. And as memory, when duly impregnated with ascertained facts, is sometimes surprisingly fertile, Mr. Snell gradually recovered a vivid impression of the effect produced on him by the peddler's countenance and conversation. He had a "look with his eye" which fell unpleasantly on Mr. Snell's sensitive organism. To be sure, he didn't say anything particular—no, except that about the tinder-box—but it isn't what a man says, it's the way he says it. Moreover, he had a swarthy foreignness of complexion which boded little honesty.

"Did he wear ear-rings?" Mr. Crackenthorp wished to know, having some acquaintance with foreign customs.

"Well—stay—let me see," said Mr. Snell, like a docile clairvoyante, who would really not make a mistake if she could help it. After stretching the corners of his mouth and contracting his eyes, as if he were trying to see the ear-rings, he appeared to give up the effort, and said, "Well, he'd got ear-rings in his box to sell so it's nat'ral to suppose he might wear 'em. But he called at every house a'most, in the village; there's somebody else, mayhap, saw 'em in his ears, though I can't take it upon me rightly to say."

Mr. Snell was correct in his surmise, that somebody else would remember the peddler's ear-rings. For on the spread of inquiry among the villagers it was stated, with gathering emphasis, that the parson had wanted to know whether the peddler wore ear-rings in his ears, and an impression was created that a great deal depended on the eliciting of this fact. Of course, every one who heard the question, not having any distinct image of the peddler as *without* ear-rings, immediately had an image of him *with* ear-rings, larger or smaller as the case might be; and the image was presently taken for a vivid recollection, so that the glazier's wife, a well-intentioned woman, not given to lying, and whose house was among the cleanest in the village, was ready to declare, as sure as ever she meant to take the sacrament the very next Christmas that was ever coming, that she had seen big ear-rings, in the shape of the young moon, in the peddler's two ears; while Jinny Oates, the cobbler's daughter, being a more imaginative person, stated not only that she had seen them too, but that they had made her blood creep, as it did at that very moment while there she stood.

Also, by way of throwing further light on this clue of the tinder-box, a collection was made of all the articles purchased from the peddler at various houses, and carried to the Rainbow to be exhibited there. In fact, there was a general feeling in the village, that for the clearing-up of this robbery there must be a great deal done at the Rainbow, and that no man need offer his wife an excuse for going there while it was the scene of severe public duties.

Some disappointment was felt, and perhaps a little indignation, also, when it became known that Silas Marner, on being questioned by the Squire and the parson, had retained no other recollection of the peddler than that he had called at his door, but had not entered his house, having turned away at once when Silas, holding the door ajar, had said that he wanted nothing. This had been Silas's testimony, though he clutched strongly at the idea of the peddler's being the culprit, if only because it gave him a definite image of a whereabout for his gold, after it had been taken away from its hiding-place: he could see it now in the peddler's box. But it was observed with like some irritation in the village, that anybody but a "blind creatur" like Marner would have seen the man prowling about, for how came he to leave his tinder-box in the ditch close by, if he hadn't been lingering there? Doubtless, he had made his observations when he saw Marner at the door. Anybody might know—and only look at him—that the weaver was a half-crazy miser. It was a wonder the peddler hadn't murdered him; men of that sort, with rings in their ears, had been known for murderers often and often; there had been one tried at the 'sizes not so long ago but what there were people living who remembered it.

Godfrey Cass, indeed, entering the Rainbow during one of Mr. Snell's frequently repeated recitals of his testimony, had treated it lightly, stating that he himself had bought a pen-knife of the peddler, and thought him a merry, grinning fellow enough; it was all nonsense, he said, about the man's evil looks. But this was spoken of in the village as the random talk of youth, "as if it was only Mr. Snell who had seen something odd about the peddler!" On the contrary, there were at least half-a-dozen who were ready to go before Justice Malam, and give in much more striking testimony than any the landlord could furnish. It was to be hoped Mr. Godfrey would not go to Tarley and throw cold water on what Mr. Snell said there, and so prevent the justice from drawing up a warrant. He was suspected of intending this, when, after mid-day, he was seen setting off on horseback in the direction of Tarley.

But by this time Godfrey's interest in the robbery had faded before his growing anxiety about Dunstan and Wildfire, and he was going, not to Tarley, but to Batherley, unable to rest in uncertainty about them any longer. The possibility that Dunstan had played him the ugly trick of riding away with Wildfire, to return at the end of a month, when he had gambled away or otherwise squandered the price of the horse, was a fear that urged itself upon him more, even, than the thought of an accidental injury; and now that the dance at Mrs. Osgood's was past, he was irritated with himself that he had trusted his horse to Dunstan. Instead of trying to still his fears he encouraged them, with that superstitious impression which clings to us all, that if we expect evil very strongly it is the less likely to come; and when he heard a horse approaching at a trot, and saw a hat rising above a hedge beyond an angle of the lane, he felt as if his conjuration had succeeded. But no sooner did the horse come within sight, than his heart sank again. It was not Wildfire; and in a few moments more he discerned that the rider was not Dunstan, but Bryce, who pulled up to speak, with a face that implied something disagreeable.

"Well, Mr. Godfrey, that's a lucky brother of yours, that Master Dunsey, isn't he?"

"What do you mean?" asked Godfrey hastily.

"Why, hasn't he been home yet?" said Bryce.

"Home? no. What has happened? Be quick. What has he done with my horse?"

"Ah, I thought it was yours, though he pretended you had parted with it to him."

"Has he thrown him down and broken his knees?" said Godfrey, flushed with exasperation.

"Worse than that," said Bryce. "You see, I'd made a bargain with him to buy the horse for a hundred and twenty—a swinging price, but I always liked the horse. And what does he do but go and stake him—fly at a hedge with stakes in it, atop of a bank with a ditch before it. The horse had been dead a pretty good while when he was found. So he hasn't been home since, has he?"

"Home? no," said Godfrey, "and he'd better keep away. Confound me for a fool! I might have known this would be the end of it."

"Well to tell you the truth," said Bryce, "after I'd bargained for the horse, it did come into my head that he might be riding and selling the horse without your knowledge, for I didn't believe it was his own. I knew Master Dunsey was up to his tricks sometimes. But where can he be gone? He's never been seen at Batherley. He couldn't have been hurt, for he must have walked off."

"Hurt?" said Godfrey, bitterly. "He'll never be hurt—he's made to hurt other people."

"And so you *did* give him leave to sell the horse, eh?" said Bryce.

"Yes; I wanted to part with the horse—he was always a little hard in the mouth for me," said Godfrey; his pride making him wince under the idea that Bryce guessed the sale to be a matter of necessity. "I was going to see after him—I thought some mischief had happened. I'll go back now," he added, turning the horse's head, and wishing he could get rid of Bryce; for he felt that the long-dreaded crisis in his life was close upon him. "You're coming on to Raveloe, aren't you?"

"Well, no, not now," said Bryce. "I *was* coming round there, for I had to go to Flitton, and I thought I might as well take you in my way, and just let you know all I knew myself about the horse. I suppose Master Dunsey didn't like to show himself till the ill news had blown over a bit. He's perhaps gone to pay a visit at the Three Crowns by Whitbridge—I know he's fond of the house."

"Perhaps he is," said Godfrey, rather absently. Then rousing himself, he said, with an effort at carelessness, "We shall hear of him soon enough, I'll be bound."

"Well, here's my turning," said Bryce, not surprised to perceive that Godfrey was rather "down"; "so I'll bid you good-day, and wish I may bring you better news another time."

Godfrey rode along slowly, representing to himself the scene of confession to his father from which he felt that there was now no longer any escape. The revelation about the money must be made the very next morning; and if he withheld the rest, Dunstan would be sure to come back shortly, and, finding that he must bear the brunt of his father's anger, would tell the whole story out of spite, even though he had nothing to gain by it. There was one step, perhaps, by which he might still win Dunstan's silence and put off the evil day: he might tell his father he had himself spent the money paid to him by Fowler; and as he had never been guilty of such an offence before, the affair would blow over after a little storming. But Godfrey could not bend himself to this. He felt in letting Dunstan have the money, he had already been guilty of a breach of trust hardly less culpable than that of spending the money directly for his own behoof; and yet there was a distinction between the two acts which made him feel that the one was so much more blackening than the other as to be intolerable to him.

"I don't pretend to be a good fellow," he said to himself; "but I'm not a scoundrel—at least, I'll stop short somewhere. I'll bear the consequences of what I *have* done sooner than make believe I've done what I never would have done. I'd never have spent the money for my own pleasure—I was tortured into it."

Through the remainder of this day Godfrey, with only occasional fluctuations, kept his will bent in the direction of a complete avowal to his father, and he withheld the story of Wildfire's loss till the next morning, that it might serve him as an introduction to heavier matter. The old Squire was accustomed to his son's frequent absence from home, and thought neither Dunstan's nor Wildfire's non-appearance a matter calling for remark. Godfrey said to himself again and again, that if he let slip this one opportunity of confession, he might never have another; the revelation might be made even in a more odious way than by Dunstan's malignity: *she* might come, as she had threatened to do. And then he tried to make the scene easier to himself by rehearsal: he made up his mind how he would pass from the admission of his weakness in letting Dunstan have the money to the fact that Dunstan had a hold on him which he had been unable to shake off, and how he would work up his father to expect something very bad before he told him the fact.

The old Squire was an implacable man: he made resolutions in violent anger, and he was not to be moved from them after his anger had subsided—as fiery volcanic matters cool and harden into rock. Like many violent and implacable men, he allowed evils to grow under favor of his own heedlessness, till they pressed upon him with exasperating force, and then he turned round with fierce severity and became unrelentingly hard. This was his system with his tenants: he allowed them to get into arrears, neglect their fences, reduce their stocks, sell their straw, and otherwise go the wrong way—and then, when he became short of money in consequence of this indulgence, he took the hardest measures and would listen to no appeal.

Godfrey knew all this, and felt it with the greater force because he had constantly suffered annoyance from witnessing his father's sudden fits of unrelentingness, for which his own habitual irresolution deprived him of all sympathy. (He was not critical on the faulty indulgence which preceded these fits; *that* seemed to him natural enough.) Still there was just the chance, Godfrey thought, that his father's pride might see this marriage in a light that would induce him to hush it up, rather than turn his son out and make the family the talk of the country for ten miles round.

This was the view of the case that Godfrey managed to keep before him pretty closely till midnight, and he went to sleep thinking that he had done with inward debating. But when he awoke in the still, morning darkness he found it impossible to reawaken his evening thoughts; it was as if they had been tired out and were not to be roused to further work. Instead of arguments for confession, he could now feel the presence of nothing but its evil consequences: the old dread of disgrace came back—the old shrinking from the thought of raising a hopeless barrier between himself and Nancy—the old disposition to rely on chances which might be favorable to him, and save him from betrayal. Why, after all, should he cut off the hope of them by his own act? He had seen the matter in a wrong light yesterday. He had been in a rage with Dunstan, and had thought of nothing but a thorough breakup of their mutual understanding; but what it would be really wisest for him to do, was to try and soften his father's anger against Dunsey, and keep things as nearly as possible in their old condition. If Dunsey did not come back for a few days (and Godfrey did not know but that the rascal had enough money in his pocket to enable him to keep away still longer), everything might blow over.

CHAPTER IX

GODFREY ROSE and took his own breakfast earlier than usual, but lingered in the wainscoted parlor till his younger brothers had finished their meal and gone out, awaiting his father, who always took a walk with his managing-man before breakfast. Every one breakfasted at a different hour in the Red House, and the Squire was always the latest, giving a long chance to a rather feeble morning appetite before he tried it. The table had been spread with substantial eatables nearly two hours before he presented himself—a tall, stout man of sixty, with a face in which the knit brow and rather hard glance seemed contradicted by the slack and feeble mouth. His person showed marks of habitual neglect, his dress was slovenly; and yet there was something in the presence of the old Squire distinguishable from that of the ordinary farmers in the parish, who were perhaps every whit as refined as he, but, having slouched their way through life with a consciousness of being in the vicinity of their "betters," wanted that self-possession and authoritativeness of voice and carriage which belonged to a man who thought of superiors as remote existences with whom he had personally little more to do than with America or the stars. The Squire had been used to parish homage all his life, used to the presupposition that his family, his tankards, and everything that was his, were the oldest and best; and as he never associated with any gentry higher than himself, his opinion was not disturbed by comparison.

He glanced at his son as he entered the room, and said, "What, sir! haven't *you* had your breakfast yet?" but there was no pleasant morning greeting between them; not because of any unfriendliness, but because the sweet flower of courtesy is not a growth of such homes as the Red House.

"Yes, sir," said Godfrey, "but I was waiting to speak to you."

"Ah! well," said the Squire, throwing himself indifferently into his chair, and speaking in a ponderous coughing fashion, which was felt in Raveloe to be a sort of privilege of his rank, while he cut a piece of beef, and held it up before the deer hound that had come in with him. "Ring the bell for my ale, will you? You youngsters' business is your own pleasure, mostly. There's no hurry about it for anybody but yourselves."

The Squire's life was quite as idle as his sons', but it was a fiction kept up by himself and his contemporaries in Raveloe that youth was exclusively the period of folly, and that their aged wisdom was constantly in a state of endurance mitigated by sarcasm. Godfrey waited, before he spoke again, until the ale had been brought and the door closed—an interval during which Fleet, the deer-hound, had consumed enough bits of beef to make a poor man's holiday dinner.

"There's been a cursed piece of ill-luck with Wild-fire," he began; "happened the day before yesterday."

"What! broke his knees?" said the Squire, after taking a draught of ale. "I thought you knew how to ride better than that, sir. I never threw a horse down in my life. If I had, I might ha' whistled for another, for *my* father wasn't quite so ready to unstring as some other fathers I know of. But they must turn over a new leaf —*they* must. What with mortgages and arrears, I'm as short o' cash as a roadside pauper. And that fool Kimble says the newspaper's talking about peace. Why, the country wouldn't have a leg to stand on. Prices 'ud run down like a jack, and I should never get my arrears, not if I sold all the fellows up. And there's that damned Fowler, I won't put up with him any longer; I've told Winthrop to go to Cox this very day. The lying scoundrel told me he'd be sure to pay me a hundred last month. He takes advantage because he's on that out-lying farm, and thinks I shall forget him."

The Squire had delivered this speech in a coughing and interrupted manner, but with no pause long enough for Godfrey to make it a pretext for taking up the word again. He felt that his father meant to ward off any request for money on the ground of the misfortune with Wildfire, and that the emphasis he had thus been led to lay on his shortness of cash and his arrears was likely to produce an attitude of mind the utmost un-favorable for his own disclosure. But he must go on, now he had begun.

"It's worse than breaking the horse's knees—he's been

staked and killed," he said, as soon as his father was silent, and had begun to cut his meat. "But I wasn't thinking of asking you to buy me another horse; I was only thinking I'd lost the means of paying you with the price of Wildfire, as I'd meant to do. Dunsey took him to the hunt to sell him for me the other day, and after he'd made a bargain for a hundred and twenty with Bryce, he went after the hounds, and took some fool's leap or other that did for the horse at once. If it hadn't been for that, I should have paid you a hundred pounds this morning."

The Squire had laid down his knife and fork, and was staring at his son in amazement, not being sufficiently quick of brain to form a probable guess as to what could have caused so strange an inversion of the paternal and filial relations as this proposition of his son to pay him a hundred pounds.

"The truth is, sir—I'm very sorry—I was quite to blame," said Godfrey. "Fowler did pay that hundred pounds. He paid it to me, when I was over there one day last month. And Dunsey bothered me for the money, and I let him have it, because I hoped I should be able to pay it you before this."

The Squire was purple with anger before his son had done speaking, and found utterance difficult.

"You let Dunsey have it, sir? And how long have you been so thick with Dunsey that you must *collogue* with him to embezzle my money? Are you turning out a scamp? I tell you I won't have it. I'll turn the whole pack of you out of the house together, and marry again. I'd have you to remember, sir, my property's got no entail on it—since my grandfather's time the Casses can do as they like with their land. Remember that, sir! Let Dunsey have the money! Why should you let

Dunsey have the money? There's some lie at the bottom of it."

"There's no lie, sir," said Godfrey. "I wouldn't have spent the money myself, but Dunsey bothered me, and I was a fool and let him have it. But I meant to pay it, whether he did or not. That's the whole story. I never meant to embezzle money, and I'm not the man to do it. You never knew me to do a dishonest trick, sir."

"Where's Dunsey, then? What do you stand talking there for? Go and fetch Dunsey, as I tell you, and let him give account of what he wanted the money for, and what he's done with it. He shall repent it. I'll turn him out. I said I would, and I'll do it. He sha'n't brave me. Go and fetch him."

"Dunsey isn't come back, sir."

"What! did he break his own neck, then?" said the Squire, with some disgust at the idea that, in that case, he could not fulfil his threat.

"No, he wasn't hurt, I believe, for the horse was found dead, and Dunsey must have walked off. I daresay we shall see him again by-and-by. I don't know where he is."

"And what must you be letting him have my money for? Answer me that," said the Squire, attacking Godfrey again since Dunsey was not within reach.

"Well, sir, I don't know," said Godfrey, hesitatingly. That was a feeble evasion, but Godfrey was not fond of lying, and, not being sufficiently aware that no sort of duplicity can long flourish without the help of vocal falsehoods, he was quite unprepared with invented motives.

"You don't know? I tell you what it is, sir. You've been up to some trick, and you've been bribing him not to tell," said the Squire, with a sudden acuteness which startled Godfrey, who felt his heart beat violently at the nearness of his father's guess. The sudden alarm pushed him on to take the next step—a very slight impulse suffices for that on a downward road.

"Why, sir," he said, trying to speak with careless ease, "it was a little affair between me and Dunsey; it's no matter to anybody else. It's hardly worth while to pry into young men's fooleries: it wouldn't have made any difference to you, sir, if I'd not had the bad luck to lose Wildfire. I should have paid you the money."

"Fooleries! Pshaw! it's time you'd done with fooleries. And I'd have you know, sir, you *must* ha' done with 'em," said the Squire, frowning and casting an angry glance at his son. "Your goings-on are not what I shall find money for any longer. There's my grandfather had his stables full o' horses, and kept a good house, too, and in worse times, by what I can make out; and so might I, if I hadn't four good-for-nothing fellows to hang on me like horse-leeches. I've been too good a father to you all—that's what it is. But I shall pull up, sir."

Godfrey was silent. He was not likely to be very penetrating in his judgments, but he had always had a sense that his father's indulgence had not been kindness, and had had a vague longing for some discipline that would have checked his own errant weakness and helped his better will. The Squire ate his bread and meat hastily, took a deep draught of ale, then turned his chair from the table, and began to speak again.

"It'll be all the worse for you, you know—you'd need try and help me keep things together."

"Well, sir, I've often offered to take the management of things, but you know you've taken it ill always, and seemed to think I wanted to push you out of your place."

"I know nothing o' your offering or o' my taking it ill," said the Squire, whose memory consisted in certain strong impressions unmodified by detail; "but I know one while you seemed to be thinking o' marrying, and I didn't offer to put any obstacles in your way, as some fathers would. I'd as lieve you married Lammeter's daughter as anybody. I suppose, if I'd said you may, you'd ha' kept on with it; but, for want o' contradiction, you've changed your mind. You're a shilly-shally fellow: you take after your poor mother. She never had a will of her own; a woman has no call for one, if she's got a proper man for her husband. But *your* wife had need have one, for you hardly know your own mind enough to make both your legs walk one way. The lass hasn't said downright she won't have you, has she?"

"No," said Godfrey, feeling very hot and uncomfortable; "but I don't think she will."

"Think! why, haven't you the courage to ask her? Do you stick to it, you want to have *her*—that's the thing?"

"There's no other woman I want to marry," said Godfrey, evasively.

"Well, then, let me make the offer for you, that's all, if you haven't the pluck to do it yourself. Lammeter isn't likely to be loath for his daughter to marry into *my* family, I should think. And as for the pretty lass, she wouldn't have her cousin—and there's nobody else, as I see, could ha' stood in your way."

"I'd rather let it be, please, sir, at present," said Godfrey, in alarm. "I think she's a little offended with me just now, and I should like to speak for myself. A man must manage these things for himself."

"Well, speak, then, and manage it, and see if you

can't turn over a new leaf. That's what a man must do when he thinks o' marrying."

"I don't see how I can think of it at present, sir. You wouldn't like to settle on me one of the farms, I suppose, and I don't think she'd come to live in this house with all my brothers. It's a different sort of life to what she's been used to."

"Not come to live in this house? Don't tell me. You ask her, that's all," said the Squire, with a short, scornful laugh.

"I'd rather let the thing be, at present, sir," said Godfrey. "I hope you won't try to hurry it on by saying anything."

"I shall do what I choose," said the Squire, "and I shall let you know I'm master; else you may turn out, and find an estate to drop into somewhere else. Go out and tell Winthrop not to go to Cox's, but to wait for me. And tell 'em to get my horse saddled. And stop: look out and get that hack o' Dunsey's sold, and hand me the money, will you? He'll keep no more hacks at my expense. And if you know where he's sneaking—I daresay you do—you may tell him to spare himself the journey o' coming back home. Let him 'ostler, and keep himself. He shan't hang on me any more."

"I don't know where he is; and if I did, it isn't my place to tell him to keep away," said Godfrey moving towards the door.

"Confound it, sir, don't stay arguing, but go and order my horse," said the Squire, taking up a pipe.

Godfrey left the room, hardly knowing whether he were more relieved by the sense that the interview was ended without having made any change in his position, or more uneasy that he had entangled himself still further in prevarication and deceit. What had passed about this proposing to Nancy had raised a new alarm, lest by some after-dinner words of his father's to Mr. Lammeter he should be thrown into the embarrassment of being obliged absolutely to decline her when she seemed to be within his reach. He fled to his usual refuge, that of hoping for some unforeseen turn of fortune, some favorable chance which would save him from unpleasant consequences—perhaps even justify his insincerity by manifesting its prudence.

In this point of trusting to some throw of fortune's dice, Godfrey can hardly be called old-fashioned. Favorable Chance is the god of all men who follow their own devices instead of obeying a law they believe in. Let even a polished man of these days get into a position he is ashamed to avow, and his mind will be bent on all the possible issues that may deliver him from the calculable results of that position. Let him live outside his income, or shirk the resolute honest work that brings wages, and he will presently find himself dreaming of a possible benefactor, a possible simpleton who may be cajoled into using his interest, a possible state of mind in some possible person not yet forthcoming. Let him neglect the responsibilities of his office, and he will inevitably anchor himself on the chance, that the thing left undone may turn out not to be of the supposed importance. Let him betray his friend's confidence, and he will adore that same cunning complexity called Chance, which gives him the hope that his friend will never know. Let him forsake a decent craft that he may pursue the gentilities of a profession to which nature never called him, and his religion will infallibly be the worship of blessed Chance, which he will believe in as the mighty creator of success. The evil principle deprecated in that religion, is the orderly sequence by which the seed brings forth a crop after its kind.

CHAPTER X

JUSTICE MALAM was naturally regarded in Tarley and Raveloe as a man of capacious mind, seeing that he could draw much wider conclusions without evidence than could be expected of his neighbors who were not on the Commission of the Peace. Such a man was not likely to neglect the clue of the tinder-box, and an inquiry was set on foot concerning a peddler, name unknown, with curly black hair and a foreign complexion, carrying a box of cutlery and jewelry, and wearing large rings in his ears. But either because inquiry was too slow-footed to overtake him, or because the description applied to so many peddlers that inquiry did know how to choose among them, weeks passed away, and there was no other result concerning the robbery than a gradual cessation of the excitement it had caused in Raveloe.

Dunstan Cass's absence was hardly a subject of remark; he had once before had a quarrel with his father, and had gone off, nobody knew whither, to return at the end of six weeks, take up his old quarters unforbidden and swagger as usual. His own family, who equally expected this issue, with the sole difference that the Squire was determined this time to forbid him the old quarters, never mentioned his absence; and when his uncle Kimble or Mr. Osgood noticed it, the story of his having killed Wildfire and committed some offence against his father was enough to prevent surprise.

To connect the fact of Dunsey's disappearance with

that of the robbery occurring on the same day, lay quite away from the track of every one's thought—even Godfrey's, who had better reason than anyone else to know what his brother was capable of. He remembered no mention of the weaver between them since the time, twelve years ago, when it was their boyish sport to deride him; and, besides, his imagination constantly created an *alibi* for Dunstan; he saw him continually in some congenial haunt, to which he had walked off leaving Wildfire—saw him sponging on chance acquaintances, and meditating a return home to the old amusement of tormenting his elder brother. Even if any brain in Raveloe had put the said two facts together, I doubt whether a combination so injurious to the prescriptive respectability of a family with a mural monument and venerable tankards, would not have been suppressed as of unsound tendency. But Christmas puddings, brawn, and abundance of spirituous liquors, throwing the mental originality into the channel of nightmare, are great preservatives against a dangerous spontaneity of waking thought.

When the robbery was talked of at the Rainbow and elsewhere, in good company, the balance continued to waver between the rational explanation founded on the tinder-box, and the theory of an impenetrable mystery that mocked investigation. The advocates of the tinder-box-and-peddler view considered the other side a muddle-headed and credulous set, who, because they themselves were wall-eyed, supposed everybody else to have the same blank outlook; and the adherents of the inexplicable more than hinted that their antagonists were animals inclined to crow before they had found any corn—mere skimming-dishes in point of depth— whose clear-sightedness consisted in supposing there was nothing behind a barn-door because they couldn't see through it; so that, though their controversy did not serve to elicit the fact concerning the robbery, it elicited some true opinions of collateral importance.

But while poor Silas's loss served thus to brush the slow current of Raveloe conversation, Silas himself was feeling the withering desolation of that bereavement about which his neighbors were arguing at their ease. To anyone who had observed him before he lost his gold, it might have seemed that so withered and shrunken a life as his could hardly be susceptible of a bruise, could hardly endure any subtraction but such as would put an end to it altogether. But in reality it had been an eager life, filled with immediate purpose which fenced him in from the wide, cheerless unknown. It had been a clinging life; and though the object round which its fibres had clung was a dead disrupted thing, it satisfied the need for clinging. But now the fence was broken down—the support was snatched away.

Marner's thoughts could no longer move in their old round, and were baffled by a blank like that which meets a plodding ant and when the earth has broken away on its homeward path. The loom was there, and the weaving, and the growing pattern in the cloth; but the bright treasure in the hole under his feet was gone; the prospect of handling and counting it was gone: the evening had no phantasm of delight to still the poor soul's craving. The thought of the money he would get by his actual work could bring no joy, for its meagre image was only a fresh reminder of his loss; and hope was too heavily crushed by the sudden blow, for his imagination to dwell on the growth of a new hoard from that small beginning.

He filled up the blank with grief. As he sat weaving, he every now and then moaned low, like one in pain;

it was the sign that his thoughts had come round again to the sudden chasm—to the empty evening time. And all the evening, as he sat in his loneliness by his dull fire, he leaned his elbows on his knees, and clasped his head with his hands, and moaned very low—not as one who seeks to be heard.

And yet he was not utterly forsaken in his trouble. The repulsion Marner had always created in his neighbors was partly dissipated by the new light in which this misfortune had shown him. Instead of a man who had more cunning than honest folks could come by, and, what was worse, had not the inclination to use that cunning in a neighborly way, it was now apparent that Silas had not cunning enough to keep his own. He was generally spoken of as a "poor mushed creatur"; and that avoidance of his neighbors, which had before been referred to his ill-will and to a probable addiction to worse company, was now considered mere craziness.

This change to a kindlier feeling was shown in various ways. The odor of Christmas cooking being on the wind, it was the season when superfluous pork and black puddings are suggestive of charity in well-to-do families; and Silas's misfortune had brought him uppermost in the memory of housekeepers like Mrs. Osgood. Mr. Crackenthorp, too, while he admonished Silas that his money had probably been taken from him because he thought too much of it and never came to church, enforced the doctrine by a present of pigs' pettitoes, well calculated to dissipate unfounded prejudices against the clerical character. Neighbors who had nothing but verbal consolation to give showed a disposition not only to greet Silas and discuss his misfortune at some length when they encountered him in the village, but also to take the trouble of calling at his cottage and getting him to repeat all the details on the very spot; and then they would try to cheer him by saying, "Well, Master Marner, you're no worse off nor other poor folks, after all; and if you was to be crippled, the parish 'ud give you a 'lowance."

I suppose one reason why we are seldom able to comfort our neighbors with our words is that our goodwill gets adulterated, in spite of ourselves, before it can pass our lips. We can send black puddings and pettitoes, without giving them a flavor of our own egoism; but language is a stream that is almost sure to smack of a mingled soil. There was a fair proportion of kindness in Raveloe; but it was often of a beery and bungling sort, and took the shape least allied to the complimentary and hypocritical.

Mr. Macey, for example, coming one evening, expressly to let Silas know that recent events had given him the advantage of standing more favorably in the opinion of a man whose judgment was not formed lightly, opened the conversation by saying, as soon as he had seated himself and adjusted his thumbs:

"Come, Master Marner, why, you've no call to sit a-moaning. You're a deal better off to ha' lost your money, nor to ha' kep' it by foul means. I used to think, when you first come into these parts, as you were no better nor you should be; you were younger a deal than what you are now; but you were allays a staring, white-faced creatur, partly like a bald-faced calf, as I may say. But there's no knowing: it isn't every queer-looked thing as Old Harry's had the making of —I mean, speaking o' toads and such; for they're often harmless, and useful against varmin. And it's pretty much the same wi' you, as fur as I can see. Though as to the yarbs and stuff to cure the breathing, if you brought that sort o' knowledge from distant parts, you might ha' been a bit freer of it. And if the knowledge wasn't well come by, why, you might ha' made up for it by your coming to church reg'lar; for as for the children as the Wise Woman charmed, I've been at the christening of 'em again and again, and they took the water just as well. And that's reasonable; for if Old Harry's a mind to do a bit o' kindness for a holiday, like, who's got anything against it? That's my thinking; and I've been clerk o' this parish forty year, and I know, when the parson and me does the cussing of a Ash Wednesday, there's no cussing o' folks as have a mind to be cured without a doctor, let Kimble say what he will. And so, Master Marner, as I was saying— for there's windings i' things as they may carry you to the fur end o' the prayer-book afore you get back to 'em—my advice is, as you keep up your sperrits; for as for thinking you're a deep un, and ha' got more inside you nor 'ull bear daylight, I'm not o' that opinion at all, and so I tell the neighbors. For, says I, you talk o' Master Marner making out a tale—why, it's nonsense, that is: it 'ud take a 'cute man to make a tale like that; and, says I, he looked as scared as a rabbit."

During this discursive address Silas had continued motionless in his previous attitude, leaning his elbows on his knees, and pressing his hands against his head. Mr. Macey, not doubting that he had been listened to, paused, in the expectation of some appreciatory reply, but Marner remained silent. He had a sense that the old man meant to be good-natured and neighborly; but the kindness fell on him as sunshine falls on the wretched—he had no heart to taste it, and felt that it was very far off him.

"Come, Master Marner, have you got nothing to say to that?" said Mr. Macey at last, with a slight accent of impatience.

"Oh," said Marner, slowly, shaking his head between his hands, "I thank you—thank you—kindly."

"Ay, ay, to be sure: I thought you would," said Mr. Macey; "and my advice is—have you got a Sunday suit?"

"No," said Marner.

"I doubted it was so," said Mr. Macey. "Now, let me advise you to get a Sunday suit: there's Tookey, he's a poor creatur, but he's got my tailoring business, and some o' my money in it, and he shall make a suit at a low price, and give you trust, and then you can come to church and be a bit neighborly. Why, you've never heard me say 'Amen' since you come into these parts, and I recommend you to lose no time, for it'll be poor work when Tookey has it all to himself, for I mayn't be equil to stand i' the desk at all, come another winter."

Here Mr. Macey paused, perhaps expecting some sign of emotion in his hearer; but not observing any, he went on. "And as for the money for the suit o' clothes, why, you get the matter of a pound a-week at your weaving, Master Marner, and you're a young man, eh, for all you look so mushed. Why, you couldn't ha' been five-and-twenty when you come into these parts, eh?"

Silas started a little at the change to a questioning tone, and answered mildly, "I don't know; I can't rightly say—it's a long while since."

After receiving such an answer as this, it is not surprising that Mr. Macey observed, later on in the evening at the Rainbow, that Marner's head was "all of a muddle," and that it was to be doubted if he ever knew when Sunday came round, which showed him a worse heathen than many a dog.

Another of Silas's comforters, besides Mr. Macey,

came to him with a mind highly charged on the same topic. This was Mrs. Winthrop, the wheelwright's wife. The inhabitants of Raveloe were not severely regular in their church-going, and perhaps there was hardly a person in the parish who would not have held that to go to church every Sunday in the calendar would have shown a greedy desire to stand well with Heaven, and get an undue advantage over their neighbors—a wish to be better than the "common run," that would have implied a reflection on those who had had godfathers and godmothers as well as themselves, and had an equal right to the burying-service. At the same time it was understood to be requisite for all who were not household servants, or young men, to take the sacrament at one of the great festivals: Squire Cass himself took it on Christmas-day; while those who were held to be "good-livers" went to church with greater, though still with moderate, frequency.

Mrs. Winthrop was one of these: she was in all respects a woman of scrupulous conscience, so eager for duties that life seemed to offer them too scantily unless she rose at half-past four, though this threw a scarcity of work over the more advanced hours of the morning, which it was a constant problem with her to remove. Yet she had not the vixenish temper which is sometimes supposed to be a necessary condition of such habits; she was a very mild, patient woman, whose nature it was to seek out all the sadder and more serious elements of life, and pasture her mind upon them. She was the person always first thought of in Raveloe when there was illness or death in the family, when leeches were to be applied, or there was a sudden disappointment in a monthly nurse. She was a "comfortable woman"—good-looking, fresh-complexioned, having her lips always slightly screwed, as if she felt herself in a sick-room with a doctor or the clergyman present. But she was never whimpering; no one had seen her shed tears; she was simply grave and inclined to shake her head and sigh, almost imperceptibly, like a funereal mourner who is not a relation.

It seemed surprising that Ben Winthrop, who loved his quart-pot and his joke, got along so well with Dolly; but she took her husband's jokes and joviality as patiently as everything else, considering that "men *would* be so," and viewing the stronger sex in the light of animals whom it had pleased Heaven to make naturally troublesome, like bulls and turkey-cocks.

This good, wholesome woman could hardly fail to have her mind drawn strongly towards Silas Marner, now that he appeared in the light of a sufferer; and one Sunday afternoon she took her little boy Aaron with her, and went to call on Silas, carrying in her hand some small lard-cakes, flat, paste-like articles much esteemed in Raveloe. Aaron, an apple-cheeked youngster of seven, with a clean, starched frill which looked like a plate for the apples, needed all his adventurous curiosity to embolden him against the possibility that the big-eyed weaver might do him some bodily injury; and his dubiety was much increased when, on arriving at the Stone-pits, they heard the mysterious sound of the loom.

"Ah, it is as I thought," said Mrs. Winthrop, sadly.

They had to knock loudly before Silas heard them; but when he did come to the door he showed no impatience, as he would once have done, at a visit that had been unasked for and unexpected. Formerly his heart had been as a locked casket with its treasure inside: but now the casket was empty, and the lock was broken. Left groping in darkness, with his prop utterly gone, Silas had inevitably a sense, though a dull and half-despairing one, that if any help came to him it must come from without; and there was a slight stirring of expectation at the sight of his fellow-men, a faint consciousness of dependence on their good will. He opened the door wide to admit Dolly, but without otherwise returning her greeting than by moving the arm-chair a few inches as a sign that she was to sit down in it. Dolly, as soon as she was seated, removed the white cloth that covered her lard-cakes, and said in her gravest way:

"I'd a baking yesterday, Master Marner, and the lard-cakes turned out better nor common, and I'd ha' asked you to accept some, if you'd thought well. I don't eat such things myself, for a bit o' bread's what I like one year's end to the other; but men's stomichs are made so comical, they want a change—they do, I know, God help 'em."

Dolly sighed gently as she held out the cakes to Silas, who thanked her kindly and looked very close at them, absently, being accustomed to look so at everything he took into his hand—eyed all the while by the wondering bright orbs of the small Aaron, who had made an outwork of his mother's chair, and was peeping from behind it.

"There's letters pricked on 'em," said Dolly. "I can't read 'em myself, and there's nobody, not Mr. Macey himself, rightly knows what they mean; but they've a good meaning, for they're the same as is on the pulpit cloth at church. What are they, Aaron, my dear?"

Aaron retreated completely behind his outwork.

"Oh, go, that's naughty," said his mother, mildly. "Well, whativer the letters are, they've a good meaning; and it's a stamp as has been in our house, Ben says, ever since he was a little un, and his mother used to put it on the cakes, and I've allays put it on too; for if there's any good we've need of it i' this world."

"It's I. H. S.," said Silas, at which proof of learning Aaron peeped round the chair again.

"Well, to be sure, you can read 'em off," said Dolly. "Ben's read 'em to me many and many a time, but they slip out o' my mind again; the more's the pity, for they're good letters, else they wouldn't be in the church; and so I prick 'em on all the loaves and all the cakes, though sometimes they won't hold because o' the rising—for, as I said, if there's any good to be got we've need of it i' this world—that we have; and I hope they'll bring good to you, Master Marner, for it's wi' that will I brought you the cakes; and you see the letters have held better nor common."

Silas was as unable to interpret the letters as Dolly, but there was no possibility of misunderstanding the desire to give comfort that made itself heard in her quiet tones. He said, with more feeling than before—"Thank you—thank you kindly." But he laid down the cakes and seated himself absently—drearily unconscious of any distinct benefit towards which the cakes and the letters, or even Dolly's kindness, could tend for him.

"Ah, if there's good anywhere, we've need of it," repeated Dolly, who did not lightly forsake a serviceable phrase. She looked at Silas pityingly as she went on.

"But you didn't hear the church-bells this morning, Master Marner? I doubt you didn't know it was Sunday. Living so lone here, you lose your count, I daresay; and then when your loom makes a noise, you can't hear the bells, more partic'lar now, the frost kills the sound."

"Yes, I did; I heard 'em," said Silas, to whom Sunday bells were a mere accident of the day, and not part of its sacredness. There had been no bells in Lantern Yard.

"Dear heart!" said Dolly, pausing before she spoke again. "But what a pity it is you should work of a Sunday, and not clean yourself—if you *didn't* go to church; for if you'd a roasting bit, it might be as you couldn't leave it, being a lone man. But there's the bakehus, if you could make up your mind to spend a twopence on the oven now and then—not every week, in course—I shouldn't like to do that myself—you might carry your bit o' dinner there, for it's nothing but right to have a bit o' summat hot of a Sunday, and not to make it as you can't know your dinner from Saturday. But now, upo' Christmas Day, this blessed Christmas as is ever coming, if you was to take your dinner to the bakehus, and go to church, and see the holly and the yew, and hear the anthim, and then take the sacramen', you'd be a deal the better, and you'd know which end you stood on, and you could put your trust i' Them as knows better nor we do, seein' you'd ha' done what it lies on us all to do."

Dolly's exhortation, which was an unusually long effort of speech for her, was uttered in the soothing persuasive tone with which she would have tried to prevail on a sick man to take his medicine, or a basin of gruel for which he had no appetite. Silas had never before been closely urged on the point of his absence from church, which had only been thought of as a part of his general queerness; and he was too direct and simple to evade Dolly's appeal.

"Nay, nay," he said, "I know nothing o' church. I've never been to church."

"No!" said Dolly, in a low tone of wonderment. Then, bethinking herself of Silas's advent from an unknown country, she said, "Could it ha' been as they'd no church where you was born?"

"Oh, yes," said Silas, meditatively, sitting in his usual posture of leaning on his knees, and supporting his head. "There was churches—a many—it was a big town. But I knew nothing of 'em—I went to chapel."

Dolly was much puzzled at this new word, but she was rather afraid of inquiring further, lest "chapel" might mean some haunt of wickedness. After a little thought, she said:

"Well, Master Marner, it's niver too late to turn over a new leaf, and if you've niver had no church, there's no telling the good it'll do you. For I feel so set up and comfortable as niver was, when I've been and heard the prayers, and the singing to the praise and glory o' God, as Mr. Macey gives out— and Mr. Crackenthorp saying good words, and more partic'lar on Sacramen' Day; and if a bit o' trouble comes, I feel as I can put up wi' it, for I've looked for help i' the right quarter, and gev myself up to Them as we must all give ourselves up to at the last; and if we'n done our part, it isn't to be believed as Them as are above us 'ull be worse nor we are, and come short o' Their'n."

Poor Dolly's exposition of her simple Raveloe theology fell rather unmeaningly on Silas's ears, for there was no word in it that could rouse a memory of what he had known as religion, and his comprehension was quite baffled by the plural pronoun, which was no heresy of Dolly's, but only her way of avoiding a presumptuous familiarity. He remained silent, not feeling inclined to assent to the part of Dolly's speech which he fully understood—her recommendation that he should go to church. Indeed, Silas was so unaccustomed to talk beyond the brief questions and answers necessary for the transaction of his simple business, that words did not easily come to him without the urgency of a distinct purpose.

But now, little Aaron, having become used to the weaver's awful presence, had advanced to his mother's side, and Silas, seeming to notice him for the first time, tried to return Dolly's signs of good will by offering the lad a bit of lard-cake. Aaron shrank back a little, and rubbed his head against his mother's shoulder, but still thought the piece of cake worth the risk of putting his hand out for it.

"Oh, for shame, Aaron," said his mother, taking him on her lap, however; "why, you don't want cake again yet awhile. He's wonderful hearty," she went on with a little sigh—"that he is, God knows. He's my youngest, and we spoil him sadly, for either me or the father must allays hev him in our sight—that we must." She stroked Aaron's brown head, and thought it must do Master Marner good to see such a "pictur of a child." But Marner, on the other side of the hearth, saw the neat-featured, rosy face as a mere dim round, with two dark spots in it.

"And he's got a voice like a bird—you wouldn't think," Dolly went on; "he can sing a Christmas carril as his father's taught him; and I take it for a token as he'll come to good, as he can learn the good tunes so quick. Come, Aaron, stan' up and sing the carril to Master Marner; come."

Aaron replied by rubbing his forehead against his mother's shoulder.

"Oh, that's naughty," said Dolly, gently. "Stan' up, when mother tells you, and let me hold the cake till you've done."

Aaron was not indisposed to display his talents, even to an ogre, under protecting circumstances; and after a few more signs of coyness, consisting chiefly in rubbing the backs of his hands over his eyes, and then peeping between them at Master Marner, to see if he looked anxious for the "carril," he at length allowed his head to be duly adjusted, and standing behind the table, which let him appear above it only as far as his broad frill, so that he looked like a cherubic head untroubled with a body, he began with a clear chirp, and in a melody that had the rhythm of an industrious hammer:

> "God rest you, merry gentlemen,
>   Let nothing you dismay,
> For Jesus Christ our Saviour,
>   Was born on Christmas day."

Dolly listened with a devout look, glancing at Marner in some confidence that this strain would help to allure him to church.

"That's Christmas music," she said, when Aaron had ended, and had secured his piece of cake again. "There's no other music equil to the Christmas music—'Hark the erol angels sing.' And you may judge what it is at church, Master Marner, with the bassoon and the voices, as you can't help thinking you've got to a better place a'ready—for I wouldn't speak ill o' this world, seeing as Them put us in it as knows best— but what wi' the drink, and the quarreling, and the bad illnesses, and the hard dying, as I've seen times and times, one's thankful to hear of a better. The boy sings pretty, don't he, Master Marner?"

"Yes," said Silas, absently, "very pretty."

The Christmas carol, with its hammer-like rhythm, had fallen on his ears as strange music, quite unlike a hymn, and could have none of the effect Dolly contemplated. But he wanted to show her that he was grateful, and the only mode that occurred to him was to offer Aaron a bit more cake.

"Oh, no, thank you, Master Marner," said Dolly, holding down Aaron's willing hands. "We must be going home now. And so I wish you good-bye, Master Marner; and if you ever feel anyways bad in your inside, as you can't fend for yourself, I'll come and clean up for you, and get you a bit o' victual, and willing. But I beg and pray of you to leave off weaving of a Sunday, for it's bad for soul and body—and the money as comes i' that way 'ull be a bad bed to lie down on at the last, if it doesn't fly away, nobody knows where, like the white frost. And you'll excuse me being that free with you, Master Marner, for I wish you well—I do. Make your bow, Aaron."

Silas said "Good-bye, and thank you kindly," as he opened the door for Dolly, but he couldn't help feeling relieved when she was gone—relieved that he might weave again and moan at his ease. Her simple view of life and its comforts, by which she had tried to cheer him, was only like a report of unknown objects, which his imagination could not fashion. The fountains of human love and of faith in a divine love had not yet been unlocked, and his soul was still the shrunken rivulet, with only this difference, that its little groove of sand was blocked up, and it wandered confusedly against dark obstruction.

And so, notwithstanding the honest persuasions of Mr. Macey and Dolly Winthrop, Silas spent his Christmas day in loneliness, eating his meat in sadness of heart, though the meat had come to him as a neighborly present. In the morning he looked out on the black frost that seemed to press cruelly on every blade of grass, while the half-icy red pool shivered under the bitter wind: but towards evening the snow began to fall, and curtained from him even that dreary outlook, shutting him close up with his narrow grief. And he sat in his robbed home through the livelong evening, not caring to close his shutters or lock his door, pressing his head between his hands and moaning, till the cold grasped him and told him that his fire was gray.

Nobody in this world but himself knew that he was the same Silas Marner who had once loved his fellow with tender love, and trusted an unseen goodness. Even to himself that past experience had become dim.

But in Raveloe village the bells rang merrily, and the church was fuller than all through the rest of the year, with red faces among the abundant dark-green boughs—faces prepared for a longer service than usual by an odorous breakfast of toast and ale. Those green boughs, the hymn and anthem never heard but at Christmas—even the Athanasian Creed, which was discriminated from the others only as being longer and of exceptional virtue, since it was only read on rare occasions—brought a vague exulting sense, for which the grown men could as little have found words as the children, that something great and mysterious had been done for them in heaven above and in earth below, which they were appropriating by their presence. And then the red faces made their way through the black, biting frost to their own homes, feeling themselves free for the rest of the day to eat, drink, and be merry, and using that Christian freedom without diffidence.

At Squire Cass's family party that day nobody mentioned Dunstan—nobody was sorry for his absence, or feared it would be too long. The doctor and his wife, uncle and aunt Kimble, were there, and the annual Christmas talk was carried through without any omissions, rising to the climax of Mr. Kimble's experience when he walked the London hospitals thirty years back, together with striking professional anecdotes then gathered. Whereupon cards followed, with aunt Kimble's annual failure to follow suit, and uncle Kimble's irascibility concerning the odd trick which was rarely explicable to him, when it was not on his side, without a general visitation of tricks to see that they were formed on sound principles: the whole being accompanied by a strong, steaming odor of spirits-and-water.

But the party on Christmas Day, being a strictly family party, was not the pre-eminently brilliant celebration of the season at the Red House. It was the great dance on New Year's Eve that made the glory of Squire Cass's hospitality, as of his forefathers', time out of mind. This was the occasion when all the society of Raveloe and Tarley, whether old acquaintances separated by long, rutty distances, or cooled acquaintances separated by misunderstandings concerning runaway calves, or acquaintances founded on intermittent condescension, counted on meeting and on comporting themselves with mutual appropriateness. This was the occasion on which fair dames who came on pillions sent their bandboxes before them, supplied with more than their evening costume; for the feast was not to end with a single evening, like a paltry town entertainment, where the whole supply of eatables is put on the table at once, and bedding is scanty. The Red House was provisioned as if for a siege; and as for the spare feather-beds ready to be laid on floors, they were as plentiful as might naturally be expected in a family that had killed its own geese for many generations.

Godfrey Cass was looking forward to this New Year's Eve with a foolish, reckless longing, that made him half deaf to his importunate companion, Anxiety.

"Dunsey will be coming home soon; there will be a

great blow-up, and how will you bribe his spite to silence?" said Anxiety.

"Oh, he won't come home before New Year's Eve, perhaps," said Godfrey; "and I shall sit by Nancy then, and dance with her, and get a kind look from her in spite of herself."

"But money is wanted in another quarter," said Anxiety, in a louder voice, "and how will you get it without selling your mother's diamond pin? And if you don't get it . . . ?"

"Well, but something may happen to make things easier. At any rate, there's one pleasure for me close at hand: Nancy is coming."

"Yes, and suppose your father should bring matters to a pass that will oblige you to decline marrying her —and to give your reasons?"

"Hold your tongue, and don't worry me. I can see Nancy's eyes, just as they will look at me, and feel her hand in mine already."

But Anxiety went on, though in noisy Christmas company; refusing to be utterly quieted even by much drinking.

CHAPTER XI

SOME WOMEN, I grant, would not appear to advantage seated on a pillion, and attired in a drab joseph and a drab beaver bonnet, with a crown resembling a small stew-pan; for a garment suggesting a coachman's great coat, cut out under an exiguity of cloth that would only allow of miniature capes is not well adapted to conceal deficiencies of contour, nor is drab a color that will throw sallow cheeks into lively contrast. It was all the greater triumph to Miss Nancy Lammeter's beauty that she looked thoroughly bewitching in that costume, as, seated on the pillion behind her tall, erect father, she held one arm round him, and looked down, with open-eyed anxiety, at the treacherous snow-covered pools and puddles, which sent up formidable splashings of mud under the stamp of Dobbin's foot.

A painter would, perhaps, have preferred her in those moments when she was free from self-consciousness; but certainly the bloom on her cheeks was at its highest point of contrast with the surrounding drab when she arrived at the door of the Red House, and saw Mr. Godfrey Cass ready to lift her from the pillion. She wished her sister Priscilla had come up at the same time behind the servant, for then she would have contrived that Mr. Godfrey should have lifted off Priscilla first, and, in the meantime, she would have persuaded her father to go round to the horse-block instead of alighting at the doorsteps.

It was very painful, when you had made it quite clear to a young man that you were determined not to marry him, however much he might wish it, that he would still continue to pay you marked attentions; besides, why didn't he always show the same attentions, if he meant them sincerely, instead of being so strange as Mr. Godfrey Cass was, sometimes behaving as if he didn't want to speak to her, and taking no notice of her for weeks and weeks, and then, all on a sudden, almost making love again? Moreover it was quite plain he had no real love for her, else he would not let people have *that* to say of him which they did say. Did he suppose that Miss Nancy Lammeter was to be won by any man, squire or no squire, who led a bad life? That was not what she had been used to see in her own father, who was the soberest and best man in that country-side, only a little hot and hasty now and then, if things were not done to the minute.

All these thoughts rushed through Miss Nancy's mind, in their habitual succession, in the moments between her first sight of Mr. Godfrey Cass standing at the door and her own arrival there. Happily, the Squire came out, too, and gave a loud greeting to her father, so that, somehow, under cover of this noise she seemed to find concealment for her confusion and neglect of any suitably formal behavior, while she was being lifted from the pillion by strong arms which seemed to find her ridiculously small and light. And there was the best reason for hastening into the house at once, since the snow was beginning to fall again, threatening an unpleasant journey for such guests as were still on the road. These were a small minority; for already the afternoon was beginning to decline, and there would not be too much time for the ladies who came from a distance to attire themselves in readiness for the early tea which was to inspirit them for the dance.

There was a buzz of voices through the house, as Miss Nancy entered, mingled with the scrape of a fiddle preluding in the kitchen; but the Lammeters were guests whose arrival had evidently been thought of so much that it had been watched for from the windows, for Mrs. Kimble, who did the honors at the Red House on these great occasions, came forward to meet Miss Nancy in the hall, and conduct her upstairs. Mrs. Kimble was the Squire's sister, as well as the doctor's wife—a double dignity, with which her diameter was in direct proportion; so that, a journey upstairs, being rather fatiguing to her, she did not oppose Miss Nancy's request to be allowed to find her way alone to the Blue Room, where the Miss Lammeters' bandboxes had been deposited on their arrival in the morning.

There was hardly a bedroom in the house where feminine compliments were not passing and feminine toilettes going forward, in various stages, in space made scanty by extra beds spread upon the floor; and Miss Nancy, as she entered the Blue Room, had to make her little formal curtsy to a group of six. On the one hand, there were ladies no less important than the two Miss Gunns, the wine merchant's daughters from Lytherly, dressed in the height of fashion, with the tightest skirts and the shortest waists, and gazed at by Miss Ladbrook (of the Old Pastures) with a shyness not unsustained by inward criticism. Partly, Miss Ladbrook felt that her own skirt must be regarded as unduly lax by the Miss Gunns, and partly, that it was a pity the Miss Gunns did not show that judgment which she herself would show if she were in their place, by stopping a little on this side of the fashion. On the other hand, Mrs. Ladbrook was standing in skull-cap and front, with her turban in her hand, curtsying and smiling blandly and saying, "After you ma'am," to another lady in similiar circumstances, who had politely offered the precedence at the looking-glass.

But Miss Nancy had no sooner made her curtsy than an elderly lady came forward, whose full white muslin kerchief, and mob-cap round her curls of smooth gray hair, were in daring contrast with the puffed yellow satins and top-knotted caps of her neighbors. She approached Miss Nancy with much primness, and said, with a slow, treble suavity:

"Niece, I hope I see you well in health."

Miss Nancy kissed her aunt's cheek dutifully, and answered, with the same sort of amiable primness, "Quite well, I thank you, aunt; and I hope I see you the same."

"Thank you, niece; I keep my health for the present. And how is my brother-in-law?"

These dutiful questions and answers were continued until it was ascertained in detail that the Lammeters were all as well as usual, and the Osgoods likewise, also that niece Priscilla must certainly arrive shortly, and that travelling on pillions in snowy weather was unpleasant, though a joseph was a great protection. Then Nancy was formally introduced to her aunt's visitors, the Miss Gunns, as being the daughter of a mother known to *their* mother, though now for the first time induced to make a journey into these parts; and these ladies were so taken by surprise at finding such a lovely face and figure in an out-of-the-way country place, that they began to feel some curiosity about the dress she would put on when she took off her joseph.

Miss Nancy, whose thoughts were always conducted with the propriety and moderation conspicuous in her manners, remarked to herself that the Miss Gunns were rather hard-featured than otherwise, and that such very low dresses as they wore might have been attributed to vanity if their shoulders had been pretty, but that, being as they were it was not reasonable to suppose that they showed their necks from a love of display, but rather from some obligation not inconsistent with sense and modesty. She felt convinced, as she opened her box, that this must be her aunt Osgood's opinion, for Miss Nancy's mind resembled her aunt's to a degree that everybody said was surprising, considering the kinship was on Mr. Osgood's side; and though you might not have supposed it from the formality of their greeting, there was a devoted attachment and mutual admiration between aunt and niece. Even Miss Nancy's refusal of her cousin Gilbert Osgood (on the ground solely that he was her cousin), though it had grieved her aunt greatly, had not in the least cooled the preference which had determined her to leave Nancy several of her hereditary ornaments, let Gilbert's future wife be whom she might.

Three of the ladies quickly retired, but the Miss Gunns were quite content that Mrs. Osgood's inclination to remain with her niece gave them also a reason for staying to see the rustic beauty's toilette. And it was really a pleasure—from the first opening of the bandbox, where everything smelt of lavender and rose-leaves, to the clasping of the small coral necklace that fitted closely round her little white neck.

Everything belonging to Miss Nancy was of delicate purity and nattiness: not a crease was where it had no business to be, not a bit of her linen professed whiteness without fulfilling its profession; the very pins on her pincushion were stuck in after a pattern from which she was careful to allow no aberration; and as for her own person, it gave the same idea of perfect, unvarying neatness as the body of a little bird.

It is true that her light-brown hair was cropped behind like a boy's, and was dressed in front in a number of flat rings, that lay quite away from her face; but there was no sort of coiffure that could make Miss Nancy's cheek and neck look otherwise than pretty; and when at last she stood complete in her silvery twilled silk, her lace tucker, her coral necklace, and coral ear-drops, the Miss Gunns could see nothing to criticise except her hands, which bore the traces of butter-making, cheese-crushing, and even still coarser work. But Miss Nancy was not ashamed of that, for while she was dressing she narrated to her aunt how she and Priscilla had packed their boxes yesterday, because this morning was baking morning, and since they were leaving home, it was desirable to make a good supply of meat-pies for the kitchen; and as she concluded this judicious remark, she turned to the Miss Gunns that she might not commit the rudeness of not including them in the conversation.

The Miss Gunns smiled stiffly, and thought what a pity it was that these rich country people, who could afford to buy such good clothes (really Miss Nancy's lace and silk were very costly), should be brought up in utter ignorance and vulgarity. She actually said "mate" for "meat," " 'appen" for "perhaps," and "oss" for "horse," which, to young ladies living in good Lytherly society, who habitually said 'orse, even in domestic privacy, and only said 'appen on the right occasions, was necessarily shocking.

Miss Nancy, indeed, had never been to any school higher than Dame Tedman's; her acquaintance with profane literature hardly went beyond the rhymes she had worked in her large sampler under the lamb and the shepherdess; and in order to balance an account, she was obliged to effect her subtraction by removing visible metallic shillings and sixpences from a visible metallic total.

There is hardly a servant-maid in these days who is not better informed than Miss Nancy; yet she had the essential attributes of a lady—high veracity, delicate honor in her dealings, deference to others and refined personal habits—and lest these should not suffice to convince grammatical fair ones that her feelings can at all resemble theirs, I will add that she was slightly proud and exacting, and as constant in her affection towards a baseless opinion as towards an erring lover.

The anxiety about sister Priscilla, which had grown rather active by the time the coral necklace was clasped, was happily ended by the entrance of that cheerful-looking lady herself, with a face made blowsy by cold and damp. After the first questions and greetings, she turned to Nancy, and surveyed her from head to foot—then wheeled her round, to ascertain that the back view was equally faultless.

"What do you think o' *these* gowns, aunt Osgood?" said Priscilla, while Nancy helped her to unrobe.

"Very handsome indeed, niece," said Mrs. Osgood, with a slight increase of formality. She always thought niece Priscilla too rough.

"I'm obliged to have the same as Nancy, you know, for all I'm five years older, and it makes me look yellow; for she never *will* have anything without I have mine just like it, because she wants us to look like sisters. And I tell her, folks 'ull think it's my weakness makes my fancy as I shall look pretty in what she looks pretty in. For I *am* ugly—there's no denying that; I feature my father's family. But law! I don't mind, do you?" Priscilla here turned to the Miss Gunns, rattling on in too much preoccupation with the delight of talking, to notice that her candor was not appreciated. "The pretty uns do for fly-catchers—they keep the men off us. I've no opinion o' the men, Miss Gunn—I don't know what *you* have. And as for fretting and stewing about what *they*'ll think of you from morning till night, and making your life uneasy about what they're doing when they're out o' your sight—as I tell Nancy, it's a folly no woman need be guilty of, if she's got a good father and a good home;

let her leave it to them as have got no fortin, and can't help themselves. As I say, Mr. Have-your-own-way is the best husband, and the only one I'd ever promise to obey. I know it isn't pleasant, when you've been used to living in a big way, and managing hogsheads and all that, to go and put your nose in by somebody else's fireside, or to sit down by yourself to a scrag or a knuckle; but, thank God! my father's a sober man and likely to live; and if you've got a man by the chimney-corner, it doesn't matter if he's childish—the business needn't be broke up."

The delicate process of getting her narrow gown over her head without injury to her smooth curls, obliged Miss Priscilla to pause in this rapid survey of life, and Mrs. Osgood seized the opportunity of rising and saying:

"Well, niece, you'll follow us. The Miss Gunns will like to go down."

"Sister," said Nancy, when they were alone, "you've offended the Miss Gunns, I'm sure."

"What have I done, child?" said Priscilla, in some alarm.

"Why, you asked them if they minded about being ugly—you're so very blunt."

"Law, did I? Well it popped out: it's a mercy I said no more, for I'm a bad un to live with folks when they don't like the truth. But as for being ugly, look at me, child, in this silver-colored silk—I told you how it 'ud be—I look as yallow as a daffodil. Anybody 'ud say you wanted to make a mawkin of me."

"No, Priscy, don't say so. I begged and prayed of you not to let us have this silk if you'd like another better. I was willing to have *your* choice, you know I was," said Nancy, in anxious self-vindication.

"Nonsense, child! you know you'd set your heart

on this; and reason good, for you're the color o' cream. It 'ud be fine doings for you to dress yourself to suit *my* skin. What I find fault with, is that notion 'o yours as I must dress myself just like you. But you do as you like with me—you always did, from when first you begun to walk. If you wanted to go the field's length, the field's length you'd go; and there was no whipping you, for you looked as prim and innicent as a daisy all the while."

"Priscy," said Nancy, gently, as she fastened a coral necklace, exactly like her own, round Priscilla's neck, which was very far from being like her own, "I'm sure I'm willing to give way as far as is right, but who shouldn't dress alike if it isn't sisters? Would you have us go about looking as if we were no kin to one another—us that have got no mother and not another sister in the world? I'd do what was right, if I dressed in a gown dyed with cheese coloring; and I'd rather you'd choose, and let me wear what pleases you."

"There you go again! You'd come round to the same thing if one talked to you from Saturday night till Saturday morning. It'll be fine fun to see how you'll master your husband and never raise your voice above the singing o' the kettle all the while. I like to see the men mastered!"

"Don't talk *so*, Priscy," said Nancy, blushing. "You know I don't mean ever to be married."

"Oh, you never mean a fiddlestick's end!" said Priscilla, as she arranged her discarded dress, and closed her bandbox. "Who shall *I* have to work for when father's gone, if you are to go and take notions in your head and be an old maid, because some folks are no better than they should be? I haven't a bit o' patience with you—sitting on an addled egg forever, as if there was never a fresh 'un in the world. One old maid's enough out o' two sisters; and I shall do credit to a single life, for God A'mighty meant me for it. Come, we can go down now. I'm as ready as a mawkin *can* be—there's nothing a-wanting to frighten the crows, now I've got my ear-droppers in."

As the two Miss Lammeters walked into the large parlor together, anyone who did not know the character of both might certainly have supposed that the reason why the square-shouldered, clumsy, high-featured Priscilla wore a dress the facsimile of her pretty sister's, was either the mistaken vanity of the one, or the malicious contrivance of the other in order to set off her own rare beauty. But the good-natured, self-forgetful cheeriness and common-sense of Priscilla would soon have dissipated the one suspicion; and the modest calm of Nancy's speech and manners told clearly of a mind free from all disavowed devices.

Places of honor had been kept for the Miss Lammeters near the head of the principal tea-table in the wainscoted parlor, now looking fresh and pleasant with handsome branches of holly, yew, and laurel, from the abundant growths of the old garden; and Nancy felt an inward flutter, that no firmness of purpose could prevent, when she saw Mr. Godfrey Cass advancing to lead her to a seat between himself and Mr. Crackenthorp, while Priscilla was called to the opposite side between her father and the Squire.

It certainly did make some difference to Nancy that the lover she had given up was the young man of quite the highest consequence in the parish—at home in a venerable and unique parlor, which was the extremity of grandeur in her experience, a parlor where *she* might one day have been mistress, with the consciousness that she was spoken of as "Madame Cass," the Squire's wife.

These circumstances exalted her inward drama in her own eyes, and deepened the emphasis with which she declared to herself that not the most dazzling rank should induce her to marry a man whose conduct showed him careless of his character, but that "love once, love always," was the motto of a true and pure woman, and no man should ever have any right over her which would be a call on her to destroy the dried flowers that she treasured, and always would treasure, for Godfrey Cass's sake. And Nancy was capable of keeping her word to herself under very trying conditions. Nothing but a becoming blush betrayed the moving thoughts that urged themselves upon her as she accepted the seat next to Mr. Crackenthorp; for she was so instinctively neat and adroit in all her actions, and her pretty lips met each other with such quiet firmness, that it would have been difficult for her to appear agitated.

It was not the Rector's practice to let a charming blush pass without an appropriate compliment. He was not in the least lofty or aristocratic, but simply a merry-eyed, small-featured, gray-haired man, with his chin propped by an ample, many-creased white neckcloth which seemed to predominate over every other point in his person, and somehow to impress its peculiar character on his remarks; so that to have considered his amenities apart from his cravat would have been a severe, and perhaps a dangerous, effort of abstraction.

"Ha, Miss Nancy," he said, turning his head within his cravat and smiling down pleasantly upon her, "when anybody pretends this has been a severe winter, I shall tell them I saw the roses blooming on New Year's Eve—eh, Godfrey, what do *you* say?"

Godfrey made no reply, and avoided looking at Nancy very markedly; for though these complimentary personalities were held to be in excellent taste in old-fashioned Raveloe society, reverent love has a politeness of its own which it teaches to men otherwise of small schooling. But the Squire was rather impatient at Godfrey's showing himself a dull spark in this way. By this advanced hour of the day, the Squire was always in higher spirits than we have seen him in at the breakfast-table, and felt it quite pleasant to fulfil the hereditary duty of being noisily jovial and patronizing: the large silver snuff-box was in active service and was offered without fail to all neighbors from time to time, however often they might have declined the favor.

At present, the Squire had only given an express welcome to the heads of families as they appeared; but always as the evening deepened, his hospitality rayed out more widely, till he had tapped the youngest guests on the back and shown a peculiar fondness for their presence, in the full belief that they must feel their lives made happy by their belonging to a parish where there was such a hearty man as Squire Cass to invite them and wish them well. Even in this early stage of the jovial mood, it was natural that he should wish to supply his son's deficiencies by looking and speaking for him.

"Ay, ay," he began, offering his snuff-box to Mr. Lammeter, who, for the second time, bowed his head and waved his hand in stiff rejection of the offer, "us old fellows may wish ourselves young to-night, when we see the mistletoe-bough in the White Parlor. It's true, most things are gone back'ard in these last thirty years—the country's going down since the old king fell ill. But when I look at Miss Nancy here, I begin to think the lasses keep up their quality; ding me if I remember a sample to match her, not when I was a fine young fellow, and thought a deal about my pigtail. No offence to you, madam," he added, bending to Mrs. Crackenthorp, who sat by him, "I didn't know *you* when you were as young as Miss Nancy here."

Mrs. Crackenthorp—a small, blinking woman, who fidgeted incessantly with her lace, ribbons, and gold chain, turning her head about and making subdued noises, very much like a guinea-pig that twitches its nose and soliloquizes in all company indiscriminately —now blinked and fidgeted towards the Squire, and said, "Oh, no—no offence."

This emphatic compliment of the Squire's to Nancy was felt by others besides Godfrey to have a diplomatic significance; and her father gave a slight additional erectness to his back, as he looked across the table at her with complacent gravity. That grave and orderly senior was not going to bate a jot of his dignity by seeming elated at the notion of a match between his family and the Squire's; he was gratified by any honor paid to his daughter; but he must see an alteration in several ways before his consent would be vouchsafed. His spare but healthy person, and high-featured, firm face, that looked as if it had never been flushed by excess, was in strong contrast, not only with the Squire's, but with the appearance of the Raveloe farmers generally—in accordance with a favorite saying of his own, that "breed was stronger than pasture."

"Miss Nancy's wonderful like what her mother was, though; isn't she, Kimble?" said the stout lady of that name, looking round for her husband.

But Dr. Kimble (country apothecaries in old days enjoyed that title without authority of diploma), being a thin and agile man, was flitting about the room with his hands in his pockets, making himself agreeable to his feminine patients, with medical impartiality, and being welcomed everywhere as a doctor by hereditary right—not one of those miserable apothecaries who canvass for practice in strange neighborhoods, and spend all their income in starving their one horse, but a man of substance, able to keep an extravagant table like the best of his patients. Time out of mind the Raveloe doctor had been a Kimble; Kimble was inherently a doctor's name; and it was difficult to contemplate firmly the melancholy fact that the actual Kimble had no son, so that his practice might one day be handed over to a successor with the incongruous name of Taylor or Johnson. But in that case the wiser people in Raveloe would employ Dr. Blick of Flitton —as less unnatural.

"Did you speak to me, my dear?" said the authentic doctor, coming quickly to his wife's side; but, as if foreseeing that she would be too much out of breath to repeat her remark, he went on immediately—"Ha, Miss Priscilla, the sight of you revives the taste of that super-excellent pork-pie. I hope the batch isn't near an end."

"Yes, indeed, it is, doctor," said Priscilla; "but I'll answer for it the next shall be as good. My pork-pies don't turn out well by chance."

"Not as your doctoring does, eh, Kimble!—because folks forget to take your physic, eh?" said the Squire, who regarded physic and doctors as many loyal churchmen regard the church and the clergy—tasting a joke against them when he was in health, but impatiently eager for their aid when anything was the matter with him. He tapped his box, and looked round with a triumphant laugh.

"Ah, she has a quick wit, my friend Priscilla has," said the doctor, choosing to attribute the epigram to a lady rather than allow a brother-in-law that advantage over him. "She saves a little pepper to sprinkle over her talk—that's the reason why she never puts too much into her pies. There's my wife, now, she never has an answer at her tongue's end; but if I offend her, she's sure to scarify my throat with black pepper the next day, or else give me the colic with watery greens. That's an awful tit-for-tat." Here the vivacious doctor made a pathetic grimace.

"Did you ever hear the like?" said Mrs. Kimble, laughing above her double chin with much good-humor, aside to Mrs. Crackenthorp, who blinked and nodded, and amiably intended to smile, but the intention lost itself in small twitchings and noises.

"I suppose that's the sort of tit-for-tat adopted in your profession, Kimble, if you've a grudge against a patient," said the rector.

"Never do have a grudge against our patients," said Mr. Kimble, "except when they leave us: and then, you see, we haven't the chance of prescribing for 'em. Ha, Miss Nancy," he continued, suddenly skipping to Nancy's side, "you won't forget your promise? You're to save a dance for me, you know."

"Come, come, Kimble, don't you be too for'ard," said the Squire. "Give the young uns fair-play. There's my son Godfrey'll be wanting to have a round with you if you run off with Miss Nancy. He's bespoke her for the first dance, I'll be bound. Eh, sir! what do you say?" he continued, throwing himself backward, and looking at Godfrey. "Haven't you asked Miss Nancy to open the dance with you?"

Godfrey, sorely uncomfortable under this signifi-cant insistence about Nancy, and afraid to think where it would end by the time his father had set his usual hospitable example of drinking before and after supper, saw no course open but to turn to Nancy and say, with as little awkwardness as possible:

"No; I've not asked her yet, but I hope she'll consent—if somebody else hasn't been before me."

"No, I've not engaged myself," said Nancy, quietly, though blushingly. (If Mr. Godfrey founded any hopes on her consenting to dance with him, he would soon be undeceived; but there was no need for her to be uncivil.)

"Then I hope you've no objections to dancing with me," said Godfrey, beginning to lose the sense that there was anything uncomfortable in this arrangement

"No, no objections," said Nancy, in a cold tone.

"Ah, well, you're a lucky fellow, Godfrey," said uncle Kimble; "but you're my godson, so I won't stand in your way. Else I'm not so very old, eh, my dear?" he went on, skipping to his wife's side again. "You wouldn't mind my having a second after you were gone—not if I cried a good deal first?"

"Come, come, take a cup o' tea and stop your tongue, do," said good-humored Mrs. Kimble, feeling some pride in a husband who must be regarded as so clever and amusing by the company generally. If he had only not been irritable at cards!

While safe, well-tested personalities were enlivening the tea in this way, the sound of the fiddle approaching within a distance at which it could be heard distinctly, made the young people look at each other with sympathetic impatience for the end of the meal.

"Why, there's Solomon in the hall," said the Squire, "and playing my fav'rite tune, I believe—'The flaxenheaded ploughboy'—he's for giving us a hint as we aren't enough in a hurry to hear him play. Bob," he called out to his third long-legged son, who was at the other end of the room, "open the door, and tell Solomon to come in. He shall give us a tune here."

Bob obeyed, and Solomon walked in, fiddling as he walked, for he would on no account break off in the middle of a tune.

"Here, Solomon," said the Squire, with loud patronage. "Round here, my man. Ah, I knew it was 'The flaxen-headed ploughboy': there's no finer tune."

Solomon Macey, a small, hale old man, with an abundant crop of long white hair reaching nearly to his shoulders, advanced to the indicated spot, bowing reverently while he fiddled, as much as to say that he respected the company though he respected the keynote more. As soon as he had repeated the tune and lowered his fiddle, he bowed again to the Squire and the Rector, and said, "I hope I see your honor and your reverence well, and wishing you health and long life and a happy New Year. And wishing the same to you, Mr. Lammeter, sir; and to the other gentlemen, and the madams, and the young lasses."

As Solomon uttered the last words, he bowed in all directions solicitously, lest he should be wanting in due respect. But thereupon he immediately began to prelude, and fell into the tune which he knew would be taken as a special compliment by Mr. Lammeter.

"Thank ye, Solomon, thank ye," said Mr. Lammeter when the fiddle paused again. "That's 'Over the hills and far away,' that is. My father used to say to me, whenever we heard that tune, 'Ah, lad, *I* came from over the hills and far away.' There's a many tunes I don't make head or tail of; but that speaks to me like the blackbird's whistle. I suppose it's the name: there's a deal in the name of a tune."

But Solomon was already impatient to prelude again, and presently broke with much spirit into "Sir Roger de Coverley," at which there was a sound of chairs pushed back, and laughing voices.

"Ay, ay, Solomon, we know what that means," said the Squire, rising. "It's time to begin the dance, eh? Lead the way, then, and we'll all follow you."

So Solomon, holding his white head on one side, and playing vigorously, marched forward at the head of the gay procession into the White Parlor, where the mistletoe-bough was hung, and multitudinous tallow candles made rather a brilliant effect, gleaming from among the berried holly-boughs, and reflected in the old-fashioned oval mirrors fastened in the panels of the white wainscot. A quaint procession! Old Solomon, in his seedy clothes and long white locks, seemed to be luring that decent company by the magic scream of his fiddle — luring discreet matrons in turban-shaped caps, nay, Mrs. Crackenthorp herself, the summit of whose perpendicular feather was on a level with the Squire's shoulder — luring fair lasses complacently conscious of very short waists and skirts blameless of front-folds—luring burly fathers in large variegated waistcoats, and ruddy sons, for the most part shy and sheepish, in short nether garments and very long coat-tails.

Already Mr. Macey and a few other privileged villagers, who were allowed to be spectators on these great occasions, were seated on benches placed for them near the door; and great was the admiration and satisfaction in that quarter when the couples had formed themselves for the dance, and the Squire led off with Mrs. Crackenthorp, joining hands with the Rector and Mrs. Osgood. That was as it should be— that was what everybody had been used to — and the charter of Raveloe seemed to be renewed by the ceremony.

It was not thought of as an unbecoming levity for the old and middle-aged people to dance a little before sitting down to cards, but rather as part of their social duties. For what were these if not to be merry at appropriate times, interchanging visits and poultry with due frequency, paying each other old-established compliments in sound traditional phrases, passing well-tried personal jokes, urging your guests to eat and drink too much out of hospitality, and eating and drinking too much in your neighbor's house to show that you liked your cheer? And the parson naturally set an example in these social duties. For it would not have been possible for the Raveloe mind, without a peculiar revelation, to know that a clergyman should be a pale-faced memento of solemnities, instead of a reasonably faulty man whose exclusive authority to read prayers and preach, to christen, marry, and bury you, necessarily coexisted with the right to sell you the ground to be buried in and to take tithe in kind; on which last point, of course, there was a little grumbling, but not to the extent of irreligion — not of deeper significance than the grumbling at the rain, which was by no means accompanied with a spirit of impious defiance, but with a desire that the prayer for fine weather might be read forthwith.

There was no reason, then, why the rector's dancing should not be received as part of the fitness of things quite as much as the Squire's, or why, on the other hand, Mr. Macey's official respect should restrain him from subjecting the parson's performance to that criticism with which minds of extraordinary acuteness must necessarily contemplate the doings of their fallible fellow-men.

"The Squire's pretty springy, considering his weight," said Mr. Macey, "and he stamps uncommon well. But Mr. Lammeter beats 'em all for shapes; you see he holds his head like a sodger, and he isn't so cushiony as most o' the oldish gentle folks—they run fat in general; and he's got a fine leg. The parson's nimble enough, but he hasn't got much of a leg: it's a bit too thick down'ard, and his knees might be a bit nearer wi'out damage; but he might do worse, he might do worse. Though he hasn't that grand way o' waving his hand as the Squire has."

"Talk o' nimbleness, look at Mrs. Osgood," said Ben Winthrop, who was holding his son Aaron between his knees. "She trips along with her little steps, so as nobody can see how she goes — it's like as if she had little wheels to her feet. She doesn't look a day older nor last year: she's the finest-made woman as is, let the next be where she will."

"I don't heed how the women are made," said Mr. Macey, with some contempt. "They wear nayther coat nor breeches: you can't make much out o' their shapes."

"Fayder," said Aaron, whose feet were busy beating out the tune, "how does that big cock's feather stick in Mrs. Crackenthorp's yead? Is there a little hole for it, like my shuttle-cock?"

"Hush, lad, hush; that's the way the ladies dress theirselves, that is," said the father, adding, however, in an undertone to Mr. Macey, "It does make her look funny, though — partly like a short-necked bottle wi' a long quill in it. Hey, by jingo, there's the young Squire leading off now, wi' Miss Nancy for partner! There's a lass for you! — like a pink-and-white posy —there's nobody 'ud think as anybody could be so pritty. I shouldn't wonder if she's Madam Cass some day, arter all — and nobody more rightfuller, for they'd make a fine match. You can find nothing against Master Godfrey's shapes, Macey, I'll bet a penny."

Mr. Macey screwed up his mouth, leaned his head further on one side, and twirled his thumbs with a presto movement as his eyes followed Godfrey up the dance. At last he summed up his opinion.

"Pretty well down'ard, but a bit too round i' the shoulderblades. And as for them coats as he gets from the Flitton tailor, they're a poor cut to pay double money for."

"Ah, Mr. Macey, you and me are two folks," said Ben, slightly indignant at this carping. "When I've got a pot o' good ale, I like to swaller it, and do my inside good, i'stead o' smelling and staring at it to see if I can't find faut wi' the brewing. I should like you to pick me out a finer-limbed young fellow nor Master Godfrey — one as 'ud knock you down easier, or's more pleasanter looksed when he's piert and merry."

"Tchuh!" said Mr. Macey, provoked to increased severity, "he isn't come to his right color yet: he's partly like a slack-bakcd pie. And I doubt he's got a soft place in his head, else why should he be turned round the finger by that offal Dunsey as nobody's seen o' late, and let him kill that fine hunting hoss as was the talk o' the country? And one while he was allays after Miss Nancy, and then it all went off again, like the smell o' hot porridge, as I may say. That wasn't my way when I went a-coorting."

"Ah, but mayhap Miss Nancy hung off like, and your lass didn't," said Ben.

"I should say she didn't," said Mr. Maccy, significantly. "Before I said 'sniff,' I took care to know as she'd say 'snaff,' and pretty quick too. I wasn't a-going to open my mouth, like a dog at a fly, and snap it again, wi' nothing to swaller."

"Well, I think Miss Nancy's coming round again," said Ben, "for Master Godfrey doesn't look so down-hearted to-night. And I see he's for taking her away to sit down, now they're at the end o' the dance: that looks like sweet-hearting, that does."

The reason why Godfrey and Nancy had left the dance was not so tender as Ben imagined. In the close press of couples a slight accident had happened to Nancy's dress, which, while it was short enough to show her neat ankle in front, was long enough behind to be caught under the stately stamp of the Squire's foot, so as to rend certain stitches at the waist, and cause much sisterly agitation in Priscilla's mind, as well as serious concern in Nancy's. One's thoughts may be much occupied with love-struggles, but hardly so as to be insensible to a disorder in the general framework of things.

Nancy had no sooner completed her duty in the figure they were dancing than she said to Godfrey, with a deep blush, that she must go and sit down till Priscilla could come to her; for the sisters had already exchanged a short whisper and an open-eyed glance full of meaning. No reason less urgent than this could have prevailed on Nancy to give Godfrey this opportunity of sitting apart with her. As for Godfrey, he was feeling so happy and oblivious under the long charm of the country dance with Nancy, that he got rather bold on the strength of her confusion, and was capable of leading her straight away, without leave asked, into the adjoining small parlor, where the card-tables were set.

"Oh, no, thank you," said Nancy, coldly, as soon as she perceived where he was going, "not in there. I'll wait here till Priscilla's ready to come to me. I'm sorry to bring you out of the dance and make myself trouble-some."

"Why, you'll be more comfortable here by your-self," said the artful Godfrey; "I'll leave you here till your sister can come." He spoke in an indifferent tone.

That was an agreeable proposition, and just what Nancy desired; why, then, was she a little hurt that Mr. Godfrey should make it? They entered, and she seated herself on a chair against one of the card tables, as the stiffest and most unapproachable position she could choose.

"Thank you, sir," she said immediately. "I needn't give you any more trouble. I'm sorry you've had such an unlucky partner."

"That's very ill-natured of you," said Godfrey, standing by her without any sign of intended depar-ture, "to be sorry you've danced with me."

"Oh, no, sir, I don't mean to say what's ill-natured at all," said Nancy, looking distractingly prim and pretty. "When gentlemen have so many pleasures, one dance can matter but very little."

"You know that isn't true. You know one dance with you matters more to me than all the other pleas-ures in the world."

It was a long, long while since Godfrey had said anything so direct as that, and Nancy was startled. But her instinctive dignity and repugnance to any show of emotion made her sit perfectly still, and only throw a little more decision into her voice, as she said:

"No, indeed, Mr. Godfrey, that's not known to me, and I have very good reasons for thinking different. But if it's true, I don't wish to hear it."

"Would you never forgive me, then, Nancy—never think well of me, let what would happen—would you never think the present made amends for the past? Not if I turned a good fellow, and gave up everything you didn't like?"

Godfrey was half conscious that this sudden opportunity of speaking to Nancy alone had driven him beside himself; but blind feeling had got the mastery of his tongue. Nancy really felt much agitated by the possibility Godfrey's words suggested, but this very pressure of emotion that she was in danger of finding too strong for her roused all her power of self command.

"I should be glad to see a good change in anybody, Mr. Godfrey," she answered, with the slightest discernible difference of tone, "but it 'ud be better if no change was wanted."

"You're very hard-hearted, Nancy," said Godfrey, pettishly. "You might encourage me to be a better fellow. I'm very miserable—but you've no feeling."

"I think those have the least feeling that act wrong to begin with," said Nancy, sending out a flash in spite of herself. Godfrey was delighted with that little flash, and would have liked to go on and make her quarrel with him; Nancy was so exasperatingly quiet and firm. But she was not indifferent to him *yet*.

The entrance of Priscilla, bustling forward and saying, "Dear heart alive, child, let us look at this gown," cut off Godfrey's hopes of a quarrel.

"I suppose I must go now," he said to Priscilla.

"It's no matter to me whether you go or stay," said that frank lady, searching for something in her pocket, with a preoccupied brow.

"Do *you* want me to go?" said Godfrey, looking at Nancy, who was now standing up by Priscilla's order.

"As you like," said Nancy, trying to recover all her former coldness, and looking down carefully at the hem of her gown.

"Then I like to stay," said Godfrey, with a reckless determination to get as much of this joy as he could to-night, and think nothing of the morrow.

CHAPTER XII

WHILE GODFREY CASS was taking draughts of forgetfulness from the sweet presence of Nancy, willingly losing all sense of that hidden bond which at other moments galled and fretted him so as to mingle irritation with the very sunshine, Godfrey's wife was walking with slow, uncertain steps through the snow-covered Raveloe lanes, carrying her child in her arms.

This journey on New Year's Eve was a premeditated act of vengeance which she had kept in her heart ever since Godfrey, in a fit of passion, had told her he would sooner die than acknowledge her as his wife. There would be a great party at the Red House on New Year's Eve, she knew: her husband would be smiling and smiled upon, hiding *her* existence in the darkest corner of his heart. But she would mar his pleasure: she would go in her dingy rags, with her faded face, once as handsome as the best, with her little child that had its father's hair and eyes, and disclose herself to the Squire as his eldest son's wife.

It is seldom that the miserable can help regarding their misery as a wrong inflicted by those who are less miserable. Molly knew that the cause of her dingy rags was not her husband's neglect, but the demon Opium to whom she was enslaved, body and soul, except in the lingering mother's tenderness that refused to give him her hungry child. She knew this well; and yet, in the moments of wretched unbenumbed consciousness, the sense of her want and degradation transformed itself continually into bitterness towards Godfrey. *He* was well off; and if she had her rights she would be well off, too. The belief that he repented his marriage, and suffered from it, only aggravated her vindictiveness. Just and self-reproving thoughts do not come to us too thickly, even in the purest air and with the best lessons of heaven and earth; how should those white-winged, delicate messengers make their way to Molly's poisoned chamber, inhabited by no higher memories than those of a barmaid's paradise of pink ribbons and gentlemen's jokes.

She had set out at an early hour, but had lingered on the road, inclined by her indolence to believe that if she waited under a warm shed the snow would cease to fall. She had waited longer than she knew, and now that she found herself belated in the snow-hidden ruggedness of the long lanes, even the animation of a vindictive purpose could not keep her spirit from failing. It was seven o'clock, and by this time she was not very far from Raveloe, but she was not familiar enough with those monotonous lanes to know how near she was to her journey's end. She needed comfort, and she knew but one comforter—the familiar demon in her bosom; but she hesitated a moment, after drawing out the black remnant, before she raised it to her lips.

In that moment the mother's love pleaded for painful consciousness rather than oblivion—pleaded to be left in aching weariness, rather than to have the encircling arms benumbed so that they could not feel the dear burden. In another moment Molly had flung something away, but it was not the black remnant—it was an empty phial. And she walked on again under the breaking cloud, from which there came now and then the light of a quickly veiled star, for a freezing wind had sprung up since the snowing had ceased. But she walked always more and more drowsily, and clutched more and more automatically the sleeping child at her bosom.

Slowly the demon was working his will, and cold and weariness were his helpers. Soon she felt nothing but a supreme immediate longing that curtained off all futurity—the longing to lie down and sleep. She had arrived at a spot where her footsteps were no longer checked by a hedgerow, and she had wandered vaguely, unable to distinguish any objects, notwithstanding the wide whiteness around her, and the growing starlight. She sank down against a straggling furze bush, an easy pillow enough; and the bed of snow, too, was soft. She did not feel that the bed was cold, and did not heed whether the child would wake and cry for her. But her arms had not yet relaxed their instinctive clutch; and the little one slumbered on as gently as if it had been rocked in a lace-trimmed cradle.

But the complete torpor came at last; the fingers lost their tension, the arms unbent; then the little head fell away from the bosom, and the blue eyes opened wide on the cold starlight. At first there was a little peevish cry of "mammy," and an effort to regain the pillowing arm and bosom; but mammy's ear was deaf, and the pillow seemed to be slipping away backward.

Suddenly, as the child rolled downward on it's mother's knees, all wet with snow, its eyes were caught by a bright, glancing light on the white ground, and, with the ready transition of infancy, it was immediately absorbed in watching the bright living thing running towards it, yet never arriving. That bright living thing must be caught; and in an instant the child had slipped on all fours, and held out one little hand to catch the gleam. But the gleam would not be caught in that way, and now the head was held up to see where the cunning gleam came from. It came from a very bright place; and the little one, rising on its legs, toddled through the snow, the old grimy shawl in which it was wrapped trailing behind it, and the queer little bonnet dangling at its back—toddled on to the open door of Silas Marner's cottage, and right up to the warm hearth, where there was a bright fire of logs and sticks, which had thoroughly warmed the old sack (Silas's great-coat) spread out on the bricks to dry.

The little one, accustomed to be left to itself for long hours without notice from its mother, squatted down on the sack, and spread its tiny hands towards the blaze, in perfect contentment, gurgling and making many inarticulate communications to the cheerful fire, like a new-hatched gosling beginning to find itself comfortable. But presently the warmth had a lulling effect, and the little golden head sank down on the old sack, and the blue eyes were veiled by their delicate, half-transparent lids.

But where was Silas Marner while this strange visitor had come to his hearth? He was in the cottage, but he did not see the child. During the last few weeks, since he had lost his money, he had contracted the habit of opening his door and looking out from time to time, as if he thought that his money might be somehow coming back to him, or that some trace, some news of it, might be mysteriously on the road, and be caught by the listening ear or the straining eye. It was chiefly at night, when he was not occupied in his loom, that he fell into this repetition of an act for which he could have assigned no definite purpose, and which can hardly be understood except by those who have undergone a bewildering separation from a supremely loved object. In the evening twilight, and later whenever the night was not dark, Silas looked out on that narrow prospect round the Stone-pits, listening and gazing, not with hope, but with mere yearning and unrest.

This morning he had been told by some of his neighbors that it was New Year's Eve, and that he must sit up and hear the old year rung out and the new rung in, because that was good luck, and might bring his money back again. This was only a friendly Raveloe way of jesting with the half-crazy oddities of a miser, but it had perhaps helped to throw Silas into a more than usually excited state. Since the on-coming of twilight he had opened his door again and again, though only to shut it immediately at seeing all distance veiled by falling snow. But the last time he opened it the snow had ceased, and the clouds were parting here and there. He stood and listened, and gazed for a long while—there was really something on the road coming towards him then, but he caught no sign of it; and the stillness and the wide trackless snow seemed to narrow his solicitude, and touched his yearning with the chill of despair. He went in again, and put his right hand on the latch of the door to close it—but he did not close it: he was arrested as he had been already since his loss, by the invisible wand of catalepsy, and stood like a graven image, with wide but sightless eyes, holding open his door, powerless to resist either the good or evil that might enter there.

When Marner's sensibility returned, he continued the action which had been arrested, and closed his door, unaware of the chasm in his consciousness, unaware of any intermediate change, except that the light had grown dim, and that he was chilled and faint. He thought he had been too long standing at the door and looking out. Turning towards the hearth, where the two logs had fallen apart, and sent forth only a red, uncertain glimmer, he seated himself on his fireside chair, and was stooping to push his logs together, when, to his blurred vision, it seemed as if there were gold on the floor in front of the hearth. Gold!—his own gold—brought back to him as mysteriously as it had been taken away! He felt his heart begin to beat violently, and for a few moments he was unable to stretch out his hand and grasp the restored treasure. The heap of gold seemed to glow and get larger beneath his agitated gaze.

He leaned forward at last, and stretched forth his hand; but instead of the hard coin with the familiar resisting outline, his fingers encountered soft, warm curls. In utter amazement, Silas fell on his knees and bent his head low to examine the marvel—it was a sleeping child—a round, fair thing, with soft yellow rings all over its head. Could this be his little sister come back to him in a dream—his little sister whom he had carried about in his arms for a year before she died, when he was a small boy without shoes or stockings? That was the first thought that darted across Silas's blank wonderment. *Was* it a dream? He rose to his feet again, pushed his logs together, and, throwing on some dried leaves and sticks, raised a flame, but the flame did not disperse the vision—it only lit up more distinctly the little round form of the child, and its shabby clothing. It was very much like his little sister.

Silas sank into his chair powerless, under the double presence of an inexplicable surprise and a hurrying influx of memories. How and when had the child come in without his knowledge? He had never been beyond the door. But along with that question, and almost thrusting it away, there was a vision of the old home and the old streets leading to Lantern Yard—and within that vision another, of the thoughts which had been present with him in those far-off scenes. The thoughts were strange to him now, like old friendships impossible to revive; and yet he had a dreamy feeling that this child was somehow a message come to him from that far-off life: it stirred fibres that had never been moved in Raveloe—old quiverings of tenderness—old impressions of awe at the presentment of some Power presiding over his life; for his imagination had not yet extricated itself from the sense of mystery in the child's sudden presence, and had formed no conjectures of ordinary natural means by which the event could have been brought about.

But there was a cry on the hearth: the child had awaked, and Marner stooped to lift it on his knee. It clung round his neck, and burst louder and louder into that mingling of inarticulate cries with "mammy" by which little children express the bewilderment of waking. Silas pressed it to him, and almost unconsciously uttered sounds of hushing tenderness, while he bethought himself that some of his porridge, which had got cool by the dying fire, would do to feed the child with if it were only warmed up a little.

He had plenty to do through the next hour. The porridge, sweetened with some dry brown sugar from an old store which he had refrained from using for himself, stopped the cries of the little one, and made her lift her blue eyes with a wide, quiet gaze at Silas, as he put the spoon into her mouth. Presently she slipped from his knee and began to toddle about, but with a pretty stagger that made Silas jump up and follow her lest she should fall against anything that would hurt her. But she only fell in a sitting posture on the ground, and began to pull at her boots, looking up at him with a crying face as if the boots hurt her.

He took her on his knee again, but it was some time before it occurred to Silas's dull bachelor mind that the wet boots were the grievance, pressing on the warm ankles. He got them off with difficulty, and baby was at once happily occupied with the primary mystery of her own toes, inviting Silas, with much chuckling, to consider the mystery, too. But the wet boots had at last suggested to Silas that the child had been walking on the snow, and this roused him from his entire oblivion of any ordinary means by which it could have entered or been brought into his house.

Under the prompting of this new idea, and without waiting to form conjectures, he raised the child in his arms, and went to the door. As soon as he had opened it, there was the cry of "mammy" again, which Silas had not heard since the child's first hungry waking. Bending forward, he could just discern the marks made by the little feet on the virgin snow, and he followed their track to the furze bushes. "Mammy!" the little one cried again and again, stretching itself forward so as almost to escape from Silas's arms, before he himself was aware that there was something more than the bush before him—that there was a human body, with the head sunk low in the furze, and half covered with the shaken snow.

CHAPTER XIII

IT WAS AFTER the early supper at the Red House, and the entertainment was in that stage when bashfulness itself had passed into easy jollity, when gentlemen, conscious of unusual accomplishments, could at length be prevailed on to dance a hornpipe, and when the Squire preferred talking loudly, scattering snuff, and patting his visitors' backs, to sitting longer at the whist-table—a choice exasperating to uncle Kimble, who, being always volatile in sober business hours, became intense and bitter over cards and brandy, shuffled before his adversary's deal with a glare of suspicion, and turned up a mean trump-card with an air of inexpressible disgust, as if in a world where such things could happen one might as well enter on a course of reckless profligacy. When the evening had advanced to this pitch of freedom and enjoyment, it was usual for the servants, the heavy duties of supper being well over, to get their share of amusement by coming to look on at the dancing; so that the back regions of the house were left in solitude.

There were two doors by which the White Parlor was entered from the hall, and they were both standing open for the sake of air; but the lower one was crowded with the servants and villagers, and only the upper doorway was left free. Bob Cass was figuring in a hornpipe, and his father, very proud of this lithe son, whom he repeatedly declared to be just like himself in his young days, in a tone that implied this to be the very highest stamp of juvenile merit, was the centre of a group who had placed themselves opposite the performer, not far from the upper door. Godfrey was standing a little way off, not to admire his brother's dancing, but to keep sight of Nancy, who was seated in the group, near her father. He stood aloof, because he wished to avoid suggesting himself as a subject for the Squire's fatherly jokes in connection with matrimony, and Miss Nancy Lammeter's beauty, which were likely to become more and more explicit. But he had the prospect of dancing with her again when the hornpipe was concluded, and in the meantime it was very pleasant to get long glances at her quite unobserved.

But when Godfrey was lifting his eyes from one of those long glances, they encountered an object as startling to him at that moment as if it had been an apparition from the dead. It *was* an apparition from that hidden life which lies, like a dark by-street, behind the goodly ornamented façade that meets the sunlight and the gaze of respectable admirers. It was his own child carried in Silas Marner's arms. That was his instantaneous impression, unaccompanied by doubt, though he had not seen the child for months past: and when the hope was rising that he might possibly be mistaken, Mr. Crackenthorp and Mr. Lammeter had already advanced to Silas, in astonishment at this strange advent. Godfrey joined them immediately, unable to rest without hearing every word—trying to control himself, but conscious that if any one noticed him, they must see that he was white-lipped and trembling.

But now all eyes at that end of the room were bent on Silas Marner; the Squire himself had risen, and asked angrily, "How's this?—what's this?—what do you do coming in here in this way?"

"I'm come for the doctor—I want the doctor," Silas had said in the first moment, to Mr. Crackenthorp.

"Why, what's the matter, Marner?" said the rector. "The doctor's here; but say quietly what you want him for."

"It's a woman," said Silas, speaking low, and half-breathlessly, as Godfrey came up. "She's dead, I think—dead in the snow at the Stone-pits—not far from my door."

Godfrey felt a great throb; there was one terror in his mind at that moment: it was, that the woman might *not* be dead. That was an evil terror—an ugly inmate to have found a nestling-place in Godfrey's kindly disposition; but no disposition is a security from evil wishes to a man whose happiness hangs on duplicity.

"Hush, hush!" said Mr. Crackenthorp. "Go out into the hall there. I'll fetch the doctor to you. Found a woman in the snow—and thinks she's dead," he added, speaking low to the Squire. "Better say as little about it as possible; it will shock the ladies. Just tell them a poor woman is ill from cold and hunger. I'll go and fetch Kimble."

By this time, however, the ladies had pressed forward, curious to know what could have brought the solitary linen-weaver there under such strange circumstances, and interested in the pretty child, who, half alarmed and half attracted by the brightness and the numerous company, now frowned and hid her face, now lifted up her head again and looked round placably, until a touch or a coaxing word brought back the frown, and made her bury her face with new determination.

"What child is it?" said several ladies at once, and, among the rest, Nancy Lammeter, addressing Godfrey.

"I don't know—some poor woman's who has been

found in the snow, I believe," was the answer Godfrey wrung from himself with a terrible effort. ("After all, *am* I certain?" he hastened to add, in anticipation of his own conscience.)

"Why, you'd better leave the child here, then, Master Marner," said good-natured Mrs. Kimble, hesitating, however, to take those dingy clothes into contact with her own ornamented satin bodice. "I'll tell one o' the girls to fetch it."

"No—no—I can't part with it, I can't let it go," said Silas, abruptly. "It's come to me—I've a right to keep it."

The proposition to take the child from him had come to Silas quite unexpectedly, and his speech, uttered under a strong, sudden impulse, was almost like a revelation to himself; a minute before, he had no distinct intention about the child.

"Did you ever hear the like?" said Mrs. Kimble, in mild surprise, to her neighbor.

"Now, ladies, I must trouble you to stand aside," said Mr. Kimble, coming from the card-room, in some bitterness at the interruption, but drilled by the long habit of his profession into obedience to unpleasant calls, even when he was hardly sober.

"It's a nasty business turning out now, eh, Kimble?" said the Squire. "He might ha' gone for your young fellow—the 'prentice, there—what's his name?"

"Might? ay—what's the use of talking about might?" growled uncle Kimble, hastening out with Marner, and followed by Mr. Crackenthorp and Godfrey. "Get me a pair of thick boots, Godfrey, will you? And stay, let somebody run to Winthrop's and fetch Dolly—she's the best woman to get. Ben was here himself before supper; is he gone?"

"Yes, sir, I met him," said Marner; "but I couldn't

stop to tell him anything, only I said I was going for the doctor, and he said the doctor was at the Squire's. And I made haste and ran, and there was nobody to be seen at the back o' the house, and so I went in to where the company was."

The child, no longer distracted by the bright light and the smiling women's faces, began to cry and call for "mammy," though always clinging to Marner, who had apparently won her thorough confidence. Godfrey had come back with the boots, and felt the cry as if some fibre were drawn tight within him.

"I'll go," he said, hastily, eager for some movement: "I'll go and fetch the woman—Mrs. Winthrop."

"Oh, pooh—send somebody else," said uncle Kimble, hurrying away with Marner.

"You'll let me know if I can be of any use, Kimble," said Mr. Crackenthorp. But the doctor was out of hearing.

Godfrey, too, had disappeared: he was gone to snatch his hat and coat, having just reflection enough to remember that he must not look like a madman; but he rushed out of the house into the snow without heeding his thin shoes.

In a few minutes he was on his rapid way to the Stone-pits by the side of Dolly, who, though feeling that she was entirely in her place in encountering cold and snow on an errand of mercy, was much concerned at a young gentleman's getting his feet wet under a like impulse.

"You'd a deal better go back, sir," said Dolly, with respectful compassion. "You've no call to catch cold; and I'd ask you if you'd be so good as to tell my husband to come, on your way back—he's at the Rainbow, I doubt—if you found him anyway sober enough to be o' use. Or else, there's Mrs. Snell 'ud happen to send the boy up to fetch and carry, for there may be things wanted from the doctor's."

"No, I'll stay, now I'm once out—I'll stay outside here," said Godfrey, when they came opposite Marner's cottage. "You can come and tell me if I can do anything."

"Well, sir, you're very good; you've a tender heart," said Dolly going to the door.

Godfrey was too painfully preoccupied to feel a twinge of self-reproach at this undeserved praise. He walked up and down, unconscious that he was plunging ankle-deep in snow, unconscious of everything but trembling suspense about what was going on in the cottage, and the effect of each alternative on his future lot. No, not quite unconscious of everything else. Deeper down, and half-smothered by passionate desire and dread, there was the sense that he ought not to be waiting on these alternatives; that he ought to accept the consequences of his deeds, own the miserable wife, and fulfil the claims of the helpless child. But he had not moral courage enough to contemplate that active renunciation of Nancy as possible for him: he had only conscience and heart enough to make him forever uneasy under the weakness that forbade the renunciation. And at this moment his mind leaped away from all restraint toward the sudden prospect of deliverance from his long bondage.

"Is she dead?" said the voice that predominated over every other within him. "If she is, I may marry Nancy; and then I shall be a good fellow in future, and have no secrets, and the child—shall be taken care of somehow." But across that vision came the other possibility—"She may live, and then it's all up with me."

Godfrey never knew how long it was before the

door of the cottage opened and Mr. Kimble came out. He went forward to meet his uncle, prepared to suppress the agitation he must feel, whatever news he was to hear.

"I waited for you, as I'd come so far," he said, speaking first.

"Pooh, it was nonsense for you to come out: why didn't you send one of the men? There's nothing to be done. She's dead—has been dead for hours, I should say."

"What sort of a woman is she?" said Godfrey, feeling the blood rush to his face.

"A young woman, but emaciated, with long, black hair. Some vagrant—quite in rags. She's got a wedding-ring on, however. They must fetch her away to the workhouse to-morrow. Come, come along."

"I want to look at her," said Godfrey. "I think I saw such a woman yesterday. I'll overtake you in a minute or two."

Mr. Kimble went on, and Godfrey turned back to the cottage. He cast only one glance at the dead face on the pillow, which Dolly had smoothed with decent care; but he remembered that last look at his unhappy hated wife so well, that at the end of sixteen years every line in the worn face was present to him when he told the full story of this night.

He turned immediately towards the hearth, where Silas Marner sat lulling the child. She was perfectly quiet now, but not asleep — only soothed by sweet porridge and warmth into that wide-gazing calm which makes us older human beings with our inward turmoil, feel a certain awe in the presence of a little child, such as we feel before some quiet majesty or beauty in the earth or sky—before a steady growing planet, or a full-flowered eglantine, or the bending trees over a silent pathway. The wide-open blue eyes looked up at Godfrey's without any uneasiness or sign of recognition; the child could make no visible audible claim on its father; and the father felt a strange mixture of feelings, a conflict of regret and joy, that the pulse of that little heart had no response for the half-jealous yearning in his own, when the blue eyes turned away from him slowly, and fixed themselves on the weaver's queer face, which was bent low down to look at them, while the small hand began to pull Marner's withered cheek with loving disfiguration.

"You'll take the child to the parish to-morrow?" asked Godfrey, speaking as indifferently as he could.

"Who says so?" said Marner, sharply. "Will they make me take her?"

"Why, you wouldn't like to keep her, should you—an old bachelor like you?"

"Till anybody shows they've a right to take her away from me," said Marner. "The mother's dead, and I reckon it's got no father; it's a lone thing—and I'm a lone thing. My money's gone, I don't know where—and this is come from I don't know where. I know nothing—I'm partly mazed."

"Poor little thing!" said Godfrey. "Let me give something towards finding it clothes."

He had put his hand in his pocket and found half-a-guinea, and, thrusting it into Silas's hand, he hurried out of the cottage to overtake Mr. Kimble.

"Ah, I see it's not the same woman I saw," he said, as he came up. "It's a pretty little child; the old fellow seems to want to keep it; that's strange for a miser like him. But I gave him a trifle to help him out; the parish isn't likely to quarrel with him for the right to keep the child."

"No; but I've seen the time when I might have quar-

reled with him for it myself. It's too late now, though.
If the child ran into the fire, your aunt's too fat to overtake it; she could only sit and grunt like an alarmed
sow. But what a fool you are, Godfrey, to come out
in your dancing shoes and stockings in this way—and
you one of the beaux of the evening, and at your
own house! What do you mean by such freaks, young
fellow? Has Miss Nancy been cruel, and do you want
to spite her by spoiling your pumps?"

"Oh, everything has been disagreeable to-night. I
was tired to death of jigging and gallanting, and that
bother about the hornpipes. And I'd got to dance with
the other Miss Gunn," said Godfrey, glad of the sub-
terfuge his uncle had suggested to him.

The prevarication and white lies which a mind that
keeps itself ambitiously pure is as uneasy under as a
great artist under the false touches that no eye detects
but his own, are worn as lightly as mere trimmings
when once the actions have become a lie.

Godfrey reappeared in the White Parlor with dry
feet, and, since the truth must be told, with a sense of
relief and gladness that was too strong for painful
thoughts to struggle with. For could he not venture
now, whenever opportunity offered, to say the ten-
derest things to Nancy Lammeter—to promise her and
himself that he would always be just what she would
desire to see him? There was no danger that his dead
wife would be recognized; those were not days of
active inquiry and wide report; and as for the registry
of their marriage, that was a long way off, buried in
unturned pages, away from everyone's interest but
his own. Dunsey might betray him if he came back;
but Dunsey might be won to silence.

And when events turn out so much better for a man
than he has had reason to dread, is it not a proof that

his conduct has been less foolish and blameworthy than it might otherwise have appeared? When we are treated well, we naturally begin to think that we are not altogether unmeritorious, and that it is only just we should treat ourselves well, and not mar our own good fortune. Where, after all, would be the use of his confessing the past to Nancy Lammeter, and throwing away his happiness?—nay, hers? for he felt some confidence that she loved him. As for the child, he would see that it was cared for: he would never forsake it: he would do everything but own it. Perhaps it would be just as happy in life without being owned by its father, seeing that nobody could tell how things would turn out, and that—is there any other reason wanted?—well, then, that the father would be much happier without owning the child.

CHAPTER XIV

THERE WAS a pauper's burial that week in Raveloe, and up Kench Yard at Batherley it was known that the dark-haired woman with the fair child, who had lately come to lodge there, was gone away again. That was all the express note taken that Molly had disappeared from the eyes of men. But the unwept death which, to the general lot, seemed as trivial as the summer-shed leaf, was charged with the force of destiny to certain human lives that we know of, shaping their joys and sorrows even to the end.

Silas Marner's determination to keep the "tramp's

child" was matter of hardly less surprise and iterated talk in the village than the robbery of his money. That softening of feeling towards him which dated from his misfortune, that merging of suspicion and dislike in a rather contemptuous pity for him as lone and crazy, was now accompanied with a more active sympathy, especially amongst the women. Notable mothers, who knew what it was to keep children "whole and sweet"; lazy mothers, who knew what it was to be interrupted in folding their arms and scratching their elbows by the mischievous propensities of children just firm on their legs, were equally interested in conjecturing how a lone man would manage with a two-year-old child on his hands, and were equally ready with their suggestions: the notable chiefly telling him what he had better do, and the lazy ones being emphatic in telling him what he would never be able to do.

Among the notable mothers, Dolly Winthrop was the one whose neighborly offices were the most acceptable to Marner, for they were rendered without any show of bustling instruction. Silas had shown her the half-guinea given to him by Godfrey, and had asked her what he should do about getting some clothes for the child.

"Eh, Master Marner," said Dolly, "there's no call to buy, no more nor a pair of shoes; for I've got the little petticoats as Aaron wore five years ago, and it's ill spending the money on them baby-clothes, for the child 'ull grow like grass i' May, bless it—that it will."

And the same day Dolly brought her bundle, and displayed to Marner, one by one, the tiny garments in their due order of succession, most of them patched and darned, but clean and neat as fresh-sprung herbs. This was the introduction to a great ceremony with soap and water, from which baby came out in new beauty, and sat on Dolly's knee, handling her toes and chuckling and patting her palms together with an air of having made several discoveries about herself, which she communicated by alternate sounds of "gug-gug-gug," and "mammy." The "mammy" was not a cry of need or uneasiness: Baby had been used to utter it without expecting either tender sound or touch to follow.

"Anybody 'ud think the angils in heaven couldn't be prettier," said Dolly, rubbing the golden curls and kissing them. "And to think of its being covered wi' them dirty rags—and the poor mother—froze to death; but there's Them as took care of it, and brought it to your door, Master Marner. The door was open, and it walked in over the snow, like as if it had been a little starved robin. Didn't you say the door was open?"

"Yes," said Silas, meditatively. "Yes—the door was open. The money's gone, I don't know where, and this is come from I don't know where."

He had not mentioned to any one his unconsciousness of the child's entrance, shrinking from questions which might lead to the fact he himself suspected—namely, that he had been in one of his trances.

"Ah," said Dolly, with soothing gravity, "it's like the night and the morning, and the sleeping and the waking, and the rain and the harvest—one goes and the other comes, and we know nothing how nor where. We may strive and scrat and fend, but it's little we can do arter all—the big things come and go wi' no striving o' our'n—they do, that they do; and I think you're in the right on it to keep the little un, Master Marner, seeing as it's been sent to you, though there's folks as thinks different. You'll happen to be a bit moithered with it while it's so little; but I'll come, and welcome, and see to it for you: I've a bit o' time to spare most days, for when one gets up betimes i' the morning, the clock seems to stan' still tow'rt ten, afore it's time to go about the victual. So, as I say, I'll come and see to the child for you, and welcome."

"Thank you . . . kindly," said Silas, hesitating a little. "I'll be glad if you'll tell me things. But," he added, uneasily, leaning forward to look at Baby with some jealousy, as she was resting her head backward against Dolly's arm, and eyeing him contentedly from a distance—"But I want to do things for it myself, else it may get fond o' somebody else, and not fond o' me. I've been used to fending for myself in the house—I can learn, I can learn."

"Eh, to be sure," said Dolly, gently. "I've seen men as are wonderful handy wi' children. The men are awk'ard and contrairy mostly, God help 'em—but when the drink's out of 'em, they aren't unsensible, though they're bad for leeching and bandaging—so fiery and impatient. You see this goes first, next the skin," proceeded Dolly, taking up the little shirt, and putting it on.

"Yes," said Marner, docilely, bringing his eyes very close, that they might be initiated in the mysteries; whereupon Baby seized his head with both her small arms, and put her lips against his face with purring noises.

"See there," said Dolly, with a woman's tender tact, "she's fondest o' you. She wants to go o' you lap, I'll be bound. Go then: take her, Master Marner; you can put the things on, and then you can say as you've done for her from the first of her coming to you."

Marner took her on his lap, trembling with an emotion mysterious to himself, at something unknown dawning on his life. Thought and feeling were so confused within him, that if he had tried to give them utterance, he could only have said that the child was come instead of his gold—that the gold had turned into the child. He took the garments from Dolly, and put them on under her teaching; interrupted, of course, by Baby's gymnastics.

"There, then! why, you take to it quite easy, Master Marner," said Dolly; "but what shall you do when you're forced to sit in your loom? For she'll get busier and mischievouser every day—she will, bless her. It's lucky you've got that high hearth i'stead of a grate, for that keeps the fire more out of her reach; but if you've got anything as can be spilt or broke, or as is fit to cut her fingers off, she'll be at it—and it is but right that you should know."

Silas meditated a little while in some perplexity. "I'll tie her to the leg o' the loom," he said at last—"tie her with a good long strip o' something."

"Well, mayhap that'll do, as it's a little gell, for they're easier persuaded to sit i' one place nor the lads. I know what the lads are; for I've had four—four I've had, God knows—and if you was to take and tie 'em up, they'd make a fighting and a crying as if you was ringing the pigs. But I'll bring you my little chair, and some bits o' red rag and things for her to play wi'; an' she'll sit and chatter to 'em as if they was alive. Eh, if it wasn't a sin to the lads to wish 'em made different, bless 'em, I should ha' been glad for one of 'em to be a little gell; and to think as I could ha' taught her to scour, and mend, and the knitting, and everything. But I can teach 'em this little 'un, Master Marner, when she gets old enough."

"But she'll be *my* little un," said Marner, rather hastily. "She'll be nobody else's."

"No, to be sure; you'll have a right to her, if you're

a father to her, and bring her up according. But," added Dolly, coming to a point which she had determined beforehand to touch upon, "you must bring her up like christened folks's children, and take her to church, and let her learn her catechise, as my little Aaron can say off—the 'I believe,' and everything, and 'hurt nobody by word or deed,'—as well as if he was the clerk. That's what you must do, Master Marner, if you'd do the right thing by the orphin child."

Marner's pale face flushed suddenly under a new anxiety. His mind was too busy trying to give some definite bearing to Dolly's words for him to think of answering her.

"And it's my belief," she went on, "as the poor little creature has never been christened, and it's nothing but right as the parson should be spoke to; and if you was noways unwilling, I'd talk to Mr. Macey about it this very day. For if the child ever went anyways wrong, and you hadn't done your part by it, Master Marner—'noculation, and everything to save it from harm—it 'ud be a thorn i' your bed for ever o' this side the grave; and I can't think as it 'ud be easy lying down for anybody when they'd got to another world, if they hadn't done their part by the helpless children as come wi'out their own asking."

Dolly herself was disposed to be silent for some time now, for she had spoken from the depths of her own simple belief, and was much concerned to know whether her words would produce the desired effect on Silas. He was puzzled and anxious, for Dolly's word "christened" conveyed no distinct meaning to him. He had only heard of baptism, and had only seen the baptism of grown-men and women.

"What is it as you mean by 'christened'?" he said,

at last, timidly. "Won't folks be good to her without it?"

"Dear, dear, Master Marner," said Dolly with gentle distress and compassion. "Had you never no father nor mother as taught you to say your prayers, and as there's good words and good things to keep us from harm?"

"Yes," said Silas, in a low voice; "I know a deal about that—used to, used to. But your ways are different; my country was a good way off." He paused a few moments, and then added, more decidedly, "But I want to do everything as can be done for the child. And whatever's right for it i' this country, and you think 'ull do it good, I'll act according, if you'll tell me."

"Well, then, Master Marner," said Dolly, inwardly rejoiced, "I'll ask Mr. Macey to speak to the parson about it; and you must fix on a name for it, because it must have a name giv' it when it's christened."

"My mother's name was Hephzibah," said Silas, "and my little sister was named after her."

"Eh, that's a hard name," said Dolly. "I partly think it isn't a christened name."

"It's a Bible name," said Silas, old ideas recurring.

"Then I've no call to speak again' it," said Dolly, rather startled by Silas's knowledge on this head; "but you see I'm no scholard, and I'm slow at catching the words. My husband says I'm allays like as if I was putting the haft for the handle—that's what he says—for he's very sharp, God help him. But it was awk'ard calling your little sister by such a hard name, when you'd got nothing big to say, like—wasn't it, Master Marner?"

"We called her Eppie," said Silas.

"Well, if it was noways wrong to shorten the name it 'ud be a deal handier. And so I'll go now, Master

Marner, and I'll speak about the christening afore dark; and I wish you the best o' luck, and it's my belief it'll come to you, if you do what's right by the orphin child;—and there's the 'noculation to be seen to; and as to washing its bits o' things, you need to look to nobody but me, for I can do 'em wi' one hand when I've got my suds about. Eh, the blessed angil! You'll let me bring my Aaron one o' these days, and he'll show her his little cart as his father's made for him, and the black-and-white pup as he's got a'rearing."

Baby *was* christened, the rector deciding that a double baptism was the lesser risk to incur; and on this occasion Silas, making himself as clean and tidy as he could, appeared for the first time within the church, and shared in the observances held sacred by his neighbors. He was quite unable, by means of anything he heard or saw, to identify the Raveloe religion with his old faith; if he could at any time in his previous life have done so, it must have been by the aid of a strong feeling ready to vibrate with sympathy, rather than by a comparison of phrases and ideas; and now for long years that feeling had been dormant. He had no distinct idea about the baptism and the church-going, except that Dolly had said it was for the good of the child; and in this way, as the weeks grew to months, the child created fresh and fresh links between his life and the lives from which he had hitherto shrunk continually into narrower isolation.

Unlike the gold which needed nothing, and must be worshipped in close-locked solitude—which was hidden away from the daylight, was deaf to the song of the birds, and started to no human tones—Eppie was a creature of endless claims and ever-growing desires, seeking and loving sunshine, and living sounds, and living movements; making trial of everything, with trust in new joy, and stirring the human kindness in all eyes that looked on her. The gold had kept his thoughts in an ever-repeated circle, leading to nothing beyond itself; but Eppie was an object compacted of changes and hopes that forced his thoughts onward, and carried them far away from their old eager pacing towards the same blank limit—carried them away to the new things that would come with the coming years, when Eppie would have learned to understand how her father Silas cared for her; and made him look for images of that time in the ties and charities that bound together the families of his neighbors. The gold had asked that he should sit weaving longer and longer, deafened and blinded more and more to all things except the monotony of his loom and the repetition of his web; but Eppie called him away from his weaving, and made him think all its pauses a holiday, reawakening his senses with her fresh life, even to the old winter-flies that came crawling forth in the early spring sunshine, and warming him into joy because *she* had joy.

And when the sunshine grew strong and lasting, so that the buttercups were thick in the meadows, Silas might be seen in the sunny mid-day, or in the late afternoon when the shadows were lengthening under the hedgerows, strolling out with uncovered head to carry Eppie beyond the Stone-pits to where the flowers grew, till they reached some favorite bank where he could sit down, while Eppie toddled to pluck the flowers, and make remarks to the winged things that murmured happily above the bright petals, calling "Daddad's" attention continually by bringing him the flowers. Then she would turn her ear to some sudden birdnote, and Silas learned to please her by making signs of hushed stillness, that they might listen for the note to come again: so that when it came, she set up her small back and laughed with gurgling triumph. Sitting on the banks in this way, Silas began to look for the once familiar herbs again; and as the leaves, with their unchanged outline and markings, lay on his palm, there was a sense of crowding remembrances from which he turned away timidly, taking refuge in Eppie's little world, that lay lightly on his enfeebled spirit.

As the child's mind was growing into knowledge, his mind was growing into memory: as her life unfolded, his soul, long stupefied in a cold, narrow prison, was unfolding, too, and trembling gradually into full consciousness.

It was an influence which must gather force with every new year: the tones that stirred Silas's heart grew articulate, and called for more distinct answers; shapes and sounds grew clearer for Eppie's eyes and ears, and there was more that "Dad-dad" was imperatively required to notice and account for. Also, by the time Eppie was three years old, she developed a fine capacity for mischief, and for devising ingenious ways of being troublesome, which found much exercise, not only for Silas's patience, but for his watchfulness and penetration. Sorely was poor Silas puzzled on such occasions by the incompatible demands of love. Dolly Winthrop told him that punishment was good for Eppie, and that, as for rearing a child without making it tingle a little in soft and safe places now and then, it was not to be done.

"To be sure, there's another thing you might do, Master Marner," added Dolly, meditatively: "you might shut her up once i' the coal-hole. That was what I did wi' Aaron; for I was that silly wi' the youngest lad, as I could never bear to smack him. Not as I could find i' my heart to let him stay i' the coal-hole more nor a minute, but it was enough to colly him all over, so as he must be new washed and dressed, and it was as good as a rod to him—that was. But I put it upo' your conscience, Master Marner, as there's one of 'em you must choose—ayther smacking or the coal-hole—else she'll get so masterful, there'll be no holding her."

Silas was impressed with the melancholy truth of this last remark; but his force of mind failed before the only two penal methods open to him, not only because it was painful to him to hurt Eppie, but because he trembled at a moment's contention with her, lest she should love him the less for it. Let even an affectionate Goliath get himself tied to a small, tender thing, dreading to hurt it by pulling, and dreading still more to snap the cord, and which of the two, pray, will be master? It was clear that Eppie, with her short, toddling steps, must lead father Silas a pretty dance on any fine morning when circumstances favored mischief.

For example: He had wisely chosen a broad strip of linen as a means of fastening her to his loom when he was busy: it made a broad belt round her waist, and was long enough to allow of her reaching the trucklebed and sitting down on it, but not long enough for her to attempt any dangerous climbing. One bright summer's morning Silas had been more engrossed than usual in "setting up" a new piece of work, an occasion on which his scissors were in requisition. These scissors, owing to an especial warning of Dolly's, had been kept carefully out of Eppie's reach; but the click of them had had a peculiar attraction for her ear, and watching the results of that click, she had derived the philosophic lesson that the same cause would produce the same effect.

Silas had seated himself in his loom, and the noise of weaving had begun; but he had left his scissors on a ledge which Eppie's arm was long enough to reach; and now, like a small mouse, watching her opportunity, she stole quietly from her corner, secured the scissors, and toddled to the bed again, setting up her back as a mode of concealing the fact. She had a distinct intention as to the use of the scissors; and having cut the linen strip in a jagged but effectual manner, in two moments she had run out at the open door where the sunshine was inviting her, while poor Silas believed her to be a better child than usual. It was not until he happened to need his scissors that the terrible fact burst upon him: Eppie had run out by herself—had perhaps fallen into the Stone-pit.

Silas, shaken by the worst fear that could have befallen him, rushed out calling "Eppie!" and ran eagerly about the unenclosed space, exploring the dry cavities into which she might have fallen, and then gazing with questioning dread at the smooth red surface of the water. The cold drops stood on his brow. How long had she been out? There was one hope—that she had crept through the stile and got into the fields, where he habitually took her to stroll. But the grass was high in the meadow, and there was no decrying her, if she were there, except by a close search that would be a trespass on Mr. Osgood's crop. Still, that misdemeanor must be committed: and poor Silas, after peering all round the hedgerows, traversed the grass beginning with perturbed vision to see Eppie behind every group of red sorrel, and to see her moving always farther off as he approached.

The meadow was searched in vain; and he got over the stile into the next field, looking with dying hope towards a small pond which was now reduced to its summer shallowness, so as to leave a wide margin of good adhesive mud. Here, however, sat Eppie, discoursing cheerfully to her own small boot which she was using as a bucket to convey the water into a deep hoofmark while her little naked foot was planted comfortably on a cushion of olive-green mud. A redheaded calf was observing her with alarmed doubt through the opposite hedge.

Here was clearly a sense of aberration in a christened child which demanded severe treatment; but Silas, overcome with convulsive joy at finding his treasure again, could do nothing but snatch her up, and cover her with half-sobbing kisses. It was not until he had carried her home, and had begun to think of the necessary washing, that he recollected the need that he should punish Eppie, and "make her remember." The idea that she might run away again and come to harm, gave him unusual resolution, and for the first time he determined to try the coal-hole—a small closet near the hearth.

"Naughty, naughty Eppie," he suddenly began, holding her on his knee, and pointing to her muddy feet and clothes—"naughty to cut with the scissors and run away. Eppie must go into the coal-hole for being naughty. Daddy must put her in the coal-hole."

He half-expected that this would be shock enough, and that Eppie would begin to cry. But instead of that, she began to shake herself on his knee, as if the proposition opened a pleasing novelty. Seeing that he must proceed to extremities, he put her into the coal-hole, and held the door closed, with a trembling sense that he was using a strong measure. For a moment there was silence, but then came a little cry, "Opy, opy!" and Silas let her out again, saying "Now Eppie 'ull never be naughty again, else she must go into the coal-hole—a black, naughty place."

The weaving must stand still a long while this morning, for now Eppie must be washed, and have clean clothes on; but it was to be hoped that this punishment would have a lasting effect, and save time in future—though, perhaps, it would have been better if Eppie had cried more.

In half an hour she was clean again, and Silas, having turned his back to see what he could do with the linen band, threw it down again, with the reflection that Eppie would be good without fastening for the rest of the morning. He turned round again, and was going to place her in her little chair near the loom, when she peeped out at him with black face and hands again, and said, "Eppie in de toal-hole!"

This total failure of the coal-hole discipline shook Silas's belief in the efficacy of punishment. "She'd take it all for fun," he observed to Dolly, "if I didn't hurt her, and that I can't do, Mrs. Winthrop. If she makes me a bit o' trouble, I can bear it. And she's got no tricks but what she'll grow out of."

"Well, that's partly true, Master Marner," said Dolly, sympathetically; "and if you can't bring your mind to frighten her off touching things, you must do what you can to keep 'em out of her way. That's what I do wi' the pups as the lads are allays a-rearing. They *will* worry and gnaw—worry and gnaw they will, if it was one's Sunday cap as hung anywhere so they could drag it. They know no difference, God help 'em: it's the pushing o' the teeth as sets 'em on, that's what it is."

So Eppie was reared without punishment, the burden of her misdeeds being borne vicariously by father Silas. The stone hut was made a soft nest for her, lined with downy patience: and also in the world that lay beyond the stone hut she knew nothing of frowns and denials.

Notwithstanding the difficulty of carrying her and his yarn or linen at the same time, Silas took her with him in most of his journeys to the farmhouses, unwilling to leave her behind at Dolly Winthrop's, who was always ready to take care of her; and little curly-headed Eppie, the weaver's child, became an object of interest at several out-lying homesteads, as well as in the village.

Hitherto he had been treated very much as if he had been a useful gnome or brownie—a queer and unaccountable creature, who must necessarily be looked at with wondering curiosity and repulsion, and with whom one would be glad to make all greetings and bargains as brief as possible, but who must be dealt with in a propitiatory way and occasionally have a present of pork or garden stuff to carry home with him, seeing that without him there was no getting the yarn woven. But now Silas met with open, smiling faces and cheerful questioning, as a person whose satisfaction and difficulties could be understood. Everywhere he must sit a little and talk about the child, and words of interest were always ready for him.

"Ah, Master Marner, you'll be lucky if she takes the measles soon and easy!" or, "Why, there isn't many lone men 'ud ha' been wishing to take up with a little un like that: but I reckon the weaving makes you handier than men as do out-door work—you're partly as handy as a woman, for weaving comes next to spinning."

Elderly masters and mistresses, seated observantly in large kitchen arm-chairs, shook their heads over the difficulties attendant on rearing children, felt Eppie's round arms and legs, and pronounced them remarkably firm, and told Silas that, if she turned out well (which, however, there was no telling), it would be a fine thing for him to have a steady lass to do for him when he got helpless. Servant maidens were fond of carrying her out to look at the hens and chickens, or to see if any cherries could be shaken down in the orchard; and the small boys and girls approached her slowly, with cautious movement and steady gaze, like little dogs face to face with one of their own kind, till attraction had reached the point at which the soft lips were put out for a kiss.

No child was afraid of approaching Silas when Eppie was near him: there was no repulsion around him now, either for young or old; for the little child had come to link him once more with the whole world. There was love between him and the child that blent them into one, and there was love between the child and the world—from men and women with parental looks and tones, to the red lady-birds and the round pebbles.

Silas began now to think of Raveloe life entirely in relation to Eppie: she must have everything that was good in Raveloe; and he listened docilely, that he might come to understand better what this life was, from which, for fifteen years, he had stood aloof as from a strange thing, wherewith he could have no communion: as some man who has a precious plant to which he would give a nuturing home in a new soil, thinks of the rain, and the sunshine, and all influences, in relation to his nursling, and asks industriously for all knowledge that will help him to satisfy the wants of the searching roots, or to guard leaf and bud from invading harm.

The disposition to hoard had been utterly crushed at the very first by the loss of his long-stored gold: the coins he earned afterwards seemed as irrelevant as stones brought to complete a house suddenly buried by an earthquake; the sense of bereavement was too heavy upon him for the old thrill of satisfaction to arise again at the touch of the newly-earned coin. And now something had come to replace his hoard which gave a growing purpose to the earnings, drawing his hope and joy continually onward beyond the money.

In old days there were angels who came and took men by the hand and led them away from the city of destruction. We see no white-winged angels now. But yet men are led away from threatening destruction: a hand is put into theirs, which leads them forth gently towards a calm and bright land, so that they look no more backward; and the hand may be a little child's.

CHAPTER XV

THERE WAS one person, as you will believe, who watched with keener though more hidden interest than any other, the prosperous growth of Eppie under the weaver's care. He dared not do anything that would imply a stronger interest in a poor man's adopted child than could be expected from the kindliness of the young Squire, when a chance meeting suggested a little present to a simple old fellow whom others noticed with goodwill; but he told himself that the time would come when he might do something towards furthering the welfare of his daughter without incurring suspicion. Was he very uneasy in the meantime at his inability to give his daughter her birthright? I cannot say that he was. The child was being taken care of, and would very likely be happy, as people in humble stations often were—happier, perhaps, than those brought up in luxury.

That famous ring that pricked its owner when he forgot duty and followed desire—I wonder if it pricked very hard when he set out on the chase, or whether it pricked but lightly then, and only pierced to the quick when the chase had long been ended, and hope, folding her wings, looked backward and became regret?

Godfrey Cass's cheek and eye were brighter than ever now. He was so undivided in his aims, that he seemed like a man of firmness. No Dunsey had come back: people had made up their minds that he was gone for a soldier, or, "gone out of the country," and no one cared to be specific in their inquiries on a subject delicate to a respectable family. Godfrey had ceased to see the shadow of Dunsey across his path; and the path now lay straight forward to the accomplishment of his best, longest-cherished wishes.

Everybody said Mr. Godfrey had taken the right turn; and it was pretty clear what would be the end of things, for there were not many days in the week that he was not seen riding to the Warrens. Godfrey himself, when he was asked jocosely if the day had been fixed, smiled with the pleasant consciousness of a lover who could say "yes," if he liked. He felt a reformed man, delivered from temptation; and the vision of his future life seemed to him as a promised land for which he had no cause to fight. He saw himself with all this happiness centred on his own hearth, while Nancy would smile on him as he played with the children.

And that other child, not on the hearth—he would not forget it; he would see that it was well provided for. That was a father's duty.

PART TWO

CHAPTER XVI

IT WAS a bright autumn Sunday, sixteen years after Silas Marner had found his new treasure on the hearth. The bells of the old Raveloe church were ringing the cheerful peal that told that the morning service was ended; and out of the arched door-way in the tower came slowly, retarded by friendly greetings and questions, the richer parishioners who had chosen this bright Sunday morning as eligible for church-going. It was the rural fashion of that time for the more important members of the congregation to depart first, while their humbler neighbors waited and looked on, stroking their bent heads or dropping their curtsies to any large ratepayer who turned to notice them.

Foremost among these advancing groups of well-clad people, there are some whom we shall recognize, in spite of Time, who has laid his hand on them all. The tall, blond man of forty is not much changed in features from the Godfrey Cass of six-and-twenty: he is only fuller in flesh, and has only lost the indefinable look of youth—a loss which is marked even when the eye is undulled and the wrinkles are not yet come. Perhaps the pretty woman, not much younger than he, who is leaning on his arm, is more changed than her husband: the lovely bloom that used to be always on her cheek now comes but fitfully, with the fresh morning air or with some strong surprise; yet to all who love human faces best for what they tell of human experience, Nancy's beauty has a heightened interest.

Often the soul is ripened into fuller goodness while age has spread an ugly film, so that mere glances can never divine the preciousness of the fruit. But the years have not been so cruel to Nancy. The firm yet placid mouth, the clear, veracious glance of the brown eyes, speak now of a nature that has been tested and has kept its highest qualities; and even the costume, with its dainty neatness and purity, has more significance now the coquetries of youth can have nothing to do with it.

Mr. and Mrs. Godfrey Cass (any higher title has died away from Raveloe lips since the old Squire was gathered to his fathers and his inheritance was divided) have turned round to look for the tall, aged man and the plainly dressed woman who are a little behind— Nancy having observed that they must wait for "father and Priscilla"—and now they all turn into a narrower path leading across the churchyard to a small gate opposite the Red House. We will not follow them now, for may there not be some others in this departing congregation whom we should like to see again— some of those who are not likely to be handsomely clad, and whom we may not recognize so easily as the master and mistress of the Red House.

But it is impossible to mistake Silas Marner. His large brown eyes seem to have gathered a longer vision, as is the way with eyes that have been short-sighted in early life, and they have a less vague, a more answering gaze; but in everything else one sees signs of a frame much enfeebled by the lapse of the sixteen years. The weaver's bent shoulders and white hair give him almost the look of advanced age, though he is not more than five-and-fifty; but there is the freshest blossom of youth close by his side—a blond, dimpled girl of eighteen, who has vainly tried to chastise her curly auburn hair into smoothness under her brown bonnet:

the hair ripples as obstinately as a brooklet under the March breeze, and the little ringlets burst away from the restraining comb behind and show themselves below the bonnet-crown. Eppie cannot help being rather vexed about her hair, for there is no other girl in Raveloe who has hair at all like it, and she thinks hair ought to be smooth. She does not like to be blameworthy even in small things: you see how neatly her prayer-book is folded in her spotted handkerchief.

The good-looking young fellow, in a new fustian suit, who walks behind her, is not quite sure upon the question of hair in the abstract, when Eppie puts it to him, and thinks that perhaps straight hair is the best in general, but he doesn't want Eppie's hair to be different. She surely divines that there is some one behind her who is thinking about her very particularly, and mustering courage to come to her side as soon as they are out in the lane, else why should she look rather shy, and take care not to turn away her head from her father Silas. to whom she keeps murmuring little sentences as to who was at church, and who was not at church, and how pretty the red mountain-ash is over the Rectory wall!

"I wish *we* had a little garden, father, with double daisies in it, like Mrs. Winthrop's," said Eppie, when they were out in the lane; "only they say it 'ud take a deal of digging and bringing fresh soil—and you couldn't do that, could you, father? Anyhow, I shouldn't like you to do it, for it 'ud be too hard work for you."

"Yes, I could do it, child, if you want a bit o' garden: these long evenings, I could work at taking in a little bit o' the waste, just enough for a root or two o' flowers for you; and again, i' the morning, I could have a turn wi' the spade before I sat down to the loom.

Why didn't you tell me before as you wanted a bit o' garden?"

"*I* can dig it for you, Master Marner," said the young man in fustian, who was now by Eppie's side, entering into the conversation without the trouble of formalities. "It'll be play to me after I've done my day's work, or any odd bits o' time when the work's slack. And I'll bring you some soil from Mr. Cass's garden—he'll let me, and willing."

"Eh, Aaron, my lad, are you there?" said Silas; "I wasn't aware of you; for when Eppie's talking o' things, I see nothing but what she's a-saying. Well, if you could help me with the digging, we might get her a bit o' garden all the sooner."

"Then, if you think well and good," said Aaron, "I'll come to the Stone-pits this afternoon, and we'll settle what land's to be taken in, and I'll get up an hour earlier i' the morning, and begin on it."

"But not if you don't promise me not to work at the hard digging, father," said Eppie. "For I shouldn't ha' said anything about it," she added, half-bashfully, half-roguishly, "only Mrs. Winthrop said as Aaron 'ud be so good, and—"

"And you might ha' known it without her telling you," said Aaron. "And Master Marner knows too, I hope, as I'm able and willing to do a turn o' work for him, and he won't do me the unkindness to anyways take it out o' my hands."

"There, now, father, you won't work in it till it's all easy," said Eppie, "and you and me can mark out the beds, and make holes and plant the roots. It'll be a deal livelier at the Stone-pits when we've got some flowers, for I always think the flowers can see us, and know what we're talking about. And I'll have a bit of rosemary, and bergamot, and thyme, because they're so sweet-smelling; but there's no lavender only in the gentlefolks' gardens, I think."

"That's no reason why you shouldn't have some," said Aaron, "for I can bring you slips of anything: I'm forced to cut no end of 'em when I'm gardening, and I throw 'em away mostly. There's a big bed o' lavender at the Red House; the missis is very fond of it."

"Well," said Silas, gravely, "so as you don't make free for us, or ask for anything as is worth much at the Red House: for Mr. Cass's been so good to us, and built us up the new end o' the cottage, and given us beds and things, as I couldn't abide to be imposin' for garden-stuff or anything else."

"No, no, there's no imposin'," said Aaron; "there's never a garden in all the parish but what there's endless waste in it for want o' somebody as could use everything up. It's what I think to myself sometimes, as there need nobody run short o' victuals if the land was made the most on, and there was never a morsel but what could find its way to a mouth. It sets one thinking o' that—gardening does. But I must go back now, else mother 'ull be in trouble as I aren't there."

"Bring her with you this afternoon, Aaron," said Eppie; "I shouldn't like to fix about the garden, and her not know everything from the first—should *you*, father?"

"Ay, bring her if you can, Aaron," said Silas; "she's sure to have a word to say as 'll help us to set things on their right end."

Aaron turned back up the village, while Silas and Eppie went on up the lonely sheltered lane.

"O daddy!" she began, when they were in privacy, clasping and squeezing Silas's arm, and skipping round to give him an energetic kiss. "My little old daddy! I'm so glad. I don't think I shall want anything else when we've got a little garden; and I knew Aaron would dig it for us," she went on with roguish triumph —"I knew that very well."

"You're a deep little puss, you are," said Silas, with the mild, passive happiness of love-crowned age in his face; "but you'll make yourself fine and beholden to Aaron."

"Oh, no, I shan't," said Eppie, laughing and frisking; "he likes it."

"Come, come, let me carry your prayer-book, else you'll be dropping it, jumping i' that way."

Eppie was now aware that her behavior was under observation, but it was only the observation of a friendly donkey, browsing with a log fastened to his foot—a meek donkey, not scornfully critical of human trivialities, but thankful to share in them, if possible, by getting his nose scratched; and Eppie did not fail to gratify him with her usual notice, though it was attended with the inconvenience of his following them, painfully, up to the very door of their home.

But the sound of a sharp bark inside, as Eppie put the key in the door, modified the donkey's views, and he limped away again without bidding. The sharp bark was the sign of an excited welcome that was awaiting them from a knowing brown terrier, who, after dancing at their legs in a hysterical manner, rushed with a worrying noise at a tortoise-shell kitten under the loom, and then rushed back with a sharp bark again, as much as to say, "I have done my duty by this feeble creature, you perceive"; while the lady-mother of the kitten sat sunning her white bosom in the window, and looked round with a sleepy air of expecting caresses, though she was not going to take any trouble for them.

The presence of this happy animal life was not the

only change which had come over the interior of the stone cottage. There was no bed now in the living-room, and the small space was well filled with decent furniture, all bright and clean enough to satisfy Dolly Winthrop's eye. The oaken table and three-cornered oaken chair were hardly what was likely to be seen in so poor a cottage: they had come, with the beds and other things, from the Red House; for Mr. Godfrey Cass, as every one said in the village, did very kindly by the weaver; and it was nothing but right a man should be looked on and helped by those who could afford it, when he had brought up an orphan child, and been father and mother to her—and had lost his money too, so as he had nothing but what he worked for week by week, and when the weaving was going down too—for there was less and less flax spun—and Master Marner was none so young.

Nobody was jealous of the weaver, for he was re-garded as an exceptional person, whose claims on neighborly help were not to be matched in Raveloe. Any superstition that remained concerning him had taken an entirely new color; and Mr. Macey, now a very feeble old man of fourscore and six, never seen except in his chimney-corner or sitting in the sunshine at his doorsill, was of opinion that when a man had done what Silas had done by an orphan child, it was a sign that his money would come to light again, or leastwise that the robber would be made to answer for it—for, as Mr. Macey observed of himself, his faculties were as strong as ever.

Silas sat down now and watched Eppie with a satis-fied gaze as she spread the clean cloth, and set on it the potato-pan, warmed up slowly in a safe Sunday fashion, by being put into a dry pot over a slowly-dying fire, as the best substitute for an oven. For Silas would not consent to have a grate and oven added to his conveniences: he loved the old brick hearth as he had loved his brown pot—and was it not there when he found Eppie? The gods of the hearth exist for us still; and let all new faith be tolerant of that fetishism, lest it bruise its own roots.

Silas ate his dinner more silently than usual, soon laying down his knife and fork, and watching half-abstractedly Eppie's play with Snap and the cat, by which her own dining was made rather a lengthy business. Yet it was a sight that might well arrest wandering thoughts: Eppie, with the rippling radiance of her hair and the whiteness of her rounded chin and throat set off by the dark-blue cotton gown, laughing merrily as the kitten held on with her four claws to one shoulder, like a design for a jug-handle, while Snap on the right hand and Puss on the other put up their paws towards a morsel which she held out of the reach of both—Snap occasionally desisting in order to remonstrate with the cat by a cogent worrying growl on the greediness and futility of her conduct; till Eppie relented, caressed them both, and divided the morsel between them.

But at last Eppie, glancing at the clock, checked the play, and said, "O daddy, you're wanting to go into the sunshine to smoke your pipe. But I must clear away first, so as the house may be tidy when godmother comes. I'll make haste—I won't be long."

Silas had taken to smoking a pipe daily during the last two years, having been strongly urged to it by the sages of Raveloe, as a practice "good for the fits"; and this advice was sanctioned by Dr. Kimble, on the ground that it was as well to try what could do no harm—a principle which was made to answer for a great deal of work in that gentleman's medical practice.

Silas did not highly enjoy smoking, and often wondered how his neighbors could be so fond of it; but a humble sort of acquiescence in what was held to be good, had become a strong habit of that new self which had been developed in him since he had found Eppie on his hearth: it had been the only clue his bewildered mind could hold by in cherishing this young life that had been sent to him out of the darkness into which his gold had departed. By seeking what was needful for Eppie, by sharing the effect that everything produced on her, he had himself come to appropriate the forms of custom and belief which were the mould of Raveloe like; and as, with reawakening sensibilities, memory also reawakened, he had begun to ponder over the elements of his old faith, and blend them with his new impressions, till he recovered a consciousness of unity between his past and present.

The sense of presiding goodness and the human trust which come with all pure peace and joy, had given him a dim impression that there had been some error, some mistake, which had thrown that dark shadow over the days of his best years; and as it grew more and more easy to him to open his mind to Dolly Winthrop, he gradually communicated to her all he could describe of his early life. The communication was necessarily a slow and difficult process, for Silas's meagre power of explanation was not aided by any readiness of interpretation in Dolly, whose narrow outward experience gave her no key to strange customs, and made every novelty a source of wonder that arrested them at every step of the narrative.

It was only by fragments, and at intervals which left Dolly time to revolve what she had heard till it acquired some familiarity for her, that Silas at last arrived at the climax of the sad story—the drawing of lots, and its false testimony concerning him; and this had to be repeated in several interviews, under new questions on her part as to the nature of this plan for detecting the guilty and clearing the innocent.

"And yourn's the same Bible, you're sure o' that, Master Marner—the Bible as you brought wi' you from that country—it's the same as what they've got at church, and what Eppie's a-learning to read in?"

"Yes," said Silas, "every bit the same; and there's drawing o' lots in the Bible, mind you," he added in a lower tone.

"Oh, dear, dear," said Dolly in a grieved voice, as if she were hearing an unfavorable report of a sick man's case. She was silent for some minutes; at last she said:

"There's wise folks, happen, as know how it all is; the parson knows, I'll be bound; but it takes big words to tell them things, and such as poor folks can't make much out on. I can never rightly know the meaning o' what I hear at church, only a bit here and there, but I know it's good words—I do. But what lies upo' your mind—it's this, Master Marner: as, if Them above had done the right thing by you, They'd never ha' let you be turned out for a wicked thief when you was innicent."

"Ah!" said Silas, who had now come to understand Dolly's phraseology, "that was what fell on me like as if it had been red-hot iron; because, you see, there was nobody as cared for me or clave to me above nor below. And him as I'd gone out and in wi' for ten year and more, since when we was lads and went halves—mine own familiar friend in whom I trusted, had lifted up his heel again' me, and worked to ruin me."

"Eh, but he was a bad un—I can't think as there's another such," said Dolly. "But I'm o'ercome, Master Marner; I'm like as if I'd waked and didn't know whether it was night or morning. I feel somehow as sure as I do when I've laid something up, though I can't justly put my hand on it, as there was a rights in what happened to you, if one could but make it out; and you'd no call to lose heart as you did. But we'll talk on it again; for sometimes things come into my head when I'm leeching or poulticing, or such, as I could never think on when I was sitting still."

Dolly was too useful a woman not to have many opportunities of illumination of the kind she alluded to, and she was not long before she recurred to the subject.

"Master Marner," she said, one day that she came to bring home Eppie's washing, "I've been sore puzzled for a good bit wi' that trouble o' yourn and the drawing o' lots; and it got twisted back'ards and fo'ards, as I didn't know which end to lay hold on. But it come to me all clear like, that night when I was sitting up wi' poor Bessy Fawkes, as is dead and left her children behind, God help 'em—it come to me as clear as daylight; but whether I've got hold on it now, or can anyways bring it to my tongue's end, that I don't know. For I've often a deal inside me as'll never come out; and for what you talk o' your folks in your old country niver saying prayers by heart nor saying 'em out of a book, they must be wonderful cliver; for if I didn't know 'Our Father,' and little bits o' good words as I can carry o' church wi' me, I might down o' my knees every night, but nothing could I say."

"But you can mostly say something as I can make sense on, Mrs. Winthrop," said Silas.

"Well, then, Master Marner, it come to me summat like this: I can make nothing o' the drawing o' lots and the answer coming wrong; it 'ud mayhap take the parson to tell that, and he could only tell us i' big words.

But what come to me as clear as the daylight, it was when I was troubling over poor Bessy Fawkes, and it allays comes into my head when I'm sorry for folks, and feel as I can't do a power to help 'em, not if I was to get up i' the middle o' the night—it comes into my head as Them above has got a deal tenderer heart nor what I've got—for I can't be anyways better nor Them as made me; and if anything looks hard to me, it's because there's things I don't know on; and for the matter o' that, there may be plenty o' things I don't know on, for it's little as I know—that it is. And so, while I was thinking o' that, you come into my mind, Master Marner, and it all come pouring in:—if *I* felt i' my inside what was the right and just thing by you, and them as prayed and drawed the lots, all but that wicked un, if *they'd* ha' done the right thing by you if they could, isn't there them as was at the making on us, and knows better and has a better will? And that's all as ever I can be sure on, and everything else is a big puzzle to me when I think on it. For there was the fever come and took off them as were full-growed, and left the helpless children; and there's the breaking o' limbs; and them as 'ud do right and be sober have to suffer by them as are contrairy—eh, there's trouble i' the world, and there's things as we can never make out the rights on. And all as we've got to do is to trusten, Master Marner—to do the right thing as fur as we know, and to trusten. For if us as knows so little can see a bit o' good and rights, we may be sure as there's a good and a rights bigger nor what we can know—I feel it i' my own inside as it must be so. And if you could ha' gone on trustening, Master Marner, you wouldn't ha' run away from your fellow creatures and been so lone."

"Ah, but that 'ud ha' been hard," said Silas in an undertone; "it 'ud ha' been hard to trusten then."

"And so it would," said Dolly, almost with compunction; "them things are easier said nor done; and I'm partly ashamed o' talking."

"Nay, nay," said Silas, "you're i' the right, Mrs. Winthrop—you're i' the right. There's good i' this world—I've a feeling o' that now; and it makes a man feel as there's a good more nor he can see, i' spite o' the trouble and the wickedness. The drawing o' the lots is dark; but the child was sent to me; there's dealings with us—there's dealings."

This dialogue took place in Eppie's earlier years, when Silas had to part with her for two hours every day, that she might learn to read at the dame school, after he had vainly tried himself to guide her in that first step to learning. Now that she was grown up, Silas had often been led, in those moments of quiet outpouring which come to people who live together in perfect love, to talk with *her* too, of the past, and how and why he had lived a lonely man until she had been sent to him. For it would have been impossible for him to hide from Eppie that she was not his own child; even if the most delicate reticence on the point could have been expected from Raveloe gossips in her presence, her own questions about her mother could not have been parried, as she grew up, without that complete shrouding of the past which would have made a painful barrier between their minds.

So Eppie had long known how her mother had died on the snowy ground, and how she herself had been found on the hearth by father Silas, who had taken her golden curls for his lost guineas brought back to him. The tender and peculiar love with which Silas had reared her in almost inseparable companionship with himself, aided by the seclusion of their dwelling, had preserved her from the lowering influences of the village talk and habits, and had kept her mind in that freshness which is sometimes falsely supposed to be an invariable attribute of rusticity.

Perfect love has a breath of poetry which can exalt the relations of the least-instructed human beings; and this breath of poetry had surrounded Eppie from the time when she had followed the bright gleam that beckoned her to Silas's hearth; so that it is not surprising if, in other things besides her delicate prettiness, she was not quite a common village maiden, but had a touch of refinement and fervor which came from no other teaching than that of tenderly-nurtured unvitiated feeling. She was too childish and simple for her imagination to rove into questions about her unknown father; for a long while it did not even occur to her that she must have had a father; and the first time that the idea of her mother having had a husband presented itself to her, was when Silas showed her the wedding ring which had been taken from the wasted finger, and had been carefully preserved by him in a little lackered box shaped like a shoe.

He delivered this box into Eppie's charge when she had grown up, and she often opened it to look at the ring; but still she thought hardly at all about the father of whom it was the symbol. Had she not a father very close to her, who loved her better than any real fathers in the village seemed to love their daughters? On the contrary, who her mother was, and how she came to die in that forlornness, were questions that often pressed on Eppie's mind. Her knowledge of Mrs. Winthrop, who was her nearest friend next to Silas, made her feel that a mother must be very precious; and she had again and again asked Silas to tell her how her mother looked, whom she was like, and how he had found her against the furze bush, led towards it by the little footsteps and the outstretched arms. The furze bush was there still; and this afternoon, when Eppie came out with Silas into the sunshine, it was the first object that arrested her eyes and thoughts.

"Father," she said in a tone of gentle gravity, which sometimes came like a sadder, slower cadence across her playfulness, "we shall take the furze bush into the garden; it'll come into the corner, and just against it I'll put snowdrops and crocuses, 'cause Aaron says they won't die out, but'll always get more and more."

"Ah, child," said Silas, always ready to talk when he had his pipe in his hand, apparently enjoying the pauses more than the puffs, "it wouldn't do to leave out the furze bush; and there's nothing prettier to my thinking, when it's yallow with flowers. But it's just come into my head what we're to do for a fence—may-hap Aaron can help us to a thought; but a fence we must have, else the donkeys and things'll come and trample everything down. And fencing's hard to be got at, by what I can make out."

"Oh, I'll tell you, daddy," said Eppie, clasping her hands suddenly, after a minute's thought. "There's lots o' loose stones about, some of 'em not big, and we might lay 'em atop of one another, and make a wall. You and me could carry the smallest, and Aaron 'ud carry the rest—I know he would."

"Eh, my precious un," said Silas, "there isn't enough stones to go all round; and as for you carrying, why, wi' your little arms you couldn't carry a stone no bigger than a turnip. You're dillicate made, my dear," he added, with a tender intonation—"that's what Mrs. Winthrop says."

"Oh, I'm stronger than you think, daddy," said Eppie; "and if there wasn't stones enough to go all around, why, they'll go part o' the way, and then it'll be easier to get sticks and things for the rest. See here, round the big pit, what a many stones!"

She skipped forward to the pit, meaning to lift one of the stones and exhibit her strength, but she started back in surprise.

"O father, just come and look here," she exclaimed —"come and see how the water's gone down since yesterday. Why, yesterday the pit was ever so full!"

"Well, to be sure," said Silas, coming to her side. "Why, that's the draining they've begun on, since harvest, i' Mr. Osgood's fields, I reckon. The foreman said to me the other day, when I passed by 'em, 'Master Marner,' he said, 'I shouldn't wonder if we lay your bit o' waste as dry as a bone.' It was Mr. Godfrey Cass, he said, had gone into the draining: he'd been taking these fields o' Mr. Osgood."

"How odd it'll seem to have the old pit dried up!" said Eppie, turning away, and stooping to lift rather a large stone. "See, daddy, I can carry this quite well," she said, going along with much energy for a few steps, but presently letting it fall.

"Ah, you're fine and strong, arn't you?" said Silas, while Eppie shook her aching arms and laughed. "Come, come, let us go and sit down on the bank against the stile there, and have no more lifting. You might hurt yourself, child. You'd need have somebody to work for you—and my arm isn't overstrong."

Silas uttered the last sentence slowly, as if it implied more than met the ear; and Eppie, when they sat down on the bank, nestled close to his side, and, taking hold caressingly of the arm that was not overstrong, held it on her lap, while Silas puffed again dutifully at the pipe, which occupied his other arm. An ash in the hedgerow behind made a fretted screen from the sun, and threw happy, playful shadows all about them.

"Father," said Eppie, very gently, after they had been sitting in silence a little while, "if I was to be married, ought I to be married with my mother's ring?"

Silas gave an almost imperceptible start, though the question fell in with the under-current of thought in his own mind, and then said, in a subdued tone, "Why, Eppie, have you been a-thinking on it?"

"Only this last week, father," said Eppie, ingenuously, "since Aaron talked to me about it."

"And what did he say?" said Silas, still in the same subdued way, as if he were anxious lest he should fall into the slightest tone that was not for Eppie's good.

"He said he should like to be married, because he was a-going in four-and-twenty, and had got a deal of gardening work, now Mr. Mott's given up; and he goes twice a-week regular to Mr. Cass's, and once to Mr. Osgood's and they're going to take him on at the Rectory."

"And who is it as he's wanting to marry?" said Silas, with rather a sad smile.

"Why, me, to be sure, daddy," said Eppie, with dimpling laughter, kissing her father's cheek; "as if he'd want to marry anybody else!"

"And you mean to have him, do you?" said Silas.

"Yes, some time," said Eppie, "I don't know when. Everybody's married some time, Aaron says. But I told him that wasn't true: for, I said, look at father— he's never been married."

"No, child," said Silas, "your father was a lone man till you was sent to him."

"But you'll never be lone again, father," said Eppie, tenderly. "That was what Aaron said—'I could never think o' taking you away from Master Marner, Eppie.'

And I said, 'It 'ud be no use if you did, Aaron.' And he wants us all to live together, so as you needn't work a bit, father, only what's for your own pleasure; and he'd be as good as a son to you—that's what he said."

"And should you like that Eppie?" said Silas looking at her.

"I shouldn't mind it, father," said Eppie, quite simply. "And I should like things to be so as you needn't work much. But if it wasn't for that, I'd sooner things didn't change. I'm very happy: I like Aaron to be fond of me, and come and see us often, and behave pretty to you— he always *does* behave pretty to you, doesn't he, father?"

"Yes, child, nobody could behave better," said Silas, emphatically. "He's his mother's lad."

"But I don't want any change," said Eppie. "I should like to go on a long, long while, just as we are. Only Aaron does want a change; and he made me cry a bit— only a bit—because he said I didn't care for him, for if I cared for him I should want us to be married, as he did."

"Eh, my blessed child," said Silas, laying down his pipe as if it were useless to pretend to smoke any longer, "you're o'er young to be married. We'll ask Mrs. Winthrop—we'll ask Aaron's mother what *she* thinks: if there's a right thing to do, she'll come at it. But there's this to be thought on, Eppie: things *will* change, whether we like it or no; things won't go on for a long while just as they are and no difference. I shall get older and helplesser, and be a burden on you, belike, if I don't go away from you altogether. Not as I mean you'd think me a burden—I know you wouldn't —but it 'ud be hard upon you; and when I look for'ard to that, I like to think as you'd have somebody else be- sides me—somebody young and strong, as'll outlast your own life, and take care on you to the end." Silas paused, and, resting his wrists on his knees, lifted his hands up and down meditatively as he looked on the ground.

"Then, would you like me to be married, father?" said Eppie, with a little trembling in her voice.

"I'll not be the man to say no, Eppie," said Silas, emphatically; "but we'll ask your godmother. She'll wish the right thing by you and her son too."

"There they come then," said Eppie. "Let us go and meet 'em. Oh, the pipe! won't you have it lit again, father?" said Eppie, lifting that medicinal appliance from the ground.

"Nay, child," said Silas, "I've done enough for to-day. I think, mayhap, a little of it does me more good than so much at once."

CHAPTER XVII

WHILE SILAS AND EPPIE were seated on the bank discoursing in the fleckered shade of the ash-tree, Miss Priscilla Lammeter was resisting her sister' arguments, that it would be better to take tea at the Red House, and let her father have a long nap, than drive home to the Warrens so soon after dinner. The family party (of four only) were seated round the table in the dark wainscoted parlor, with the Sunday dessert before them, of fresh filberts, apples and pears, duly ornamented with leaves by Nancy's own hand before the bells had rung for church.

A great change has come over the dark wainscoted parlor since we saw it in Godfrey's bachelor days, and under the wifeless reign of the old Squire. Now all is polish, on which no yesterday's dust is ever allowed to rest, from the yard's width of oaken boards round the carpet, to the old Squire's gun and whips and walking-sticks, ranged on the stag's antlers above the mantel-piece. All other signs of sporting and out-door occu-pation Nancy has removed to another room; but she has brought into the Red House the habit of filial rev-erence, and preserves sacredly in a place of honor these relics of her husband's departed father. The tankards are on the side-table still, but the bossed silver is undimmed by handling, and there are no dregs to send forth unpleasant suggestions: the only prevailing scent is of the lavender and rose-leaves that fill the vases of Derbyshire spar. All is purity and order in this once dreary room, for, fifteen years ago, it was entered by a new presiding spirit.

"Now, father," said Nancy, "*is* there any call for you to go home to tea? Mayn't you just as well stay with us?—such a beautiful evening as it's likely to be."

The old gentleman had been talking to Godfrey about the increasing poor-rate and the ruinous times and had not heard the dialogue between his daughters.

"My dear, you must ask Priscilla," he said, in the once firm voice, now become rather broken. "She man-ages me and the farm, too."

"And reason good as I should manage you, father," said Priscilla, "else you'd be giving yourself your death with rheumatism. And as for the farm, if anything turns out wrong, as it can't but do in these times, there's nothing kills a man so soon as having nobody to find fault with but himself. It's a deal the best way o' being master, to let somebody else do the ordering, and keep the blaming in your own hands. It 'ud save many a man a stroke, *I* believe."

"Well, well, my dear," said her father, with a quiet laugh, "I didn't say you don't manage for everybody's good."

"Then manage so as you may stay tea, Priscilla," said Nancy, putting her hand on her sister's arm affectionately. "Come now; and we'll go round the garden while father has his nap."

"My dear child, he'll have a beautiful nap in the gig, for I shall drive. And as for staying tea, I can't hear of it; for there's this dairymaid, now she knows she's to be married, turned Michaelmas, she'd as lief pour the new milk into the pig-trough as into the pans. That's the way with 'em all: it's as if they thought the world 'ud be new-made because they're to be married. So come and let me put my bonnet on, and there'll be time for us to walk round the garden while the horse is being put in."

When the sisters were treading the neatly-swept garden-walks, between the bright turf that contrasted pleasantly with the dark cones and arches and wall-like hedges of yew, Priscilla said:

"I'm as glad as anything at your husband's making that exchange o' land with cousin Osgood, and beginning the dairying. It's a thousand pities you didn't do it before; for it'll give you something to fill your mind. There's nothing like a dairy if folks want a bit o' worrit to make the days pass. For as for rubbing furniture, when you can once see your face in the table there's nothing else to look for; but there's always something fresh with the dairy; for even in the depths o' winter there's some pleasure in conquering the butter, and making it come whether or no. My dear," added Priscilla, pressing her sister's hand affectionately as they walked side by side, "you'll never be low when you've got a dairy."

"Ah, Priscilla," said Nancy, returning the pressure with a grateful glance of her clear eyes, "but it won't make up to Godfrey: a dairy's not so much to a man. And it's only what he cares for that ever makes me low. I'm contented with the blessings we have, if he could be contented."

"It drives me past patience," said Priscilla, impetuously, "that way o' the men—always wanting and wanting, and never easy with what they've got: they can't sit comfortable in their chairs when they've neither ache nor pain, but either they must stick a pipe in their mouths, to make 'em better than well, or else they must be swallowing something strong, though they're forced to make haste before the next meal comes in. But joyful be it spoken, our father was never that sort o' man. And if it had pleased God to make you ugly, like me, so as the men wouldn't ha' run after you we might have kept to our own family, and had nothing to do with folks as have got uneasy blood in their veins."

"Oh, don't say so, Priscilla," said Nancy, repenting that she had called forth this outburst; "nobody has any occasion to find fault with Godfrey. It's natural he should be disappointed at not having any children: every man likes to have somebody to work for and lay by for, and he always counted so on making a fuss with 'em when they were little. There's many another man 'ud hanker more than he does. He's the best of husbands."

"Oh, I know," said Priscilla, smiling sarcastically, "I know the way o' wives; they set one on to abuse their husbands, and then they turn round on one and praise 'em as if they wanted to sell 'em. But father'll be waiting for me; we must turn now."

The large gig with the steady old gray was at the front door, and Mr. Lammeter was already on the stone steps, passing the time in recalling to Godfrey what very fine points Speckle had when his master used to ride him.

"I always *would* have a good horse, you know," said the old gentleman, not liking that spirited time to be quite effaced from the memory of his juniors.

"Mind you bring Nancy to the Warrens before the week's out, Mr. Cass," was Priscilla's parting injunction, as she took the reins, and shook them gently, by way of friendly incitement to Speckle.

"I shall just take a turn to the fields against the Stone-pits, Nancy, and look at the draining," said Godfrey.

"You'll be in again by tea-time, dear?"

"Oh, yes, I shall be back in an hour."

It was Godfrey's custom on a Sunday afternoon to do a little contemplative farming in a leisurely walk. Nancy seldom accompanied him; for the women of her generation—unless, like Priscilla, they took to outdoor management—were not given to much walking beyond their own house and garden, finding sufficient exercise in domestic duties. So, when Priscilla was not with her, she usually sat with Mant's Bible before her, and after following the text with her eyes for a little while, she would gradually permit them to wander as her thoughts had already insisted on wandering.

But Nancy's Sunday thoughts were rarely quite out of keeping with the devout and reverential intention implied by the book spread open before her. She was not theologically instructed enough to discern very clearly the relation between the sacred documents of the past which she opened without method, and her own obscure, simple life; but the spirit of rectitude, and the sense of responsibility for the effect of her conduct on others, which were strong elements in Nancy's character, had made it a habit with her to scrutinize her past feelings and actions with self-questioning solicitude. Her mind not being courted by a great variety of subjects, she filled the vacant moments by living inwardly, again and again, through all her remembered experience, especially through the fifteen years of her married time, in which her life and its significance had been doubled. She recalled the small details, the words, tones, and looks, in the critical scenes which had opened a new epoch for her by giving her a deeper insight into the relations and trials of life, or which had called on her for some little effort of forbearance, or of painful adherence to an imagined or real duty—asking herself continually whether she had been in any respect blamable.

This excessive rumination and self-questioning is perhaps a morbid habit inevitable to a mind of much moral sensibility when shut out from its due share of outward activity and of practical claims on its affections—inevitable to a noble-hearted, childless woman, when her lot is narrow. "I can do so little—have I done it all well?" is the perpetually recurring thought; and there are no voices calling her away from that soliloquy, no peremptory demands to divert energy from vain regret or superfluous scruple.

There was one main thread of painful experience in Nancy's married life, and on it hung certain deeply-felt scenes, which were the oftenest revived in retrospect. The short dialogue with Priscilla in the garden had determined the current of retrospect in that frequent direction this particular Sunday afternoon. The first wandering of her thought from the text, which she still attempted dutifully to follow with her eyes and silent lips, was into an imaginary enlargement of the defence she had set up for her husband against Priscilla's implied blame. The vindication of the loved object is the best balm affection can find for its wounds: —"A man must have so much on his mind," is the belief by which a wife often supports a cheerful face under rough answers and unfeeling words. And Nancy's deepest wounds had all come from the perception that the absence of children from their hearth was dwelt on in her husband's mind as a privation to which he could not reconcile himself.

Yet sweet Nancy might have been expected to feel still more keenly the denial of a blessing to which she had looked forward with all the varied expectations and preparations, solemn and prettily trivial, which fill the mind of a loving woman when she expects to become a mother. Was there not a drawer filled with the neat work of her hands, all unworn and untouched, just as she had arranged it there fourteen years ago—just, but for one little dress, which had been made the burial-dress? But under this immediate personal trial Nancy was so firmly unmurmuring, that years ago she had suddenly renounced the habit of visiting this drawer, lest she should in this way be cherishing a longing for what was not given.

Perhaps it was this very severity towards any indulgence of what she held to be sinful regret in herself, that made her shrink from applying her own standard to her husband. "It is very different—it is much worse for a man to be disappointed in that way: a woman can always be satisfied with devoting herself to her husband, but a man wants something that will make him look forward more—and sitting by the fire is so much duller to him than to a woman." And always, when Nancy reached this point in her meditations—trying with pre-determined sympathy, to see everything as Godfrey saw it—there came a renewal of self-questioning. *Had* she done everything in her power to lighten Godfrey's privation? Had she really been right in the resistance which had cost her so much pain six years ago, and again four years ago—the resistance to her husband's wish that they should adopt a child?

Adoption was more remote from the ideas and habits of that time than of our own; still Nancy had her opinion on it. It was as necessary to her mind to have an opinion on all topics, not exclusively masculine, that had come under her notice, as for her to have a precisely marked place for every article of her personal property: and her opinions were always principles to be unwaveringly acted on. They were firm, not because of their basis, but because she held them with a tenacity inseparable from her mental action.

On all the duties and proprieties of life, from filial behavior to the arrangements of the evening toilet, pretty Nancy Lammeter, by the time she was three-and-twenty, had her unalterable little code, and had formed every one of her habits in strict accordance with that code. She carried these decided judgments within her in the most unobtrusive way: they rooted themselves in her mind, and grew there as quietly as grass. Years ago, we know, she insisted on dressing like Priscilla, because "it was right for sisters to dress alike," and because "she would do what was right if she wore a gown dyed with cheese-coloring." That was a trivial but typical instance of the mode in which Nancy's life was regulated.

It was one of those rigid principles, and no petty egotistic feeling, which had been the ground of Nancy's difficult resistance to her husband's wish. To adopt a child, because children of your own had been denied you, was to try and choose your lot in spite of Providence; the adopted child, she was convinced, would never turn out well, and would be a curse to those who had wilfully and rebelliously sought what it was clear that, for some high reason, they were better without. When you saw a thing was not meant to be, said Nancy, it was a bounden duty to leave off so much as wishing for it. And so far, perhaps, the wisest of men could scarcely make more than a verbal improvement in her principle. But the conditions under which she held it apparent that a thing was not meant to be, depended on a more peculiar mode of thinking. She would have given up making a purchase at a particular place if, on three successive times, rain, or some other cause of Heaven's sending, had formed an obstacle; and she would have anticipated a broken limb or other heavy misfortune to any one who persisted in spite of such indications.

"But why should you think the child would turn out ill?" said Godfrey, in his remonstrances. "She has thriven as well as child can do with the weaver; and *he* adopted her. There isn't such a pretty little girl anywhere else in the parish, or one fitter for the station we could give her. Where can be the likelihood of her being a curse to anybody?"

"Yes, my dear Godfrey," said Nancy, who was sitting with her hands tightly clasped together, and with yearning, regretful affection in her eyes. "The child may not turn out ill with the weaver. But, then, he didn't go to seek her, as we should be doing. It will be wrong; I feel sure it will. Don't you remember what that lady we met at the Royston Baths told us about the child her sister adopted? That was the only adopting I ever heard of; and the child was transported when it was twenty-three. Dear Godfrey, don't ask me to do what I know is wrong; I should never be happy again. I know it's very hard for *you*—it's easier for me—but it's the will of Providence."

It might seem singular that Nancy—with her religious theory pieced together out of narrow social traditions, fragments of church doctrine imperfectly understood, and girlish reasonings on her small experience—should have arrived by herself at a way of thinking so nearly akin to that of many devout people whose beliefs are held in the shape of a system quite remote from her knowledge; singular, if we did not know that human beliefs, like all other natural growths, elude the barriers of a system.

Godfrey had from the first specified Eppie, then about twelve years old, as a child suitable for them to adopt. It had never occurred to him that Silas would rather part with his life than with Eppie. Surely the weaver would wish the best to the child he had taken so much trouble with, and would be glad that such good fortune should happen to her; she would always be very grateful to him, and he would be well provided for to the end of his life—provided for as the excellent part he had done by the child deserved.

Was it not an appropriate thing for people in a higher station to take a charge off the hands of a man in a lower? It seemed an eminently appropriate thing to Godfrey, for reasons that were known only to himself; and by a common fallacy, he imagined the measure would be easy because he had private motives for desiring it.

This was rather a coarse mode of estimating Silas's relation to Eppie; but we must remember that many of the impressions which Godfrey was likely to gather concerning the laboring people around him would favor the idea that deep affections can hardly go along with callous palms and scant means; and he had not had the opportunity, even if he had had the power, of entering intimately into all that was exceptional in the weaver's experience. It was only the want of adequate knowledge that could have made it possible for Godfrey deliberately to entertain an unfeeling project; his natural kindness had outlived that blighting time of cruel wishes, and Nancy's praise of him as a husband was not founded entirely on a wilful illusion.

"I was right," she said to herself, when she had recalled all their scenes of discussion—"I feel I was right to say him nay, though it hurt me more than anything; but how good Godfrey has been about it! Many men would have been very angry with me for standing out against their wishes; and they might have thrown out that they'd had ill-luck in marrying me; but Godfrey has never been the man to say me an unkind word. It's only what he can't hide: everything seems so blank to him, I know; and the land—what a difference it 'ud make to him, when he goes to see after things, if he'd children growing up that he was doing it all for! But I won't murmur; and perhaps if he'd married a woman who'd have had children, she'd have vexed him in other ways."

This possibility was Nancy's chief comfort; and to give it greater strength, she labored to make it impossible that any other wife should have had more perfect tenderness. She had been *forced* to vex him by that one denial.

Godfrey was not insensible to her loving effort, and did Nancy no injustice as to the motives of her obstinacy. It was impossible to have lived with her fifteen years and not be aware that an unselfish clinging to the right, and a sincerity clear as the flower-born dew, were her main characteristics; indeed, Godfrey felt this so strongly, that his own more wavering nature, too adverse to facing difficulty to being unvaryingly simple and truthful, was kept in a certain awe of this gentle wife who watched his looks with a yearning to obey them. It seemed to him impossible that he should ever confess to her the truth about Eppie: she would never recover from the repulsion the story of his earlier marriage would create, told to her now, after that long concealment. And the child, too, he thought, must become an object of repulsion: the very sight of her would be painful. The shock to Nancy's mingled pride and ignorance of the world's evil might even be too much for her delicate frame. Since he had married her with that secret on his heart he must keep it there to the last. Whatever else he did, he could not make an irreparable breach between himself and this long-loved wife.

Meanwhile, why could he not make up his mind to the absence of children from a hearth brightened by such a wife? Why did his mind fly uneasily to that void, as if it were the sole reason why life was not thoroughly joyous to him? I suppose it is the way with all men and women who reach middle age without the clear perception that life never *can* be thoroughly joyous: under the vague dulness of the gray hours, dissatisfaction seeks a definite object, and finds it in the privation of an untried good. Dissatisfaction seated musingly on a childless hearth, thinks with envy of the father whose return is greeted by young voices—seated at the meal where the little heads rise one above another like nursery plants, it sees a black care hovering behind every one of them, and thinks the impulses by which men abandon freedom, and seek for ties, are surely nothing but a brief madness.

In Godfrey's case there were further reasons why his thoughts should be continually solicited by this one point in his lot: his conscience, never thoroughly easy about Eppie, now gave his childless home the aspect of a retribution; and as the time passed on, under Nancy's refusal to adopt her, any retrieval of his error became more and more difficult.

On this Sunday afternoon it was already four years since there had been any allusion to the subject between them, and Nancy supposed that it was forever buried.

"I wonder if he'll mind it less or more as he gets older," she thought; "I'm afraid more. Aged people feel the miss of children: what would father do without Priscilla? And if I die, Godfrey will be very lonely— not holding together with his brothers much. But I won't be over-anxious, and trying to make things out beforehand: I must do my best for the present."

With that last thought Nancy roused herself from her reverie, and turned her eyes again towards the forsaken page. It had been forsaken longer than she imagined, for she was presently surprised by the appearance of the servant with the tea-things. It was, in fact, a little before the usual time for tea; but Jane had her reasons.

"Is your master come into the yard, Jane?"

"No'm, he isn't," said Jane, with a slight emphasis, of which, however, her mistress took no notice.

"I don't know whether you've seen 'em, 'm," continued Jane, after a pause, "but there's folks making haste all one way, afore the front window. I doubt something's happened. There's niver a man to be seen i' the yard, else, I'd send and see. I've been up into the top attic, but there's no seeing anything for trees. I hope nobody's hurt, that's all."

"Oh, no, I daresay there's nothing much the matter," said Nancy. "It's perhaps Mr. Snell's bull got out again, as he did before."

"I wish he mayn't gore anybody then, that's all," said Jane, not altogether despising a hypothesis which covered a few imaginary calamities.

"That girl is always terrifying me," thought Nancy; "I wish Godfrey would come in."

She went to the front window and looked as far as she could see along the road, with an uneasiness which she felt to be childish, for there were now no such signs of excitement as Jane had spoken of, and Godfrey would not be likely to return by the village road, but by the fields. She continued to stand however, looking at the placid churchyard with the long shadows of the gravestones across the bright green hillocks, and at the glowing autumn colors of the Rectory trees beyond. Before such calm external beauty the presence of a vague fear is more distinctly felt—like a raven flapping its slow wing across the sunny air. Nancy wished more and more that Godfrey would come in.

CHAPTER XVIII

SOME ONE opened the door at the other end of the room, and Nancy felt that it was her husband. She turned from the window with gladness in her eyes, for the wife's chief dread was stilled.

"Dear, I'm so thankful you're come," she said, going towards him. "I began to get . . ."

She paused abruptly, for Godfrey was laying down his hat with trembling hands, and turned towards her with a pale face and a strange unanswering glance, as if he saw her indeed, but saw her as part of a scene invisible to herself. She laid her hand on his arm, not daring to speak again; but he left the touch unnoticed, and threw himself into his chair.

Jane was already at the door with the hissing urn.

"Tell her to keep away, will you?" said Godfrey; and when the door was closed again he exerted himself to speak more distinctly.

"Sit down, Nancy—there," he said, pointing to a chair opposite him. "I came back as soon as I could, to hinder anybody's telling you but me. I've had a great shock—but I care most about the shock it'll be to you."

"It isn't father and Priscilla?" said Nancy, with quivering lips, clasping her hands together tightly on her lap.

"No, it's nobody living," said Godfrey, unequal to the considerate skill with which he would have wished to make his revelation. "It's Dunstan—my brother Dunstan, that we lost sight of sixteen years ago. We've found him—found his body—his skeleton."

The deep dread Godfrey's look had created in Nancy made her feel these words a relief. She sat in comparative calmness to hear what else he had to tell. He went on:

"The Stone-pit has gone dry suddenly — from the draining, I suppose; and there he lies—has lain for sixteen years, wedged between two great stones. There's his watch and seals, and there's my gold-handled hunting-whip, with my name on: he took it away, without my knowing, the day he went hunting on Wildfire, the last time he was seen."

Godfrey paused: it was not so easy to say what came next.

"Do you think he drowned himself?" said Nancy, almost wondering that her husband should be so deeply shaken by what had happened all those years ago to an unloved brother, of whom worse things had been augured.

"No, he fell in," said Godfrey, in a low but distinct voice, as if he felt some deep meaning in the fact. Presently he added: "Dunstan was the man that robbed Silas Marner."

The blood rushed to Nancy's face and neck at this surprise and shame, for she had been bred up to regard even a distant kinship with crime as a dishonor.

"O Godfrey!" she said, with compassion in her tone, for she had immediately reflected that the dishonor must be felt still more keenly by her husband.

"There was the money in the pit," he continued— "all the weaver's money. Everything's been gathered up, and they're taking the skeleton to the Rainbow. But I came back to tell you: there was no hindering it; you must know."

He was silent, looking on the ground for two long minutes. Nancy would have said some words of comfort under this disgrace, but she refrained, from an instinctive sense that there was something behind—that Godfrey had something else to tell her. Presently he lifted his eyes to her face, and kept them fixed on her, as he said:

"Everything comes to light, Nancy, sooner or later. When God Almighty wills it, our secrets are found out. I've lived with a secret on my mind, but I'll keep it from you no longer. I wouldn't have you know it by somebody else, and not by me—I wouldn't have you find it out after I'm dead. I'll tell you now. It's been 'I will' and 'I won't' with me all my life—I'll make sure of myself now."

Nancy's utmost dread had returned. The eyes of the husband and wife met with awe in them, as at a crisis with suspended affection.

"Nancy," said Godfrey slowly, "when I married you, I hid something from you—something I ought to have told you. That woman Marner found dead in the snow—Eppie's mother—that wretched woman—was my wife: Eppie is my child."

He paused, dreading the effect of his confession. But Nancy sat quite still, only that her eyes dropped and ceased to meet his. She was pale and quiet as a meditative statue, clasping her hands on her lap.

"You'll never think the same of me again," said Godfrey, after a little while, with some tremor in his voice.

She was silent.

"I oughtn't to have left the child unowned; I oughtn't to have kept it from you. But I couldn't bear to give you up, Nancy. I was led away into marrying her—I suffered for it."

Still Nancy was silent, looking down; and he almost expected that she would presently get up and say she would go to her father's. How could she have any mercy for faults that must seem so black to her, with her simple severe notions?

But at last she lifted up her eyes to his again and spoke. There was no indignation in her voice—only deep regret.

"Godfrey, if you had but told me this six years ago, we could have done some of our duty by the child. Do you think I'd have refused to take her in, if I'd known she was yours?"

At that moment Godfrey felt all the bitterness of an error that was not simply futile, but had defeated its own end. He had not measured this wife with whom he had lived so long. But she spoke again, with more agitation.

"And—O Godfrey—if we'd had her from the first, if you'd taken to her as you ought, she'd have loved me for her mother—and you'd have been happier with me; I could better have bore my little baby dying, and our life might have been more like what we used to think it 'ud be."

The tears fell, and Nancy ceased to speak.

"But you wouldn't have married me then, Nancy, if I'd told you," said Godfrey, urged, in the bitterness of his self-reproach, to prove to himself that his conduct had not been utter folly. "You may think you would now, but you wouldn't then. With your pride, and your father's, you'd have hated having anything to do with me after the talk there'd have been."

"I can't say what I should have done about that, Godfrey. I should never have married anybody else. But I wasn't worth doing wrong for—nothing is in this world. Nothing is so good as it seems beforehand—not even our marrying wasn't, you see." There was a faint, sad smile on Nancy's face as she said the last words.

"I'm a worse man than you thought I was, Nancy," said Godfrey, rather tremulously. "Can you forgive me ever?"

"The wrong to me is but little, Godfrey: you've made it up to me—you've been good to me for fifteen years. It's another you did the wrong to; and I doubt it can never be all made up for."

"But we can take Eppie now," said Godfrey. "I won't mind the world knowing at last. I'll be plain and open for the rest o' my life."

"It'll be different coming to us, now she's grown

up," said Nancy, shaking her head sadly. "But it's your duty to acknowledge her and provide for her; and I'll do my part by her, and pray to God Almighty to make her love me."

"Then we'll go together to Silas Marner's this very night, as soon as everything's quiet at the Stone-pits."

CHAPTER XIX

BETWEEN EIGHT AND NINE o'clock that evening, Eppie and Silas were seated alone in the cottage. After the great excitement the weaver had undergone from the events of the afternoon, he had felt a longing for this quietude, and had even begged Mrs. Winthrop and Aaron, who had naturally lingered behind every one else, to leave him alone with his child. The excitement had not passed away: it had only reached that stage when the keenness of the susceptibility makes external stimulus intolerable—when there is no sense of weariness, but rather an intensity of inward life, under which sleep is an impossibility. Any one who has watched such moments in other men remembers the brightness of the eyes and the strange definiteness that comes over coarse features from that transient influence. It is as if a new fineness of ear for spiritual voices had sent wonder-working vibrations through the heavy mortal frame—as if "beauty born of murmuring sound" had passed into the face of the listener.

Silas's face showed that sort of transfiguration, as he sat in his arm-chair and looked at Eppie. She had drawn her own chair towards his knees, and leaned forward, holding his hands, while she looked up at him. On the table near them, lit by a candle, lay the recovered gold—the old long-loved gold, ranged in orderly heaps, as Silas used to range it in the days when it was his only joy. He had been telling her how he used to count it every night, and how his soul was utterly desolate till she was sent to him.

"At first, I'd a sort o' feeling come across me now and then," he was saying in a subdued tone, "as if you might be changed into the gold again; for some times, turn my head which way I would, I seemed to see the gold, and I thought I should be glad if I could feel it, and find it was come back. But that didn't last long. After a bit, I should have thought it was a curse come again, if it had drove you from me, for I'd got to feel the need o' your looks and your voice and the touch o' your little fingers. You didn't know then, Eppie, when you were such a little un—you didn't know what your old father Silas felt for you."

"But I know now, father," said Eppie. "If it hadn't been for you, they'd have taken me to the workhouse, and there'd have been nobody to love me."

"Eh, my precious child, the blessing was mine. If you hadn't been sent to save me, I should ha' gone to the grave in my misery. The money was taken away from me in time; and you see it's been kept—kept till it was wanted for you. It's wonderful—our life is wonderful."

Silas sat in silence a few minutes, looking at the money.

"It takes no hold of me now," he said ponderingly—"the money doesn't. I wonder if it ever could again—I doubt it might, if I lost you, Eppie. I might come to think I was forsaken again, and lose the feeling that God was good to me."

At that moment there was a knocking at the door; and Eppie was obliged to rise without answering Silas. Beautiful she looked, with the tenderness of gathering tears in her eyes and a slight flush on her cheeks, as she stepped to open the door. The flush deepened when she saw Mr. and Mrs. Godfrey Cass. She made her little rustic curtsy, and held the door wide for them to enter.

"We're disturbing you very late, my dear," said Mrs. Cass, taking Eppie's hand, and looking in her face with an expression of anxious interest and admiration. Nancy herself was pale and tremulous.

Eppie, after placing chairs for Mr. and Mrs. Cass, went to stand against Silas, opposite to them.

"Well, Marner," said Godfrey, trying to speak with perfect firmness, "it's a great comfort to me to see you with your money again, that you've been deprived of so many years. It was one of my family did you the wrong—the more grief to me—and I feel bound to make up to you for it in every way. Whatever I can do for you will be nothing but paying a debt, even if I looked no further than the robbery. But there are other things I'm beholden—shall be beholden to you for, Marner."

Godfrey checked himself. It had been agreed between him and his wife that the subject of his fatherhood should be approached very carefully, and that, if possible, the disclosure should be reserved for the future, so that it might be made to Eppie gradually. Nancy had urged this, because she felt strongly the painful light in which Eppie must inevitably see the relation between her father and mother.

Silas, always ill at ease when he was being spoken to by "betters," such as Mr. Cass—tall, powerful, florid men, seen chiefly on horseback—answered with some constraint:

"Sir, I've a deal to thank you for a'ready. As for the robbery, I count it no loss to me. And if I did, you couldn't help it: you aren't answerable for it."

"You may look at it in that way, Marner, but I never can; and I hope you'll let me act according to my own feelings of what's just. I know you're easily contented: you've been a hard-working man all your life."

"Yes, sir, yes," said Marner, meditatively. "I should ha' been bad off without my work: it was what I held by when everything else was gone from me."

"Ah," said Godfrey, applying Marner's words simply to his bodily wants, "it was a good trade for you in this country, because there's been a great deal of linen-weaving to be done. But you're getting rather past such close work, Marner: it's time you laid by and had some rest. You look a good deal pulled down, though you're not an old man, *are* you?"

"Fifty-five, as near as I can say, sir," said Silas.

"Oh, why, you may live thirty years longer—look at old Macey! And that money on the table, after all, is but little. It won't go far either way—whether it's put out to interest, or you were to live on it as long as it would last: it wouldn't go far if you'd nobody to keep but yourself, and you've had two to keep for a good many years now."

"Eh, sir," said Silas, unaffected by anything Godfrey was saying, "I'm in no fear o' want. We shall do very well—Eppie and me 'ull do well enough. There's few working-folks have got so much laid by as that. I don't know what it is to gentlefolks, but I look upon it as a deal—almost too much. And as for us, it's little we want."

"Only the garden, father," said Eppie, blushing up to the ears the moment after.

"You love a garden, do you, my dear?" said Nancy,

thinking that this turn in the point of view might help her husband. "We should agree in that: I give a deal of time to the garden."

"Ah, there's plenty of gardening at the Red House," said Godfrey, surprised at the difficulty he found in approaching a proposition which had seemed so easy to him in the distance. "You've done a good part by Eppie, Marner, for sixteen years. It 'ud be a great comfort to you to see her well provided for, wouldn't it? She looks blooming and healthy, but not fit for any hardships: she doesn't look like a strapping girl come of working parents. You'd like to see her taken care of by those who can leave her well off, and make a lady of her; she's more fit for it than for a rough life, such as she might come to have in a few years' time."

A slight flush came over Marner's face, and disappeared, like a passing gleam. Eppie was simply wondering Mr. Cass should talk so about things that seemed to have nothing to do with reality, but Silas was hurt and uneasy.

"I don't take your meaning, sir," he answered, not having words at command to express the mingled feelings with which he had heard Mr. Cass's words.

"Well, my meaning is this, Marner," said Godfrey, determined to come to the point. "Mrs. Cass and I, you know, have no children—nobody to be the better for our good home and everything else we have—more than enough for ourselves. And we should like to have somebody in the place of a daughter to us—we should like to have Eppie, and treat her in every way as our own child. It 'ud be a great comfort to you in your old age, I hope, to see her fortune made in that way, after you've been at the trouble of bringing her up so well. And it's right you should have every reward for that. And Eppie, I'm sure, will always love you and be grateful to you: she'd come and see you very often, and we should all be on the look-out to do everything we could towards making you comfortable."

A plain man like Godfrey Cass, speaking under some embarrassment, necessarily blunders on words that are coarser than his intentions, and that are likely to fall gratingly on susceptible feelings. While he had been speaking, Eppie had quietly passed her arm behind Silas's head, and let her hand rest against it caressingly: she felt him trembling violently. He was silent for some moments when Mr. Cass had ended—powerless under the conflict of emotions, all alike painful. Eppie's heart was swelling at the sense that her father was in distress; and she was just going to lean down and speak to him, when one struggling dread at last gained the mastery over every other in Silas, and he said, faintly:

"Eppie, my child, speak. I won't stand in your way. Thank Mr. and Mrs. Cass."

Eppie took her hand from her father's head, and came forward a step. Her cheeks were flushed, but not with shyness this time: the sense that her father was in doubt and suffering banished that sort of self-consciousness. She dropped a low curtsy, first to Mrs. Cass and then to Mr. Cass, and said:

"Thank you, ma'am—thank you, sir. But I can't leave my father, nor own anybody nearer than him. And I don't want to be a lady—thank you all the same" (here Eppie dropped another curtsy). "I couldn't give up the folks I've been used to."

Eppie's lip began to tremble a little at the last words. She retreated to her father's chair again, and held him round the neck: while Silas, with a subdued sob, put up his hand to grasp hers.

The tears were in Nancy's eyes, but her sympathy with Eppie was, naturally, divided with distress on her husband's account. She dared not speak, wondering what was going on in her husband's mind.

Godfrey felt an irritation inevitable to almost all of us when we encounter an unexpected obstacle. He had been full of his own penitence and resolution to retrieve his error as far as the time was left to him; he was possessed with all-important feelings, that were to lead to a predetermined course of action which he had fixed on as the right, and he was not prepared to enter with lively appreciation into other people's feelings counteracting his virtuous resolves. The agitation with which he spoke again was not quite unmixed with anger.

"But I've a claim on you, Eppie—the strongest of all claims. It's my duty, Marner, to own Eppie as my child, and provide for her. She's my own child: her mother was my wife. I've a natural claim on her that must stand before every other."

Eppie had given a violent start, and turned quite pale. Silas, on the contrary, who had been relieved by Eppie's answer, from the dread lest his mind should be in opposition to hers, felt the spirit of resistance in him set free, not without a touch of parental fierceness. "Then, sir," he answered, with an accent of bitterness that had been silent in him since the memorable day when his youthful hope had perished—"then, sir, why didn't you say so sixteen year ago, and claim her before I'd come to love her, i'stead o' coming to take her from me now, when you might as well take the heart out o' my body? God gave her to me because you turned your back upon her, and He looks upon her as mine: you've no right to her! When a man turns a blessing from his door, it falls to them as take it in."

"I know that, Marner. I was wrong. I've repented of my conduct in that matter," said Godfrey, who could not help feeling the edge of Silas's words.

"I'm glad to hear it, sir," said Marner, with gathering excitement; "but repentance doesn't alter what's been going on for sixteen year. Your coming now and saying 'I'm her father,' doesn't alter the feelings inside us. It's me she's been calling her father ever since she could say the word."

"But I think you might look at the thing more reasonably, Marner," said Godfrey, unexpectedly awed by the weaver's direct truth-speaking. "It isn't as if she was to be taken quite away from you, so that you'd never see her again. She'll be very near you, and come to see you very often. She'll feel just the same towards you."

"Just the same?" said Marner, more bitterly than ever. "How'll she feel just the same for me as she does now, when we eat o' the same bit, and drink o' the same cup, and think o' the same things from one day's end to another? Just the same? That's idle talk. You'd cut us i' two."

Godfrey, unqualified by experience to discern the pregnancy of Marner's simple words, felt rather angry again. It seemed to him that the weaver was very selfish (a judgment readily passed by those who have never tested their own power of sacrifice) to oppose what was undoubtedly for Eppie's welfare; and he felt himself called upon, for her sake, to assert his authority.

"I should have thought, Marner," he said, severely— "I should have thought your affection for Eppie would make you rejoice in what was for her good, even if it did call upon you to give up something. You ought to remember your own life's uncertain, and she's at an age now when her lot may soon be fixed in a way very different from what it would be in her father's home: she may marry some low working-man, and then, whatever I might do for her, I couldn't make her well-off.

You're putting yourself in the way of her welfare; and though I'm sorry to hurt you after what you've done, and what I've left undone, I feel now it's my duty to insist on taking care of my own daughter. I want to do my duty."

It would be difficult to say whether it were Silas or Eppie that was more deeply stirred by this last speech of Godfrey's. Thought had been very busy in Eppie as she listened to the contest between her old, long-loved father and this new, unfamiliar father who had suddenly come to fill the place of that black featureless shadow which had held the ring and placed it on her mother's finger. Her imagination had darted backward in conjectures, and forward in previsions, of what this revealed fatherhood implied; and there were words in Godfrey's last speech which helped to make the previsions especially definite. Not that these thoughts, either of past or future, determined her resolution— *that* was determined by the feelings which vibrated to every word Silas had uttered; but they raised, even apart from these feelings, a repulsion towards the offered lot and the newly-revealed father.

Silas, on the other hand, was again stricken in conscience, and alarmed lest Godfrey's accusation should be true—lest he should be raising his own will as an obstacle to Eppie's good. For many moments he was mute, struggling for the self-conquest necessary to the uttering of the difficult words. They came out tremulously.

"I'll say no more. Let it be as you will. Speak to the child. I'll hinder nothing."

Even Nancy, with all the acute sensibility of her own affections, shared her husband's view, that Marner was not justifiable in his wish to retain Eppie, after her real father had avowed himself. She felt that it was a very hard trial for the poor weaver, but her code allowed no question that a father by blood must have a claim above that of any foster father. Besides, Nancy, used all her life to plenteous circumstances and the privileges of "respectability," could not enter into the pleasures which early nurture and habit connect with all the little aims and efforts of the poor who are born poor: to her mind, Eppie, in being restored to her birthright, was entering on a too long withheld but unquestionable good. Hence she heard Silas's last words with relief, and thought, as Godfrey did, that their wish was achieved.

"Eppie, my dear," said Godfrey, looking at his daughter, not without some embarrassment, under the sense that she was old enough to judge him, "it'll always be our wish that you should show your love and gratitude to one who's been a father to you so many years, and we shall want to help you to make him comfortable in every way. But we hope you'll come to love us as well; and though I haven't been what a father should ha' been to you all these years, I wish to do the utmost in my power for you for the rest of my life, and provide for you as my only child. And you'll have the best of mothers in my wife—that'll be a blessing you haven't known since you were old enough to know it."

"My dear, you'll be a treasure to me," said Nancy, in her gentle voice. "We shall want for nothing when we have our daughter."

Eppie did not come forward and curtsy, as she had done before. She held Silas's hand in hers, and grasped it firmly—it was a weaver's hand, with a palm and finger-tips that were sensitive to such pressure—while she spoke with colder decision than before.

"Thank you, ma'am—thank you, sir, for your offers—

they're very great, and far above my wish. For I should have no delight i' life any more if I was forced to go away from my father, and knew he was sitting at home a-thinking of me and feeling lone. We've been used to be happy together every day, and I can't think o' no happiness without him. And he says he'd nobody i' the world till I was sent to him, and he'd have nothing when I was gone. And he's took care of me and loved me from the first, and I'll cleave to him as long as he lives, and nobody shall ever come between him and me."

"But you must make sure, Eppie," said Silas in a low voice—"you must make sure as you won't ever be sorry, because you've made you're choice to stay among poor folks, and with poor clothes and things, when you might ha' had everything o' the best."

His sensitiveness on this point had increased as he listened to Eppie's words of faithful affection.

"I can never be sorry, father," said Eppie. "I shouldn't know what to think on or to wish for with fine things about me, as I haven't been used to. And it 'ud be poor work for me to put on things and ride in a gig, and sit in a place at church, as 'ud make them as I'm fond of think me unfitting company for 'em. What could *I* care for them?"

Nancy looked at Godfrey with a pained questioning glance. But his eyes were fixed on the floor, where he was moving the end of his stick, as if he were pondering on something absently. She thought there was a word which might perhaps come better from her lips than from his.

"What you say is natural, my dear child—it's natural you should cling to those who've brought you up," she said mildly; "but there's a duty you owe to your lawful father. There's perhaps something to be given up on more sides than one. When your father opens his home to you, I think it's right you shouldn't turn your back on it."

"I can't feel as I've got any father but one," said Eppie, impetuously, while the tears gathered. "I've always thought of a little home where he'd sit i' the corner, and I should fend and do everything for him: I can't think o' no other home. I wasn't brought up to be a lady, and I can't turn my mind to it. I like the working-folks, and their victuals, and their ways. And," she ended passionately, while the tears fell, "I'm promised to marry a working-man, as'll live with father, and help me to take care of him."

Godfrey looked up at Nancy with a flushed face and smarting dilated eyes. This frustration of a purpose towards which he had set out under the exalted consciousness that he was about to compensate in some degree for the greatest demerit of his life, made him feel the air of the room stifling.

"Let us go," he said, in an undertone.

"We won't talk of this any longer now," said Nancy, rising. "We're your well-wishers, my dear—and yours, too, Marner. We shall come and see you again. It's getting late now."

In this way she covered her husband's abrupt departure, for Godfrey had gone straight to the door, unable to say more.

CHAPTER XX

NANCY AND GODFREY walked home under the starlight in silence. When they entered the oaken parlor, Godfrey threw himself into his chair, while Nancy laid down her bonnet and shawl, and stood on the hearth near her husband, unwilling to leave him even for a few minutes, and yet fearing to utter any word lest it might jar on his feelings. At last Godfrey turned his head towards her, and their eyes met, dwelling in that meeting without any movement on either side. That quiet mutual gaze of a trusting husband and wife is like the first moment of rest or refuge from a great weariness or a great danger—not to be interfered with by speech or action which would distract the sensations from the fresh enjoyment of repose.

But presently he put out his hand, and as Nancy placed hers within it, he drew her towards him, and said:

"That's ended!"

She bent to kiss him, and then said, as she stood by his side, "Yes, I'm afraid we must give up the hope of having her for a daughter. It wouldn't be right to want to force her to come to us against her will. We can't alter her bringing up and what's come of it."

"No," said Godfrey, with a keen decisiveness of tone, in contrast with his usually careless and unemphatic speech—"there's debts we can't pay like money debts, by paying extra for the years that have slipped by. While I've been putting off and putting off, the trees have been growing—it's too late now. Marner was in the right in what he said about a man's turning a blessing away from his door: it falls to somebody else. I wanted to pass for childless once, Nancy—I shall pass for childless now against my wish."

Nancy did not speak immediately, but after a little while she asked—"You won't make it known then, about Eppie's being your daughter?"

"No: where would be the good to anybody?—only harm. I must do what I can for her in the state of life she chooses. I must see who it is she's thinking of marrying."

"If it won't do any good to make the thing known," said Nancy, who thought she might now allow herself the relief of entertaining a feeling which she had tried to silence before, "I should be very thankful for father and Priscilla never to be troubled with knowing what was done in the past, more than about Dunsey: it can't be helped, their knowing that."

"I shall put it in my will—I think I shall put it in my will. I shouldn't like to leave anything to be found out, like this about Dunsey," said Godfrey, meditatively. "But I can't see anything but difficulties that 'ud come from telling it now. I must do what I can to make her happy in her own way. I've a notion," he added, after a moment's pause, "it's Aaron Winthrop she meant she was engaged to. I remember seeing him with her and Marner going away from church."

"Well, he's very sober and industrious," said Nancy, trying to view the matter as cheerfully as possible.

Godfrey fell into thoughtfulness again. Presently he looked up at Nancy sorrowfully, and said:

"She's a very pretty, nice girl, isn't she, Nancy?"

"Yes, dear; and with just your hair and eyes: I wondered it had never struck me before."

"I think she took a dislike to me at the thought of my being her father: I could see a change in her manner after that."

"She couldn't bear to think of not looking on Marner as her father," said Nancy, not wishing to confirm her husband's painful impression.

"She thinks I did wrong by her mother as well as by her. She thinks me worse than I am. But she *must* think it: she can never know all. It's part of my punishment, Nancy, for my daughter to dislike me. I should never have got into that trouble if I'd been true to you—if I hadn't been a fool. I'd no right to expect anything but evil could come of that marriage—and when I shirked doing a father's part, too."

Nancy was silent: her spirit of rectitude would not let her try to soften the edge of what she felt to be a just compunction. He spoke again after a little while, but the tone was rather changed: there was tenderness mingled with the previous self-reproach.

"And I got *you*, Nancy, in spite of all; and yet I've been grumbling and uneasy because I hadn't something else—as if I deserved it."

"You've never been wanting to me, Godfrey," said Nancy with quiet sincerity. "My only trouble would be gone if you resigned yourself to the lot that's been given us."

"Well, perhaps, it isn't too late to mend a bit there. Though it *is* too late to mend some things, say what they will."

CHAPTER XXI

THE NEXT MORNING, when Silas and Eppie were seated at their breakfast, he said to her:

"Eppie, there's a thing I've had on my mind to do this two year, and now the money's been brought back to us, we can do it. I've been turning it over and over in the night, and I think we'll set out to-morrow, while the fine days last. We'll leave the house and everything for your godmother to take care on, and we'll make a little bundle o' things and set out."

"Where to go, daddy?" said Eppie, in much surprise.

"To my old country—to the town where I was born—up Lantern Yard. I want to see Mr. Paston, the minister; something may ha' come out to make 'em know I was innicent o' the robbery. And Mr. Paston was a man with a deal o' light—I want to speak to him about the drawing o' the lots. And I should like to talk to him about the religion o' this countryside, for I partly think he doesn't know on it."

Eppie was very joyful, for there was the prospect not only of wonder and delight at seeing a strange country, but also of coming back to tell Aaron all about it. Aaron was so much wiser than she was about most things—it would be rather pleasant to have this little advantage over him. Mrs. Winthrop, though possessed with a dim fear of dangers attendant on so long a journey, and requiring many assurances that it would not take them out of the region of carriers' carts and slow wagons, was nevertheless well pleased that Silas should revisit his own country, and find out if he had been cleared from that false accusation.

"You'd be easier in your mind for the rest o' your life, Master Marner," said Dolly—"that you would. And if there's any light to be got up the yard, as you talk on, we've need of it i' this world, and I'd be glad on it myself, if you could bring it back."

So on the fourth day from that time, Silas and Eppie, in their Sunday clothes, with a small bundle tied in a blue linen handkerchief, were making their way through the streets of a great manufacturing town. Silas, bewildered by the changes thirty years had brought over his native place, had stopped several persons in succession to ask them the name of this town, that he might be sure he was not under a mistake about it.

"Ask for Lantern Yard, father—ask this gentleman with the tassels on his shoulders a-standing at the shop door; he isn't in a hurry like the rest," said Eppie, in some distress at her father's bewilderment, and ill at ease, besides, amidst the noise, the movement, and the multitude of strange indifferent faces.

"Eh, my child, he won't know anything about it," said Silas; "gentlefolks didn't ever go up the Yard. But happen somebody can tell me which is the way to Prison Street, where the jail is. I know the way out o' that as if I'd seen it yesterday."

With some difficulty, after many turnings and new inquiries, they reached Prison Street; and the grim walls of the jail, the first object that answered to any image in Silas's memory, cheered him with the certitude, which no assurance of the town's name had hitherto given him, that he was in his native place.

"Ah," he said, drawing a long breath, "there's the jail, Eppie; that's just the same; I aren't afraid now.

It's the third turning on the left hand from the jail doors—that's the way we must go."

"Oh, what a dark, ugly place!" said Eppie. "How it hides the sky! It's worse than the Workhouse. I'm glad you don't live in this town, now, father. Is Lantern Yard like this street?"

"My precious child," said Silas, smiling, "it isn't a big street like this. I never was easy i' this street myself, but I was fond o' Lantern Yard. The shops here are all altered, I think—I can't make 'em out; but I shall know the turning, because it's the third."

"Here it is," he said, in a tone of satisfaction, as they came to a narrow alley. "And then we must go to the left again, and then straight for'ard for a bit, up Shoe Lane: and then we shall be at the entry next to the o'erhanging window, where there's the nick in the road for the water to run. Eh, I can see it all."

"O father, I'm like as if I was stifled," said Eppie. "I couldn't ha' thought as any folks lived i' this way so close together. How pretty the Stone-pits 'ull look when we get back!"

"It looks comical to *me*, child, now—and smells bad I can't think as it usened to smell so."

Here and there a sallow, begrimed face looked out from a gloomy doorway at the strangers, and increased Eppie's uneasiness, so that it was a longed-for relief when they issued from the alleys into Shoe Lane, where there was a broader strip of sky.

"Dear heart!" said Silas, "why, there's people coming out o' the Yard as if they'd been to chapel at this time o' day—a weekday noon!"

Suddenly he started and stood still with a look of distressed amazement that alarmed Eppie. They were before an opening in front of a large factory, from which men and women were streaming for their midday meal.

"Father," said Eppie, clasping his arm, "what's the matter?"

But she had to speak again and again before Silas could answer her.

"It's gone, child," he said, at last, in strong agitation—"Lantern Yard's gone. It must ha' been here, because here's the house with the o'erhanging window—I know that— it's just the same; but they've made this new opening; and see that big factory! It's all gone, chapel and all!"

"Come into that little brush-shop and sit down, father—they'll let you sit down," said Eppie, always on the watch lest one of her father's strange attacks should come on. "Perhaps the people can tell you all about it."

But neither from the brush-maker, who had come to Shoe Lane only ten years ago, when the factory was already built, nor from any other source within his reach, could Silas learn anything of the old Lantern Yard friends, or of Mr. Paston the minister

"The old place is all swep' away," Silas said to Dolly Winthrop on the night of his return—"the little graveyard and everything. The old home's gone; I've no home but this now I shall never know whether they got at the truth o' the robbery, nor whether Mr. Paston could ha' given me any light about the drawing o' the lots. It's dark to me, Mrs. Winthrop, that is; I doubt it'll be dark to the last."

"Well, yes, Master Marner," said Dolly, who sat with a placid listening face, now bordered by gray hairs; "I doubt it may. It's the will o' Them above as a many things should be dark to us, but there's some things as I've never felt i' the dark about, and they're mostly what comes i' the day's work. You were hard done by that once, Master Marner, and it seems as you'll never know the rights o' it; but that doesn't hinder there *being* a rights, Master Marner, for all it's dark to you and me."

"No," said Silas, "no; that doesn't hinder. Since the time the child was sent to me and I've come to love her as myself, I've had light enough to trusten by; and now she says she'll never leave me, I think I shall trusten till I die."

CONCLUSION

THERE WAS one time of the year which was held in Raveloe to be especially suitable for a wedding. It was when the great lilacs and laburnums in the old-fashioned gardens showed their golden and purple wealth above the lichen-tinted walls, and when there were calves still young enough to want bucketfuls of fragrant milk. People were not so busy then as they must become when the full cheese-making and the mowing had set in; and besides, it was a time when a light bridal dress could be worn with comfort and seen to advantage.

Happily the sunshine fell more warmly than usual on the lilac tufts the morning Eppie was married, for her dress was a very light one. She had often thought, though with a feeling of renunciation, that the perfection of a wedding-dress would be a white cotton, with the tiniest pink sprig at wide intervals; so that when Mrs. Godfrey Cass begged to provide one, and asked Eppie to choose what it should be, previous meditation had enabled her to give a decided answer at once.

Seen at a little distance as she walked across the churchyard and down the village, she seemed to be attired in pure white, and her hair looked like the dash of gold on a lily. One hand was on her husband's arm, and with the other she clasped the hand of her father Silas.

"You won't be giving me away, father," she had said before they went to church; "you'll only be taking Aaron to be a son to you."

Dolly Winthrop walked behind with her husband; and there ended the little bridal procession.

There were many eyes to look at it, and Miss Priscilla Lammeter was glad that she and her father had happened to drive up to the door of the Red House just in time to see this pretty sight. They had come to keep Nancy company to-day, because Mr. Cass had had to go away to Lytherly, for special reasons. That seemed to be a pity, for otherwise he might have gone, as Mr. Crackenthorp and Mr. Osgood certainly would, to look on at the wedding-feast which he had ordered at the Rainbow, naturally feeling a great interest in the weaver who had been wronged by one of his own family.

"I could ha' wished Nancy had had the luck to find a child like that and bring her up," said Priscilla to her father, as they sat in the gig; "I should ha' had something young to think of then, besides the lambs and the calves."

"Yes, my dear, yes," said Mr. Lammeter; "one feels that as one gets older. Things look dim to old folks:

they'd need have some young eyes about 'em, to let 'em know the world's the same as it used to be."

Nancy came out now to welcome her father and sister; and the wedding-group had passed on beyond the Red House to the humbler part of the village.

Dolly Winthrop was the first to divine that old Mr. Macey, who had been set in his arm-chair outside his own door, would expect some special notice as they passed, since he was too old to be at the wedding-feast.

"Mr. Macey's looking for a word from us," said Dolly; "he'll be hurt if we pass him and say nothing— and him so racked with rheumatiz."

So they turned aside to shake hands with the old man. He had looked forward to the occasion, and had his premeditated speech.

"Well, Master Marner," he said, in a voice that quavered a good deal, "I've lived to see my words come true. I was the first to say there was no harm in you, though your looks might be again' you; and I was the first to say you'd get your money back. And it's nothing but rightful as you should. And I'd ha' said the 'Amens,' and willing, at the holy matrimony; but Tookey's done it a good while now, and I hope you'll have none the worse luck."

In the open yard before the Rainbow the party of guests were already assembled, though it was still nearly an hour before the appointed feast-time. But by this means they could not only enjoy the slow advent of their pleasure; they had also ample leisure to talk of Silas Marner's strange history, and arrive by due degrees at the conclusion that he had brought a blessing on himself by acting like a father to a lone, motherless child. Even the farrier did not negative this sentiment; on the contrary, he took it up as peculiarly his own, and invited any hardy person present to contradict him. But he met with no contradiction; and all differences among the company were merged in a general agreement with Mr. Snell's sentiment, that when a man had deserved his good luck, it was the part of his neighbors to wish him joy.

As the bridal group approached, a hearty cheer was raised in the Rainbow yard; and Ben Winthrop, whose jokes had retained their acceptable flavor, found it agreeable to turn in there and receive congratulations; not requiring the proposed interval of quiet at the Stone-pits before joining the company.

Eppie had a larger garden than she had ever expected there now; and in other ways there had been alterations at the expense of Mr. Cass, the landlord, to suit Silas's larger family. For he and Eppie had declared that they would rather stay at the Stone-pits than go to any new home. The garden was fenced with stones on two sides, but in front there was an open fence, through which the flowers shone with answering gladness, as the four united people came within sight of them.

"O father," said Eppie, "what a pretty home ours is! I think nobody could be happier than we are."

Afterword

AFTERWORD
Silas Marner

George Eliot said that *Silas Marner* came to her "first of all, quite suddenly, as a sort of legendary tale suggested by my recollection of having once, in early childhood, seen a linen-weaver with a bag on his back." The novel which developed from this simple *donnée* touches on many aspects of life, but its special achievement is the momentary recapturing of the vision of childhood. With memory as one of its principal subjects, it is in the form of an extended reminiscence, a poignant musing over the sad, humorous, bitter but irrevocably lost world of childhood. *Silas Marner* is, unlike many modern novels, a *tale told;* we feel always the presence of the novelist-narrator, wise and tolerant, recreating and commenting on the past, heightening the implications of her moral fable. The village of Raveloe, the world of the novel, represents not only the individual past of recollected childhood, but the historical past, that rural England which was industrialized out of existence in George Eliot's own lifetime. The legendary tale is embedded in solid circumstance; a geographical region (the English Midlands) and a historical period (the early years of the nineteenth century) are faithfully rendered. The novel, small as it is, communicates on more than one plane: the plot, so "unlikely"—as befits a legend—is surrounded by realistic social observation; the extremely simple story— it could be told in a few sentences—carries a moral burden which only mature wisdom can appreciate

fully. Much of the interest of this innocently sophisticated novel comes from the incongruity between the
apparent simplicity of its form and the complication of
its meaning.

The action of *Silas Marner* is defined by two narrative threads, the story of Silas, the miserly weaver, and
the story of the Cass family. The plot is made by the
intersection (not the interweaving) of these two
threads. The fable offers a set of moral paradoxes, a sort
of spiritual balancing of loss and gain. Silas, for example, is robbed of his gold, but finds the golden-haired
Eppie and through her recovers his humanity. The
brutish Dunstan Cass loses his way in the dark, but his
blind wanderings fulfill a larger purpose. George Eliot
said that she wanted her novel to set "in a strong light
the remedial influences of pure, natural human relations." And indeed one of its messages is that man pos-
sesses only what he gives away and finds himself only in
love and care for others. The plot depends on what
might be considered an excessive use of coincidence,
but this is in keeping with its fabulous aspects. The door
of Silas's cottage, for example, happens through a set of
unusual events to be unlocked at the moment at which
Dunstan comes by; later when Molly appears with her
baby the weaver's door is open because he had recently
"contracted the habit of opening his door and looking
out from time to time, as if he thought that his money
might somehow be coming back to him." It would
be foolish to object to such plot devices on the grounds
that "real life" is not like that. Coincidence in literature
is an irony of action, and must be judged not by the
accuracy with which it reflects ordinary events, but by
the quality of the insight it gives into human experience. The coincidences in the plot of *Silas Marner*
are charming in a fairy-tale way, but they also embody

a moral reality. The door of Silas's cottage, open to evil and to good, is deeply significant: the literal fact that first Dunstan and then Molly come to the door at exactly the right moment illustrates the moral fact that what they represent is always outside the door, ready to enter. The irony evoked by George Eliot's plot has meaning as the sign of some deeper reality of which the reader ultimately becomes aware.

In a novel that is as much like a poem as *Silas Marner* is, imagery plays an important part. The image represents a non-physical reality by a sign apparent to the senses. Therefore Silas's open door is more than a literal event. The gravel-pit next to Silas's cottage is, to begin with, a perfectly real pit, there is a reason for its being where it is, the people in the story can—and do—fall into it; but it has a significance that goes beyond this: the pit corresponds, in a way that ordinary language cannot state, to the gulf within each of us; it is the pit which lies in the path of every wayfarer and conceals evil. This dimension of meaning is so well established that when Dunstan Cass's skeleton is at last discovered, his living brother Godfrey is, as it were, stripped, and the secret that lay within him is also revealed.

Silas's strange spells are also reflections of a moral reality. At the beginning of the novel he is described as "a dead man come to life again," and for the townspeople the fits which make him appear dead are both the sign and the cause of his alienation. This repeated pattern of dying and returning to life enhances the fact of redemption, which is the main theme of the novel. The most important quality, however, in all the imagery of *Silas Marner* is its naturalness. It rises easily out of the literal context of the story; there is no straining for complicated symbolic significance, no display of the author's ingenuity.

Much of the reader's pleasure in this novel comes from the surrounding events which are not essential to the action, but which modify our responses to it. The life of the Raveloe community is evoked through a series of festivals; in the background of the action are the rites of Sunday church-going, the convivial pint at the Rainbow, the celebrations of Easter, Christmas and the New Year. The narrator, describing the New Year's feast at the Squire's, remarks that "the charter of Raveloe seemed to be renewed by the ceremony." This pattern of ritualized renewal expresses the function of ceremony in actual life as well as in *Silas Marner*. By its rites a society assures its survival, and it is appropriate that a novel about alienation and the life of the community should stress the repeated affirmation of that social unity from which Silas was for so long detached. But ritual ceremonies are also a way of marking time through the unfolding of the individual life and the passage of the year. In its feasts, the church has always followed the plow. By reminding us of the continuing changes in the life of man and the earth, the novelist roots her fictional action in a surrounding world. "It is the habit of my imagination," George Eliot once said, "to strive after as full a vision of the medium in which a character moves as of the character itself." In the light of such an intention the celebrated chapter on the Rainbow tavern is seen to be more than a piece of *genre* description. The scene is rendered with Shakespearian fullness, and like similar scenes in Shakespeare's plays (one is reminded of *Henry IV, Part 2*) it stands for the eternal background of ordinary human affections against which our individual dramas play themselves out.

The abundance and complexity of life which surround the central action of George Eliot's novel are especially impressive when *Silas Marner* is compared with other modern fables. Hemingway's *Old Man and the Sea*, for example, is as ambitious in conception as *Silas Marner* and, in its different way, as intensely moral. The story is beautiful, but its action is stripped down to the point where it has no matrix of surrounding life. The agon is so essentialized, so detached from all that does not directly concern it, that the novel seriously lacks interest and richness.

What a good novel *says* is inherent in its style and structure. And yet, no matter how purely formed a literary work may be, it inevitably expresses a definable attitude on the novelist's part and offers ideas to which the reader responds. We are not justified in assessing the scientific truth of a writer's ideas, but we are compelled to judge their adequacy as a coherent interpretation of life. Certainly *Silas Marner* invites us to formulate the moral view which it implies, and having done so we must test it against our experience and perceptions. The first question we might ask is whether the novelist's whole conception is not vitiated by sentimentality. The story, indeed, presents great dangers, some of the most noxious commercial fictions in our language exploit the redemptive powers of golden-haired infants; and the notion of the crabbed recluse, brought back to happy community life by love and kindness, invites derision. But sentimentality arises from a writer's treatment, not from his materials: there is not much difference between the substance of an archetype and of a stereotype. In the fictional world of the sentimentalist people do not achieve virtue, but have it thrust upon them; moral difficulties are easily solved, glorious results achieved with no significant effort. Action in the sentimentalist's world does not involve learning. George Eliot, however, never slips into such delusions; for her, life—in the words of a modern philosopher—is not a feast or a spectacle, but a predicament.

Eppie, it is worth noting, is not allowed a sentimental reincarnation to a higher social sphere. She marries Aaron and continues her accustomed way of life. Human relations, as we see them in this novel, are not particularly easy; people have a hard time of it, but most of them rub through life, decently making the best of things. It must be said too that George Eliot avoids not only sentimentality of the Pollyanna variety, but that reverse kind which presents the universe as blackly menacing, and life as a situation in which things consistently and necessarily go wrong. In the world of Raveloe there are possibilities of achievement; satisfaction is found in minor, even trivial activities—in doing a job well, in helping a neighbor, in setting a good table. If we accede to the meanings of the novel we conclude that there is an ultimate good, but that to gain wisdom is to diminish expectation.

Finally, *Silas Marner* affirms a philosophical position and poses questions as to the origins of evil and the existence of a providential plan. The young Silas, cast out by the Lantern Yard congregation, declares "there is no just God that governs the earth righteously, but a God of lies, that bears witness against the innocent." And throughout the novel we are made to feel the existence of evil, to be aware—even in pastoral Raveloe —of the "hidden life which lies, like a dark by-street, behind the goodly ornamented facade that meets the sunlight and the gaze of respectable admirers."

One answer to Silas's denial of a just God is represented by the simple faith of Dolly Winthrop: ". . . there's trouble i' this world and there's things as we can niver make out the rights on. And all we've got to do is to trusten, Master Marner—to do the right thing as fur as we know, and to trusten. For if us as knows so little can see a bit o' good and rights, we may be sure as there's a good and a rights bigger nor what we can know—I feel it i' my own inside as it must be so." Without entirely accepting Dolly's intuitive faith, Silas eventually agrees: "There's good i' this world— I've a feeling o' that now; and it makes a man feel as there's a good more nor he can see, i' spite o' the trouble and the wickedness. That drawing o' the lots is dark; but the child was sent to me: there's dealings with us—there's dealings." But the Winthrop theology is not to be taken as the "message" of the novel. Nancy Cass, for one, has her own Hebraic code, making for righteousness, and the novelist-narrator affirms a tentative, humanistic position. In one of the asides to the reader it is said that in old days there were angels who led men away from the city of destruction: "We see no white-winged angels now. But yet men are led away from threatening destruction: a hand is put into theirs, which leads them forth gently toward a calm and bright land, so that they look no more backwards; and the hand may be a little child's."

But to attempt a flat statement of the ethical views implicit in George Eliot's novels is to make her work sound too portentous. *Silas Marner* does, I think, illuminate some of the most perplexing questions of good and evil, but what it offers more immediately is the suspenseful interest (not to be despised) of highly plotted fiction, the color of a regional tale, and the limpid inevitability of a fable. The chief impression it makes on the reader is of easiness, the impression of a novelist completely in command of her materials and technique, who always surprises by making every element of her novel yield more than one expects to find.

G. ROBERT STANGE

Minneapolis, 1962

Biographical Note

FURTHER READING

BIOGRAPHICAL NOTE

Mary Ann (later Marian) Evans, who was to write under the name of George Eliot, was born on November 22, 1819, in a country house at Nuneaton in Warwickshire. Her native region, the English Midlands, furnishes the typical landscape of her novels; a country of broad plains and rich fields of grain, it is the countryside of Raveloe in *Silas Marner* and the Loamshire of *Adam Bede*.

George Eliot's formal education was completed at two small girls' schools, and then at an academy at Coventry. When she was quite young she was converted to Evangelical Christianity, and though she was to lose her faith in later years, her cast of thought and all her work were influenced by Evangelical teachings. When she was twenty this young provincial intellectual went to London and found a job as assistant editor of the *Westminster Review*, an organ of advanced liberal opinion. She became acquainted with George Henry Lewes—a journalist, scientist, playwright, novelist, critic—and fell in love with him. Though Lewes's wife had abandoned him, there was no possibility in Victorian England of a legal divorce. In 1854, defying convention, the couple left London to live together as man and wife. Their union lasted until Lewes's death in 1878 and was so obviously responsible and productive of happiness for both of them that even their most strait-laced contemporaries came to treat them as a married couple.

In 1856, and at Lewes's urging, George Eliot began to write fiction. Her first work, *Scenes of Clerical Life*, appeared as three sketches in *Blackwood's Magazine* in 1857, and as a book in the following year. It was for this publication that she assumed her pen name: George in honor of Lewes, and Eliot because it was "mouth-filling" and "easily pronounced." This first book had a considerable success and George Eliot, diffident about her powers, was encouraged to continue writing. *Adam Bede* appeared in 1859, *The Mill on the Floss* in 1860, and *Silas Marner* in 1861. The three novels form a group, since they all make use of childhood recollections and of the rural world of Warwickshire.

Romola (1862—63) is a sort of preface to the later phase of the novelist's work; it is followed by *Felix Holt the Radical* (1866), a political novel, and by *The Spanish Gypsy* (1868), a dramatic poem. In 1871—72 *Middlemarch*, George Eliot's masterpiece, was published. Her last novel, *Daniel Deronda*, appeared in 1876. In these last two novels the field of interest is much more extensive than in the earlier novels and, in *Middlemarch* at least, the humor and pastoral inspiration of the earlier work is fused with the social and moral interests of the novelist's later career.

After Lewes's death in 1878 George Eliot devoted herself to preparing his unfinished work for publication. Of her own writings she published only a volume of essays, *The Impressions of Theophrastus Such*. In 1880 she married an old friend and devoted admirer, the American banker, J. W. Cross. In December of that year the Crosses moved into a new London house, and on December 22, 1880, George Eliot died.

Further Reading

The most interesting work for the study of the novelist is *The George Eliot Letters*, edited by Gordon S. Haight, 7 volumes, 1954–55. This carefully annotated collection amplifies J. W. Cross's *George Eliot's Life as Related in Her Letters and Journals*, 3 volumes, 1885.

Valuable critical discussions of the novels are to be found in F. R. Leavis, *The Great Tradition*, 1948; Joan Bennett, *George Eliot: Her Mind and Art*, 1948; Barbara Hardy, *The Novels of George Eliot*, 1959; and W. J. Harvey, *George Eliot*, 1961.

G.R.S.

POETRY from WASHINGTON SQUARE PRESS ^{WSP}

General Anthologies

THE POCKET BOOK OF VERSE. Edited by M. E. Speare—250 favorite British and American poems — W • 0241/45¢

IMMORTAL POEMS OF THE ENGLISH LANGUAGE. Edited by Oscar Williams—400 poems from Chaucer to Dylan Thomas — W • 0909/75¢

THE NEW POCKET ANTHOLOGY OF AMERICAN VERSE. Edited by Oscar Williams—from colonial days to the present — W • 0908/75¢

A POCKET BOOK OF MODERN VERSE. Edited by Oscar Williams—English and American poetry of the last one hundred years — W • 0910/75¢

STORY POEMS. Edited by Louis Untermeyer—narrative verse from medieval times to the twentieth century — W • 0911/75¢

Critical Anthologies

MASTER POEMS OF THE ENGLISH LANGUAGE. Edited by Oscar Williams—over one hundred classic poems, each with a critical essay by a leading poet or critic — W • 1446/$1.45

A CONCISE TREASURY OF GREAT POEMS. Edited by Louis Untermeyer—including biographical and critical prefaces — 75061/75¢

THE MAJOR ENGLISH ROMANTIC POETS — W • 1443/$1.45

THE MAJOR VICTORIAN POETS — W • 1444/$1.45
Edited by William H. Marshall, University of Pennsylvania—with biographical and critical introductions to each poet

THE SONNET. Edited by Robert M. Bender, Brooklyn College, and Charles L. Squier, University of Colorado—from the Renaissance to the present — W • 1084/90¢

Collections and Individual Works

CANTERBURY TALES OF CHAUCER. Translated by R. M. Lumiansky — W • 0913/75¢

SHAKESPEARE'S SONNETS. Folger Library edition edited by Louis B. Wright and Virginia A. LaMar—facing-page notes — W • 0132/45¢

THE COMPLETE ENGLISH POEMS OF JOHN MILTON. Edited by John D. Jump, University of Manchester — W • 1009/90¢

IDYLLS OF THE KING. Alfred Tennyson—facing-page notes — W • 0914/75¢

THE WHITMAN READER. Edited by Maxwell Geismar — GC • 25/50¢

COLLECTED LYRICS. Edna St. Vincent Millay — W • 0550/60¢

COLLECTED SONNETS. Edna St. Vincent Millay — W • 0551/60¢

ROBERT FROST'S POEMS. Edited by Louis Untermeyer—100 poems with editorial commentary — W • 0912/75¢

WSP

The FOLGER LIBRARY General Reader's
SHAKESPEARE

Distinguished editions of the plays and poems edited by Louis B. Wright, Director, and Virginia A. LaMar, Executive Secretary, Folger Shakespeare Library, Washington, D.C.

The text is printed on right hand pages only, with notes on the facing pages keyed by line number for easy reference.

Each edition contains an introduction, biographical information, a discussion of the Shakespearean theatre, summaries of each scene, and illustrations from the Folger collection.

EACH VOLUME 45¢

Comedies

All's Well That Ends Well	W • 0104
As You Like It	W • 0106
The Comedy of Errors	W • 0107
Cymbeline	W • 0126
Love's Labor's Lost	W • 0114
Measure for Measure	W • 0127
The Merchant of Venice	W • 0116
The Merry Wives of Windsor	W • 0128
A Midsummer Night's Dream	W • 0117
Much Ado about Nothing	W • 0129
The Taming of the Shrew	W • 0122
The Tempest	W • 0123
Twelfth Night	W • 0124
The Two Gentlemen of Verona	W • 0130
Troilus and Cressida	W • 0103
The Winter's Tale	W • 0102

Poetry

Shakespeare's Sonnets	W • 0132

Tragedies

Antony and Cleopatra	W • 0105
Coriolanus	W • 0125
Hamlet	W • 0108
Julius Caesar	W • 0112
King Lear	W • 0113
Macbeth	W • 0115
Othello	W • 0118
Pericles	W • 0139
Romeo and Juliet	W • 0121
Titus Andronicus	W • 0141
Timon of Athens	W • 0140

Histories

Henry IV, Part I	W • 0109
Henry IV, Part II	W • 0110
Henry V	W • 0111
Henry VI, Part I	W • 0134
Henry VI, Part II	W • 0135
Henry VI, Part III	W • 0136
Henry VIII	W • 0137
King John	W • 0138
Richard II	W • 0119
Richard III	W • 0120

Shakespeare for Everyman

By Louis B. Wright. An illuminating introduction to Shakespeare for the general reader. Annotated bibliography, index, extensive illustrations from the Folger collection. W • 1081/90¢

WSP
Ⅲ WASHINGTON SQUARE PRESS, INC.

If you are unable to obtain these books from your regular dealer, you may order them by sending the retail price, plus 10¢ per book for postage and handling, to: Mail Service Department, WASHINGTON SQUARE PRESS, INC., 1 West 39th Street, New York, N.Y. 10018. Please enclose check or money order—*do not send cash.*

WSP 1/7

The Iron Tree

MARTIN BOOTH

The Iron Tree

SIMON & SCHUSTER

LONDON·SYDNEY·NEW YORK·TOKYO·SINGAPORE·TORONTO

First published in Great Britain by
Simon & Schuster Ltd in 1993.
A Paramount Communications Company

Copyright © Martin Booth, 1993
The moral rights of the author have been asserted

This book is copyright under the Berne Convention
No reproduction without permission
All rights reserved

Simon & Schuster Ltd
West Garden Place
Kendal Street
London W2 2AQ

Simon & Schuster of Australia Pty Ltd
Sydney

A CIP catalogue record for this book is
available from the British Library
ISBN 0-671-71783-9

Typeset in Sabon 11/13 by
Hewer Text Composition Services, Edinburgh
Printed and bound in Great Britain by
Butler & Tanner Ltd, Frome

Not very far from here is a small temple.

It is not an elaborate place of worship, nothing like the gaudy, extravagant spots the tourists visit, disembarking from coaches with cameras slung around their necks, the women in floral print dresses and straw hats with the men in slacks and open-neck shirts, their hip pockets well buttoned. It has no message of welcome in English at the door, no sign prohibiting or encouraging photography, no request that the visitor respect it as a house of religion. There are no obtrusive alms boxes or grasping beggars, no hawkers selling Kodak film, boxes of out-of-date colour slides or dog-eared postcards. Indeed, if you did not know the temple was there, you might well pass it by in the street and, if you looked in its direction, you might assume the forecourt, in which there grows a low, wide banyan tree and a number of shrubs in dark-brown glazed pots surrounding a stone bench, was nothing more than a little garden set aside by the authorities to relieve the cramped panorama of tenements and shops, factories and street stalls.

The building is not in the least pretentious. It has a roof of green glazed pantiles with a frieze of dragons and mythical heroes along the ridge, all badly in need of repainting and hidden from the street by the banyan. On either side of the door, the scarlet paint of the wooden plaques has dulled with time and traffic fumes to a deep red, like that of arterial blood. The gold characters have also tarnished to a dark brazen yellow.

Once inside, the atmosphere is thick with the smoke of joss sticks dropping, heavier than air, from the coils of sandalwood incense suspended from the rafters. The usual temple trappings stand dusty and mystical in the shadows of the side aisles: the scarlet and yellow drum with its taut hide skin, the bronze bell hanging in its squat

1

frame like an inverted tulip head and, just inside the door, a huge model of a sailing junk in full sail protected behind a glass screen, the bottom right-hand corner of which is cracked.

It is always twilight in the temple. The sun may be beating down outside without a vestige of mercy but, in here, it is invariably semi-dark. The only illumination, apart from an early afternoon beam of sunlight cutting through the roof and the clouds of incense smoke, comes from a few guttering flames in lamps before the altars and a neon strip light tucked in behind the canopy hanging in front of the god to whom the temple is dedicated.

I frequently visit this place.

Sometimes, I light a few joss sticks and, placing them between my hands, make several noncommittal bows before sticking them in the urn of sand and ash which stands in the centre of the temple. On or just before festival days, I may light a red wax candle on a bamboo splint and, at Chinese New Year, I make sure to bring an offering of a miniature bottle of snake wine and four oranges which I place on the altar in the form of a little pyramid. There is an alms box hidden away beside the junk: I never fail to put a dollar in it, thrusting the note down through the slit in the top not because I feel anyone might come along and fish it out but just to make sure that it falls safely to the bottom and cannot be lost.

It is a peaceful place. Walking in from the day's heat, it is always cool, the thick walls killing the incessant sound of traffic. The incense also eradicates the dubious smells of the city.

If I have time, I sit in the temple. There is a folding stool to the right of the altar, just beside the statue of one of the guardians of heaven, a life-size warrior carved of wood. His eyes, the white made of bone and the iris of black soapstone, glare ferociously. His spear, tipped with a blade like a Victorian butter knife, is gilded. There is usually a spider's web connecting the tip of this weapon to the point in the centre of his elaborate helmet.

The old woman who is the temple caretaker knows me: she has seen me come here for years. As well as sweeping the stone flags and cleaning out the urn, tidying the offerings and getting rid of the ashes of burnt paper money offered to the god, she operates a tiny stall selling joss sticks, candles and small talismen shaped like fish or birds and carved out of plum stones. I am possibly her most

2

regular customer and certainly her only regular European visitor. This fact, that I am a *gweilo*, no longer bothers her. The first time I visited the temple, she must have thought I was a tourist who had lost his camera and his way but now she knows I am a local resident and unquestioningly accepts me.

On occasion, she speaks to me. Her voice is weak from age and possibly from spending much of her later life inhaling the pungent joss stick fumes. Our conversation is always the same. She asks if I am well, I reply affirmatively and ask after her health which she always reports to be fair, except for her rheumatism. Next she asks me where I live and I tell her: just a few streets away, near the rickshaw rank. To this information, she nods: yes, she confirms, she knows of it. It is not that she has forgotten where my home is, it is just good manners to enquire. This ritual over, she briefly comments upon a topic of the day. It might be the failure of her chosen horse to win at the races or the proximity of the next typhoon. It never concerns the temple, its fabric or its deity. They can look after themselves. More often than not she just nods to acknowledge my presence, sells me a bundle of joss sticks wrapped in red cellophane and leaves me to my own devices.

I think of nothing when I am sitting in the temple. I am certainly not a worshipper for I am done with gods. It is more that it is one of the few places left in the world where I can be alone with myself and forget my life. No one disturbs me. No one looks to wonder who or what I am. I am quite anonymous. Time ceases to pass and I can pretend, for a short while at any rate, that I am at peace.

In the winter, the Nine Dragon Hills of Kowloon catch fire.

By day, the only hint of this conflagration is a weak haze of grey smoke hanging above the skyline, disseminating into the clear blue of the heavens. It has no more substance than a wash of water colour seeping into a heavy woven paper.

Sometimes, an eagle soars in the fire's thermals: more often the dots that endlessly wheel over the hillsides are shite hawks on the lookout for rodents flushed out of the ground, snakes making good their escape, the stones under which they nestle becoming hotter than the winter sun usually makes them. Below the shite hawks smaller birds dive and turn, picking off insects on the wing. They dart through the smoke, oblivious to the discomfort or proximity of danger. Some, the more agile or foolhardy, dip almost to ground level in their search to feed and their abiding desire to get the choicest morsels.

When night falls, the burning hills change. As the sun lowers, they shift from their daylight cloak of khaki into first a hint of purple then a blackness so deep that, unless it is a starry night or the moon is high and filling, their silhouette is lost. And it is when the darkness descends that the fires appear.

Each hill bears a ring of orange lights. From far away, a casual observer might assume them to be a newly opened road illuminated by sodium lamps. Yet watch them for a minute and they will be seen to part, disappear then suddenly rejoin themselves. And they flicker. This movement might be misconstrued as the last of the day's heat haze playing its shifty games but it is not. It is the greedy fire climbing inexorably up the slopes, consuming dried grass, scorching bushes and temporarily surrendering only when coming upon a bare gully or an outcrop of boulders.

Who is responsible for this orological arson is unknown. The police never arrest anybody. The fire brigade invariably fails to apprehend a suspect. When the tenders arrive and the firemen reach the blaze, there is never anyone about. It is said that arsonists like to remain to watch the chaos and calamity their handiwork creates, but in the case of the burning mountains they do not.

It might be that the grass self-combusts. Perhaps a shard of broken glass amongst the rocks sets it off, or a thoughtlessly discarded cigarette end thrown away by a lorry driver crawling up the Tai Po Road: perhaps a charge of static electricity does it. No one can tell.

All that is a surety is that the hills of Hong Kong – and many others, throughout China, when the winter wind whips down from the Siberian north – catch fire once a year. For years I have pondered this puzzle. It is not the cause that is of curiosity to me: I am sure it is people who do it and that their actions are deliberate. It is their reason I want to discover.

I have asked others why the hills are torched and everyone has a different answer.

Mr Wu claims it is done by those whose ancestors are buried on the hills or whose bones are kept there in lines of urns. If, he deduces, they have relatives there, they would set the grass alight to clear the hillside so that, at the Festival of Ching Ming, when they went to tidy the graves, polish the bones and leave their annual offerings, they could more easily find their family plot.

On the other hand, Tsoi says it is the work of vandals. He laments the fact that Chinese teenagers listen to the music of Elvis Presley and that this is driving them away from their roots. They have to let off steam, he declares, because the music is made of destructive rhythms and contains no life force other than that of the primeval. The best way to release these emotions, he states, is to burn the hills. That the slopes have burned periodically for centuries seems not to dent his argument.

Other suggestions put forward are that the hills are set alight by the fire brigade to give their men practice, by the Urban Services Department to clear the brush, by charcoal makers or by the police in an attempt to smoke out opium factories. I have, however, discounted all these theories as either being too far-fetched or too simplistic. Besides the best explanation, in my opinion, is that suggested by Mrs van der Poehl.

She lives a floor down from me with a nondescript cat, a budgerigar and a pug dog she calls Pu Yi, so named because she once played tennis in Shanghai with the last emperor of China and declares he played the game like a lap-dog. He also, she recalls, swam like one with his arms paddling under him, but that is hearsay. I suspect much of what she says may be hearsay but that does not deter me.

'I will tell you why they set light to the hills,' she told me. 'It's to kill off the dragons.'

'Dragons?' I said.

I have for decades now had an abiding loathing of dragons.

'Kowloon hills!' she exclaimed. 'Stands to reason, man. *Kow loon*. Nine Dragons. They live up there. And they can do a lot of damage.'

'What about clearing the grass from graves?' I asked, playing devil's advocate to see if I could shift her attractively plausible line of reasoning.

'Graves? Up there? You've been on those hills?'

I nodded.

'You see graves there?'

I shook my head.

'Exactly! The *fung shui*'s lousy. No one wants to be buried on those hills. No necromancer would risk his reputation recommending it. No,' she lowered her voice conspiratorially, 'you mark my word, they're burning out dragons.'

And that is what I have chosen to believe.

Sometimes, on a winter's night, I sit quietly on the roof watching the necklace of destruction gradually rising to the peaks. I have never spied a dragon taking off, seen a shite hawk swoop on one in the dusk, watched one running with its back undulating like a carpet of scales being shaken, but that is by the way.

I choose to believe in her hypothesis, and that is enough.

Sometimes, to enter the tenement in which I have my dwelling, I must ring an electric buzzer to summon Chiu. He is the day- and night-watchman, always on duty and invariably to be found in a cubby-hole beneath the stairs, which space he has made his own by erecting a plasterboard wall and running into it an electric cable from which he operates a light, a small transistor radio and a single ring cooker. He has not installed a door for the simple fact that doors cost more than walls, requiring not just board and nails but also hinges, locks and handles. In lieu of such a convenience, he has hung a curtain of several layers of hessian sewn together with twine. His furniture is minimal: he has a narrow iron bed frame covered with a quilt, a folding stool, a wide shelf fixed to the wall with iron brackets which he uses as a table and several cardboard boxes which he keeps under the bed.

In this cubicle, he lives his life as happily as any man who might own a grandiose mansion. Unlike most of the residents, he pays no rent and his electricity is free for his cable is connected illegally to the street side of the junction box. No one begrudges him his luck. He has succeeded in part where we have failed and that's all there is to it.

Chiu is a quiet man, about forty years of age with thin, delicate hands. Plainly, he has never seen manual labour. When he looks at you, his eyes show a deep cavern within him where there might be a laugh echoing towards silence. His face is round and his eyes narrower than those of many Chinese, but he is not ugly in the fashion, say, of a Korean and his skin is pallid for he seldom ventures out of the building, even at night. He has made his little world under the stairs and is content with it.

He is always ready with a smile to unlock the street door after checking the bona fides of the would-be entrant by peering at him through the crack between the hinges. He has been given the keys not by the landlord but by Mr Pao, the middle-aged proprietor of the typewriter and cash register repairing workshop on the first floor. It is in his interest to see no thieves enter the building, break into his business and steal either the tools or the considerable stock of parts he maintains. It is also Mr Pao who pays the bulk of Chiu's salary.

Every Thursday evening, Chiu waits expectantly for the work-shop to close. As Mr Pao leaves, he stops by the cubby-hole and a small ritual commences. Mr Pao reaches inside his jacket and removes a worn crocodile-skin wallet down the centre of which is a row of rounded scales. He opens the wallet, unzips a compartment and removes fifty dollars in ten dollar bills, held together by a paper clip. These he hands to Chiu who smiles broadly and makes a little bow. Mr Pao then utters a single phrase and Chiu bows again and says, '*Doh tse! Doh tse!*' which is the required response when one is given a gift.

This done, Chiu holds open the street door for Mr Pao and, as he walks away towards the rickshaw rank, makes a show of locking up behind him, rattling the bolt and loudly snapping the locks.

If I am present, I wait until Mr Pao has gone and then I give Chiu twenty dollars. At some time during the evening, so do Mr Wu, Mrs van der Poehl, Tsoi and the woman called Pei whom I do not like who runs a secretarial agency in Flat 22 on the second floor. From time to time, we may also give Chiu food – some fruit or a bag of dried fish, some tea or a catty of rice – or some clothing we no longer require. The food he eats, the clothes he either stores in one of his cardboard boxes to be worn later or sells.

For everything, he is very grateful. Unlike many men, his gratitude is not expressed in the hope of receiving a greater benefaction. He smiles his thanks, bows to each of us and mutters his '*Doh tse!*' in a quiet whisper. These are the only words I ever hear him say.

In my own way, I love this diffident, gentle man. He makes no demands of life, accepting whatever good fortune it might toss his way and being pleased his lot is better than it otherwise might have been. And I envy him. I would be as stoic if I could.

Like me, I am certain that Chiu has been through all the vicissitudes that human experience can provide. He arrived in our building in 1949, not long after the fall of China to the Communists, one of the tens of thousands who fled ahead of the Red Army, afraid of the doctrines, diatribes and cold revenges of Mao Tse-tung. Yet he seems unaffected by it all. He has taken the misery and loss in his stride, accepting his lot with as much resignation as a dog who, abandoned by one owner, takes up with the next. I cannot be like him, no matter how much I wish it. Where I am concerned, I have spent decades trying to reason, to seek to explain what I have seen, to set it in a context of history and belief. I have failed. He has not even embarked upon such a quest and is happier for his naiveté.

The street door of which Chiu is in charge is a sturdy affair made of steel sheets riveted onto a welded metal frame. It is held shut by two mortise locks and an industrial bolt with a hasp. It was painted silver some time ago but that has become chipped with age and the bottom is rusty. On the pavement beside the door is a tiny shrine like that to be found outside every building or shop in the street. It contains a small, brightly painted porcelain statue of Kwan Tai, a minuscule bowl of dusty rice wine and a tin can filled with dirty sand from which poke one or two glowing joss sticks. A shrivelled orange stands on the pavement in front of the wine bowl and incense. Chiu is responsible for the shrine as well as the door: it is up to him to see the god is never without sustenance and the joss sticks never extinguished except at night, after everyone is asleep.

Whenever I stand by the door, press the button and wait for Chiu, the blue cords of smoke rise into my face until the draught from a passing pedestrian or taxi disperse them. The aroma mingling with the scents and smells of the street reminds me of wooded mountains and mysterious forests, of tiny villages and dark houses, of obscure gods squatting on their haunches with malevolent sneers and fat, jovial Buddhas in curio shop windows. It brings back the past, the first months I spent in China, a time of wonder and of happiness. And of sorrow. It also reminds me of death.

As happens these days with increasing frequency, I am startled by a voice on the stairs.

Sometimes the voice may be one I recognise but that still does not reduce the level of surprise. I find I am becoming susceptible to sudden noises, that they increasingly catch me off my guard. There is no explanation: I have never suffered from shell shock or tinnitus and loud noises have never made me jump.

'*San foo*, my old friend. How you doing?'

I remove the key from my door and turn to find Mr Wu standing a few steps up from the landing. Quite often, the startling voice is his. I sometimes wonder if he does not lurk on the stairway waiting to pounce on me although I know this to be nonsense.

In the flat glow cast by the light over the lift door his face looks as if it is covered in parchment stretched across a frame of angled bones. Upon his nose is balanced a pair of circular spectacles with thin, black frames. They are not positioned squarely but askew, the right lens a good half an inch lower than the left.

'I'm doing okay,' I reply. I slip my key into my trouser pocket, placing my handkerchief over it as a defence against the light-fingered street operators one may encounter in the evenings. 'And you?'

Mr Wu has not been well for several months. He does not

confide in me exactly what is wrong, but he drops occasional hints so I might be in a better position to sympathise. He thinks that as I am old like him I will offer him a greater sympathy than he might get from a younger man. He may be right and he may be wrong. I have never considered the matter.

'Better, better,' he responds.

When we meet, he likes to talk in English. This is not a pretension for his command of the language is good. He does it because he thinks it makes me feel at home. I have told him, over and over, it is not necessary. My home is here, I tell him, in Hong Kong. In China. He smiles benignly and nods his head but I can tell he only half believes me. Like many Chinese, he hopes to return to some distant nook or cranny in Kwangtung or Kwansi provinces to die with his ancestors and he mistakenly assumes Europeans will ultimately do likewise, going back to a leafy village churchyard in the shires of England to let their bodies rot in the mother soil whence they sprang.

'I been to see my doctor,' he continues. 'He has given me a prescription.'

He holds up a piece of flimsy paper on which I can make out printed red lines and a dense passage of characters in black ink. The paper has a similar texture to his skin.

'What is it?' I enquire, pressing the button for the lift.

'Herbs, spices. Deer's tail . . .' Mr Wu squints over his spectacles. 'You know, *san foo*, I can't see so well these days.'

I reach over and straighten the old man's glasses.

'That will not improve it. But thank you.'

'You need new glasses,' I say, not for the first time. 'You've had these for eight years at least.'

Mr Wu calculates time in his head.

'Now is 1961. I bought them in 1952. But they do me, my old friend. I need no more. New eyes, perhaps.' He holds the piece of paper out. 'See if you can read it.'

'Deer's tail is there,' I confirm, surveying the characters written with a calligraphic brush. 'And anis, ginseng, some other things I don't know the English for.'

'Do you think it will do me good?' Mr Wu enquires.

'I'm sure it will.'

'This is strange,' Mr Wu remarks, smiling at me. 'I am Chinese and you are a *gweilo* and I have to ask you to read my own language and then I ask you if you think the medicine will be good. You who do not believe . . .'

'I believe,' I interrupt him. 'I have seen Chinese medicine working many times. Do not assume, because I am a *gweilo*, I take only aspirin.'

A tinny bell pings to announce the arrival of the lift and the doors rattle open. A metal grating sound can be heard: the lift is never serviced. I put my hand against the safety bar to prevent the door closing, signalling Mr Wu to go in first and we step into the lift.

'I should do that for you, my old friend. By your standards, I am a youngster. Why! When you first came to China, I could have been your pupil. Learned my English speaking from you.'

'You could not,' I answer, pressing the ground-floor button. 'You are the wrong sex. I taught only girls.'

I look up in silence at the numbers flicking slowly on and off. It is not my custom to discuss my affairs, even with those whom I know well, unless I choose to do so. There has to be a proper time and place for such intercourse and a lift is not one of them. A man must keep himself to himself unless he wishes his life to become public property. Not that I think Mr Wu would start blabbering about me. We have a certain secret in common which ensures we neither of us spill the other's beans. It is just that lift shafts carry sound, especially in an old tenement, with the efficacy of a tannoy.

'What were you doing on the roof?' I ask. 'In the daytime.'

'Nothing,' Mr Wu replies defensively. 'Nothing at all.'

He stares at the door as if willing it to open. I look at his profile and consider how much more quickly Chinese age than Europeans. Mr Wu is much my junior at seventy-three yet we look quite similar, racial physiognomy apart.

The old Chinese lives alone in Flat 36, third floor, one of the less salubrious quarters of the building for it looks out not on to the busy street crowded for eighteen hours a day with pedestrians and traffic but on to an alleyway at the rear in which dubious characters meet to carry on their suspect business and which, when there is no human presence, is the domain of some particularly large rats. Sometimes he curses these rodents and sometimes he feeds them. It all depends upon his mood or whether or not he wants to earn a credit in the account books of the gods. He has the idea that, if he shows compassion for his enemies, the gods might treat him kindly when he comes into their company. The rats being enemies, he sees feeding them as a good opportunity to be charitable.

The lift stops abruptly, my legs momentarily giving way then regaining their strength.

'Where are you going, *san foo*?' Mr Wu asks.

'You know,' I say, 'I am not a *san foo* any longer. That was a long time ago. I do wish you would call me something else.'

'What do I call you?' Mr Wu rejoins. 'There is nothing else. I am always a tailor, Tsoi will always be a cook, you will always be a *san foo*.'

Deciding not to follow this line of conversation, for it is one we have at least once a week without resolution, I say nothing. Mr Wu chuckles, a soft gurgling laugh I have grown to know well. At the street door, we part company. Mr Wu waves as we set off in different directions.

'I shall see you later?' he asks me.

'Later?' I consider his words. 'No, I think not.'

'You should come,' Mr Wu calls after me. 'Need to relax. You are too busy for an old man.'

Yet I have made up my mind, wave and walk away.

There are times when I do not want Mr Wu's company, and others when I need it. Tonight is one of the former. I seek only my own company in the presence of strangers, wish to be alone in the crowds, just another European wandering the streets.

Now it is evening, the tourists are out in force in Tsim Sha Tsui: their day excursions are over, they have had their hotel dinners and their guides have gone home. Left to their own devices, they have embarked upon a shopping spree in the brightly lit streets, pausing in front of camera and jewellery shops, being accosted by touts wanting to sell them silk ties and leather wallets. I mingle with them, watch and listen as they are persuaded, beguiled and cheated. One American, his tropical shirt decorated with palm trees and hula-hula girls hanging down over his belt, a Leica camera suspended around his neck, enquires into the price of a pair of binoculars.

'Six hund'ed eighty dollar,' the shopkeeper tells him. 'Good price. For you, first customer tonight, I say six hund'ed fifty. You wan' buy?'

'Six hundred,' the American bargains.

He has been told no one pays the asking price. It is the done thing, the guidebooks instruct him, to dicker with vendors, ignore the marked price on the label and go for the deal.

'Six forty,' the shopkeeper suggests. 'I make little p'ofit.'

'Six twenty,' the American demands.

'You hard man. Strike good bargain,' the shopkeeper congratulates him, smiling sheepishly. 'Okay! Six twenty.'

He grimaces, pretending to be a loser. The American grins and winks at his wife who is standing behind him clutching her handbag. He starts to remove traveller's cheques from his wallet, laying them out on the glass counter next to his purchase.

'Honey, give me a pen.'

'Okay. I got a pen,' says the shopkeeper and takes one out of his pocket.

The American's wife looks relieved. She does not want to open her handbag: she has read the Orient is awash with thieves.

'Say,' the American asks, 'is that US or Hong Kong dollars?'

'US dollar,' the shopkeeper says.

So the American signs six hundred and twenty US dollars' worth of cheques for an item he could have purchased for six hundred Hong Kong. I glance across the street at a money-changer's shop: the rate is four Hong Kong dollars and ten cents to the American buck. It occurs to me there should be another beatitude: blessed are the fleeced and suckered for they shall remain in blissful ignorance of their own stupidity.

In the side-streets, others are looking for a different deal. These would-be customers carry no cameras and are not accompanied by their wives. They walk in twos and threes, comrades-in-arms facing the thrill of the Oriental night. Some are visiting businessmen but most are sailors from the cruise ships, stewards from the airliners or soldiers posted to Whitfield Barracks in Nathan Road or Kowloon Tong.

Here, where the streets are narrower and the traffic slow moving, pimps are out in force. They are less strident than the silk tie hawkers but no less insistent.

'You want girl?' they enquire, walking beside a potential client for a few steps. 'Good girl. Young girl. Speak goo' English. Free beer for you.'

Some accept and are hustled down alleys: some refuse and are left alone for a few yards before another pimp confronts them. Only a few make it to the end of the street undecided or unmolested.

I am not accosted. I do not look right and am therefore left alone by both touts and pimps. There is something about me these canny operators can sense. Perhaps, in their eyes, I am too old. They think I am past it, have purchased all the silk ties a man can require in one lifetime and am too decrepit to lie with a woman young enough to be my great-granddaughter.

My perambulation is not to strike a hard bargain or to rent young flesh for an hour or two. I do not look upwards at the neon signs advertising the *Bayside Night-club* and *Eddie Shiu: Tailors*, *Rolex* and *Longines*, *Zeiss Ikon* and the *Opal Factory*. I am not here to swim vicariously in the wake of the more adventurous or foolhardy but simply to watch, to be with my fellow man as he makes an ass of himself, degrades himself, surrenders himself to base instincts. I do not criticise him nor try to prevent him going along the course he has set: I am not a judge or a jury, merely a lone spectator sharing in the quandaries of human existence, looking for truths which I know, deep within myself, I have never owned nor shall ever find.

Once, the tenement in which I live had been a chic apartment block in the modish style of its times: the corner of the building between Nanking Street and Woosung Street is rounded, this feature drawing much consternation from local residents. Sharp angles are bad luck and encourage evil spirits but a smooth curve makes life hard for them. Their talons cannot get a grip.

What seemed even more amazing to the local populace was the fact that the curved end of the building contained windows. It was a topic of considerable discussion in the local tea-houses and cooked food stalls as to how the building did not fold like a pile of rice wafers when the corner had no visible means of support.

It is five storeys high, six if you count them in the Chinese fashion where the ground is the first floor, with a communal flat roof. The whole structure was originally faced in cream-coloured concrete designed not to glare in the tropical sun like white-painted surfaces but to still keep the interior cool. The structural design allowed for no verandas but this did not deter residents: no one would want to sit out overlooking a street. Balconies were for those with gardens. Each apartment, in the old Colonial style, had a servants' quarters at the rear and spacious rooms. In the days before air conditioners, it was considered the bigger a room was, the cooler it would become in the hot months. The stairs were wide and there was no lift but the architect installed a winch system at the back to raise heavy loads into the apartments. It was by this route furniture arrived.

Each apartment had parquet floors, wide windows with typhoon-proof metal frames, solid mahogany doors and well-appointed kitchens. The bathrooms contained both a bath and a shower, and a western-style, sit-down water closet. The roof was paved with red quarry tiles and had an area set aside, with drain holes in the floor, where wash-amahs could hang the laundry and sit about to chatter.

The edifice was considered a marvel but I did not live here then. At the time, I rented two rooms in an wooden building in Western District, not far from the market and abattoir. Nanking Street, in those days, was above my station. By the time I moved into Flat 42 on the fourth floor, the building had come down in the world: it was no longer an apartment block but had become a tenement.

Today, the servants' quarters are self-contained flats occupied by families of up to six. The roomy apartments have been sub-divided into two, sometimes three, and the stairwell has shrunk by the addition of the now decrepit lift which was installed up the centre, cutting out all light from the stairs and causing them to be rebuilt in a square spiral. Above each floor, a corrugated iron rooflet has been added over the windows: I suppose once the rooms were reduced in size, they became hot in the summer. The iron has rusted, staining the concrete facing which is no longer cream but blotchy grey and the window frames of every apartment, without exception, have also decayed, making their typhoon-proof abilities a matter for conjecture.

Mr Li, my neighbour in 43, realising the building's deficiency in balconies, has knocked a window into a door and bolted onto the outside of the building a metal cage lined with steel mesh. It is three-feet deep, six wide and high, with a metal floor and a tin roof upon which the rain drums deafeningly and which, like the corrugated iron, has rusted. It can just accommodate him for, like his flat, it is chock-full with four kumquat and azalea bushes in pots, a green-and-white striped plastic chair, a folding table and a wooden crate in which there live two clucking hens and an indignant cockerel.

On the roof, the landlord has allowed an old woman to erect a shanty in the corner where the laundry area had been. It is a meagre, two-room shack of timber planks and packing cases nailed together under a sloping roof of plywood covered in flattened off-cuts filched from a metalworking business in Saigon Street. Once I saw her in the dead of night scurrying about the alley behind the workshop, tying aluminium sheets together with bamboo twine. In front of the shack is a small area of potted plants including a clump of bamboo which she claims is from the grove before her father's house near Swatow.

In the early hours of summer mornings, when the street is empty and the traffic temporarily stilled, the building hums with the spinning of old air-conditioner motors, the dripping of water sucked from the air, the buzz of neon lights with faulty connections and the belligerent, if muffled, crowing of the cockerel, which always begins its noise an hour before dawn. Not that it has much territory to protect nor any serious threat from an interloper. The nearest competition for his two scruffy hens is over two hundred yards away in Pak Hoi Street where there are a number of poultry sellers. Furthermore, the cockerels there are transients, en route for the cooked food stalls.

Yet I do not curse the bird. He has his life to live, just as we all do and, like us, is making the best of it.

My flat is not large but I am one of the lucky residents of the tenement for it incorporates one of the smooth corner windows. This has distinct benefits and equally manifest disadvantages. On one hand, it affords me a panoramic view of the junction between Nanking and Woosung Streets, brings morning sunlight into my abode and keeps the place cool in summer. On the other, the frames do not fit. Those sceptics who pondered on the wisdom of having an unsupported corner were right: the evil spirits cannot get a grip but neither can the concrete. The building has sagged under its own weight and buckled the window frames, some of which do not open, those which do opening too easily and letting in draughts when shut.

I live, by tenemental standards, in a plush residence of four rooms. What is more, I own it, having purchased the flat from Mr Poon on a fifty-year lease. He was a serious man with a limp who, like so many Chinese, was addicted not to opium or nicotine, alcohol or concubines but to gambling. He bet quite effectively on the horses and was a cool, quick-witted mah-jong player and these two sports, the one of kings and the other of coolies, brought him a steady if unspectacular profit. Yet, like any gambler, he was never satisfied: his life was empty without the big win and he could not understand, although I warned him, there was no such thing as the ultimate pot.

'I wan' one million dollars,' he confided one day as we met at a food stall in Temple Street.

'And then?' I asked.

'I stop, buy one more building, rent more flats. Maybe buy a Chrysler car. Big one. Sen' my son to school in America.'

He spooned his fish soup and noodles into his mouth as I watched him. There was a gambler's faraway stare in his eye.

'You cannot stop gambling,' I said. 'It is in your blood. It is a part of you, like doing business.'

'Sure, can do,' he answered, putting his bowl down on the wooden table. 'When I a rich man what I wan' to gamble for? I got my money.'

'No man gambles to win,' I replied. 'They gamble for excitement, for the thrill. Like drinking strong wine or having good sex.'

'How you know?' Mr Poon laughed. There was a hint of mockery in his words. 'You no gamble. You no drink too much. You no have woman.'

Yet I knew for I had seen the world and Mr Poon had not. His son never went to school abroad and he never bought another tenement. He gradually slid further into debt with the loan sharks and, one Sunday, after he had lost heavily at the Happy Valley races, he approached myself, Mr Wu and Mrs van der Poehl to offer us our flats. The asking price was below the going rate. He was desperate. We each spent the next day raising the money in our respective ways and, that evening, became the owners of our flats. We had attained the dream of everyone in the street – to own our own place, beyond the reach of rent rises and devious landlords. Mr Poon, however, did not pay off his creditors. He went immediately to Macau where we assumed he lost it all playing *fan tan* in the casino. He never returned. Rumour said he had made his fortune, cut and run, yet I know he did not. He loved his son too much if not his wife and daughter. He was probably killed by the loan sharks or at his own hand, going into the hills and swallowing caustic soda. One man's misfortune is another's good luck. That's the way it is.

The flat is not lavish. I have chosen not to live extravagantly. My needs are not excessive nor are my desires beyond more or less immediate satisfaction: at my age, the latter are reduced to the few plain luxuries which an old man might want to keep to ensure his life is made less difficult. A roof, sufficient food and adequate clothing are all I now demand of the world. And, of course, the security of mind to know these are mine without fear of imminent loss. I have a few friends whom I can trust or sit beside without endlessly talking cant and the good fortune to live where the sunlight is never chill and the world never boring. What is more, I have the inestimable luck of never being idle unless I so choose. An idle man dies quicker than a busy one.

However, I admit to having some weaknesses. I like beer in moderation and there is, of course, my occasional nocturnal indulgence with Mr Wu. These I consider my delicious little sins, weaknesses proving I am still alive. Should the time come when I no longer regard them in such a light, then that would be the hour to shuffle off this mortal coil and head for the next way point in eternity.

My home consists of a shower-cum-wc cubicle, an equally minute kitchen, a bedroom and a sitting room which is L-shaped. The latter is the only room with windows, the corner ones forming the heel of the L. I do not own a television although I have a third-hand air conditioner which keeps me awake just as the heat it is meant to combat does: it rattles incessantly and, after running for an hour or so, takes on the character of an old car, the motor stuttering as if changing gear. My furniture is simple – a bed and chest of drawers, a small round table to eat or read at with four chairs, some bookshelves, a cracked leather armchair I seldom sit in, a battered cane table with a glass sheet across the top and a matching chair which is my favourite, a scratched roll-top bureau and a large camphorwood chest. On the window sill is a kumquat plant in an ochre glazed pot whilst on the round table is a plastic cloth: on the cane table I keep a chipped Ming bowl and a pink-and-black soap-stone ashtray full of melon seeds.

I have allowed myself the luxury of a small refrigerator which does not come from the same stable as the air conditioner. The latter I bought from a stall in the market, the former from an electrical goods store in Sham Shui Po.

The floors are parquet making the place cool and I keep the wooden blocks polished therefore having no need of carpets. Having said that, I own a light blue Tientsin carpet in front of my arm chair. Just for decoration.

I am not a man for possessions. The older one grows, the less one wants. The collecting phase of one's life ceases after fifty, objects replaced by memories. The mental trappings of the long voyage through the years are enough. Objects remind one of the past and in this they are beneficial for one can give them away and it is like shedding history. Memories are more cruel: they cannot be given away, only shared.

I have, however, retained three specific items from my past which sit on the bookcase. They are little mementos, totems of where I have been in my travels towards today. I do not need them as reminders. Why I keep them I do not really know for I am not sentimental. Sentimentality is a surrender to base emotions which I will not allow.

One of these *memento mori* is a trade dollar. On the face stands Britannia, her trident sharp and her Union Jack shield bold in her left hand. Her cloak billows in the wind. In the distance is a sailing ship, the might of commerce nestling under her protection. Beneath her feet is the date of issue – 1899. My *annus mirabilis*. The obverse is a geometrical design of curlicues and whirls set in a ring of Persian design with a central Chinese motif. The value is given in Arabic and Chinese and the coin is forged in silver, the figure of Britannia having lost its finer detail.

Next to the coin is a six-inch-high opium oil lamp with a thick glass bulb, brass fittings and a burnt wick protruding from the oil reservoir. From a distance, it looks like a small medicine bottle for the barrel of the straight sides is dark green: this is not glass but quality jade.

I rarely use the lamp and I cannot spend the coin. They are both, like myself, antiques. No one accepts trade dollars and few bother with the traditional rigmarole of opium smoking. Today's chasers of dragons make do with matches or a Zippo cigarette lighter.

And the third item: that is also jade, an exquisite carving no bigger than a thumb joint. The jade is off-white, the colour of clouds after they have shed their rain. It has a smooth, waxy touch: collectors refer to this as mutton-fat jade. Perfect in every detail, it is a tortoise's shell. The creature has left it: all that remains is the dome and flat base with a thin hole through the centre so one might pass a cord through and wear it.

This is not an ornament nor a piece of jewellery. It is grave jade. At some time in its past, it has adorned a corpse.

I do not wear such things. Not yet, anyway.

There are other possessions I own but, like unwanted relatives, I have farmed them out and they reside now in the vault of the Hongkong & Shanghai Bank. There they may remain. I am unable to bring myself to cast them off. Like unwelcome relatives, they are affiliated to me by blood. Not the blood that runs in my veins for this is but a convenient metaphor: their blood has already been spilled.

The bookcases are laden mostly with paperbacks. I mention this because the best judge of a man is to know what he reads: and what point is there in listing my few belongings if not to give an insight into my soul.

If a man reads nothing, he is a hollow creature: if he reads detective fiction, he has an errant mind and would prefer a puzzle to a truth: a reader of romances is a dolt unable to find love: an aficionado of adventure stories is a tired man who lacks the imagination to leave his room and run a risk: one who indulges in scientific works is a dullard. All may be acceptable fellows and staunch friends, their weaknesses indicated by their reading matter but not a cause for avoidance.

The only man to eschew is the one whose shelves bear books about religion, for he is a seeker after eternity, a pious fool, a self-righteous bombast and a moralistic toad. He may read this tripe, but be assured as readily as there are fish in the sea he has a mistress or a young boy in his past, has thieved or cheated, connived or killed. He cannot be trusted for he is lost and one lost man drags others after him into oblivion.

My shelves bear none of these although I admit that once they did: a Bible and the Apocrypha, religious treatises, *The Life of Christ* and *The Life and Works of St Paul* by Farrar, both volumes of Caird's *The Evolution of Religion*, Bartoli's *The Primitive Church and The Primacy of Rome*. No longer. I was lost but now am found.

At the end of the top shelf, on the right hand side, out of reach unless I climb onto a chair, a precarious action at my age, is a book bound in black leather. I have placed it second in from the end of the shelf so that I might never see the gold blocked numbers on the cover. There is no title visible on the spine, so one might assume it to be a prayer book.

I rarely take it down: in fact, I have not touched it for years, not even to dust it. I do not bother with the top shelf. No one sees the agglomeration of dead flies, desiccated mosquitoes and grey exuviae. And yet I know it is there, am unable to forget or ignore it. It squats above my room, above my life, like a small dark incubus which, every day, draws my eye to torment me.

I have not the courage to destroy it. I have thought to set it alight, watch as the brittle pages flare and char, or drop it over the side of the Star Ferry, not looking round as it floats away in the wake, but it holds too much I cannot refute, contains too many days I want to forget yet dare not. If I were to utterly destroy it, I would achieve nothing, for what it holds is in me, moving relentlessly about in me like cigarette smoke marbling in the still air of an empty room.

The gold numbers read 1900.

It is the diary of just one year of my life.

The hull of the steam pinnace *Lucky Moon* was black with a gold stripe and two golden entwining dragons painted on either side of the bow. They were not pretentious Chinese dragons with huge eyes, forked tongues and curving tails like scaly hawsers but small and discreet, somehow suggestive of considerable power. The black funnel was tall and thin with a brass collar which, being as highly polished as the deck fittings, looked golden: even the belching smoke was solidly black, not greyly ephemeral.

There was no cabin. Instead, aft of the boiler, there was a well deck stretching to the stern covered by an awning of blancoed canvas supported by a steel cross-frame which could be folded flat and transformed into a sort of shack by pulling a roof of wooden slats over the metal framework. The bench seats opened into beds, the lockers beneath them storing bedding and personal possessions.

She had a crew of two, a captain and a boy. The former was in his late middle-age and wore the threadbare remnants of a British naval officer's jacket with tattered epaulettes and a high collar he could not button up because of the prominence of his Adam's apple. Unlike most Chinese men, whose heads were shaven back to their long cues, he had a Western-style haircut with a few long wisps of bristle growing from a mole on his jaw.

His responsibility was the sailing of the vessel, watching pressure gauges, taking the wheel, navigating and uttering guttural remarks to the boy between humming a tuneless music, his tongue making sonorous bell-like noises.

The boy was not more than thirteen, with his hair in a cue. His clothes were not as threadbare as his master's but just as incongruous, being a dark-blue Chinese jacket worn over a British soldier's pair of shorts which, being much too large, had been folded in a tuck in front and were held in place by a leather thong. What the captain did not do, the boy took on, swabbing decks, polishing pipes, stoking the boiler, coiling ropes and stowing painters.

The only other person aboard the craft, other than myself, was Ah Fong. It was he who had welcomed me aboard that morning. I had arrived by rickshaw at the dockside just before seven to be greeted by him bowing low at the foot of the gangplank.

'Goo' morning, master,' he had said, tilting his head back so he could see me. 'Me Ah Fong. Serwant, frien', compan-ee-on for you to go China side.'

His cue of hair slid to one side and he flicked it deftly out of the way as he straightened his back.

'Good morning, Ah Fong,' I answered and held my hand out to him. He shook it firmly, just the once, the sleeve of his black cotton jacket swishing against his wrist.

'You come now, master,' he instructed, taking charge of my baggage and stowing it away in two lockers. 'Come on *Lucky Moon*. We go now.'

'How long is our journey?' I enquired as I stepped on to the gangplank.

'One two day, master. But goo' sea. Goo' wind. No rain, no womit.'

'Womit?' I replied.

'Womit, master. Womit.' He stretched his neck and gave a mime of retching. 'Womit. Chow come back topside. If sea too big. But now no big sea. No womit.'

I settled in the well deck as he indicated. The captain tinkered with some valves, the boy cast off, the steam whistle shrilled and the screw began to turn, threshing the water. We departed the dock, crossed through lines of sailing vessels riding at anchor then set off along a channel between rock-strewn, grassy hillsides falling steeply to the sea. Little beaches and headlands of boulders slid by until, after an hour or so, we passed a conical mountain to starboard and headed into the wide estuary of the Pearl River. Thus had begun the last stage of my journey from Dublin, upon which I had embarked three months previously.

For some time I stared pensively at the swirling wake but watching its convolutions made me feel slightly giddy. I turned my attention to the captain at the wheel, his jacket hazy through a jet of escaping steam: the boy knelt by the boiler operating a secondary firebox the door of which was open to display a trapped hell of glowing coals. Ah Fong stood over him.

We crossed the Pearl River estuary in three hours and, although the sea was not smooth, the swell was low and I was not discomforted. By one o'clock, the sun beating on the awning and striking off the sea, we entered channels of the river delta south west of Canton, passing a Chinese fort, the wide-mouthed cannons poking through battlements, bright red triangular pennants flying from bamboo poles which whipped in the breeze.

'For fighting,' Ah Fong had announced. 'Plenty bad men here in riffer. He name pywrat.'

'Shall we be troubled by them?' I asked apprehensively.

The pirates' reputation was bloody and extensive: given the opportunity, they would attack a sixty-gun man-o'-war. Only a few months before a band of brigands had stormed a Yokohama-bound clipper, murdering the crew, looting the vessel then setting her alight.

'No,' Ah Fong reassured me. 'We too small. No got much. He wan' catch big junk, big ship. Plenty people, plenty money.'

The delta lands were monotonous. Small fishing and cargo sampans drifted by, the banks lined by dense groves of bamboo with small matshed houses built by fishing nets suspended from poles. The further from the sea, the thicker the bamboo became and it was half an hour before we came upon a village. It was little more than a hamlet of low, grey stone houses under roofs the eaves of which curled upwards at the corners. By a mud and shingle landing place grew a tree with branches hanging into the water reminding me of the scene depicted upon willow-pattern plates.

A mob of children, hearing the thump of the engine, ran down to the muddy shore to gaze at the vessel yet not one child waved and I felt sad. On the voyage out, wherever the ship had berthed, children had appeared to wave, beg, cat-call and laugh. They had gathered around me, their hands outstretched and their faces alight with smiles appealing for baksheesh, offering to be guides to mosques or iniquitous dens of pleasure. If the ship lay offshore they had swum out to dive for coins, their lithe nut-brown bodies disappearing under the sea like otters. Yet these children stood in a mute, solemn group, their eyes fixed on the *Lucky Moon*, following it intently as it passed. I waved to them yet drew not the least response.

Ah Fong stepped across the deck with a bowl of rice, an oval platter of fish and vegetables and a cup of tea. The eating utensils were a pair of bamboo chopsticks.

'I sowwy chow late come, master,' he apologised, placing the food beside me. 'No good cook before. Water too big.'

'That does not matter,' I said then, noticing his food was by the firebox, added, 'Get your food and sit with me. I want to talk to you.'

With Ah Fong squatting on the deck before me, I began to eat. The vegetables were a sort of pointed boiled mushroom the shape of an ink-cap, sliced crisp bamboo shoots and long strands of green leaves which looked like spinach but tasted delicious. The fish contained an inordinate number of bones which I found difficult to separate from the flesh with chopsticks. I watched Ah Fong to see how he managed.

It was quite simple. He picked up a piece of the fish with his chopsticks, noisily sucked the flesh from the bones then spat the detritus over the side of the boat. I did likewise which produced a quick sideways glance from him which I construed as approval.

The fish and vegetables eaten, I was left with rice in my bowl, flavoured by a thin gravy. Ah Fong tackled this by placing his bowl to his lips, shovelling the rice into his mouth with a rowing motion of his chopsticks. I copied him.

'D'ink tea now,' Ah Fong suggested.

I picked up the cup which was like the rice bowl only smaller. It was hot and my fingers tingled as I sipped cautiously.

'Too hot for you, master? No matter. You d'ink, make noise. Make cold.'

Ah Fong took my cup, put it to his lips and slurped loudly.

'Now I get nuffer one.'

He went off and poured a second cup taken from a basin by the firebox. The tea was clear, weak and scented with jasmine flowers which hung above the tea leaves like tiny fish.

'Ah Fong,' I asked after imitating his slurp, 'why did those children not wave?'

'He no wafe. He af'aid.'

'Afraid?' I puzzled. 'Have they not seen a steam boat before?'

'Oh, he see. Plenty time see. *Lucky Moon* go up down Wuchow two time one mumph.'

'Do they think this a pirate boat?'

'No!' Ah Fong laughed. 'No pywrat boat! All pywrat Chinese man got junk. No engine.'

'So why are they afraid?'

'He af'aid you,' Ah Fong replied bluntly.

'Of me! They don't know me.'

'You fowener. Not Chinese man. You *gweilo*. Fowen devil. So he no wafe. If he wafe, you look him, can steal his soul.'

In mid-afternoon the hazy sky cleared to a hot blue and the delta countryside gave way to mountains. They were not a thousand feet high, as yet unweathered by time or sculptured by men. The steep slopes were wooded and the valleys cultivated with small paddy-fields. Villages appeared and the river, after going through a gorge a few miles long, widened to half a mile. The captain kept the *Lucky Moon* near the centre.

We made less headway, the engine straining against the current, the pistons vehemently hissing, the funnel gouting gobbets of smoke. About three o'clock, we passed a small town on the outskirts of which stood a seven-storey pagoda, its walls painted white with red piping, the roof crowned by a golden orb.

'What is that building for?' I asked Ah Fong, who was leaning over the side rinsing the food bowls by lowering them into the wake in a bucket pierced with holes.

'What for?' He was puzzled. 'Is pago-dah.'

'Yes, but why was it built?'

'To stop riffer d'agon,' he replied.

'River dragons?'

He pulled the bucket in, hanging it from a davit to drain in the scuppers.

'Water home for d'agon,' he explained. 'You see riffer bend come go? Because his tail bending.'

'How does the pagoda stop the dragon?' I enquired.

He pondered the question before answering, 'Pago-dah tell d'agon no come here, we know you, you no make t'ouble for us or we kill you.'

Just as the sun was settling upon the mountains, the pinnace turned a bend to steam across a wide bay on which there was another town with a pagoda in its centre: on the opposite bank stood a second. The pinnace altered course to avoid a long, low barge-like vessel sailing up-river under a single brown square sail as ribbed as a bat's wing. When our bow swung round, the sun silhouetted the sail and hull, the river behind it a shifting cascade of gold light cast between the two pagodas.

I caught my breath and felt the strong desire to pray, to give thanks for such beauty at the end of a day that had seen me safely journeying into China. I knelt on the deck, placed my hands together and raised my face, the last rays of the sun warm on my skin. It was as if God were touching me.

'Thank you, Lord,' I said, 'for Your guidance and strength this day, for Your protection as I sail at Your command up the Si Kiang river to do Your bidding.' I paused for a moment before adding, 'And I offer my thanks also for this beautiful evening which is a manifestation of Your Holy Glory.'

Interrupting my devotions, Ah Fong called out, 'Master, here two pago-dah. Because too many d'agon in riffer.'

When Ah Fong served the evening meal, a thick broth in which floated pieces of anonymous gristly meat, I asked him when we would reach Wuchow.

'Long time, master,' was the reply. 'Next day we come Wuchow. Afternoon.'

As darkness fell, the river came alive with lights. At first, I thought these were houses on the shore but as we drew nearer they moved and soon we were in the thick of a fleet of small sampans hung with lanterns.

'He fishing,' Ah Fong explained. 'Make light. Fish come see light, like moff. When he come, fisherman catch him. Easy work.'

'Are we stopping tonight?' I enquired.

'We stop. But no here. Too many fisherman. Stop small time more, up near mountain.'

He pointed ahead: set darkly against the night was a range of hills. They could not have been more than a few miles away but it was an hour before we reached them, the captain throttling back the engine and turning the *Lucky Moon*, allowing her to drift with the strong current into a narrow creek grown over with tall bamboo and edged by reedbeds.

Once we were stationary in the creek, Ah Fong transformed the well deck into a cabin, covering the bench with a quilt.

'Sleep now,' Ah Fong said unnecessarily, as the boy attended to the boiler, raking out the hot ash to drop it hissing into the river. 'Tomorrow, we go before sun come.'

'I should like to stretch my legs,' I said. Ah Fong did not understand the colloquialism. 'I should like to walk. My legs,' I rubbed my thigh, 'are very sore.'

Ah Fong nodded and went into a huddle with the captain. They talked for several minutes before he said, 'Can do. But no go long way. No must meet people. If you see people, must hide. Capting say good you wear black cassock. No can see you easy. But if you see people hide come back quick quick. No talk him.'

The boy pushed the gangplank onto the bank, jamming it between some thick trunks of bamboo.

'Jus' here,' Ah Fong pointed through the bamboo, 'one parf. You walk parf, go only on parf. Go here.' He pointed up-river. 'No here.' He swung his arm down-river. 'How long you go?'

'Half an hour,' I suggested.

'Half hour can do. No more.'

I stepped along the gangplank but, as I reached the bamboo, Ah Fong advised, 'If you hide, look down you shoes. Put hand in pocket. White skin can see. People t'ink you ghost. No good be ghost.'

Struggling through the bamboo, I discovered the path and set off along it. I thought the need for caution to be overstated but appreciated from reports in Hong Kong that the hills harboured bandits. My baggage would constitute ripe pickings and, as a European, I could be held for a substantial ransom.

The moonless sky was clear, my eyes soon adjusting to the starlight. I could plainly see the path and was confident that if I were to meet someone I could easily step unseen into the bushes and bamboo thickets along the way.

I had walked for about ten minutes and was considering turning back when I smelt wood smoke. The path, which was narrow and not well-frequented near the *Lucky Moon*, was joined here by another coming up from the river, the two forming a well-used thoroughfare. Past a clump of bamboo I found myself suddenly at a gate set in a fence of wooden planks.

Quickly, I stepped back and studied the gateway. The two pillars were made of stone across which was a wooden beam a foot square. Several vertical planks were set into a slot in the beam and a groove cut in the step which was carved of natural rock. In the centre of the beam was a circular mirror on either side of which was carved a Chinese character.

Through the gate, about thirty feet away, was a square, single-storey house before which was a hard, beaten-earth courtyard. To one side was a small shed of bamboo matting such as I had seen by the fishing nets on the river. Leaning against the building was a crude wooden plough next to which glowed several incense sticks poking out of a small glazed pot. The house was windowless but a faint light emanated from an open doorway.

I stood quite still and listened. Somewhere in a tree behind the house, a cicada was making its loud intermittent insect chirruping. From the shed came a restless shuffling which I assumed to be livestock of some sort. From the doorway came a low hum of voices punctuated by the sound of a liquid being poured. One voice was momentarily raised and someone laughed. They were male voices.

In the doorway appeared a woman. She materialised so

quickly and so silently I had somehow not seen her. One moment the doorway was empty, the next she was standing there holding a lantern. I stepped into the shadow of the gate pillar. By the lamplight, I could make out her features. She was short and slim, wearing baggy trousers with a dark smock-like blouse. Her hair was raked back and shone across her scalp as if oiled. Her cheekbones were high but her eyes wide and not at all narrowed.

She moved to one side, set her lantern on the ground and, from the shadows, produced a small stool on which she sat. A child then came out of the house carrying a baby which it handed to her. Neither of them spoke and the child returned the way it had come.

The woman unbuttoned a flap at the shoulder of her blouse and, folding it back, lifted her breast out and gave it to the infant which began to suckle. I could see the soft white of the woman's skin and hear the contented suck of the baby. For several minutes, I watched this scene, captivated by its beauty, simplicity and wonder. Here was the work of God at its most basic: a mother feeding her child. All they needed, I considered, was to know the Word of the one God and have His Light shine upon them.

Another lantern appeared at the door held by an older woman. She rasped a curt command to the young mother who immediately put her breast away and, with a quiet word, handed the baby to the other who cuddled it. Then, by the old woman's side, appeared a dog. It sniffed the air, stepped onto the courtyard, sniffed again and growled in my direction.

Anxious not to alarm the animal, I stepped away. My sleeve snagged on a short sapling of bamboo but I was unaware of this: I continued to move until the thin stem broke free and snapped upright, rattling against the broader trunks of the parent plant like a pair of castanets. The dog began to bark furiously, raised voices accompanying it.

My cassock slapping against my legs, the sleeves flailing in the air, I ran. The heavy material snagged on thorns and snared on branches. I fled so quickly I missed the point where I had to turn down to the *Lucky Moon* and was obliged to retrace my steps for fifty yards, sweating with fear that I might meet a group out looking for me. When I reached the boat, I was breathless.

'You make dog bark,' Ah Fong whispered.

'Yes,' I stuttered, trying to find my breath. 'I don't think they followed me.'

'He no follow,' Ah Fong said matter-of-factly. 'Night time no follow. Too many ghost, too many d'agons.'

In the starlight, I could see Ah Fong and the captain grinning broadly.

'No more walk,' Ah Fong then stated quietly. 'Now sleep.'

I removed my outer garments and, in my underwear, wriggled under the quilt. I had the cabin space to myself, Ah Fong lying on the deck, the boy curled up and wheezing softly in his sleep by the engine: the captain sat on the gangplank listening to the night.

Just after dawn, I was disturbed from my slumbers by a gentle hissing of steam as the pinnace started to edge backwards. The roof and sides of the cabin were gone, the awning back in place. A faint wisp of smoke drifted out of the funnel to hang in the thick white mist settled upon the river.

'No noise,' Ah Fong cautioned me, pressing his finger horizontally along his lips rather than vertically across them. 'After you sleep, fisherman come look see for boat . . .'

As the *Lucky Moon* edged clear of the creek, the pull of her hull dragged a limp body out of the reeds. The figure lay face down, dressed in a blue jacket and trousers, a long cue of hair floating out from the head at right angles. Around the neck was a red weal where, I assumed, a garrotte had tightened. The body pirouetted about as it nudged a bed of weed. Twenty feet out from the bank a current took hold of the body, spun it ninety degrees and towed it quickly away.

'No good swim in riffer,' Ah Fong observed, as I watched the body vanish. 'D'agon take you downside. Eat you.'

A run of cold blood flowed down my spine: I could feel the hair rise on my nape. It was not the horror of death that filled me with such dread but the terrible matter-of-factness in Ah Fong's voice. Death was unequivocally accepted by him and the dragons were as real as the daylight.

'Did you have to kill him?' I asked.

'Must do. If no, people come, kill you, kill me.'

I looked at the river and thought of what I had witnessed the night before, the mother suckling her infant: if I had not gazed upon the sight, had not been so self-indulgent, the man would be alive and the infant would still have a father or an uncle.

'But will they not miss him?'

'He no know where he gone. They shout but no look. Too af'aid.'

'Will they not know it was us?'

'He no know!' Ah Fong said dismissively. 'He say d'agon eat him.'

Looking up at the funnel, I saw blacker smoke beginning to appear. The captain pressed a lever and the pistons began to hiss and spit, the propeller turning once more with its rhythmical thumping.

'They will hear the engine. They will smell the smoke,' I said.

'No, master. He say it d'agon. No can see boat, can smell fire, hear noise like snake. Like d'agon . . .'

I crossed myself and muttered a quick prayer for the poor heathen's soul but Ah Fong gave it no further thought and, as soon as we were under way, set about preparing a breakfast of thin gruel-like soup, little dumplings stuffed with fish and a cup of thick, dark tea.

'Man die ve'y quick, master,' he commented as he served the food. 'Captain ve'y good man. No noise, no pain.'

'He was not a dog,' I remonstrated, angry he could be so utterly ruthless and puzzled how a convert to Christianity could be so merciless.

Ah Fong, not understanding the analogy, said, 'No kill like dog. Hit dog with big stick on the head to kill him. Sometimes must hit five, six times before dog die. This one no hit. Just one touch and he finish.'

For the whole day, the *Lucky Moon* steamed up-river, the currents in places so strong the vessel barely made any headway against the flow, the captain standing in the prow to find a slower running channel. With him on lookout, the boy took the wheel, holding the vessel steady, a bright puerile grin of pleasure lighting up his face. Other vessels journeying upstream were overhauled very slowly whilst those going down-river sped by, their oarsmen struggling to keep the line of their course. The sun beat down and, although there was a brisk easterly breeze, it was hot and carried no relief.

Throughout the day, I either sat and watched the mountain landscape move inexorably by or stood in the bow gazing ahead. I could not take from my mind the fact that a man had died so my own life might be spared.

It was true that I had not done the deed: indeed, I had been oblivious of it. Yet I could not escape the realisation that, even unwittingly, I had been the cause of the man's murder and that, if the divine plan to which I had submitted my life was that I come to China to bring the heathens to Christ then this was a very sorry start, and no mistake. It would have been better if I had been killed: as it was, an ignorant fisherman, trying to protect his family, had died without blessing, without salvation and, therefore, without hope.

The afternoon drew on to early evening. The sun set behind the hills, the sky turning the colour of ducks' eggs and, just as I was wondering if we were to spend another night moored secretly in a bywater, Ah Fong called out.

'Master! Wuchow come soon.'

I eased my back and, stretching my arms, massaged my fingers together. Every bone in my body seemed tuned to the throb of the pistons: my mouth tasted of soot and my skin felt grimy even though I had washed myself with a bucket of river water just after noon.

'Soon see Wuchow,' Ah Fong declared as I joined him in the bow. 'You see island?'

Straining my eyes against the dusk, I could just make out a small island about a mile and a half away. It was rocky by the shore but wooded higher up. From within the trees shone a surprisingly bright light.

'Yes, Ah Fong, I can see it.'

'He name D'agon Island.'

'Because a dragon lives there?' I asked with a hint of irony.

'D'agon live there sometime,' he confirmed.

'And the light is the dragon's eye, is it?'

'No, no d'agon eye.'

'His fiery mouth?' I suggested.

'No,' Ah Fong repeated pedantically, 'no mouth. D'agon mouth got flame. Got yellow light, not white light. Light come from Customs post.'

Remaining at the bow, I watched the island draw closer as the crew readied for arrival. The boy lowered painters over the gunwales, tidied the deck and re-coiled the ropes. The captain began to jostle the craft against the currents, spinning the wheel, speeding up or slowing down the engine. Ah Fong lit several lamps, stowed the eating utensils and removed my baggage from the lockers, lining it up on the deck.

The town was on the right bank, glimmering lights indicating its extent: on the opposite shore was a featureless darkness with only a few sparse, dim lights showing at the water's edge. Behind Dragon Island, their bows facing up-stream and their masts outlined against the sky, were three large sailing vessels, obviously trading up from Hong Kong or Macau, and a number of junks riding at anchor. All showed running lights whilst at the stern of one of the former was displayed a row of illuminated windows.

In less than half an hour, the captain spun the wheel and the pinnace veered in to the right shore. Although it was now dark, I could see the bank was high and steep with a long flight of stone steps leading up to a sort of promenade which was lined for a hundred yards with a throng of chattering people, many of whom carried lanterns. At the foot of the steps was a wooden pontoon upon which were gathered five or six men.

As the *Lucky Moon* slid alongside, the boy jumped onto the planking, securing a line to a wooden bollard. Once the gangplank was out, I stepped onto the jetty and two figures detached themselves from the group to walk towards me, one behind the other: the second was a Chinese with a lantern hung from a pole which he tilted forward over the other's shoulder so that it swung, casting a mobile shadow across his face.

As he came nearer, I could see that the first man was short and ruddy-faced, wearing a black cassock. Around his waist hung a black silk girdle whilst about his neck was a silver cross suspended by a chain of the same metal. Despite the jetty being made of planking, he moved silently and, glancing down, I noticed he was not wearing the shoes of a European but the soft slippers as worn by Chinese men.

'Welcome to Wuchow, Father Stephen,' he said as he drew closer. 'It's good to see you delivered safely from your journey and the ravages of the river dragons. I doubt not that Ah Fong here's been regaling you with tales of submarine monsters breathing fire and stealing virgins from their beds.'

I could not help smiling.

'We have had mention of them,' I asserted, adding 'but we have been mercifully spared an encounter.'

Yet no sooner had I spoken than I saw again in my mind the heathen's body turning in the river and, with an awesome feeling of apprehension, considered that perhaps we had, after all, come close to one but had, this time, escaped its clutches.

The man offered me his hand and said with a slight Irish lilt which time and China had not quite eradicated, 'As you will have guessed, I'm Father Callaghan. To be sure but it's good to see you.'

I halt by the flower stall at the entrance to the alleyway where I frequently stop, having done so for more years than I care to consider. It is on a short cut I occasionally take from the waterfront to Nanking Street and visiting it is almost a ritual, perhaps a part of growing old.

The stall consists of a trellis of makeshift wooden shelves arranged against the wall of a coffin-maker's shop, under an awning of moth-eaten tarpaulin stretched between the iron bracket of the shop sign, the framework of an asthmatic air conditioner and a lamp-post to which is attached a small galvanised cylindrical box for the collection of dead rats. The air conditioner is switched on, dripping morosely onto the tarpaulin, a steady trickle finding a hole and pock-marking the pavement.

Fumbling in my pocket for a fifty-cent coin, I smile benignly at the old crone who sells the flowers, squatting on a low three-legged stool out of range of the drips. She glances at me then, recognising me, stares wide-eyed as if surprised to see me. I raise my eyebrows in greeting but do not speak. This, too, is a part of our ceremony.

My hand shakes as I sort out coins in my pocket. They have begun to quake a little more recently and although this does not unduly worry me, for I accept it as a further sign that I am finally growing old, it annoys me. I tug my fingers free of the lining with an impatient jerk, grasping loose change.

'Good afternoon,' I greet the old woman, my voice calm now I have overcome my frustration.

My first words are always in English. There is no logic behind this for she speaks not a word of it.

Her response is to giggle: it is the giggle not of an old woman but of a young girl. I can see, in my mind's eye, how she must have looked as a domestic *saw hei* amah, vowed to celibacy and a life dedicated to the service of foreigners. Perhaps those words in English stir happy memories of polished floors and riding in varnished rickshaws, of missy in her cocktail dress, master in his white shorts and shirt, little missy with her hair in bunches and young master riding his tricycle. And of having a full rice bowl.

'*Nei ho ma?*' I enquire next, reverting to Cantonese.

She stops giggling and smiles, the lined skin about her eyes folding like those of an ancient reptile, two gold teeth glinting between her thin lips. Her arthritic hands lift from her lap. One half-waves to me, the other involuntarily stroking her tightly combed grey hair where it is severely dragged into a taut bun held by a jade and bone pin. The jade is weak green and semi-translucent: cheap jade, the sort coolie women wear.

'And what small, heavenly faces have you today?' I ask.

My Cantonese accent is so colloquial it might be a Chinese living within my body who speaks.

'Smiling faces, sad faces, sleeping faces,' the flower-seller responds. 'What do you want?'

She stops stroking her hair, her hand vaguely gesturing in mid-air in the direction of the shelves.

'What do you recommend?'

She ponders this problem, her eyes scanning her wares

propped in tin cans, some carrying labels marked *Heinz, Cow and Gate* or *Crosse & Blackwell.* As always, I follow her gaze along the lines of multicoloured petals, bunches of asparagus fern and twigs of peach blossom not yet open. Her gaze halts on some spikes of yellow and pink blooms.

'*Wong keung,*' she declares, seeing me looking at the same tin can.

I consider the ginger flowers. They are waxy, like the death lilies one sees on altars at Easter and I catch their heady, sinful scent even above the reeking perfume of Liuchow pine sap from the coffin-maker's shop and the faint, omniscient stench of drains which haunts the alley.

'*Kei toh?*'

There is no need for me to enquire for every bloom is always fifty cents. No matter if it is an Australian imported rose, a tiger lily from the market gardens near Yuen Long or a sprig of wild camellia picked on the hills behind Kowloon, it is invariably half a dollar, the sum the old woman assesses I am good for: it is not so much as to put me off buying but it is not so low as to dent her profit margins. I know she pays not more than fifteen cents for the blossom and that, had I been a Chinese, the cost would have been twenty-five cents.

'*Ng saap sin,*' she declares, confirming the price at fifty cents and looking me straight in the eye as if daring me to haggle.

Yet it does not matter. I do not begrudge her a living and I know any other European would be charged seventy-five cents and an American sailor a dollar or more.

'*Hai,*' I agree abruptly, shrugging to imply she has got the better of me. This is another part of the custom of our commerce.

The old woman turns on her stool and pretends to choose the best of her stock, rejecting several perfectly fine blossoms, clicking her tongue and muttering incoherently. Finally, she decides on the one I should purchase and wraps it in a funnel of Chinese news-paper, sealing the base of the stem with a rubber band. She does not need to ask how many flowers I want: I always purchase just one.

'*Ng saap sin,*' she demands again, holding the flower out with her left hand.

Opening my fingers, I display the coin and her right hand comes out, palm turned upward with her gnarled fingers bent not to grasp the money but from age, decades of laundering clothes and ironing uniforms, dusting ornaments and making beds, serving at table and minding a small, blonde-haired child she loved as if it had sprung from her own womb.

As her hand meets mine, I think how both of them have touched so much in their many years, blessed and cursed, struck and stroked, held other hands, chopsticks, rice bowls – all the impedimenta of three score years and ten, and a good few more beside.

She takes the money and passes over the flower. There is a sense of propriety in the exchange: we might have been making the trade-off at the end of a long kidnap or protracted marriage brokerage. Lifting the bottom hem of her white blouse, she inserts the coin in a canvas money belt. It chinks against other coins.

I nod and she smiles again. It is a golden smile not only because of her two eighteen-carat teeth but also because, in those lines of age, there still resides the tenacity to live, the soul of a young girl waiting to die: and I wonder if, in my own face, people can read my own past, assess my current state of mind.

The ginger flower in hand, I turn away from the bright array of flowers to face the dismal alleyway. It occurs to me that the flower stall is perhaps a little evil, a gaudy but deceitful display which camouflages the entrance to the dissolute world for which the alley stands with its garbage bins and detritus of human existence. If I gave credence to such thoughts, I might believe it had been placed there by Satan himself as an enticement into Hades, the old flower seller one of the fallen angels in disguise. For a moment, I pause and survey the way ahead.

It is not a long alleyway, perhaps twenty yards from the flower stall to the next street. On either side are tenements rising to four or five storeys. From some windows project bamboo poles resting on wrought-iron brackets and hung with drying laundry. As the alley is only ten feet wide, the poles reach almost to the opposite wall. It being early evening, the hanging flags of clothing are mostly dry: had I arrived earlier, I would have needed an umbrella to reach the far end without being soaked.

Doors lead into the tenements. Some are of metal construction and some wooden but all are substantial and carry hasps and padlocks or are fitted with double deadlocks; several have iron sliding lattice security gates across them. One, leading into the rear of a gold merchant's shop, is a grey-painted steel door like the door to a companionway on a warship. It might have been pilfered from such a vessel being broken up in the Lai Chi Kok scrap yards for it has lugs which could have taken watertight screw-clamps. The few windows at ground-floor level are grimy, glazed with frosted glass strengthened with wire or protected by iron grills. Wreathes of rusty barbed wire decorate the drainpipes.

Down the centre of the alley runs an open sluice leading to a grating. It never ceases to flow with a noxious, black liquid in which, over the years, I have seen floating, along with the usual effluent, drowned kittens with their fur spiked by the water, sleek grey rats with their spines snapped, khaki-coloured rubber prophylactics, two-inch long cockroaches trying to swim clear, dead geckoes and, once, an aborted human embryo not much bigger than a small doll and curiously misshapen.

I hate the alley for I can never enter it without recalling, even for the briefest moment, that half-made infant. I had cried at the time and, taking a length of plank from beside the coffin-maker's door, had stopped the stream in order to quickly bless the little corpse, making the sign of the cross over it and muttering what I could recollect of the Latin text of the Extreme Unction. I felt I had to do something to mark its passage from reality towards eternity.

That done, I had removed the plank and the build-up of filth washed the little body away, rolling it over and over towards the sluice opening and out of sight. There had been no grating then to halt its progress under the streets and into the harbour where the fishes would consume it.

It is a hot afternoon for so early in the year. I am slumped in the battered cane chair, my head tilted forward with my chin on my chest, my right arm folded limply in my lap, my left hanging out over the side. I am bare to my waist.

I am not asleep, nor yet am I fully awake. I am in that delicious limbo where the mind is alive but still divorced from the body. Transcendentalists spend hours trying to reach such a state. I can do it in minutes, on a hot afternoon, with the air conditioner off and the window ajar, the warm breeze wafting in the familiar reassuring sounds of Nanking Street.

As I have always been, I am a thinker. I was trained as such, taught to ponder the imponderable, my duty in life to grasp philosophical problems and seek to solve them. All the other responsibilities placed upon me I have long since shirked, cast off or ignored. Yet this, the act of thinking, is the one I have retained: it is the only one worth keeping.

When I indulge myself in these moments of quiet, one of the problems I pose myself is to consider the notion that a dying man sees, in his penultimate instant as a thinking being, his life flash before him. I do not subscribe to the theory.

Instead I believe that in the weeks leading to his final day he remembers his past: not all of it in some glorious fashion, like a cinema film being projected with interludes in which he may relieve or refresh himself. He merely sees incidents from it which recapitulate his personal history so he has an idea of what he has achieved, or failed to accomplish, found or lost along the way.

If my surmise is correct, then I have been dying for years.

My past does not flash before me but comes slowly by, dragging its heels, every action slowed so I might be aware of my every stupidity, every error, every fault laid bare, so I might look at it and know myself.

Perhaps this is a punishment, a chance at redemption in that, by seeing these scenes, I might renounce them or apologise for them. Yet it is too late for all that. I am an old man and those to whom I owe apologies have long since gone before me into oblivion.

My old leather-bound travelling clock rings. I come fully to myself, my mind joining my body again. I fumble for the switch, turning the clamour off and catching my finger in the clasp on the case. I am not yet in total command of my flesh. It will take a moment or two. I replace the clock a little too heavily on the table and a thin fluted vase with the now bedraggled ginger flower in it teeters dangerously. I make no effort to steady it. I would only knock it over.

The air in the room is sultry. I twist my head, casting an eye over the round, formica-topped table with its four chairs, the shelves of leaning books and the dark shadow of the passageway that leads to the door of my flat. Through the bedroom door I can see the upright wooden chair at the foot of my bed, my dark brown shoes resting one upon the other beneath it and my favourite cream jacket draped over the back.

Nothing has changed whilst I have been away.

I vigorously massage my neck: in dozing I have cricked a muscle below my left ear, tightening the flesh in a spasm which tics irritatingly. My skin is tanned but loose-fitting, as if I am shrinking within it. During my dozing, I have loosened my belt, undoing the top button of my trousers which have slid down to my groin, showing the elastic waistband of my underpants. My feet are unshod, my toes long and thin as if they have never been confined by shoes. As I breathe, I make a soft hushing sound, my chest barely moving. At my age, breathing takes little effort. I do not need the rush of oxygen demanded by the blood of young men.

I am not sure how long I have sat here. There have been occasions, occurring with increasing frequency of late, when the passage of minutes has gone by without recognition, without impinging itself upon me. Sometimes, I pause in the middle of an everyday action, like walking along the street, and realise I have not the slightest notion of what has occurred during the last few minutes. I look down the street at, say, a coolie in a conical rattan hat struggling under the swaying weight of his pole and baskets and find that I cannot remember having seen him pass me.

Tiny sections of my life are becoming blanks: it is like reading a book and discovering certain lines have been omitted, requiring the reader to make up what has occurred in the narrative in order to maintain the continuum of sense. These lapses do not worry me. They are a curious symptom of growing old, beyond my governance and therefore impassively accepted.

I glance at the clock. The numbers have lost their luminosity, the phosphorescent paint as pellucid as the eyes of a blind beggar. The enamel face is chipped beside the 4 and the hour hand has lost its point. The glass is beginning to oxidise, too, in the region of the 11 and 12.

'Half past four,' I remark. 'The boy'll be here soon.'

Quite often, I talk to myself. It is a trait I learned long ago and is not a sign of increasing senility or loneliness. It cannot be the former for I am fully aware of my action and do not seek to reply to myself. I make statements, not being so stupid as to pose questions. And it cannot be the latter for I am not lonely. Besides, self-conversation is not a wasted gift for it not only fills empty hours but often helps to reason out problems, assures and gives confidence. All it cannot do is quell fears.

I am hot, more so than I realised sitting still. Sweat runnels from my neck down the hollow of my sternum to my stomach. It tickles and I slap at it as if it is an annoying insect.

'Still firm!' I congratulate myself.

I smite my stomach again, the flat of my palm making a loud hollow report on the damp skin.

'Loose, maybe. Old. But not flabby. Not like one of those flaccid, languishing old pedants in the Kowloon Cricket Club. Bar-proppers. Mere *boulevardiers* . . .'

There is a knocking on my door.

'The boy,' I declare.

I tug up my trousers and, reaching under the table, fumble for my shirt, pulling it on. The cotton sticks to my skin. Finally, buttoning it up, I walk down the short, narrow passage to the door. There is a repeat of the knocking.

'A moment, please,' I call out, a little exasperated.

Quickly, I check my flies are closed, discover my trousers are still open and hastily do them up.

'Never do to see the young gentleman whilst in semi-disarray,' I murmur as I slide the chain off the door.

Twice a week, I teach a private pupil. His name is Gerald Nelson and he comes to me for Cantonese lessons. He is English, a European, a *gweilo* like myself, about seventeen years old and a pupil at King George V School. It would be foolish to be discovered by him dishabille, as it were. That sort of thing can give one a reputation and Hong Kong is little more than a village where the earning of dubious celebrity is concerned.

I open the door.

'Good afternoon, sir,' the boy says.

He is fair-skinned with blond hair in a quiff hanging over his forehead with the rest combed back to what is called a duck's-arse at the rear. It is a fashion made popular by the film star Tony Curtis and adopted by many of the popular rock and roll singers. His eyes are intensely blue and, in spite of being fair, his skin is well tanned. Like my own.

'Good afternoon. Come in.'

I hold the door open and study him as he goes down the passageway. He is wearing his school winter uniform of a smart chocolate-brown blazer with a blue-and-gold badge of a rampant lion attached to the breast pocket, a white shirt and a blue-and-brown banded tie. Despite the heat, the boy seems not even to be warm: the crease in his trousers is still evident although he must have been wearing them all day. In his left hand is a small square wicker basket like a woven bamboo briefcase. He glances at his wrist-watch.

'I'm sorry I'm late, sir. The buses were held up in Waterloo Road. By an accident. A taxi had . . .'

'You could have got off there and walked,' I interrupt. 'It's not far.'

'Yes, sir. I'm sorry.'

The boy seems, to me, genuinely apologetic. I decide to let the matter rest. He is polite and appears considerate.

'Never mind,' I say curtly. 'Let's get on with your instruction. Enough time's been wasted.'

The boy looks quickly around the room then sits uninvited at the round table, putting his basket on the floor and, sliding aside the bent rattan clasps, opening the lid which creaks. From within he takes out a textbook and a black-and-red hardback notebook of the sort Chinese students use: from the breast pocket of his blazer he produces a Parker fountain pen.

'Page 15. Entering tones. Begin at the top.'

For a moment, the boy is silent as if gathering himself for some kind of performance. Then he commences.

'*Sik. Sìk. Sík. Tsuk. Tsùk. Tsúk.*'

'Stop!' I order. 'Stop! Think, boy, think. Not *Sík*. Not *Tsúk*. What is it . . .'

The boy is silent. I watch his face. It is as impassive as that of a Chinese lad yet I can tell that, underneath, there is a struggle going on.

'Well? Do you not remember, boy? *Sík?*' I wait a moment then, staring at the boy, say exasperatedly, '*Sîk*. And *Tsûk*.'

The boy avoids my stare.

I am impatient with him and cannot help it. I suppose I like the boy: at least, I do not dislike him. He means well, does his best but he sometimes lacks concentration, lacks the dedication such a study demands.

'Say them.'

'*Sîk. Tsûk.*'

'Again.'

'*Sîk. Tsûk.*'

'Good. Now note them down. Something written is never forgotten.'

Screwing the end off his pen, he opens his notebook. I sense he is glad to be given the opportunity to do something to show willing. He is not an unpleasant boy, unlike some pupils I have had: young bank or trading-house executives fresh out from public school in England with an imperious air about them; bored housewives who wanted to pass the time and communicate more accurately with their amahs and cook-boys; colonial civil servants struggling to master Cantonese before seeking promotion. Yet the boy is slow and forgets the basics too readily: in this failing he annoys me.

I cannot explain the reason for my vexation. Perhaps the boy's watch and fountain pen make me jealous, although I do not wish to own such prodigalities; perhaps it is his inability to remember his lessons, to apply himself and differentiate between a high-rising or low-rising tone, which anger me; perhaps it is an envy of his youth and future which I shall never see. There again, it might just be my character. Whatever the reason, I find the boy in turns infuriating and a frequent test for my patience.

The boy stops writing and lays his pen on the table, glancing briefly at me, avoiding my eye, seeking no contact.

'Done?'

'Yes, sir.'

'Very well. And remember – *sik* is the noun *colour* while *sîk* is the verb *to eat*. Tones in Cantonese – all Chinese dialects – are of vital importance. Don't forget this. Now continue, boy.'

'*Fat. Fàt. Fât. Kuk. Kùk. Kûk.*'

For an hour, I take the boy through tone exercises and simple sentences which use them. The sun leaves the room and the sky lightens as if making a final effort to cling on to the day before surrendering to evening. I do not switch on the light and the lesson ends just as it becomes too dim to see the text exercises.

'That will do,' I declare, turning my head pointedly in the direction of the travelling clock.

The boy, without speaking, pulls a leather wallet from his hip pocket and removes forty Hong Kong dollars in ten-dollar bills.

'Thank you, sir,' he says, giving me the money.

'Practise the tones before your next visit,' I reply, counting the bills with my fingers yet without looking at them.

'Yes, sir,' he replies.

From a single drawer in the table, I take out a pad of receipt forms and a plastic ballpoint which I bought in a stationery shop in Yunnan Lane. The pad is a cheap item made of flimsy paper with one page printed and the next blank. Between the two is inserted a square of blue waxed carbon paper. I inscribe my name at the head of the page then, printing carefully, I write *Rec'd HK$40 (four-oh) in full pymnt for lesson*, followed by today's date. Over this I scribble what passes for my signature, fold the sheet and hand it to the boy. He says nothing but puts it in his wallet, gathers up his books and pen and places them in his basket.

As we part, he looks quite closely at me, as if studying my face for the story of my life. He does not stare rudely and the inspection lasts only a moment but it is positive and, as long as it exists, is deep and inquiring. There are times when I swear there may be more to him than meets the eye and I get the sense he wants more of me yet dares not ask.

As I close the door on the boy, I sigh. I am tired. My afternoon doze has not refreshed me and I feel an uncomfortable restlessness stirring in me, welling deep down inside like a hatred long felt and suppressed.

Or it might be a new kind of as yet nameless fear.

At the other end of the flat tenement roof from the old lady's lean-to stands the small concrete building housing a storeroom and the lift mechanism. The former is empty, a source of surprise to me that the landlord has neither let it nor has an enterprising person moved in to establish a small factory there. A similar construction three doors down Woosung Street contains a fluorescent plastic ribbon maker and the building beyond has a man who renders fat installed on the roof. I am thankful I do not live below his workshop: one can smell his operation in the street.

The roof space on the far side of the lift mechanism housing, away from the door, is ideal for Mr Wu and myself, being secluded and not overlooked. It faces north-west and there are no taller buildings between our tenement and the Yau Ma Tei typhoon shelter. The seclusion is aided by the fact that it is most awkward to reach: one has to squeeze between the housing and a large, rusting, galvanised tin ventilator hood, then edge along a parapet retained by a low wall.

I do not have a head for heights and whenever I make my way along this little rampart I feel the space over the wall calling silently to me. Its words are never distinct but I know their drift, heeding them if I do not accept their invitation.

Over several years, Mr Wu and I have equipped the space as our own little pleasure garden, installing two parallel benches three feet wide and made of planed deal planks: they resemble the ancient Chinese *k'ang*, with boxed in sides and a tiny lip around the edge, yet no source of heating beneath them. Around the area we have placed plant pots in which we grow chrysanthemums, marigolds, salvias and fuschias which Mr Wu tends: at his own admission he has a green thumb, an expression he has learnt from reading gardening books. By contrast, he states I have a brown thumb. What he touches grows whilst what I touch withers. Or so he claims.

We meet here at least once or twice a month but not by prior arrangement. We are both old men and that would be to tempt fate. We either knock on the other's door, suggesting we go up to the roof there and then or we meet during the day and agree we shall come together at a mutually acceptable time that evening. Also, we might go up alone: Mr Wu frequents the place more often than I do for his need is greater.

Today, we met in the market where he was purchasing some socks. He usually wears drab Chinese clothes – a jacket with a high collar buttoned by embroidered knots and loops, traditional trousers and a white vest with the label sticking out of the neck marked *Fruit of The Loom*. Mr Wu enjoys American underwear if he can afford it. His footwear, around his flat, is the traditional felt slipper: only when he is walking the streets does he wear leather shoes. Socks, however, are his indulgence.

'Well, *san foo*, what do you think?' he asked me as I came upon him at a stall selling socks, ladies' stockings and assorted hosiery.

He was holding a pair of knee-length woollen socks in brilliant yellow embroidered on the side with small red, white and blue sailing yachts.

'They are ostentatious,' I replied. 'Not befitting a man of your age.'

I took the socks from him and turned them over in my hand. The wool was of a good quality mixed with cotton. They would certainly keep his feet warm.

'Imperial yellow,' Mr Wu commented. 'If there were still an emperor of China, he would wear these socks.'

'With yachts?' I exclaimed.

Mr Wu studied them.

'Yes,' he admitted cautiously, 'the boats may put him off. But,' he brightened, 'he could order a different decoration.'

'You, however,' I reminded him, 'are not the emperor of China. And you cannot buy these socks. How can a man of your age – of our age – command respect dressed in these? They are . . .'

I was, unusually, momentarily lost for words.

'. . . young!' Mr Wu snapped.

'Young,' I agreed.

'Well, there is a famous Chinese saying. An old peacock may draw the young hen if his feathers catch the sun.'

Mr Wu frequently does this. When he fears he is losing an argument he reverts to a maxim allegedly passed down through the ages from some wise old cove a thousand years before who had, by good chance, anticipated such a discursive problem.

'That is not an old Chinese saying,' I replied. 'That was invented by you this moment to support your argument. I know you too well, my friend. And you – a peacock! What hen do you hope to attract? There is another saying' – it was my turn to be inventive – 'which goes as follows: an old crow on a sturdy bough is better than a young crow on a twig. Which would you be at your age?'

He laughed then, taking the socks, rolled them up and placed them in their cellophane band. I believed I had won the argument but he took out his wallet and bought the loathsome things.

'What does it matter, *san foo*? I may have these bright feathers but I shall keep then hidden under my trousers.'

'I am not *san foo*,' I reminded him crossly.

I was annoyed he had got the better of me but he ignored my reprimand. He cannot or will not alter his ways if he thinks he can use them to score a point over me. Whenever he is like this I am glad we are not bridge partners.

As we left the market, he suggested, 'Tonight, *san foo*?'

I looked at the clear blue sky, the sun shirking behind a cloud. The air was warm, a light breeze blowing through the stalls, ruffling the hanging clothing and agitating the tarpaulin covers and awnings.

'Very well,' I answered. 'Eleven o'clock?'

'Eleven o'clock,' Mr Wu concurred and studied his watch.

And so, now, we are in our little garden, safe from prying eyes and noses. A few minutes ago, a huge moon moth flitted past on pale, lazy wings, heading towards the lights of the street. It lingered for a moment over our plants, searching out any wayward blossoms but, disappointed, it vanished over the parapet. It is the first of its kind I have seen this year, a signal summer is coming.

'Will you go away tonight?' I ask, breaking a silence of some minutes.

'I think I shall,' Mr Wu answers falteringly then, as if gathering determination, says, 'Yes, *san foo*, I shall go away tonight.'

'Do you know where?'

'I do. Far away.'

'Tell me of your journey,' I ask.

'Well,' he begins, 'I shall fly. Not in the aeroplane. On the back . . .' He pauses to consider his transport. '. . . of an owl. A white owl with black eyes. So black, they might be the onyx buttons on an old lady's coat. We shall not go high.'

'Where will you go?'

'To see my wife,' he says. 'To check she is well.'

'How was she the last time?' I enquire.

'Well. My offerings were welcome. The gods look kindly upon her. She has a new house. And a new servant. There are,' he adds as if to reassure me, 'no problems in heaven.'

'I am glad.' I say. 'And then?'

'My duty done for her, we shall visit the cloud country. You know the place?'

'I do not. Tell me.'

'There, everything is white. Not the same white, you understand. If that was the case, how could you see anything?'

He laughs very softly, like a young man in the first stages of seduction by someone he wants to love him.

'From there?'

'From there, I leave the owl and take a butterfly. The one we see in Hong Kong. Black with azure eyes upon its wings and emerald sparks set into its body. It will take me from the white place to the gardens. Here there is no white, just colours. Every colour. Colours with no earthly names. This, *san foo*,' he says quietly, 'is why I go to the cloud country first. To prepare for the colour.'

We fall silent. There is nothing we wish to convey to the other. We are lying side by side on our respective *k'angs*, which are close together so they are almost, but not quite, touching. Mr Wu is stretched out on his back staring at the sky whilst I am lying on my side looking at his profile. His face is outlined by the glow of the street lights. He is breathing shallowly but I am not worried. This is a way of preparing himself for his journey. I, on the other hand, take deeper, more spaced breaths.

Both of us have a Chinese pillow under our heads, a block of lacquered papier maché with an indented centre. Mine is decorated with bamboo sprigs upon which perches a bird of indeterminate species: Mr Wu's has a white crane flying over an imagistic cloud.

'Are you ready now, *san foo*?' Mr Wu asks, sitting up and slowly swinging his legs over the far side of his bench.

'Yes. I am ready,' I say, propping myself up on my elbow. 'Let us go.'

Lifting a wooden case the size of a shoe box from the floor, Mr Wu puts it next to me, lying down on his bench. From the box, the wood of which is scratched and stained, he removes a small porcelain oil lamp which he lights with a match and places between us. The flame is at first smoky but quickly clears, its glow lighting up our faces. He then produces a pair of bamboo stems and two minute china pipe bowls which he fits to the stems, handing one to me.

Mr Wu keeps his opium in an ivory box with a sliding lid. It was not intended for such a use being in fact a chop box. Over a hundred years old, the ivory is yellowed with exposure to sunlight and carved with the relief of two copulating figures. I watch as he slides the lid and, by the lamplight, I can see the opium. It is a dark rich brown and looks like a mixture of bees'-wax and honey. I marvel something so innocuous-looking can produce such wonders.

With a little silver spoon, Mr Wu scours a scoop of opium from the box, slides the ivory lid shut on his opium container and puts it to one side. Rolling the drug into a ball between his finger and thumb, he holds it in the spoon over the flame until it begins to melt: then he deftly divides it in two with his thumb nail, pressing half into my pipe and the remainder into his own. We both lie down on our sides, facing each other, taking turns to hold the bowl of our pipe inverted over the lamp flame.

The opium is of good quality, of Thai origin. Mr Wu is never foisted off with sub-standard dope. He does not purchase his supply from the heroin makers and the coolie suppliers but from a man of our acquaintance of whom we seldom speak.

The pipe lasts about twenty-five seconds: I suck in its promises with three long breaths. Mr Wu prepares another. As I suck again, a deep relaxing calm moves over me. My muscles do not so much slacken as grow light. If this is how the drug affects Mr Wu, I think, then the owl and the butterfly will carry no heavy burden this night. Staring at the plant pots, they are larger than before. If the moon moth was to appear now, I might hitch a lift on it. The downy hairs on its thorax would be a fine blanket in which to snuggle to keep warm as we gained altitude.

With the third pipe, the concerns of living and dying evaporate. I am a free man. All fear has suddenly abandoned me.

More relevant to the moment, I have no worries about being discovered smoking opium. A fleeting logical thought tells me we are safe, Mr Wu and I, for the perfume of the molten drug in my pipe is drifting away in the sky, lost amongst the myriad smells, scents and stinks of the city. It would be a different matter if we indulged our desires in our flats. The Pei woman with the secretarial agency would sniff us out and call the police: that is her way.

My pipe is empty and I put it down, the hot bowl hanging over the crack between our benches. Mr Wu has put his down too. His eyes are shut with his face devoid of expression. If he were not breathing I might think him dead.

I lie on my left side, my head on the hard pillow and tuck my right arm under my neck.

The crane on Mr Wu's pillow seems to be considering flight but, just as the thought occurs to me that it is about to follow the moon moth, it disappears and, in its place, I see an angel.

'These are some of the girls' quarters,' Father Callaghan explained.

We entered a spartan room with four bunks bearing only sleeping mats and quilts folded beside calico sheets. On each bunk was a square head-rest. I picked one up. It looked heavy but was as light as a loaf of bread. Painted on the end was an angel with a Chinese face and a faint white halo, not wearing the traditional smock of a heavenly being but the flowing robe of a wealthy Chinese woman.

'The girls decorate their own pillows,' Father Callaghan remarked. 'Just as they would if they were at home.'

Under one of the bunks was a wooden case which Father Callaghan pulled out. It was divided into four partitions each containing a few clothes. Beside the box were four pairs of wooden sandals with leather straps. On the wall hung a small crucifix and, pasted to the door pillar, a red paper prayer-strip three feet long with gold characters written upon it.

'Is this not pagan?' I asked, pointing to the paper strip.

'It's a prayer flag,' he agreed, 'but it doesn't worship the God of War or the Goddess of Mercy.' He paused and smiled to himself. 'Well, in a way, I suppose it does. But not Kwan Yin.' He rang his finger down the characters, translating as he went. '*May the Blessed Virgin Mary, Mother of Jesus Christ, guard me safely as I sleep.*'

'Why not hang a sampler there?' I enquired. 'This is an heretical . . .'

'My friend,' Father Callaghan broke in, 'you will see and hear many . . . How shall I put it? . . . unorthodox things in China. In this mission. Not all might be approved by Rome. But I say this to you – is it not better to meet the people halfway than to be a dogmatist? Surely Our Lord doesn't mind how His message gets across. I see nothing wrong with using the ways of the heathen to preach the ways of God. Did not Our Saviour do just this?'

'Yes,' I began, 'but . . .'

'There's not a but about it. It's the way we must be. Did not the Jesuit Ricci, three centuries ago, permit his converts to worship their ancestors and images – and even Confucius – on the condition there was a holy cross upon the altar beside the idols?'

I made no response. His words were anathema and confusing to me yet I knew, in my heart of hearts, he must be right. Father Callaghan had lived in China for decades and I had to bow to his knowledge and experience.

We walked down a long corridor, descending a flight of stone steps at the end. As we went, there grew ahead of us the clamour of voices. They were young, lively and, it occurred to me as we approached, innocent and happy. Near the bottom of the steps, we stopped before a double set of doors closed against us.

'This is something which may shock you,' Father Callaghan warned as he turned the polished brass handle. 'Not at first but . . . Well, you shall see.'

I wondered what I was about to be shown: a roomful of lepers perhaps, or malformed cripples with misshapen limbs and the faces of mongoloid idiots.

As the door began to open, a silence fell. The merry chattering voices died away, the only sound remaining being a mechanical clacking noise. Father Callaghan entered and I stepped after him. The clacking sound slowed and ceased.

The room was large with open windows down one wall through which I could see the hills across the river. Seated at one end, on a dais, was an old woman wearing a Chinese jacket and trousers but with a starched, white wimple upon her head. The sight of her took me aback: I had not expected to see a nun in Wuchow.

'Sister Margaret,' explained Father Callaghan, 'speaks not a jot of English but has a command of Latin would shame many a monsignor. She was converted in Amoy in 1858. I guess her to be in her mid-sixties, but I can't be sure and neither can she. All she claims with conviction is she was born in the Year of the Horse. That comes round every twelve years in the Chinese calendar, and 1858 was a Horse Year, so I reckon my assumption is correct. She would have been converted about the age of twenty-four or five.' He paused, lowering his voice as if she could understand him. 'It's often hard to tell with them.'

Sensing she was aware we were speaking of her, I smiled at her and she gave me a gap-toothed smirk in return.

'Of course,' Father Callaghan went on, 'by saying she was born in a Horse Year she might be referring to her conversion. Born to Christ from her heathen past. In which case, she could be any age from about sixty to seventy-five. I try not to give such a quandary much consideration. There are sufficient conundrums in the Orient without adding another ephemeral one.'

Seated at rows of tables before the old nun was a large class of children ranging from the age of six up to about fourteen. They were dressed in a uniform of white Chinese blouses, black trousers and black slippers or wooden clogs with leather thongs. All had their hair tied back into a cue.

'*Cho san*!' Father Callaghan said in a loud voice.

'*Goo' more-ning, Farfer Ka Lai Hon*,' the children replied in a perfect chorus.

Father Callaghan laughed and replied in English, 'Excellent! Excellent! Carry on, my children, carry on.'

He waved his hand in the air with an almost grandiloquent gesture.

'*Yes, Farfer Ka Lai Hon*,' they responded as one and returned to their work, every one of them bowing their heads.

The clacking of the machine recommenced from the rear of the room and I saw it emanated from a battered foot-treadle sewing machine operated by one of the elder pupils.

'What do you notice about them?' Father Callaghan asked me.

Not quite understanding the import of the question, I suggested, 'They are very obedient. And very diligent.'

'Nothing more?'

'Very neat, very polite, very . . .'

'Come, come! Look at them.'

I looked but all I saw were bent heads and busy hands.

'They're girls,' Father Callaghan pointed out. 'Every Jill and Jane of them. Not a boy in the lot.'

Casting my eye over them again, I realised they were indeed all girls. Although they wore their hair in cues, none had a partially shaved head as was customary amongst males and, here and there, I noticed one or two were developing breasts, their bosoms being pressed upwards as they leaned against their tables. In other respects, to my untrained eye, they could have been males. Their clothes seemed lacking in sexual variation.

'Do the poor Chinese not educate their sons?' I replied with some surprise: it was not what I had been led to believe in the seminary. There we had been instructed that Chinese boys were afforded the best education their parents could afford: indeed, they were given the best of everything possible.

'Sons they nurture and educate,' Father Callaghan confirmed, 'and molly-coddle and spoil and indulge and as near as worship. Girls,' he went on, 'they throw away if surplus to requirements.'

I stared at him. I was not sure if I had heard him correctly for the sewing machine, which had momentarily fallen still, had started up again and was joined by another.

'I beg your pardon. I don't . . .'

'It's simple,' Father Callaghan interjected. 'Boys carry on the family, the clan. They're the men of the future. Girls are good for nothing but household chores and the begetting of sons, to use a Biblical phrase. If you marry one off, you have to pay a match-maker's fee, a dowry and the Lord Himself knows what else. So daughters are unwanted.'

'And these?' I enquired.

'These are the lucky ones. They were all abandoned as babies . . .'

'Abandoned?'

'Dumped like rubbish,' Father Callaghan retorted curtly. 'In doorways, in the street, in the courtyards of temples. Wherever they see fit, I suppose.'

'And they are lucky!' I exclaimed.

Father Callaghan's voice dropped to a quieter, more sombre tone.

'Yes, Father Stephen, they're the lucky ones. Most, you see, are killed at birth. Infanticide is one of the biggest of Satan's arts rife in the Heavenly Kingdom.' He spoke with bitterness. 'And when I say killed, I don't mean quickly despatched as one might wring a chicken's neck or drown unwanted puppy-dogs. They're usually left out in the open, to die of exposure. Sometimes, their mothers love them and put them where they might be found and supported. For example, on doorstep.'

'And what happens to them then?'

'Sometimes they are taken in, raised then set to work as domestic servants. A few — the comely ones — may become concubines. At other times, they're ignored and instead of dying in the fields, they die in the streets.'

He moved towards the door and I followed him. I thought we might be leaving, but he stopped beside it.

'When I first came to China, I saw a dead infant girl in the street. That was far away, in Kukong, but it matters not: it might just as well have been here. The poor little mite had been dead some time, I should guess. A part of it had been consumed. By dogs, I suppose. There are a lot of dogs in Chinese towns . . .'

I glanced at his face. There were tears lingering in his eyes, even after so many years. Then he rubbed his lower eyelid with his index finger, his mood brightening.

'Some, however, are saved by rich men. Of that I am certain. I know of at least two in this town. Living as servants but safe, well-fed and, in their own way, treasured by their masters.'

'Or saved by a mission,' I suggested.

'Yes, to be sure! I sometimes think Our Lord sent us here not to convert the heathen hordes but to save the little children and suffer them to come unto Him. And,' his voice was suddenly hard and cruel, 'may God rot the blasted population.'

He briefly looked upwards at the ceiling by way of apology.

'What are they doing?' I asked, looking at the rows of studious girls.

'They're learning to sew. Some of them to embroider,' Father Callaghan explained. 'Sister Margaret's teaching them. When they've become proficient and are about fifteen years old, we pack them off down the river to Canton, Hong Kong, Macau and our brethren there find them employment as sew-sew amahs. Some drift away, of course. They become whores or *mu tsai*. That's a sort of servant-cum-concubine. But the majority, I'm delighted to say, get gainful work and support themselves.'

Father Callaghan clapped his hands in a smart slap. Immediately, the work stopped, the girls sat upright in their seats and the sewing machines ground to a halt.

'There!' he said. 'Look at them, Father. Did you ever see such faces of innocence?'

I surveyed the room. Some of the girls were very pretty, some plain and a few ugly. As my gaze fell upon each of them, they smiled and shyly lowered their eyes. A few giggled. Father Callaghan then started to speak to them in Cantonese, his fluency such he sounded exactly like a Chinese with the words rising and falling, stretched out or clipped short in an exotic, linguistic music. As he spoke, the girls looked at him, occasionally glancing for the fleetest of moments in my direction, smiling and giggling again.

'What did you say to them?' I asked as Father Callaghan fell silent.

'I told them you were here to help us and I informed them of your name,' he said. 'At least, your Chinese name. Mine, you will have noticed, is *Ka Lai Hon*.'

'What is mine?' I enquired.

'Yours is *See Faat Han*. Stephen. It must be changed a little as there is no *st* phonetic in Cantonese.'

'*See Faat Han*,' I repeated, testing the name on my tongue.

No sooner had I spoken than a fit of giggles once more rippled round the room. A few of the girls nudged each other: others hid their faces behind their hands. As I looked at them, they turned away, giggling all the more.

'Why do they laugh?' I asked.

'They mean no harm,' Father Callaghan said. 'They are simple peasant girls, every one of them.'

'Are they laughing at me?' I enquired. I felt uneasy, embarrassed and sensed my cheeks beginning to warm and redden.

'Not at you, Father Stephen. Not at you.'

And he, too, chuckled, which set off another spasm of girlish titterings.

I thought for a moment then asked, 'What does *Ka Lai Hon* mean?'

'Nothing. It has no meaning. It is just a phonetic rendition.'

'And *See Faat Han*?'

There were more giggles verging upon being laughter.

'Itchy anus,' Father Callaghan replied, his face straight but his eyes laughing. 'It's a colloquial expression, not as unpleasant as it sounds. Quite often, it's a term of endearment of a mother for her child.'

He put his hand on my shoulder and guided me out of the doors which he closed behind us. The giggling subsided and the noise of sewing began again.

'You'll soon learn their language,' Father Callaghan said, adding reassuringly, 'then you'll discover other names have not so pleasant meanings.'

We went down the stairs, out of the building and across a smaller courtyard at the rear of the mission. The sun was warm but not oppressive. We approached another building, an ancient structure with no windows and a wooden door on either side of which were pasted more prayer flags, the sunlight glinting on the gold lettering.

'And these?' I asked, touching one.

'The same. Why not ask Christ to protect the place instead of Kwan Tai? What difference does it make in the long run?' He stopped with his hand on the wooden bar holding the door closed. 'I suggest to you, Father Stephen, we should ourselves have been better Christians, better men and done a better job had we heeded such concepts when we sought to convert the indigenous peoples of the South Americas.'

He raised the bar, leaned it against the wall and pushed upon the thick timbers of the door. As it swung back, I saw a short passage with a closed door to either side. The scent of burning pine and old stone hung in the air but there was no sound to be heard.

'Over a thousand years old,' Father Callaghan said in little more than a whisper. 'Once, it was a wealthy merchant's home. Our mission stands in what was the gardens. The man disgraced himself and his family, committing suicide and losing the family its position. The house is therefore considered unlucky, which is why we have been able to take it over. No one gives a farthing for what bad luck we foreign devils have dropped upon us.'

At the end of the passage we walked into a courtyard thirty feet square into which the sun was not shining, Father Callaghan pointing upwards. The yard was half-roofed with pantiles resting on bare, ancient trusses and spars. In the centre the sky could be seen but it was partially obscured by a drift of wood-smoke. As my eyes grew accustomed to the shade, I noticed many of the beams were intricately carved and blackened by decades of soot. A door opened and a young Chinese woman stepped into the yard, bowing to us.

'This is Ah Mee,' Father Callaghan said. 'She's one of our waifs but she came to us at about fifteen which makes her now twenty-six. She was not deserted but orphaned. Her parents – like so many others – were killed by brigands. She's our baby-amah. Follow me.'

I went after him as he stepped through the doorway, Ah Mee taking up the rear. Before us, against the wall, was a row of wooden cribs, in six or seven of which slept babies wrapped in swaddling sheets.

'Our nursery,' Father Callaghan explained quietly, a hint of pride in his voice, much the same as one might hear from a father pleased with his children's successes. When I looked at him, I could see his face softly smiling, reminding me of the half-smile upon the face of the Christ in a portrait by Alma Tadema, suffused with an inner joy he knew no one else could despoil or steal.

'Girls?' I asked.

'Girls,' he confirmed.

'How do you feed them?'

'You mean, how do *we* feed them?' Father Callaghan corrected me. 'They are your babies now, too.' He reached into one of the cots, gently stroking the sleeping infant's cheek. 'The Chinese don't drink milk. There are no cows in China. But they keep buffalo for ploughing and as beasts of burden. We buy their milk. Mostly though, we employ wet nurses, peasant women from outside the town who're glad to do it for a few grains of rice and a bit of dried fish. They feed our babies and we feed them. It's a fair business deal to me. And may God forgive me for saying this, but our girls are lucky there's still such infant mortality in China. Now,' he moved towards the door, pointing the way out, 'come and look at this.'

He led me into the courtyard and across to a high door barred with three thick beams. The timbers were studded with iron bolts and showed signs of charring.

'This leads to the *hutong* at the rear of the mission. By the way, that means alley. We never open it. The Tai Ping Rebellion,' he remarked, 'did the damage you see. The merchant's godown was set afire in the uprising and this was its main door. I had it placed here when we built the mission. You would not believe it but it weighs over a ton and took seventeen coolies with . . .' He abruptly stopped talking, putting his finger to his lips. 'Listen,' he whispered, 'to China's sorrow.'

I stood quite still. At first, no sound came to me except the trilling of a bird on the roof and the barking of a dog some way off. Then, gradually, I heard a soft sobbing coming from the other side of the door. Father Callaghan crossed himself and I did likewise, although I did not know why. For over a minute, we remained in silence while the sobbing continued.

'Should we not do something?' I urged finally in a whisper. 'There is someone in trouble . . .'

'There's nothing we can do, Father Stephen,' he replied quietly. 'The matter's in God's hands.'

At last, we heard footsteps in the *hutong* and the sobbing began to fade away.

'What was that?' I asked.

'A poor woman,' Father Callaghan responded, his voice filled with sadness. He pointed to a wooden box beside the door. 'What do you suppose this is for?'

I studied it. It was an oblong wooden box mounted into the wall, a simple handle on one end whilst the other was hidden in an opening in the stonework.

'You'll not guess,' Father Callaghan declared. 'Watch.'

He held a carved peg away from the side and pushed. The box slid through the wall on waxed wooden runners. Sunlight shone into it as it cleared the outside. After waiting a moment, he pulled it back in again, the peg falling in place to lock it shut and, at the same time, a length of string attached to it rang a small bell hanging on a coil spring. It was like the servant's bell one found in well-to-do houses in Europe.

'This contraption,' he said, 'was brought here by Sister Margaret from her convent in Amoy. They're common in nunneries in the north but I've seen few so far south.'

'What is it?' I asked.

'This,' said Father Callaghan, 'is a baby girl deposit box. It's here we collect our girls, posted to us like letters. And what we have just listened to was an incompleted delivery, one that will not come unto Christ.'

'What will happen to it?'

'That one, I fear,' Father Callaghan answered ruefully, 'will go the way of the puppy-dogs.'

I left my flat at ten and descended alone in the lift to the first floor where one of Mr Pao's minions entered it, carrying a cash register. He nodded to me and we continued down to the ground together where I held the lift door open for him and he thanked me politely. On the pavement, he loaded the register onto a hand cart, setting off down the street with it, the cart wheels squeaking, taxi drivers blaring their horns at him. Despite the modernity of Hong Kong, the streets still bustle with coolies carrying goods suspended from poles, rickshaws, hand carts, and even old-fashioned wheelbarrows with solid wooden wheels. The sight of a National Cash Register riding on a bamboo raft mounted on small iron wheels and being pulled along by a rope is but one of the paradoxes of the place.

After watching him disappear, I made my way to Pak Hoi Street, where there are half a dozen poultry stalls and shops, intending to buy a pullet and two eggs. One of the glories of Chinese shopping is one may buy just what one needs. There is no demand, as in European shops, for customers to purchase more than they require. Items are not sold in packs but singly. There is no waste and no shortage.

As I neared the street, I met increasing numbers of people carrying their purchases — clucking hens with their wings and feet trussed, complaining ducks and wicker baskets filled with a scrabbling clamour of feet and feathers. Fowls are sold live: an animal which still breathes, eats and defaecates is not going to deteriorate before it reaches the pot. For all their inventiveness, their discovery of comets, mathematics, gunpowder and magic, the Chinese never devised refrigeration.

I patronise one stall in particular. The man who runs it, whose name I do not know, has lost his left eye. He has not obtained a glass replacement nor does he wear a patch to cover the hollow orbit. Instead, he merely has a cavity in his face into which the eyelid has fallen and atrophied, giving him a grotesque appearance. He enhances this bizarre visage by occasionally fitting into this space a new fifty-cent coin. He then tilts his head to catch the bright light from the electric bulbs which illuminate his stall. Men laugh at this exhibition, women recoil from it, their children gawping in stunned amazement or hiding behind their mothers. Yet his customers return again and again. His showmanship is part and parcel of his trade, his inevitably Oriental way of turning a disability into an advantage. They may be revolted by his act but his clientele remembers him, which is the secret of successful business. If he had the money, no doubt he would install a flashing neon sign above his stall: but, being unable or unwilling to go to such extravagance, he has a flashing eye instead.

When I arrived at his stall, he was busy piling crates of hens on top of one another, catching them adroitly as they were tossed from a parked lorry at the kerb. A number of other would-be customers waited nearby for the delivery to be completed, and I joined them, surveying his stock.

One-eye does not sell only chickens. If it has feathers, a beak and a culinary use, then he sells it: which is to say he deals in every type of bird that does not have a fine song. Those are available from the song-bird sellers in Shek Lung Street. This morning, One-eye's cages and crates contained a wide assortment of fowl for the weekend is drawing near and he sells not only to housewives but also to restaurants.

By my shoulder were crates of common brown hens but next to these was a box of white silkies, chickens with long, hair-like feathers about their feet and delicate crests on their skulls lending them a supercilious expression: they reminded me of twenties flapper-girls bedecked in ostrich plumes. To the left of the silkies were two crates of ducks. These were not ordinary ducks but brilliantly plumaged teal shipped down from the far north of China. A common brown hen was priced at four dollars: one of these ducks would cost between thirty and fifty-five, according to the label hanging from the bars, depending on the sex and colour of the plumage. Another box contained several Lady Amherst's Pheasants.

This bird has my deepest admiration. Its plumage is brilliant with a red crown, silver and black cope on its neck, sea-green body, white breast, black wings and, at the base of the tail, a scarlet and yellow rainbow as if there was a fire encapsulated there from which the long white-and-black barred tail might be a petrified plume of smoke tugged out by a strong wind. Yet it is not the bird's appearance which captures my admiration but its courage. The other fowl cower, resigned to the chopper. This creature refuses to be cowed. It stands all the while, thrusting its head out of the bars, calling raucous defiance at One-eye.

At least, such is one interpretation of it – the romantic in me speaking. The other might be that the bird is a fool and cannot guess from the blood and entrails in the gutter what its fate will be. Or perhaps it has entered into an unholy alliance with One-eye, taking a side part in his fifty-cent coin advertising gimmick.

The birds in the top cages are comparatively well off but, as one descends the pile, the worse the conditions get. Birdshit filters down through the barred floors, the cut-down tins serving as water containers grimed with dried guano and discarded belly feathers. Those at pavement level are a sorry lot and priced the cheapest.

I am inured to this state of affairs. Living in China for six decades has shown me far worse.

One-eye has to pay rent for his stall. It is erected on the public pavement and he has a hawker's licence but he also has to pay other dues, not a levy imposed by the government but by the 14K, the local triad gangsters who make their living operating cheap whores in Temple Street, selling drugs, conducting numbers games or mah-jong schools and running protection rackets. They own the streets around my tenement, no shop-keeper free of their graft. All profit margins take into account, hidden in the balance sheet, tea money, which is the colloquialism for pay-offs. This is the way of China, has been so and will remain so forever, regardless of who sits on the Heavenly Throne or which party flag flies over the police station.

It was obvious to me this morning One-eye has not kept up his tea money for, as I waited to purchase my pullet – in the third level down: not too expensive yet not too besmirched with shit as to be the cheapest – a *fei jai* approached him. Like spivs the world over, be they pimps or politicians, he walked with a swagger, his wristwatch the latest Rado on a steel bracelet, his shirt crisp and clean. He wore well-creased tailored trousers and his hair was trimmed, greased back then flipped up at the front.

There were only two customers left to be served at the stall, myself and a woman with a sleeping infant strapped to her back in a brightly coloured sling. She was half-way through her transaction and the spiv, waiting for this to end, began to study the cages in the polite, obliquely menacing way powerful men have of letting others know they are subordinate. He stroked a pheasant's head, felt the breast of a duck and, as One-eye watched him, purposefully knocked a water tin over, spilling the rank contents on a hen in the box underneath. The woman dealt with, One-eye glanced at me then turned to the rent collector.

'You've forgotten,' said the spiv, his voice quiet with menace: he spoke in Cantonese on the assumption I would not understand their intercourse.

'I have not forgotten, sir,' One-eye replied obsequiously. 'The money is coming. Business is not so good. Prices of chickens at Tuen Mun . . .'

'Four hundred dollars,' the spiv demanded. 'Pay me now.'

'I do not have four hundred.' One-eye fumbled in his jacket. 'I've got two hundred.'

'No good. Four hundred.'

The spiv was calm and I knew violence was imminent. I have seen this ploy so often.

'Tonight,' One-eye said. 'I borrow some.'

'Who you going to borrow from?' the spiv enquired.

'*Way Foong*,' came the prompt reply.

One-eye was quick with his answer. He named the bank because he knew, had he not, he would have been forced to borrow what he owed from the spiv: loan sharking is another of the triads' multifarious businesses.

'Okay,' the spiv said in English then, after considering his reply, continued in Cantonese, 'Six o'clock. Four fifty.'

One-eye nodded and the spiv turned to go. As he passed the end of the cages, he reached into one of them taking out a speckled Chinese partridge hardly bigger than a thrush. With a deft clenching of his fingers, he squeezed it to death. It chirped once then, despite the passing traffic, I heard its miniature bones shatter. Dropping the mangled carcass on the pavement and without looking back he departed. One-eye's face was blanched.

Human cruelty is far worse than that of the world of nature, which is to say the world of God if you believe in such a thing. It is gratuitous, premeditated and obscene. The cruelty which gods exact is more perfected, refined: that of man is crude, lacking the beauty of divine cunning.

For many years, I was taught man was fashioned in the image of God. Believe that and you will understand the situation as I see it.

The street in Kowloon Tong is a cul de sac ending in a low hill, the side perpendicular where rain and sun have in turn loosened and eroded it. On the top is a stand of pine trees behind which drift high clouds. All the houses are tucked behind concrete walls, the tops of which are lined with broken glass, rolls of barbed wire or spikes. They are low, two-storey buildings with deep verandas and broad-leafed sub-tropical trees shading the stonework. Every property has wrought iron gates, one bearing a steel shield painted gold and emblazoned with a rampant Chinese lion, its paw on a pearl. The tarmac is covered in fine gravel washed from the hill, which sparkles like semi-precious stones in the sunlight. From where I am standing under the shade of a bauhinia tree, I consider that if they were diamonds and not quartz, I would be a rich man with a huge responsibility. I am glad, therefore, they are worthless: such a weighty responsibility is not something I wish to bear. Life is better simplified into the day-to-day gratification of basic needs and petty desires.

A dark anonymous bird glides down from the pines to settle in the bauhinia. It does not sing but flits silently from bough to bough uttering a soft, almost inaudible weep. It knocks one of the blossoms, lilac-and-white petals fluttering down to the pavement.

I am not alone in the street. Where it joins another, wider road, is a gathering of twenty amahs wearing their customary uniforms of white smock tops and black, loose trousers. They chatter and laugh in high-pitched voices, their gestures stilted and unnatural as if their lives are a sham. Not one of them is over thirty-five and they look quite sexless: they might be eunuchs rather than spinsters.

Next to them is parked a tricycle on the saddle of which balances a man wearing a blazer besmirched by dust and worn through to the point of stripping into tatters. His machine consists of a single rear wheel with two forward, larger ones upon which is mounted a tall aluminium box. This had once been painted with a background of white with blue Chinese characters and the outline of a snow-capped mountain peak stencilled over it but it is now scratched, the peak having lost its summit. The corners are dented and the lid does not fit for a wisp of white mist is eking out of it. He has his feet up on the handle bars with his back resting on the wall behind him and is studying the back pages of a Chinese daily newspaper. I try to read the headlines, printed in red characters, but he is too far away.

From the other side of the concrete wall across the street, an electric bell sounds: it is not so much a ringing as a metallic tattoo of hammer on cracked steel.

Before it stops, the amahs fall silent, suddenly demure and the tricycle rider is seated upright in his saddle, the newspaper folded and tucked into the springs. The bird in the bauhinia squawks and zips away, jinxing in flight over a tangle of barbed wire.

The gates in the opposite wall open and Chinese children aged six or seven begin to issue from it. A few run or skip with the sudden freedom of their release, but most seem unperturbed by the fact school is over for the day. Each carries a satchel or a bundle of books held together by a canvas strap and they all wear a uniform of white shirts and blue trousers or skirts. The boys have short, tidy haircuts, the girls wearing little pony-tails or bobs tied with coloured twine. From the colour of their uniforms they might be somehow related to the company owning the tricycle.

A number of the children set off on their own or in pairs along the street, holding hands with a touching innocence, disappearing as they reach the next road. Others go to the group of amahs from which each steps in turn, says something and takes a child's books or satchel. Then they, too, walk out of sight. Others cross to the tricycle. The rider opens the lid, pushing aside blocks of fuming dry ice and selling them small cylindrical popsicles on sticks, stripping the paper wrappers off before handing them over and dropping the ten cent coins into a pouch tied to the cross-bar of his machine.

I watch and wait in the shade of the bauhinia. There are only four amahs left. Suddenly, a little girl appears at the gate on her own. Pausing for a moment, she surveys the street as if expecting to see someone waiting for her, visibly shrugs her shoulders and sets off in the direction of her schoolmates.

As soon as she has turned the corner, I follow, leaving the shade, my feet crunching on the gravel. As I pass the gate, I give a quick glance at a brass plate screwed onto the pillar. It reads *China Coast Catholic Mission Society – Kindergarten.* Above the lettering is etched a cross and a Sacred Heart.

Out of the protection of the tree the late sun's rays, low over the roof-tops, blind me and I shield my eyes with my hand.

The child passes through a number of streets of well-to-do residences until she reaches a very wide main road down the centre of which runs an open nullah. The breeze wafts the acidulous stink of sewage issuing from the putrid stream flowing in it.

Crossing the nullah by a stone bridge, the child heads north, towards the foothills of Kowloon. In the haze of late afternoon, the ragged outline of Lion Rock juts defiantly at the coming sunset.

After a quarter of an hour, the child reaches the end of the road by a bus stop at which is parked an empty bus. Here, she starts up a pathway towards the hills. I stop at the foot of the path and watch as the child climbs higher between scrubby bushes, disappearing at last into a gully. From higher up in the hills comes a drift of wood-smoke but it is too far away for me to pick up even a slight trace of its perfume.

For some moments I wait, my eyes set on the point where the child has vanished, then I retrace my steps to the bus stop and, checking it is a number 7 service, board the vehicle and sit heavily on the wooden slats of the seat by the door. As if he had been waiting for me, the driver starts up the engine and the conductor pulls the sliding bars of the gate closed across the entrance, tugging on a cord running along the ceiling. A bell chimes twice and the bus sets off.

As it drives along by the nullah, the bus passes the popsicle vendor pedalling slowly along, his back bent with effort and sweat streaming down his neck to soak into his vest and blazer collar.

'One day,' I say to myself, 'I'll buy her a popsy.'

Yet I know that is not possible. I shall never be able to approach the child for to do so would be to give too much away of myself.

The mission was not situated upon one of the town's main streets but in a *hutong* lined with buildings, many of which were as ancient as the mission nursery. Some were built of grey stone and others of dull red brick, but none was more than two floors tall. No windows faced the street except for a narrow grill or shuttered hole through which no passer-by could peer, its function being not so much to let light in as smoke out and to act as a spy-hole to study who might be at the door.

The *hutong* was dirty, with leaves, spilled rice and chewed sugar-cane stalks lying on the flat cobblestones. Down the centre ran an open sluice which, judging from its contents, served as the only provision for sanitation to the houses.

'It smells a bit,' Father Callaghan declared as he stepped over the drain. 'Especially now, in the hot months. In winter, it's nothing like so bad. These little nullahs are also a good reason for wearing native costume. One is forever picking up the hem of one's cassock otherwise. Nothing worse than discovering a damp hem on returning home.'

Had there been a window or casement of glass in any of the properties, I should have liked to have seen my reflection. At Father Callaghan's recommendation, I had given up my clerical dress and had attired myself in the costume of a Chinese gentleman, consisting of a jacket called a *sam* and baggy, loose trousers referred to as *fu*. These were not fitted with a tight buttoned waistband or belt, as were clothes of European cut, but by a wide strip of white material which Father Callaghan told me was called the *fu tau*, or head of the trousers.

'Sometimes,' he had said as he showed me how to fold this

strip, tucking the loose ends in and tightening the material about my midriff, 'it is called the *baak tau do lo*. This means the white head and old sage. It implies the wearer wishes to live a long time.'

'Why do we dress in native fashion, Father?' I had enquired. 'Surely it is best to wear our cassocks. They will then know us as priests.'

'Don't you worry,' he had laughed, 'they know who we are and what we are. Whether we wear the black or the white habit of our calling, the smart suit of the merchant or the outfit of the shopkeeper, they know us. I wear Chinese clothes because they make me comfortable in the heat. Those long cassocks were made for a penance, I'm sure of it. Besides, if we wear their dress, they'll feel we are closer to them. And that's what we must be, if we're to do the Lord's work. Be closer to them. Be a man amongst their men, not a foreign devil in his weird get-up stalking the streets like a predator. They think we hunt for their souls as it is.'

The two garments were made of black gummed silk which was shiny and a little stiff to the touch and yet not abrasive against the skin. Upon our heads we sported black skull caps with matching buttons in the centre and, upon our feet, we wore white socks and black cotton shoes, through the thin soles of which I felt every bump and stone on the ground.

Just down the *hutong* from the mission entrance was a wooden building with carved beams and a balustraded balcony. I paused in front of the house to admire the carved flowers, leaves and, as I now realised, inevitable dragons. From the balcony hung prayer flags which moved gently in the warm breeze and by the door was a shrine, in front of which guttered a red wax candle on the end of a splint, looking somewhat like a bizarre fruit. The door into the building was made of wide planks studded with iron bolts, reminding me of the church doors one finds in rural Italy. There was no handle to turn but a wooden latch which was well-polished by what I assumed to be centuries of pressing fingers. The timber of the building was, like the roof of the nursery yard, blackened by age and smoke. Although the house looked rickety, I could tell it was solid and somewhat forbidding.

Father Callaghan, who had walked on unaware I had halted, came hurrying back and took me by the arm.

'Don't pause,' he advised. 'Look, by all means, but show no interest unless you are so invited to do. Some regard us as harmless dolts, some think of us with charity but there are many who believe we cast an evil eye.'

We walked on in silence. Although the sun was now hot upon our heads, I felt surprising cool in the Chinese clothing and the slipper-like shoes were not only comfortable but also gave me a good grip upon the steps descending at the far end of the *hutong* towards a main street. The stones were worn smooth, angled dangerously in places and I was glad for the confidence the footwear afforded me. My own leather-soled shoes would have sent me tumbling for there was no handrail.

So far, we had not seen a single living creature but, as we neared the street, the sounds of commerce and life grew louder. Ahead, I could see people passing and re-passing the *hutong* entrance, going by like figures in a magic lantern show.

'Now remember,' Father Callaghan said as we reached the street, 'don't stare. Look about you but don't linger on any one sight. Look back again a minute later but – well, don't stare. That's the cardinal rule.'

The street was very wide and paved with bricks and flags. The buildings were two or three storeys high with colonnaded arcades on the ground floor under which the pavement ran although most people were walking in the street. Upon the pillars of the arcades, six feet from the ground, were mounted stout iron rings.

'They tie their mule's heads up high,' I remarked.

Father Callaghan laughed and said, 'Those are not for mules. Nor even horses. You'll not find many mounts in southern China. They're for boats.'

'Boats?' I queried.

The street was at least several hundred yards from the river which I could see in the distance down a gentle incline.

'Boats,' Father Callaghan said again. 'Sampans mostly but I've seen bigger craft moored to them.'

'Why do they drag their boats all this way up from the river? Are there no mudbanks upon which to beach them?'

'They don't drag their craft up here. The river does it for them. You see, Father Stephen, in the summer months, the river floods something terrible. It can rise ten feet an hour and it's not unknown for it to flood three quarters of the town. You've come at a peculiar time for in a normal year the river is fifty feet higher than you see it now. The drought this year is exceptional. You might have arrived in a boat to the very end of the *hutong*. I've known the waters to come up so far.'

As we continued on our way I tried to imagine what the town must look like inundated by the Si Kiang and pondered on whether or not the people believed that, when the river rose so far, the dragons entered their houses and shops.

The pedestrians mingled, crossed and re-crossed the street, weaving in and out of each other with the alacrity of fish whilst, within the shadows of the arcades, were stalls selling vegetables, kindling, charcoal and small clay pots, everything contained in rattan or wicker baskets of various sizes. The vendors squatted by their merchandise, calling out to attract custom or haggling vociferously with would-be clients.

Within a few minutes, I had seen two old crones with crooked spines arguing with an equally aged man over the price of living, grey-green fish flapping in a wet basket, young men in smart and intricately embroidered silk jackets walking together in animated conversation, coolies loping by with their poles bending under the weight of loads of sugar cane, stringy-looking cabbages and squealing piglets trussed up in rattan cylinders. Children ran by with hoops of bamboo. In the centre of a street, a solemn little boy stood holding a triangular paper kite made of brown rice-paper stretched over a bamboo frame. By a cobbler's stall, the air punctuated with the tap-tap of his hammer upon a wooden clog, I bumped into two young women strolling purposefully along. Each had a baby strapped to her back by a brightly dyed square of cotton secured in the front by straps, pushing the women's breasts apart. I smiled my apology, prompting giggles from them as they raised their hands to their mouths and averted their eyes.

'So, what do you think?' Father Callaghan enquired as we reached a part of the street not lined with the stalls of peasant farmers and therefore not quite so crowded.

'I don't know,' I answered. 'It's all so . . .' I searched without success for an appropriate word, '. . . unusual.'

'Yes, it is,' Father Callaghan agreed. 'I've lived here – in China, that is – for nearly twenty years and I never cease to be astounded. Not one day passes when I don't see or hear something new.'

He turned into the shade of the arcade and I followed him. It was much cooler out of the sun.

'Where are we going?' I asked.

'You shall see. We shall take just a short perambulation so you might get to know the town. This is the Street of The Cranes and our alleyway goes between this and *Bei Shan*, the North Mountain – that's the hill behind the town. *Shan* is Cantonese for mountain. The next street we come to is the Street of Heavenly Happiness. You'll soon get to know them by their Chinese names and recognise the characters for them. You'll pick it up. I shall give you a few lessons. It's not as hard as it seems.'

'As it sounds,' I said.

'True, Father. The sounds are often more important than the words.'

We arrived at the junction between two streets and turned left, keeping to the arcade. The Street of Heavenly Happiness was wider than that which we had just quit yet not as busy.

As we passed, I glanced in the shop doorways observing what I could without slackening my pace: a rice shop with polished wooden barrels and hessian sacks, stone tubs and a cat asleep upon a bale of straw; a tea shop with its casks of different teas ranging in colour from light green to matt black; a herb shop, its ceiling hung with a dense array of roots and dried leaves. Some of the premises were workshops where craftsmen beat out copper cooking vessels, turned clay on foot-propelled wheels or cut planks with two-handed saws.

Not only the sights impressed themselves upon me: so too did the smells. The rice shop smelt merely of dryness and the incense burning in a shrine on the wall at the rear, but the tea shop was scented with a tart fragrance, the herb shop emitting such a confusing cascade of sweet perfumes and acrid odours they made me sneeze. Even the potter's shop had aroma all its own, of wet earth and linseed oil.

A few of the shop-keepers acknowleged my quick glances into their businesses. The herbalist, a crouched man wearing steel-rimmed spectacles with several strands of thin hair issuing from a mole on his lower jaw, looked up from a set of hand scales to leer at me. I smiled back and looked at the brass pan hung by small chains from the scale bar. The concoction in it consisted of dried bark, gnarled roots and flakes of what looked like crushed leaves.

'Snakeskin,' Father Callaghan said, as he saw my attention taken by the scales. 'Snakes have a powerful medicinal value to the Chinese.'

A little further on, the proprietor of an egg stall tucked into a doorway beckoned to me to make a purchase. I stopped for a moment to study his stock. The eggs were of three varieties: the first were ordinary eggs, their shells pallid and clean, the second were coated in what appeared to be chopped wheat straw bound with dried clay and the third were black with a soot-like covering. Several of the latter had been scraped with a blade so they appeared striped.

'This is Kung,' Father Callaghan said, adding a quick burst of Cantonese to the egg-seller. 'He's one of ours.'

Kung bowed and spoke to me for at least thirty seconds without taking a breath.

'What does he say?' I asked when the tirade was over. I was afraid I might have somehow offended the man.

'He says, broadly translating,' Father Callaghan replied, 'he welcomes you to his stall and the town of Wuchow. He wishes the Lord go with you in your business. He also asks you to buy his provender.'

'Are his eggs good?'

'Generally. He supplies the mission.'

'Then perhaps we could buy some?' I suggested.

'Ah Fong does all our buying,' Father Callaghan said. 'He's our compradore, our go-between with merchants and the like. I cannot go over his head. He'd lose face. But . . .'

He spoke briefly to the stallholder who picked up one of the black eggs and commenced scraping the covering off, which fell to his feet in lumps. Had I known Father Callaghan better, I might have been alerted by the quick, mischievous glint in his eye. When the egg was more or less clean, the vendor rapped it against the wall by his head and started to peel the shell away.

At the end of the street, two dogs were snapping and snarling at each other, arguing over a scrap of entrails thrown into the thoroughfare from a butcher's shop. No one attempted to separate them.

'Quite a delicacy, this,' Father Callaghan remarked, looking down the street as if distracted by the dog fight. 'It's called a one-hundred-year-old egg.'

Kung dipped the egg in a small bowl of yellow sauce and held it out to me: I was not sure whether I should accept and eat it or admire its longevity. My uncertainty was allayed when the Chinese pushed his arm further outwards in a motion of offering and Father Callaghan felt in the pocket of his jacket for a coin which he placed on the stall.

'A hundred years old?' I mused.

'That's what they say,' Father Callaghan said, adding by way of assurance, 'but of course that's just a metaphor. It's no more than a few weeks old. I'd bet my belt on it. I'm sure it's the fashion of the preparation gives them their name and distinct colouration.'

I looked at the proffered egg. It was a dark translucent green, reminding me not so much of an egg as the bulbous indentation at the base of a wine bottle.

'You see,' Father Callaghan continued, 'to the Chinese, everything is either a hundred years old or a thousand years old. As a nation, they are somewhat given to hyperbole.'

I glanced at the egg. The colour made me feel slightly nauseous.

'The yellow sauce,' Father Callaghan concluded, 'is a variety of mustard but not as hot as our Colman's.'

I took the egg. It was firm yet pliable as if it had been hard-boiled. I held it up to my face and sniffed surreptitiously at it.

Anticipating my next concern, Father Callaghan said, 'It is cooked. Kung has prepared it in the manner of hay-box cookery. It is not so much hard-boiled as hard-baked. One eats it in one mouthful,' he added, his face still averted in the direction of the dogs which had now ceased growling and taken to a tug-o'-war with the offal.

Considering it best to get this experience over with as quickly as possible, I placed the whole egg into my mouth, closed my lips and bit into it: it was as if every swamp east of Suez had been emptied into my throat. My nostrils burned with the stink of rotten egg and my tongue smarted from the sauce. The white of the egg, if it could be called such, slithered unpleasantly down my gullet whilst the yolk was dry and clung like ashes to the sides of my oesophagus.

'They are rather fine, aren't they?' Father Callaghan commented.

As quickly as I could I swallowed the egg and did my best to smile at Kung who grinned at the evident pleasure his egg had given.

'Well done!' Father Callaghan exclaimed as we walked on. 'A rare delicacy. However, I allow they are an acquired flavour.'

'Yes,' I replied, the taste still lingering strongly in my mouth and the smell at the back of my nose, 'they are.'

We arrived in the central square of the town. It was a broad area around the edge of which were market stalls. In the centre was a stone dais upon the plinth of which were pasted a number of public notices, written in black ink upon white or yellow paper.

'Edicts,' Father Callaghan explained, cursorily reading one. 'This one emanates from the Peacock Throne. It says foreigners may not trade in jade discs. Not something to affect mendicant friars like us, eh Father Stephen?'

'Is the platform where the town crier stands?' I asked as we moved across the square.

'No. They don't have town criers,' Father Callaghan replied. 'That's primarily used for public executions.'

We were still halfway across the main square when I felt the waistband of my trousers suddenly loosen. I stood stock still and spread my legs apart.

'What is the matter?' Father Callaghan asked. 'Are you not feeling well? The egg, perhaps?'

'It's not that,' I said, my voice somewhat hushed. 'I think my trousers are falling down.'

I looked around in despair for cover. There was none. The nearest side of the square was at least a hundred feet away.

Father Callaghan put his hands on his hips, threw back his head and roared with laughter. A number of passing coolies turned abruptly and stared at him.

'It's not in the least bit amusing,' I retorted peevishly.

My words made no impact. Father Callaghan continued to laugh, if a little less raucously, the tears streaming down his cheeks. He wiped them away with the broad sleeve of his jacket, the wet patches marking the silk. At last, his mirth subsiding, he beckoned to me to follow him. My hands in the pockets of my *sam*, gripping at the folded material at the sides of my trousers, I limped after him towards a tea-house behind a row of trees.

Once inside, Father Callaghan led me into a cubicle and, while the waiter fetched us tea, he unbuttoned my jacket and refolded my trousers, showing me again how to shape the *fu tau* so it would not work loose.

When the tea arrived, I took a long drink of it, disregarding the fact it was piping hot. It burned my lips and scorched my tongue.

'You're suppose to sip it,' Father Callaghan said. 'That's the etiquette.'

'I'll obey it next time,' I promised, taking another pull and risking swilling it round my mouth.

'The egg?' Father Callaghan suggested.

I nodded.

'You'll learn, Father Stephen,' he declared, sipping at his own cup. 'In time. The east is not as inscrutable as they make out back home, you know. And I'm sure you'll enter into the spirit of China.'

'I will?' I wondered, sucking my lips and tugging nervously on the trousers to see if I could unravel the folds.

'Oh, for certain,' Father Callaghan said with utter conviction. 'You will. You will, Father, for sure.'

I am a man of habit.

I do not live by a timetable but there is a certain round I follow, if not regularly then at least frequently. I am not adventurous, preferring that which I know and like to that which is new. It is better at my age to stay within the boundaries of the familiar than to investigate some other landscape. The times are passed for such indulgences: I did all that as a young and foolish man.

A man is not what he is because of what he does, but where he goes, whom he meets. Any police officer will tell you a criminal is judged not only by his crimes but also by his friends and the places in which he may be found. If I am to be assessed in such a fashion, I may be seen to be an ordinary man with quotidian desires and common vices. And this would be right, for I am an ordinary man, was always thus although, when younger and naive, I considered myself extraordinary, an arrogance within me born from blind ignorance: but that was long ago, before manhood put its fist down on my table, rattled my windows with its loud voice and told me to stop being a buffoon.

One of those whom I regularly meet is Sam Kwan. At least once a week, often twice, we happen to cross on our paths to oblivion. We do not talk much. He is often preoccupied with his work and cannot spare the time to chat. We are just in each other's company which gives me a sense of familiar well-being and him the idea he has an ally at hand, albeit one who, in a pinch, can do nothing more than lift the telephone and call for help.

It is always evening and I always approach our meeting in the same fashion, walking round the corner by the rice shop and looking up and down the street. My actions are a reflex. I am not afraid someone might see me, report my behaviour to higher authorities: besides, were there a snoop about seeking to muddy my pond, I am confident I could bluff my way out of trouble.

I do not feel ashamed of or regret my association with Sam nor of my going to his place. If I were, I would not look from side to side but upwards as was once my nature but is no longer.

Only last evening, I paid a visit to Sam. It was already dark. The bright bulbs hanging in the rice shop illuminated deep mahogany rice tubs with bands of polished brass. The red characters on the label boards jammed into the contents of each, denoting quality, variety and price per catty, glistened as if painted with fresh blood. A small brazier down the street guttered with flames lifting feathers of burnt paper into the air: someone was either burning garbage or lucky money to a dead relative, paying their rent in heaven.

At a fruit stall, the proprietor leaned against a pile of crates reading a Chinese comic whilst a young boy flicked a feather duster of orange cockerel plumes over the display. Under a neon light, his merchandise appeared more like artificial fruit than edible produce, the pomeloes sickly yellow as if curiously jaundiced, the near-ripe mangoes as red as if blushed by rouge, the guavas pink as cheap plastic dolls and the star-fruit inesculent. As I walked past, the furniture maker's shop was closed but through the stencil-cut holes in the steel shutters came diamonds of light, the pungent smell of French polish, varnish and camphorwood, the deep drone of conversation and the slap of mah-jong tiles on a table.

From the outside, Sam's — how shall I put it? — *establishment* looks little different from any of the other hundred or so joints scattered throughout Wanchai. The frontage contains no windows as a protection against brawling matelots. The wooden door, painted scarlet with a writhing golden dragon spitting yellow flames, looks like a panel stolen from a Taoist temple. It automatically swings shut but was propped open as I drew near, the entrance hung with a new curtain of red-and-blue plastic beads. On the pavement beside the door is the inevitable miniature shrine.

Projecting twenty feet into the street, vying for space with those of neighbouring shops, is the signboard. Sam is particularly proud of it for it cost several thousands of dollars and is an indication his business is doing well.

Fifteen feet long and eight high, it is suspended from a dubious steel framework bolted into the building. Shaped in neon strips, it portrays a large black cat in a top hat with a supercilious grin on its face, standing on its hind legs with a martini glass in one paw: the other is placed around the shoulders of a smaller, pink cat with long eye-lashes and a cheeky smile which is intended to be sexy. She is wearing a ballerina's tutu and is seated on a bar stool. The two figures ride a chariot of neon lettering which spells out the name of Sam's place – *The Black Pussy Bar & Nite Club*.

I looked up at these two felines. I always do for they seem not only loftily orgulous but also ridiculing and I like to feel I am the subject of their mockery. It does one good to be occasionally humbled. As I glanced up at them, the garish sign sputtered into life with a few pops of electricity, the explosion of light alarming sparrows which had been roosting on the framework. With twittering complaints, they took to the wing, darting into the sky, twisting in mid-flight to weave over the roof-tops. I drew aside the plastic beads and entered.

The bar is large with a set of stairs at the rear beside a green plastic sign reading *LA ATORY*: the *V* has dropped off and in its place some wit has scored in the letters *VD*. An internal toilet is not common: many bars direct clients to the gutter at the rear, despite the demands of the urban council inspectors. However they, like the police, can be persuaded to turn a blind eye to the finer vagaries of the by-laws. This indoor convenience is another object of Sam's pride.

Once within, I halted for a moment. My eyes smarted from the neon sign and the interior was dark, the only lights I could see being those in the winking jukebox, one behind the face of a wall clock advertising Johnnie Walker scotch whisky and an ultraviolet strip over the bar.

I feel vaguely uncomfortable whenever I am in that dimness, like a blind man coming into a place with which he is not familiar. I need fear nothing but, nevertheless, the feeling always persists for a moment. Perhaps it is some long-lost guilt trying to surface and not quite making it. I give it little thought and, as my eyesight adjusts and I notice more detail, it fades.

The room is slightly angled, the bar itself a curved counter at one end, not far from the entrance. Around the walls are cubicles of dark-stained wood, not unlike those of a traditional tea-house. They each contain a table and seating for four to six people. The cubicle walls are lined with padded benches of dark red leatherette: the individual chairs are of substantial construction.

Just as a steak-house will fail with blunt knives so would a bar if the chairs are not capable of supporting two people, one on the other's lap. Lighting is provided by cast-iron Chinese-style lamps securely screwed onto the tables which, like the chairs, are bolted to the floor as insurance against serious injury in a brawl. Sam knows all this. He designed the place. He has been in the business man and boy and is *au fait* with all the tricks.

In the centre of the room is an area of polished planking fifteen feet square which serves as a dance floor, music provided by the jukebox. It is a bizarre contraption of yellow-and-red lights, rows of illuminated buttons and, protected by a perspex dome like the helmet of a space comic hero, the turntable and record selection equipment.

Behind the bar counter stood Sam. He is a middle-aged Chinese and always wears a white shirt which looks lilac under the ultraviolet strip. Upon his wrist he has a Japanese imitation of a Rolex watch whilst on the second finger of his right hand is a twenty-four carat gold ring set with an oval of bright green jade. The gold is so pure it looks like costume jewellery.

'Hi, *san foo*!' he called out, careful in his enunciation. 'How are you?'

He is fluent in English but as he frequently has to communicate with drunks he has developed the pedantic style of a schoolmaster.

I looked at him. He was, as always when someone entered his bar, smiling broadly.

If you did not know it, that smile could be construed as a sign of friendship. Where I am concerned it is. Yet it is also a vital aid to good business, as seminal as the smile a doctor makes to a patient, a teacher makes to a new pupil or a priest makes to a stranger entering his church.

It is a smile with which I have had acquaintance for six decades, being both a recipient of it and the source of its congenial benefaction. I am as expert at it as Sam. He knows this for he believes we are both members, if disparate ones, of the same fraternity and therefore accepts the smile as part of my bag of tricks just as it is his own.

'You know, *san foo*,' he once said to me, 'you and me alike. Two pea on one pod.'

At the time the bar was empty of customers: a typhoon was brewing so the warships had sailed to ride out the storm at sea, the soldiers confined to barracks.

'Why do you say that?' I asked him.

'You a priest: me, I own a girlie bar.'

'I was a priest,' I corrected him, 'but go on.'

'Both make a living the same way, make promise we cannot keep, earn our money selling dream and we both want salvation when we die. Both want to be forgiven for broken promise, bad dream . . .'

There is, he believes, very little basic difference between a priest and a pimp. I tend to agree with him: we are both peddlers of fantasies which do not last and I cannot fault his thesis, of which the smile is an integral aspect.

It is not a smile of invitation and certainly not of a man about to charge $8 for a bottle of San Miguel lager which may be purchased in a hotel lounge for $5.50 and a shop for $3. More, it is a smile to put any newcomer at his ease, to let him know he is amongst friends, to inform him, no matter what happens, he has a pal, someone on whom he can rely, with whom he may share petty confidences and private miseries. It is a smile of universal provision guaranteeing alcohol, sympathy and, for a side charge, companionship.

'Hello, Sam, how are you?' I replied.

I have never discovered if Sam is a diminutive of Samuel or an abbreviation of his Chinese names. Perhaps he chose Sam as it sounded good with Kwan. Sam Kwan. It has a ring to it.

'Okay,' he said carelessly. 'I getting older, like you. Soon, we be old man together.'

'You will need to hurry,' I said, 'if you are to catch me up.'

Sam laughed, 'You are a funny man, *san foo*. Should take a job in a bar. In a night club. Tell funny stories. Make good money.'

I lifted myself onto a stool at the end of the bar, leaning against the wall and hitching my heels behind the foot rest. The stool seems a fraction higher each time I come, proof perhaps of the statement one passes through life from childhood to childhood: chairs which were tall at eight are tall again at eighty.

'What you want to drink?' Sam asked. 'San Mig.? Whisky? Gin?'

'San Mig.,' I replied.

'Okay. No sweat! One San Mig. comin' up!' Sam exclaimed and he turned to a fridge under the counter.

From my elevated position on the stool, I surveyed the bar. Sam and I were not alone. In the farthest cubicle from the door sat six young Chinese women huddled in conversation, whispering and giggling. All were dressed in tightly tailored brocade *cheong sams* with the slits in the sides reaching far higher up their thighs than Chinese decorum would usually permit.

'One San Mig. Ice cold.' Sam lowered his voice as if afraid the girls might overhear him. 'Four dollars, *san foo*. But pay when you leave. Credit is good for you.' He followed my gaze. 'You looking for good time?' he enquired. 'Can do. No too much for you. Early evening . . .'

'No. Not tonight,' I answered, turning away from the girls. 'I don't feel up to it.'

Sam laughed again. This is an old joke we share between ourselves. He knows I am not interested in his girls – his little ladies, as he calls them – but he always asks. Perhaps he hopes one day to see me succumb, vanish up the stairs over the la-atory for half an hour of rented bliss, one of the fake fantasies he or I are able to arrange. Yet he is aware I forswore the carnal long ago.

After about a quarter of an hour, there came from the street a curt, raucous shout followed by loud laughter. No Chinese would make such a public display: it meant the evening's first clients were on their way.

When the bead curtain parted, five American sailors entered. Their uniforms were starched white and upon their heads they wore those hats which remind me of steamed *dim sum* dumplings. These they removed as they sauntered across the room, tucking them into their belts. They were suddenly silent after the noise in the street, each one of them surveying the bar, the lines of bottles and the girls.

Sam was smiling his proprietary smile.

'Hi, you guys!' he greeted them. 'Welcome to *The Black Pussy*. What's your poison?'

'Beers,' one of the sailors replied bluntly. 'Not that San Mig. shit. You got any good American beers?'

'Ah!' Sam chuckled. 'You been to Hong Kong before! Okay. I got Schlitz, Bud, Coors, Miller . . .'

'Five Buds.'

Sam began to prise the tops of the bottles. The sailors eyed the girls. I watched. There was an almost tangible atmosphere of expectancy in the air. How often have I observed such a scene. It is as ritualised as the courtship of birds, as strictly adhered to as a catechism.

One of the girls stepped forward, putting her hand on the arm of the first sailor she came to. She did not say anything but looked up into his eyes, smiling: yet this was not a Sam-like friendly smile but a covetous, enticing, beautiful smile. It was exactly the same smile as Adam saw on the face of Eve, promising paradise but delivering only bleak earthly joys.

'Beers up!' Sam said jovially and he placed five tall glasses on the counter, one after the other, as if setting up targets in a coconut shy.

'Forty dollar,' he said.

'Put it on a tab,' said the sailor who had ordered the round.

'No tab. Pay as you drink.' Sam laughed lightly. 'Pay now, no angry later. All's fair in *The Black Pussy*.'

The sailors paid up and drifted away to the cubicles, each with a girl. One, who had not been forward enough to get herself a sailor, sat at the end of the counter from me. She sipped a glass of iced tea and, when the girls called for drinks, acted as waitress.

By nine o'clock, the *Black Pussy* was doing a brisk business. More American sailors had arrived and a number of new girls had walked in to accommodate them. The jukebox played continuously, sailors dancing with the girls. It was the last night the US fleet would be in port and the sailors, forbidden alcohol on board ship, were eager to make up for anticipated lost drinking time. Those with brief romances were keen to take them to their limit, those with money anxious to spend it.

The air was fogged with cigarette smoke, the door propped open to give ventilation, the bead curtains never still from a coming and going of sailors on the lookout for friends or girls with whom they had struck up an acquaintance.

As Sam served the drinks, gave the girls their pass-out chits and collected the money, I sat quietly, in my usual fashion, surveying the machinations of the clientele and considering my motivation for being there.

I come to The *Black Pussy* because it is my place to do so, to be amongst the sinners and the fallen, those who have failed or are failing in their lives, the dispossessed and the disappointed. I am not here to offer them salvation, as once I might have been. I am here, as they are, to avoid looking truth in the eye.

Just along the bar from me stood a sailor. Perched beside him on a stool was one of the bar-girls. She was barely five feet tall and he was at least six: more a gangling youth not quite yet a man. It was obvious this was his first encounter with a tart. I can tell a virgin in the *Black Pussy* just as readily as I could a sinner in the pews. It is a matter of having the eye trained for the tell-tale signs which say *I am lost*, or *I am afraid*, or *I have sinned, father, forgive me*.

The sailor was drinking beer, the girl at his side having a Sam Special in a shorts glass. Sam's smile is not the only front-of-house con. He mixes cold tea with sherry at a ratio of five to one and when a girl asks a sailor to buy her a drink, she requests this noxious concoction. It costs Sam about seventy cents a glass.

Once I had asked Sam why he added sherry: surely, I reasoned, cold tea would be cheaper. He had frowned and said, 'Maybe, *san foo*. But if I put sherry in, it cover the tea taste.'

'So what?' I replied. 'The girls aren't going to complain.'

'No. But the sailor maybe complain. See, *san foo*, I charge five dollar. Good profit! The girl get twenty five per cent. She glad for this. Good money for her, too. The more she drink, the more she earn. Even if the sailor don't take her out. But if you were sailor . . .' He poured the rest of my beer into my glass and dropped the empty bottle into a waste bin where it broke '. . . what you do if you found out you buying shorts glass of tea for five bucks?'

'I wouldn't find out,' I said.

'You could, *san foo*. You could. You lean over and you say,' he put on a mock American accent. '"Hey, baby! Wot you drinkin', eh?" And you take a sip. If it's tea you get angry. You come to the bar. "Wotthehell, you ass hole!" you shout. Make trouble. Maybe hit me, maybe break some things. But, if you taste sherry mix with tea, you say to your friend, "Jesus, Mother of Mary, Hal! You taste the crap these girls got? Christ, I'm glad I don't drink this Chinese wine shit."'

I had laughed, had to admire Sam's artfulness, his sheer audacity. Sam had then passed me one of the little glasses.

'You try, *san foo*. Maybe you like.'

Putting the glass to my lips, I drank it in one, rolling it round in my mouth. It was dark brown, had a film upon the surface like oil on rain puddles and tasted like sweet acid.

'It's foul,' I remarked.

'I no like it,' Sam answered truthfully. 'But the girls don't complain. So . . .'

He had shrugged his shoulders, corked the sherry bottle and set about wiping the bar down.

The bar-girl's hand was on the young sailor's thigh, caressing it and creasing the material of his white uniform trousers but she did not let her fingers wander up to his groin. That next move would only come if he gave her a sign of his intentions to pay her out of the bar for a quarter of an hour.

After a minute or so of her palm massaging his leg, she took her hand away and said, 'You want buy me another drink, John?'

At first, they are always John: John or perhaps, sometimes, Joe.

'No, I . . . I don't think so,' the sailor replied. He stuttered slightly, looking obliquely at her and smiling a little sheepishly.

'My name Rosie,' she said, undeterred. 'What you name?'

'Gary. My name's Gary,' he replied, quietly.

'Okay!' she exclaimed enthusiastically. 'Is a good name. Ga-wy. Like Gah-wee US Bonds. You know him? Good singer. You know him song?'

She started loudly to hum the opening bars of *New Orleans*, a popular song on the jukebox.

'Yes,' the sailor said. 'I know him.'

He looked over her shoulder. In one of the cubicles sat a more experienced sailor, his companion's face buried in his neck, her fingers pushed well down the front of his pants.

Rosie ceased her humming, drained her tea and sherry cocktail and put her hand on Gary's arm.

'You buy me one drink, Gah-wee,' she wheedled. 'No' too much. Jus' one drink. Five dollar.'

I looked at Sam who was reaching for a tray of ready-filled glasses.

'No,' the sailor reiterated. 'Maybe later.'

'Why not now?' she cajoled. 'I can give you good time.'

The sailor shook his head yet he still smiled at her in a shy fashion. She became confused: willing punters smiled, dismissive clients bluntly told her to sod off. Her disconcertion made her angry.

'Why you smile if you no want fuck?' she demanded. 'You see something funny?'

'No,' the sailor said anxiously. 'I see nothing funny.'

He was afraid, an amalgamated fear of being seen to be a fool in front of his peers, of being embarrassed in front of a woman. It was also a fear of God, or the clap, or the ship's doctor and the rumour of his long needle, or simply not being able to do it. It was the fear of the unknown from which all men suffer.

'So! I no pretty girl?' Rosie suddenly exploded.

Sam, who was putting some coins in the till, slammed the cash drawer shut. The report drew Rosie's attention for a moment. She caught his reproving eye.

'You're a real pretty girl,' the sailor assured her.

'Maybe . . .' She spoke in a quiet undertone. 'Maybe you no can do.' She slid down from the stool. 'Maybe you think you cock drop off,' she added sarcastically and stomped off.

With her gone, the sailor hunched forward, concentrating on his beer. He cast a cautious glance at his shipmates but they were giving their undivided attention to their own girls and had not noticed what had happened. After a few minutes, there was an outbreak of giggling from one of the cubicles where Rosie had joined a friend with another customer: her voice could be heard saying loudly, 'Maybe not drop off. Maybe him arse-bandit!'

The sailor stared at his beer, blushing.

'Bar-tender,' he addressed Sam who was looking disapprovingly in the girls' direction, 'give me a beer.'

Sam opened a bottle of San Miguel and poured it into the sailor's glass.

'How much?'

'Have this one on me,' I offered, leaning over and nodding to Sam. I felt sorry for this awkward youth and his clumsy attempts to accomplish what he thought would make him a man.

He did not know what it really takes to face up to the demands of manhood. Laying a whore is not even the most minute part of the process, not even a preliminary requirement for entry into the first stage of the initiation that will not be over in a day or a month, like admission to a select club or basic military training, but which evolves until the day life ceases. Manhood is not something one ever attains. It is an impossible goal like trying to resist temptation. One can dream of it but never achieve it.

I wished I could have told him this yet I knew I could not surrender the information. Even if I had had him in the confessional my words would have gone unheeded.

'Cheers!' I said, as the sailor raised his replenished glass.

'Thanks,' he said then, after a pause, added, 'but I don't need no sympathy.'

I replied, 'I'm not giving you sympathy. I'm giving you a beer.'

One of the girls thumbed a ten cent coin into the juke-box and walked straight across the dance-floor to him.

'Hi!' she said cheerily. 'You no listen Rosie. Rosie no good.' She lowered her voice, taking his hand in hers. 'You no upset. I know you cherry boy.'

The sailor took a long pull of his beer, looked at his reflection in the mirror behind the bottles and asked in soft voice, 'What's your name?'

'My name Lindy,' she answered. 'You like me.'

It was not a question but a statement.

The jukebox started to grind out a song by a singing duo called the Everly Brothers. It was entitled *Ebony Eyes*: I have heard it often in the past weeks for it is this girl's favourite. Intertwining her fingers in his, Lindy gently tugged at his arm.

'Come on, John. You dance, no buy me drink.'

He left the bar and the girl put her arms round him, hugging herself against him, her face level with his chest. As they began to move slowly over the planking, she began to sing along with the record.

'*My ebony eyes was coming to me, F'om out of d' skies on f'ight twel'e oh free . . .*' Her voice was reedy and thin, strangely sad. 'Is a good song?' she remarked as the singing became a spoken refrain. 'Is about a girl who die in plane crash.'

Nothing really changes. Sailors' uniforms alter and the ships in which they serve get larger and are better armed: fashions in drink shift from rum to scotch to beer: tastes in music move from jazz to rock and roll: strains of venereal disease come to the fore before surrendering to a stronger antibiotic. Otherwise, things are as they have always been with young men afraid of the future and of losing their virginities, of stumbling clumsily into petty sin.

This is the way life is. I know it, accept it. It is a catalogue of experiences which makes the man. I have had a thousand of them, am accustomed to their hollow tauntings, petty triumphs and inconsequential failures.

The easel rocked slightly on the floor and the corners of the blackboard were no longer square. Decades of usage in a Jesuit school in Dublin had chipped and scarred them until they were now crudely rounded. The black surface had been freshly primed before shipping but was now beginning to wear thin so the chalk screeched jarringly. On the other hand, the pegs upon which the blackboard rested were brand new, but very unlike the originals, being hand-carved by a Wuchow carpenter with the bosses neatly fashioned into little birds.

Before the girls arrived, I had prepared my lesson on the board by drawing four simple pictures, filling them in with coloured chalk and hiding them under lengths of cloth draped over the top. On the desks I placed squares of card face downwards beside tablets of coarse rice paper, brush pens and ink pads. This done, I opened the shutters, decided the sunlight was too strong, closed them again then opened them halfway. I was as nervous as an apprentice fighter before his first bout in the bare-knuckle ring, fussing about the room until I heard the girls' footfalls in the corridor.

As they filed into the room, the girls did not look at me but went straight to their places, keeping their eyes lowered. Sister Margaret entered with them, standing next to me by the blackboard. When all were assembled, she clapped her hands once and the girls looked up, their hands at their sides.

Not sure what to do next, I said in what I hoped were unwavering tones, 'Let us think of the Lord and trust in His help with our work.'

I put my hands together. There was a soft rustle of cloth from the girls' sleeves as they followed suit.

'Lord,' I prayed, 'look down upon us, Your humble subjects, and guide us with Your strength and wisdom.'

The girls made no response until Sister Margaret said loudly, '*Ah-meng*!' which they imitated with gusto.

This preliminary over with, the old nun nodded briefly to me and walked towards the door. At her every step, I felt my spirits sinking, my fears rising pro rata. By the time her fingers grasped the door handle, I was near panic. With her outside the room, however, and the door closed, I sensed a surge of confidence which, at the same time, I knew was quite unjustified.

'My name,' I began very slowly, 'is Father Stephen. I have come from Ireland.'

The girls looked blankly at me, uncomprehending and docile. They did not fidget or attempt to look at the squares of cardboard, did not stare rudely yet nor did they seem to be giving me their attention. I was confused and nonplussed. If ever I had wanted an angel to materialise before me and give me divine inspiration, it was now: please God, I begged, give me some guidance but no light flashed in the sky and no revelation appeared. The sun continued to shine through the half-open shutters, dust dancing in the beam. From the *hutong* outside came the call not of a friendly God but of a street vendor.

I had no idea how to start to break through to them. I spoke only a few words in Cantonese which I had quickly tried to commit to memory all the previous night from a dog-eared booklet Father Callaghan had given me. It was called *A Merchant's Guide to The Language of Cantong-nese*. The publication date on the fly-leaf was 1846 and the booklet appeared to have been published in Macau. It contained little of use to me: words and phrases such as *fiscal, godown, compradore, held in bond* and *contractual obligation* were not relevant to priests or teenage girls destined to become sew-sew amahs in rich men's houses.

'I am your teacher of English,' I continued painfully slowly, mouthing each word with the exactness of the most expensive elocution mistress. 'I am your teacher,' I repeated. 'I will teach you to speak English.'

They still stared blankly at me.

'Me *sin shaang*,' I said, deciding to risk one of the useful words of Cantonese I had discovered in the glossary to the book. '*Sin shaang*, teacher.'

The girls tittered at my pronunciation. They quickly glanced at each other then, as if afraid I might be angry, stopped suddenly and looked in my direction again. I felt the panic returning.

'On the board,' I pointed to the blackboard, 'there are some pictures. Today, we will look at some words.'

I was about to lift one of the pieces of cloth when a pupil in the front row stood up. She was one of the older girls, her hair not tied in a cue but gathered into little bunches behind each ear. Her white smock shone brightly with the sunlight.

'*Fuffer See Faat Han*,' she began.

The other girls tittered and she glanced round, smiling nervously at her classmates: then she seemed to pluck up her courage again.

'You come' – she pointed at me, – '*Eye-lun*. Me'– she pointed at herself, – 'come Wuchow.'

For a moment, she remained standing as if not sure what to do next then sat down, blushing and looking sideways at her companions for support. The other girls all looked apprehensively at me.

'Thank you,' I said, bowing slightly to her. '*Dor jay*.'

The girls broke into peals of light, happy laughter, their merriment infectious. I joined in with them which pleased them all the more. When, after a few minutes, the laughter died I was confronted with smiling, trusting faces. No planning on my part, I was sure, could have so reached through to the class and I thought how God had not abandoned me but answered my plea in his inimitable fashion. I gave him quick and silent thanks as I turned to the blackboard.

For over an hour, the lesson progressed with my feeling more at ease with my charges. I uncovered the drawings on the board one by one, each being greeted with surprised giggles and broad smiles. When the chalk screeched on the board, the girls sucked their teeth and grimaced.

The pictures on the card squares produced as much hilarity as my chalk drawings. They had been prepared for a Catholic educational missionary society by a kindly lady whose knowledge of China was restricted to what she had gleaned from the pages of the *Illustrated London News*. Her drawings were artistically exact, her depictions accurate but she had no concept of the fact Chinese girls did not wear layered petticoats, Chinese housewives did not use saucepans and the European cow did not resemble, save in its number of legs and horns, a Chinese buffalo. When the girls turned over their sixth card to be confronted with a drawing of a black and white Friesian, they exploded into such laughter I was momentarily afraid I might lose control of the class.

By the time the lesson ended, the girls were convinced all Western dogs had patches over their eyes, all Western men had hairy faces and all Western houses must be very cold and full of evil spirits because they had so many windows. Yet they knew the words for cow, cat, mouse, dog and rat: and I also knew the equivalents in Cantonese.

When at last I released the class back into the charge of Sister Margaret and the girls filed out of the room, I leaned against the window sill with a feeling of intense exhaustion tempered by considerable joy. I had done it, survived my first lesson. Below me, in the courtyard, the girls passed by on the way to their sewing class. As they moved into the sunlight and it reflected off their smocks, I realised I had perhaps been visited by an angel after all, possibly by a whole assembly of them. They were wingless but had, I believed, invisible haloes and I felt an intense love for each and every one of them swell in me until it was so unbearably vast

I had to look away, busy myself with wiping the blackboard clean and collecting up the cardboard squares to take my mind from its enormity.

'So how did it go, Stephen?' asked Father Callaghan as we strolled along the high bank of the river in the late afternoon.

'Well,' I reported, adding, 'I think.'

'Don't be modest. You were a great success. The girls spent the rest of the morning chattering about you. I overheard them and Sister told me you had made a great impression.'

'I think I may have made a bit of a fool of myself,' I confessed. 'I tried a bit of Cantonese.'

'And they loved it. You didn't pronounce it right, mind you. I won't tell you what you said. Just be sure it wasn't what you thought. But you broke the ice.'

'No, I didn't,' I quickly admitted. 'One of the girls did.'

'They're good little creatures,' Father Callaghan remarked as we stepped aside to allow two coolies pulling a large cart to pass. 'They mean and do well. You'll not have any trouble from them.'

We reached the confluence of the two rivers that joined at Wuchow, the Li Kiang which flowed from the north and the Si Kiang which ran from the west eastwards towards the sea at Canton. The river water was so brown with silt that the sun, now down in its afternoon descent, did not sparkle upon the surface. I gazed at the swirling and eddying where the currents vied with each other for dominance.

'A dangerous spot,' Father Callaghan remarked. 'That's where they say the river dragon lives. His tail causes the whirlpools. With the river this low, it doesn't look so bad but you wait until after the monsoon. Then it'll look like the maelstrom itself.'

'Always dragons,' I said, thinking aloud.

'Oh, yes! Always dragons. There are other evils in the Chinese bestiary but the dragon's the one to watch for. Yet they're not all bad, you know. Some are beneficial. China's a land of opposites, of checks and balances. The *yin* and the *yang*. Gods and devils.'

'Where do the dragons come from?' I asked.

'Everywhere. You get them living in hills, in forests, in rocks and rivers, in the sky . . .'

'I mean, where does the legend come from? What foundation has it? All legends are based upon some truth.'

'That's a fact.' Father Callaghan answered. 'Did you ever hear a banshee? Back in Ireland.'

'I did not,' I replied.

'I have heard it. In Galway, one winter, when I was a lad.' His eyes took on a brief far-away stare. 'But, you know, I didn't believe the old folk so I went to look for it.'

'Did you find it?'

'I did, for sure. It was the wind blowing off the Atlantic through a hole in a stone wall. And do you know, from that moment I wanted to be a priest. Dispel the myths of evil and show how they're all God's harmless work when you look closely at them.'

'And the dragons?'

'It's my theory, in ancient times, there dwelt along the coasts and rivers of China a breed of crocodile. Sea-living ones such as they have in the Dutch East Indies. It's died out now, but the memory of its man-eating lingers in the collective consciousness of the people. They're simple folk so if a man's sucked under by the tow of the current why not say a crocodile – that is, a dragon – has him? The poor soul's dead whatever took him.'

We walked on in silence for a short way before Father Callaghan spoke again.

'We – you and I, Father Stephen – are in the myth business, you know. All those miracles Our Lord performed. Myths, really. It's our job to explain them, place them in context. They've all a basis in truth.'

'You sound like a heretic,' I said.

'Heresy's a frame of mind,' he replied. 'If you're true to God and seek the truth what difference does it make if you question a few things? Take the burning bush. A wonder, they said. But I've seen a bush catch fire of its own on a sweltering dry Chinese day. And if I had a silver dollar for every farmer hereabouts who's seen his hayrick catch alight of its own accord, I'd be richer than all the compradores from here to Shanghai.'

I looked across the river and up the wooded slope of a steep hill on the opposite bank.

'*Bak Hok Shan,*' Father Callaghan said following my gaze.

'White Crane Hill. Can you see the building through the trees? The British Resident's house, that is. A fine mansion built like a cross between a Chinese pavilion and an Indian *dak* bungalow. Trust him to arrange for his house to be built on a site with the best view of the town and river. You know, I think along with Latin and Mathematics, they teach Strategics in English public schools.'

Towards us along the path came a figure dressed in a saffron gown slung over his shoulder toga-fashion, the material held in place by the strap of a brown cloth bag. His head was completely shaven, his feet shod in leather sandals. In his hand was a rice bowl.

'Buddhist monk,' Father Callaghan said. 'They're itinerant, like our mendicant brothers before us.'

He nodded to the monk who squinted vaguely at us, smiled distantly and raised his free hand in greeting. At that moment, a door opened in a building facing the river and a woman appeared with a cooking vessel. The monk abruptly held out his bowl, the woman ladling some rice into it. The monk muttered something, took a spoon from his bag and started to eat quickly. He made no attempt to squat down to enjoy his repast as any coolie might. Without speaking, the woman re-entered her house, firmly closing the door behind her.

'That's her duty for the day done,' my companion remarked. 'One step closer to a sure place in heaven.'

When the monk had finished his brief repast, he sucked his spoon clean, wiped the inside of his bowl with his finger and then, stooping to the ground, put a handful of grit into it which he scoured round the inside. This done and the grit discarded, he placed both articles in his bag and walked off, his eyes turned down at the ground before him.

'There's so very little difference between religions, when you come down to it,' observed Father Callaghan. 'All the world over, the clergy depend upon charity and the congregations upon their consciences.'

Moored along the river were sampans and low barge-like vessels. We halted under the shade of a broad-leafed tree to watch the activity of the people, Father Callaghan hoisting up the legs of his *fu* and going down on his haunches like a native. I leaned against the smooth bark of the trunk, feeling its coolness through the cotton of my *sam*.

The bows of the vessels all faced the shore, coolies unloading them, carrying their cargoes up the steep bank on poles. Everyone was stripped to the waist and wearing a rattan hat with an oval crown and a down-turned brim which cast their faces in shadow. Stray dogs wandered about gleaning whatever they might whilst small children played at the water's edge.

Whereas the bows of the boats were theatres of frenzied mercantile activity, the sterns were calm, domestic areas. Women rinsed clothes in wooden buckets or prepared food over small braziers. Babies tottered about with a rope round their waists to prevent them falling overboard, the seats of their little pants cut out in a hole. Several men were engaged in fishing with lines. On one sampan, a man was plucking a hen, the feathers drifting down to the water to be snatched and whisked away by the current.

'The rivers are the life's blood of our town,' Father Callaghan observed, watching a line of coolies carrying tree-trunks up from one of the barges. 'If there were no rivers, there'd be nothing here but a few shacks and a tumble-down temple.'

I considered his words. He referred to it as our town and, at that moment, I believed he was right: a strange place halfway round the world, filled with superstition and lost to God where he had found his home and where I hoped to establish mine. Beneath that shade tree overlooking the Li Kiang, I felt I had discovered what I wanted in life, a desire beyond even that to serve my God: it was to be with these people whose lives were so fascinating me, whose ways were so mysterious.

There was no revelation about my awareness. It was not a sudden realisation but the coming together of random, unspoken thoughts and feelings, a culmination of many factors – of the poverty of Ireland which I had left behind me and felt I could do nothing about, the misery of those without God who were doomed to damnation, the need to be a new man myself. Being in China, standing with the river flowing by and the coolies calling out to each other in their strange tongue, gave me the same feeling of rebirth and rejuvenation as I had experienced on the day of my ordination. It was as if a bright light had come into the darkness of my life and shone upon the path to a new future.

What I wanted more than anything else was to start again with new purpose in a new land which I could call my home and China afforded it to me.

'Do you know,' Father Callaghan interrupted my reverie, 'Wuchow was a city long before the Blessed Carpenter walked in Bethlehem? It received its present name in the Tang dynasty. In the year of Our Lord, 621. In the Sung dynasty, the poet Su-shi wrote of this place, *Every night, the moonlight on the river is beautiful: every dawn the cloudy hills look different.* Understand, of course, the poem loses a lot in the translation. But, you know Father Stephen, when I'm here and look across at *Bak Hok Shan*, I can imagine the poet sitting on this very spot and looking at just the same view. Save for the British Resident's bungalow . . .'

On the river bank, there erupted a commotion. Coolies dropped their loads to run pell-mell down to the sampans, shouting and bellowing. Women screamed, children started to cry with bewilderment at the pandemonium. The man who had been plucking the chicken had fallen into the river. He was already thirty or forty feet from his sampan, flailing his arms in the water and shouting in a high-pitched voice.

I started to run down the bank, struggling to unbutton my jacket as I went, Father Callaghan a few steps behind me. None of the coolies was making any attempt to save the man. They hollered and screamed: some of the women beat metal cooking utensils they had picked up from the sampans, yet no one made any effort to find a rope or jump in to the rescue.

Thrusting my way through the clamouring throng, I leapt onto a sampan, the deck heaving down under my weight and almost tipping me off balance. I was on the flat stern deck, pulling off my jacket when Father Callaghan gripped me so firmly by the arm it hurt.

'No, Father!' he said sharply.

'We've got to save him!' I shouted through gritted teeth. 'We can't just let him drown. And they're doing nothing.'

The man was now another ten yards away, his head turning

this way and that as an undertow started to twist him around. He continued to shout, pointing at me.

'What's he shouting?' I demanded to know, still trying to get my arm free of both Father Callaghan's grip and my *sam*.

'He is saying, "Barbarian! Barbarian! Save me!"'

At that moment, the man's head disappeared under the surface. I watched the spot and prayed hard he would reappear. He did not. The crowd of coolies fell silent and then, as if nothing had occurred, returned to their labours.

'You should have let me . . .' I began angrily.

'. . . let you drown yourself?' Father Callaghan interrupted. 'You couldn't rescue him. None of us could.'

'I am a strong swimmer,' I complained, shrugging my *sam* back on.

'Not strong enough. The currents where the rivers meet are dangerous. You'd have gone under with him.'

'I should've tried.' I was irate, almost shouting. A small gathering of coolies and women looked on from the bank. 'What are we here for if not to save the likes of him?'

'We're here to save the living, my son,' Father Callaghan said coolly, 'not the dead. They've already gone to their gods and are beyond our touch. We're here for the abandoned, not the lost.'

His voice calmed my rage. I saw the reason behind his words but found them hard to reconcile. With my jacket back on, I started to make my way towards the prow of the sampan, stepping over some fishing nets and domestic utensils.

'Why didn't they do something?' I asked bitterly, looking up at the little crowd which was dispersing and at the coolies along the bank raising their loads to their shoulders once more. 'Throw him a rope or at least a plank of wood. And quite what banging cooking pots would do to help him I cannot say. There was no need to raise the alarm. Everyone saw what was going on.'

'They didn't bang pots and pans to attract the attention of would-be rescuers but to drive away the evil spirits and the dragons.'

'I've heard enough of damned dragons already!' I retorted exasperatedly.

'And they dared not save him,' Father Callaghan continued.

'If they had, the spirits of the river might have taken one of them in his place.'

'That's ridiculous!' I exclaimed.

'It is,' he replied, 'superstitious, yet it's also logical. They know the treacherous waters. Why risk two men when one will do? Why orphan two sets of children? You must learn, Father Stephen, to be a realist. Temper your faith with practicalities. None of us can survive in China without pragmatism.'

I was shaken by the event and it was some minutes before I felt I wished to speak to my companion again. I found I was angry with him for preventing my actions and with myself for doing nothing. If I had jumped in and drowned, it would not have mattered: it would have been the will of God. I looked back at the spot in the river where the man had drowned. There was nothing to show for this tragedy but the vortex of brown water and, near his sampan, some white hen's feathers spinning around and around in a miniature whirlpool.

One of the scavenging dogs approached us, growling ferociously. Father Callaghan bent to the ground as if to pick up a stone and raised his arm. The dog, conditioned by years of experience, slunk quickly off.

'Beware of the dogs. They may be rabid,' he advised. 'So may some of the animals in the market. It's best not to touch them. Hydrophobia's not a pleasant way to die.'

We had walked on in silence for a quarter of a mile, each of us lost in our own thoughts. The river widened slightly, the bank below us no longer crowded with sampans or barges but with long, thin vessels resembling houseboats: whereas there had been a lot of bustle about the sampans, there was hardly a body to be seen here.

'These are flower boats,' Father Callaghan remarked.

'Flower boats?' I replied.

There was no sign of any flowers on their decks nor any coolies on the bank attempting to sell them.

'A colloquialism, Father. They're whorehouses. Floating brothels. If we did not save those girls we have, some of them would be down there now, plying their trade.'

As he spoke, a door on one of the houseboats opened and a young woman emerged onto a short length of deck. She was dressed in the lavish style of a Chinese lady, her full-length *cheong sam* embroidered in intricate detail with clouds and phoenix birds. Her black hair glistened and was worked into an extravagant coiffure piled upon her crown and hung with small pendants of pearls.

'She's heard our voices,' Father Callaghan commented, 'and come out to see if we might be her customers. In each of those benighted vessels there may be up to six or seven more like her. She's but the madam of the establishment.'

'Would she . . .' I paused, not sure of an appropriate verb to use, 'would she cater for us? For foreign devils?'

'For anyone, Father Stephen, who can pay the price. The Chinese may wish to keep our God and our customs at arm's length, but where the carnality of man is concerned, there are no racial barriers. Their natural xenophobia does not extend to the level of the courtesan.'

The woman looked up and down the bank. She could hear foreign voices but could not see us, expecting as she was men in tropical suits and tall hats rather than Chinese costume. When at last she realised which of the figures walking on the high bank were us, she turned away inside the boat, her footsteps short and unsteady.

'You see how she walks?' Father Callaghan said.

'Yes.'

'Do you know why?'

'She is a cripple?' I ventured.

'No, Father Stephen. Either she's in an advanced stage of syphilis which has attacked her nerves or her feet are bound.'

I knew of bound feet: infant girls had their feet from the toes to the ankles wrapped tightly in cloth bandages from an early age, misshaping the foot as it grew into a tiny, useless appendage which would bring pain and discomfort to its owner for as long as she lived. Yet I also knew this cruelty was exacted upon girls in wealthy families, not upon the poor: I assumed those who were whores came from poor families.

'I know what's in your mind, Father Stephen. But these whores – some of them – come from good backgrounds. They are not all waifs and strays, peasant girls with pretty faces. You see, when a man dies in China – a husband, that is – the chances of his widow remarrying are slim. Other men, the bachelors, regard her as sullied goods and will not seek to court her no matter how fair her features or her personality. She has only two real options open to her. The first is to remain in her husband's family where you can bet your very breath she'll be as like as not treated as a slave by her mother-in-law. The second is to leave, but to go where? Her own family will not take her back. She's an extra and unproductive mouth to feed. So she ends up as a tart in a boat.' There was a distinct hint of disgust in his voice. 'Mind you, there is a third option and those who are unable to resist take it.'

'A third?' I said.

'Suicide,' Father Callaghan answered bluntly. 'The Chinese are a sophisticated nation. They have some quite remarkably ingenious ways of killing themselves.'

We had by now reached almost to the outskirts of the town. The road along the bank petered out, becoming less of a highway and more a well-worn dusty track hardly more than a cart wide.

'Let us turn back,' Father Callaghan suggested. 'But I recommend you come this way yourself some time. Just beyond the trees, where the path bends, you'll find a place to interest you. And instruct you, I dare say, in more of the ways of China.'

Mr Chan's shop is halfway along Hankow Road, one of the thoroughfares traditionally and continually infested with tourists: only on Chinese New Year, when the shops close for four days, are they absent. His business is called the Hing Loon Curio and Jewellery Company and is announced, as are all the others, by a large wooden sign hanging in the forest of other, similar boards suspended over the roadway.

The shop is one of a kind that is gradually disappearing. It does not sell tourist garbage. The curios on offer are genuine antiques or antiquities, not fakes or fifty-year-old items dirtied up to look a good deal older than they are, and the jewellery is of a high standard. His rings do not wear through in months, the clasps of his brooches do not snap in weeks, his pearls do not lose their lustre nor the gemstones in his pendants drop free in hours. What is more he has not, as have many of his neighbours, concentrated his trade upon one area of activity. Most of the other shops in the street have become dedicated jewellers, watch-sellers, camera dealers, cultured pearl merchants or what I term kelter traffickers. He has not succumbed to the mid-twentieth century ailment of specialisation and the result is a shop of the kind that is truly Chinese, has existed for centuries and is a joy to enter.

I have known Mr Chan for many years and love him. He is a quietly humorous, gentle and generous man for whom the world is not just a place in which to make money but also to spread slivers of happiness.

The first time I went into his establishment, I was not seeking to purchase anything. Indeed, I was hunting out places where I might sell rather than buy. There are, of course, pawn shops aplenty in Hong Kong but the operators frown as soon as a *gweilo* enters: they are meant for the poor Chinese and a European face in front of the high counter raises suspicion, doubt and, on occasion, animosity.

Seated on a red leather stool before one of Mr Chan's glass-topped cabinets was an auburn-haired English woman. To her right was an expensive handbag resting against her foot whilst, to her left, there stood her son. He was about six years old, dressed in buckled sandals, white ankle socks, a pair of khaki shorts and a white short-sleeved shirt to which was attached by metal poppers a yellow and brown school badge. She was leaning forward, directing Mr Chan's finger under the glass.

'This one. No, next. Up one. No, other way. Yes!'

He removed from the display a sapphire ring set in rose gold. The strip lights under the glass top and the bare bulbs hanging from overhead split in the gemstone.

'Maybe.' She was undecided and pointed to another ring. 'What is that?'

'Alexand'ite,' Mr Chan informed her, removing a second ring from the cabinet.

I noticed he did not replace the sapphire ring but left it on the counter. This was most unusual. Shopkeepers, ever on the look-out for being cheated or robbed, rarely leave two items out simultaneously.

'This stone change colour,' Mr Chan remarked. 'If you put in neon light, go one colour, but in plain go different.'

He handed it to the woman who moved the ring from side to side, to catch the various light sources, and I watched as the stone translated itself from a delicate mauve to a rich blue.

'I think . . . Let me see an aquamarine,' the woman requested, placing the alexandrite next to the sapphire.

Mr Chan, leaving the second ring on the counter also, started to rummage about in a drawer behind the counter, opening packages of folded paper, studying the contents then refolding them.

Apart from four glass counters and some stools, the shop is also furnished with tall, sombre cabinets made of dark-stained wood which give the place an air of solid if dusty history. This atmosphere of age is increased by the fact the cabinets are not illuminated and therefore contain an aura of mystery. They are crammed to overflowing with curios, the shelves so full it is almost impossible to see to the rear of them: I have known him to open a door and catch an item falling out.

Leaving him to continue serving the woman, I wandered towards one of the cabinets, peering into it. On the shelf just before my face were Buddhas carved of ivory or rosewood, ivory horses and elephants, soapstone still-lifes of karst mountains with little men climbing them on precipitous paths, glass snuff bottles with pictures painted on the inside, ancient pottery bowls, red-and-gold carved wooden temple tablets, cloisonné-handled paper-knives, black lacquerware boxes and cups, porcelain goddesses and a fifteen-inch high model of a sea-going fishing junk in full sail, complete in every detail down to the blocks through which the rigging ran. Upon the shelf below, surrounded by hand-painted eggshells in glass boxes and miniature fretwork landscapes cut from layers of cork, was a complete elephant's tusk intricately carved into a frieze of classical Chinese figures walking through a panorama of plum trees and pavilions.

'I can help you?' Mr Chan enquired, leaving the woman to decide upon her purchase.

His voice was soft, unhurried yet not unbusinesslike.

'Yes,' I replied in Cantonese. 'Do you only sell or will you also buy from individuals? I have some items I no longer wish to keep.'

For a very brief moment, he showed surprise at my fluency but this did not last.

'I do buy some things,' he said cautiously in his own language, 'but it depends upon the quality. If you bring the items to me I can see if we may do business. Are these Chinese items?' he asked as an afterthought. 'I do not usually buy Western things.'

'They are all Chinese,' I assured him, 'or of Chinese origin.'

'Are they made of gold?'

'No,' I said. 'Some are made of silver, others are jade but many are as you have in the cabinets.' I raised my hand to strengthen my point. 'Curios, antique items. Things I have picked up over the years.'

'Good,' he said warmly, 'I am sure I can do some business with you.'

He glanced in the direction of his lady customer. She was still trying to make her mind up, slipping the rings one by one onto her fingers, comparing them at arm's length with her hand outstretched. The little boy was growing restless at his mother's indecision. He was of the age when to be still for more than a few minutes is the equivalent of a session of severe torture in adulthood.

Mr Chan excused himself from me and went across to the child, going down on his haunches so they might be face to face.

'Little boy,' he said in English, 'you come.' He beckoned to him.

'Can I?' the boy asked his mother.

Not turning round, she said testily, 'Of course you can. Mr Chan isn't going to eat you.'

Taking the boy's hand, Mr Chan stood and led him to the rear of the shop, unlocking one of the sombre cabinets, pushing the door wide and steadying a vase teetering on the edge of the third shelf up.

'When you born?' he enquired of the child.

'September,' he replied shyly.

'No, not this. What year you born?'

The boy considered this question then said a little doubtfully, 'Nineteen forty four.'

'You sure?'

'Yes.'

'Ah! Then I know you!' Mr Chan exclaimed. 'You a monkey.'

He laughed quietly and, reaching in to the cabinet, took out a two-inch high jade figurine of a monkey upon a small wooden base. The animal was depicted sitting with its hands before its face, holding a fruit of some kind.

'This for you.'

Mr Chan held it out to the boy who was not sure whether to accept it. His face was filled with puerile doubt and unhappiness.

'He's giving it to you as a present,' I explained, sitting on a stool by the child.

'But he called me a monkey,' the boy stuttered, close to tears.

'No, he did not,' I said. 'He did not mean you were a monkey. He meant you were born in the Year of the Monkey. Each year in China has an animal to represent it.'

The child looked doubtful.

'I was born,' I went on, 'in the year of the Ox or Bull.'

The boy considered this. He was not at first sure if I was telling him the truth or spinning him some fantastic lie but, gradually, his doubt dissolved into the joy of being given the jade figure.

'You like it?' Mr Chan asked, sitting on another stool.

'I like it,' the boy admitted, holding it in both his hands. 'Thank you. Thank you very much.'

Unable to keep the fact of being given his own gift to himself, he ran across the shop to his mother.

'Mummy! Look what Mr Chan's given me. It's because I am a monkey boy.'

Whenever I pass the shop, I recall that act of simple kindness. It was not commissioned by a desire to close a deal with the boy's mother, or to impress, or to be some kind of advertisement, although it achieved all three. It was done simply because Mr Chan is a good man, one of those rare humans who, when he sees a petty suffering, tries to alleviate it. It is the likes of him who restore my faith in human nature, tell me there are good men in the world if only one is fortunate enough to discover them.

Over the years since that morning, I have sold perhaps two dozen items to Mr Chan. He is the only person with whom I have carried on such a trade; he has never once cheated me, has always given me a truthful evaluation of the object I have presented to him and not played upon my ignorance of its worth. Furthermore, he has always paid me in cash, in full and once, when he sold something obtained from me for considerably more than he expected, he insisted on giving me a percentage of the windfall profit.

This does not smack of bad business practice but basic honesty and such integrity is something I value more highly than any other human achievement. It is true, as one ancient maxim states, a display of honesty in any business is the surest way to prosper just as another apothegm declares the most certain way to remain poor is to be honest. Yet one does not grow rich in coin alone and poverty may take many forms.

The sun was not yet up, a vague grey light hanging in the room like a mist, slipping through the wooden slats of the shutters. It had been a muggy night and I had slept with the glass casement open but, on the recommendation of Father Callaghan, with the shutters firmly bolted, even though my room was on the third floor.

'They can be mighty wily devils!' Father Callaghan had remarked when he discovered at breakfast on the morning after my arrival that I went to bed with the window open. 'If they can't climb the walls or get themselves a ladder they'll as like throw up a grappling hook and shin in your room all the same. It amazes me,' he went on, breaking off a piece of bread and cramming it into his mouth, his next dozen or so words delivered with a light blizzard of crumbs falling upon the black cloth of his cassock, 'the further one travels East the more ingenious becomes the mind of the native pilferer.'

I swung my legs over the edge of the bed and scratched my shin. I had had a restless night, waking when an insect bit me just before dawn. I hoped it was not a mosquito: I was far more afraid of the malaria than a burglar. To combat the former threat, both Father Callaghan and I were sure to take a nightly dose of quinine disguised in a tumbler of gin and lime juice.

'Best drink in the world,' Father Callaghan declared when first introducing me to the bitter concoction. 'The quinine kills the parasites in your blood, the lime stops scurvy and the gin gives the evening a merry little glow.'

The drink was so sharp that, at first, I had found it hard to swallow.

'My advice,' Father Callaghan offered, 'is to wrinkle up your nose, praise God for the discovery of the drug and grit your teeth.'

Following his advice did not alleviate the bitterness: nor did the addition of sugar syrup which I tried at the suggestion of Ah Fong.

'Would it not be possible to take it with something else?' I enquired.

'I've tried,' Father Callaghan said. 'Rum does not disguise the quinine. Rice wine and quinine turns the stomach and I'll not adulterate Irish whiskey with the stuff for any price. Or even Scotch. Gin's the only thing, but don't you worry, Father Stephen. You'll acquire the taste.'

'Like the eggs?' I replied.

'Exactly!' he retorted. 'Why, in a year you'll be asking, "Ah Fong, we've not had any of those ambrosial hundred-year-old eggs of late. How about a serving of them tomorrow?"'

I had to smile. He was a jolly man and doing his best to cheer me up.

'What's more,' he finished, 'if you were in Hong Kong, you'd be a man of society drinking this liquor. It's quite the thing to drink it thus – they call it gin and tonic.'

I unlatched the shutters. In the morning mist, the roofs of Wuchow looked like the scaly backs of reptiles. Slowly, I washed my face and upper torso in a basin of chilling water poured from a pitcher covered with a square of muslin on the night-stand. The leather-bound travelling clock on the bookshelf beside my Bible showed it was just after six.

I was nearly through with my ablutions when, over the splashing of the water, I heard a gentle knocking.

'Master? Master?' a voice muttered. 'You 'wakey, master.'

'I 'wakey,' I replied: speaking in pidgin English eased communication.

The door opened and Ah Fong entered carrying a steaming earthenware jug.

'For shafe,' he declared.

Before I could thank him, Ah Fong put the jug down and, taking the basin, tossed the cold soapy water out of the window without so much as a glance to see who might be passing in the *hutong* below. He rinsed the bowl, threw that water after the dirty and filled the basin.

As I shaved, I heard a strange, brief sound from outside. It was a cross between a slurping, animal noise like a dog lapping and the rill of water over rocks. My face half lathered, I went to the window and peered down into the *hutong*. At first, I could see no one, the alley being in shadow, as if an hour of the night was lingering in it. It was not until a movement caught my eye I saw the source of the noise.

Below was a man with a hand cart. He was dressed in shabby clothes and walked with a stoop. Hanging down his back, over his cue, was a conical hat tied in place round his neck on a cord. Upon the cart were a number of barrels over several of which was placed a crude lid of split canes lashed together with bamboo strips. The man, bent in the shafts of his vehicle, was pulling the cart along the *hutong*, the wooden axles creaking and the wheels thumping on the cobbles. Just past the window, he stopped, lowered the shafts on uprights so the cart did not tip and hobbled to a doorway. I saw the man was either a hunchback or had been bent by years of labour.

From the doorway he carried a bucket which, having removed the lid, he poured into one of the barrels, making the sound I had heard. I was still pondering what on earth the man was doing when an atrocious and odious stench hit me. I reeled back from the window, almost knocking over the empty jug, pressing my hand to my mouth. Holding my breath, I closed the window and, before finishing my shave, rinsed my mouth out in case the stench carried some pestilence of which I was ignorant and to which, being a newly arrived foreigner, I could not hope to be immune. The stink seemed to linger in me as had the taste of the accursed egg.

When I was dressed in my cassock, I descended to the chapel and, after genuflecting before the altar, made my way to Father Callaghan's side. I must have looked white in the face for he commented, 'Are you well, Father Stephen?'

I recounted to him what I had seen, and smelled.

'That was what we call the honey-cart you saw,' Father Callaghan informed me. 'Old Quasimodo and his chums collect – how shall I put it? – family waste, including ours and take it out to the countryside. The polite phrase for this ordure is night-soil.'

'And then?' I asked.

'They spread it on the fields. There's few animals in China to manure the crops – not many horses or mules, few kine. And the droppings of chickens don't go far. All that leaves is the most plentiful animal – mankind.'

'Is this not a terrible source of pestilence?' I suggested.

'Indeed, it is,' Father Callaghan replied firmly. 'Especially of the cholera. And typhoid. This is the reason for thoroughly washing all vegetables before cooking. And perhaps why the Chinese have not invented the habit of eating a salad. You may like to know, Father Stephen, our annual expenditure of permangate of potash crystals is in excess of thirty pounds by weight. All you can trust to wash your greens in.'

The doors opened and the girls entered in silent rows. It was a quarter to seven, the sun not yet visible through the mist yet their white smocks filled the room with light as if a holy presence had surreptitiously arrived. They filed into the pews and sat down, Sister Margaret chivvying a few along a bench with a flap of her hand.

Father Callaghan genuflected, faced the altar and began in a booming voice, '*In nomine Patris, et Filii, et Spiritus Sancti . . .*'

I looked up. The girls were kneeling with their heads bowed, their hands together at their breasts. Their hair was so black, so sleek where it was combed into short plaits. One or two, in the front row, wore little wooden crosses. Before them, on the tiled floor, were copies of their missals bound in black covers with gold Chinese characters embossed upon them.

In this room, I considered, lay my future. I had put Europe behind me, set my sail to the East and here I was, in a heathen land, doing the bidding of my calling. I wanted to feel proud I had made such a sacrifice. I might, I considered, in another age have been one of the ancient ascetics who wandered off into the desert to live as hermits in a life of contemplation. Yet my pride, which I knew was a vanity I should not allow myself, was in any case overcome by my feelings of humility.

I have given myself to God, I thought, surrendered myself to His mercy, to follow His path and bring His blessing to these poor, benighted heathens.

I had forgone the company of my own kind, the security of a parish living in Dublin or Cork, a caring congregation and a fine church, not to mention the chance to attend concerts, wander quietly through the art galleries or the park on a sunny afternoon. Yet what, I considered, had these girls surrendered? Certainly, they had been cast out yet they had gone so much further. They had denied their own gods for my God, had taken to living in the company of foreign devils, of eating their food, relying upon their charity and doing their bidding. Theirs, I considered, was the greater sacrifice and I, for my part, must honour it by giving myself to them.

When they sang the *Gloria*, the musical score was familiar to me but the words were incomprehensible. Father Callaghan had translated them from Latin into Cantonese, another example of the unorthodoxy of which he had warned me. I tried to sing along in Latin but could not so took to humming the tune instead, the words passing in my head.

It was, I thought, like my first day as a child at the brothers' school when I had felt so completely alone, unknowing and afraid.

I remembered what I had done, as a small boy living in a village near Cork. My grandfather had recommended it to me on the morning I had left for school for the first time, riding in a dog-cart driven by Mr O'Hara, the butcher.

'When you're afraid, Stevie,' the old man had said to me, picking bits of pipe tobacco out of his whiskers, 'when you're truly afraid not of the sword or the fist but of the whole world, take my advice and ask for His help. You don't need to pray. No kneelin' and puttin' your palms together. Just look up for a moment and think, "God, will you not help me now I'm so scared?" And he will, Stevie, he will.'

I looked up. The ceiling of the chapel was bare to the rafters. I was, I think, about to ask for help with the incomprehensible *Gloria* when I saw something move. I narrowed my eyes. On one of the beams was what appeared to be a small dragon. I could clearly see its head. It was ten inches long with a broad, flat skull and yellow eyes. As I watched, it shifted onto the side of the beam clinging there with wide-toed feet, its tail hanging down. Its skin was grey with spotted markings which, even in the gloom, were brilliantly scarlet.

Suddenly, it vanished: one second it was there, the next it was not. All thought of Cantonesified Latin, prayer and fear was gone, replaced by a fascination in the creature.

The service continued under Father Callaghan. I played my part when it was required of me. Just as the final words were being spoken, from high in the rafters came a curt shrill call. *Tok-eye*, it went, then repeated itself twice. *Tok-eye! Tok-eye!* It was a penetrating sound like the metallic click of the tin frogs to be found as prizes in stalls at fairgrounds and it made me jump.

Father Callaghan, his back to the congregation, glanced upwards and, noticing my consternation, whispered over his shoulder to me, 'Gecko. Noisy as the devil but they keep the cockroaches down.'

With Mass over and my fast broken, I went around the town on my own, getting used to finding my way about. It was a daily routine that one of us should wander the streets, watching out for those who may need our help, be brought to Christ or just befriended. The sooner I had a grasp of my bearings the sooner I could take my share of the burden of God's calling.

For the whole morning I wandered the streets, mentally noting landmarks by which I might know my specific location in the future until, at about noon, I reached a wide street in which there was a thriving animal market. The stallholders sat on low three-legged stools next to bamboo cages, some shaded by the buildings, others by umbrellas of wax paper.

The first stall I came upon was selling cats: a few were domestic cats but others were larger, spotted leopard-like cats with sleek coats and rounded ears which spat and hissed at the feet of passers-by. In one cage was a palm civet with a black-and-white striped face like a badger's and a long tail which hung out of the bars.

'Buy cat?' asked the vendor hopefully.

I was taken aback at his speaking English: it was the first words I had heard uttered all morning that were not in Cantonese. I should not have been surprised for there were over twenty Europeans living in Wuchow, merchants and their wives, expatriate officers working for Chinese customs authorities and the British Resident: the trader, I assumed, probably sold them pets.

'You speaky English?' I asked.

'Small small.'

I shook my head and replied, 'No buy cat.'

'*Ho sik*! *Ho sik*!' the cat-seller said, smiling broadly. He pointed to the cat and tapped his teeth with an inch-long fingernail.

It was then I realised the cats were on sale not as household pets or the hunters of vermin but as food. I looked down at a tabby in a bamboo basket. It was hunched up, its eyes half closed against the bright sun, its tail curled around its side. It might have been basking in front of a hearth.

Moving on, I passed cages of tusked, bristle-haired wild boar trussed with bamboo thongs, small ginger-pelted deer with short horns crammed into boxes with their forelegs broken to prevent escape, tubs of giant salamanders and golden-shelled turtles, buckets of frogs and leather or canvas sacks tied at the neck. The contents of the latter thrashed and writhed: I guessed they contained snakes. At the end of the street, I came upon two cages erected in the shade. Whereas most were on the ground, these were set up on trestles, protected from the sun by two umbrellas and a length of hessian.

Inside were a dozen monkeys. They sat at the rear of the cages, huddled together, several clutching each other. Every one of them had such a deep human sorrow in its face I was immediately affected. Reaching forward, momentarily forgetting Father Callaghan's warning about hydrophobia, I put a finger through the bars. One of the monkeys stared at it then grasped hold of me. Its own little fingers were like a child's, the palm cold. It was shivering despite the midday heat.

I wanted to buy them all, set them free in the hills and watch them swing into the branches, chattering excitedly at their unexpected liberty. Yet I knew this was impossible. I could not transport them and, besides, it would most likely be only a few days before they were recaptured, imprisoned and waiting once more for a fate of which I believed they were fully conscious.

As I left the animal market, thoroughly depressed and still wondering how I might rescue the primates, I met Father Callaghan in the company of Ah Fong. They were doing their rounds, looking to follow Christ's bidding.

'So how are you finding Wuchow, Father Stephen?' asked Father Callaghan as I joined them.

'Interesting,' I replied thoughtfully.

'But disturbing?'

'Yes,' I allowed.

'It's the strangeness, Father Stephen. You'll become used to it. To the sights and sounds. Oh! And the smells,' he added. 'Not all as unpleasant as your early morning encounter.'

I made no response and he sensed there was more on my mind for, after a few minutes, he touched my arm and said, 'You've seen the animal market.'

'Yes, I have.'

'All for food, you know.'

'Yes,' I repeated.

'You'll come to understand it,' Father Callaghan remarked as we turned a corner. 'It's a cruel, hard world here but that's for the better. If it wasn't we should have no job to do. As for the Chinese, they're good folk. They mean well and they work hard. Industrious and pious in their own way. Respectful of . . .'

He stopped abruptly, took a firm hold of my arm, catching me off-balance and making me stumble. At the same time, he uttered a curt command to Ah Fong who was walking a few steps to our rear.

About a hundred yards down the street was a small crowd listening to a man standing on an up-turned wooden tub. He was tall for a Chinese, with his head half-shaved, his cue hanging down his spine. Around his forehead was wound a red scarf. He waved his arms as he spoke at the top of his voice, his head turning this way and that as he addressed the people before him.

'Well, most of them,' Father Callaghan added as a codicil to his praise and then he pushed me into a doorway. Ah Fong joined us but not quite so precipitously.

'What is it?' I asked.

'Bad man,' Ah Fong said. 'He no good for you, for me.'

'A revolutionary of sorts,' Father Callaghan added. 'And, as Ah Fong rightly says, potential trouble.'

'A revolutionary?' I questioned.

'*I Ho Ch'üan*,' Ah Fong declared.

Father Callaghan was listening intently at the corner of the doorway.

'A Righteous Harmony Fist,' he said.

I was none the wiser but I did not speak. Instead, I listened. The Chinese was clearly a skilled orator, the tone of his voice at one turn haranguing the crowd, at the next cajoling, pleading or reasoning with it. He seemed to be able to talk without pausing to catch his breath, reminding me of one of my fellow noviciates in the seminary who had been able to recite the whole of the *Ordo Missæ* in just the same way, a feat he had performed as a party piece until one of the priests caught him doing it and severely reprimanded him.

'What is he saying?' I enquired after some minutes.

'He is saying,' Father Callaghan replied, 'it is time China was cleansed of the Pale Ghosts. And that, Father Stephen, is the likes of you and me. And when we go, be sure as hell is a hot place, the Holy Ghost'll come with us.'

We slipped from the doorway, making for a narrow passage-way. I glanced in the direction of the orator. His audience had swelled threefold since we had ducked out of sight.

Caution being the better part of valour, we returned to the

mission and, on Father Callaghan's advice, I did not set foot from it again until, early in the evening, I left the gate, walked along the *hutong* and attempted to retrace my steps of the morning. Ah Fong accompanied me, at Father Callaghan's instigation: he would, my superior explained, know what he saw and would steer me safely from trouble.

It was a balmy end to the day. Birds sang in cages hanging from the eaves of the houses or the branches of trees under which their owners sipped tea, smoked and conversed. Although it was not yet dusk, lanterns had been lit in some of the tea-houses and shops, bathing the interiors with soft light as if the air was somehow bending the last of the sun in through the doors.

No one gave me a second glance. Sedan chairs passed by, their small doors or cloth hangings closed against the last of the day, the chair coolies shouting to clear the way of pedestrians. I was eager to see the sights of the city and felt supremely but unjustifiably confident no one would wish to do me harm.

There seemed to be more children playing in the streets than there were during the day. A toddler carrying a colourful paper fish on the end of a stick caused one chair to halt, the coolies bellowing at him and so scaring him that, rather than run, he stood his ground petrified. The child's mother appeared from a doorway, shrieking abuse: when she saw the chair, she was instantly silent, kow-towed and lifted the little boy out of the way.

The games the children played fascinated me. They were quite unlike those of their counterparts in Europe. Here there was no hop-scotch or skipping. Instead of rolling hoops or playing tag, they kicked a feathered shuttlecock into the air with their heels or tossed coins against a wall. On a street corner, a group of older boys squatted in the last of the sunlight coming through a gap in the mountains, playing what Ah Fong informed me was *Hsiang-Ch'I* chess, the white counters embossed with black and red characters.

As we turned into a side street leading to the animal market, we found our way blocked by an angry crowd of some thirty people. I was immediately on edge, fearing an encounter with another of the revolutionaries.

'We go other way?' I asked Ah Fong.

'No. Can go here,' he assured me.

The crowd's ire was not directed at either myself or a revolutionary. Indeed, several people nodded respectfully to me as I went by. To them I made the obligatory return, a slight tilt of the head.

Reaching the front of the crowd I saw a young man squatting against a wall, his face a picture of misery and embarrassment, his clothing shoddy and his feet bare. His hair was not plaited into a cue but hung in dirty clumps from his head, although his crown had been shaved, whilst around his neck was fastened a cangue, a heavy platform of boards through holes in which projected his head and hands. About his ankles were thick iron manacles attached to a short length of chain which would allow him to walk only at a shuffle. Pinned to the upper surface of the cangue was a notice.

'What does it say?' I asked Ah Fong.

'He feef,' reported Ah Fong. 'Take no belong him.'

'How long he stay like this?'

'Long time, master.'

'How long? One week? One month?'

Ah Fong looked in my direction.

'I no know,' he whispered. 'He die.'

'They execute him?' I asked.

'What *ex-ee-koot*?'

'Kill him.'

'No, master. No kill him. People no give him food. He die.' He turned from the sight. 'Come, master. We go. No good stay long time. People no like you look see long time.'

For another hour, as we wandered through the city, I could not cease contemplating the living death I had witnessed. Finally, as the twilight began to deepen, we started back towards the mission.

In the town's main square, a sort-of small circus was performing by the light of pine torches mounted on poles. Their flames burned with a yellow light, sparks falling in showers to the ground. A large gathering had congregated around two acrobats who were leaping into the air, turning cartwheels and prancing about with mock Chinese swords flashing in the light. Peddlers mingled with the crowds selling toys. One had a tray of cup-and-ball games fashioned from wood, another offering ladder puzzles with the steps cut out of polished bone and the strings made of twisted silk yarn. A third displayed carved miniature acrobats, imitations of the real thing nearby, which tumbled head over heels at the turn of a little wheel.

The centre of attraction, however, was a kiosk like a Punch-and-Judy show, the puppets operated by poles rather than strings. One was a mandarin in a fancy costume of red and gold: he appeared to me to be the hero of the pageant. Another was the fair maiden with a pretty costume from the head of which protruded the eye of a peacock feather. There was also a dragon. The theme of the play centred on the dragon wanting the girl for a meal and the mandarin wanting her for a bride. There was much jumping and fighting, to the accompaniment of a small gong and a high-pitched penny-whistle-like instrument played by two young boys at the side of the kiosk.

For fifteen minutes, Ah Fong and I watched the performance, the light of the torches throwing shadows from the puppets and giving the play an added drama. Subsidiary characters appeared – a peasant, a god, a ghost and an old crone – and the action became a little more heated. Suddenly the dragon, which had been on stage throughout the performance, vanished. In its place stood a figure dressed entirely in black with a round, dish-like hat on its head. The mandarin, the fair maiden, the god and the peasant started to shout at the black puppet. The gongs banged more frequently and the music rose an octave and quickened its pace. The black puppet was driven to the very edge of the stage by the peasant which hit it repeatedly on the head with a hoe. He beat it down until it hung over the front of the kiosk, struggling to regain its balance. Around its neck was a white circle and, painted on its front, was a cross. The audience was laughing.

No one had taken the least notice of me, but I suddenly knew I was in danger: then, before I could address this feeling, the gong bashed loudly, the mandarin puppet screamed and the entire gathering fell silent, turned as one and stared at me.

'We go, master,' Ah Fong whispered and touched my sleeve. 'Go now. No good.'

We turned and walked sedately away. I wanted to run but knew I dared not. For a moment, there was no reaction to our departure, then the audience began to shout. Some hurled what were plainly obscenities at Ah Fong who coloured up but ignored them.

'Mus' turn o'er cheek, master,' he said and walked stolidly ahead, not looking either to left or right.

We turned a corner into the Street of Heavenly Happiness and quickened our pace, but the crowd did not follow. I heard the gong begin to strike again and the penny whistles pick up their tune once more.

'I understand from Ah Fong you saw a criminal?' Father Callaghan remarked as we sat later together on the roof of the mission, watching the moon rise and sipping our gin and quinine.

'Yes. A thief, according to Ah Fong.'

'That's right. He was caught stealing a hen. From the house before which he was pilloried.'

'Just a hen?'

'A mere chicken. I saw him this morning. He's not a town-dweller but a countryman. You could tell from his clothes. He's just a hungry peasant. There's a degree of famine in the land. Because of the drought,' he added.

'Ah Fong says he'll starve to death.'

'That's right,' Father Callaghan said. 'Or they might execute him by strangulation.'

'They will hang him?' I asked incredulously.

'No. They'll strangle him by hand with a knotted rope. Only the worst criminals are beheaded. In the eyes of a Chinese, there is no worse fate than to die incomplete, as it were. This is why, when eunuchs leave the emperor's employ, they are given back their genitals which have been stored in special boxes. They may then be buried whole and be men once more in the after-life.'

'It's a barbaric land I have come to,' I said.

'It's a land where Our Lord's as much a stranger as we are,' Father Callaghan said, 'and it's our work to introduce Him to it and the people to His glory and His love.'

Hsiao has his pitch and, indeed, his home opposite the tea-house I occasionally frequent in Prince Edward Road. It is a wide street and the traffic invariably heavy so, unless there is an accident or roadworks, I only see him for a glimpse at a time as the buses and lorries zip by.

The tea-house is a modest establishment. The half a dozen tables are of the small round folding type, each of which can accommodate up to five people without becoming cramped. In the early morning, it is packed with workers on their way to the factories in Sham Shui Po or the offices in Central but when I visit it in late morning it is usually doing a slow trade of old men like myself taking their constitutionals or on their way to a mah-jong game.

There are four urns in the tea-house, each made of polished brass with Chinese characters set upon them in copper. They gleam like the statuary in the gold dealers next door but three: if this were a temple, they would be the most important idols for miles around. One of them hisses from a slight leak: it has done this for as long as I can remember. The air is aromatic with the competing scents of different teas and the counter is stacked with little green, red or yellow cartons and tins of tea.

Nowhere in the tea-house is there a single word of English except upon the tea packets and that is very small. This is one of the reasons I like the place. It is utterly Oriental without so much as the merest hint of the Occidental. One does not find tea-houses in Europe – cafés, bars, cantinas, bistros, coffee-shops and even tea-shops there are, but no tea-houses. This place does not serve little sandwiches or dainty cakes, or the Chinese equivalent thereof. It sells tea to refresh the mind, rejuvenate the body, enliven the parts that are failing and cure the others which are ailing. It is a serious place for thought and health, not gossip and banter.

My tipple is gunpowder tea. The name is not indicative of some punch hidden it in, such as lies in rice wine. It is a raw tea which comes looking like little grey pellets of seventeenth-century gunpowder, hence the name. I like to watch as the water is added to the pot, the pellets swirling and opening slightly, looking like tadpoles: then they quickly spread out into thick, dark leaves and a delicate perfume lifts from the surface. At that point, I put the lid on the pot to keep the heat and flavour in.

The tea is the colour of plasma, a straw-yellow which, when it is warm but not hot, slips down the throat like molten honey. It lifts my spirits and clears my head.

Sitting at the front table, I can see Hsiao. He is a wizened stick of a man with untidy, short grey hair and a pinched look who wears rimless pince-nez which lend his countenance a vaguely professorial appearance. Always dressed in what we term a Mao jacket, for it is like that worn by the arch tyrant of Peking (as Mr Wu calls him), he sits all day long on a stool by his wares at the mouth of an alley which he has made his own.

At the entrance is his stall selling magazines and paperback books. By the pavement the racks, which are nailed to the wall of a tenement, carry copies of *Mad* magazine, *Time* and *Newsweek*, *Life* and *Paris Match*, *Punch* and *Vogue*, *Vanity Fair* and the *New Yorker*, and American comics which retell the classics in abridged, picture form.

When I first discovered Hsiao's pitch, I could not for the life of me see how he could make a living from such publications. This is not an area often visited by Europeans, save those tourists who have lost their way or police officers doing the rounds with their Chinese constables. To understand Hsiao's business success and acumen, one has to quit the pavement and go into the alley.

Next to the international publications of repute, a little further from the street but not too far, are displayed copies of *Playboy* and *Men Only*, some Chinese girlie magazines with the titles or captions carefully placed so as not to offend the eye of passers by and thin pamphlets with plain covers.

I remember very well my first call on Hsiao. Stopping at the rack nearest the pavement, I took down a comic entitled *A Tale of Two Cities*. The front cover showed a colour illustration of Sydney Carton riding in a hay wagon, hand in hand with the little seamstress: across the foot of the page was pasted a sticker in English and Chinese stating 'Air Mail Copy – $5'. From the grimy state of the cover and the faded colour of the label, I deduced it had not recently been flown in, although I was sure five dollars would still be the asking price. I opened the comic at random and read the bubble coming from the mouth of a pretty young woman in a poke bonnet, her blonde tresses showing under the small crown at the back of her head.

'As a wife and mother,' I read aloud, 'I implore you take pity on me, Madame Defarge. Oh, sister-woman, think of me.'

Hsiao left his stool and came to my side, looking up at me over the top of his pince-nez. His spine is curved by years of sitting on the stool in all weathers with nothing against which to rest his back. I am not a tall man any longer but I still tower over him.

'You wan' buy?' he hissed in English.

Looking up from the tragic face of Lucie Manette, I studied Hsiao at close range. His face was not only pinched but hard and I guessed he had not long to live: I was, of course, wrong. He is still going strong, like a buffalo in a paddy-field one thinks must long ago have lost the power to pull a plough through such cloying mud.

'No wan' buy,' I answered.

Before I could replace the comic on the rack, he snatched it from me and, straightening a crease on the cover which I had not made, said curtly, 'No buy, no read.'

I took a few steps down the alleyway and, reaching to the top rack, removed a magazine on the front cover of which were two lines of Chinese characters over the photograph of a naked Chinese girl smiling coyly at the camera, her arms crossed over her chest, which was also partially hidden by a strategically placed price label: a large Ming vase hid her body from her waist down. I opened the magazine at a page depicting two other Chinese girls, their backs to the camera, playing with a bright beach ball. Their bottoms were small, their buttocks clenched.

The old man, having been angered at my fingering the comic, was not so upset at my handling this merchandise.

'Make in Taiwan,' he stated. 'Chinese girl. Guruntee good pikchur. You want B'itish girl? Can do. Also can do Japonese. Black girl okay.'

'Maybe,' I said, more out of curiosity than a desire to

purchase any of his trash, and returned the magazine to its slot on the rack.

'Got more,' Hsiao volunteered, pointing to the rear of the alley. 'You wan' see? No charge.'

I briefly nodded and he led the way down the alley to what any casual observer unused to the ways of Kowloon back-streets would have assumed was a pile of rubbish awaiting collection but which was, in fact – and remains to this day – Hsiao's residence.

He lives in a very large wooden crate which, according to the writing burned into the timber, had been used to transport a German loom from a factory in Stuttgart to another in Tsuen Wan. He has improved upon it by giving it a covering of tar-soaked canvas and fitting to it a heavy door with a brass Chubb padlock which would do credit to a bank vault. The electric light within has been wired to the public street lamp: a tap just by the door provides running water. Behind the crate, at the dead end of the alley, is a cubicle erected from corrugated iron which is Hsiao's personal convenience.

Unlocking the door, he swung it wide, banging it back against the crate wall.

'You go in. I come.'

The interior, in which I had to bow my head but Hsiao did not, was cramped yet surprisingly homely. Against the rear of the crate was a folding bed. Shelves nailed to the walls carried Chinese books, eating and cooking utensils and a few ornaments of the tacky tourist variety. A minuscule table for one stood under a calendar for the Chinese year, a pictorial map of South East Asia cut from a *National Geographic* and a colour portrait photograph of Her Majesty, Queen Elizabeth II in a cheap beaten-tin frame.

'Queen ve'y good,' Hsiao declared, tapping the picture with his knuckle. 'Look Hong Kong good. No Commooneest come if Queen.'

He pulled out a stool and a folding chair, inviting me to sit. I did so as he squatted on the stool and, from under the bed, pulled out three cardboard boxes, flicking on a bulb hanging by a flex from the centre of the ceiling.

'You wan' photo? Book?' he enquired. 'I got good books. Make in Holland. Make in Singapore. Hot stuff!'

Without waiting for my reply, he rummaged in one of the boxes, pulling out a lurid publication, on the cover of which was a totally naked European girl unadorned by price labels or Ming vases. She was bending backwards over a chair and looking between her breasts at the camera. Her legs were spread apart, one of her hands resting inside her thigh.

'Dis a good one. Ve'y popular. Plenty people buy. Fifty dollar. But for you,' Hsiao paused as if doing some mental arithmetic, 'thirty-five dollar.'

'I don't think so,' I replied.

'Okay. No sweat,' he answered lightly, undeterred by my negativity. 'Got more.'

From another box, he took out a thicker book, handing it to me. The photographs were interspersed with text printed in German. The early pages carried a series of photographs of a fornicating couple: after page twenty they were joined by another woman dressed in a military uniform.

'Come f'om Germany. Very good. Good pikchur.' He took the book back and flicked through the pages with his thumb. 'All colour pik-chur. No black-an'-white. Good story. Forty dollar for you. First sale for today. Good p'ice.'

'I don't want anything,' I said in Cantonese.

Hsiao was immediately cautious. My speaking Cantonese was what put him on his guard: I was no idle, elderly tourist but a *gweilo*.

'You policeman?'

I laughed briefly and, reverting to English to put him at his ease, said, 'I look like a *chaai yan*?'

'No . . .' he replied pensively, then added, 'What you wan'?'

'Nothing.'

He became cross with me, annoyed I had apparently wasted his time and he was not going to make a sale.

'So! You *chun chu*! Stupid man! Like pig!'

He began to wave his arms about.

'Okay! You go. No buy, no come.'

I rose to my feet and left the crate. He followed me to the street, muttering and swearing in Cantonese. As I reached the pavement, I suddenly stopped and removed a copy of *Time* from the rack.

I turned round. Hsiao halted dead in his tracks: he reminded me of a dog that is brave when its quarry retreats but unsure of itself when confronted.

'*Kei toh*?' I asked.

'*Sze mun*,' he snapped.

I gave him four dollars, crossed the road, entered the tea-house and, sitting down, ordered a pot of gunpowder tea and read the magazine. Every so often, looking up, I saw him watching me.

Sometimes now, he looks out for me. When I pass his stall, he greets me and I buy a magazine from him about once a month. He also continues to study me from across the street. When I have read the magazine over my tea I always leave it on the table and I am told by the waiter that, as soon as I have disappeared, Hsiao scuttles through the traffic and takes it back again for resale. He has not told me this, but I know the waiter occasionally charges him a dollar for the buy-back which he begrudgingly pays.

At the moment, Hsiao is not glancing in my direction. He is sewing. Across his knees is a pair of trousers in which he appears to be repairing a rent. Possibly a previously undiscovered nail in the crate has snagged his clothing.

I feel sorry for Hsiao. Not in a moralistic sense. I declare no interest whatsoever in his soul. My days of worrying over another man's place in the immortal kingdom – heaven, nirvana, Zion, paradise or whatever – are long since ended. If he wishes to make his living purveying pictures of copulating couples and girls with their buttocks taut with embarrassment I care not a jot.

My sympathy for him is beyond definition. Perhaps it is his crate home that causes me to feel something for him, or his utterly hopeless situation, for he will never rise out of it. Pornographers make big money but their salesmen remain poor. It is the same in any business. As Americans say, the bosses strike rich and the bums strike out.

Perhaps I should have befriended him, my sympathy not for him but for myself for not doing so, for losing the opportunity of knowing another man whose friendship might have amused me.

The message reached me this morning just before eight o'clock. I have no idea who delivered it – as, indeed, I never have on these occasions – but it was contained in an envelope upon which was written the words *By Hand* in that particular cursive script taught as standard in Chinese schools. Above this was printed *Golden Phoenix Film Production Co. (HK) Ltd.* and the company's address some ten minutes' walk from my home. I slit the envelope open with my finger. The sheet of paper within was crisp and headed *Golden Phoenix Films*: *from the Desk of Desmond Tan*.

I have known Desmond Tan for four years. He is a would be mogul in the movie world, his dream to be the equal of Run Run Shaw, with his own studios in the New Territories, a gold-painted Rolls Royce and a house in the countryside overlooking the sea. Whenever we meet, he tells me he is one step nearer to fame and fortune: always a little step, he assures me, but he qualifies this by saying that babies take little steps to practise for the bigger ones of adulthood.

The truth of the matter is he will never be the tycoon he wishes for he does not think big. Roughly translated, for much nuance and imagery is lost in the transposition from one language to another, there is an old Chinese saying: the sparrow would be an eagle but he does not stretch his wings.

Desmond is a sparrow. He picks up the crumbs from the rich men's tables. He does not produce films, nor does he direct them: he would like to, of course, but that takes talent, capital, ambition and vision. He lacks three of these seminal necessities. Instead of producing films, he dubs them. He is what is known in the parlance of his trade a facilities house, which is to say a pretty low but essential bird in the pecking order. In short, a sparrow.

I like him for he is a man not unlike myself, one who dreams. He has no real vision, and I have lost mine, so that sets us together. He takes life as it comes, harms no one deliberately or not, at least, maliciously and has a sense of justice. That is rare.

The note read,

Dear Stephen,
 I am able to offer you some work today.
Can you be ready at ten o'clock for the rest of the day? Usual
rate but with overtime because no time to stop for lunch.
Sanwitchs will be provided with tea and beer if you prefer.
 If you can not come, let me know on receetp of this note.
Otherwise, see you at ten o'clock.

It was signed, *Your buddie, Desmond Tan.* His signature is large and full of flourishes: at least he has developed the handwriting for the job.

His studio, which is to grace the establishment with a grander word than it deserves, is on the seventh floor of a fairly modern tenement building in Mong Kok. It was intended as a light industrial factory unit but Desmond has reconstructed it as the start of his movie-making empire.

The entrance is through a glass door into which has been etched the name of the company under a stylised phoenix rising from flames and flecked with gold dust. Beyond this is a square of red carpet (with another phoenix woven into it) and a polished plywood desk which looks as if it was designed by the same person who made Sam's bar counter. Behind this sits the receptionist, a pretty Chinese girl who obviously shares Desmond's dream of making it big in the movies one day for she keeps her hair trimmed and cut in what she deems to be the latest Hollywood fashion (this month her mentor appears to be Doris Day) and makes sure her blouse is tight enough for even a casual observer to notice the curve of the top of her exceedingly small breasts. Her name is Audrey, after Hepburn.

I pushed open the door and stepped across the carpet. Audrey looked up and smiled at me as if I might be coming to offer her a first-class Pan-Am ticket to Los Angeles, Sunset Boulevard and stardom.

'Morning, sir,' she greeted me. 'Goo' to see you again, sir.'

She has developed a sort of American vocabulary and accent which makes her hard to understand in a sustained conversation. Earlier this year, I was present when an American producer, in Hong Kong to make a film on location, visited Desmond to discuss using his studio to look at unedited film. In what he believed to be Hollywood style, Desmond had laid on rather good quality *sanwitchs* and, from a friend in the hotel trade, had borrowed a cocktail waiter. I was asked to attend to lend, in Desmond's words, an air of sophisticated internationality to his business: in other words, I was to stand around, pretend I was one of his partners or a man of greater stature than I am in the world, and make small talk to the American's assistant. For this, I was paid $280.

All went well at first. The American was impressed by Desmond's equipment and apparent knowledge of operating it; the viewing studio was comfortable; the studio seemed efficient and, by Los Angeles standards, was not far from the producer's hotel. I made small talk with the producer's aide, a somewhat delicate young man in a lilac shirt and a pair of denim jeans that fitted him like a glove and had been permanently creased. At a lull in the conversation, one of those silences that occurs every now and then when more than four people are talking together, Audrey saw her chance.

'Yall seen *Solijer of Forchoon*?' she piped up. 'Weal goot moowie. Cluck Gabul an' Soosun Haywoot. Soosun Haywoot weal goot actwess. You guys mus' see it.'

There was a stunned silence. The American producer stared at Audrey. So did his fey assistant. So did Desmond but whereas the others were somewhat bemused, he was plainly unamused. Audrey smiled delicately at the Americans then caught Desmond's eye and scuttled from the room.

'She one of your staff?' the American enquired.

'She make the tea,' Desmond lied.

The two Americans exchanged glances.

'She is a school girl,' I chipped in, hoping I was lying convincingly: it has never been part of my repertoire. I am truthful to the point of bluntness and generally don't give a damn what I say.

'School student?' the aide asked.

'Yes,' I said. 'We employ her when she has time off. To help her improve her English.'

'Been here long?' the producer wanted to know.

'Six month,' said Desmond.

126

'She's finding the language hard then,' the American observed and sipped at his cocktail.

Desmond was awarded the contract and, for eight weeks, his studio was one step nearer to the back lot of Metro-Goldwyn-Mayer and he was half an inch nearer his Rolls Royce.

'Morning, Audrey,' I replied, adding, 'which door today?'

'Stoo-dio B,' she said, pointing down to the left. 'They waiting for you.'

I could not get lost in Desmond's establishment for there is only one corridor and two studio suites, A and B. The light outside the door to A glowed red meaning a film was being worked upon inside. The light by the door to B was green. I pulled on the handle and entered the sound lock between the corridor and the studio. Through a glass pane in the door I could see Desmond and several other people standing together.

'Hi, Stephen,' he welcomed me as I entered, the door closing on a wheezing hydraulic hinge.

We shook hands. Desmond is tall for a Chinese, nearly six foot, and he always wears a pin-stripe suit, which gives him the illusion of being taller still. On his right wrist he has a gold-link bracelet, partly because this gives him a sense of status when in the company of other Chinese, indicating he is wealthy, and partly because the American producer wore one. He has a jade-and-gold ring on the little finger of his left hand for the same reason.

There were four other people present. One was a European woman in a tight black skirt and white blouse, two were European men in their twenties whom I took to be soldiers from one of the barracks earning a bit on the side and the fourth was a short, dapper Chinese man in a tweed jacket.

'Everybody. This is Stephen,' Desmond introduced me adding in his best Hollywoodese. 'He's an old pro at the dub game.'

I smiled distantly and we all exchanged nods.

Desmond left the studio and the European woman began to talk to me. I felt she believed she was obligated to do so, my being the last to arrive and not yet an integral member of the group. In this respect she was like those spinster women who linger at parochial church functions, eager to see no one is left without a cup of tea and a bun.

'Hello, I'm Barbara,' she said. 'So you've done this before?'

'Yes,' I told her, 'many times.'

'It's my first,' she confided. 'I'm a little nervous.'

'There's no need to be,' I reassured her, 'if you keep your wits about you.'

'I don't mean just the dubbing. It's – well, not the usual thing, is it? I am, I admit, beginning to have second thoughts.'

'The usual thing?' I replied.

'Well, the sort of thing . . . This is Hong Kong. As soon as my name appears in the credits . . . Bang goes invitations to Government House, for a start.'

She glanced at me for a moment, her eye running me up and down. I was wearing an old padded *sam* and she was nonplussed at seeing a European in semi-Chinese attire.

'Then don't use your real name,' I said. 'I seldom put my name on the films I dub. I use a fictitious one. A pseudonym. Sometimes, I am Peter Hansard, sometimes Bruce Carter, at other times Raymond Leung. What does it matter? I get paid.'

'But,' she began, then she paused.

'But?' I asked.

'Well, forgive me but you are a . . . I don't mean to be nasty, but you aren't one of us, are you? I mean, you've,' she paused and was plainly embarrassed but knew she had to finish her statement, 'rather – how can I say this? – gone native.'

I laughed and this put her a little at her ease. I think she was expecting me to be either angry or distantly aloof.

'I can assure you,' I said, 'I am one of you. More or less. You're English and I'm Irish but that's the extent of our differences, gender apart. As for going native . . . Well, my dear, I have lived in China since the early summer of 1900 and I have not once, as you would put it, gone home. Indeed, China is my home.'

She stared at me almost in disbelief and asked, 'Have you never wanted to?'

'Not once,' I confirmed and it is the truth. 'I came out here leaving nothing behind me and I have stayed.'

'But how have you made a living?'

'This and that. Buying a little, selling a little. I taught

English for many years, teach Cantonese and I dub Desmond's movies. I am, I admit, quite immodestly, a dab hand at kung fu fighting ones.'

'Were you in the forces when you came out?' she enquired. 'In 1900, I mean.'

'No,' I answered, relishing what was coming next, 'I was a Roman Catholic missionary.'

The look on her face was one of shock, her hand even going halfway up to her mouth. She may well have been the heroine of one of Desmond's corny romance films.

Just then, Desmond returned, clapped his hands and Audrey appeared carrying a pile of cardboard folders, handing us one each. She smiled sweetly at her boss and I wondered, just for a fleeting moment, if she was sleeping with him in the true Hollywood manner: I would not have been surprised. They might both have been practising for the future.

'Today just first twenty-six pages. Fifteen-minute read then we make a run-through. Each person marked for them,' Desmond declared officiously and he left, tailed by Audrey.

I sat on one of the tall stools in the centre of the room and pulled the reading shelf projecting upwards from one of the legs round in front of me, latching it in place with a little brass bolt. I placed the folder on the shelf and peered at it. On the cover was typed *Lord Yuan and The Merciful Lady*. I opened it, removed the script and began to read the outline.

The story was not out of the ordinary. Lord Yuan wanted to marry Lily Flower but she was betrothed to Hwang, an evil war-lord. She planned to elope with Lord Yuan and wed him in the mountains, where he had been forced to live in a fortress cave ever since Hwang had killed his father and usurped his lands. Hwang heard of Lily Flower's plan and kidnapped her. He was now holding her in his impregnable castle on the plains. Lord Yuan was bent on recovering his lands, eradicating the evil Hwang and marrying his true love. Where the Merciful Lady came into it I could not tell as we did not have pages relevant to her part but I am sure it was she who aided Lord Yuan in getting into Hwang's base, guiding him to Hwang's chambers, having drugged the guards either with a potion or with magic. Hwang, of course, would be awake being too strong or too evil to be affected by the poison or the spell.

I was to play two parts: an Old Sage who was Lord Yuan's adviser and Leaping K'uo, a character into which the Old Sage metamorphosed for a few minutes at a time when he touched a magic jewel he kept in a pouch around his neck.

My reading done, I sat and looked about the studio as a technician entered and began to position microphones, adjusted reading lamps on poles and placed vertical sheets of black cardboard here and there to deaden echoes.

Each dubbing suite is divided into two, the recording studio and the control room, separated by a double-glazed window. The walls are painted black but, here and there, the paint is peeling to display the last colour scheme, which seems to have been brilliant yellow. The ceiling is also painted black and is lined with an acoustic material consisting of irregular peaks and troughs of foam rubber. The floor is covered in a thick carpet which is worn threadbare by the door. The viewing screen is like those one sees in lecture theatres, mounted on the wall and capable of being rolled away into an oblong box.

Through the soundproof window I could see Desmond sitting at a table in the control room with Audrey standing behind him. He was reading and she was gazing vacantly into space. Two technicians, dressed in trousers and vests, busied themselves with a projector and a console of knobs and meters.

'All Okay?' came Desmond's voice through a crackling loudspeaker somewhere behind the screen.

We all nodded except for Barbara, who smiled nervously at me and whispered, 'I'm Peach Flower. The girl warrior in Lord Yuan's band.'

'Don't worry,' I answered. 'Next time, you may well be Lily Flower or the Merciful Lady.'

'I'm not sure I can do this,' she said quietly.

'You'll be all right,' I said. 'Just follow the counter on the film and relate your speeches to the character on the screen. You don't have to be too exact. Just so long as you don't speak when your character's mouth is shut.' She seemed unconvinced, so I added, 'This isn't Shakespeare, you know.'

She smiled wanly, the ceiling lights dimmed, the reading lamps came on and the film began to roll. Upon the screen appeared a number of warriors in seventeenth-century costume. Lord Yuan was young and handsome, Peach Flower young and beautiful, the five followers young and strong and the Old Sage wrinkled and hunch-backed. He was dressed in what looked like old military blankets and carried a staff: for a moment, I had a fleeting vision of Quasimodo, the honey-cart operator. Peach Flower wore baggy trousers, a tight bodice and had a sash tied around her head.

The action in the film consisted of brief bursts of conversation, followed by long, intense fights with Hwang's henchmen in which Peach Flower killed up to four men with one swing of her sword, Lord Yuan fought with two different types of weapon, one in each hand, and the Old Sage either grunted and ducked or metamorphosed and leapt over trees with his staff flailing. The dialogue consisted mostly of shouts of warning, curt commands and short lines of explanation to keep the plot, such as it was, evolving. One of my lines, addressed to a Hwang bandit, was *'Where is the Lady Lily Flower?'* to which he replied *'In my lord's castle, safe from the hands of scum like you'* which was the only indication to the audience as to where the maiden was being held.

As is usually the case, I became involved in this puerile story. For three hours, apart from a twenty-minute interlude for Coca Cola and *sanwitchs*, I was the Old Sage and Leaping K'uo. I delivered my lines and saw myself not as an aged man on a stool before a microphone but as an ancient hero combating injustice and righting wrongs three hundred years old. When the work was done, the final dub made and the lights switched on once more, I felt exhausted as if I had not been the voice of the actor but the body as well. I might have done all that metamorphosing, leaping and staff-play, I was so tired.

As I left the building Barbara called out, walking quickly to catch up with me.

'Would you like a cup of tea?' she asked.

'I'm afraid I can't,' I lied. 'I've another appointment.'

I did not want to be with her. It was not a matter of dislike, just wanting to be on my own.

'I hope I didn't hurt your feelings,' she said. 'About going native and so on. It was impertinent of me and I'm sorry.'

'No, you did not hurt me,' I replied to put her at her ease. 'And your apology is not required. I'm not bothered by what you or anyone else might think of me. I am what I am.'

I carried on down the street thinking she might leave me but she kept up.

'May I ask you something?' she requested.

I nodded.

'In his office, I caught a glimpse of some pictures from one of Mr Tan's other films. They were quite,' she searched for an appropriate phrase, 'rude.'

'He does blue movies,' I confirmed.

'And do you – I mean, do you dub those, too?'

'Sometimes,' I admitted.

She thought for a moment then went on, 'The fighting films with mythological sorcerers and lords and so on I can understand but how can you, as a missionary – a priest – justify dubbing such immoral – such . . .?'

'Pornography?' I suggested. 'Quite easily. First, I'm not a retired priest. I'm a former priest. There is a distinct difference. You see, I gave up my vows. Second, I don't see such a film as either moral or immoral. If anything, it's beyond morality. A mere sequence of pictures to give pleasure to others. The pleasure may be dubious, but it is not for me to judge. Indeed, I'm not one to judge any man.'

'I do not understand,' she began but I cut her short. I had no intention of standing in a busy street justifying myself even to someone who had attempted to show me a kindness after inadvertently speaking their thoughts.

'To be a judge, one must be above others. I'm not. Even you consider me below you. An old man gone native. And I am below you. I'm on the lower levels of humanity but I do not worry about it. It's a condition in life to which I promoted – perhaps demoted might be more apt – myself and where I'm quite happy. As for morality, I don't believe in it. It's a man-made set of judgements, fashioned by each society to validate its own actions.'

'Surely morality comes from God?' she submitted.

'God,' I told her, 'is the most immoral of all. Or amoral, depending upon your point of view. And before you ask me why, I shall tell you. Because he disregards his creations.'

A coolie came between us pushing a low hand-cart on rattling metal wheels. Upon it was a cylindrical wicker basket containing a live pig. Its ears and curling tail stuck out through the wickerwork against which its snout was pressed: the animal's feet were folded up under its belly and tied in place.

'You see,' I pointed out as the man passed with his load and we were able to move together again, 'even pigs are abandoned by their gods.'

'Shall I see you again?' Barbara inquired as we arrived at the bus stop.

'I am sure you will,' I replied, holding out my hand and shaking hers. 'Desmond will be calling upon our services again. And quite soon. We've yet to reach the Merciful Lady, who may well be you. So practise another voice before then.'

She smiled and hailed a taxi.

'Can I give you a lift?' she asked as a red Mercedes Benz slid to the curb.

'I shall take the bus,' I said, 'but thank you.'

The rear door of the taxi sprang open on the automatic lever operated by the driver and Barbara got in. I heard her tell the driver to go to the Star Ferry. As it drove off, I could see her glancing at me through the rear window. She was plainly puzzled. I was, for her, another enigmatic and paradoxical aspect of life in the Orient and would, I knew for certain, be the subject of cocktail party conversation before the week was out.

Now, back in my flat in the evening twilight, the glare of the street lights slicing through the venetian blinds and the last of the day glowing in the sky, the drone of traffic and voices in the street, I feel somehow disembodied as if I have returned from another life, where I was not old and moving towards death but old and in command of that magic gemstone.

I look around my room, my cell in the middle of the twentieth century and wonder what the Old Sage's corner of the fortress cave looked like. And I think how, when I was young, vibrant and eager like Lord Yuan and Leaping K'uo, like Luo the swordsman and

Gong-sun the fire-master, I saw people like them. Not characters on a screen or actors on a stage but real, walking the streets.

I glance up at the bookshelves, at the thin black leather-bound notebook near the end which I never touch. As if I am outside myself, an actor escaped from Desmond's studio and alive in my flat, I rise from my chair, moving it to the bookshelves. Balancing upon it, I reach up and take hold of the book. It is jammed tightly between the others as if it does not want me to take it down. I pull a little harder and it suddenly gives way as if it has lost its grip upon its companions. I sit at the table and, not opening it, look at it in my hands.

The black leather is blotched by damp and mould: the spine is split where the leather has become brittle. I have never attempted to repair it just as I have never put an annual coating of dubbin on the leather to keep it supple: the Oriental climate is unkind to books.

I cannot account for my actions. There is no need for me to remove it from its place.

I open it at random.

The page is for a day in the early summer of my first year out East. The exact day is of no concern. The first part of the entry reads simply: *Vy. hot. Sun high and glaring. Air dry, no humidity. Town swelters. No cloud. Drought severe. Will rain come? The land and people need it.* That is all. Two dozen words with no narrative. A telegrammatic statement best written on a postcard sent to an ageing aunt. Anyone reading this would judge nothing from it. Yet I remember it all so well.

I had, I recall, written my entry in the early afternoon and was lightly snoozing, dressed only in baggy Chinese trousers. The sun beat down on the roof and the air was sultry and oppressive. The heat made me lethargic, causing my eyes to grow heavy and my back ache. The entry on the page was as banal as the day was acheronian.

It was one of those fulcrums in time upon which my life tottered before swinging the way it has. It was one of the days which began to shape me.

The sun was just touching the hills when Father Callaghan and I settled into our sedan chairs to set off through the town in the direction of the Li Kiang. Although it was not customary, I left my chair open, confident that no passers by could see in for the shadows were deepening.

Proceeding down a narrow street, we came upon a group of some forty people standing silently before the wooden façade of a building. Father Callaghan's chair continued past but my bearers halted, lowering my chair to the ground. The one in front started to gesticulate and I, assuming he wanted me to dismount, began to clamber out. This greatly agitated him and, muttering what might have been curses, he thrust me roughly back into my seat, tearing the curtain across. He muttered something again under his breath, the chair rose and we set off once more.

Needless to say, I was curious to see what it was the bearer would rather I did not and, as we passed the gathering, slowed to less than walking pace by the crush, I reached forward to edge the curtain aside.

Before the semi-circle of people was a tall, T-shaped perch, upon which balanced a common monkey with greyish fur, a pink face and staring eyes of the same species I had observed in the animal market. Beside it stood what I took to be the owner. He was a sturdy young man, his head wrapped in a flaming red turban which held his cue in place, coiled like a ship's rope upon his crown. Red ribbons were tied around his bare ankles and wrists and around his waist was a brilliant red sash, all the brighter for being set against the white cloth of his jacket. In his hands he nonchalantly swung a curved sword which reminded me of a paper-knife owned by the priest in charge of noviciates in the Dublin seminary I had attended: there, however, the similarity ended for Father Ciano's knife was so blunt he had to slash at envelopes whilst this weapon was razored so finely I could almost feel its sharpness upon my flesh.

The monkey was dressed in clothing as well. At first, I did not take these in but then realised its garb was an approximation of a European suit, with a jacket, trousers and waistcoat.

As I watched, the young man flung back his head and bellowed a single word into the sky: I could not understand it yet I knew it to be terrible. His lips contorted like those of a snarling cur, his eyes wide and empty. Then, with a movement so lithe he could have learned it in a dancing academy, he spun on his heels and sliced the monkey's head off as neatly as a man picking off the top of a boiled egg. The little body remained for a few seconds upright on the perch, blood fountaining from its shoulders: then it dropped to the ground. The head smashed against a nearby wall.

The crowd made no move nor did a sound rise from it. I let the curtain drop, my hand shaking and my cheeks turning cold with the drainage of blood. The chair gathered speed as the bearers worked clear of the crowd.

At the river bank, my chair was lowered to the ground and I joined Father Callaghan already seated in a sampan. A woman in a broad rattan hat started to row us across the river, standing up to work a pair of long oars projecting over the sides near the stern. Towards the centre of the river, she began to row harder and I recalled with a chill running down my back the sight of the drowning man. We were not a hundred yards from the point where he was sucked under.

'You'd not be thinking of dragons, would you, Father Stephen?' Father Callaghan asked.

'Yes,' I admitted, 'in part, I would.'

'Well, you need not,' he replied. 'We've the good Lord looking down upon us and if His efficacy isn't sufficient, which I'm sure it is, we've this good lady's little god to guard us, too.'

He nodded towards the prow of the sampan where, tucked under the gunwale, was a shrine no bigger than a pocket missal containing a wooden idol painted in red and gold and some little paper flags.

'I'd say that was blasphemous, Father,' I remarked.

'What is?'

'Saying if the Lord Jesus doesn't do a good enough job then that little effigy will do the rest.'

Father Callaghan laughed and said, 'Father Stephen, I'm sure the Lord knows when I'm joking and when I'm serious. Regardless of what monsignors and cardinals might tell us, I'm sure God has as good a sense of humour as the rest of us.'

I wanted to mention what I had witnessed in the town but felt I could not for, somehow, the sight was an intensely personal one. I believed – I cannot say why – fate had deliberately staged the murder of the little primate so I might understand something of which I was still ignorant, something about China, the Chinese and, maybe, also about myself.

On the far bank another pair of chairs was waiting which took us up the hill to the British Resident's house, our names being called out by the bearers as we passed the sentry at the gate, who made a curt response. I saw the guard was not a British soldier but a Chinese wearing felt slippers, puttees, baggy trousers and a wide waistband under an embroidered jacket. He held a carbine to his side and stood to attention.

The building was a large stone bungalow with a veranda running all the way round it, its walls painted imperial yellow with scarlet footings. The gardens were neat with trimmed bushes, paper lanterns hanging from the trees. A light breeze, rising from the town, swayed them gently. From the veranda, a European man in his mid-thirties appeared, walking towards us as we alighted from the chairs.

'Fathers! Good evening!' he said, extending his hand. 'And how are you, Father Michael?'

'Tolerable, tolerable,' said Father Callaghan.

'And so you are Father Stephen,' the European went on turning to me. 'Robert Morrisby, I'm the Resident. And I'll bet,' he continued as we shook hands, 'you're already known as *See Faat Han*. That'll be the nearest in Cantonese I think they can get.'

'I am,' I replied, 'and I have been apprised of the meaning.'

Morrisby laughed and gave my hand a final shake.

'A sign of respect, Father. Endearment. I always say, never trust a schoolmaster who doesn't have a nickname, eh? No moniker, no character. Now, come and join the others. We're not a large community in Wuchow, Father Stephen. Indeed, you see half of our number before you.'

Upon the veranda, sitting under a string of lanterns, were a dozen Europeans, only three of the assembly being women. Some of the men stood in a group looking out over the garden whilst the women, dressed in long skirts and blouses, with lace collars and cuffs, sat together. A Chinese servant in black trousers and a white jacket handed me a drink. I knew before putting it to my lips it would be the same gin and quinine concoction Father Callaghan and I drank each evening.

'Sit next to us, Father,' one of the women said, beckoning to me. 'I am Mrs Elizabeth Tremlett – but do call me Betty. And this,' her hand waved over her compatriots, 'is Mrs Harriet Blair and Miss Alice Trowell.'

Looking from one to other, I took in the details of each as I remembered, a little balefully, the warning I had received from Father Piazzoli, the Vicar Apostolic in Hong Kong. The night before I set sail in the *Lucky Moon*, he had taken me aside in his house and, after praying with me for a short while, gave me several pieces of advice.

'Remember, my son,' he had said in his rich Italian accent, his hand upon my shoulder, his full beard twitching as he spoke, 'three important things in China. First: take care of your feet. There is much walking to do in China, in the path of Jesus Christ. If your feet are hot they will grow big and sore. Keep them cool. Second: take care of your soul. There are many temptations in China for a young man. Our greatest enemy, Satan himself, works his black wonders there on the most staunch of souls. And third: beware of colonial women. I do not mean this in a carnal sense. But you should know they are like society ladies where there is no society. They will commandeer you. A priest is of fascination to them.' He rubbed his long nose. 'Why, I cannot tell. It is a mystery God has not yet shown to me.'

Mrs Tremlett was a small woman with the angled features of a bird. Her chin and nose were sharp, her eyes small and porcine and her hands, where they projected from the lace of her cuff, thin-fingered and active. On the other extreme, Mrs Blair was a formidable and buxom woman, broad-hipped and looking better suited to a shooting party in the English countryside than a sundown party in the wilds of the Orient, whilst Miss Trowell was petite and delicate yet singularly unattractive. Indeed, all three of them held little I felt would have encouraged carnal desire in any man: were I not celibate, I was sure I should not have been tempted by any one of them and would rather have talked to the men than associated with what I was afraid might be mindless prattle, yet convention controlled me and, heedful of the Vicar Apostolic's warning, I joined them.

'You are the new Catholic father,' Mrs Blair remarked unnecessarily, adding to my first introduction, 'Mrs Tremlett's husband is a merchant here in Wuchow whilst my husband is in the Chinese Customs Service.'

'And I am Betty's sister,' Miss Trowell chipped in. 'I'm on my way to Japan. To be married.'

Mrs Tremlett frowned at her sister and said, 'I am sure the Father is not at all interested in that, my dear.' She turned to me. 'Her beau is a missionary in Honshu. A Protestant, I fear, Father . . .' She was clearly embarrassed to make this declaration and, taking her glass from the table beside her to cover her discomfort, went on, 'But enough of that! Now, you must tell us all about what is going on in the big, wide world. We are quite out of touch here.'

'I'm afraid,' I responded, 'I know as little as you. I'm not one for reading the newspapers.'

'You priests are too unwordly, Father,' declared Mrs Tremlett, straightening her back and rearranging a cushion in her chair. 'So! You will have to entertain us. But first, did you see the criminal near the ferry?'

'I saw a man in red and white with a monkey,' I said.

'That was a Boxer,' Mrs Blair informed me. 'Just a trouble-maker. I think what we are referring to is the man in the cangue. A nasty piece of work. Dirty as the soles of your shoes. You know,' she continued, 'I feel we should still treat our criminals so. It's no use imprisoning them. A drain on the exchequer. We should bring back the village stocks. I'm sure it would be cheaper and more effective.'

'The criminal in the cangue,' I said quietly, 'I saw near the animal market. He is going to die.'

'No, no. That board thing they put on him doesn't kill him,' Mrs Blair interrupted. 'It merely hampers him.'

'He cannot feed himself,' I said patiently, putting on my best priestly tone, 'and the people will not feed him. He will die of starvation.'

The three women exchanged glances.

'I'm sure you can't be right, Father,' said Mrs Tremlett.

'I assure you I am,' I answered and there was a long pause.

'Do you know,' said Mrs Blair, changing the subject, 'what the Chinese call Bruce?'

'Who is Bruce?' I asked.

'Bruce is my Jack Russell terrier,' Mrs Blair informed me. 'I had him sent out from England.' Her voice softened. 'He's such a jolly little chap! Anyway,' her tone became brusque, 'do you know what they call him? They call him a rat. Because he's small, you see,' she went on as if an explanation was needed. 'They don't seem to grasp the fact that anything other than their damnable Esquimaux chow-chows can be a real dog.'

After a quarter of an hour of listening to almost continuous feminine babble, I excused myself and stood on my own at the edge of the veranda. The last of the day's light was pencilled along the mountains, a bat flying silently in and out of the lanterns, picking off insects attracted to the flames.

'Father Stephen?'

I turned to discover an elderly man in a black suit with a pair of bifocals pinned to his nose.

'Arthur Doble,' the man said, offering me his hand. 'I'm a merchant here in Wuchow.' He cast a quick glance at the women. 'You seem to have mercifully escaped the tirades of banality.'

'That I have,' I agreed, 'and feel I've done my Christian duty by them.'

'Forgive my lack of charity, but I'm sure Our Lord would consider five minutes with the ladies to be sufficient penance for all but the most heinous of sins.' He looked through the trees and suggested, 'Shall we take a walk? The Resident has a fine garden and the view can be quite beautiful on a calm evening such as this.'

We set off through the bungalow grounds, passing neatly manicured bushes and stately trees.

'A pity you can't grow real grass in China,' Doble remarked

as we went by an area of beaten earth in the centre of which was a boulder, the crannies planted with miniature trees, giving the appearance of a mountain in classical Chinese paintings. 'I do so miss lawns. And croquet. One cannot play croquet on earth. Or anything except that game of French bowls and horseshoe throwing. But where can one get a horseshoe in southern China?'

'Perhaps,' I suggested, 'Mrs Blair could be persuaded to import some with her next pet, perhaps?'

Doble laughed and said, 'You've a wicked mind, Father. A devious, wicked mind!'

At the end of the garden, we reached a steep drop to the river at the top of which was a small pavilion. We entered it to look across at the town on the opposite bank.

'China's a fascinating land,' Doble said, sipping at his gin. 'Just look at that.'

The town was a mass of pinpricks of lantern light, the haze in the warm air making them glitter and wink. Smoke rose in vertical columns, not disseminating for perhaps a hundred feet. The occasional call of street traders and the buzz of human commerce drifted over the river to us whilst far out in the dark mid-stream bobbed fishing lanterns.

'That's a scene unchanged for a thousand years,' Doble remarked. 'Perhaps two. Who can tell? But it will change. Oh, yes, it will all change.' There was a sadness in his voice. 'The railways and steamboats will alter it irretrievably. We shall change it, the pale ghosts from the west. And it is our job – yours and mine – to see change is done in a Christian way, the barbarism of the Orient replaced by the Love of God.'

I nodded and looked up the Li Kiang to the flower boats moored upstream from the cargo sampans and barges and thought again of the drowned man.

'I love China,' Doble said, interrupting my thoughts. 'Been out here for twenty-two years next month. Traded first in silk then shifted to tea, cotton and porcelain. Dabbled in opium.'

I looked at his face. He was gazing down on the town but I could tell he was not seeing it. Like a man making a confession, his thoughts were far away in the history of his life, of his sins and sinning.

'That was long ago,' he went on. 'Bought it in India, sold it in Whampoa. Had a little godown there in partnership with a Scotsman. Sold some of it back to London. Medicinal purposes. Useful to promote the literature of our land. Ah,' he paused, 'I apologise, Father. You're Irish. I mean, of my land.'

'Promote literature?' I asked, wondering if he used the profits from his opium trading to patronise writers.

'Oh, yes. Keats, Shelley, Coleridge, Wilkie Collins. All took laudanum. All had the dreams that made good writing. Xanadu where Kublai Khan his stately pleasure domes decreed is not in China, it is in the misty countryside of the narcotic.'

'Do you take opium yourself?' I ventured.

'Not the done thing, Father,' he said quickly. '*Gweilos* do not imbibe of native vices. Yet, as you are a priest, I confess to you that I do, from time to time. But you are beholden to keeping the secret. Oath of the confessional, or whatever it is called. I am not, Father, a Catholic.'

I laughed to put him at his ease, assuring him his secret was safe.

'You should try it once in a while. Taken in moderation, it's not addictive. And it does less harm than alcohol.'

I drained my drink, sucking my cheeks in at the tartness of the quinine. I had not agitated my glass whilst standing talking and a residue had collected near the bottom.

'Have you been back to England since you came to China?' I enquired.

'Once, eight years ago. I found it – how shall I put it? – bland. There was nothing to it. In London, you know what you will find around the next corner. And, I dare say, it is the same in Dublin. Or Paris. Here, each turn of the path has a surprise.'

'Father Callaghan told me as much,' I remarked. 'He said he never ceases to be astounded, not for one day.'

'He's right. Even after nearly a quarter of a century, China still holds surprises for me.'

'And is that why you love China?' I asked.

'Yes. And also because it fascinates me. In China is all of humanity, all we, as a species, are. The people are . . . Well, beyond description. There are depths to them, Father, our race has yet to devise. It comes from thousands of years of civilisation. When the Romans were building their first road, the Chinese had mapped the heavens. And as for us, in the British Isles!' He shrugged his shoulders and emptied the remains of his drink into a bush by the pavilion steps. 'We were dressed in fatty animal hides when the Chinese hung themselves about with silk.'

'I am beginning to feel as you do,' I admitted.

My reason for coming East was not to fall in love with the people but to bring them to Christ, to the ways of humans in which I believed lay not only religious but also social salvation. Yet, at that moment, standing in the pavilion with the lights of Wuchow coruscating before me, I felt God to be almost a side issue in my life: I had not sailed half way around the world merely to do His bidding but to discover new horizons for myself. In short, I was not seeking to save the Chinese, to alter their way of life thousands of years old, but to save something in myself which I knew existed but which I could not name.

This self-revelation, if such it was, made me profoundly afraid, a fear so deep-rooted my skin contracted as if I were suddenly transported from a balmy South China evening to one of the frozen poles. I was not ready to deny my mission and my Saviour: yet something deep within me was touched, something I could not reach down and undo.

An intuition, it can have been nothing more, told me it was not Satan at play in that dark corner of my being but another power, neither good nor evil, one beyond morality or religion. It had no rigid doctrines, inflexible dogmas. It was devoid of ideology and theology. I struggled to know what it was and then, as if it had been waiting for the right instant to introduce itself, it did so. It was reason, reality, the cold rationale of intellect, the same power which told me there were no dragons living in the river, no spirits existing in the rocks and, consequently, possibly no God in heaven.

In a fleeting instant, I saw an awesome question loom within me, offering no solution but doubting the premise of my God, challenging the very fundamentals upon which I had based my life. That I wanted to do good for my fellow creatures was as firm a purpose within me as my desire to draw my next breath:

what was different now was that I wanted to do this in my own name, for my own reasons.

'I'm not in the least surprised, Father,' Doble said quietly, stopping my confused race of thoughts, 'China works upon a man such as no other country.'

Above the mountains briefly flickered a flash of lightning. It might have been a charge set off in my soul and seeking release in the heavens.

'There's a storm coming,' I observed.

'On the contrary, Father,' Doble replied, smiling, 'there is no storm coming. You won't have seen this before. It is heat lightning, presaging not rain but heat. We are, I fear, in for more rainless weeks.'

There was another flash but no accompanying thunder.

'Have you yet travelled to the north?' Doble asked.

'This is my only experience of China,' I said.

'Not the north of China, Father. The north of the world. Many years ago, before coming East, I went to Russia. Beyond St Petersburg, into the far bleak north. There I saw one of the wonders of the world. It was as if a vast hand was painting the sky. They call it the aurora borealis. The sky is hung with curtains of the most delicate nature – blues and greens and reds – which shimmer as if they were a heavenly veil of chiffon. Have you ever seen this?'

'I have not,' I said.

'I think,' Doble went on as another flicker of lightning appeared, 'that if the Northern Lights may be the gift of gods then this heat lightning is the doing of devils.'

Somewhere far off in the trees, a night bird called with a strange, melodic music. Another bat flitted through the pavilion and out into the air above the river, weaving this way and that in its crazy flight.

'Hot summers here spell drought,' Doble said at length. 'The rivers are already much lower than usual. And, in China, drought means starvation.'

I thought of the thief in the cangue. Such a sight would become a commonplace, I considered, if Doble's prediction came true.

'If there's a flood or a drought,' he continued, 'it is thought by the people the Emperor has done wrong, displeased the gods and jeopardised the Throne of Heaven. In that event, the people must overthrow him or he must appease the spirits to avert their wrath being visited upon the nation. Yet, should such a turn of events come to pass this year, I do not see the Emperor or the Old Buddha being de-throned'.

'The Old Buddha?' I queried.

'Tzu-hsi, the Dowager Empress,' he explained. 'An evil woman, that one. You mark my words Father: it is my belief the tables will turn not on the Emperor or her but upon us. There is already much feeling against foreigners. Being whipped up by ne'er-do-goods.'

'I saw a street entertainment the other day,' I replied. 'In it a Catholic priest was beaten by a Chinese Mr Punch.'

'Or Anglican, Father. Or Anglican. You Catholics do not have a monopoly on martyrdom.'

From the town came the sudden rattle of exploding fire-crackers. A street near the waterfront was illuminated with a series of brilliant flashes. In the last of the twilight, a dense column of smoke rose into the sky, blotting out the lanterns behind and spreading as it climbed higher. As the echoes died away, dogs could be heard barking hysterically, through which din came the muffled dull boom of a gong.

'Fireworks and gongs tonight,' Doble said, 'I fear it may be gunfire or grenadoes tomorrow.'

In the rock-strewn, scrubby foothills of the Nine Dragons, north of Kowloon, tucked between the city and the uninhabitable slopes, tens of thousands of people live in anticipation and hope. Known as squatters, they have erected shacks and lean-tos wherever the gradient is sufficiently short of the perpendicular to allow con-struction. Their towns are illegal, regarded as dangerous by the fire brigade, unsanitary and disease-ridden by the health authorities, corrupt by the police – even the education department lists them as places of ignorance and low literacy: yet this is to misconceive the situation, to fail to appreciate the tenacity of the Chinese.

The buildings in the squatter areas are made of the detritus of the city, much like Hsiao's shack or that of the old woman on the roof of my tenement, but often with considerably greater ingenuity. Hsiao, after all, only lives in a converted crate. The hill squatters do not adapt, they construct. Their buildings are fashioned from rough timber, sheets of corrugated iron, tin or aluminium: the windows contain glass or waxed paper and the doors ride on hinges of iron or leather. Between them run a maze of passages, alleys, and narrow streets, a few crudely paved but most bare earth trodden hard by feet. Dogs lie in corners, chained to the walls which look so flimsy one might assume the dog, taking umbrage at a passer-by and straining on its leash, might cave the wall in or tug the building with it. In addition to dogs there are innumerable cats and, here and there, hens, ducks and even pigs in minute pokes.

Between the ramshackle buildings run ditches serving as sewers: these are noxious little nullahs, foul-smelling even on the coolest of days, jammed with garbage and effluence which are only flushed when there is a rainstorm. The chickens scratch on the banks of these filthy drains but the ducks and dogs know better and keep away.

These derelictions are sturdy. They withstand the high winds of typhoons, the chilly blasts of winter. Many are cosy within, snug hovels which are the homes of extended families of up to ten folk, each with a job to do and a purpose in life.

The grandparents mind the shack, sweep the floor and hang out the laundry, feed the dog its daily bowl of rice and watch its spine gradually arch like their own for want of a proper diet. The women cook, mind the children, wash clothes and sometimes labour as coolies on the building sites of the city. The men also do hard labour or work in the factories of Tsuen Wan dyeing cloth, rolling material, setting looms or driving trucks. The teenagers attend school, the toddlers sit on their grandparents' knees and hear of what it was like in China in the old days, when the Kuomintang held sway and the Communists were just a rabble army in the far north.

I could tell them of those times.

Not all the buildings are hovels. Some are large, with a

146

second storey, divided into two or three rooms, have kitchens and storerooms, lined with metal to protect against the weather and vermin rather than thieves: few rob each other in these places. Some of the buildings are thriving industries devoid of safety regulations, unregistered and untaxed, unknown to the factories inspectorate. I have seen men rendering fat collected from the meat markets and turning it into cooking oil, hair cream, soap or temple candles: other businesses I have come across make plastic flowers, metal washers, fish-balls, biscuits and egg rolls, boiled sweets, paper kites and latex rubber penises for export to sex-shops in Japan. Other shacks are cinemas, shops, restaurants, gambling and opium dens, whorehouses for coolies and unlicensed schools.

Once or twice a month, I make my way to the squatter area north of the airport called Tsuen Shek Shan, or Diamond Hill. The residents know me by sight and I no longer draw anxious looks for they appreciate I am not a resettlement officer, health inspector, charity worker or policeman. Quite what my motives are they must wonder at but they are too polite to ask and I do not tell them when I stop to chat, buying a glass of tea or a sticky, sweet cake.

I have a number of contacts in Tsuen Shek Shan whom I would not class as friends and yet they are more than mere acquaintances.

One of these is Mr Yee, to whom I was first introduced by Mr Wu: he is our opium supplier. A portly man of about fifty, he is the chairman of the Tsuen Shek Shan *kai fong* association, the committee of residents which governs the shanty town, elects representatives to speak on their behalf to the authorities and decides matters of social interest. As Mr Yee is also the Dragon Head of a local triad society he is in a good position to wield power over the locality. He controls the water standpipes, the illegal electricity supply and the network of coolies which the assorted factories are obliged to employ to transport their goods to the nearest highway. In addition, he owns a barber's shop, two eating-houses and a general store, none of them licensed, which front for an opium den he operates at the farthest point in the squatter area from the road. To assist him, he has a band of some one hundred followers in different ranks of the triad hierarchy:

of these, seventy-seven are always Red Poles, the soldier rank. He maintains this number for it is not only militarily sufficient but also very lucky. He was, he has informed me, born on the seventh day of the seventh moon, which is why he has done well in life.

In short, he is a powerful, well-connected man to whom the squatters are bound by fear or allegiance and upon whom they rely.

Do not assume he is an arrogant or selfish man. He takes his responsibilities very seriously. An electricity failure is repaired more quickly than it might be by the China Light and Power Company. If the water ceases to flow, he is quickly onto discovering the leak and having it repaired. He is also in charge of the town plan of the area: he decides where huts will be erected, factories opened up and the sewage ditches dug. He is no expert in town planning but he is logical and does his best. In other words, he is part master criminal, part businessman and part mayor: in this respect he is no different from any other local politician the world over.

It is to his barber's shop that I go to get my hair cut. It operates in a larger than average shack made of one-inch sawn planks under a roof of beaten aluminium. Some years ago, an aircraft missed the airport approach, crashing on the mountains. By the time the rescue services reached the site, the dead crew had been respectfully removed from the wreckage, their bodies covered by sheets and the cargo – rumoured to be gold bullion – had vanished. A section of the aircraft was also missing: that is now the barber's shop roof.

Within are seven barber's chairs in shining chrome and white enamel, seven stainless steel basins and taps, seven mirrors and shelves lined with ranks of bottles of hair oils, perfumes and other impugnable unguents. His staff are equipped with the latest German electric trimmers and a comprehensive range of scissors, combs or cut-throat razors which they strop in turns on a length of wet leather attached to the wall. A haircut, shampoo and curl costs one dollar and fifteen cents. Not being a young Chinese man-about-town, I forego the curling and pay ninety-five cents.

If Mr Yee is not in his opium den, he is in the barber's behind which he has a little office. When my hair is trimmed, he usually invites me to take tea with him. So it was today.

'How you?' he asked as I got out of the chair and paid

for my haircut with a dollar bill, dismissing the change as a tip, something which always pleases the staff: the local Chinese seldom offer gratuities.

'I am well,' I replied in Cantonese. 'And you? How is business?'

'Business is good. Will you take some tea with me? Or are you, perhaps, in a hurry?'

He always says this: he does not wish to intrude upon my time. I always accept.

His office is a room about ten feet square containing a steel desk, a filing cabinet and three upright chairs. Upon the shelves are file boxes and upon the desk is a shining black telephone. It is, I am sure, the only room in the entire squatter area that has a smooth concrete floor.

'Come! Sit down!' He indicated a chair and called through the door for tea. 'Or would you prefer a Coke?' he enquired as an afterthought.

'Tea,' I assured him, sitting by his desk, out of the beam of sunlight coming in through the window which was open but covered by a fine mesh of the sort one saw in the old days lining meat safes.

'Good!' He smiled beneficially and sat down behind the desk. 'Cola is for the young. We are not young. We are older and wise.' He leaned forward conspiratorially. 'Let me tell you something. You, I can trust. You will not run to the police. Near to Shek Kip Mei, I have heard of a man who is a counterfeiter. He makes fifty-cent coins. They look very real until you drop them – then they do not chime. When they come from the press they are dull. So do you know what he does? He puts them in a *kong* of Coca Cola. This polishes the coins so they look new. Then he rubs them in a little graphite – from pencils. The finished article – perfect! Unless you drop it.'

'Has he made many?' I enquired.

'Over twelve thousand. That is six thousand dollars.'

The tea arrived, brought in by the man who had cut my hair. I wondered, as he poured it from a rice-pattern teapot into my glass, if Mr Yee had invested in the coining operation.

'How is our mutual friend, Mr Wu?' Mr Yee asked. 'I have not seen him for ten days.'

'Well, he is well.'

'And have you and he chased dragons lately?'

'Not for some days,' I replied, smiling and slurping at my tea in the best fashion.

Mr Yee drank from his glass. He looked at me over the rim and I wondered if he was looking for a way to get some kind of a hold over me. Yet no sooner had the thought occurred to me than I dismissed it as preposterous. I had nothing he wanted and, besides, I know more about him than he will ever know about me. Maybe this lay at the root of his comment: he wished to redress the situation somewhat.

When we had finished our tea Mr Yee offered to walk with me to the road and we set off, walking down the hillside through the densest areas of occupation. On the way, we halted at Mr Yee's shop, where he spoke for some minutes with the shop-keeper. I stood in the doorway, glancing over the well-stocked shelves laden with boxes of matches, packets of needles, cakes of soap and tubes of Palmolive toothpaste, tins of lychees in syrup and, incongruously, corned beef and Irish stew. Elsewhere were wooden tubs of rice and beans, bags of brown raw sugar, bundles of sugar cane and piles of cabbages, whilst from the ceiling hung Chinese sausages, shiny flattened ducks and dried fish. A counter carried bottles of *mai tai*, San Miguel beer, *sam she chiu* snake wine and the ubiquitous Coca Cola.

Mr Yee's business concluded, we made our way down a path stepped with wooden boards zig-zagging back and forth upon itself.

'How is the girl?' I asked.

'You always enquire about the girl,' he replied. 'Why?'

'As you know, I have my interest,' I said.

Mr Yee halted by a lean-to selling fruit, absentmindedly helping himself to two oranges, one of which he passed to me. The vendor made no attempt to elicit payment: such is Mr Yee's position in the community.

'Tell me, why do you have this interest? The family can be nothing to you. You do not know them. You cannot benefit. Or perhaps,' he scratched his ear and peeled his orange, 'you maybe knew the mother.'

I was not insulted: it was natural for him to assume there might have been another reason for my actions.

'No,' I assured him, 'I never knew the mother. Indeed, I have never known any woman. That is, in the way you imply.'

'Then you are either a very foolish man or a very guilty one.'

I did not reply immediately. Like all successful men of business, Mr Yee is a good judge of character. He knows I am not foolish and his comment was not intended as a sleight but a probe.

'Guilty, I expect,' I admitted.

'What have you to be guilty of?' he retorted. 'You were a priest.'

'A priest is not excluded from the luxury of sinning,' I said, 'and I have lived a long life. There has been plenty of time for me to do wrong.'

'That is so,' he agreed, 'but usually the sins of a priest are surely small. Little indiscretions. Nothing big.'

I did not answer but let him guess the magnitude of the errors of my ways, what it must have been which made me, in his opinion, so guilty.

'Maybe you would like me to find you another little girl? There are many here who would benefit from your interest.'

'Perhaps, but not yet. I am not a rich man.'

He dropped his orange peelings on the ground and a scrawny hen made a rush at them.

'Is there not a saying in the Bible,' Mr Yee remarked, 'it is easier for a poor man to pass through a needle hole than a rich man to enter heaven?'

I nodded and said, 'Yes, there is. Have you read the Bible?'

'No. I am not a Christian. But I went to a Methodist school in Shanghai. The masters taught us such things. Maybe,' he continued, 'you want to be poor so you can go to heaven and, by spending your money in this fashion, you will make it easier.'

'I do not wish to go to heaven,' I said.

'Then you will go to hell.'

'Nor shall I go there,' I responded. 'There is neither heaven nor hell. I shall simply pass into the void.'

'Become an ancestor?'

'Quite possibly.'

'Ah!' Mr Yee said, putting an orange segment in his mouth. 'Then you do this so there will be someone to burn gifts for you at Ching Ming.'

'As I do not know the girl except by sight and as she has no idea about me, how can she make offerings for me? Besides, those gifts go to heaven, do they not? And I shall not be there.'

'You puzzle me,' Mr Yee admitted, spitting out the pips and attracting the attention of two more chickens. 'You are not like men I know. You act without reason.'

'I do not. I have a very good reason, but you have not yet found it.' I smiled at him and added, 'You have still not told me how she is.'

'She is well.'

'Her mother?'

'Her mother is well. Her father is working with the company clearing the hills in Ho Man Tin. He was a general coolie but now he is in charge of the dynamite charges. He is the one you will see on Waterloo Road, beating the gong as the time draws close to press the detonator.'

'And the other child?' I asked.

'The elder daughter works in a factory in Sai Ying Pun.'

'And the baby?'

'Born last month. Another girl,' he replied. 'They are not lucky people. No sons.'

As I approached the door to Father Callaghan's room, I could hear him talking. At first, I thought he was praying, but the tone of his words seemed not to be that of a priest talking to God but of a man angry with a child he was reprimanding. I knocked on the panelling and he fell silent. I knocked again, less loudly, for fear of interrupting him. It occured to me perhaps he had someone in the room with him.

'*Pin kòh-ah*?' I heard his voice enquire.

'Father Stephen,' I said in reply, assuming he was asking after who was visiting him.

There was a shuffling, followed by soft footfalls. The door opened. Father Callaghan was dressed in his cassock but it was unbuttoned to the waist. His chest was shiny with perspiration.

'I wondered if I could see you a moment, Father?' I asked. 'But not if I disturb you.'

'No,' he said quickly, 'no, you're not disturbing me. Come along in.'

He pushed the door wider and I entered his room for the first time. I was surprised how bleak it was. My own quarters were hardly lavish but his were positively ascetic. His bed bore no thin quilt, the only covering being a straw mat with no pillow block. There were two upright chairs made in the square style of Chinese furniture and a table with a wooden crucifix, Christ's figure cast in steel, and an open missal. The bookshelf, above a brass-bound sea chest, carried a number of small indeterminate ornaments and not more than a dozen books bound in black leather. Beneath the shelf hung two sets of ecclesiastical clothes and four Chinese-style suits. Beside the window was a small Madonna, carved in wood and painted in subdued colours. Upon the floorboards by the table were two dark stains which I realised were damp marks where he must have been kneeling for some time, the sweat running down his legs.

'Please, sit down,' he suggested, indicating one of the chairs.

I sat as he bade and he perched on the edge of his bed.

'I thought,' I began, glancing round the room, 'that you might . . .'

'. . . that I was holding a discussion with someone. Well, in a manner of speaking, I was. With myself.'

'I see,' I said, not quite sure how to respond to his revelation.

'Let me tell you something, Father Stephen,' he went on. 'As you know, you're the first priest to join me in a number of years. I've been ministering on my own since '94. Not just here in Wuchow but also to the north, far to the north. Anshun, Kwei Yang and a God-forsaken spot called Hsüyung. No one to talk to up there, not in my own mother tongue. So I took to talking to myself.'

'I see,' I said again, finding his admission a little embarrassing.

'There's nothing wrong with it,' he continued, looking at me sharply. 'Indeed, I'd say it was a prerequisite of being a priest and I recommend the habit to you. The only people you can really talk to, other than a brother or sister in God, is yourself or The Lord. Quite often, I talk to myself not because I'm going mad but because, by making what I'm thinking into a dialogue instead of a soliloquy, I can reason all the better. After all, what's prayer if it's not just that?'

'Were you never lonely?' I asked.

'To be sure,' he began but then paused a moment. 'Well, no,' he mused, 'not lonely. I always had Christ as a companion. But I did sometimes yearn to hear a Western voice. Yet now, in Wuchow, where there are others of my own kind, so to speak, I still like to talk to myself for a few minutes every day. It gets things straight in my mind.'

'You may always talk to me,' I offered.

Father Callaghan laughed quietly and replied, 'I know Father Stephen. And I will, I will. But you must still allow me my little indulgence. Just so long as you don't think I'm losing my mind. If that was to have happened, believe me, it would have happened in that accursed Hsüyung.'

'May I ask what you were talking about?'

'You may. We have no secrets, you and I, Father Stephen. I was confessing to myself.'

I stared at him in surprise.

'Well, what do you expect?' he continued. 'Up there in the north, I had no one to hear my confession. I couldn't call around the next village, knock on the priest's door and say, "Father O'Brien" or "Father Kelly, will you pause for a moment to hear my confession?" The nearest Catholic father to me was over two hundred miles away. But now you are here, Father Stephen, I'll come to you. When you're not busy. But I may still confess to myself, if you don't mind. It's nothing against you, of course. But when I confess to myself, I sense I'm doing it directly to God.'

He put out his hand, briefly touching mine where it was resting on the arm of the chair. It was an action of neither friendship nor love but one of compassion, of companionship perhaps, and I sensed he did it more for his own benefit than for mine.

'Surely,' I said, 'we are instructed that just the desire to repent is sufficient.'

'That's true,' he agreed, 'just as it's also true I cannot give myself absolution. But you know, I gain a strength from putting it all into words. A thought is such an easy thing to accomplish. The voicing of it takes a bit more determination. Anyway, I've no great sins to confess. Only the usual little ones every man has and cannot seem to rid himself of. Unless he's a saint. Now,' he straightened his back, pressing his hands down upon the mat on his bed, 'what is it you want of me?'

'I have a need to confess.'

'I see.' He grinned at me. 'And you've not been here long enough to hear your own. Shall we go down to the alter?'

He began to button up his cassock.

'Would it be possible for you to hear it here?'

'Of course. God does not listen only in the confessional.'

I knelt on the floor before Father Callaghan and admitted to him and Our Lord that I had sinned.

'Tell me of your sin, my son,' Father Callaghan ordered.

Settling my knees again, for the floor was hard and there were knots in the boards, I told him of my stupidity on the night of my journey up the river, of how I had gone ashore to satisfy my own indulgence and how I had eavesdropped upon the occupants of the house and had fled for my own safety rather than their privacy, how I had startled the dog and how a search party had been sent out to find me and the captain had killed the villager.

'Is there something more?' Father Callaghan enquired when I eventually fell silent.

'No, Father,' I replied but he sensed I was lying.

'Are you sure? Quite sure?'

'Yes,' I said. 'Quite sure.'

I should perhaps have admitted my doubts to him, the

confused thoughts I had experienced in the pavilion of the Resident's garden which had so logically resolved themselves in a way contrary to the well-being of my faith yet I believed I need not. Kneeling before my confessor, I did not view them to be a sin. They were, I considered, perhaps a failure of my character, a perverse twist in my mind but not a sin: for I was not casting God out of my presence, denying His existence or slighting Him but casting myself away from Him.

'Very well,' Father Callaghan said.

I felt his eyes looking hard upon the top of my head as if willing me to confess further but I resisted him. Reason took control of me, overriding emotion and theology. If there was a wrong involved, I thought, it was against myself and not Jesus Christ: that I could and would bear.

For a few minutes, Father Callaghan did not speak again. At length, he stood up from his bed and went to one of the windows, looking across the town bleached by a high sun. He remained there for several minutes, a black silhouette against the scorching day. When he turned back to the room, he sat in one of the chairs behind where I was still kneeling awaiting his – or perhaps God's – criticism or forgiveness.

'Get up, Father Stephen.' When he finally spoke, his voice was quiet and gentle. 'Sit with me a moment here.'

I took the other chair, wondering when or if he was going to absolve me, forgive me. I was repentant. The death of the man had weighed upon me. What I needed was to be given a penance and absolution for this terrible wrongdoing.

'Father Stephen,' Father Callaghan said, 'I know your feelings and, for whatever sin you've done, you're forgiven if you are truly remorseful. And I know you are, so that's all there is to it. But . . .'

He was not looking at me but at the window again. A small bird had landed upon the sill and was watching us. It was a dull-coloured little creature with a short, black beak and a bead of an eye catching the sunlight, sparkling like a pebble of jet.

'There's something you must learn now you're in China,' Father Callaghan resumed. 'Here, the value of life is much cheaper than we consider it. A man's death is not regarded as important as, indeed, we saw with the poor soul who drowned. For us, life's precious even if we are in expectation of the glories of heaven. We seek to nurture it, encourage it. But the Chinese do not share this concern. Death and life are but parts of the turning of fortune's wheel. For them, life's not unique. Today they are men, tonight they die and become either revered ancestors in heaven or are resurrected, according to their faith.'

The bird piped a single, shrill note as if to lend its weight of native opinion to Father Callaghan's statement.

'But I was the cause of the man's murder,' I said. 'If I had not been so proud as to take an evening walk . . .'

'Fate, Father Stephen. Nothing more. You did not kill the man. Nor did your pride. He was a victim of circumstance.'

I could not believe Father Callaghan, a guardian of discarded girls and a Christian priest who had forgone the company of his own kind in order to dedicate himself to bringing the Catholic faith to heathens, could be so callous.

'Father,' he said, interrupting my thoughts and once more touching my hand, 'I know what you're thinking. Yet consider this: we are here to show the Chinese the word of God but we cannot change their ways nor, I think, should we. In time, they may follow our example but, until then, the Chinese must live as they do and we must relieve their suffering where we may.'

He then gave me absolution, his voice soft and low. '*Ego te absolve in nomine Patris* . . .' I heard him say, but my attention was captured by the bird.

It remained on the sill watching us until, just as Father Callaghan completed his absolution, it imparted its brief whistle again and flitted from sight. I wondered if it had been a deliberate witness sent by Our Lord to check up on us, an insignificant brown angel already flying high on the thermals above Wuchow, preparing his report.

'Would you kill a man?' I asked as I rose from my knees.

'I would not!' he exclaimed. 'But nor would I prevent another's hand. Not here. Not in China. If I were in Dublin it would be different but I am not. I am in Wuchow. Every day the opportunity arises for me to save a man from another's hand: consider the thief in the cangue. It would be nothing to step forward, cut free the wood, bless him and preach brotherly love on the spot to the onlookers. Teach them compassion and mercy. But, I ask you, is it worse to starve a man to death in the cangue than to steal him from his loved ones and transport him to the Australian colonies, send him and his family to the poor house for the theft of a silk kerchief which, to its owner, is a mere bauble? It is a matter of priorities, customs and attitudes. No, Father Stephen, I believe we may observe and relieve suffering, teach by example, but we may not go beyond. We may not interfere.'

There came a tapping on the door.

'*Pin kòh-ah?*' Father Callaghan said again.

'What does that mean?' I asked.

'It means *who*. It implies *who is there?*' He smiled kindly. 'You are learning, Father Stephen. That's the way to be. Curious, inquisitive. Find out all you can. Of language and life and death. And if you live a hundred years you will still not know more than a smidgin of this land and its people.'

A voice outside the door called, 'Master. Ah Fong here. Food on table.'

'Come,' Father Callaghan suggested, 'it's time for us to eat.'

He completed the buttoning of his cassock, stood up and held the door open for me. As we descended the stairs, I could hear the shuffling of feet as the girls made their way towards the refectory.

'You've not given me a penance,' I said as we reached the refectory entrance.

'I've not,' he replied, 'and it's remiss of me. Well, I'll give you one shortly.'

We made our way to our places at the head of the long table. After Father Callaghan had said grace, he beckoned to Ah Fong, speaking in a louder than necessary voice, considering his proximity. The Chinese left the room to return with a small box which he opened and placed on the table. Had we been gentlemen in the smoking room of our club, sitting together with a decanter of port, the box might have contained cigars. Instead it appeared to hold a number of shrivelled grey-brown pebbles.

'What are these?' I enquired.

'*Wah mui*,' Father Callaghan replied but offered no translation. 'Try one, but beware for it contains a large pip.'

'Try it?' I said.

'Eat it, Father, eat it.'

'What is it?'

'Have faith, Father. Pick one up and eat it.'

Thoughts of the execrable egg returned to me but I did as he instructed. The *wah mui* was hard and rough to the touch. I placed it cautiously in my mouth. Instantly, there was a slight sensation of sweetness upon my tongue.

'Put it in your cheek and suck it,' Father Callaghan advised, 'as you would a cough lozenge.'

All down the table, the girls were craning their necks, watching me avidly. Sister Margaret, at the far end, was leaning forward, so intense was her attention. Ah Fong stood close by with a deadpan expression.

I sucked. A peculiar sweetness came off from the thing: then, suddenly, the back of my mouth was hit by a terrible saltiness. I felt my throat muscles contract under the shock. I wanted to spit the thing out. Instead, I sucked harder. Now the sweet and the salt were mingled and the flavour, though tart, became bearable, even slightly pleasant.

'So?' Father Callaghan enquired.

'It is . . .' I was lost for words to describe the taste.

'Now, I'll tell you what it is. A *wah mui* is a salted plum,' Father Callaghan informed me, 'a favourite sweet of the Chinese. The plums are picked when ripe then pickled in salt water for some days. When shrivelled by their immersion, and the salt permeated into them, they are spread out to dry in the sun. Usually', he added, 'on the pavements of the town.'

I chewed the flesh of the sweet and swallowed it, removing the large stone from my mouth with my fingers and placing it on the table beside my rice bowl. I smiled at the girls who all broke into giggles. Sister Margaret clapped her hands, not to halt their mirth but in applause at my having eaten the thing.

'That was your penance,' Father Callaghan said, 'and you must be truly repentant for you were not nauseous. I have known others rush from the room on their first encounter with a *wah mui*.'

'It was not as bad as the egg,' I replied.

'No. You're right,' Father Callaghan declared. 'That was my mistake. I should have saved the egg for your first confession in China.'

Mrs van der Poehl is a short, etiolated woman who wears just too much make-up to be decent. She has no disfigurement to hide, nor is she trying to retain her youth: she likes to stretch the bounds of propriety to their limits. In colonial society, she would be regarded as outrageous, one of the select company whom it was fun to invite to a dinner party if one wished to shock the other guests, but whom one decidedly did not invite to a cocktail party where there might be children under fifteen years of age. She is the sort who would have been known, in the years preceding the Second World War, as NBHE – Not Before His Excellency.

In Chinese society, however, the community of the back streets, the fellowship of the tenements, she is regarded not as a semi-pariah but as an eccentric who, being elderly, commands respect.

I see her almost every day, although not necessarily to speak to: I spy her walking in the streets, taking her pug dog, Pu Yi, across Nathan Road and up the path to King's Park where she lets it off its lead to defaecate upon the grass around the blocks of government quarters there. She dresses in the style of the 1940s, disdains hats and sun creams with the result that the backs of her hands, and possibly her face under the just-too-liberal coating of cosmetics, are dried, the skin having a papery texture, like that of brown manila envelopes. Her hair was once, I guess, ash blonde but is now a sort-of ash grey and she wears it wound into a bun. I have never seen her without a string of pearls at her neck which, like her face, is also well besmirched with powder.

To sum her up, she is a character and for this I admire her. She fights convention. In a society such as that of a British colony, she is brave – courageous, even – to be the way she is. Many women better than her have been destroyed, and their husband's careers terminated or stagnated, by the vindictiveness of tennis court chitter-chatter in the Ladies Recreation Club, the censure of tight corsets in the tropical sun and the sneering snobbery of those for whom individuality is a threat and a sense of independence a trait unbecoming in a female.

She has done just as I did many years ago: she has assessed the mundane, found it not to her liking and rebelled against it. She has not won, and she cannot win just as I have not, but she fights on with the dogged determination that would have earned a soldier accolades but has afforded her acrimony.

Furthermore, like myself, she is in love with the East. This is not a rational love nor one based upon emotion. It is a fact, built upon necessity. Mrs van der Poehl has abandoned her past, all that history and birth have given her and chosen to live as she does. And she is trapped, as inescapably as I am, in this place.

Both of us, I am sure, could buy ourselves a ticket to leave: we could go to the airline desk in the Peninsula Hotel, hand over sufficient in cash and take a taxi to Kai Tak. There, we would present our docket to the hostess, place our bags upon the conveyor belt and, at the appointed hour, step onto the concrete, mount the steps of a BOAC airliner and vanish.

Yet we do not. There is something in us which prevents us going, something we love and yet which we hate, something it is better to live with than to escape from, something with which we have come to terms. We have deemed it desirable to maintain the status quo rather than stir things up. Perhaps it is something we hate in ourselves.

Be that as it may, in the case of Mrs van der Poehl, she has not only abjured her past and her own kind but has positively taken on the side of the Chinese against the European.

Once, some years ago when I was getting to know her, I met her in a market on the praya of the Yau Ma Tei typhoon shelter. This is an artificial harbour behind a high breakwater which, in times of impending inclement weather, is packed with the smaller, fragile craft the storm would destroy like matchwood. When the weather is fair, it is the haven for these craft when they are not out in the harbour, or the South China Sea, plying their various trades. It is like a floating city of fishing and cargo junks, sampans, wallah-wallah boats, lighters and the smallest of the coastal traders. The whole ragamuffin fleet, with the exception of the lighters, has one thing in common – every vessel is made of wood.

On the praya, when the authorities are not about, there exists an impromptu market in which a number of commodities may be purchased without let or hindrance from the street trading laws, the hawker legislation and the strictures of public hygiene. Seafood is landed without going through the fish markets: goods brought down the coast from China, regardless of border regulations, are also traded – I have done business there over the years in raw silk, white and green tea, unrefined opium, poor quality firecrackers, matches with too high a phosphorus content, antiques and old jade and fake copies of Sheaffer fountain pens which may all be bought if the price is right and the dealer knows the customer well enough to appreciate they are not in the pay of the police, the triad cartels that operate the street markets or the health authorities.

Mrs van der Poehl and myself are the only Europeans who visit the place. Our faces are known. We are *gweilo* folk but we may be trusted.

On this occasion I was there buying fish. The prices are much lower than in the organised markets or the streets. There are no middlemen involved: the man who hauls the nets offers his catch for sale from buckets and tin-lined trays. My aim was to purchase shrimps and I was walking along the quay looking into the assortment of plastic and tin buckets when I saw Mrs van der Poehl ahead of me waving her arms at what I took to be a fisherman. She was speaking in rapid, fluent and colloquial Cantonese, her voice raised and her ire clearly up.

'What are you doing? What *are* you doing? You blockhead! You utter blockhead!'

I remember quite clearly she used the phrase *mok tau* several times.

She took no notice of me as I drew closer, so intense was her attention to the object of her tirade, a Chinese man crouched by a large wooden tub of live squid. The animals were swimming round in the water, delicately changing colour from brown to an off-pink as if occasionally feeling intense embarrassment at her pronouncements. A crowd began to gather, consisting of fishermen, children from the sampans, women in wide-brimmed Hakka hats, stevedores and coolies. They all stood by in a respectful silence, bemused at this elderly European woman creating hell.

Whenever the Chinese began to speak he was drowned out by her.

'You fool! What right have you to do this? These squid . . .'

At that point I wondered if she was one of those kind- yet ignorant-hearted people who will not see an animal treated in a manner which they believe to be cruel and who, if they lived in China, would exist in a permanent state of angst. Glancing into the tub, I could see nothing wrong with the squid at all save that they were bound for the *wok*.

'These squid . . .' the man began, rising to his feet, but it was as far as he got.

'These squid . . .' Mrs van der Poehl erupted at him. 'One and a half catties of these squid are going to be sold to me. You cannot prevent me from buying them and you will not prevent him from selling them to me.'

She waved her hand cursorily in the direction of a second, barefoot man standing nearby, dressed in trousers rolled up above his knees and bare to the waist, his front besmirched with fish blood and scales, his hands clutching a thin, much-sharpened shiv.

'It is his right to sell these to me. To me! To me or to any of these people here.'

She swung her arm around the crowd, some of whom edged a little backwards as if she was about to strike them.

'Hong Kong is a free trade port. An entrepôt port.' She spoke the word *entrepôt* in English. 'You will not – I repeat, *not* – interfere.'

It was at this point I noticed that the Chinese man who was the object of her attack was holding a clipboard. A plastic ball-point pen dangled from a piece of string tied to a hole drilled in the board.

He reached for the pen and caught it.

'You can forget that! Don't you dare write a single word. Not so much as one character!'

The man let go of the pen and attempted once more to speak.

'Go!' Mrs van der Poehl shouted regally, pointing to the distant hills. 'Go! Do not interfere here again. I shall have words with your superiors. You may count on this.'

At this juncture, the people parted suddenly and a European man dressed in a white shirt, white shorts, long white socks and brown brogues appeared. He was tall and tanned: his hair was blonde, cut short and he wore a pair of American-style sunglasses which he removed as he approached the centre of the crowd, tucking them into his breast pocket.

'What's going on here?' he shouted in Cantonese: then he spied Mrs van der Poehl and reverted to English. 'May I help you, madam?'

'Yes,' snapped Mrs van der Poehl. 'This upstart here has had the temerity to prevent me from purchasing these squid.'

'I see. If you'll wait a moment?'

He went to the Chinese with the clipboard and they spoke in hushed tones for some minutes: there was much gesticulating upon the part of the Chinese whom the European tried to calm down. At last, he returned to Mrs van der Poehl who, in the meantime, had chosen the squid she wished to buy, had had them caught by the man with the scaly chest and had paid for them. The fisherman had placed the animals in a plastic bag of water.

'Madam,' the European began, 'may I explain? This fisherman is contravening the law by selling his produce on the praya. He has . . .'

'I'm not interested . . .' Mrs van der Poehl started but the European raised his hand.

'If you would be so kind as to let me finish, madam,' he said tersely. 'This fisherman, and indeed all these traders, are operating without licences. They are therefore committing an offence by trading on the praya and it is the duty of my inspector here to prevent them from so doing.'

'I don't give a jot,' Mrs van der Poehl returned, her fingers tightening on her plastic bag of squirming squid.

'Madam,' the European continued, 'these laws are here to protect you. Those squid,' he nodded in the direction of the bag, 'may not comply with the hygiene regulations.'

'Dear God!' Mrs van der Poehl said, raising her eyes momentarily to the skies as if for divine encouragement. 'Do you think I give a sod about that? Let me tell you, young man,' she went on, a certain irony in her words, 'when I was a prisoner-of-war in Hong Kong, I ate rats roasted on a shovel over a fire of driftwood, seaweed and dried shit. And I am still here. What is more, there were young children in the camp who shared the same *menu de la maison japonaise* and they are still with us, hale and hearty. So . . .'

'That notwithstanding,' the European butted in, 'my inspector has rules to apply and apply them he will. These traders are operating without licences. They are therefore committing an offence . . .'

'*Diu lei lo mo!*' Mrs van der Poehl hollered.

An approximate translation for this common colloquialism might be fuck your mother. An American might use it to imply the object of the abuse was a mother-fucker. The crowd, now at least an hundred strong and for the best part ignorant of what had been said since Cantonese had been abandoned as the language of the contretemps, hissed with amazement. A few of the coolies and stevedores laughed. I sensed their humour was almost nervous.

Somewhat nonplussed, the European took a step back and sideways but Mrs van der Poehl was not to be stopped. She dropped her bag of squid onto the stone flags of the quay and went for him, her arms flailing. She hit him hard in the middle of his chest and he attempted to grasp her wrists but without success. To avoid her, he next stepped backwards again and Mrs van der Poehl, seeing her chance, rammed into him with her shoulder. The European arched over backwards and disappeared. There was a muted splash. The crowd surged forwards, leaving a respectful space around Mrs van der Poehl: one of the coolies retrieved her bag of squid and almost reverentially handed it to her. She was breathless with indignation and exertion.

Gazing over the side of the praya, I saw the European in the water, floundering about in a thick wadge of flotsam in which I could see floating some offcuts of wood, rice straw, a discarded plastic sandal, a broken rattan basket, some sheets of paper, a small drowned rodent and several anonymous brown lumps I took to be human excreta. A man on one of the sampans was pushing a thick bamboo pole out towards the European, who began to swim clumsily towards it.

'Are you all right, Mrs van der Poehl?' I asked, moving to her side.

'Quite!' she replied, adding in the direction of the swimmer, 'Bumptious little bugger!'

I was out following Father Callaghan's suggestion, that I should go north along the river past the clump of trees: I was eager to discover the place he had said would interest and instruct me in the ways of China.

The road along the waterfront was crowded with coolies. Upstream from the flowerboats, a larger than average barge was moored side on to the bank, unloading a cargo of stone. The blocks were several feet square and each took two men with a substantial bamboo pole slung between their shoulders to lift it. These pairs of men struggled up the steep bank with the blocks, their breath coming in starved gasps by the time they reached the road, their horny bare feet kicking up dust as they staggered off into the town.

Pausing for some minutes, I watched the procession, wondering what the life expectancy might be of these near-slaves. They could not be able to look forward to long lives and it was of no surprise to me the British had found it so easy to addict the Chinese to opium. Anyone with such an existence would want frequent release into a better world.

The copse stood out from a tall, rock-strewn bank which over-hung the road at the point where it deteriorated into a wide path, on the left of which was a precipitous drop of sixty feet to the river below. Conscious of the currents and afraid of the state of the pathway on the edge of the brink, I kept well in to the rocks, in the crannies of which scuttled lizards. For a moment, I stopped and studied one of the creatures. It was not a big-headed, awkward looking reptile like the lizard I had seen during Mass but lithe and streamlined with a black body decorated by yellow stripes and a bright blue tail. It rustled the leaf litter as it scampered away from my presence.

Once past the trees, the path ran in a straight line along the river bank with groves of dense bamboo growing on the right, behind which were scattered some houses and terraced fields rising up a low hill. None of the buildings was situated on the pathway save one, around which was built a six-foot-high stone wall painted dark red and topped off with green glazed tiles. In the centre of the wall, facing the river, was a wide roofed gateway with two smaller ones to either side, one of which was open. As I approached, I caught the perfume of incense on the wind.

Above the central gate was a carved wooden plaque of several characters surrounded by a curling dragon. It meant nothing to me, but by the open gate was a square of board hanging from a nail, upon which someone had written, presumably for the benefit of the *gweilo* residents of Wuchow, *Lung Mo Dagon Mothr tempul*. I smiled at this enterprise: clearly, the temple priest realised foreigners visited temples and, out of a felt obligation if nothing else, left offerings of money just as trippers in Europe did when visiting holy shrines or cathedrals.

I looked through the gate. There was no one about and, as the gate was open and the notice a virtual invitation, I mounted the raised step and entered.

In the centre of a beaten-earth courtyard, between the main gate and the equally large front door of the temple, which was also closed, there stood a massive bronze urn a foot taller than myself. The legs were bowed like those on Jacobean tables and cast as the shins and feet of a dragon. From the top of the vessel projected a few dozen smouldering joss sticks casting a bluish mist into the sunlight. On either side of the main door, as in the case of the gates, were two smaller entrances. I walked past the urn and entered the building.

I found myself before a side altar: had this been a Christian place of worship, the room might have been a lady chapel. The altar was a simple affair consisting of a table draped in scarlet-and-gold cloth upon which was standing a number of brass open-flame oil lamps of the sort one saw in children's picture-books, illustrating the story of Aladdin. They were all lit and guttered fitfully. Some fruit and little cakes were piled on dishes before the idol, which was a small, unimpressive statue of a nondescript figure of a woman positioned under a canopy of similar material to the altar cloth.

There were no pews, but before the altar were a number of low wooden stools to assist kneeling worshippers. Apart from these the only other furniture was a large bronze bowl on a stand in the middle of the room. It was filled with water, the metal sides tarnished but the rim highly polished. Another little notice hung from the stand. I raised it and read, *Empuroar Good Luk Boll. Puss fingr on edge, make noise in watr. If round good you got good luk.*

Following the instructions, I placed my finger on the rim and began to slide it round the bowl. Nothing happened so I pushed a little faster. Suddenly, the metal began to hum then whistle an incessant whine. In the water, ripples appeared in perfect circles radiating out from a point in the very centre of the bowl where the liquid danced and bubbled as if boiling. I stopped abruptly, the ripples vanishing and leaving no waves but just a mirror-flat surface.

The main part of the temple was reached through an archway, from the other side of which I could hear noises. I wondered if I should pass through, encroach upon someone at prayer, yet I knew temples were not like churches. There were no set services at specified times and visitors could come and go as they pleased: in a Hong Kong temple, I had watched two men praying whilst a sweeper flicked a duster over the altar before their very faces.

Casting my concern aside, I passed through to discover myself in a far more opulent and colourful shrine. Incense coils were suspended from the roof with bright red prayer flags, curtains and triangular banners hanging down to the floor: joss sticks burned in profusion from two urns filled with dusty earth and, on either side of the altar, were positioned two seven-foot statues of fiercesome-looking gods with scimitars and ornate spears. The walls were decorated from roof to floor with embroidered tapestries depicting clouds and mountains, writhing snakes and dragons, delicate cranes and squat phoenixes, snarling lion-dogs and ferocious tigers. In front of the tapestries were a large gong and a massive drum shaped like a beer barrel but half as big again, both suspended in black wooden frames. At the rear, behind the altar, stood a flamboyant palanquin which, I assumed, was used to parade the effigy of the god round the town at festivals, in the same manner we processed saints through the streets.

Where the side chapel had contained the *good luk boll*, the main shrine displayed a table draped in an imperial-yellow silk cloth laden with offerings – fruit, cakes, bowls of rice and even coagulated dishes of stew. One platter held a complete, cooked fish. All these comestibles were beyond the point of consumption and only the thick incense smoke killed the stench of the rotten fish and kept the flies at bay. All the rice was spotted with either mould or ash from the overhead coils.

I had to rub my eyes for they were smarting from the smoke, my cheeks damp from tears of discomfort: my nostrils prickled as if I was on the verge of contracting influenza.

The main altar was magnificently arrayed with red and gold brocades, more Aladdin's lamps and scarlet wax candles. The effigy was life-size, a goddess with a wooden face immaculately painted but not aloof or vacant in her expression. She was made not to look down upon her worshippers but out through the main door. Upon her head was a crown of gilded metal and she wore the silk gowns and robes of a wealthy dowager.

In front of the altar knelt an old woman. Her short grey hair cropped at her nape was swept back and her feet, although not bound, were small in black cotton slippers. She was otherwise dressed as a peasant in a dark blue woman's *sam* and black *fu*.

I did not wish to disturb her devotions and stepped back, half hidden by two of the prayer banners. She kept her head bowed, kow-towing several times to the idol, all the while muttering a low incantation in a monotonous tone. Her hands were placed together in the fashion of a Christian but, between her fingers, she held two or three joss sticks and she moved her hands up and down in front of her breast in supplication.

Just as I was about to leave to explore the third section of the temple, through yet another archway, the old woman completed her worship and rose unsteadily to her feet. She stuck her joss sticks in a small container on the altar and turned to go.

It was Sister Margaret. For a moment, I stared at her then hid myself behind the banner. She passed within a yard of me, oblivious of my presence. When she was gone, I just stood in the smoke-filled twilight and considered her actions. It was blasphemy. She, a nun in holy orders, was paying service to a heathen deity.

After a period of time and deeming it to be safe, I left the temple and, in the courtyard, sat upon a step to consider what my next actions should be. Obviously, I had to tell Father Callaghan. He would, in turn, have to notify the Vicar Apostolic in Hong Kong, and he in due course, would have to notify Rome. Sister Margaret would then be excommunicated.

And yet, I realised, the due process would take months. In the meantime, she could hardly return to the society of her countrymen which she had long since given up and, furthermore, she was needed in the mission to look after the girls.

I set off towards the town, keeping to the land side of the path and walking slowly so as not to catch her up and to give myself time to ponder further on the situation. When I reached the mission, I went directly to Father Callaghan's room.

'Where've you been, Father Stephen?' he enquired. 'You look as if you've taken a bit of the sun.'

'I've been to the temple by the river,' I replied. 'When I was there . . .'

'The Dragon Mother temple,' Father Callaghan replied. 'The story is there was a mother and her son who lived here a thousand years ago – well, what other time span would there be in a Chinese story! – and fought the dragon that made the river flood. Whether they won or not, I cannot say. The river still floods. Anyway, they were deified and the temple was erected to them by a pious general whose name I forget. Did you go in?'

'I did,' I said, 'and . . .'

'And did you try your luck on the bowl?'

'I did but there is something else I must tell you,' I answered, all in one breath to try and halt his garrulity.

'What's that, Father?'

'When I was there, there was a worshipper . . .'

Father Callaghan raised his hand to silence me.

'I know what you're about to say.'

'You do?' I rejoined, annoyed he had, once again, interrupted me.

'For sure I do. You saw Sister Margaret there.'

I was speechless and stood before him open mouthed.

'You look like a fish,' he said. 'A carp,' he added.

'I don't know what to say . . .' I began.

'Then say nothing.'

'But you knew!'

'I've known for years. She visits the Dragon Mother once a month.'

'Why? She's a Christian.'

'She's also a Chinese,' Father Callaghan said, 'and she's covering her bets just as any pragmatic Chinese would. I don't blame her. I don't condone her actions, mind, but I'll not chastise her nor will I inform on her. She may not have given her soul entirely to Jesus Christ, but she has her life and that's good enough for me. If she wants to back two horses, then let her. The time will come for her to make her peace with God and that's her affair, as far as I'm concerned. And as far as you are, too. The matter is between us, her and Our Lord. Let it rest there.'

He closed a book on the table which he had been reading, his action emphasising his words.

'I told you,' he said quietly, 'you would see some unorthodoxies here in China and a few of her mysteries if you went to the temple. Now, I think, you understand a little more?'

'I do,' I admitted and I left his room.

I learned an important lesson that morning and it had been taught me by Sister Margaret: it is not necessarily what one believes in but what one does with one's life that is important.

☯

All day, I have been following the little girl, who is on a school outing with classmates, travelling by bus from Sham Shui Po in the company of a young Chinese lady teacher and a not-so-young Chinese nun in a white wimple and grey habit.

Their destination was the beach at the 11$\frac{1}{2}$ milepost on the Castle Peak road, where they congregated by the bus stop, chattering loudly, eager to get onto the pale sand and discover another corner of the world. The teacher and the nun, after taking a register, ordered them into a crocodile and marched them down the steps to the sand.

I had dismounted from the bus ahead of them and was already settled on the beach with the daily edition of a Chinese newspaper, my shoes off and my toes dug into the sand which, although it was only ten o'clock, was warm from the sun.

The children sat in a circle at the far end of the beach, the nun in the centre and the teacher on the outside. They removed their shoes and socks, as I had done, and lined them up in neat rows.

I was not close enough to hear what was said but it seemed they were listening to some kind of religious instruction, for the nun frequently paused in her diatribe, the children bowing their heads. This went on for fifteen minutes, ending in a prayer and a hymn in Cantonese which sounded distant and ethereal when sung in the open air by their tiny flute-like voices. After the prayer session, the nun quit the circle and, walking off a little distance in my direction, sat under the shade of a bush to engross herself in a book. Judging by the cover it was not a religious volume: the front was decorated by a lurid picture, although I could not quite make out what it was. Perhaps she was looking for the realities of life the nunnery had forbidden her. If this was the case, her confessor would have some interesting listening and she would be busy with a number of Ave Marias.

It is strange how even the most devout Christian must sin. It is not a matter of slipping into evil, for they do not sin to be wicked, but to show their goodness. If they deliberately sin they can deliberately repent and, in recanting, display their fealty to God. It is the responsibility of the pious to be sinful in order to maintain fidelity: no religion survives upon prayers but upon heresies.

The nun's book may well have been salacious. She sat with her back half-turned towards the children, shielding the cover illustration with her hand, her palm spread across it to form a little lectern of flesh.

With the nun engaged in her dubious recreation, the teacher took charge of the class, the little girls sitting on the shore side of the circle, the boys with their backs to the sea. For some minutes, she gave out instructions and asked questions, to which a forest of arms shot up. This phase of the lesson completed, the children jumped to their feet, formed lines then, at a clap of the teacher's hands, broke off into pairs and sped to a cardboard box from which they took plastic jars and toy nets. Thus equipped, they ran to the far end of the beach to paddle in a stream emptying from the hills into a series of sandy rock pools. At their departure, the nun closed her book, walked to the lines of shoes and socks and sat by them, guarding them like a hunched bird of prey. Once settled, she opened her book again.

The nature-study class continued for an hour, the children gathering specimens, shouting with glee at their discoveries. The teacher encouraged and laughed with them, wading through the pools, helping them catch elusive fish. One of the little boys, straying away from the pools with his partner and coming along the water's edge towards me, found a crab with a leg span of five inches and, egged on by his companion, succeeded in picking it up, its legs and pincers flailing infuriation, its mouth blowing bubbles and its swimmerets paddling hard against the boy's arm.

The child was terrified, his face screwed up with fear, tears running down his cheeks. Yet he was afraid to let it go. Perhaps he thought it might turn and attack him, drag him into the sea and under the waves, storing him forever in its submarine caverns.

The teacher did not see this little drama being played out and the nun was ignorant of it for she was still, even after an hour, engrossed in her sinning, which she had not ceased with the exception of one occasion when a child returned to the cardboard box.

I got to my feet, placed my shoes on the newspaper to prevent it blowing away and walked towards the boys. The one with the crab was petrified and sobbing quietly, not moving for fear of enraging the crab further. His comrade was casting scared looks in the direction of the pools: they had evidently been told not to wander away and he was considering which might be worse, the teacher's wrath or the crab's fury.

'Are you in trouble?' I enquired in Cantonese.

They gazed at me in silence.

'Do you want to let the crab go?' I asked.

The boy holding it made no move but his friend said, in a small voice, 'Yes. It is a dangerous animal.'

'I will take it from you,' I said and, sliding my hand over the boy's, gripped the crab's carapace between my finger and thumb, instructing the boy to let go and remove his hand backwards.

'Do not let it go near the claws,' I told him, 'or the crab will bite you and we shall have to kill it.'

He did as he was told, his hand moving slowly so as not to alarm the crab.

'There!' I exclaimed. 'You are free of the crab and all is well.'

'Now you have it,' said the boy.

'But I am not afraid of it. And you should not be. Now,' I said, kneeling on the sand, 'let us look at him. Or her. For,' and I pointed to the rear of crab, turning it upside down, 'this is a lady crab. This mass of orange pips are her eggs.'

There was a shout from along the beach and the second of the two standing in front of me shouted, 'Look! Look!'

All the children came running, their teacher taking up the rear. Only the nun did not rush in my direction, but she did put down her book.

With the children gathered, I said, 'This is a crab. It's Latin name is *Ocypode* but in English they call it,' – and I momentarily reverted to that language – 'the large ghost crab. This is not because it is a ghost but because it is white. Like a ghost. And, like a ghost, it comes out at night but, if there are not too many people on the beach, they also come out in the day.'

'What do they eat?' enquired a child standing beside me.

'They eat dead fish, little sea animals and other crabs.'

'Where do they live?' asked another.

'They live in sand holes,' I replied, looking up.

It was the little girl. She was staring straight into my face. For a moment, I was silent, awed by her attention. Her proximity seemed so strange, so dangerous. I had never been so close to her and wanted to say something more to her, tell her how glad I was that she was doing well in school, to inquire after her sister in the factory, request she give my regards to her family. Yet I knew none of this was possible: I must stay as a distant observer.

Mercifully, at this moment, another child spoke up.

'Where are its eyes?'

The spell was broken and I embarked upon a quick tour of the creature's anatomy, pointing out its eyes and mouth-parts, the clever hinges of its limbs and, with the aid of the teacher's pencil, its powerful claws.

The questions over, I put the crab close to the sand and let go of it. It stood stock-still for a second then fled, running sideways into the water where it started fidgeting with its legs to bury itself.

'Thank you, sir,' the teacher said in English, the children crowding the water's edge to see the little pit in the sand under which the crab was cowering.

'Not at all, it was a pleasure,' I told her.

She smiled and called all the children away and into a circle once more. The nun joined them and there followed a session of note-taking and drawing, the children silently concentrating on their work.

I collected my newspaper, put on my shoes and walked up the steps towards the road, turning right and setting off along the verge. Glancing down, I saw the children engrossed in their work, the teacher moving from one to another giving advice. Only the nun glanced up, watching me with that look one sees in sinners who know they have been found out.

It is not long to go until four o'clock. The warm sun is glinting off the harbour: one window in a house on The Peak is glimmering, giving the impression of someone hiding in the lush greenery with a heliograph.

The rickshaw coolies are hunkered down in the shafts of

their vehicles by the Star Ferry, smoking and talking or sleeping uneasily in the contorted positions only the poor in tropical lands can achieve, their spines made supple by poverty and heat. A few squat on the pavement playing *tien kow* with strips of card. The exhaust fumes from the red-and-cream painted buses hang poisonously in the air and the taxis, swinging round to join the rank, screech and rattle.

Although I cannot see them I know that, in a doorway or dock gateway down Canton Road, there will be other rickshaw pullers sitting in the shade, not to escape the high sun but to hunt out some privacy in which they can chase the dragon, lighting small balls of opium in tea spoons or squares of silver paper gleaned from discarded cigarette packets, sucking the fumes hungrily, waiting as the drug soothes their lives, irons the wrinkles of their worries away.

It is still comparatively early in the year but the afternoon sky is already harsh and iron-like with heat as I stride out from the shade of the ferry pier: according to the necromancers in the Chinese press, it promises to be a hotter than usual summer.

Wiping my brow with a damp handkerchief, I set off along Salisbury Road, dodging the traffic of lorries, taxis and hand-carts heading up Canton Road towards the docks. I welcome the arrival of the next area of shade opposite the general post office, cast by overhanging creepers and trees growing along the top of a rock-face halfway between the driveway to the marine police headquarters and the fire station, but I do not slow my pace. I have never been one to saunter.

By the fire station, under the last tree, an old man with a shaved head and wearing thick tortoiseshell-framed spectacles has stationed himself on a storm culvert under a black umbrella. The rock behind him, faced with concrete to prevent erosion, is scrawled with a disorderly pattern of characters drawn in charcoal varnished in a feeble attempt to extend their life. One inscription is in English. It reads, *Buy Grashoper Make by Hand with Leaf Good Luck Good Fortune Grashoper $1.*

The old man is weaving coarse grass leaves and strips of green bamboo bark, his fingers crooked but agile as they twist and fold, bend and tuck in corners. Beside him on the culvert is a row of variously sized green grasshoppers, whilst others are pinned to the surface of his umbrella.

'You buy?' the old man asks me as I pass by.

'*M'hai*,' I say, shaking my head, '*Mo cheen*. No money.'

It is a universal phrase used to dismiss persevering street peddlers and insistent beggars.

'You go' money. Pleng-ty money,' the grasshopper-maker replies adding, '*Jah maang*. G'ass-hopper. *Wan lai-ga*. For luck. *Ho wan ah-ma*.'

Yet he does not press the matter. It is hot and there will be tourists along soon. A large white cruise ship has berthed in the docks around the corner. The first battalion of passengers has already come ashore, trodden the streets and returned laden with packages: now lunch has been served on board, another wave will soon disembark and head for the camera shops and jewellers, the curio houses and the tailors, most of them passing this way.

Once more, I look at the sign on the concrete. There is no need for me to feel in my pocket. I know how much I have on me – thirteen dollars and eighty cents. But I have lived in China for so long the introspective caution of the European is reduced to a few seconds' inconsequential nag. Like every Chinese, I am inured to the acceptance of fate and the grasshoppers might be, in some oblique and unfathomable way, an omen I should not dismiss lightly.

Reaching forward, I pick up the smallest grasshopper. It is cleverly crafted, the emerald leaves lending a lifelike appearance and the intertwining of the various constituents so fashioned they might almost be the casings of an actual insect's carapace. Only the eyes are not made of vegetable matter, but red glass-headed pins.

'Sixty-five cents,' I suggest.

The old man ignores me. This is a ploy and I know it – and he knows I know it.

'Seventy cents.'

'Sevung-ty-fi'e,' the old man says.' Small wung. Small g'as-hopper, small luck.'

I take a dollar bill out of my pocket and hand it to him.

'One dollar. You buy big one.'

'No. Jus' small one. Small luck good for me. Got no luck now,' I tell him.

The old man shrugs, removes twenty-five cents from a leather pouch on his belt and drops the coins into my hand.

'Okay. You get luck, come back, buy big one.'

The grasshopper nestling in my hand as if it is a living creature which might take flight, I cross Hankow Road and enter the main lobby of the Peninsula Hotel, a bell-boy in a pork-pie hat holding the door open for me.

From time to time, I like to come in here. The ornate ceiling is thirty feet high, supported on pillars decorated in gold leaf. It is as much like the interior of a baroque Catholic cathedral as it is the lobby of an hotel. To left and right are comfortable chairs and polished tables standing on carpets with a rich pile and sombre pattern. Waiters in Chinese-style white jackets and black trousers move silently on slippered feet between the furniture, carrying silver trays laden with tea pots and bone china. Above, in one corner of the ceiling, a chamber quartet ensconced in a little gallery plays subtle music. At this moment, they are playing Bach.

Choosing a table, I order afternoon tea and request a newspaper, which arrives held between a pair of wooden strips screwed tightly together by butterfly nuts. Printed upon the gleaming wood in gold, cursive lettering are the words *Peninsula Hotel: Hong Kong – Do Not Remove*.

I cursorily start to scan the paper. I do not read it: I am not in the least bit interested in the news. It is just that the newspaper gives me something with which to occupy my hands and disguise my eyes as I wait for my tea to arrive. Long ago, I learnt that a man doing nothing attracts attention, but he who is seemingly busy is ignored.

From my vantage point behind the paper, I observe.

There are three types of people present, the Chinese staff excepted. I do not use the word class for Hong Kong is a classless society: there are no lords and lackeys but only the rich, the not-so-rich and the poor. In the lobby of the Pen, as the hotel is colloquially known only the former are present yet there is on view all three varieties of the sub-species.

At the next-but-one table are gathered three European ladies wearing neat dresses and jackets with low-heeled shoes. They are not adorned with lavish jewellery but the one nearest me has on her left wrist a solid gold lady's Rolex. Although they drink their tea and have eaten some of the sandwiches on a tiered rack, they have not touched the dainty cakes in frilled paper cups.

I do not look at them, but I listen to their conversation. They are discussing their servants, the merits of Ah Wong against those of Ah To, the advantages of having one's own sew-sew amah versus employing a freelance when there is darning to be done or a child's fancy dress costume to be made.

Scattered about the lobby are a number of other little cliques of European women no doubt discussing similar topics, the latest fashions out from Paris, the information about who is sleeping with whom and which marriages are on the rocks. These women are remainders from the old days when it was common to ask each other to tiffin and spend winter afternoons chasing native Chinese foxes in the Lam Tsuen valley with imported English hounds.

Six tables away is an example of the second group of wealthy folk. These are Chinese women. They wear tight skirts and high heels and are hung about with jewellery: one wears a diamond the size of a pea which shards the sunlight into a tiny prismatic explosion. I cannot tell of what they are speaking; even were I sitting closer I should not know for they lean together conspiratorially. Their faces are immaculately made up, their eyes outlined in mascara, their cheeks smooth as porcelain. They have eaten all their cakes but not touched the sandwiches.

The third variety of the rich are represented by just one table: there, sitting close together but not so close as the Chinese women, are four Chinese men. Their suits are made of shiny grey silk, their socks are black with embroidered motifs at the ankles and their ties are dark blue or green. Their wristwatches are heavy, ostentatious and gold. They sip their tea but ignore the sandwiches and the cakes. They too are out of earshot yet I know they are talking of money, of how to increase their wealth, of what the day's rate is of the Hong Kong dollar *vis à vis* the pound, the yen, the American dollar.

The waiter brings my tea. I fold the newspaper and, when he has unloaded his tray, thank him in Cantonese, which takes him aback. He is not sure how to respond and says in English, 'You are welcome, sir.'

I pour out my tea into the bone china cup with the hotel crest printed upon it, stirring it with a silver spoon. I eat one of the sandwiches: it is almost as thin as a communion wafer and has a filling of anchovy paste.

The reason I visit this lobby is not because I wish to return to the world of European mores and fashions, nor is it because I wish to indulge myself in luxury. I come for the same reason that I visit *The Black Pussy* – to be amongst the sinners and the lost, to know that I am not alone.

For, as I chew on the fine white bread and sip the Earl Grey tea, I consider how, not a mile away from the oblivious and unforgiving rich, my tenement flat awaits my return, One-eye is selling chickens to pay off his extortionist's debt and how, two miles beyond that, there are shacks on the hillsides the residents of which pay homage – and tithes – to Mr Yee.

This irony is something I savour. It is the paradox of the human condition, the enigma some call justice and others injustice but which I refer to as fate, as destiny.

Here, genteel folk take afternoon tea to the strains of Bach. Two hundred yards away, men sit in the shadows and chase dragons.

Arthur Doble's house was on the outskirts of the town, built on the side of a steep hill overlooking the river directly opposite Dragon Island. It was a Chinese house with heavy wooden double doors set in a windowless wall of dark grey stone and, from the pathway up from the river, appeared no different from the home of any well-to-do Chinese trader. The doorway gave on to a flagged courtyard and it was here that he welcomed Father Callaghan and me on the evening of 13 June 1900.

'I'm so glad you could both make it,' he said, as we alighted from our sedan chairs. 'I've two friends from Hong Kong whom you must see. Come,' he beckoned to us with an open hand, palm downwards in the Chinese fashion, 'and meet them.'

The reception room, which in a European home might be the drawing room, was large and lit by oil lanterns, the furniture traditionally Chinese but, as a concession to European comfort, the seats were lined with brocade cushions. The tables were low and in one corner was a massive wooden trunk carved with a view of Hong Kong Island in bas-relief. The only item not of Chinese manufacture was an enamel-faced carriage clock standing upon one of the tables under a scroll showing an intricate landscape devoid of perspective. We passed through to a second, larger room, in the centre of the ceiling of which was a square hole. Directly beneath this was a hearth in which a fire was burning without flames but giving off a column of smoke rising to eddy along the ceiling towards the hole.

'Sandalwood,' Mr Doble said as I sniffed the smoke-scented air. 'A pleasant aroma but, best of all, it keeps mosquitoes at bay. The little beggars tend only to feed between four and eight o'clock, so if we keep the embers glowing and the smoke billowing until eight-thirty it will greatly reduce our chances of being consumed by itching. Now,' he guided us around the hearth, 'let me introduce Mr Ronald Pearsall and Mr Eric Nicol.'

We all shook hands, exchanging pleasantries. Mr Pearsall was a tall man with very long limbs and a small, pinched face whilst Mr Nicol was shorter, more rotund and with fat hands. The former worked for W. Powell & Co., a trading firm in Hong Kong, whilst the latter owned a small printery. All three were dressed in dinner suits, as if they were not in the heart of Southern China but in the smoking-room of a London club, whilst both myself and Father Callaghan were in our clerical clothes. It was only the second time I had worn ecclesiastical garb outside the mission since my arrival in Wuchow.

'Arthur informs us you are new to China, Father Stephen,' Mr Pearsall remarked as we relaxed on wide settles around the fire.

'Just a few weeks and still wet behind the ears,' Father Callaghan said before I could reply. 'But you're learning fast,' he added, looking at me through the smoke. 'Already, he can fix his own *fu* so that they don't fall down and he's had his first thousand-year-old egg.'

The others laughed, Nicol asking, 'And have you had your first salt plum?'

'Indeed, I have,' I admitted.

A young Chinese lad entered and handed me a glass of whiskey.

'This is Ah Ping,' Mr Doble explained. 'He is my makee-learnee house-boy. An orphan picked up in the gutters of Whampoa when he was eight. Or so. He's been with me for four years. You see,' he went on, 'you holy men don't have a monopoly on the waifs and strays of China.'

'The Lord will look down kindly on you,' Father Callaghan responded, sipping at his whiskey in the savouring, luxurious way only an Irishman can.

'He may, Father,' Mr Doble replied, 'but I'm not looking to score points with the Almighty. I am merely doing another poor, benighted human a favour and gaining, I hope, a lifelong servant into the bargain.'

Mr Pearsall continued, talking to me, 'I'll not ask you what you think of Wuchow, or China come to that, for I'll bet every white man and woman you've met has sought the same information. But I will ask you if you think you will make it your home.'

'My home?' I said.

'When I first came to the Orient in '86, that was the question posed to me by the manager of Powell's. He didn't quite phrase it that way, mind you. He actually said, "Well, my boy, you're stuck out here for six years without sight of the White Cliffs of Anywhere. Do you think you'll be able to stand it?"'

'I think I shall,' I replied.

'Understandable,' Mr Nicol observed. 'Unlike us mere business wallahs, you've the strength of your convictions to give you backbone.'

'On the contrary,' I responded. 'It may be true that the Lord Jesus will give me the courage I need to persevere but that is not to say it will make me happy and settled. It is one thing to be at home in a place and quite another to want to be in it. Yet I believe I shall make my home here. Happily and willingly.'

'You sound confident,' Mr Doble said.

'I am,' I replied firmly. 'Quite confident.'

And I believed myself. The realisations I had experienced when we first met were firming to resolute intention as the days passed.

Our conversation drifted into the realm of inconsequentials, topics such as expatriate men anywhere in the world might discuss – trade, colonial politics and the petty vagaries of colonial administrators, news from Europe that was weeks old. At precisely eight o'clock, as the delicate chimes of the carriage clock rang out, Ah Ping returned and, with a small gong in his hand, struck it once with a leather-padded hammer.

'Supper is ser-wed,' he announced.

We were led through a door onto a terrace where a circular table was set as for a Chinese meal under a number of red and gold paper lanterns hanging from beams entwined with creepers. Beyond was a small garden sloping towards the river and Dragon Island with its bright light shining upon the water.

'You've a fine place here,' Pearsall congratulated our host. 'Quite the best house I know in China outside Hong Kong.'

'I am fortunate,' Doble acknowledged, 'though for how much longer I cannot say.'

'Are you leaving Wuchow?' I enquired, sitting down as indicated by an elderly manservant who held the chair for me.

'I would not doubt it if we aren't all going to leave Wuchow in the not-too-distant future,' Pearsall said. 'There's trouble brewing.'

'The *I Ho Ch'üan*,' Father Callaghan commented, lifting his chopsticks and taking a small piece of chilli-pickled cabbage from a dish before him.

'Those are the fellows,' Doble said. 'Righteous Harmony Fists. Boxers. Causing a lot of problems in the north and there's a few down around here.'

The elderly manservant re-entered and placed an oval iron platter of meat on the table, resting it on a block of wood. From the dish rose a cloud of steam which smelled of ginger.

'They've the tacit permission of the Empress Dowager,' Nicol remarked. 'They refer to themselves as the Buddhist Patriotic Society. I saw one of their banners in Hong Kong, brought down from Shantung by an army chap. It was, of course, scarlet and had written upon it *Feng Chi Mieh Kiao*.'

The others nodded sagely, Father Callaghan frowning.

'What does it mean?' I queried.

'By Imperial Command exterminate the Christian religion,' Father Callaghan said.

There was silence about the table. The steam rising from the platter had decreased and Doble, picking up his chopsticks, leaned forwards.

'Let us eat,' he suggested, 'or else the food will spoil. We've fourteen courses ahead of us . . .'

We began to help ourselves in the Chinese fashion, the meat tasting unlike anything I had ever known, the manservant going round the table filling small cups with rice wine.

'I was at a ball in Weihaiwei last December,' Pearsall said after we had started eating, 'and there were a number of Chinese present affecting European dress. It's becoming a bit of a fad amongst some of them, when they mix with foreigners. They manage the swallow-tail coats and black trousers without much difficulty although some have theirs tailored with fur linings. Traditional Chinese winter clothes in the north are always fur-lined, the houses seldom being heated with more than a brazier. Must be hellish hot to wear such an evening suit at a legation party. Anyhow, as I was saying, they have no trouble with the coat and pants but the shirt confounds them. The studs and collars are a bit unusual for them. One old boy was having an awful time with his. It was several sizes too big for him and kept sticking out of his waistcoat. I noticed this – and so did the French consul. After about half an hour, the Frenchie said to me out of the blue, "When I return home, I shall sack my laundryman." "Why?" I asked. It was so sudden a statement and bore no relation to what we had been talking about. "*Cet homme*," he started in French, so angry was he, "*il* . . . The man there is wearing my shirt. My crest is sewn into it, under the starched front. Now I know why my shirts stay so long in the laundry. My servant is hiring them out!"'

We all laughed, a little over-zealously: the story expunged

our sombre thoughts of the *I Ho Ch'üan*, setting the evening on a pleasant course once more. The meal continued for about three-quarters of an hour when, as we began on the eighth or ninth course, the manservant returned and whispered something to Mr Doble.

'Gentlemen,' he announced as the Chinese stood back, 'Ah Ching informs me we must go to the end of the terrace and observe something. He does not say what.'

We left the table, guided along the terrace by the elderly manservant and his master. The view down to the river, through some sparse conifer and willow trees, was as clear as if it had just rained, although not a drop had fallen for several months. At a low wall was gathered Ah Ping, two house amahs and the cook-boy with a white apron around his waist. They were standing in a silent and apprehensive huddle.

A full moon was rising along the course of the Si Kiang, about a third of its orb having appeared over the mountains. It was huge, filling a quarter of the lower quadrant of the sky, every crater and mark upon its face etched with an awesome clarity: and this was no ordinary grey, cool moon for it was as blood red as a setting sun.

No one spoke. Mr Doble put his hand upon Ah Ping's shoulder and one of the amahs took the boy's hand. I noticed the child was silently sobbing and the cook was shivering with fright.

Father Callaghan, standing next to me, crossed himself and muttered something in Latin under his breath which I could not comprehend.

'A bad omen,' Mr Doble murmured. 'Most inauspicious for us all I fear.'

'*Yat nin yau shâp yêe kôh yûet.*'

The boy was leaning forward, his shoulders hunched, his arms crossed on the edge of my table. The quiff of hair had fallen over his brow and, from time to time, he ran his fingers through it to push it clear of his eyes. He struggled with the tones again and with his accent.

'*Kòh yùet*,' I said, 'not *kôh yûet*. Try the next sentence.'

He took a deep breath as if about to submerge himself in freezing water.

'*Yat kòh yùet yau saam shâp yât.*'

He stressed the first three words, desperately trying to get them right, to gain my approbation.

'Good,' I said.

He smiled faintly at me. We were reaching the end of our hour's tutoring and he was flagging. So was I. Yet he was trying today, striving hard and this did not raise my ire, frustrate me as has been the case on occasions in the past.

'Now the next.'

'*Yat yat yau yêe shâp sày tún chung.*'

'Not quite. Not *Yat yat* but *yat yât*.'

I closed my copy of our textbook.

'Enough for today. You have worked hard and progressed. Practise on your own. Don't talk to your house servants in the kitchen Cantonese they expect of you. Communicate with them precisely. Tell them to correct you if you are wrong. You don't lose face and they, being servants, will not gain any. Indeed, you will gain face.'

'Yes, sir,' he replied.

I pushed my book to one side and, from the drawer, removed my invoice pad. I opened it at the bookmark, a strip of bark fallen from my grasshopper.

For several days, I have had the air conditioner on the whole day: we have been having an unusually warm, humid spell for this time of year. The result is that the fabric of the grasshopper has dried out and begun to shrivel. First to go was a foreleg, then a piece of its carapace. Yesterday, a section of wingcase came free and it is this I am using as a marker.

'A receipt is not necessary, sir,' the boy said.

'I beg your pardon?'

'A receipt, sir. It's not necessary.'

'I am sure,' I answered, 'your father will require some proof of payment and I feel I must have the security.'

'But I trust you, sir. And as for my father, this has nothing to do with him. He does not pay for my lessons. I pay for these from my own money. My spending money, sir,' he added as if an explanation might be required.

I did not know what to say. I closed the receipt pad and pressed the little plastic nipple on the end of my biro, retracting the point. For some reason, I had assumed the boy was taking Cantonese lessons at the insistence of his parents. It was not unknown for colonial fathers to press such instruction upon their offspring: it assured a higher entry level into business or the colonial administration.

'I see. In other words, you have chosen of your own volition to learn Cantonese.'

'Yes, sir.'

'May I ask why?'

For a quick moment, I ran over the possibilities: he has a Chinese girlfriend, he wants to pre-empt his father's intentions, have another qualification to stand him in good stead with a prospective employer, he wishes to know what is being said about him when walking in the street. These have been reasons others of my former students have held.

'So I might speak to the Chinese, sir.'

His reply was put in the matter-of-fact fashion of a person as yet to learn of the guile and deceit of men.

'Why should you want to speak to them?'

He paused. I sensed my question was unexpected.

'Well, sir . . .' he began. 'I . . . Well, how else can one communicate? If I can't speak Cantonese, how can I learn from them?'

'Learn from them?' I asked. 'Learn what from them?'

Again, he was momentarily at a loss.

'But . . . Well, everything, sir.'

It occurred to me this boy did have more to him than I had appreciated after all. I looked at him, with his Tony Curtis film-star quiff and his tanned young skin, his blue eyes, his expensive gold fountain pen, his starched white shirt and I did not see a young boy living towards the middle of the millennium but another in a heavy cassock walking through history at the turn of the nineteenth century.

From his wallet, which he tugged from his tight hip pocket, he removed my fee, which he placed on my receipt pad. I could see he had more money in the wallet, a season ticket for the Kowloon Motor Bus Company and impressed into the leather of one of the inner compartments was a narrow oval. This, I knew from occasional glances at the contents of sailors' wallets in *The Black Pussy*, was a condom.

'May I ask you a question, sir?'

Now it was my turn to be taken aback. We have never spoken in this fashion before. He has always arrived, been polite, attended to his studies with more or less application and then, having settled the bill, left as politely as he arrived. Save for his occasional glance at my face, he has never sought to discuss anything other than the finer points of Cantonese tones.

'Yes, you may.'

'Why does the man who lives downstairs call you *san foo*?'

He pronounced the words correctly. I should have been mildly pleased: we had never gone over them.

'How do you know that?' I snapped.

'It's in my vocabulary book,' he replied.

'I mean,' I said, brusquely, 'how do you know what he calls me?'

'I met him once. In the lift. He wears round glasses . . .'

'And? Get on with it, boy,' I demanded.

He blushed and blustered.

'He asked me if I was going to see *lung wong hau*. I said I was visiting you. He then smiled and said you were *san foo*.'

'His name is Mr Wu,' I informed the boy. 'He is . . .' I was going to say friend but decided otherwise. '. . . an acquaintance of mine.'

I was hoping this would be the end of the conversation but it was not: the boy was determined to get the answer he wanted.

'So may I ask, sir, why he calls you that?'

'Do you know what it means?'

'It is the noun for a priest.'

'I was a missionary in China,' I replied, adding in the hope this would silence the boy, 'at the Catholic mission at Wuchow. On the West River.'

'Why are you not a priest now, sir?' he asked. 'I thought if you were once a priest . . .'

'That's none of your business,' I retorted sharply.

He blushed again and I felt sorry for him, regretted my curtness.

'I am not embarrassed by your prying,' I went on, 'but you must learn there are some things you do not ask of another man. If someone wants you to know something, they will tell you.'

'Yes, sir. I'm sorry.'

'There is no need for you to apologise.'

He stood and placed his books in his rattan briefcase.

'When were you at Wuchow, sir?' he enquired, his voice quiet as if, by not speaking loudly, he might not offend with his continued interrogation.

'A long time ago. A very long time ago. A considerable length of time before you were born. Or your parents, I doubt not.'

'Would you . . .?' he began but I cut him short.

'I don't talk about it. Indeed,' I lied, 'I seldom think about it. It is in the past and that's an end to it.'

I do not know what it was told me this but I knew he was not only not satisfied but would, given the chance, return to his delving into my life when he felt the moment opportune.

He finished putting away his books, pressing them down on top of some sports clothing in his basket, shifting aside a pair of tennis shoes to make room.

I did not want to alienate him. He is, after all, a source of my income and I admit to preferring to teach him than to coaching colonial civil servants striving to gain promotion.

'Do you play much tennis?' I enquired.

'Yes, sir. At the Kowloon Bowls Club.'

An uneasy silence fell then he was ready to leave. I accompanied him to the door of my flat.

'Before I go, sir . . .' he started again.

'Yes?' I responded.

I wondered what he was going to come out with next: ask me if I had fallen from grace with a woman and been excommunicated, been caught with a choir-boy behind the vestry cupboard.

'What does *lung wong hau* mean?'

His pronunciation was weak but I decided not to make a point of it for I understood him.

'Queen of the Dragons,' I told him. 'I believe Mr Wu was referring to the other European resident of this tenement.'

'There is someone else?' the boy said with amazement.

'An elderly woman. But not as old as myself.'

He asked no more questions and I watched him walk to the lift, pressing the black call button. A green light behind a cracked perspex disc came on and I could hear the mechanism start to grind high up the lift shaft.

'Good afternoon, sir,' he said as the lift doors slid gratingly open.

I made no reply and closed my flat door.

That was over two hours ago. It is now late evening and I am sitting alone at the table. I have not put my Cantonese book away, nor even the receipt book, which remains with the boy's money untouched upon it. I am thirsty but I have not risen from the table to fetch myself a drink of water from the flat-sided Gordon's gin bottle in my little refrigerator.

Ever since the boy left, I have thought about him. He is so like me. I hate to admit it but the fact is plain. He is not learning Cantonese for any other reason than he has committed himself to China. Just as I did. He has found his home and wants to settle into it, merge with it so he can be a part of it, be accepted by it despite his blond hair and blue eyes.

What is more, he is burning to question me about China, knows I have a lifetime's knowledge of its geography, its people: he also appreciates I have experienced it, have come across its every mood and mannerism, have seen, he thinks, all it can show.

As I realise this, I simultaneously understand I should tell him nothing, should not risk colouring his judgement, giving him preconceptions he will use to formulate responses, assess his own experiences, come to terms with his own excitements and disappointments. He should discover the future and its landscape for himself, learning of it the hard way, the painful way.

It occurs to me, sitting in the last of the evening with the glow of the street lights and shop signs cutting coloured bars on my ceiling through the plastic venetian blinds, that he is my successor, the next generation of old China hands.

I do a little mental arithmetic. If he is seventeen now, which assumption must be fairly accurate give or take a year, he will be fifty-five years old when the century turns, my age in the year two thousand and twenty-eight.

By then, China will be a different land, as radically altered from what it is today as the present is from how I found it when I stepped off the *Lucky Moon* onto the pontoon at Wuchow.

A pang of terrible sadness strikes me through. How I wish, at this moment, for immortality. I should like to be here to see what the future holds in store, to share in its fortunes and vicissitudes. However, there are no deals for immortality, no devils with whom to make a pact: that is the stuff of fancies, literature and miracles.

There are no such things as miracles.

Yet, when the Dalai Lama dies, the exact moment of his last breath is recorded and monks are sent throughout the Buddhist world to find a boy child born at that exact moment in time and he is taken to Lhasa to be declared the new leader of his faith. In a similar fashion, my boy pupil is to be my successor. I am certain of it. He must inherit my past even though he knows nothing of it.

I cannot justify my certainty. It is one of those thoughts, those realisations that come to a man which he knows to be incontrovertibly right without having any logical basis whatsoever for his assumption. In this respect, it is not unlike belief and I am familiar with that and its dangers.

Standing upon my chair, I take down the thin volume of my life, looking at the cover, at the gold leaf lettering – *1900*. Some men give their heirs fortunes in money or stocks, estates, wealth counted in precious stones and rare metals. I have none of these. My estates are the passing of time, my wealth is counted in pebbles.

I do not open the diary. Instead, from the drawer in which resides the receipt book I remove a brown manila envelope. The flap bears no gummed strip: instead there is a length of twine tied to an eye, a replica of which is attached to the back of the envelope. I slip the diary in, twisting the twine around the second eye, sealing the flap.

Although I know I should not do it, on the front of the envelope I write with my biro *Gerald Nelson – by hand* and, with the receipt book and the cheap pen, place it back in the drawer.

Through my dozing, I heard what I fancied was the slap of wet fish on marble slabs: it might have been the striking of sopping clothing against a laundry stone. It was at first a cool sound but it developed into the frantic drumming of a fist upon my door. I sat bolt upright, instantly awake with sweat dripping down my forehead and the small of my back. A voice began to shout.

'Mas-ter! Mas-ter!'

It was Ah Fong's voice.

'What do you want, Ah Fong?' I called out, suppressing my irritation at being abruptly woken.

'Big t'ouble! Big t'ouble! You come quick chapel-side.'

The patter of his feet receded down the passageway and I heard him descending the stairs, several steps at a time.

I struggled into my clothing, the material sticking to my damp skin, thrust my feet into my cloth slippers and went after him.

From the chapel came the sound of a woman crying. It was not the soft, pitiful sobbing of a Chinese woman, such as I had heard by the baby posting box, but a strident, breath-catching weeping between gusts of strangled words trying to form themselves.

Pushing open the chapel door, I discovered Father Callaghan standing over a huddled form in the front pew, his hand resting gently upon it. He was bent slightly forward. At my entrance, he looked up.

'Father Stephen,' he greeted me, 'it's a terrible thing has happened.'

At that moment, the person in the pew looked up. It was Mrs Blair. Her hair was awry, her face streaked with tears which had run in eddies through a light coating of dust on her cheeks.

She put her hand up to try to bring some order to her coiffure but all she did was make it more bedraggled. The sun, coming through one of the windows, glinted in the gemstones of her necklace.

'Mrs Blair,' I said, nodding politely to her.

I seemed incapable of any other response. I could feel no rapport nor sorrow for this meretricious woman in her bejewelled if dusty condition.

She began to sob again, her face in her hands, her body wracked with sorrow.

'It's a tragedy,' Father Callaghan declared, quietly. 'An awful tragedy.'

'Yes,' I replied. Having yet to be appraised of the situation I could not think what else to say.

'He's been shot,' Father Callaghan went on. 'By one of the Residency guards. Just an hour ago.'

The muscles about my spine tightened. If Mr Blair had been injured in a shooting incident it could bring about serious political consequences. Even now one of the ships moored along the southern praya could be slipping her lines and sailing for Hong Kong. She could be there in a day and a half with the currents behind her, sooner with a westerly wind to fill her sails. After that, a week at the most would have a British man-o'-war anchored off Wuchow, her cannon aimed at the town. There was no telling then where it might end.

'Was it an accident?' I wondered aloud.

'No,' Mrs Blair whimpered. 'It was not. It was cold-blooded, deliberate murder . . .'

'He's dead?' I asked: in my mind, Mr Doble's foreboding and remarks at the bloody moonrise echoed hollowly.

'Dead,' Father Callaghan said dully.

Mrs Blair sobbed more loudly, blowing her nose in her handkerchief, which was already sodden.

'Where is he now?' I asked, assuming Father Callaghan wanted me to attend to the body whilst he comforted the widow.

'We don't know,' Father Callaghan explained. 'As soon as he was shot, the guard grabbed him and carried him off. Harriet,' he squeezed Mrs Blair's shoulder gently as she broke into another bout of sobbing, 'is afraid the guard will . . .'

Behind Mrs Blair's back, Father Callaghan mimicked with his free hand the picking up of something with chopsticks and transporting it to his mouth.

'Eat him?' I said incredulously, staring at my companion.

'Eat him,' Mrs Blair wailed in confirmation.

I put my hand on the back of a pew to steady myself. I could think of nothing more horrific.

'Do they do that? The Chinese?' I asked disbelievingly.

'They do,' Father Callaghan replied, 'but usually only in the winter months. For this reason, I am sure the guard will not do so now. In this weather . . .'

'My poor Bruce!' Mrs Blair howled.

'Bruce?' I said, puzzled. 'I thought Mr Blair . . .'

'You dolt!'

Mrs Blair was standing in the pew. She had got to her feet with such alacrity I had not seen her move. A snake could not have struck more rapidly.

'I'm sorry . . .' I began but she cut me short.

'You bloody fool! Not my husband, you dunderhead! My Jack Russell. That bloody Chink has shot my dog.' Her rage suddenly collapsed and she dropped back into the pew as if she had been a puppet of which the strings had been cut. 'Now he'll eat him.'

'I'm sure he will not,' Father Callaghan comforted her. 'I'm sure we shall find him. Now, come along, dear lady. Come and rest. Let us see what we might do.'

He helped her to her feet. After her sorrow and rage she quickly became meek and apologetic.

'I'm sorry to come to you,' she said in a near whisper. 'My husband . . .'

She looked from Father Callaghan to me then lowered her eyes.

'It doesn't matter,' Father Callaghan said softly. 'Now you come along with me.'

We assisted Mrs Blair to Sister Margaret's room, Ah Fong was sent to fetch tea and rice cakes to revive her and Father Callaghan lent her his smelling salts in case she should feel faint. When at last she was lying on the bed, her face turned to the wall and her soul lost in grief, we left her and climbed to the mission roof. The sun was fierce so we sat in the shade of the bell.

'There'll be hell to pay,' Father Callaghan remarked as he settled himself on the stone steps under the bell pergola. 'Tell me, did Ah Fong not tell you what had happened?'

I sat next to him. The stones were remarkably cool in the shadow.

'He just hammered on my door shouting, *Big t'ouble!*'

Father Callaghan chuckled.

'And you thought the old man had bought it?'

I nodded.

'Well, that's a rare one, that is!' he laughed quietly. 'If it had been Mr Blair, I doubt there would have been so many tears shed. Save in the name of decorum.' He tapped his nose with his finger. 'I'll not break the secrecy of the confessional but Mr and Mrs Blair do not see eye to eye on a number of subjects. Religion and dogs are but two of them.'

'What shall we do?' I asked.

'Nothing, Father. We shall do nothing. We can only wait.'

'Wait for what?' I asked. 'Surely, at the end of the day, it's only a dog. The guard'll get fined or something. Did he shoot it for no reason?'

'He had a reason, to be sure,' Father Callaghan said, 'and in my mind a good one. Apparently, and Ah Fong's told me so it can't be far from the truth, the dog had been barking at the guard off and on for days. His comrades had teased him about it. You know they called the dog a rat?'

'Yes,' I remembered, 'she had mentioned it.'

'Well, the other guards took the rise out of him. Chinese are afraid of dogs. Hardly surprising, so many of their own curs being rabid. But this one – why be afraid of a rat? Anyway, the man had had enough of this teasing. He was losing face, so he took his gun to the creature.'

The sun was shifting and my foot was out of the shadow, my toes beginning to itch in the heat. I pulled my foot in, repositioning myself on the stone step. Looking out over the rooftops, the wood smoke of cooking fires rose in columns through the hot air before breaking to hang in a haze high above the town.

'If we can do nothing, what will happen next?'

From the *hutong* came the delicate sound of a hand-gong, its chime dulled by the heat. Father Callaghan nodded in the direction of the sound.

'We're about to find out,' he said, pushing his hands down on his knees to assist himself in standing: he might have been endeavouring to push his frame up through the day's dense heat. 'That's the mandarin paying us a house call.'

We went quickly downstairs, arriving in the yard as Ah Fong swung the doors open to allow the entry of a grand, four-bearer palanquin preceded by two men carrying a gong and a flag, four men holding coiled bull-whips and ten others carrying oblong plaques painted red with gold characters drawn upon them.

'He's the *fu tai*,' Father Callaghan whispered as we bowed low. 'The governor of the district. We're to be on our best behaviour. And,' he added, 'he speaks some English so be discreet.'

The palanquin was constructed of highly polished rosewood, the shafts smooth bamboo and the curtains red and gold brocade embroidered with chrysanthemums. The roof was made of lacquered rattan, domed with a wooden spire at the apogee, the corners curled upwards, the supporting pillars carved with dragons and mythical animals.

As the bearers lowered it to the ground, a short, tubby Chinese ran round from behind and hurriedly parted the curtains. He was joined by two other minions, one carrying a fan of black cloth and bamboo, the other an ornate umbrella. Just inside the gates two guards armed with long-bladed swords positioned themselves, their weapons unsheathed. From outside came the sound of feet shifting about. Looking to my left, I could see Ah Fong bending so far over I was surprised he did not topple forward.

'Welcome to the Catholic Mission of Wuchow, Your Excellency,' Father Callaghan greeted the mandarin in English. 'We apologise for our humble abode and hope you will forgive our unpreparedness.'

'*M'gan yiu*,' the mandarin said peremptorily. '*Dui ngoh mo m'fong been-ah.*'

Father Callaghan and I straightened ourselves.

'What did he say?' I whispered.

'He said,' Father Callaghan muttered, 'it is of no consequence and does not inconvenience him. He's a very formal person. They all are at his rank.'

Carefully, but not obviously, I studied my first mandarin. He looked very much as I expected from the illustrations I had seen in a volume on Chinese costume. About five feet six inches tall, he was approximately forty years old with a smooth, expressionless face and dressed in a blue silk *ch'I fu* richly embroidered with gold dragons and swirling clouds. The base of the garment, reaching to his cloth shoes, was decorated with diagonal gold and blue bands under a border of rounded billows. Around his waist was a tight girdle, held in place with a mother-of-pearl clasp from which hung a rosewood fan case, an ivory snuff bottle, a thin bamboo tube which I knew from my reading on Chinese costume contained a pair of chopsticks and, incongruously, a silver pocket watch on a chain with an onyx fob. Across his shoulders was a *pi ling*, a stiff flared collar attached to the top front button of the *ch'I fu*. It, too, was adorned with woven dragons and a two-inch border of gold thread. His hat was a small cone of split bamboo held in place by a red cotton string under his chin. From the finial on the apex, a button of opaque jade, hung two peacock feathers attached to the hat by a small jade cylinder.

'You do not know our new priest, Excellency,' Father Callaghan said. 'May I introduce you? This is Father Stephen.'

The mandarin, who had been busying himself with one of his entourage, stared myopically at me. I kow-towed as low as I dared.

'I know 'bout you,' the mandarin remarked in English, adding noncommittally, 'People tell me 'bout you in Wuchow.'

'To what do we humble priests owe the unexpected pleasure of your company, Excellency?' Father Callaghan said, continuing, 'I hope we have not unwittingly transgressed a law. It is not our intention to break the peaceful, law-abiding nature of the town of Wuchow.'

'You have Miss-us Bwair?' the mandarin enquired.

'She is indeed here, sir. She is resting in our quarters.'

'Fetch her,' the mandarin ordered. 'I wan' talk her.'

Father Callaghan signalled to Ah Fong, who bent low yet again then ran into the mission.

'May we offer you refreshment, Excellency?' Father Callaghan suggested. 'Our food and drink is humble but we have tea.'

The mandarin shook his head very slightly and, with a show of reaching down and stretching out the loose sleeve of his *ch'I fu* to its fullest extent, studied his watch. I sensed he was not doing this to discover the time so much as to pass it. The watch was less a timepiece and more an ornate piece of jewellery.

Ah Fong returned, Mrs Blair walking behind him. She had tidied her hair but her face, without make-up, looked ethereally white. She stepped towards the mandarin then, at a discreet distance from him, bowed as we had done. I had somehow expected her to curtsey.

'Miss-us Bwair,' the mandarin began, taking his fan out of its case, 'a message come say you dog shot by guard.'

'Yes, Your Excellency,' Mrs Blair replied softly, 'this morning.'

'The dog small dog,' the mandarin went on, toying with his fan, opening and closing it. 'The dog call *lou siu gau*.'

Mrs Blair nodded bleakly.

'You dog good dog,' the mandarin declared. 'Do his job good. Must guard also. Like tiger. Guard also like man for you. So! Dog must be gife honour. You come East Side . . .' He studied his watch again. '. . . one hour, one half hour.'

'Yes, Your Excellency,' Mrs Blair said.

'You come, *san foo*,' the mandarin added, pointing to Father Callaghan and myself with his fan. 'Must come. Important you come. I leave solijer help you.'

He motioned to one of his men and an order was barked out. Two of his personal guards stepped away from the palanquin, stationing themselves outside the mission gate. They were joined by a third liveried Chinese carrying a whip.

'One hour, one half hour,' the mandarin repeated, snapped his fan shut in the palm of his hand with an act of finality and turned to get into his palanquin.

Everyone quickly kow-towed and the procession, preceded by the gong, flag and whip bearers, marched down the *hutong*, scattering the crowd gathered there, children fleeing and adults hastily kow-towing in the dirt. Those who were slow to show their obeisance were cracked with the whip.

'What does he mean by the East Side?' I enquired as Ah Fong closed the gates.

'He means the cemetery,' Father Callaghan replied.

'Cemetery?' I queried.

'When we came here – the Europeans – we were given a plot of land outside the town. On the hillside overlooking the river. They don't want us buried in their places. Where we have our final resting place does not have good *fung shui*. In other words, it's not a propitious spot. The balance of nature is out of kilter there. The wind and water – the *fung* and the *shui* – are not quite right.'

'Why does he want us there?'

'Only the Lord knows. But be sure it's not an invitation we can ignore. And we'll have to don our best robes. This is going to be an official afternoon.'

Exactly an hour and a half later, I stepped out of my chair to see the mandarin's party gathered on a hillside terrace lined with low stone graves and wooden crosses, some of them askew, others bleached by the sun. There must have been nearly a hundred Chinese present, many wearing the mandarin's livery. Some were guards, others I assumed to be secretaries, household staff or local Chinese dignitaries who had been obliged to attend. All were attired in formal finery regardless of the beating sun.

Our small group of the Blairs, Mr Morrisby, Father Callaghan and myself made its way slowly towards the assembly up the earth steps cut in the hillside, the mandarin impassively awaiting our arrival under an ornate umbrella. Before him had been dug a small square hole. As we drew near, there was a succession of kow-towing before the mandarin made it known, with a flick of his fan, he wished the proceedings to commence.

The throng parted and a servant appeared carrying the corpse of the Jack Russell on a lacquer tray. He laid it at the feet of Mrs Blair, bowed to her and stepped back. The dog was already semi-rigid, its legs stuck out at right angles, its jaws slightly apart showing a pink tongue and its eyes open but glazed. In its shoulder was a small black hole, the only sign of blood upon the little corpse a dark stain in the leather collar.

Mrs Blair looked down upon the dog and began to sob. Father Callaghan put his hand on her arm, whispering something to her whilst her husband took her other hand. A large fly buzzed over the wound. I flicked it away with my hand. It seemed the least I could do in the circumstances. The motion of my hand wafted a slight, sickly perfume of putrefaction towards my face.

At a signal from the mandarin, the servant stepped forward again, lifting the tray and taking it to a diminutive old man who produced a small pine box from within the crowd. With some ceremony, the dog's legs were folded and held in place with red silken cords. This done, it was wrapped in a sheet of white silk and placed in its coffin which was lowered into the hole. A Chinese in working men's clothes carrying a shovel was ushered forward and, after kow-towing, commenced to fill in the hole.

I watched all this in a detached way, wondering what Father Callaghan was thinking. It was not right that a dog should be buried in the Christian cemetery and it occurred to me the mandarin might have ordered this ceremony by way of a slight against the foreigners. And yet, I considered, he had praised the dog's good qualities.

Throughout the ceremony, the mandarin neither looked at the dog, the grave nor the people around him. With a stolid stare, he gazed into the distance, at a pagoda on the far bank of the river and the hills behind, vague in the haze.

The dog buried, I assumed that would be end of the matter but it was not. With the earth mound above its coffin smoothed over, the mandarin stepped back, giving a brief sign with a flick of his hand. The crowd opened to allow two guards to push another man forward. Mrs Blair gasped and put her hand to her mouth.

'What is it?' I muttered to Father Callaghan under my breath.

'The Residency guard,' Father Callaghan whispered.

Stripped to the waist, the guard looked dejected and ashamed. He was a young man with firm muscles, his cue tied in a circle around his brow. He was thrust in front of the mandarin, to whom he kow-towed deeply, going down on his knees and pressing his forehead to the ground. The mandarin let him do this for several minutes before giving a curt speech in rapid Cantonese.

'What is he saying?' I asked softly.

'He's saying the guard did not do his duty and brought shame upon himself and his master,' Father Callaghan translated. 'By that, he means himself, not Mr Morrisby. He says he must now pay his respects to the dog. It's about the most insulting thing he could order him to do. He'll lose a lot of face.'

The guard shifted round on the ground until he was kneeling before the dog's grave. He looked quickly about then began to kow-tow to the mound of earth, bobbing his head up and down.

I did not see what signal was made, nor by whom, but as the miscreant bobbed up for the sixth or seventh time, one of his erstwhile comrades stepped abruptly forward and, with a swift single swing of his sword, decapitated him.

Mrs Blair screamed once, turning into her husband's shoulder. The Chinese crowd did not flinch. The mandarin continued to gaze distractedly at the faraway hills. Father Callaghan muttered what I assumed was a brief blessing for the dead man.

As for myself, I could think of nothing. I know I should have reacted somehow, joined my fellow priest in prayer, felt pity or horror. Even fascination, in the circumstances, might have been acceptable. Manic laughter would not have been amiss, would later have been forgiven. Yet I did nothing. I just stared, my mind a total blank, at the severed head lying on its cheek next to the dog's grave, the man's cue unravelled and his neck pumping the last of his blood into the freshly dug soil.

Last week, I had an accident. Of sorts. I have tried to ignore it but it nags, which I find most annoying.

It was a hot night and I could not sleep. I had lain for hours, tossing and turning with the sighing, rattling air conditioner turned off. Finally, in a restless fidget, I dressed in my pyjama trousers and went up to the roof.

Stepping carefully through rows of shrubs and flowers grow- ing in pots tended by Tsoi, and ducking the washing lines strung between metal Y-shaped poles, I sat on the low wall surrounding the roof top. Glancing down into Nanking Street, all the cooked food stalls but one were shut and it was doing a brisk trade, steam billowing from the cooking range on the pavement, the sound of shallow frying exploding over the rise and fall of conversation at the makeshift tables.

There were a few clouds overhead upon which the lights of the city reflected but no moon, the stars invisible so the night sky seemed foreboding and sullen. The Kowloon hills were indiscernible against the darkness, but, as I peered into the night, I became aware of a band of orange hanging along their upper slopes.

'They are burning the hills again,' I remarked to myself.

I moved from the wall to a wooden tea chest in the middle of the roof in which Tsoi keeps his gardening tools and propagates cuttings to sell for a few cents in the markets. It is not that he needs the money: he needs the work rather than the income for, like me, if he stopped being active he would stop living.

A dark gap appeared in the line of fire. I watched it intently for some minutes: the fire brigade had arrived or the flames met with a rocky outcrop. Yet, in a short time, the flames had joined hands again, inexorably climbing higher.

'They're burning out the dragons!' I exclaimed, as if I had suddenly stumbled upon the *raison d'être* for the fire-raising. 'They're burning out the mountain spirits. Chasing the ghosts away.'

Unsteadily, I climbed onto the tea chest to get a better view. The wood creaked under my weight, but I was somehow unaware of my precarious position and became light-headed with a kind of exhilaration I had not experienced before.

'Go on!' I heard a voice mutter from somewhere in the sky. 'Get the bastards! Burn them out! Drive them away into the sky to be frozen by the clouds. Freeze their pointed tails off. Put their murderous eyes out.'

I shook my fists at the hills, but they were no longer fists but cudgels. My body seemed not to belong to me. Some kind of divine divorce had occurred and I was another entity, an observer watching an old fool totter on a tea chest in the middle of a flat roof on a hot night, surrounded by pots of mute flowers.

I assume I lost my balance.

One moment I was secure, the next I was falling. I seem to recall a dragon pushing me. Bars of fire seared across my ribs, a terrible pain running through my arms. I thought I was dying, that this was what it was like. When life left the body, it was drawn out like cords of twine being pulled through the flesh.

The next sensation I felt was an intense warmth. I opened my eyes to be confronted by a brilliant light. Trying to shield my eyes was useless: something was holding my right arm. I squinted and slowly became aware of my surroundings. Three feet beneath me were rows of chrysanthemums. Somehow, I was floating over them as if in a flying dream when a motion of the arms sets one swimming, soaring and gliding through the air.

It was a minute before I realised I was suspended above the plants on a mesh of washing lines. The warmth was the early sun. I tried to free my right arm but found I was well and truly hog-tied. Then I heard a voice from somewhere out of sight over the top of my head.

'So! Look at you, you old sod! How on earth did you get into such a bloody pickle, eh! My god! The ways and whims of ancient fools.'

It was a woman's voice, rich not with mockery but laughter.

I screwed my head round. Standing by the edge of the garden of pots, the sun behind her, was a woman. I seemed to know her and yet I seemed not to. My mind was confused. I remember thinking if I was dead then this was no angel. She was short, slightly bent, with grey hair tied into a straggling bun, her face lined not so much by exposure to the passage of years as to the rigours of harsh sunlight. Her nose was prominent, Jewish and her eyes small, dark and shrewd like those of a clever rodent.

'Who's that?' I asked with alarm. I became aware my genitals were in full view, my pyjama trousers having twisted themselves around me so the buttonless fly was wide open.

'Who do you think it is, you old buffoon!'

'I don't know,' I said, discovering my left arm was free after all and struggling to reposition my clothing.

'Stella!' the woman retorted.

I thought for a moment, my mind still befuddled.

'Stella what?'

'What do you mean, Stella what?' the woman replied in the impatient tones of a crabby schoolmistress. 'Stella who! Stella van der Poehl! Christ almighty, man! Who the hell do you think it is? You've so many old women in your life?' She paused, then added, 'Plenty of young tarts perhaps, but no old harridans. Now,' she stood with her arms akimbo, 'what shall we do with you?'

'Cut me down,' I suggested, gathering my wits.

'We could leave you there.'

'We?' I exclaimed.

I turned my head further. Standing behind the woman were Mr Wu, Tsoi and a young man stripped to the waist holding a long knife which glinted in the sunlight. I recognised him as one of the workers from the butcher's shop along the street.

'What you doin'?' Mr Wu enquired.

'I fell,' I said lamely. 'At least, that's what I think happened.'

'So we see,' Mrs van der Poehl observed sarcastically, 'although God alone knows what you were up to.'

'I was watching them fighting dragons,' I answered, my memory clearing.

Mrs van der Poehl grimaced impatiently and nodded to the others. Tsoi moved all the pots away from beneath me then, with Mr Wu's help, they lowered me as the butcher's boy cut the washing lines, one by one. At last, I was standing vertically once more upon the roof top.

'You were bloody lucky,' Mrs van der Poehl said, pointing to the chrysanthemums. 'Another foot and you'd've been impaled upon Tsoi's garden.'

I looked at the pots: every plant was tied to a length of bamboo thicker than a pencil. The sight of the stakes weakened me and I felt my legs giving way. The butcher's boy caught me and assisted me to the lift and down to Mrs van der Poehl's flat.

'I can look after myself,' I protested as he lowered me into a worn leather armchair positioned directly in front of a television set. 'I don't need molly-coddling.'

'Nonsense!' Mrs van der Poehl snapped. 'Be quiet, you old goat, and say thank you to the good souls who not only found you but cut you free. I couldn't have done it.'

I meekly obeyed, nodding my thanks to the butcher's boy

who, smiling profusely but saying nothing, left. I noticed he had a curling dragon tattooed on his right shoulder-blade. It was not a crude picture such as sailors have but an intricate portrait drawn with careful artistry, not the result of a twenty-minute needle session but of hours of painful craftsmanship. The creature's eyes were incredibly evil, its claws and scales, the pointed edges to its spinal fins outlined in the finest detail. I wondered vaguely to which of the local triad gangs the boy owed allegiance.

Mrs van der Poehl draped a towel around my shoulders and began vigorously to massage my neck.

'They thought you were dead, you know,' she remarked as she manipulated my muscles, twisting my head in a circular motion. 'A goner. You weren't moving. Just hanging there. How long had you been there?'

'Since about two, I think,' I answered, 'and you're hurting my neck.'

'It'll do you good. Nothing worthwhile comes of lethargy. The best things in life are borne of pain. You're a priest. You should know that.'

'I *was* a priest,' I remonstrated.

'Once a good man always a good man. Or bad. Men don't change. Mr van der Poehl,' she spoke as if he was not a relative but a passing acquaintance, 'was just the same. Started life as a little shit and ended it as a bigger turd. Only size alters, not character.'

I put my hand up, grabbing her wrist.

'That's enough! I want to be able to hold my head up without having a brace on my neck. If you must massage something, do my legs. They've got pins and needles.'

Mrs van der Poehl pulled a low stool from under the table upon which the television stood and knelt before me. She rolled my pyjamas up and began manipulating my toes as if they were not part of a living man but of an inanimate doll.

I looked around the room. I had not entered Mrs van der Poehl's flat before although I had been afforded a glimpse of the interior from time to time through the door. The rows of books she kept on a set of shelves by the television leaned against each other as if exhausted from being read, the gaps between them indications of where she had sold volumes to raise money. The curtains were faded to a uniform khaki. Under a day bed slept a tabby cat, oblivious to a blue budgerigar in a bamboo cage suspended from a hook in the ceiling which had once held up a ceiling fan. A vase of daisies on a sideboard might have been newly picked, had they not been plastic: I guessed they had been rinsed to shift the dust forever ekeing through the windows.

On the day bed above the cat was the pug dog, Pu Yi. It was an even uglier sight at close range than it was from a distance in the street. The animal was asleep on its side, its feet jutting out and the folds of skin on its face all the more contorted for being wedged up against a cushion. Its pose reminded me of the terrier's corpse from long ago.

In the stillness of the room, the scent of the obnoxious beast and the cat mingled with that of Mrs van der Poehl's perfume, which rose from where she knelt before me, bringing back an uneasy memory of supplicants, psalms and the stifling fumes of censers. Had I not been used to the street smells of the Orient, the waft of different effluvia from shops, drains and obscure foods, I am sure I would have recoiled from the curious odour.

Hanging upon the wall was a red lacquer frame containing the photograph of a dashing man in uniform. About thirty years old, he had a bushy moustache and his cap was tilted, giving him a debonair rather than raffish look. The portrait was faded from exposure to sunlight, the bottom so deteriorated that a dedication in black ink stood out starkly. The writing was cursive and effeminate. Under the photograph was a small glass-fronted box in which hung five medals, the metal tarnished and the ribbons, like the photograph, faded from sunlight.

'My husband,' Mrs van der Poehl said, following the direction of my gaze.

'Yes, I guessed it was.'

'He was a little prick!' she replied, not looking up from my foot.

I squinted at the photograph. The figure seemed to be wearing a Sam Brown belt.

'Was he in the British Army?'

'HKVDF,' she said adding, 'Hong Kong Volunteer Defence

Force. Not a real soldier. He was Dutch, you know. From Java.'

'You've kept his photo,' I remarked. I might have added, despite what you think of him, but I did not: my bluntness does not extend to cruelty.

'Yes, I've kept it,' she answered glumly. 'God knows why.'

I knew why. Just as I have not destroyed my diary or those few possessions I have in the bank, so has she not discarded her husband's photograph. I suspect she feels as I do about memory. A vision of him will remain in her mind until the moment of death so the photograph is superfluous: why chuck it out with life's other trash? And yet photographs are such handy items for they refresh vision, keep alive memories in the mind's eye. Perhaps, I thought as I looked at him, she was keeping this picture because she preferred to think of him as a little shit rather than what he became. There again, it might have been love.

The budgerigar came to life, hopping from perch to cage bars and whistling. The cat raised its head languorously then went back to sleep.

Her flat is not unlike my own. It is untidy, filled with the petty detritus of a long life in a foreign land. The furniture is plain and cheap, such as one might find in the down-market shops in Mong Kok, the only Oriental piece positioned away from the window. It is a temple table, a narrow wooden trestle supported by curved legs which end in balls gripped by carved talons. It was originally painted in deep scarlet and gold but time has darkened it the colour of plum juice. Upon it, amidst a debris of old letters, a tea cup stuffed with pencils, a brown glass San Miguel beer ashtray containing loose change and a paperback book, there stood a head of Buddha carved from a light, rich wood.

It was not a Chinese Buddha with a sublime smile on its round chubby face, which I take to be the grin of an imbecile rather than a deity, but an Indian or Burmese one. At least a foot tall, the eyes were hooded so the bust looked demurely downwards. It might have been reading the letters or casting a disapproving glance at the mess strewn around it. The god's chin was slightly pointed, the nose thin and the mouth like a young girl's with the hint of a pout. In the middle of the figure's forehead was a tiny spot.

'The third eye,' I said without thinking.

'I'm sorry? What did you say?'

I stared for a moment at Mrs van der Poehl. Despite her having left my feet to work upon my shins, her fingers tugging my flesh, I had forgotten her presence. Once again, this time only briefly, I had wandered away from myself.

'Your Buddha . . .' I began.

'My husband's Buddha,' she corrected me. 'What about it?'

'It's a fine piece,' I said. 'Made of sandalwood?'

'It is. Rub it and the fragrance comes off to this day. Over a hundred years old. I don't know where he bought it. Or won it. Or stole it.'

'The mark in the forehead is where the third eye hides,' I said.

'Who needs a third eye!' Mrs van der Poehl exclaimed. 'I see too bloody much with a pair of the damned things. If god had intended us to see more, he'd have arranged it. You should know. You're a priest.'

'I *was* a priest,' I corrected her again. '*Was*, not *is*.'

We fell silent. I listened to the sounds drifting in from outside. A hawker was calling out his wares. The horn of a passing lorry wheezed asthmatically. A coolie carrying a heavy load shouted '*Wei! Wei!*' as he pushed through the pedestrians, his shouting punctuated by the rattle of the steel shutters going up in the butcher's shop.

Closing my eyes, I imagined the people passing below. By doing so, focusing on specific realities, I hoped to cease my mental drifting.

The coolie with the load would be dressed in ragged shorts, bare to the waist with his muscles bunched under the weight of his pole and load. The hawker would be similarly dressed, but instead of having bare feet would be wearing a pair of old tennis shoes or flip-flop plastic sandals made to look like leather. Down the street, towards the junction with Ning Po Street, a police constable in a khaki uniform, his silver buttons gleaming and his revolver snug in a leather holster so polished it might have been glazed, would be filling in his beat notes, putting them in the grey galvanised box nailed to the wall of the herbalist's shop. The old man who operated a key-cutting service from a pavement stall like a wooden pulpit would just be setting out his tools: he would be wearing a pair of worn dark trousers and a white vest so bright and clean it would catch the sun.

I opened my eyes and found I was watching the cat. Its paws were twitching in a dream of chasing rats down the alleys or getting to grips with the budgerigar.

'I dream of dragons,' I admitted.

'We all dream of strange things,' Mrs van der Poehl replied, massaging my left knee. 'It's what comes of being old. We've seen it all, the likes of you and me . . . We've been there, done that and sent the postcard.'

The cat got up, idly stretched, left the shadow of the day bed and, leaping nimbly onto the window sill, settled there to await the sunlight.

'How do your legs feel?' Mrs van der Poehl enquired.

'Good. They feel good.'

'It's just a matter of restoring the circulation.'

'What do you dream of?' I asked.

'Me!' she retorted lightly. 'What makes you think I dream? That's a luxury only the innocent can afford.' Then, after thinking for a moment, she went on, 'I dream sometimes. Of handsome young men who dance with me all night long and give me diamonds.'

'Do you know these men?'

'No, not one of them. Figments of the imagination. But,' and her voice took on a hard edge, 'I can tell you there isn't a single man jack of them wears a soldier's kit.' She glanced fleetingly at the photograph on the wall. 'Sailors, airmen, young bucks in well-cut suits. And it's always in the twenties. When I was a girl.'

I looked at Mrs van der Poehl. Her grey hair was wispy where it was escaping from the bun which moved as she worked her hands against my flesh. It was not difficult to imagine her as a flapper girl. Despite her large nose, she must have been pretty, her eyes darkly seductive before the years filled them with caution, her skin soft before the Oriental sun sucked it dry.

'The other night,' she continued, 'I did the Charleston with a blonde, pretty lad decked out in one of those hideous shirts tourists wear. All printed palm trees and beaches. Awful dress sense. But what a beautiful boy he was . . .'

'My dragons are real,' I said. 'I've never seen a dragon, of course. But I know they're genuine. Somewhere, they lurk as alive and real as that cat of yours.'

'Just age!' Mrs van der Poehl rejoined. 'Your dragons are no more real than my dandies.'

'They seem it.'

'So they should! What use is a dream if it doesn't seem like reality?'

She finished her massaging and pulled my pyjama trouser legs down.

'Feel better?' she asked, not waiting for a reply. 'You should slow down, you know,' she went on. 'You're past it. Give up your pupil. I'm sure you could get by. I do.'

'It's not just that. I need to be active. You know what the Bible says? The devil finds work for idle hands.'

I looked into Mrs van der Poehl's eyes. There was no hint of condemnation, no suggestion of criticism.

'I have to keep on working,' I explained. 'If I stop, I'll die. I'm like . . .' I searched for an appropriate image '. . . like a shark. If it stops swimming, it drowns.'

'I know,' she said. 'It's the same with all men. Once you start to slow down, you think you're redundant and it scares the hell out of you. But you're wrong.'

She opened the window a fraction, warm air blowing in, ruffling the cat's fur.

'I'll tell you a story,' she said in a mock patronising tone. 'I'm sure it's one you know, being an old China hand. Like me!'

She brushed some cat hairs off the day bed, pushed the dog's malodorous hindquarters aside, smoothed her skirt under her buttocks and sat down. The bed creaked and the budgerigar, assuming the sound to be an intruder flying in through the window, set up a belligerent twittering.

'Once upon a time,' she began, as if recounting the tale to a child, 'there was an emperor of China called Tai Lung. He lived in the Forbidden City surrounded by henchmen and mandarins, eunuchs and concubines and guards. One day, worrying about an uprising by a distant warlord, he was walking in the gardens, deep in thought, when a peacock strutted towards him. It was a magnificent bird. Its feathers were azure and emerald, glistening in the sunlight like a box of gems. To the emperor's surprise, the bird perched before him on a rock statue and began to speak. "You are old and worried about your kingdom just as I am old and was concerned about mine," squawked the bird. "What know you of the affairs of state?" Tai Lung said sharply. "Everything," the peacock replied. "I have subjects I must appease, the whole of the Imperial Gardens to rule over. Just as you have China. But it was getting beyond me. I could no longer chase the younger cocks away, no longer tread the peahens as I did." This struck a nerve with Tai Lung who had resorted to his herbalist of late to remedy a certain lacking in the Imperial bedroom department. His favourite concubine was growing sullen. "So what did you do?" the emperor asked. "I let the young cocks take charge of the garden," answered the peacock. "They chase the sparrows and sort out their own squabbles. I concentrate on my harem of hens and leave them the rest. That way, I still rule but I don't have all the cares." The emperor thought it over, called his council and delegated responsibility for the warlord to his princes. The herbalist was dismissed and the concubine smiled once more.'

'No doubt,' I remarked, 'the herbalist was executed and the emperor ate the peacock.'

'Perhaps,' Mrs van der Poehl agreed. 'Peacock is delicious. But the lesson was learned. You should heed it. Slow down. Let younger men take on the world. It's theirs, you know. Not ours. Not yours. We've had our turn and made a bloody mess of it.'

'That's not a true story,' I said. 'There's never been an Emperor Tai Lung. Big Dragon. You made it up.'

'What does it matter?' Mrs van der Poehl replied. 'The moral holds water even if the narrative leaks like a colander.'

I rose to my feet. My legs felt stronger than they had for days.

'I must go,' I said. 'I've things to do . . .'

I went to the door of the flat and turned the handle.

'We should stick together, us old hands,' Mrs van der Poehl said. 'We're a dying breed.'

'Yes,' I agreed pensively. 'We are.' I opened the door and stepped out into the hallway. The air was cool and smelt of disinfectant and dust. 'Thank you for bringing my legs back to life,' I said.

'Don't go dreaming of dragons on the roof again,' Mrs van der Poehl advised. 'And remember you can't fly. Only Peter Pan and the angels can.'

As soon as the words left her mouth I saw, as clearly as if I was there again, the girls entering the yard in Wuchow, a lifetime away, their white blouses catching the rays of the hot, high sun.

'Stephen! Stephen!'

It was Father Callaghan's voice, urgent and insistent. I put down the censer I was polishing, folded my rag and screwed the top on the Brasso bottle, genuflected quickly to the altar and ran to the chapel door. Just inside the mission gate was a figure sitting on the ground with its back to the stonework. Ah Fong was by its side with Father Callaghan standing over the pair of them.

'What is it?' I called out.

'Come!' Father Callaghan shouted. 'Lend a hand, will you?'

On joining him, I saw Ah Fong was tending a Chinese youth wearing the remnants of a uniform.

'One of the mandarin's cohorts?' I asked.

'No,' Father Callaghan said, 'he's a soldier. There was a detachment in the town yesterday. Moved on now. Something to do with the prefect. Help us carry him in.'

I put my arm round the soldier. He was little more than a boy, perhaps seventeen or eighteen years of age. His clothing stank of sweat and smoke but there was also a faint, acrid stench about him I could not place. With Father Callaghan, I lifted him by the shoulders: I was surprised he was so light. We carried him into our little infirmary, a room once used as a store but equipped to take any of the sick who might come to us. We laid him face down on a *k'ang*. As soon as his skin touched the quilt he began to shiver in rapid spasms, his eyes rolling and his tongue incessantly licking his lips. Beads of perspiration appeared on his nape.

'Malaria?' I suggested.

'No,' Father Callaghan said and, turning to Ah Fong, ordered, '*Dung shui*, Ah Fong.'

This, I knew from the smattering of Cantonese I was picking up, meant cold water. Ah Fong ladled some into a bowl whilst Father Callaghan unlocked our medicine box and rummaged in it. I wiped the youth's neck and he ceased shivering, craned round and, looking up into my face, muttered something I did not comprehend.

'What he saying?' I asked Ah Fong.

'He say you good man. *San foo* good man.'

'Cut the legs off his *fu*,' Father Callaghan instructed. 'Above the knee.'

I took a pair of scissors to the material and cut round his thigh. It was not until I went to his feet to pull the tubes of cotton clear I smelt the unidentifiable stench again, a little stronger.

'Take off his shoes,' Father Callaghan commanded. 'Be gentle.'

I put my hand on the sole of one shoe and pulled carefully. The youth thrashed his arms on the *k'ang* and hissed through his teeth.

'I hold him,' Ah Fong said. 'You pull quick-quick, master.'

I did as I was told and a wave of noxious gas hit my face so strongly that I reeled backwards, the bile rising to my throat.

'Gangrene,' Father Callaghan said ominously. 'Take off his other shoe.'

Holding my breath, I did as requested. Both the young man's feet were pussed. What was not livid red was a glutinous pale green.

'Can we amputate . . .?' I began but Father Callaghan shook his head.

'If we were the most learned surgeons in Dublin, we'd be at a loss. There's nothing we can do for the poor soul except make his last days a little more peaceful.'

For the next twenty minutes, as Ah Fong held the youth down and talked continuously to him in a monotone, Father Callaghan and I cleaned the wounds on his feet as best we could. Although the flesh was putrid to just above the ankles there seemed no break to the skin except on the soles of the feet.

'He must have walked a long way,' I observed, 'to have so injured himself.'

'Oh, he crawled here,' Father Callaghan said. 'Look at his knees. Raw. He's not walked for some days. The wounds on his feet were not caused by marching. He has committed some trifling wrong and this is his punishment.'

'His punishment?' I replied.

Father Callaghan started to dab iodine on the wounds. I expected the young man to start writhing as the medicine stung but he remained quite still.

'He can't feel it,' Father Callaghan remarked as if reading my thoughts. 'The local nerves are gone. Long gone.'

'What was his punishment?' I asked.

'An age-old one. They lie the miscreant on his front and tie him down. Then a man with a light switch of flat bamboo starts to tap lightly on the skin. Tap, tap, tap. For four or five hours, the administrator of the punishment changing as the arms tire. It does not hurt at first. This is nothing like a caning from a schoolmaster. Thrash, thrash and over with. Oh, no! After a time, all the little veins under the skin rupture. The bamboo carries on its tap, tap, tap. The flesh swells and the bruising spreads so the complete sole will lose its nerves. Then, in no time at all, gangrene sets in. Sometimes it's done to the soles of the feet, sometimes to the thighs and sometimes to the fleshy part at the base of the buttocks. It's called the *light bamboo punishment*. It's a death sentence, though.'

'And his crime?'

'Nothing grand,' Father Callaghan answered, 'you can be sure. Perhaps he disobeyed an order he did not hear. Dropped his gun, perhaps. This is China, Father Stephen, not the Household Cavalry of the Queen of England.'

The wounds cleaned and bandaged, Father Callaghan gave the young man an opium pill and he was soon asleep.

'Surely,' I suggested as we left the infirmary, closing the door behind us and leaving one of our girls to look over the patient, 'we could cut his feet off.'

'No, Father Stephen, we could not.'

'But they do it at sea,' I interrupted. 'They get the sailor drunk, in a stupor, cut off the damaged limb, cover the wound in boiling tar and leave it. The pitch sets and . . .'

I wanted so much to save this man, to bring him back from the door of death, rescue him from the barbarity of his punishment. I could not believe a life could be so discarded because of a petty misdemeanour. Perhaps I also wanted to save him to atone for the captain's victim.

'We're too late. The corruption'll be right through his system by now. Besides, if we cut his feet off and he survived – then what? Another cripple begging in the streets of Wuchow. Another man living in torment and fear of death because he knows he'll go to his ancestors incomplete. No, Father Stephen, we can do nothing but pray for his soul.'

I returned to the chapel and the censer I was polishing, feeling a terrible, bitter rage deeper than any I had ever known. I hated not the Chinese, nor their barbarity. It was not the cruelty I abhorred.

It was my God who had looked down upon His world, at His creation fashioned in His own image and let this abomination happen.

This morning, I took myself along to the forecourt of the temple where I installed myself, sitting quite peacefully on the stone bench, and set about reading today's edition of *Wah Kiu Yat Po*, the oldest of Hong Kong's Chinese newspapers.

I have purchased a copy almost every day since it was first published in the summer of 1925. It is an ironic title where I am concerned for it translates as *Overseas Chinese Daily News*. The implication is that Chinese who live in Hong Kong are exiled from their native lands, which is bunkum. If anything, Hong Kong is more like the true China than its vast neighbour, now the latter has ejected its emperor, its Taoist and Buddhist religions and its village culture and replaced it with a chairman, the doctrine according to

Marx and the commune system. In Hong Kong, temples thrive that would, over the wire border, be derelict shells: the hillsides of Hong Kong are scattered with tombs swept clean each year by the living in respect for the dead which, in China, would be just hollows in the bracken.

This aside, it is even more ironic I should read this paper. I am not an overseas Chinese. I am an adopted one.

The newspaper costs me twenty cents. I buy it from a news-vendor who runs a stand in the entrance to a stairway in Ning Po Street. He may be found there only in the morning, until half past nine, his main trade being office and shop staff on their way to work. He does not call out headlines to attract trade, nor does he hang a billboard in the street with the main news hurriedly scribbled upon it with the thickest of writing brushes but relies entirely upon those who know he is there.

His stall is little more than a narrow box of planks screwed into the wall of the hallway which, when not in use, folds flat against the plasterwork so as not to hinder those who use the building. Even when operating, the fold-down shelf projects no more than a foot from the wall.

I know the news-vendor as Lam: his given names are unknown to me. He is in his late twenties and tubercularly thin with a malformed left hand, his fingers being mere stubs of flesh projecting from a club of bone where his palm should be. As if to compensate for this flaw, his right hand is equipped with slender, sensitive fingers like those of a musician. Had he two such hands he could be an accomplished *pipa* player. Not only is his left hand defective but he is also exceedingly short-sighted and wears spectacles with large lenses which look like those of an old-fashioned bicycle lamp. These give him an owlish appearance, magnifying his eyes to at least twice their natural size: when he blinks he might be pulling blinds down over the windows of his mind rather than flaps of skin to clean the street grit from his vision.

Lam is a gentle character, soft-spoken and kind. One morning, I saw him feeding a lame sparrow with crumbs from a bun he had half-eaten. The bird had only one leg upon which it hopped, effectively but clumsily. I was sure this was Lam's only repast that morning and was so moved as to be prompted to speak to him.

'My friend,' I said as I handed over two ten-cent coins, 'I think you spoil the sparrow.'

'How is that?' he replied.

'In this city there is much food to be had by birds. To be served with a fresh sweet bun rather than having to hunt for it is indeed a luxury.'

'That is so,' he said, 'but there is no harm in it. When I am done, the bird will still be able to find his food. Let him share my good fortune for once.'

I left with my newspaper under my arm, humbled and filled with a sense of privilege that I had been fortunate to see such noble justice, a crippled man dividing his precious luck with a crippled bird.

For months after Lam set up his business, I wondered how on earth he made a living from it. He sells about 300 newspapers a day, stocking not just *Wah Kiu Yat Po* but also *Sing Tao* and *Kung Sheung* with a number of lesser, more esoteric broadsides and Chinese comics, but these cannot bring in a living wage when one considers he must pay rent to the landlord of the building for use of the hallway and protection money to the local Red Poles to ensure his wooden lock-up shelves remain attached to the wall. So concerned was I for this gentle young man I once, some time ago, surreptitiously followed him after his close of business.

At nine thirty, he folded away his shelving, sold at a discount what remained of his morning delivery to a store on the corner of Shanghai Street and disappeared in the direction of Mong Kok. I shadowed him to a back alley in Tung Choi Street, where he met a man standing by a large aluminium cabin trunk. Money changed hands and Lam was presented with a wooden box the size of a large attaché case. It was painted green with Chinese characters stencilled on the side but I was too far away and could not make them out.

The case in his right hand, Lam went to Nathan Road and boarded a bus going south: I was fortunate enough to catch another immediately behind his own. At the Star Ferry, he left the bus and travelled across the harbour on the lower deck where coolies and the poor are obliged to ride: it is against the ferry by-laws for cargo to be taken onto the upper deck. Once in Central District, Lam made his way to Peddar Street, where he squatted on the pavement, opened the box and wrapped a black, stained cloth around his club hand, holding it in place with a thick rubber band cut, I should think, from a bicycle inner tube. This done, he undid some catches and, as if performing a magician's trick, transmuted the box from an attaché-type case into a shoe-shine stand complete with a foot-rest. Within minutes, he was in business.

I laughed at myself, at my stupidity, at my allowing emotions to cloud my certain knowledge of Chinese acumen: that is, wherever there is life there is business to be done.

Today's edition of *Wah Kiu Yat Po* held little to capture my attention. The front page carried news of a bicycle-bomb attack in Saigon, general South-East Asian politics and a report of a kidnapping attempt on Hong Kong Island which had been bungled. The sun was warm but not yet too hot. The old lady in the temple was busy sweeping the stone floors, the scratching swish of her broom loud enough to overcome the traffic. I put the paper down on the bench beside me and leaned forward with my forearms on my legs. As I was wearing my *sam* and *fu*, albeit with an ordinary shirt, and having had my grey hair cut short as Chinese men of my age do, I very much doubt if anyone but the most eagle-eyed observer would have seen I was anything other than Chinese.

When I sit like this in the temple precinct, I let my mind empty. If I were more energetic, or less creaky of joint, I might do a bit of *tai chi*, shadow-boxing in slow motion with the elements of earth, air, fire and water. It has the same effect, clearing the brain of extraneous thoughts in preparation for meditation or peaceful, detached consideration of the metaphysical problems and obstacles of human existence.

My mind thus blank for a while, I became aware of a brief, quick movement on the ground beneath one of the shrubbery pots across the forecourt. I concentrated on the shadow of the pot. It was not until it moved again that I saw the gecko. It was two inches long and coloured in the dull khaki of its kind, its head raised and its front legs holding its forequarters clear of the ground. Aware the reptile is primarily nocturnal, I wondered what it was doing in the mid-morning, risking the presence of sharp beaks and heavy feet.

It bobbed its head a few times: this was the motion which had caught my eye. I looked around the ground near the creature, careful to move my eyes but not my head. There were no tasty insect morsels in view.

Quite suddenly, I saw a second gecko. It was near the base of the banyan tree and facing the first. It, too, was bobbing its head. A cloud shifted across the sun and, as soon as the shadow was over the temple forecourt, the banyan gecko went for the pot gecko, streaking over the open ground between them with such speed my eye could scarcely follow it. The creature skidded to a halt a few inches from the pot and they faced each other. The sun came out and the banyan gecko, realising it was in the sunlight, shifted its stance into the shade which, I presumed, the other thought its own. This was too much for the pot gecko which lunged at the newcomer. They thrashed together, a minuscule haze of dust rising from their conflict.

The confrontation was over quickly. The banyan gecko fled across the open ground towards my bench. I shifted my foot deliberately and it swerved in mid-flight to vanish under another of the pots. The victor, meanwhile, stood his ground then, with less haste, moved under the base of his own pot.

I considered this little contretemps for some minutes, drawing the same conclusion I do whenever I watch sparrows jousting on the tenement roof, dogs circling each other in the side-streets or cats spitting a warning to other feline intruders in the alleyways.

It is this: in the world of nature, where the animals live and rule, you may observe them conducting elaborate rituals but never see them going through the absurd, indecorous fooleries of religion. They have no time for the mystical, the magical, the marvellous. They are not governed by gods or goals. They exist for the sake of living, going about their business of survival without question.

Only men engage in such gratuitous nonsense, abiding by ceremony, governing themselves with liturgies and theologies. Some would say it is the price they pay for being intelligent. I suggest it is the cost of being not sufficiently intelligent to see through it all.

I have today purchased a new dressing gown, a full-length garment in heavy, crimson silk brocade with wide collars and, as it was tailored for a *gweilo*, it is large and generous. I have lost some weight over the past few years and can consequently wrap it substantially around my frame.

The shop in Mody Road from which I purchased it is owned by a man called Lau Kui-shing, whom I first met through Mr Wu. It seems they share the same ancestral village, somewhere in Kwangtung province, and the same vice.

Lau is a jolly man in his early sixties, short and curiously plump, which is uncommon for a Chinese. As they grow older they tend to become sinewy, wiry men, their bones bending as if not designed to carry even such a little flesh for so many years.

In this respect as in many others, I am like a Chinese: for that is what is happening to me. It pleases me. I regard myself as a Chinese for I have lived three-quarters of my natural life in China, spent my years eating the food and drinking the drink, breathing the air and speaking the language. What is more, although I suppose there is sufficient reason for me to wish otherwise, I am proud of it. I do not want to be a European, some high-and-mighty conqueror of the native masses, a patronising colonial with his all-too-perfect laws and his universal language, his wide-eyed pseudo-innocence and his grasping fingers, his hygienic, risk-free life and impeccable gods. I prefer to be one of those men who has discovered enough to know his own mind, to know he wishes to change and be another.

Lau's shop is crammed with merchandise. It is what he calls a general tourist mart, having seen the word in an advertisement in *Life* magazine: it showed a photograph of a Buick car before a glossy showroom over which were emblazoned the words *Stark's Car Mart*. Cars are one of the few items Lau seems not to purvey although I suspect, if you wanted one, he would know a man who could provide it at a discount for cash.

The window of the shop is a rich kaleidoscope of padded

cotton coats and brocade smoking jackets, lace blouses, embroidered slippers, sandalwood fans, small boxes of round ivory balls which, it is said, reduce tension if fondled, rattan coolie hats and children's skull-tight red and black silk hats with pom-poms on the top, octagonal card wastepaper baskets with appliqué cotton Chinese dolls on the side and lingerie. A hand-written sign reads *Many good price – pleas appley within.* The counters and shelves carry miniature ancient sword paper-knives in bone and brass scabbards, carved sailing junks ranging in size from a few inches to three feet tall, toys made of cheap plastic and racks of postcards depicting rickshaws, the Star Ferry, a crowded Tsim Sha Tsui street, the Peak Tram, the Hongkong and Shanghai Bank, a temple forecourt (cleared of beggars by the photographer) and two infants squatting on the deck of a sampan shovelling rice into their mouths.

'Good morning,' Lau said brightly as I walked in. His head was bent over an invoice book and a parcel wrapped in green tar-paper tied around with cord. The address on it was in Australia: he conducts a mail order business for former customers.

'Please,' he went on. 'Sit down. Take the weight off.' That is a phrase he picked up as he did *mart*. 'You wan' a beer, soft drink? San Mig? Green Spot orange?' Then he looked up and recognised me. 'Hi, *san foo*! Morning! *Nei ho ma?*'

'*Ho, ho.* I am well. And you? How's business?'

'Business good!' he exclaimed emphatically. 'One week, four cruise ship. Much business done. I run out of cotton hand-kercheefs. Never before.'

'That's bad,' I observed.

'No p'oblum. More coming from Tsuen Wan today. I got a friend . . .'

His voice tailed off and he winked. So much business is conducted in Hong Kong through friends and friends of friends. Lau will have paid a little over the odds to buy up someone else's order.

'So! You wan' a beer?'

'I'll have a Green Spot,' I replied.

He shouted out to the rear of the shop and an old woman came hobbling in with a bottle in one hand and a straw in the other. She had bound feet, her legs ending in stubs encased in what looked like painted wooden blocks.

'My mother,' Lau remarked.

I nodded politely to the old lady and made some comment of respect but she merely smirked toothlessly, put the drink on the counter, handed me the straw and hobbled off.

'She no can hear.' Lau touched his ear. 'Deaf. No sound. Good woman.'

I put the straw in the bottle and sucked. The orange juice was sickly sweet.

'So, what can I do for you?' Lau asked.

'A dressing gown,' I said. 'I want a dressing gown.'

'Silk? Cotton? Cotton polyester? Wool cotton mix? Very warm. I got good cotton one. Make in China.'

Before I could reply, he had whisked a packet from a shelf, ripped the cellophane open and spread the garment across the counter. It was light blue with the character *sow*, meaning *long life*, stitched in navy on the back.

'Good quality cotton. From India. Not Madras, not so good. Twelve dollars, for you seven. Old frien', old customer. *Gweilo*, not tourist. Live Hong Kong long time.'

'It's good,' I commented, feeling the cloth, 'but I want silk. Silk brocade.'

'Ah! You got good taste!' Lau exclaimed.

I picked my dressing gown from a choice of four. Two were deep blue, one black and the other crimson. They were all heavy, with double thickness sashes and intricate embroidery. The black gown portrayed clouds and hills and was a sober-looking piece, more befitting a man of my age and position, but the crimson one had a highly detailed pattern of trees and lakes, houses hidden in pine copses, people on sampans, temples on islands and bamboo groves beside cottages. Whereas the predominant colour in the pictures on the black item was silver with some blue, the crimson gown was realistic, with greens and browns, yellows and greys. I picked the latter.

'Good choice,' Lau congratulated me, wrapping the gown in brown paper and sealing it with sticky tape. 'Usually fifty-five dollar but for you, thirty-five.'

I handed over the bills. He did not count them. He trusted me just as I trusted him. A tourist would be unwise to do so.

Now, back in my flat, I am sitting in the cane chair, naked except for the gown. It is mid-afternoon and I feel decadent. I might be a latter-day Noël Coward. The silk is cold against my warm flesh despite the fact I have been wearing it for twenty minutes. Silk has a wonderful capacity, like jade, to stay cool, to lose heat quickly when removed from a source of warmth.

The dressing gown becomes me. I would gladly wear it in the street if I were not certain to be justifiably gawked at and, later, arrested. Yet I did not purchase it in preference for the black gown because of its flamboyance or garishness. I bought it because it reminds me of something long lost in the mist of years, something I should not wish to recall for, like so much in life, the joy was tinged with sorrow.

This is a weakness in me. I should not be prone to such madcap purchases. I am not that wealthy a man. The cotton dressing gown with *sow* on the reverse would have done me just as well even if the character displayed on my back would have been not a little ironic. It would just as effectively have covered my scrappy body, given me some modesty should someone enter my flat and it too would be cool to wear. I should reprimand myself. I suppose, by recognising my weakness, I am doing so.

The fact remains it brings back to me, as if it was only yesterday, the sight of Mei-ling in all her finery.

And I bought it because it reminds me of one of God's broken promises.

In the mission yard, between the chapel and the nursery, there hung a barometer in a heavy oak frame beneath which was a thermometer. As I passed it, I tapped the glass with my knuckle: the needle did not shift from a reading of 30¾ inches of mercury. The silver column in the thermometer registered 89°.

In the shade of the eaves by the nursery door, Ah Mee was

223

sitting on a low stool, a sleeping infant in her arms. She, too, was dozing, her eyes shut and her head drooped forwards.

The heat was intolerable. Although I was dressed in my Chinese garb, sweat dripped between my shoulder-blades and soaked through the armpits of my dark blue cotton *sam*. I peered into the water butt which collected rainwater from the chapel roof: it was empty save for a stagnant inch at the bottom, under the surface of which flicked mosquito larvæ.

As I passed the window to the mission office, I heard Father Callaghan talking Cantonese. His voice was quiet as if he was afraid to be eavesdropped upon. The person with him spoke in a gruff, guttural voice from which I could not determine the owner's sex.

My shadow must have darkened the stretched paper pane of the window for, no sooner had I passed than I heard Father Callaghan call me. Without hurrying, for the heat was telling upon me, I made my way to the office.

'Come in,' Father Callaghan said as I knocked upon the door, which was ajar.

On entering, I saw he was in the company of an elderly Chinese woman. She wore the ordinary clothing of a peasant but the material was of a superior quality silk and she wore a fine jade bracelet.

'Please, sit down,' Father Callaghan invited. 'I have some news you must hear.' He said a few words in Cantonese to the woman who nodded in my direction, studying my face as Father Callaghan spoke. 'This woman is a matchmaker. She has come to us with a proposition.'

For a moment, I wondered what a woman was doing making matches and asked, 'What do we want with more matches? We have a dozen boxes in the store. Swan Vestas . . .'

Father Callaghan grinned and said, 'I think you misunderstand, Father Stephen. She is not a manufacturer of lucifers but an arranger of marriages. All marriages are so conducted in China.'

I laughed slightly at my foolishness and went on, 'All the more reason she should have no business here.'

'On the contrary,' Father Callaghan replied, 'she wishes to arrange a marriage between one of our girls and a young man.'

I was at a loss as to what to say. It was my impression our girls did not leave us for marriage but for employment in Hong Kong or Macau.

'The girl in question,' Father Callaghan continued, 'is Mei-ling. You will not know them all as yet by name, but she is one of our more comely maidens, in the Chinese concept of beauty, and certainly one of our most accomplished. She is also one of those who has offered herself to Christ Jesus.'

'You mean she wishes to be a nun?' I asked.

'No. Not that. Just she has professed her faith in Our Lord.'

I considered the situation for a moment: to marry one of our saved Christian girls to a heathen was a quandary for which I had not been prepared in the seminary.

'Who is the intended husband?' I enquired.

'The eldest son of Kung whom you, Father Stephen, will remember as the purveyor of those particularly fine eggs and who is the temporary employer of this good lady before us.'

He grinned and I could, just for an instant, taste the vile thing once more in my mouth, feel the consistency of the pellucid green-glass-like albumen slide down my gullet, followed by the dry cloying of the yolk.

'I do recall him,' I admitted.

'Kung is a Christian and so is his son. A sturdy young man of twenty-three. He keeps the chicken farm from which his father obtains his eggs. The lad has taken the name of Matthew in addition to his Chinese name. He is thus either Kung Chi-ching or Matthew Kung.'

'What shall we do?' I said: I was not sure if Father Callaghan would be in favour of the marriage. 'Need we contact the bishop?'

'No, of course not. It's up to us. To me, as you are so newly come amongst us. And it's my opinion to give the union our blessing. What better way to cement the foundations of our faith than to see it rising from the holy state of matrimony? Do you not agree with this?'

I was in no position to reply in the negative: furthermore, I agreed it was a perfect means by which to bring Christ to the people.

Father Callaghan then entered into a lengthy conversation with the matchmaker. She was not only the broker but also the comptroller of the timetable, the fixer of arrangements and the bringer together of the many strands of the complex affairs of love. The couple, she reported, requested a Christian marriage but along the lines of the Chinese fashion. The right date had been ascertained by studying the two parties' horoscopes and the almanacs, the auspicious day being the following Wednesday week.

In the spirit of compromise I had seen him display over the prayer-flags in the mission, Father Callaghan agreed to all the old woman's suggestions, which greatly pleased her. The wedding, it was decided upon, would be a Chinese service in every respect but the actual religious content.

When the matchmaker had departed, Father Callaghan called Ah Fong and Sister Margaret into the office. There was a discussion lasting several hours, each of us given a series of tasks in preparation for the big day. Sister Margaret was to draw on the mission funds and procure the bridal gown, Ah Fong was to act as the go-between with the Kung family and I was to find a dowry.

This was by no means an easy matter. For several days I spent every spare minute I could afford avidly reading through both volumes of Dr Doolittle's detailed publication, *Social Life of the Chinese*, seeking out what tradition and etiquette demanded be in a dowry purse. I questioned Ah Fong several times an hour and, eventually, decided it was best to put some money aside in the form of *lai see*, coins placed in a vermilion envelope as a gift. And yet I felt, if the marriage was to be at least partly Occidental, I should also provide a bride's drawer. I purchased a fine cotton quilt, some cooking utensils, two hard lacquer pillows and an assortment of lesser domestic items, placing these in a rattan hamper Ah Fong produced from a store-room. By the day before the wedding, I was ready.

The chapel was cleaned from top to bottom by the girls, who were in an increasing frenzy of excitement as the day drew nigh. The stone steps were swept and even the *hutong*, where it passed the mission, was cleared of the garbage usually accumulated in it.

On the evening before the wedding day, Father Callaghan

and I sat together on the mission roof, close to the bell, our gins and quinine in our hands. The sun was down, a pale moon low in the sky.

For a long time, we were silent, each of us keeping our own council, watching the twilight deepen and listening to the night sounds. Even though the air was hot, we could hear the call of the boatmen on the river, the cry of peddlers and the humming sound of distant conversation at the food stalls in the street at the end of the *hutong*. At last, Father Callaghan broke our silence.

'You know, Father Stephen,' he said in a quiet voice, 'I feel a strange man tonight. Somehow, I believe this marriage is not just a matter of the old biddy fixing things up, nor is it merely a matter of two young people falling in love – if, indeed, they've seen each other at all, save in a service here or walking in the street. It's not in the nature of the Chinese for intended partners necessarily to know one another. Quite often, they depend solely upon the descriptive powers of the matchmaker. No,' his voice fell even quieter as he gazed into the looming night, 'I think there's more to it.'

'How do you mean, Father?' I asked.

'When that old woman entered my office, I know I should have felt a repulsion. After all, she is little more than a pimp in the service of Venus. And yet, as she came in, I felt a wondrous calm befall the room. When she spoke, she was reason itself which surprised me greatly. We stand in her way with our practices. If Christianity became strong in China, her sisters in the guild of marriage brokers would soon be out of business. And, take my word for it, she's not a poor woman from her employ.'

He sipped his drink, sneezing at the tartness of the quinine: he had felt a twinge of fever that day and had doubled his evening dose.

'Where I should have felt evil, I felt goodness,' he went on. 'I'm sure she's as wicked as the prong on Satan's tail, but she came to us as a messenger of the Lord. Albeit unwittingly. You know, I'm convinced this marriage upon which we embark tomorrow is one truly made in Heaven.'

I looked at his face. There were tears in his eyes. He sensed me looking at him.

'It's the quinine,' he said, his voice marginally louder. 'It brings not only an itch to the nose but water to the eyes as well. Come, Father Stephen,' he stood up, 'we'd best get down to our beds. It's a long day tomorrow.'

We made our way along the girls' corridor. It was a hive of activity, of happy laughter and giggles. Mei-ling was sitting upon her bunk in the company of a Chinese woman whom I had not seen before: she was certainly not one of our number.

'Who is this?' I enquired.

'She's the wife of the tea-house owner where you did your pants up,' Father Callaghan said. 'I've asked her to do us this service.'

As I watched, the woman entwined two red threads about a hair on Mei-ling's forehead and then, with a deft pull, tugged it free by the roots.

'What is she doing?'

'*Hoi min*,' Father Callaghan explained. 'It is a ritual which means *showing the face*. The hair is pulled out so the bride may be more open to her bridegroom.'

'Why not ask Sister Margaret to perform the deed?'

Father Callaghan laughed briefly and said, 'She somewhat lacks the qualification. For the sake of the bride, it should be done by someone who has borne many sons. The tea-house owner has fathered seven boys. And not a single daughter. I could hardly find a better woman for the job.'

I took to my bed, lying upon my quilt naked save for a towel folded about my waist: this was not a matter of modesty but of wisdom for if the stomach was bare it was considered an invitation to the fever. The night was hot and I fell into an uncomfortable sleep, occasionally bothered by the hatchlings from the water butt.

The following morning, at about eleven o'clock, the ceremony of the wedding commenced. Had we been conducting a Chinese religious marriage, the bride would have gone by sedan chair to her groom's family home but this was dispensed with: instead, the groom came to the mission but not to the girls' building. Instead, he lingered before the chapel door, wearing a black coat on top of a blue *cheong sam* with a red cotton sash draped over his shoulder and tied at the waist: on his head he had a black hat with a red tassel upon it.

'He is wearing five articles of attire,' Father Callaghan said to me as we waited inside the chapel door, 'in accordance with the principles of *yin* and *yang*. Being a male, he must have an odd number whilst she must have even. He has two pieces of underclothing, a pair of *fu* you cannot see, his *cheong sam* and his jacket.'

Mei-ling was to arrive from the girl's quarters as if it was her home. Ah Fong had arranged a sedan chair be hired for this very short but crucial journey. At the time decreed by the matchmaker in collaboration with a Taoist necromancer, the chair appeared around the corner of the building and halted by the chapel door. Matthew Kung knocked on the side of the chair with a fan, the curtain opening to allow Mei-ling to step out.

I was speechless at her beauty. She wore a scarlet embroidered skirt with a long black silk overcoat and an elaborate wide collar such as the mandarin wore. On her head was balanced an ornate, intricate head-dress of silver and gilt inlaid with small pearls and the azure feathers of a kingfisher. Over the whole of this was draped a red gossamer veil of thin silk.

Father Callaghan smiled much as I would guess a father might at the wedding of his favourite daughter.

The bridegroom lifted the veil and I saw Mei-ling's face was heavily made up with cosmetics, her skin whitened and her eyes and lips accentuated by dark powder and red paste.

Ah Fong, standing to one side, ignited a string of firecrackers which produced an acrid cloud of smoke and a blizzard of charred confetti. The explosions were amplified in the *hutong* so it sounded as if the whole of the thunder stored in the heavens was echoing to celebrate the occasion. Sister Margaret appeared with a tray of smouldering charcoal which she placed upon the steps to the chapel. The groom lifted Mei-ling off her feet and, carrying her, stepped over the fire whilst, above her head, Ah Fong contrived to hold a tray containing a rice bowl, some chopsticks, a tea cup and a small dish such as one spits bones into at a meal.

'All this would normally be done at the home of the groom,' Father Callaghan stated, 'but we decided it should be done here. We cannot entirely avoid their traditions. Besides, they're entering their house here. The house they share with Our Lord.'

'I wonder what Rome would think,' I suggested.

Father Callaghan grinned the same kind of smirk he had when I ate the groom's father's egg.

'They would disapprove, Father Stephen. Be quite certain of it. But, you know my friend, I really don't give a tinker's curse!'

The congregation entered the church. The couple were led to the altar where they knelt. I did not take a part in the service but watched, listening as Father Callaghan stood before Christ on his Cross and uttered the words so familiar to lovers at the time of the consummation of their love before God, albeit in a tongue I could not understand.

'Father,' he began in Cantonese, 'when you created mankind you willed that man and wife should be one. Bind Mei-ling and Matthew Chi-ching in the loving union of marriage and make their love fruitful so that they may be living witnesses to your divine love in the world . . .'

After the service, in accordance with Chinese tradition, tea and sweetmeats were served. Had this been a heathen Chinese wedding, the repast would have been given in the bridal chamber, but our refectory served the purpose instead. Gifts were made, the dowry presented. Each of the mission girls paraded before the bride and presented her with *lai see* provided by Father Callaghan from the sea chest in his room wherein he kept the mission funds. Eventually, at about four o'clock, the wedding party left and the mission became suddenly silent.

'Our first,' Father Callaghan remarked as the sound of the newly-weds and their guests disappeared from the end of the *hutong*.

'First?' I answered.

'Our first marriage. The first, I pray, of many. What a fine start we could have witnessed today, Father Stephen. How good it would be if all our girls could be so accommodated instead of, most of them, heading for a world of servitude.'

'Are you suggesting we start a matchmaking service of our own?'

'Heavens above, no!' he laughed, then, after a moment said, 'But it's an idea. Just think of it! We'd find happiness for all our poor girls, spread the work of Our Lord and earn a good matchmaker's fee for the mission coffers. We could kill a lot of little birds with that one stone.'

We went into the chapel to tidy the altar and make ready for Mass. Father Callaghan went down on his knees before Christ.

'Give them years of happiness in the Light of Your Love, Lord,' I heard him say. 'Let them be an example of Your Goodness to their fellows and bring others unto You.'

It was twelve days later when I next saw Mei-ling. She was lying on the flags in the mission yard, Father Callaghan at her side, her head resting in Sister Margaret's lap and surrounded by all the girls. In her hair was a white woollen flower fashioned like a chrysanthemum. She was fighting for breath.

'What is it?' I asked, falling to the ground by Father Callaghan's side.

'She's killing herself,' he whispered.

'How?' I said. I could not understand it. 'Why?'

'Matthew Kung's been killed. Butchered,' he answered. His voice was dense with anger as he touched the blossom. 'This is the custom of mourning. It is called *dai hau*.'

As I gazed down upon her bloodless cheeks, I remembered his comment to me by the flowerboats: the Chinese are in possession of remarkable methods of self-murder.

'Who killed him?'

'The Harmony Fists. He was found this morning in the paddock where they keep the hens.'

He took the flower out of her hair and handed it to me.

'But why?' I asked.

Father Callaghan made me no answer at first then, through clenched teeth, he said, 'Because he was one of us.'

Putting his hand upon Mei-ling's brow, he stroked it gently and started to recite the Extreme Unction in a quiet, almost inaudible voice.

Mei-ling was sucking hard at the air, her face contorted with effort. Already her skin was as pale as the white woollen flower in my hand, had the translucent quality of a corpse. The inside of her mouth seemed to glisten in the sunlight. About us, all the girls sobbed quietly.

Looking up to Ah Fong who was standing by me, I asked, 'Can we not revive her?'

'No can do, master,' he said.

'We must try.'

'No good. She eat gold.'

'Gold?'

'Gold paper, master. Thin-thin. Go inside her, make air hard to swallow. No can take in air.'

In fifteen minutes, she suffocated and was gone.

Once more, there are American sailors in port. They are not from the main fleet but off three supply ships which are here, according to the *South China Morning Post*, to re-provision and allow the crews some R&R – Rest and Recreation. Sam declares this should be called R&P – Rum and Procreation.

He stocked up the bar of *The Black Pussy* with bottles of good quality bourbon – *Jack Daniel's Old No.7* and *Jim Beam* – bringing in a supply of bread rolls and hot dog sausages. In addition, he employed two friends to act as waiters and a young lad to stand on the pavement by the Fenwick Street pier where the liberty boats dock handing out flyers which I have written and for which Sam paid me $50.

The flyers have been printed on stiff white card edged with gold leaf in order to look like invitations and read as follows:

> *The Black Pussy Bar and Nite Club*
> *where dames, dancing and dawgs*
> *last the night through.*
> *Free first drink – bear or liquor.*
> *Free jukebox.*
> *Live Band Music after 10 pm.*

On the reverse is a map on how to reach the bar from the pier, the address and the telephone number. Only the printers' error in the fourth line detracts somewhat from the invitation's authenticity.

'No sweat,' Sam said when I pointed it out to him. 'Nobody

expect *bear*. He want beer. Anyway, these guys sometimes no can spell so good anyway.'

He also asked me to be in attendance in the bar. Quite why, I do not know. I can do nothing but I sense he likes me there to add a bit of colour: I suppose an old China hand sitting at the counter lends the establishment a certain *je ne sais quoi*. I am not just an old man but an artefact of the East, as much of an attraction in my own way as the bar-girls and the Hong Kong-brewed lager.

When he requested my presence, and said the drinks were on him, I questioned his uncharacteristic benevolence towards his clientele.

'You aren't usually this generous. With me you're kind, but this seems somewhat extravagant. What are you up to?' I enquired.

Sam tapped his nose: he has learnt this sign from the cinema. He is an avid devotee of the American movie.

'Good business,' he replied, winking.

'How much are you spending? The printing, my fifty, free drinks. Free music. Waiters and the lad at the jetty. And a band! You've never had a band in here before.'

'Must spend money to make money,' he answered obliquely and would not be drawn further.

So, last night, I was in the bar, sitting on my usual stool at the end of the counter waiting to see what was on the cards: Sam was up to something and I was more than curious.

I arrived just before seven o'clock, as he was preparing for the hectic hours ahead.

'Big night,' he announced, pouring my first lager.

'Big night,' I agreed, raising my glass in a toast and saying, '*Yam sing.*'

'Tonight, make good money,' he predicted. 'I do good, girls do good. Everybody do good. Even you, *san foo*, maybe can do good.'

'When do you expect the first customers?' I asked, wondering how he believed I might profit from the evening's activities.

'Eight o'clock. First boat in half past seven. Boy down at the pier now. He ready. Plenty of invitation card.' He rubbed his hands on a length of towelling. 'Tonight, good night.'

I looked at the Johnnie Walker whisky clock over the bar shelves: it was already a quarter past seven.

'Got in good stock of cigarette. All American. *Lucky Strike, Chesterfield, Camel*, king-size *Peter Stuyvesant*. Good quality.'

From under the bar he took out a carton of the latter, split the seal open with his thumb nail and proceeded to place a handful of cigarettes in half a dozen whisky glasses.

'Free cigarettes as well?' I said, not a little amazed.

'Not so free. Jus' until the glass empty. Get people going. Make him feel my bar the best in Wanchai.'

I sensed at that point there was more to this unprecedented evening than met the eye and wondered if Sam was looking to do a competitor out of business, had received a sharp rise in his rent or demands for protection money by the Chiu Chow triads who ran the area. Yet I did not pry: it is best to let a man get on with his own affairs. If he wanted to tell me about it, he would.

As the clock hands shifted to seven-thirty, I thought of the first liberty boat pulling alongside, the sailors checking their wallets, chewing on antibiotic sweets that looked like *LifeSavers* candies, slapping each other on the shoulder and premeditatively boasting about conquests to be made during the next six hours. Those for whom this was a first visit to Hong Kong would be listening to the experienced ones, anticipating the broads, the beers and the bars.

I drained my glass as Sam placed a new bottle by my elbow. I drink my first lager fairly quickly, thereafter pacing myself, sipping slowly, exchanging the odd word with Sam, one of the girls or a client. On rare occasions, one of the latter engages me in conversation: he might be a young sailor afraid of whores, an old one who came ashore just for a drink, a faithful one not wishing to cheat on his sweetheart or a queer disappointed by the shortage of young boys, unaware that colonial culture and Chinese tradition do not openly accept homosexuality.

The curtain of beads rattled and someone entered. I looked up. It could not be a sailor for it was too early: even an Olympic sprinter could not get from the Fenwick Street pier to *The Black Pussy* in under five minutes.

As I surmised, it was not a sailor. It was the boy to whom I tutor Cantonese. For a moment, I did not recognise him, for he was not wearing his school uniform but a pair of tight black trousers, a pink shirt with a wide collar and a scarlet waistcoat with brass buttons. His shoes were black and highly polished, the toecaps pointed and the heels stacked.

His eyes unadjusted to the gloom, he did not see me but waved to Sam standing under the ultra-violet lamp.

'Hi, Sam!' he called out.

'Hi, Gerry!' Sam replied. 'You okay?'

The boy nodded and crossed to the jukebox. One of the bar-girls quit her seat in the end cubicle – all the girls, as usual, were crowded in there, playing cards and chattering to each other like pullets in a coup – and went to his side, putting her arm about his shoulder. This, I considered, was perhaps one reason for his wishing to speak Cantonese, after all.

He thumbed a coin into the jukebox and I expected him to dance with the girl: but he did not. Instead, he entered a cubicle and started to furiously scribble on a piece of paper. When it stopped playing, he returned to the jukebox and, inserting another coin, played the same tune over, returning to his scribbling. He was, I realised, writing down the words of the song. I listened to them. The singer had a falsetto voice.

As I walk along, the jukebox pumped out, the bass thumping, *I wonder what went wrong with our love, a love that was so strong. And as I stroll on down I think of the things we've done, together, while our hearts were young. I'm a-walking in the rain . . .*

'Del Shannon,' Sam said loudly in my ear. He had come along the bar, placing the cigarette glasses. 'New American singer. Many people listen to him.'

The song ended, the boy chose another record. It was a song I have heard played often by the sailors and whores. It is entitled *Are You Lonesome Tonight?* by Elvis Presley: this is the singer Tsoi claims is responsible for encouraging Chinese youths to set light to the hills. As the slow opening bars issued from the loudspeaker, two of the girls left their cubicle, dancing together. Their arms entwined about each other's waist, pulling them together. I could imagine what was going through their minds: for the duration of the lilting tune, they were not bar-girls in a dive awaiting a groping hand and thrusting pelvis but film stars, happy young women in the embrace of a loved one, rich and contented.

Just as Mr Poon was a gambler so are these whores. He chanced his money and his life: they play with the future, throwing their bodies like dice and holding their breath for the six that never rolls.

The boy looked up from his scribbling and saw me. For a long moment, he just stared and, even in the gloom, I could tell he was very surprised. He put away his pen, folded the paper, left the cubicle and, skirting the dancers, came towards me.

'Good evening, sir,' he said.

'Good evening,' I replied.

I did not add anything more. I wanted to see how he would handle our meeting and was, in a mild way, enjoying not so much his embarrassment, but his amazement.

'I was . . . was . . .' he stuttered and, even by the ultra-violet strip light, I could tell he was colouring.

'Not aware I came here?' I suggested.

My words saved him. I could tell, for I have seen it often, he was going to make a confession, a denial or an excuse for being in such a place at such a time.

'Yes, sir.' There was a distinct relief in his voice. 'I usually come early in the evening. Before . . .'

Once more, he was lost for words and I waited a moment before replying, savouring his predicament.

'Before business really starts to get under way. As for myself,' I went on, 'I usually come later in the evening.'

He was silent, not quite knowing what to say next.

'Sam,' I called out, 'one more beer.' Looking the boy in the eye, I asked, 'You do drink beer, don't you?'

'Yes, sir. Thank you.'

Sam poured out a San Miguel and I reached for my wallet.

'Okay. Beer free for Gerry, too. I got an agreement with him.'

'You seem to know Sam very well,' I commented, lifting my glass.

The boy raised his own, tilting it towards me to signal his thanks, sipping the froth off before replacing the glass on the counter.

'Yes. I come here at least once a week, usually just after the US Navy's been in. That's the best time. Sam doesn't mind. There's no law against it. So long as I'm over sixteen.' He was suddenly voluble, like every sinner when he sees a chance to justify himself, or repent. 'I don't come here for the girls. I know them, of course, and they know me but I'm not a . . .' He paused, perhaps to catch his breath or to find an appropriate word.

'A customer?' I suggested.

'Yes, a customer,' he concurred.

'So you aren't learning Cantonese in order to communicate with these young ladies of the night?' I answered.

'No, sir. Besides,' he said, smiling briefly, 'they all speak English. After a fashion. They have to for . . . for their business.'

'That's true,' I replied, 'so why do you come here?'

'To get the lyrics of the latest songs. You see, sir, Sam has the best jukebox in Wanchai. Probably the best in Hong Kong. He's famous for it. Some of the records are put in it within a week of appearing in the Billboard Hot 100. Like *Runaway*. That was the first I spun just now.'

'And why,' I enquired, 'do you want these lyrics?'

'To sing the songs, sir. To play them. You see,' he sipped at his beer again, 'I'm in a group.'

'A group of what?' I asked.

'Well, a group,' he replied, somewhat nonplussed. 'A group. A band. I'm in with four friends. We call ourselves the Intercontinentals. Because we're from different nationalities – I'm English, the lead's American . . .'

'The lead what?' I interrupted.

This was not a conversation I had expected. The boy, usually so quiet when involved with his studies at my table, was quite talkative, forthcoming even. I found myself taking a distinct liking to him.

'Lead guitar,' he explained. 'We are a rock group – a rock-and-roll group,' he added for my elucidation. 'I play rhythm, the American plays lead, a Swedish friend plays bass guitar, the drummer's a Filipino and the singer's English like me. But, in fact, we all sing at some time or another.'

'And you put on concerts, I suppose,' I said.

'Not exactly. We play at school dances, parties and now,' he looked about himself, 'night clubs.'

'This is hardly a night club,' I began, then it dawned on me. 'You mean,' I continued, 'you are Sam's live band?'

'Yes. We start at ten.'

'And is your father aware of your evening's activities?'

The boy avoided my eyes, scanning the dance floor where two more girls were moving sinuously against each other to the tune of the same record.

'Not exactly. He knows we have a band and knows we do parties and things. He thinks this is a party.'

'In a manner of speaking,' I remarked, 'it is. After all, there were invitations printed.'

I had one folded in my pocket, having brought it with me in case Sam insisted it be shown at the door to comply with some obscure by-law. Taking it out, I smoothed the crease and gave it to the boy, who held it at an angle to the ultra-violet strip light and read it.

'May I keep this, sir?' he asked.

I nodded: he wanted it to lend some veracity to his story should his parents discover where he was performing and I saw no harm in assisting him in his petty deception.

The plastic beads of the curtain rattled and five American sailors entered, standing on the edge of the dance floor and surveying the scene.

'Hey,' one said loudly, 'this where the party's at?'

'Come on in, boys!' Sam called from behind the bar. 'Welcome to *The Black Pussy*.'

Over the next three-quarters of an hour, other sailors arrived until the bar was more crowded than I had ever seen it. Sam dispensed a free drink to each sailor on presentation of his invitation which, once the drink was served, Sam tore up. Those who had lost their cards were given their free drink but Sam, not to be cheated, stamped the backs of their hands with a small ivory chop engraved with the two cats from the neon sign.

Most of the time, the boy was lost to my sight in the mêlée but I occasionally noticed, through the mass of sailors and bar-girls – of whom more had arrived, paying a one-night-only permission fee to Sam – a number of figures erecting a drum kit at the far end of the room.

Nobody talked to me. I sat quite alone at the end of the bar, enjoying my drink. Sam and his two part-time waiters were kept busy serving drinks and, after nine o'clock, hot dogs smeared with mustard from a large pot.

As I observed the action around me, I saw one thing that so amazed me I watched for it again. Sam was giving credit to a sailor.

He was a young man, barely out of his teens, with crew-cut blonde hair and a fresh face. This was clearly his first visit to Hong Kong for he was less than au fait with how to handle whores in both the physical and metaphysical interpretations of the word: indeed, he was so forward with one of them that she abandoned him. This was not from prudery but because he had not bought her out: as the girls put it in the vernacular of *The Black Pussy*, no can pay, no can play.

When he arrived at the bar to buy a drink or place an order for his friends, Sam personally served him. This was a deliberate action for, if one of the waiters was approached by this sailor, he directed him to Sam. At one point, he stood next to me.

'What your poison?' Sam asked, cursorily wiping the bar with a cloth.

'Two San Migs., two chasers, Sam,' the sailor called out over the ruckus of the jukebox.

'Comin' up, Pete!' Sam replied and set about opening bottles.

The sailor nodded to me.

'How're ya doin'?' he enquired.

'I'm fine, just fine,' I said.

He looked at my glass. His face was flushed and not just with the heat of the place.

'You wanna beer, pal? Have one on me. Hey, Sam, one more beer down here.'

'Thank you,' I said.

I was surprised at his generosity even though I knew it to be the benevolence of the merry and soon-to-be-smashed rather than an exuding of the milk of human kindness.

'How much?' the sailor asked as Sam delivered three beers and two bourbon chasers.

'On the tab, Pete. No sweat. Pay later.'

As the sailor left the counter, I could not believe what I heard. Sam was running a slate. I interpreted this not as a sign of his growing weak nor an extension of his evening's already astonishing generosity. There was another reason but I was damned if I could figure it out.

By nine thirty, I felt hot and tired and, leaving my stool, made my way towards the door at the rear of the bar which leads onto a rear alley. The door was unlocked, the little battery operated light above it illuminating a plastic fire exit sign, one of the few acts of compliance with the law to which Sam pays more than lip service.

The alley was cool and, as the door shut on a spring the sounds were cut short, quiet. Somewhere overhead, a radio played Cantonese opera, the singers wailing to the clash of gongs and cymbals. At the end of the alley, traffic passed by, the vehicles momentarily loud as they came into view. In the tenement opposite some kind of machine was running, its movements punctuated by a hiss, a sliding of metal, two more hisses and a clunk followed by the first hiss once more.

Leaning against the wall beside a stack of empty beer crates and boxes, I found myself breathless, as if I had been walking quickly for a long distance. I put my hands to my chest, pressing gently in and out to aid my lungs. I was not panicked for I am on occasion breathless, although admittedly only after exertion. The wall behind me vibrating slightly from the music within, I put my condition down to the dense smoke-filled air, the tightly packed crowd, the noise and the heat.

The door opened and Sam appeared.

'*San foo?*' he called, looking round. '*San foo.* You okay?'

'Just tired,' I assured him. 'And hot.'

'If you inside, must drink plenty. If you body get dry, you ill.' He called through the door, '*Wei! Foh gei! Ho lok!*' Then, turning to me again, he said, 'Soon fix you up, *san foo.*'

A hand appeared through the door holding a green fluted Coca

Cola bottle. Sam wiped the mouth of the bottle with his hand and gave it to me.

'Drink, *san foo*. Get water in you, sugar. Then you be okay.'

I swallowed the chilled sweetness and felt immediately revived. 'Okay now?'

'Yes,' I answered. 'Fine.' I took another swig before continuing, 'Sam, what are you up to?'

'The party? Easy! These sailors work on supply ships, go to all the other ships in the US fleet. You know, sailors like men in a club. All from one ship, talk to his friend there and go ashore with him. But he often don't see other sailors. These guys,' he jerked his thumb in the direction of the door, 'see all the ships and when they go to them, taking supplies, they have a coffee and talk. So! What they talk about? About the last R&R.'

He grinned, putting his hand on my shoulder. It was the touch of friendship: the ex-priest and the whorehouse bar-man joined in amity.

Sam is no fool. This party might cost him a drop in profits but it will spread his reputation. Like every Chinese, he is a shrewd and usually successful businessman at heart, his eye open for opportunity and his energy charged to realise it. I admire this tenacious determination. Other nations lack it in various degrees: the British are idle complainers, the Italians too keen on a walk in the sun after lunch, the Spanish too fond of the *siesta* and the French too set in their ways. The Germans work hard but they are sterile, lack colour and have only gritted teeth: they do not smile.

'That's not what I meant,' I said. 'I understand all that. What's the scam you're running on the sailor?'

I used the word because Sam would appreciate it. He knows this one from the movies, too.

'Scam?' he repeated.

'Scam. Sting. You're running numbers on a sailor called Pete.'

'You clever man, my old frien',' Sam laughed, 'got eyes like an eagle. You see too much!'

'So what's the game?'

'I tell you. I trus' you. But it's a secret,' he exclaimed, moving his hand and stroking my shoulder. 'You tell nobody or I lose money.' He shifted closer to me, resting his elbow on a crate. 'First night the ship in port, I choose one sailor, not too stupid, not too clever. All night, give him credit. Plenty drink, for him and for his frien', something to eat and, later, free girl. I pay for her. She give him quick time only. Ten minute. No more. After, she bring him back and I say, must pay now. But I know he not got enough money.'

'That sounds like poor judgement,' I commented, but knew it was not.

'No, good judgement, *san foo*. I pretend to be cross. Shout, "You got no money, you drink so much. Have girl. Have a good time and now you cheat me. I call the Shore Patrol, Hong Kong Police. Call my frien's. Got tough frien's."' He winked at me. 'He get afraid. Then I say, "Okay. You got no money so must pay me another way." He say he do it so I say, "You bring me record from your ship mess jukebox. All new record only. One just come in from US. You see, *san foo*, every week the US Navy send new records for sailors. All the new hits. And he do it.'

Sam shrugged his shoulders and grinned.

'So that's how you've the best jukebox in Wanchai,' I congratulated him.

'Best in Hong Kong, Gerry tell me.'

It was impossible not to laugh. His scheming was so preposterous, artful, well planned and skilfully executed.

'But,' I went on, 'what if he doesn't? What if he goes to the Shore Patrol and says he was rolled? What if he goes back on his ship and stays there?'

'He don't,' Sam replied confidently. 'If he call the Shore Patrol, the US Navy want no trouble so they pay. And if he go to the ship he don't want to stay there. His friend' go ashore, he want to go too. But he can only come ashore at Fenwick Street. My guard can see him.'

'Who's your guard?' I asked.

'The boy who give out the invite card.'

The door opened and the waiter called to Sam.

'Now mus' go back in. You comin', *san foo*?'

We returned to the smoke and din but I did not stay to hear

the boy's band or see the outcome of the scam yet I am sure it worked. Sam will have selected Pete with all the forethought of a corporate manager deciding who to appoint to a trustworthy position. Men who run whorehouses and bars have all the skills of a top industrialist, a senior manager or a priest. They can smell a sucker, a sap, a sinner and a sound man at fifty paces.

There is no man alive who, given the chance, would refuse to discover his future and there are as many charlatans about selling this information to him as there are priests offering to bless him or save him from himself. The daily newspapers, both English language and Chinese, publish horoscopes whilst the magazines print advice according to the planetary alliances. The temples are invariably busy with fortune-tellers and fortune-hunters, especially before a race day at Happy Valley or at the time of a major festival when people take stock of their lives, assess their sins and make resolutions they know they cannot keep.

Sometimes, when I am out taking the air in the evening, I walk towards the waterfront and, on my way, pass along a street where fortune-tellers congregate to ply their trade.

They are a motley band, yet all cultivate certain qualities which it is beholden of them to maintain, attributes which give them veracity. None of them is under forty years of age for the reading of the future is an old man's game: indeed, some of them have worked upon appearing old so, although their real ages are indeterminate, they look sage-like with long thin beards or Fu Manchu moustaches, straggling hair reaching to their collars and, of course, two-inch-long fingernails to prove they are not manual workers but thinkers, philosophers and poets. They always wear traditional Chinese clothing, the *ma kwa* waist-length jacket over a loose man's *cheung sam* or black *fu*. Several wear skull caps with pom-poms on the top and none wear Western shoes but traditional slippers, even if the street is wet. Each man has a small collapsable kiosk on the pavement, little bigger than a telephone box and equipped with a folding seat for the fortune-teller, a small table or shelf and a stool or two for clients.

The inside walls of the kiosks are hung with palmists' charts, phrenologists' diagrams, testimonials from satisfied customers and photographs of the individual fortune-teller's master, the man who taught him the arts of divination. These, too, always show sages or learned-looking men dressed as their disciples are in old-fashioned clothing. A few of the photos have lit joss sticks wedged in their frames.

I am on nodding acquaintance with one of these men. He is called Mr Ng, speaks good English and has a degree in History from the University of Canton. Our friendship is not of a client-based nature. I do not indulge myself in his business. I know my future.

This evening, I was making my way to the waterfront with no intention in mind other than to stretch my legs before retiring, when I came upon Mr Ng setting up his stall.

'My friend,' I said, stopping to help him press home a particularly tight metal clasp holding the side wall to the rear, 'how are you?'

'Good. I am good,' he replied, adding, 'Thank you. The metal is bent. Last week – a lorry – ' he slapped his hands together '– boom! Into my stall.'

'You were not hurt?'

'No. No worry for me but much for the driver. I saw his face. He was unhappy. I could tell his fortune. It was not good.'

He unfolded the shelf in his kiosk, arranged the seats and called to a shop nearby for two glasses of tea.

'You sit with me?' he invited, pointing to the stool.

'I don't want to take away your custom,' I replied but he waved his hand in the air dismissively.

'Too early. Nobody will come before eight o'clock. Too many people are eating now.'

A boy arrived with the glasses of tea and I paid for them. Each had a pink plastic lid and red roses stencilled on the side. Mr Ng picked his up, removed the lid and slurped noisily.

'You want your fortune told?' he enquired, his tone joking.

'No. I know where I am going.'

'So do I. You are going to the waterfront at the typhoon shelter, you will walk along it some way, you will go back to your home by another route and you will sleep. I mean, do you want news of your next week or month?'

'At my age,' I declared, 'one does not want to know what is coming. To guess is enough.'

'You will die,' Mr Ng said quite matter-of-factly, as if it was perfectly normal for him to give such information out. 'In the next three months. Already you are tired. Your body is not ill but it is going more slowly. You are like a car with the petrol getting less.'

'Perhaps,' I answered and I sipped at my tea.

'You will go to heaven,' he then declared.

'Possibly,' I said.

'No. You will go,' Mr Ng said with utter conviction. 'I know this because the iron tree flowers.'

At that moment, as if he was standing somewhere over my shoulder, I heard a man's voice say, quite distinctly, 'After nearly a quarter of a century, China still holds surprises.'

Despite myself, I glanced over my shoulder. Had I seen Mr Doble standing there with his glass of gin and quinine in his hand, I should not have been in the least astonished: what I did see was an elderly woman walking past holding her grandchild by the hand. The child was a little girl dressed in a crimson padded silk jacket with a bonnet on her head from which two rabbit's ears stuck upwards.

'You heard someone,' Mr Ng announced as I turned round again. 'A man from your past.'

'Yes,' I said. 'I did. How could you tell?'

'It is my job,' he smiled. 'Would you expect me to give you the secrets of my work?'

'No, I would not.'

He smiled again then, his face becoming expressionless, he said, 'This is a sign you will die soon.'

I was not unnerved either by the spirit voice of Mr Doble or Mr Ng's prediction. What will be, will be. There is nothing I can do, nor want to do, to slow down the clock of my life. A second is a second and that's all there is to it.

'What is an iron tree?' I asked.

'It is a special plant,' Mr Ng responded. 'A little like a cactus but with leaves.'

'Do you have one?'

'I know of one. Not here. In the New Territories, in the valley beyond Tso Shan. They are very rare.'

'And what has this iron tree to do with me?' I said.

'The iron tree only flowers every hundred years. Unless a good man is about to die. Last week, I went to this place and there was a flower upon the tree.'

'Perhaps it is a century since it last bloomed,' I suggested.

'This is not the case.'

'Then what,' I said, 'makes you think it foretells my death?'

'You are a good man.'

'I may dispute that,' I rejoined, 'but even if I were, what is there to say the tree was giving its sign about me? Am I the only good man in Hong Kong who will die in the next few months?'

Mr Ng smiled politely and sipped his tea again before saying, 'No. You are not. But this tree is your tree.'

I did not question the logic and, my tea drunk, got to my feet to leave. Mr Ng also rose, holding his hand out to me. The nail on his middle finger is as long as a talon.

'I will not see you again,' Mr Ng declared as he shook my hand. 'I am going to Macau. My mother is there, come down from China. Do not be afraid.'

'I am not afraid of anything,' I replied and he smiled again.

'That is the way to die.'

I left his stall and passed by the other fortune-tellers, some of whom were busy with clients, reading palms, touching heads and studying charts, holding tortoiseshells out or watching as their customers shook bamboo splints out of wooden cups. At the end of the street was a man with a trained finch which, when touched by a customer, hopped from its cage, pulled a card from a deck, accepted a grain of seed from its master and then, with a trust verging upon the inane, hopped back into the cage instead of taking flight for the sky.

At the waterfront, I sauntered slowly along, observing the domestic life of the sampan-dwellers. Children were sleeping on quilts in the arched fabric cabins, men squatted smoking on the decks whilst women busied themselves with chores. The steamy smoke of boiling and frying fish wafted on the gentle breeze, clouding densely as it blew across the glass chimney of an oil lamp.

When I reached the end of the dockside, I halted and sat on a concrete bollard. At my feet were stretched the mooring hawsers of a large junk from the spars of which hung drying fishing nets and racks of gutted fish, their salty stink touching my nostrils.

Mr Ng is right. I am dying although I did not need him to tell me. There have been other signs. I do not refer to the incident on the roof: that was just a coincidence or secondary factor. What does assure me my death is nearing is that, deep inside myself, there is an enceinte quietness. It is the kind one expects at any minute to hear filled with voices, the sort of stillness one experiences when talking to someone with a bad stammer. It is a noiselessness waiting for a noise to fill it.

Everyone, drawing slowly towards death, has this kernel of silence in them. I am certain of it.

What I shall find in mine I cannot tell. Perhaps this is the void I shall hear filled with the song of angels. But there again, it might be filled with the hush of dragons' wings, the hiss of their fiery mouths. Or simply nothing, nothing at all.

On a day-to-day basis, I am all right.

I am not late for appointments and, being a man of some method, I keep an exact mental note of what engagements are forthcoming. The only diary I have ever kept started and ended in the summer of 1900. I reinforce my memory with the aid of a desk calendar, one of those page-to-a-day affairs with the date written large in both English and Cantonese, weekdays in black and Sundays or religious holidays in red, held in place on a plastic stand with metal hoops. Every morning, I tear off the previous day's page and discard it.

Long ago, I learned the future is an unfriendly country filled with disappointment. As for the past, that is best not recorded. In any case, it lingers in the memory, no matter how one tries to eradicate it: it is like an unwanted guest who refuses to leave after all the others have bade farewell. It takes no hints and heeds no pleas, will not put on its coat and stagger off into the darkness.

Today, however, I had another accident, not as drastic as my rooftop interlude and yet, in its own way, more alarming. I was not fighting dragons, nor had I been chasing them. I was merely going about my business, on the way to the market.

It was just before noon. I was making my way up Shanghai Street, keeping to the shadows of the arcades. The sun was high yet it was pleasantly cool in the shade despite the passing traffic: even the din of the motors and the exhaust fumes was unable to filter into the arcades where people walked and shopped, bartered and gossiped.

I was strolling along quite slowly with no need to hurry: life at my age has a certain inevitability.

On the corner with Tung Kun Street, a large crowd was gathered, blocking the pavement and slowing the traffic. Lorry drivers impatiently blared their horns, gesticulating out of their cab windows; cyclists jangled their bells, rickshaw coolies yelled for a clear passage, leaning back in the shafts of their vehicles to brake, but no one paid them attention.

As I approached, I wondered if there had been a minor traffic accident: yet there were no police in evidence. It takes only the slightest diversion to draw a crowd of Chinese onlookers. They are a nation of observers, avidly assembling to watch anything from a public execution to two men with a jack hammer digging up the road.

All my efforts to squeeze past the crowd were in vain. It was packed firmly into the arcade and stationary, everyone chattering and staring in one direction. Having no other alternative, I joined the throng and followed the general gaze.

The centre of attention was a shoe shop across the road. Suspended over the front of the building, three storeys high and twenty feet wide, was a huge decorated *pai lau* of garishly coloured paper flowers and red and gold characters mounted on a bamboo frame. To either side, running from the roof six floors up to the pavement, were two or three dozen strings of firecrackers.

'New shop,' a man standing next to me said in English, in case I was a tourist. 'Opung to-day.'

From his hand dangled two white hens, their feet and wings trussed by twine. They were trying to raise their heads and clucking with indignation. I wondered vaguely if they had been purchased from One-eye.

On the pavement in front of the shop stood the proprietor with a Taoist priest dressed in yellow robes, a black cap tied to his head by a scarlet chin-strap. He was holding an almanac and, when he raised his hand, the shop owner lit a master fuse on the pavement. A rush of sparks ran along the gutter, igniting the base of the firecracker strings which started to explode up the building with an ear-shattering racket. Red flecks of paper fluttered out across the road, blizzarding down on the traffic, thick grey-blue smoke billowing into the air obscuring the front of the building and the *pai lau*. Every other sound was drowned out by the cacophony.

The noise, which I have heard a thousand times without a flinch, began to ring in my head, growing to a painful throbbing. I put my hands over my ears but it continued. I felt giddy and reached out to grasp the arm of the man next to me, missed it, struck the chickens which started to thresh about and fell against one of the arcade pillars. A panic rose in me, my breath came in short gasps and I knew I had to get away from the shattering pandemonium.

Looking round, I saw my best escape was to turn right down Tung Kun Street and into Temple Street. Using my elbows, I fought my way through the crowd and made off at a stumbling jog, working my way through the traffic which was now brought to a standstill. I kept my hands to my ears, drawing curious glances from passers-by: I did not care if I lost face for I was inexplicably frightened.

Turning the corner into Temple Street instantly reduced the sound level of the explosions to an acceptable, distant din. I lowered my arms. My hands were shaking and my head pulsated. I needed a glass of water. Looking round, there was no stall or tea-house but I noticed a snake restaurant on the other side of the street.

The establishment was open but not yet catering for clients. The neon lights were on, the chairs taken off the tables and the frontage open to the pavement but the waiters were dressed in vests and trousers, yet to don their white uniform jackets. The traffic moving slowly once more, I crossed through the vehicles, avoiding being run down by a man on a bicycle with a front platform piled high with bolts of cloth, and stepped towards the rank of glass aquaria along the restaurant wall. They were positioned close to the pavement so they not only provided the snakes with air but were also a means of advertising the menu.

The proprietor and waiters were preoccupied with laying the round tables, spreading white cloths over them and noisily dropping bowls, spoons and chop-sticks by each place setting. Overhead, two brass and mahogany ceiling fans desultorily stirred the air. At the rear, a elderly woman vigorously scrubbed a cooking range while a youth in his teens ran a mop smelling tartly of disinfectant over the white and red tiles of the floor.

Most of the tanks contained an immobile knot of snakes, one species to each tank. They did not move except for an occasional flick of the tongue tasting the air. In a smaller tank huddled a group of large lizards, their skins green with minute yellow spots. Their eyes were huge and filled with a great simplicity. If reptiles could be innocent then these knew nothing of the cruelty of the world, were ignorant of what was soon to befall them.

As I looked at them, a sense of terrible foreboding spread over me, centred upon the unfathomable recesses of the soul beyond the reach of the most intricate self-searching. It was followed by a startling feeling of *déjà vu*, the hair on my nape rising as if a tentacle of ice was run across my neck.

From one of the tanks came a sound I had not heard for many years. *Tok-eye!* it went. *Tok-eye!* I turned sharply. The tank from which the sound came was empty.

Feeling faint, I rested my hand against the nearest tank in which there was a single snake, a variety of python three feet long. It was a light emerald creature marked with delicate, random black patterns, the colouring so subtle it might have been painted with water-colours, have been the work of a divine artist dripping indian ink on a green background while the paint was wet.

The distant explosions came to an end. I pressed my hand to my forehead, the skin hot and dry. My cool fingers unaccountably dissolved my fear.

The next tank contained a tangle of many-banded kraits. Their brilliant black-and-yellow or white rings were dulled: in one corner of the tank, a single snake was curled in a patch of white mucus. It was, I guessed, dead and therefore of no use. No Chinese will eat a snake he hasn't seen wriggling before it reaches the cooking pot.

'What you want?' the proprietor asked belligerently in pidgin English, his suspicion aroused by a European in his snake shop. It is rare to see a *gweilo* in such an establishment.

'This snake kill one man,' I replied, pointing to a krait lying close to the glass at the front of the tank. 'Get more money for him.'

The restaurateur was a little taken aback by my response.

'He kill one man,' he confirmed. 'How you know?'

'This snake *ngun keuk tai*. In English call many-banded krait. He tail stop in black band,' I said. 'Chinese say if tail black at end then he kill a man.'

The Chinese laughed and said, 'You know too much!'

'This one,' I pointed to a yellow-and-black snake in another tank, '*kum keuk tai*. Gold leg band snake.'

Moving to a tank to my right, the restaurateur tapped his fingernail on the glass. One of the inmates flashed its head around at the noise.

'What he call?' he asked.

I put my hand to the glass, rapidly bunching and opening my fist. The snake reared up, spread its hood and struck at the glass, a thin stream of venom running down in a colourless trickle like glutinous spittle.

'*Kwoh shan fung*,' I replied adding as a translation, 'More fast mountain wind snake. Very dangerous. In English, we say king cobra.'

'Good snake!' the restaurateur remarked, giving a thumbs-up to lend credence to his statement. 'Can sell for much money.'

'How much?' I enquired.

'Too much. You must have good money for him.'

'*Kei toh?*' I enquired once more, using Cantonese.

'Fi' hundred eightee dollar,' the owner of the snake replied in English, perhaps not believing I could speak more than a few phrases and name a few snakes.

I pretended astonishment and replied, '*Yau mo gau chor ah*!'

At this, the restaurateur and the waiters fell into fits of laughter. Even the woman at the cooking range stopped work to join in and the youth leaned on his mop to share in the joke.

'You speak Cantonese ve'y good. How long you live Hong Kong?'

I looked into the cobra's tank. The perceived threat removed, it had shrunk its hood and lowered its head, but it was still alert, its tongue flicking and its head swaying slightly as if sizing me up for another strike. I wondered how old the snake was. Cobras can live for thirty years: it was not inconceivable to think they might last longer. As I was moving inexorably towards death at the hand of time, so was the reptile doomed, its fate sealed by the first customer to walk in with five hundred and eighty dollars and a desire to fortify his blood, improve his sexual prowess or live longer.

'*Luk saap yat neen*,' I said.

'*Ay-yah*!' the Chinese exclaimed, thought for a minute then added, 'Sixty-one year! So long! You old man now!'

I felt suddenly weak and my head began to throb again. I reached out and held on to the back of a chair by the nearest table.

'Yes,' I agreed, 'a very long time. A very long time, indeed.'

I turned the chair around and sat down heavily in it.

'You Okay?' the Chinese asked.

'Yes. Okay. I buy one glass tea.'

The restaurateur signalled to a waiter who disappeared into the back of the premises. I could hear crockery being moved and reached into my pocket for some coins but the restaurateur waved his hand.

'Tea no charge. Free tea for old man live long time in China.'

Smiling my thanks, I leaned forward and stared at my feet. I felt dizzy and rested my arm on the table, knocking over a rice bowl with my elbow. The room shifted as if it was on a pendulum and I was the only fixed point. The snake tanks swayed and, for a moment, I wanted to reach out and steady them in case they should fall, shatter and the irate inhabitants attack me. In a detached way, I wondered what it would be like to be bitten by a deadly snake.

'Take tea slowly,' the Chinese advised. 'You get better soon. You wan' Green Spot orange? Wan' Seven-up? Wan' a Coke?'

'No, no thank you,' I said. 'I be all right.'

The youth with the mop had not yet reached this area of the room and, around my feet, I could see the congealed remains of the snakes which had provided the previous evening's menu. The waiter arrived with the tea in a glass tumbler.

'*Chai*,' he said, placing it in my hands.

Although it was hot, I held the glass and sipped noisily at it. It did not refresh me but it calmed me, stopped the room moving so violently.

Hunched forward with the glass in my hand, my mind gradually filled with disjointed images and vague, half-recollections which passed before me as if seen through an insubstantial dawn mist, the sort that hung in river valleys before the sun could soak them up. I saw a distant fire burning though what was fuelling the flames I could not say: it might have been old car tyres or engine oil for the smoke was thick, black and acrid. From the heart of the fire came a curling dragon. It was not a scaly monster such as one could see on a temple façade but a soft-skinned creature with sad eyes in which I could tell it knew it was going to die. The dragon rose into the sky and as soon as it had disappeared into the mist it was replaced by a butterfly. It was a dark-winged insect but in the centre of each hind wing was an iridescent blue circle which winked on and off as it flew slowly before me, blotting out the fire. As it moved by me, its wings seemed to stroke against my cheek, soft as rich velvet. It reached what I assumed was an iron tree and, as I watched, the tree burst into anonymous, indescribable blossom. I felt a warmth spread through me at the sight of the flowers. The mist disseminated and a hot sun shone out of a blue sky, which I was observing through a screen of tall yellow bamboo stems shot through with green lines, the leaves rustling in the breeze and brushing slightly against me.

The visions ended when I was touched gently on the shoulder:

I thought at first it was either the butterfly returning to caress me or the leaves but, when I turned, it was the snake restaurant owner.

'You Okay?' he enquired again.

I straightened my back. My spine ached at the waist but otherwise I felt quite refreshed. The dizziness was gone.

'Yes, I'm okay.'

Yet I could hear the leaves of the bamboo still, rustling in the breeze. The restaurateur stepped aside. Behind him was one of the waiters. His left hand was wearing a thick glove from which dangled a hissing rat snake.

'This for you. Make you strong.'

The waiter put his right hand around the snake's neck and, with a deft downward strike, opened its skin up the length of its body with a razor blade gripped between his fingers. He might have been unzipping the creature. The intestines fell out. Another waiter pushed a small basin under the snake with his foot, the dripping blood collecting in it. The snake's internal organs were cut out and dropped into the basin, which the restaurateur picked up, placed on the table and started to stir rapidly with a pair of chop-sticks, the plastic banging against the metal sides.

Putting my glass of tea down, I was surprised to see I had drunk less than a third of it.

An inch of the snake's blood was poured into a tall wine glass, to which was added red wine from a bottle on the label of which was a dragon similar in appearance to the one in my vision. A waiter stirred the drink with a steel spoon and handed it to me.

I put the glass to my lips and drained it in one. It tasted of sweetness and iron with a bitter tang.

'Good,' the restaurateur said. 'Make you live long time.'

'I already live long time,' I replied after a moment's thought. 'No good for one man live too long. If you live too long, you see too many things. No be happy see too much.'

As I stepped on to the flat roof of the mission, Father Callaghan was standing beside the bell, his left hand resting on the metal, his right in his pocket: we had just celebrated Mass and he was still wearing his cassock. At the sound of my foot-steps he turned sharply and I had the ridiculous impression he was afraid of me.

'Ah Fong said you wanted me, Father,' I enquired.

'Yes,' he said hurriedly, glancing over my shoulder. 'Come by my side, Father Stephen.'

I was puzzled. He was not usually brusque.

'Is there something wrong, Father?'

'There may be,' he replied enigmatically. 'This is why I wanted to speak to you up here. I don't want to alarm the others.'

I felt a twinge of anxiety and wondered what it was he would wish to keep from Ah Fong and Sister Margaret.

'Before Mass,' he began, 'I went into the *hutong* at the rear. The baby posting box was jammed in its runners and I went to free it. Sometimes the wood sticks. There's a worn slide.'

His procrastination increased my anxiety. This, too, was out of character and I wondered if I had done something terribly wrong, upset a local Chinese who had lodged a complaint against me with the mandarin. I could not imagine what my sin might have been but my ignorance of local custom made such an error quite feasible.

'I reached the *hutong* and all looked quite normal,' he continued. 'It is narrow back there and I could not see the box until I was close to it. It was not jammed shut by malfunction. A large splint of wood had been rammed into the side of it, hammered in so firmly I could shift it only with two hands and some mighty tugging. The box, I fear, is now defunct for the splint has cracked the slide. We shall not see so many little souls coming to Christ through our letter-box.'

'Can we not have it repaired?' I suggested.

'Not now. There is no carpenter in the town who will undertake the job.'

'I do not understand . . .' I started to say, but Father Callaghan interrupted me.

'I fear our days in Wuchow, Father Stephen, are numbered.'

'But who would have done such a thing?' I cut in, not appreciating the import of his words through my anger.

'It's not a matter of who,' Father Callaghan said 'but why.'

He took his right hand out of his pocket. In his fingers was a light brown sheet of Chinese paper, coarse and containing the husks of the rice pulp from which it was manufactured.

'This was attached to the splint,' Father Callaghan said and he handed the document to me.

It was written in characters with a brush pen dipped in red ink, the vertical lines neat and ordered.

'What is it?' I enquired.

'I translated it,' Father Callaghan said, ignoring my question. 'Before Mass.'

He took the paper back from me and held it in both hands as if it was a proclamation and he the crier about to shout its message.

'It says, "May the gods assist the *I Ho Ch'üan*." That is the heading. It goes on, "The foreign devils disturb the Middle Kingdom urging people to join their religion, turn their backs on Heaven and do not venerate the gods and ancestors. Foreign devils are not produced by mankind. If you doubt this, look carefully at their eyes. They are blue." There follows a passage of insults. Then it carries on, "No rain falls in the Middle Kingdom. The moon is made of blood. The earth is dry. The rice fails to grow. This is because the Christian religion has stopped up the heavens."'

Father Callaghan let his hand drop and looked up at the sky. The sun was gaining in height and there was not a cloud to be seen.

'It goes on to make other preposterous claims. One is that we take in babies to steal their eyes to sell. Another is that we cause others to eat them as a part of our rites. A third is that any man who takes the *I Ho Ch'üan* oath shall be impregnable against the bullets of the foreign devils' rifles. And so on. There is more . . .'

There were beads of sweat upon his brow but he made no attempt to wipe them away, blinking as they seeped through his brows to sting his eyes.

'Yesterday,' he said quietly, 'as I was walking towards the river, I met Mrs Tremlett. I think you know her from our party at the Residency?'

I nodded.

'She was accompanied by her two children. Sarah is five, her brother Ambrose three. Their baby amah was with them. We stopped by the market where they sell songbirds. Mrs Tremlett wished to buy some golden finches. I engaged her in conversation as the children looked at the birds. Suddenly, a man appeared from behind the bird stall and, without any warning, slapped their amah so hard across the face she tottered sideways, upsetting a pile of cages. I was astounded for this is quite unlike Chinese behaviour. As the amah picked herself up, Mrs Tremlett assisting her, the man berated the poor servant. "You wicked woman," he screamed, "Look at these children!" He called them *siu kwei-tsi* which means little devils. "Their eyes are as blue as the big devils." He tried to hit her again but Mrs Tremlett was in the way. For a moment, I thought he would strike her but he desisted. Then he shouted in the most insulting of tones, *"T'ien Chu Kiao,"* spat on the amah's *sam* and disappeared as quickly as he had arrived, ducking behind the bird stall.'

'What does *T'ien Chu Kiao* mean?' I asked.

'It means Roman Catholics,' Father Callaghan replied.

I sat on the step beneath the bell. Strangely, I was neither afraid nor indignant. My flesh had grown cold yet I was inwardly calm and composed.

'We shall have to take care,' he said after a long moment of silence. 'I spoke to Morrisby last evening. He had already telegraphed Hong Kong. It was just as well I did, for the lines went dead less than an hour later, before he could receive a reply.'

'What shall we do now?' I asked.

'I think our best option,' he almost whispered, 'is to pray that Jesus Christ will look over us and bring us to safety. We are in, I am sure, for a rough time.'

During the night, there has been a squatter fire in the Kowloon foothills. I did not know of it until this morning when I bought my daily paper from Lam, saw the headlines and discovered, according to a sketch map, where the conflagration had occurred. Without bothering to read the article, I walked quickly into Nathan Road and caught the first number 7 bus to come along. It was packed with pupils on their way to school. I squeezed onto one of the wooden slatted seats and was about to unfold the newspaper to read of the disaster when a voice spoke to me from behind.

'Good morning, sir.'

I turned. It was the boy.

'Good morning,' I replied.

'Are you reading about the fire, sir? We saw it from The Peak. It was in the hills behind Kowloon Tong.'

'I am going there,' I told him. 'I have . . .'

I was going to add I had acquaintances there but decided not to admit to this: the boy, however, was thinking ahead of me.

'Friends there, sir. I thought you might.'

He moved aside a little so I could see a very pretty girl standing next to him.

'This is Roxy,' he said, 'Roxy Drawdale.' Then, turning to her, he added, 'This is Mr Galvin, my Cantonese teacher.'

The girl smiled charmingly and asked, 'How d'you do?' in a West Coast American accent, adding, 'Are you going to see they're okay?'

'My friends?' I answered, a little distracted by this sudden conversation. 'Yes. Yes, I'm going to see if they need help.'

'We're going to set up a fund at school,' the boy volunteered. 'Roxy will be in charge of it. For the homeless,' he added.

'That's very noble of you, Gerald,' I replied and realised, I do not quite know why, it was the first time I had ever used his name in addressing him.

The bus lurched into Waterloo Road. By the public mortuary next to the fire station, a funeral cortege was gathered. It was not a grand affair but the ceremony of a poor person. There was only one band equipped with silver trombones, trumpets and tubas, two funereal wreaths mounted on the front of tricycles and one paper orb on a pole through which the devils might escape. A group of about twenty mourners, the deceased's immediate family dressed in white cloaks with the others, the paid mourners, in black, mingled by the door of an ancient Ford hearse. The sight was not a good omen.

'We're hoping to raise money by paying to see our teachers

jump into the harbour,' the girl declared. 'A lot of the kids'll pay to see that. We reckon on getting $4,000.'

'A handsome sum,' I said. 'I hope you'll reach your target.'

'We will,' she stated confidently. 'I reckon we'll go over but it's best not to be too optimistic.'

The bus drove under a railway bridge and pulled into a stop. The boy and his girlfriend disembarked, waving to me as the vehicle drove off. I felt touched they should have spoken to me and the encounter, brief though it was, greatly impressed upon me the boy's sincerity.

At the end of the route, the road where the bus usually turned round was blocked by police and fire brigade vehicles. Over a dozen hoses snaked up the path from two hydrants and a water tender on the pavement beside a parked ambulance, its rear doors open and the stretcher missing. Some British soldiers in fatigues were busy nearby sorting out boxes of clothing and military two-man tents.

No one attempted to prevent me from going up the path although there were a number of Chinese being held back by several police constables with whom they were having a heated argument. I suppose, being a *gweilo*, the police thought I was a government official or an aid worker.

I followed the hoses until I came to the edge of what had, until the night before, been a thriving shanty town. Now it was just a smouldering, blackened landscape with hardly any structure remaining standing. Fragments of clothing, charred wood, twisted lengths of corrugated iron, the skeletal frames of chairs, beds and bicycles, and warped or partially melted aluminium cooking utensils were scattered throughout the desolation. The air smelled of singed hair, burnt feathers, wet charcoal and sodden earth, for the ground was soft underfoot from the use of the hoses.

Through this bleak panorama about a hundred people were moving, heads down looking at the ground, sifting through the detritus of their lives, prodding about with sticks, occasionally stooping to pick something up and put it in a straw bag or cardboard box.

Everything was eerily silent. The people did not speak and there was not a single bird in the sky. Even here and there, where there were still a few tiny flames or glowing embers showing, causing no risk and therefore of no concern to the fire brigade, the fire made no sound. Nothing crackled or hissed or spat. It was as if the fire had not only burned down the houses but the very sounds which had emanated from them.

I made my way along what had been a thoroughfare through the shanties. The ground was beaten so hard from the passage of feet that it had not yet broken up under the flow of water. At a junction, I passed the remains of a small shop, the ground littered with broken glass and pottery jars: next to it was what had been a little workshop. The remains of a machine stood in the rubble, surrounded by a scattering of metal discs the size of tap washers but without holes drilled in them: they were discoloured from the heat and I wondered if this had been the site of Mr Yee's counterfeiter.

Ahead of me up the hill was a gathering of men huddled in conversation. They were all Chinese but several wore suits and ties and one carried a briefcase. These, I assumed, were the committee of the local *kai fong* association. As I looked at them, a man detached himself from the group and came towards me, walking gingerly through the ashes. It was Mr Yee.

'*Cho san, nei ho ma*?' he greeted me, holding out his hand which I shook.

'*Ho, nei ho ma*?' I answered.

He nodded, casting a look around us.

'*Kei toh koh yan . . .*?' I began, but he interrupted me.

'*Yee maan . . .*' he said and shrugged, adding in English, 'Not a good place to see today.'

'Twenty thousand people?' I said.

'Maybe more. How can you tell? More than four thousan' house gone.' He rubbed his hands together as if he was cold. 'I expect to see you come.'

'You know I had to come . . .' I started to say.

'They are okay.'

'Are you sure?' I asked.

'Sure. You see up the hill? Some house not burning. Maybe fi've hund'ed people. They got their house up there.'

His news made me feel immensely pleased, as if I had

personally been responsible for stopping the fire from sweeping higher up the mountainside. I would have liked to have sat down for I felt a little weak now: the urgency which had been pumping itself through me was now abated.

'Not all bad news,' Mr Yee said, once more looking about the devastation. 'All the people here now got new houses. New flat some place. Soon, more people come, build new houses and can live here.'

'And when they come?' I replied.

Mr Yee is a businessman. He may not seek to profit from the misfortunes of others but, should those misfortunes place him in such a position as to be able to assist them and himself at the same time, he will be quick to seize the opportunity.

'When they come, business like before. I can get wood, make places here flat for a house, bring in water pipe – even power. I can lend money for him if he want to start his factory. Make something.' He kicked at the discs on the ground. 'Maybe fifty-cent coin,' he added and grinned.

'Did you lose anything here, Mr Yee?'

'Some money. Some small company burn. Five, six, not too many. But no way I can get my investment back. It's a loss. All businessmen mus' make a loss sometimes,' he said stoically and laughed briefly.

'And this fire?' I enquired.

'Maybe start by accident. Somebody knock down a cooking pot, maybe. You know, jus' down the hill there was a factory making soap, hair cream and another making,' he searched for a moment for the English but did not know it, '*yin fa.*'

'Fireworks,' I said.

'Yes. Small one made of gunpowder inside a little ball of earth. For children. They throw them in the street. *Pang*! No too much danger. The name,' he stirred the air with his hand to encourage the words, 'cher-wy bomb.'

'And one of the factories caught fire?'

'Maybe,' he declared.

Yet I could tell he knew this was the official reason which would appear in the fire brigade report: the true reason was that it was caused by deliberate, premeditated and publicly – if secretively

— advertised arson. Everybody was aware the best way for a family to be rehoused was to be made homeless. The squatters knew this but were reluctant to risk their homes and livelihoods: Mr Yee and his triad society knew it and were more than conscious of how they might benefit: the authorities knew it but were powerless to do anything about it.

The ploy was simple. As soon as a new block of low cost housing was completed, but just before it was occupied, the local triad societies put their heads together and decided it was time for a squatter blaze. Someone would be tipped off to begin it, setting light to his flimsy shanty after he had removed his most valuable possessions. Invariably, he would tip off his friends and relatives who, in turn, would warn their friends and kin. At the appointed hour, usually late in the evening of a day that had been sunny and bright with, if possible, a brisk onshore breeze, the inferno would commence. The timing was important: a rainy or humid day would mean the fire would not spread as quickly as it might, the breeze was needed to fan the holocaust and the hour of the fire was vital because it would slow the fire brigade arriving through the evening traffic. Furthermore, no one wanted to be made homeless when there was the chance of a rain shower.

Inevitably, ten people might perish in the blaze but that was the cost of having ten thousand relocated into proper abodes. These were odds Mr Yee and his businessmen partners were prepared to back.

'You come an' see me soon?' Mr Yee asked.

'When I need my hair cutting,' I said and we shook hands again.

He walked back towards his group of cronies and I started to wend my way down through the ruins towards the road.

I should hate Mr Yee. He is a manipulator of human lives, a ringmaster in the circuses of joy and tragedy.

Yet I am not one to umpire his little games. When I was young and idealistic, I used to spend my time manipulating people with just as much self-interest as he does, if not for so much profit. All men use and exploit their fellows. It is a part of nature and I know, when the time comes to put the rest of this hillside of shacks to the torch, he will assure my interests are protected just as he will his own.

I have spent this afternoon in Tiger Balm Gardens in the hills behind Causeway Bay. It is a bizarre place described in the tourist guide books as a 'quaint pleasure garden in which a number of tableaux depict scenes from Chinese mythology and religion'. Quaint is not quite the adjective I would choose: macabre might be more apt.

Arranged in the shadow of a tall, white pagoda, the gardens are tucked into a hillside which has been shaped into a series of grottoes, in each of which are hollowed out caverns containing scenes from hell. Half life-size demons, the occupants of the dreams of madmen and murderers, have been fashioned out of clay or plaster of Paris and garishly painted. Some have vermilion dog's faces, puce-and-green snake's heads or the visages of bears and tigers painted royal blue or bright yellow and mounted upon the shoulders of human bodies dressed if not in classical Chinese robes then in the scales of a reptile, with the tail of a shark or the shaggy fur of a wild man and the feet of a beast. These creatures are all armed with tridents, Chinese pikestaffs, swords with serrated blades or spears with wave-edged double-sided points: and every one of them is torturing a living soul, a man or woman who, through some slight folly unworthy of the attentions of the underworld, is being made to pay for their sins. Their faces are contorted with fear, their eyes staring and their mouths wide with silent screaming. Some of these poor unfortunates are shown as past the point of caring about their torture. They have been beheaded, dismembered and are being cast into the flames of eternal damnation, into pits of sulphur from whence there are no exits.

The gardens were erected by a Chinese millionaire from Singapore called Aw Boon Haw who made his money from a medicinal paste he invented which is considered to be a cure-all for a wide range of ailments. It is purveyed in little hectagonal glass jars with a green label upon which, in an orange oblong, is portrayed a leaping tiger. It is a petroleum wax-based ointment and contains menthol, oil of cloves, camphor and tincture of peppermint: it is rumoured to contain opium, too. The lid of the jar is golden like every promise ever made by one man to another. And like all promises, it tarnishes.

I use the balm quite regularly. It has a pungent smell which is not unpleasant and may well be addictive over time but I find it soothes my muscles and, if I have slight catarrh, it clears my nose in minutes even if it also makes my eyes stream.

I am fascinated by these gardens partly because of their utter tastelessness and partly because they profoundly amuse me with their infantile barbarity and simplistic moralising. It also never escapes me that the presentation of all this distress and horror was financed by a medicine which eradicates pain. Perhaps the founder wanted to press home the argument that he could cure the ailments of the flesh but not the ills of the soul.

One of the tableaux is entitled *The Barbarity of Wicked Men*. It depicts the usual scene of torture and disembowelment and is overlooked by an incongruous eight-foot-high white rabbit with bulging eyes and wearing a top hat. He seems to have escaped from an Oriental interpretation of *Alice's Adventures in Wonderland*.

Ignoring the rabbit's thyroid stare, I studied the plaster figures but quite dispassionately. Barbarity is not something which worries me: I have seen too much to be affected by it. I am more concerned with the barbarity upon which God and all his churches depend. If it was not for the barbaric threat of amaranthine damnation the promise of heavenly bliss would be a shabby counterfeit, not worth the striving of being good.

And I do not hate barbarous men. What I really despise is God's barbarity. He promised justice, prophesied peace, held out his hand and offered goodness. He pledged to banish pestilence, expel starvation and ostracise evil. I was bedazzled by his reason, fell for his patter and trusted his word when I should have been on my guard. I assumed that, as he was not a man, I was safe. That was my mistake for God and men are too close for comfort: I have often wondered whether man was made in God's image or men made God like themselves.

Yet another of the plaster scenes has a small notice before it in a wooden frame. Rain and humidity have seeped behind the glass so that the writing has run. It states *A Compassionate Scene in Heaven*. Several vaguely angelic spirits, painted entirely in white with stark blue eyes and red mouths, stand over a sinner who has, presumably, recanted. He bears the marks of the brutality from, perhaps, the tableau by the White Rabbit.

I dislike the compassionate. In compassion there is a grotesque piety I cannot abide, those who show pity seeing themselves as blessed. In their hearts, they relish the misery of others for it affords them an opportunity to earn the attention and praise of their fellows and the generosity of their gods. They are without shame, obloqious vultures without honour or grace.

Only the man who has no god can be truly compassionate for he can have no ulterior motive of pathos up his sleeve, no deceit hiding in his kind words and actions.

For him, such displays are not compassion. They are merely an in-built animal response to the plight of another of his kind in dire straits.

I would be deemed kind by those who do not share my interpretation, would be considered compassionate and kind-hearted. They would be fooled. I merely do what I believe should be done to protect the order of things, for I am not a sympathetic man but a realist who, on occasion, would soften the impact of reality upon those who deserve better.

The Street of Righteous Enlightenment led from the river to the main square, passing on the way the *kong kwan*, the official inn used by guests and visitors to the mandarin whose yamen was situated next door. Of all the thoroughfares of Wuchow, this was the most pleasant, a wide boulevard with a cobbled way running down the centre and broad sidewalks under an avenue of flame trees. The street was seldom crowded for no market stalls were permitted there and the few shops in the street catered for the richer inhabitants. Whereas in other parts of the town a pedestrian had to side-step barrows of produce, tables of fish, sleeping dogs, rickshaws and laden coolies, here the only obstacles were the trees, loose cobbles, the occasional passer-by and, if he should be on the move, the mandarin in his palanquin.

The gateway to the yamen was an imposing structure fifteen feet high, a square arch with heavy wooden doors, a glazed tiled roof with curved eaves beneath which was suspended an ornately carved rosewood plaque the size of a narrow bed announcing the name and status of the place. Beside the gate stood two guards. They were not erect, soldierly figures such as one might find in a foreign army but comparative slouches. Admittedly, they did not go so far as to squat on the ground, but they leaned on the wall, chatting or playing toss-the-coin against the curbing stones. Their uniforms consisted of a conical hat tied under the chin by a cord, a cotton jacket died saffron, a pair of short black trousers tucked incongruously into what looked like knee-high puttees and slippers. They were armed with a muzzle-loading rifle and a small sword each. Although they were short men, they were well muscled and held themselves, as soldiers do anywhere in the world, with a certain arrogance.

With Ah Fong accompanying me, I was making my way through the town on one of the circuits Father Callaghan had drawn on a map. Although dressed as a Chinese, I wore my cross about my neck on a silver chain and carried in my hand a woven straw basket in which there were some rice cakes, several packets of dried fish and half a dozen of Mr Kung's aged eggs. It was my business to discover needy souls and present them with the food, bless them in the name of Jesus Christ and tell them briefly of the mission. I had already found two beggars on the river side, had fed them in the name of Our Lord and was walking up the Street of Righteous Enlightenment on my way to the square.

Neither Ah Fong nor I expected to find any needy folk in the street. The town's sick or lame kept away from it for they knew they were likely to be harangued by the mandarin's guards if they appeared. The comparative reduction in the number of pedestrians also gave the street the reputation of being a poor begging spot.

As we approached the gateway to the *kong kwan*, it opened and a most beautiful woman appeared from within, riding in a palanquin with the door curtains tied back. This was so unusual a sight Ah Fong stopped in his tracks and stared, forgetting for a moment to kow-tow. She was dressed in the finest of brocades, the material coloured ultramarine blue shot through with silver and embroidered with birds and clouds. Her face was impassive behind a heavy layer of alabaster white cosmetics, only her eyes and small red lips accentuated by colour, her hair piled high and draped with a string of pearls: she reminded me of the goddess to which Sister Margaret made her sly devotions. Her feet were bound and contained in wooden clog-like shoes with silk uppers, no bigger than those of a small child.

She was in the company of several officials, one of whom screamed at Ah Fong who rapidly bowed as low as he could, bending at the knees to make himself look even smaller. I followed suit but we still received a verbal tongue lashing as the little procession passed by, another official slapping the curtains closed.

'Who she?' I asked Ah Fong after they had disappeared from the end of the street and we straightened up once more.

'Lady for mandarin,' he replied. His face was red from bending over. 'Famous lady. He got many son with her. Wife no got son.'

'What her name?'

'Her name I no know. Mandarin secret.'

We followed in the direction of the palanquin, passing the yamen guards who leered silently at us. The dusty ground bore the flat, slapped footprints of the palanquin bearers and the shod imprints of the officials.

About thirty yards past the yamen was a *hutong* going off at right angles to the street. It was in deep shadow, for the sun was not yet sufficiently high enough to illuminate it. I gave a studied look into the darkness, increased in blackness by my eyes being accustomed to the bright light. Father Callaghan had, since the attack upon Mrs Tremlett's amah, suggested we keep a cautious eye open for trouble. Neither Ah Fong nor I were armed with so much as a penknife.

The *hutong* appeared empty: I could see, at the far end, the oblong of sunlight where it gave onto the next street, figures criss-crossing it. Yet, as I looked down the alley, I heard a groaning noise of the sort made by animals in pain rather than humans.

'What is that?' I wondered aloud, not so much as a question to Ah Fong as an exclamation of my own curiosity.

Starting towards the *hutong*, I slid the handles of my basket over my shoulder to free my hands. I did not expect to be attacked but it was best to be prepared.

'We be care,' Ah Fong said, as if reading my thoughts. 'No good see bad men,' he went on unnecessarily.

The shadows were cool and the *hutong* seemed to contain no living creature save a cat curled up on an inverted tub halfway to the next street. Some doors opened onto the alley but these were all firmly shut as were the few windows. There was no breeze, a few prayer banners hanging from a lintel not so much as twitching.

My stepping into the alley caused the groaning to cease abruptly. The cat, sensing my presence or awakened by the cessation of the noise, got up. It arched its back, hissed menacingly at me then, appreciating I was no threat, circled about and settled once more to continue its repose.

'There is nothing here,' I remarked to Ah Fong and was about to turn when a movement behind some firewood stacked against the wall of a house caught my attention.

I moved carefully forwards, the space behind the boxes gradually becoming visible. If there was a robber there, or one of the rebellious bandits, I wanted to be ready either to repulse his attack or flee to the street, where I hoped the yamen guards might come to my rescue. Such an expectation was, of course, without foundation: the mandarin was hardly likely to have instructed his soldiers to act upon my behalf and yet he had punished one of his own race over the death of the terrier.

These thoughts rushed through my mind as I edged along the *hutong*, conscious I was disregarding Father Callaghan's advice.

What first came into sight was a bare foot covered in grime and several large scabs. The leg above it was equally dirty, the skin blotched whilst the thigh, when it came into view, was covered by the filthy material of a rolled up *fu*. Just as I was about to take another step a hand appeared trying to smooth down the material. It was an adult-sized hand but devoid of fingers: in their place was a row of gnarled stumps like the roots of an old tree.

Ah Fong, a few steps behind me, whispered, 'What you see, master?'

'I have,' I said in my normal voice, 'discovered a poor soul suffering from leprosy.'

'What *lee-pro-see*?' Ah Fong enquired.

The Cantonese for the sickness was one of the words I had come upon only that morning: I had taken to learning by heart ten nouns every day before Mass, recapitulating them afterwards. If they survived my attention to the Latin of the service, I could be confident they were mine.

'*Ma fung*,' I replied, starting forwards again but Ah Fong grabbed me by the waistband.

'*Ay-ah*! No look see, master.' His voice was filled with alarm. 'No look see. No good look see. We go. Go! Go!'

Leprosy was one disease every Chinese knew: it was more feared by them than any other. They would rather have faced all the dragons of the countryside than expose themselves to it. They were, however, ignorant of its two varieties and regarded every leper as evil, a person who was carrying the punishment of the gods upon himself, a reminder to others of what might befall them if they, too, were to grievously sin. In the eyes of the people, they were so damned even the gods would not let them go to their deaths with their bodies intact. Beggars could expect alms, a bowl of unhusked rice or one or two cash from the sympathetic: a leper had to scavenge like a stray dog, expecting nothing but curses and revulsion.

So firm was Ah Fong's grip, so solid his determination we should leave the *hutong* immediately, I had to struggle to make progress towards the leper. As soon as I took a step, Ah Fong leaned away from me, digging the heels of his soft shoes into the dirt.

'Ah Fong!' I remonstrated with him, trying to twist my head. 'Let me go.'

'*Ma fung* no good. Much bad. You no go, master,' he pleaded at the top of his voice.

Reaching behind, I managed to get hold of Ah Fong's hands

and began to prise his fingers off my *fu tau*. The more I sought to loosen his grip the firmer it became. At last, I surrendered, allowing him to pull me into the street.

'We go now, master,' he demanded hopefully once I was back in the sunlight.

'Listen, Ah Fong,' I said, calming him down by putting my hand on his shoulder, 'I am going to see the leper. The man with *ma fung*. This is my work. You do not need to come with me. I understand. But you do not need to be afraid.'

'Mus' be af-aid, master!' he answered loudly. 'If you touch *ma fung beng yan* you too *ma fung*. You finger fall off. You toe fall off. You nose fall off.'

'No,' I said sternly, 'not with this *ma fung beng yan*. He has dry leprosy. Only wet leprosy is contagious.'

Ah Fong did not understand the meaning of the word *contagious* but it did not matter. He was not to be convinced and as I started towards the entrance to the *hutong* he begged me once more to leave well alone.

'No go, master. Please, no go.'

'I must go,' I said. 'This is my work.'

I entered the *hutong* and walked to the pile of firewood. The leper was huddled behind the wood wearing the filthiest rags I had ever seen. His *sam* was in such tatters I wondered if he had deliberately scissored it as beggars were known to do, to enhance the chances of benefaction. Yet, looking at his hands, I knew this was not the case: he had too few appropriate fingers left to use a pair of scissors.

At the sight of me, he cringed against the wall and gibbered something that might have been words but sounded more like the bestial noises of a subterranean creature. Bubbles of saliva formed at his mouth, growing as large as plums before bursting.

'I am come with the Light of Jesus,' I told him in English, with as gentle a tone as I could manage, although I knew he was unable to comprehend a single word I spoke. 'Let His Mercy come upon you.'

I stretched out to lay my hand on the poor wretch but he must have thought I was going to strike him, for he instantly swung his arms over his head and cowered against the firewood, knocking over a bundle of kindling. So as not to alarm him further, I put down my basket and, opening it, removed a rice cake which I held out to him. He eyed it cautiously, uncertain whether to reach for it or not.

A soft voice began to speak over my shoulder but I could only make out a few of its phrases and these meant nothing to me.

'*Sùng lai . . . Lai mât . . .*' it said.

Turning, I found Ah Fong close behind me. He was smiling down at the leper who, encouraged by hearing his own tongue, put out both his stump hands and, grasping the cake between them, thrust it towards his mouth and began to bite into it. He ate in the manner of a rat, his two hands at his face: but he no longer owned the dexterity of either a man or a rodent, crumbs falling down his clothing.

'You touch no get *ma fung*?' Ah Fong asked.

'No get,' I assured him, slipping back into pidgin myself. 'What you say him?'

'I tell him you got present. Can take.'

Once more, I reached out. The leper did not flinch but sat quite still as I put my hand upon the crown of his head. His hair was patchy, such as one might find the coat of a mangy dog, the skin beneath dry and flaking.

'May the Love of Our Saviour, Jesus Christ, come to you, relieve your suffering and bring you to His Eternal Glory,' I whispered.

The leper's head moved under my palm and he gazed up at me. He had not raised his face until now and, as he turned his countenance upwards, I saw his nose was disfigured and his upper lip withdrawn back across his teeth in a permanent, hideous smirk. I felt instantly repelled but fought the emotion and looked into his eyes. The pupils were black but the whites bloodshot and sore.

'*Yee thoo*,' he said, spittle spraying from his mouth onto the front of his *sam*, his tongue grotesquely sticking out below his upper jaw. '*Yee thoo. Gai du. Gai du.*'

'Master,' Ah Fong whispered in my ear, 'he say *Yeh so Gei duk*. Is Cantonese for Jesus Chri's.'

The leper muttered something else and Ah Fong, moving

between me and the woodpile, put out his hand and placed it next to mine on the man's scalp.

I made the sign of the cross upon the leper's forehead then, as I began to give him the blessing, there came a clamour from the far end of the *hutong*. A tight throng of people was rushing towards us. At the forefront was a man with a red cloth tied about his brow.

'Master, we go! *Fie di! Fie di!*' Ah Fong shouted, grabbing me by the arm.

I turned without so much as a thought and ran after him, down the *hutong* towards the Street of Righteous Enlightenment. As we reached the sunlight, I looked back. The crowd had halted, the leper having crawled into the centre of the *hutong*, where he was kneeling up with his back towards us, his pathetic arms outstretched on either side so that he almost touched each wall. It seemed as though he was protecting us with his hideous illness, knowing the mob would not so much as brush against him. But his delaying tactic was short: the leader grabbed a length of firewood from the pile and, using it as a stave, smashed it down upon the side of the leper's head. He crumpled and the crowd surged forward again, jumping over the prone, misshapen body and kicking my basket aside so the contents spilled over him.

Ah Fong and I had to seek safety and quickly. We spun to our right, fleeing for the gate to the yamen: if we could enter it, we would come under the protection of the mandarin and no canaille would dare enter his premises.

Running at full tilt, we sped up to the two yamen guards who, hearing the approaching shouts and seeing us sprinting towards them, had picked up their muzzle-loaders and stationed themselves on either side of the gate. Ah Fong yelled at them to open the gate but they stood firm and did not respond. Drawing nearer, he hollered again but the only response he got was from the nearest guard who, unsheathing his sword and shaking his head, shouted curtly back at us.

'The *kong kwan*, Ah Fong!' I bellowed, seeing the yamen door was not to open for us. 'Go *kong kwan* side!'

We sped past the guards and on to the second door. It was not open but I hammered upon the wood and the gatekeeper inside, not able to judge what was going on in the street, slid the wooden bar across, pulling the door ajar. I rammed my shoulder against the timbers and we slid in. The gatekeeper was too flabbergasted to stop us. I slammed the door shut, ramming home the retaining beam.

For a moment, all was quiet then there drew near a screaming cacophony and a thumping on the door. The gatekeeper wanted to open up but Ah Fong took him roughly by the arm and demanded he do nothing. I could not tell what was being said but the gatekeeper kept looking in my direction so I guessed Ah Fong was telling him some lie about my importance, my being held in high esteem by the mandarin and so on. At last, the argument was won and the gatekeeper, slipping an iron hasp across the gate as added security, led us across a courtyard and into the inn.

We were shown into a lofty room, large and swept clean but devoid of any furniture with not even so much as a straw mat. After a minute or two, however, several heavy upright chairs were brought in by the gatekeeper, who was accompanied by a young boy with a tray upon which was a pot of tea and two bowls.

'We lucky people,' Ah Fong remarked as he poured the tea. 'If we outside, *I Ho Ch'üan* kill us.'

'Yes,' I answered distantly.

My mind was not on the thought of my danger and escape but upon the sacrifice made by the leper. I could see him still, a vivid and terrible picture in my mind, his arms outspread as if inviting crucifixion, holding back our would-be assassins with nothing more than the abhorrence of his disfigurement and the evil of his awful disease.

'You should buy yourself one like this, *san foo*. Such a thing brings joy to old lives.'

I glance up at the bamboo cage in which Mr Wu keeps his song bird. A light breeze blowing through the tea-house window gently rocks it, sending the bird hopping from perch to perch, trilling and fluttering its wings. It is a pretty little creature, not three inches long with a crimson beak and orange patches of feathers on its cheeks as if a miniature clown had been given instructions in colouring it. Beneath its neck, the plumage is grey with black lines whilst down its sides are rich brown stripes dotted with white spots culminating in a long black-and-white tail.

'So you are pleased with your new acquisition,' I reply. 'Tell me, my friend, what is it?'

'A zebra finch. From Australia,' he informs me. 'Not very expensive. Fifteen dollars.'

'What does it eat?'

'Just seeds. Tiny seeds. Very cheap. And it drinks water. Very easy to keep. Live three, maybe five years.'

Mr Wu's bird has no name. He is not into calling his companions by anthropomorphic titles. To him it is just a bird and, when he communicates with it, he does so by clicking his tongue and half-whistling.

A waiter stops by our table, replacing our empty tea pot with a full one from his tray. I tap the middle finger of my right hand on the table: this is a sign of thanks, saving on words. At times, the Chinese can be very economical with words whilst, at other times, they are profligate.

The tea-house is, as usual for late afternoon, full of men with their cage birds. There is not a single woman in sight, not even as a menial employee of the tea-house, for this is a man's place. It is not because the conversation is smutty, bawdy or esoterically masculine: it is because, traditionally, men bring their birds here. It is spacious and light with iron-framed windows and seating for a hundred patrons. The waiters are efficient, the range of teas is wide and the sweetmeats are expensive.

Every cage is suspended from a hook, each table having four hooks hanging above it and four seats. The reason for this is so that, as the men sit to chat or gossip, the birds may become acquainted overhead, chirping and singing to each other. As I do not own a bird, Mr Wu's finch has to try and butt in on the avian intercourse two tables away, where an aloof mynah is intermittently squawking in disregard of two canaries.

'The song of birds brings peace to the soul,' Mr Wu announces with quodlibetic authority. 'It is the music of spirits. As the playing of an Indian's flute can calm the snake so can the music of birds soften a man's hardness.'

'The snake is mesmerised by the waving of the flute, not the sound. Snakes have no ears,' I respond pedantically.

Mr Wu is not daunted by the fact. He is old and reality, like truth, is to be avoided when it suits the moment: an old man, like a young boy, prefers fantasies to facts for they are not only more romantic but more convenient. I am old too, so I should know.

'I like to hear the bird sing, *san foo*, because it is free.'

'Your bird,' I say, 'is hardly free. You do not so much as let it out of its cage to fly about your flat.'

'The bird is free,' Mr Wu insists. 'Its spirit is free. Do you know the poetry of Emily Dickinson?'

I admit I do not so Mr Wu sips his bowl of tea, swills the liquid around in his mouth, swallows it noisily and grunts to clear his throat.

'No ladder needs the bird but skies,' he recites, his eyes closed to aid memory, 'to situate its wings, nor any leader's grim baton arraigns it as it sings.' He opens his eyes. 'The song of the bird cannot be reproached. It is like a pure idea, come from the gods, unable to be argued with. What matter if the bird is in a cage so long as its spirit is free?'

I look out of the window by our table. In the street below is a thriving market, a slow-moving wedge of pedestrians flowing by the stalls, eddying where there is a bargain on offer or a parked vehicle causes an immovable obstacle. The view makes me consider how much like life the scene is, a slow progress past temptations and obstructions which are not so much to be resisted as to be smoothed over or avoided.

'Are you afraid of death, *san foo*?'

The suddenness of Mr Wu's question takes me by surprise.

'No, I am not,' I answer with some emphasis.

Mr Wu shrugs and says, 'It was a foolish question. If you have a god you are not afraid.'

'I do not have a god,' I respond somewhat tetchily. 'One does not need such a thing in order to face a reality. Death is merely an unavoidable fact.'

Looking out of the window again, I notice that another at

the same level across the street, partially obscured by a large blue-and-yellow neon sign announcing in English and Chinese characters *The Penguin Suit & Garment Mfct. Co. Ltd.*, gives upon a dentist's surgery. In the white-enamel and black-leather chair is seated an elderly woman in a green-and-beige check jacket, her cheeks pushed out with rolls of cotton wool and a chromed tube hanging over her lower jaw. She is gesticulating in the air to the dentist, whom I cannot see for the factory hoarding.

'A dentist I do fear,' I continue, nodding in the direction of the window, 'because he is avoidable. But death? I give it no thought.'

This is a lie.

Death concerns me for it is unknown and the unknown disturbs me. That this ignorance is a condition *sine qua non* of my life is a further reason for worry for I can no more come to eradicate it than ice can embrace a flame. To know it, I must cease to exist: the horror of death is not the act of dying but the irreversibility of it, the finality from which I cannot return any the wiser. When breath stops so does knowledge. That is my ultimate fear.

When I was young, the great mystery was not death but God: I wanted to know him, to be able to recognise him when I saw his signs or words, when I watched an event unfolding and knew his hand was in it. But now that I am old, the mystery is no longer of God but of death and its proximity to me for soon we shall be one.

'Once a *san foo* . . .' Mr Wu begins, impinging upon my thoughts, but I cut him short.

'We are all dying,' I interrupted him. 'Our whole life is but a journey towards death. From the moment we are born, we are on the slide. In the middle of life we are in death. Indeed, we cannot live if we do not accept death. You,' I go on, chiding him, 'as a Chinese should know this. You visit with death twice a year, when you go to the graves of your ancestors. And do not call me *san foo*. I am not a priest and, in retrospect, I was never a priest.'

'You took your vow.'

'I did,' I admit curtly. 'And you promised your wife not to be unfaithful to her. But I'll bet you had a concubine.'

I look into his face, detect the glimmer of memory one sees in the faces of the aged which tells me I have hit the quick.

'I'm not criticising you,' I continue. 'It is not my place either as your friend or, as you will keep on insisting, even as a priest. I'm merely stating a fact. You were not unfaithful to her any more than I was to my supposed faith. At the moment of taking the vow, you and I believed in what we were doing. It is just that men change. Their ideas, hopes, beliefs, moralities alter. It's a fact of life. And death. What does it matter?'

Mr Wu smiles and gazes up at his bird, which is singing noisily and without cessation. Another finch of the same species has arrived, its cage hanging above the next table where two young men in their late twenties are talking animatedly.

'I would be like my bird,' he admits quietly.

'My friend,' I reply, 'you and he are one, both in a cage of which no one opens the door. His cage,' I glance up, 'is made of bamboo and yours – and mine – is made of time. His door will not open until a hand goes in to remove his corpse and our door will not open until, for us, the clock stops.'

He refills our bowls and we both slurp our tea, fresh from the pot and just too hot for our old mouths. The remains of some honey-coated nuts and melon seeds lie in a dish between us, all that is left of the snacks we have eaten.

It is only a matter of time now. I look across at Mr Wu and I know in the instinctive way I suppose any animal knows, that my death is not far off. It can only be a matter of weeks, perhaps days. I have not long to get my house in order, sort out my affairs.

I am sure we do not die at what the doctor or lawyer would term the moment of death. I believe we die by degrees, mouldering away over the weeks before, gradually degrading, faculty by faculty slipping away. We must seek to break our attachments bit by bit for a man should not face eternity encumbered by the trappings of living. We do not die but are torn, part by part, from our existence.

'Forgive me for calling you *san foo*,' Mr Wu says. 'I mean no harm by it. It is habit and a habit is a thing of comfort in old age.'

I smile and he knows he is forgiven.

The zebra finch stops singing. The two young men have finished their intent conversation and are leaving, the one with the bird having unhitched the cage which he now carries at arm's length as if it was an offering.

'I am not an old man,' Mr Wu declares. 'Outside, I am ancient but, within, there are no lines in my skin or a tired heart. Inside, I am a young man.'

At his words, I think of the old flower-seller in the alley and I am suddenly immensely saddened.

The headquarters building of the Hongkong and Shanghai Banking Corporation faces onto Des Voeux Road, across Statue Square and the Cenotaph and, beyond these, to the Star Ferry pier. At least, the rear doors do. Most of those entering the bank through this most popular of portals do not realise they are going in through the tradesman's entrance: the front door of the bank is in Queen's Road which has no view save of the trees surrounding the government offices and the old French Mission building.

Such an enigma could only exist in China: for a business to be successful, the laws of *fung shui* must be obeyed. These dictate that the main door may not face the sea and must be higher than the rear door. Failure to comply with these basic rules ensures instability, insecurity and anxiety, three factors with which no bank may contend.

Beside the rear doors are two bronze statues of lions, each thrice lifesize. They are bold, magisterial creatures, true colonial beasts with solid-sounding British names – Stephen and Stitt, after former senior managers of the firm. Stitt is to the right of the entrance, proudly demure, whilst Stephen is to the left and has his mouth open in a growl. Both statues are pockmarked with shrapnel scars from the Japanese invasion of 1941 and have highly polished paws, for it is customary to stroke them for good luck. I restrain myself from caressing Stitt's paws, preferring to associate with my namesake. He does not sit and watch life pass him by but makes a comment upon it.

Entering the building, I climb some stairs to the banking hall, a lofty, grand temple to Mammon. No matter what the weather, it is always five degrees cooler in here. The marble and the presence of so much money chills the air.

Vast, dark square pillars support a barrel-vaulted ceiling decorated with a huge mosaic portraying the themes of trade and industry between the Occident and the Orient, the God of Wealth surveying steelworkers and aircraft builders, brocade embroiderers and tin beaters, sedan chairs and automobiles.

Often, I momentarily crane my neck to admire the beauty of this roof, remembering it was not made by a famous artist, a Michaelangelo of our age but by a man not unlike myself, a White Russian émigré called Podgoursky who had been eking out a living in Shanghai before his talent and temperament were discovered. I met him once, in the thirties, just as he was about to commence work upon this masterpiece. He was a sad man with a quick wit and a mistress half his age, afraid of something in himself. Perhaps it was his artistic skill scared him so. Art is a god of sorts.

Today, however, I have no time to pause: I am here on business and have not come empty-handed. In one of the narrow lanes – it must have been Li Yuen Street East for there was an inordinate number of stalls selling ladies' lingerie there – I have purchased a cheap suitcase. Where a more expensive item would have leather, this has plastic and the locks are feeble things that could be split open with a flick of the wrist and a twenty-five-cent screwdriver. This weakness is not important. I am not going anywhere. I merely need the case for temporary transportation. After today, I shall give it to Chiu to use as a store for his clothing: he will be pleased to be rid of one of his cardboard boxes.

The enquiries desk is to my left and I head for it, leaning against the counter as a clerk quits his seat to speak to me.

'May I help you, sir?' he asks in a polite voice from which he has striven to remove as much as he can of his Chinese accent.

I want to tell him not to be ashamed, to speak as he would if he were addressing me in the street and selling me dried fish rather than in this austere magnificence and selling me his services.

'I have an appointment to open my deposit box,' I inform him. 'My name is Galvin.'

He runs his finger down the page of a thick ledger and says, 'Mr S. Galvin? Yes.' He places a tick next to my name, swings the book around and asks, 'Will you sign here, please, sir?'

I scribble my initials and a messenger appears at my side to usher me to a private viewing room. Here, in a cubicle with leather upholstered chairs and a walnut veneered shelf, I am presented with a black steel box, upon the lid and end of which are stencilled white numbers.

The messenger makes no comment but leaves me to my business, quietly closing the door behind me. Putting my fingers under the box, I lift it a little. It is not heavy, weighs not more than ten pounds, not much to show for the end of a life in the Orient. I would wager there are other boxes in the vaults, perhaps right next to mine on the strong-room shelves, which contain fortunes in silver or gold, rubies or emeralds, works of art and treasures carved of ivory, jade and agate.

The lock is easy to open. My key slips in and turns without a snag, the mechanism well oiled.

Opening the lid is a terrible thing for me. I have not done this since Mr Poon offered me the ownership of my flat.

The box is divided horizontally into two halves by a metal tray. The top contains little of importance: my birth certificate, my passport (which must be long out of date for I cannot remember when I last sought to renew it), the deed to my flat which I never need to see and shall soon no longer require, a faded photograph of myself in a cassock, as a smug young man in control of himself and his world and an envelope containing assorted papers, the exact contents of which I have forgotten.

Before I remove this tray, I add to it a new envelope sealed with paper tape over which a Chinese chop has been stamped, the mark of a Chinese lawyer who practises in Saigon Street. Upon the front of the envelope, in a delicate, cursive script, is written *Last Will and Testament*. I do not place this on top of the items but smuggle it in underneath the old envelope. I do not wish to see it again.

My hands shake as I hook my index fingers into the metal loops at the side of the tray and lift it clear.

The contents in the bottom are wrapped in pieces of felt. One by one, I unwrap them, placing them on the shelf, moving aside an inkwell and dip pen to make room. They are all made of silver: two single candlesticks, a paten ten inches in diameter and a plain chalice with a simple cross engraved upon the side, the gilding on the interior faded and patchy as though struck by metallic serpigo. I handle them gently as if they were made not of precious metal but eggshell porcelain or Venetian glass, liable to shatter at the least touch.

Beneath them is another package, also wrapped in felt. I open this and remove two small wooden jugs. Their sides have split with age and the dry atmosphere of the bank vault whilst the handle of one of them, originally an intrinsic part of the vessel, for they were carved from single blocks of wood, has snapped off at the base and warped badly. Any polish they may once have displayed has long since dulled, soaking into the surface. The inside of the damaged one is lightly coloured whilst the other is stained black.

I place them next to the silver items, removing the box to put it on the floor by my chair, the interior tray resting across the top. This done, I carefully wrap all the objects but one in their felt coverings again and place them in my cheap suitcase. Only the broken jug is to remain in the bank.

My leaving it has nothing to do with its value although it is true it is worth very little in financial terms. It is simply that I do not want to lose it. The chalice, paten and candlesticks mean nothing to me now, but the secular jugs are somehow special, simple Chinese peasant items. What may happen to the broken one after my death I can neither guess at nor care about yet, whilst I am alive, I want it safe. It is a matter of nostalgia more than anything else, a splinter of sentimentality jammed in the thumb of my thoughts, not to be shifted with the needle of sensibility.

The re-wrapping completed, I lift the box back onto the shelf and remove from it the last item it contains. This is wrapped not in felt but in thin tissue paper which was once white but has turned cream with time. Carefully, I spread open the crisp sheets of tissue to reveal a priest's stole folded neatly along creases that have formed themselves over the years into permanent lines. The material is still white and has not gone the way of the tissue paper.

I unfold it until I see the gold and light blue embroidery of a cross: then, I stop.

If I were to continue to open out the stole I should come upon a black patch which resembles a neat ink stain. It is stiff as if made by indian ink, the liquid evaporated and the lampblack left. Yet I do not. I stop, lean forward and very lightly, as if the material was the head of an infant or the brow of a sick friend on their death-bed, I kiss it. My mouth remains closed. It is less of a kiss and more of a touch of the lips.

This done, I quickly replace it and the tray in the box, close the lid and snap the lock shut. The messenger comes at my call and the box is taken away on a little trolley to its secret hiding-place beneath the building.

Suitcase in hand, I leave the bank by the back door and cross the street, taking care to avoid the creaking, squealing trams. At the Star Ferry, I pay my fare, pass through the turnstile, climb the steps and board a ferry, tugging the wooden back of a row of seats across so I can sit facing the direction of travel. Facing backwards makes me feel queasy. At the Kowloon pier, I walk to the rickshaw rank and, leaning back in the seat with my arm firmly on the suitcase wedged in beside me, watch the pectoral muscles of the rickshaw coolie flex and relax, flex and relax as he pulls me homeward through the afternoon traffic.

There are no cruise liners in port, no American warships riding at anchor and only three British naval vessels alongside in the dockyard of HMS Tamar: one is a black, sleek submarine, one a destroyer and the third an unarmed supply vessel. As a consequence, the streets are more thinly populated by tourists than usual.

This state of affairs has both advantages and disadvantages. The benefits are that one is not surrounded by sun-pinked buffoons armed with Baedeker guides and all-but-useless teach-yourself-Cantonese phrase books, sporting clothes they would never wear in their native countries and speaking in louder than normal voices.

One does not have to eschew their meandering strolls along the pavements, pausing momentarily to avoid stepping into the frame of their photographs. What is more, with the reduction in potential targets, there are fewer pickpockets and professional beggars abroad and prices are lower. Of the disadvantages, the main one is that the shop touts are out in force competing strongly for customers in order to maintain their cash flow. Shops in Tsim Sha Tsui succeed on high turnover rather than high profit margins.

One tout I particularly dislike. He is an Indian who owns a tailor's shop down the street from Mr Chan's emporium. Most of these store sentinels maintain a station at the entrances to their businesses, calling out to would-be clients as they pass. They may step out of their doorway to press home the point of the magnificence of their wares but nothing more.

This Indian, however, if he believes he has espied an easy sucker, not only berates him from the doorstep but follows him down the street, even going so far as to tug a sleeve. He offers silk ties, silk shirts, tailor-made suits 'to the finest fashionable cut this side of Bombay, sir', Madras cotton vests and sweaters of the purest cashmere.

It is impossible to lightly dismiss this man's pesterings with the usual curt negative response or a wave of the hand. He will not be so easily put off. Trailing a step behind and to one's right, he leans forward to edge himself into the corner of the line of one's sight and blathers.

'Why will you not come in my shop and see for yourself? There is no obligation to buy, sir. No obligation, sir. If you can find nothing you like, please to go. Never mind.' He shakes his head in the falsely deprecating way Indians have. 'What can you lose by visiting the shop, sir? Only a few minutes. Please.' It is at this moment he touches the sleeve or presses his hand against one's arm. 'This way. Just a few steps. I have new Thai silk ties in stock. Just come from Bangkok. Only yesterday.'

He was at it this morning and, to my surprise, attempted to persuade me to enter his shop: after the last time he tried this with me, I would have thought he would remember my face and stay clear but it seems his memory, like my own, is not without voids.

'Sir,' he called from the shop front. 'Good ties, silk shirts, cotton socks, finest quality.'

'No,' I said bluntly and kept on walking, my straw basket in my hand.

He should have been able to judge I was a resident, not a tourist. No visitor carries a locally made bag with the handle repaired with parcel string: but, as well as being forgetful of a face, he is unobservant. Abandoning his doorway, he kept pace with me along the pavement.

'Come, sir. I have very good quality cotton – South Sea Island. Can make you a shirt in two hours. Guaranteed top quality. Your initials embroidered on the pocket for no extra charge.'

'No,' I repeated, a little more assertively.

'If you don't want shirts, I can make waistcoats, smoking jackets. All pure silk from China, made by hand . . .'

I stopped but did not immediately turn around. He thought I was caving in.

'This way, sir, just a few steps . . .'

I rounded on him and said, with as much invective as I could muster, '*M'hai! Ngoh wâ m'hai, m'hai, m'hai. Lun hoi!*'

He reeled back, cursing me under his breath in Hindustani but I knew I had got the better of him. A number of Chinese shop owners in front of their windows laughed and the Indian, having lost face, skulked away. I walked on, pleased at having silenced him.

As I entered the Hing Loon Curio and Jewellery Company, Mr Chan rose from an old armchair at the rear of the shop and came forward to greet me, folding a daily newspaper.

'*Cho san,*' he said, smiling his welcome. 'How are you today?'

'I'm well,' I replied and sat on one of the stools. 'How is business?'

'Not so good,' he confided in me. 'No ship in the docks. Maybe Sunday better.' He rustled the newspaper, dropping it on the counter. 'Big ship coming on Sunday. Two thousan' passengers.'

Along the edge of the underside of his glass counter top are wedged fifty or sixty business cards. I studied them as he moved behind the counter to sit on his own wooden stool, which is marginally higher than those provided for customers. It is considered good psychology for the trader to be taller than the purchaser.

In Mr Chan's line of trade, he comes across every kind and condition of tourist for visitors to Hong Kong always buy curios: it does not matter if they are sailors, businessman, honeymoon couples or elderly folk taking a retirement cruise – whatever they are, they purchase trinkets and, if they have a card, Mr Chan collects it and puts it in his counter. The few I read proved the range of his clientele: *David L. Rodgers, Capt. USN*; *William Corman, Corporate Finance Division, The Bank of Australia*; *Allan Browning, South-East Asian Affairs, The Daily Sketch/London*; *Frederick Fisher, Accountant* and *Peter Lowry, Lowry Bells and Diving Equipment, Djakarta*.

'You brought something for me?' Mr Chan asked, nodding in the direction of the basket.

'Yes, I have,' I answered.

'Let me see.'

I lifted the basket on to the counter and opened the handles, removing the contents. Mr Chan unwrapped the felt to display the two candlesticks, paten and chalice. He stroked the latter then, removing a yellow duster from a drawer, began to polish it.

'Where you get this?'

'I have had them a long time,' I said.

I did not look at the four items. It seemed just then to be an act of betrayal to part with them.

'Yes, but where you get them?' he reiterated.

'I got them when I was a young man. In China. They are very old. The chalice – the cup you are holding – was made in 1838. In Italy.'

'They are make of good silver,' Mr Chan commented, turning the chalice over in his hands, 'but they belong to a church. How you get them?'

'When I was a young man,' I admitted, 'I was a priest. A *san foo*. These were mine then.'

One of the few tourists walking the street entered the shop and started to mooch about, gazing at the cabinets. He had the obligatory camera hanging over his shoulder, a parcel wrapped in brown paper under his arm.

'I can help you?' Mr Chan enquired.

'Just looking,' responded the tourist.

Mr Chan, out of deference for my privacy, spoke in Cantonese.

'*Hái pin shùe?*' he asked.

'*Lai pàai t'ong hái Wuchow,*' I said, adding, '*T'ien chu kiao.*'

The tourist's wife appeared in the door and called out, 'I'm through here, honey.'

'Okay,' he called back and left the shop without saying a word to us.

Mr Chan reverted to English.

'Why you take these things?'

'No one would want them,' I said. 'The church itself was finished.'

'What year was this?'

'Nineteen hundred,' I replied.

Mr Chan fell silent and, putting down the chalice, picked up the paten which he studied closely, holding it up to his face and running his finger around the rim.

'This one make in England. See,' he pointed to the base, 'got a hallmark. The silver is very good quality. Not Chinese silver. European silver. Chinese silver got too much tin. But I can't sell it like it is. No one want to buy church silver. But, if you don't mind, I can buy f'om you and sell to a silver merchant. But he will melt it down to make something new.'

I did not care. Not any longer. They were useless to me and meaningless to anyone else. If they were reduced and made into tourist baubles or chopstick rests, cheap brooches, dollar note clips or tie-pins, what difference did it make? None to me.

'No, I don't mind,' I said and any feeling of betrayal lingering in me was dispelled.

Mr Chan brought out a set of scales and weighed the four items together. This done, he opened his newspaper to see what the day's silver rate was and, with a quick flicking of his fingers over the beads of his abacus, made me an offer.

There was no doubt I would take it. He knew I would accept

whatever he decreed but he was not to know that had he offered me ten dollars and a glass of beer I should gladly have parted with them.

He removed the money from a thick wad of notes he had in a drawer, slid it into an envelope and snapped a rubber band around to keep it shut. I did not bother to re-open the envelope and count the contents. I merely pushed it well down into the inside pocket of my jacket for safety.

'I see you again soon?' he enquired as I stood up.

'Soon,' I promised.

'Okay. Nex' time you come, we maybe go take tea.'

I smiled and told him I would accept his invitation: and yet I was not sure when I would come his way again for I had nothing left to sell. The well of my life is now empty except for the mud at the bottom.

The chapel was lit by oil lamps, one hanging at each station of the cross and, upon the altar, two candles burned, their light reflecting off the silver of the chalice and paten to the side. The shadows of the roof beams shifted imperceptibly to and fro as the flames moved to the touch of draughts of warm air blowing in through spaces between the pantiles. There was that night, for the first time in over a week, a warm breeze blowing up from the river, carrying on its shoulders the scents and stinks of the banks.

'I wonder if we should not go down on our knees and thank the Lord for this wind,' Father Callaghan remarked, entering the chapel carrying a bottle of wine and some wafers in a porcelain rice bowl. 'After days of having the air as still as it is inside an alms box, it is a blessed relief, to be sure, to have it here tonight. Hot it may be, and distinctly nidorous, but at least it stirs the night.' He placed the wine on the side table. 'So long as it doesn't stir the residents of our fair city.'

'Should it?' I asked, curious to know if the coming of an evening breeze had some supernatural properties for the Chinese.

'Not ordinarily,' he said. 'But these days, who can tell? This drought is doing more than just drying up the land and killing the rice.'

He began to take the wafers out of the bowl, arranging them in the paten and pouring the wine into one of the two wooden jugs that stood behind the chalice.

'When a natural catastrophe strikes the Chinese,' he began, talking as much to himself and the altar as to me, 'such as a drought like this or a flooding of the Yangtse Kiang, they put it down as an act of their gods. Which, I suppose, is fair enough: after all, we speak ourselves of such things in just the same fashion. See the insurance contract on any ship: acts of God are a common commercial risk, it would seem. However, if we suffer a drought, which in Ireland is as likely as a typhoon in Tipperary, we put it down to bad luck. Here, it is considered a visitation from the gods to tell the people that something is wrong. They, in turn, do not blame themselves but the emperor. It is his fault for he has, in their eyes, executive powers in the kingdom of heaven. And so he must atone, fix things so that it doesn't happen again.'

'How does he atone?' I asked.

'Not how you'd think, Father Stephen. Indeed not. You would guess that he'd have a big festival and so on. Mollify the spirits. And that does happen. But it's not that simple. He must be seen by the people to be doing something. The populace, it would seem, are more for appeasement than the gods. Emperors in the past have lost their thrones and their lives because of a month of heavy rainstorms two thousand miles to the west of Peking.'

'So what do they do?'

'Do? They give to the poor to show their humility: of course, they raise taxes to generate the revenue for this generosity. Or they stir up trouble over which they can hold sway, start a fight they know they can win. Or they find a scapegoat.'

He finished laying out the wafers and pouring the wine, ramming the cork back into the bottle and checking that I had done my appointed task of filling the second jug with water.

'That's where we come in,' he continued. 'We are the scape-goats. The *gweilos* in general. The *yang kwei tsi*, the *yang ren*. Which is to say foreign devils and foreigners in general. And especially the *T'ien Chu Kiao* and the *Ye Su Kiao*. The Catholics and the Protestants.'

'How are we to blame?' I said.

'In their eyes, we have come to China with our religion and our One True God and we have upset the lords of heaven. The gods, the spirits, the ancestors are all angry that we are here. The fact that we *T'ien Chu Kiao* first arrived in China in the year 1246 does not seem to dawn upon them. Admittedly we were thrown out a century later, but we've been back ever since the middle of the sixteenth century when the blessed Francis Xavier arrived in Macau. Of course, we've been persecuted but that's all a part of it, isn't it, Father Stephen?'

He placed the wafers upon the altar and put the chalice next to them.

'Now, I fear, we are to be persecuted again. We are seen as the bringers of this drought and, no doubt, the instigators of this hot breeze which you and I know is just air rising off the land but which, to the town's-folk, is the sour tincture of our anger, or the curse of the gods, or the breath of the dragons come to burn their houses if they don't burn ours.' He pulled his watch out of his pocket and, holding it to one of the oil lamps, said, 'Twenty minutes. We had best go and get ourselves up to look like Christians. I'm sure Our Lord would not mind us conducting Mass in *sams* and *fus* but I don't somehow think we should let things go that far. Not yet, in any case.'

We left the chapel, parting on the stairs beside the oil lamp that hung halfway up. I looked briefly at his face as we separated. It may have been the influence of the oil lamp but I believed it was lined more deeply than I had realised before.

As I opened the door of my room, a warm blast blew past me. It was so hot I thought, for a moment, that perhaps Father Callaghan's warning had come true and the building had been set on fire. I rushed to the window but there were no flickering lights outside.

The town seemed unusually still. It was only the early evening but I could not hear the usual clamour that drifted up to the mission from the busy streets. The faint aura of light over the rooftops was there, the smoke of the evening fires wafting through it, but there was no hum of life. I wondered if the hot air was suppressing the sounds but then, to dispel this query, a gong began to sound far away from the direction of the Lung Mo temple. I left the window, lit my own lamp and started to remove my *sam* and *fu*, putting on my cassock and albe.

As I dressed, I considered Father Callaghan's warning that we were to be the next persecuted. He was right. I knew it, had known it in my heart for days although I had not let my awareness or apprehension voice itself to me. I sat in the chair by the table, my cassock unbuttoned, and thought over the events of the past few weeks, closing my eyes the better to concentrate my mind, deliberately conjuring up pictures of those signs I knew foretold our doom – the puppet and the beheaded monkey, the conversations at the Residency and Mr Doble's house, the bloody moon.

When I opened my eyes, they were tuned not to the faint light of the lamp in my room but to the night outside. I gazed across the roofs and wondered then if I was doing the correct thing, if my life was following a pathway that was just and true. I was filled with a surety that my seeking to cure the sick, guide the blind and heal the lame was moral and right but I felt rising in me a terrible question which made me doubt the ultimate purpose of my vocation. I was suddenly filled with an all-encompassing scepticism: it was wrong to bring an alien god to these people.

It occurred to me, looking out over the ancient roofs at the view that must have changed little since the poet Su-shi gazed upon them, that I was not unwelcome here because of my seeking to do good by the people: I was hated because of what I insisted they take in order to accept the goodness I could offer them. In the eyes of the local people, it was not my medicine, my compassion, my sympathy and my desire to assist them against which they reacted. It was my religion.

The gong, which had fallen silent, started up again. It was a monotonous, deep sound, exotically threatening and yet at the same time captivating and exciting. It was like a heartbeat far off in the night, the heartbeat of a people and their history.

Standing up, for the time was drawing nearer to go down to Mass, I commenced buttoning up my cassock. The collar was tight and I had to twist my fingers to get it fastened. When it was closed, it was so firm about my throat that it might have been throttling me.

I contemplated that the Chinese were no more cruel than we. Father Callaghan had intimated as much but the more I thought about it, the more I saw little difference. What was more, any difference I could discern between their cruelty and that of not only my own race but also my own brethren in Christ was insignificant.

Reaching onto my bookshelf, I removed a volume on the history of our faith in China and started to thumb through the pages. It was an old book which had been in my room upon my arrival and must have belonged to Father Callaghan. Bound in brown leather with gold tooling and marbled end-papers, it had suffered much from its time in the East. The covers were mottled with mould, the end-papers separating from the boards and the pages dog-eared from much reading and fingering. Somewhere, there was a reference I needed to read, that would prove my point to me. It was no longer a question of doubting morality but requiring documentary proof to back it up. Sure enough, in the fifth chapter, I found the words I sought.

St Francis Xavier, I read, his name in the text followed by a small × to denote his canonisation, *landed upon St John's Island at Amacao in that year, but his plans of spreading the teachings of Christ were thwarted by the jealousy of his own countrymen and he died thereupon without ever setting foot upon the main land of China.* I flicked several pages over, the paper crisp with age and brittle to the touch: from the edges, the gold dust flaked off upon my fingers. In the next chapter was another passage to confirm my thesis. It went, *After the death of the Jesuit, Matteo Ricci in the Year of Our Lord 1610, there began the prominent controversy concerning the nature of the worship of ancestors by the Chinee. It was undecided whether or not this was idolatrous. The controversy raged for 132 years. An appeal was made to the Holy Father in Rome who sent forth to China his legate, but the Bishop in Macau sequestered him and held him fast with forty priests within the dungeons of the fortress there in which he was detained without favour until his death.*

Closing the book, I placed my albe about my shoulders and

left the room, blowing out the lantern. My mind was in turmoil and yet never for an instant did it occur to me that I should go down on my knees and ask God for His advice. Somehow, I knew what it would be: stay and preach, spread the word, change the history of five thousand years. This was not what I wanted to hear. I was beyond divine persuasion.

The girls were already in their places in the pews as I entered. Father Callaghan was standing to one side, the light of a lamp casting its glow down upon him. Behind it, painted on the wall, was a portrait of Christ carrying the burden of his cross to Calvary. The colours were faded and there was a section of the picture missing by his right foot where damp had undermined the plaster.

Sister Margaret was in her usual place near the rear, where she could keep an eye on her charges, and Ah Fong was in the front row, his hands resting demurely in his lap. Another thirty or so Chinese were also present and, amongst them, I caught sight of Mr Kung. He looked haggard, a tired old man without any of the glint in his eye that I had seen when he presented me with his foul egg.

If, I realised as I walked past him, he was not a Christian – that was, if we had not converted him – his son would now be minding his chickens, married to Mei-ling whom we saved from serfdom that she might instead die in agony, suffocating on gold.

Glancing around, the beauty of the scene struck me. The soft light of the oil lamps shone on the girls' hair where they sat in silence, their heads slightly bowed and the gentle movement of the shadows seemed to add an ethereal wonder to the chapel but, whereas a week before I might have said that this was the work of God I now regarded it as a wonder of nature, as a quirk of physics, as a delight accidentally shaped by the hand of man.

Why, I tried to guess, did these people come to the mission, bend their knee to a strange god? What was it that made them dissatisfied with their own ancestors, the ghosts in the hills and the gods in the temples who had served them and their spiritual needs for a thousand years longer than Christ had offered his release to my own kind?

There was something immensely sad about the congregation

I had joined. They were, I realised, searching for a dream they felt they could not find in their own world yet which I knew mine could not provide for them. In the course of their search, they had abandoned their history, their people and cast themselves out to be ostracised and martyred.

It was wrong to put these simple people in such jeopardy. They were to die – had already died, in the case of Matthew Kung, who had taken a disciple's name in the place of his own – for a cause they did not understand, which was extrinsic to them and to which they had sold their souls just as much as their neighbours had given theirs to their predecessors or Confucianism, Buddhism or Taoism.

The girls were the ones I felt most for: they had been rescued from death but they had had, with no other choice, to follow Christ. In keeping their lives they had inadvertently traded their souls. They were as much used by myself and my church as Faust was used by the devil. They had been corrupted.

Father Callaghan began the service but I could not keep my mind on it.

This was not what I wanted to do. I had come to China to save people from themselves and I found myself condemning them.

With his back to the congregation, Father Callaghan stood and faced the altar. The embroidery on his stole shone like dull gold in the lamplight then, as I looked, it seemed to fragment and come loose, drift into the air just as the leaf from the ancient book had come off upon my fingers. For a moment, I was puzzled by this then realised that it was not the gold that was flaking but the light reflecting off it being destroyed by my tears.

Wiping my eyes with the knuckle of my finger, I heard Father Callaghan embark upon the Penitential Rite. He spoke in Cantonese and the response from the people came in the same language but I responded in Latin.

'*Confiteor Deo omnipotenti et vobis, fratres,*' I intoned, the words coming out of my mouth like honeyed lies, '*quia peccavi nimis cogitatione, verbo, opere et omissione: mea culpa, mea culpa, mea maxima culpa . . .*'

I had sinned sure enough. I was guilty of misleading the Chinese towards a foreign god that would not defend them any more than the oaths and rites of the *I Ho Ch'üan* would protect the movement's malcontents from the bullets of the *gweilos'* rifles.

Striking my breast, I continued, '*Ideo preor beatram Mariam semper Virginem, omnes Angelos et Sanctos, et vos, fratres, orare pro me at Dominum Deum nostrum.*'

I did not want my Chinese brothers and sisters to pray for me. I wanted them to rise as one and rush out from the chapel, disappear into the night and find their own gods again, ask their forgiveness if needs be and, later, return to secrete me away with them.

Today, my legs have been inexplicably weak. I have not taken any excessive exercise nor have I used the stairs in the tenement in preference to the elevator, but it took me longer to walk from the bus stop to the school than usual. I was obliged to halt twice and would dearly have liked to sit down to relieve the dull hurt in my shins.

Although it was only two o'clock, the popsicle seller was already on station at the corner of the street, seated in the saddle of his machine but dozing with a white pith helmet on his head. When ice cream vendors begin to wear such headgear, one can be sure the really hot months are only just around the corner. I was sorely tempted to purchase one of his popsicles but resisted: it would not have done to go to my interview with a bright red, green or yellow mouth.

The gravel on the street was slippery. I had to cross with extreme care and wished there was something on to which I might hold not so much to retain my balance as to gain some degree of confidence. The individual crystals of quartz on the road flashed in the sunlight: whilst it applies that all that glitters is not gold nor is it so that all which appears beautiful is benign.

I reached the pavement and stood for a moment by the gate. The brass plate had been furbished within the hour for there was a residue of the liquid polish collected in the screw holes which was not yet dry. What is more, the cross and Sacred Heart have been touched up since my last visit to the street, the drops of holy blood crimson and grotesquely shining with gloss paint.

The gate to the school playground is about eight feet high and made of sheets of iron riveted to a frame. This, too, has been recently repainted light grey, the name of the school being written upon it in a wide arc of lettering. Underneath the words *Mission Society* there is a door in the steel beside which is an electric button.

I placed my hand on the gate to steady myself but the metal was so hot from the sun that I quickly removed it and jammed my finger on the button. A buzzer sounded not far away to be followed by soft footsteps. A lock rattled and the door was opened by an elderly Chinese man.

Nodding to him politely, I said in Cantonese, 'I have an appointment with Sister Joseph. At a quarter past two,' adding in case there were two Sister Josephs in the place, 'the headmistress.'

He looked at his watch and beckoned me in.

'Go through that door,' he said, pointing to the entrance of the school, 'and report to the office.'

I set off across the playground, the concrete partitioned with white lines marking out a basketball and badminton court: in the centre was an arrangement of coloured boxes for a game with which I was not familiar. On the inside of the curtain wall by the street was painted a series of circular targets much marked by the impact of rubber balls.

The wide steps up to the main door were shallow and I easily negotiated them. They reminded me of steps in the seminary, so made that priests might mount them without tripping over the hems of their cassooks. Once inside, the building was cool. The walls of the entrance lobby were decorated with infantile paintings and a stone tub in which had been constructed the model of a Chinese garden with miniature trees, little baked-clay houses and pavilions, a larval rock filled with holes and a waterfall down which a trickle was tumbling. It vaguely reminded me of the garden of the Resident's bungalow in Wuchow.

To my left, opposite three low leatherette chairs, was a glass sliding window over which a sign projected from the wall. It was made of lime-green plastic with lettering stuck to it: it stated in both English and Chinese, *School Office & Enquries*. The missing *i* made me think incongruously of the *Black Pussy*. I knocked upon the glass and a Chinese woman slid it open.

'Mr Galwin,' she said somewhat officiously, not looking at me but running her finger down a register.

'Yes,' I confirmed. 'I have an appointment . . .'

'Please,' she interrupted me, 'sit down. Sister will see you in a few minutes.'

I stepped back and sank gratefully onto one of the chairs. My right leg was getting pins and needles just above the knee and I rubbed it vigorously to try and get the circulation going once more. From somewhere deep in the building there started up a chanting. It could not have been a religious intoning for there was a lightness about it, a rhythm that was airy and free. A hum of conversation could be heard too but it was unlike that of adults. Somehow, it was more lively, more joyous.

For a moment, I closed my eyes and no sooner had I done so than I saw, as if in an opium dream, the rows of bent heads of girls long since lost and heard the clack of the foot-treadle sewing machines and, although I could not see her, I could hear Sister Margaret chivvying the girls into Mass.

'Good afternoon, Father,' a voice said but it was not hers.

'Good afternoon,' I replied and, opening my eyes, discovered a nun standing in front of me. She was a European, her wimple as white as her skin and her habit light grey, not more than a shade removed from the colour of the school gate.

'It is good to see you again. Do come into my office,' she invited me. She spoke very clearly with the upper-class accent of a well-to-do colonial madam, yet her tone indicating that she was indeed pleased to welcome me.

I tried to get up but the chair was too low and my legs just would not accept the task of getting the rest of me vertical. My shoes slipped on the polished tiles of the floor and I was stranded.

'Here, let me help you, Father,' the nun said and, with the efficiency of a trained nurse, she shoved one hand under my armpit and the other in the small of my back. With one movement, she had me up.

'Thank you,' I said, a little unsteady but feeling stronger. 'I'm afraid the flesh is somewhat weak.'

'It is the spirit that counts,' she answered, and led the way down the corridor to her study.

It was a bright room, the walls painted in soft yellow and hung with both devotional pictures and more artistic efforts done by the children. Before a wide steel-framed window, through which I could see a small grassy lawn lying in the shade of several trees, were several chairs and an old wooden desk upon which was a black telephone, a stack of exercise books, a section of bamboo standing up like a vase and filled with coloured pencils, a letter tray and a small statue of the Virgin Mary, beside which there stood a slightly larger effigy of Kwan Yin, the goddess of mercy.

Sister Joseph stepped to the window and lowered a light blue venetian blind halfway down the window. The sun was coming in through the mottled shade of the trees outside. As she turned, she must have noticed me looking at the idol.

'A present from one of the girls,' she explained. 'Her father makes them in a little factory at Lai Chi Kok.'

'I knew a priest once who would have approved,' I said.

'Oh!' she exclaimed dismissively. 'It is only a piece of tourist pottery.'

Sister Joseph indicated one of the chairs to me and I sat in it, expecting her to move behind her desk but she did not, coming instead to sit next to me.

'Tell me, Father, how are you keeping? It has been a long time since you were last here. You are, you know, always in our prayers.'

'Well, they seem to be working,' I replied a little facetiously, 'for I am still about and hearty if not hale. But, Sister, you know you must not call me Father. I gave all that up long ago.'

'You have not been . . .'

'Excommunicated, defrocked, call it what you will. No, that is quite true. I am still on the register of holy fathers tucked away in some dusty dossier in the Vatican. But I am no longer a priest so you must not address me as one.'

My speech did not come with any degree of anger nor did I display any petulance.

I am so tired now. It seems hardly worth bothering.

As with Mr Wu, this is a topic she is keen to broach on the rare occasions when we meet, insisting in that stubborn way nuns have of calling me Father. I always refute it, wondering why on earth she does it: probably, she hopes to bring me back to Christ before I shuffle off my mortality and head for the boneyard. How often have I seen priests convince themselves that they see a sign of life in a corpse – on one occasion, in a cadaver – just so that they may absolve the soul and prepare it for heaven with a few quick words. Sister Joseph, I assume, thinks she has more time for I am not yet cooling.

'What may I do for you today then, Father?' she enquired, changing the subject and totally ignoring my request just as she would the unreasonable demands of one of her more fractious pupils.

'I wish to make a provision into the future for the girl,' I told her. 'With the best will in the world, I shall not go on much longer.'

'You are not ill?' Sister Joseph responded with a touching urgency.

'If, by that, you mean am I suffering a specific medical condition then the answer is no, I am not. I am simply getting old and starting to fall apart. It happens to old machines and the human body is nothing more than a machine.'

She opened her mouth to rebut me.

'No argument, Sister. You must leave an old man with his own ideas or, if you will, delusions. But I no longer ascribe to the theory that the human body is a wondrous work of God. Leonardo da Vinci dispelled that one and I agree with him. As for being made in the image of our God – well, if that is the case, I feel sorry for him. My legs don't work properly. What his must be like at his age I dare not think.'

To give her her due, Sister Joseph laughed slightly, though she might have been patronising an old man rather than sharing in his sense of humour.

'I was informed of your natural history lesson,' she said, avoiding a direction of conversation she wished not to follow. 'That was very kind of you. The boy was quite terrified of his catch. Miss Chow, our biology teacher, was most interested and amazed at your knowledge of shore creatures.'

'Your attendant nun was somewhat occupied at the time,' I informed her, hoping my voice contained a hint of criticism. 'She was engrossed in a book.'

Sister Joseph smiled a little bleakly and replied with a somewhat tight lip, 'I could certainly believe it. Sister Margaret is quite a bookworm.'

There was nothing else I could do. I leaned back a little in the chair to give my lungs space and I laughed. For at least a minute, I could not stop myself. Sister Joseph looked worriedly at me: my laugh these days is less of a sound of joyous release and more of a sort of chesty rattle devoid of pain.

'Are you sure you're all right?' she asked earnestly as my laughter subsided.

I nodded to put her mind at rest, gathered my breath and leaned forward again.

'I am sure. It is just that I knew a Sister Margaret once.' I chuckled briefly at the memory.

'Was she a great reader?'

'I don't know. But she was a remarkable woman,' I allowed. 'I met her once in a temple at Wuchow in the summer of 1900. The Dragon Mother temple, it was called.'

'What was she doing there? I know of a fascinating treatise written by a Sister Margaret in, I think, 1911. She came, I recall, from Eastbourne. An Englishwoman who was the daughter of a missionary in Africa. Her essay was about Taoist temple architecture. I wonder if this could be the same woman.'

'I think not,' I said. 'This nun was Chinese and a good age, though not perhaps as venerable as myself. As for what she was doing, she was praying.'

'My Sister Margaret would never, I am sure, do such a thing. She would never bow her knee to another altar.'

I thought that perhaps it was true in that she would never pay her respects to an heathen idol: yet she did, it seemed to me, prostrate herself before the altar of cheap fiction to the detriment of her responsibilities to her pupils if not to her god. For that I criticised her but I was not going to inform on her to the extent of reporting on the quality of her literary taste. Her weakness made her more of a human and less of a nun in my eyes.

'As I was saying,' I began, returning to the reason for my visit, 'I wish to make provision for the girl. To this end, I have here a sum of money to be placed by you in trust for her. If there is any residue remaining after she completes her schooling, please use it for another girl. And, of course, it must be a little girl, as in the past. No boys.'

'You know, Father, I have always wondered about that,' Sister Joseph remarked.

'About what?' I asked.

'About your stipulations. Under any circumstance, no boys. And no mention of who their benefactor might be.'

There was, I thought, no harm in telling her now. It is after all a petty reason really, a mere whim if you like.

'Girls,' I explained, 'because, when I first came to China I taught girls. Not for long. Just a few months. They were strays, orphans or babies abandoned by their mothers. You know how it was.'

'How it still is,' Sister Joseph interrupted. 'Times do not change that quickly in the East, Father.'

'No,' I concurred, 'they do not.'

The telephone on the desk rang once but Sister Joseph ignored it.

'So I have chosen just to help girls,' I went on. 'They are, I suppose, disadvantaged and it is for their weakness that I feel sympathy.'

'You, Father, are a sentimentalist.'

I frowned at her and said, a little sharply, 'You, Sister, are the only person I would allow to get away with such an insult. I am most certainly not a sentimental man. I am a realist. That is why I am no longer a priest. And boys can fend for themselves.'

'And your anonymity?' she asked, impervious to my disapproval.

'That is more complex. But if I remain unknown I am afforded the liberty of being an observer. Such as I was at the beach the other week.'

'Do you often follow her about?' Sister Joseph enquired.

'I catch sight of you sometimes outside the gates as school ends. Under the bauhinia tree, just up the street from the ice cream man.'

'Not very often. Just sometimes. I follow her . . .'

There were so many reasons for my actions. Some I could explain quite easily: some I cannot even interpret to myself.

'I follow her because I like to see her happiness,' I said at last. 'There is a joy in children that we have lost. Both you and I, Sister. Lost forever.'

There were other rationales for my actions of which I did not tell her, dared not even: how my paying for the little girl was in part an absolution, how my anonymity allowed the child to be detached from me, receiving my benediction without the strings of friendship or the obligations of God.

Feeling in my jacket pocket, I removed the envelope Mr Chan had given me and handed it to Sister Joseph. It still had its rubber band around it.

'Open it, Sister.'

She slid the rubber band off it and pulled the wad of notes free.

'It is not very much,' I remarked, 'but I think it is sufficient.'

'It will be more than sufficient,' she replied. Her voice was quiet. 'Will this leave you . . .' she paused to consider her words, '. . . without means?'

'No, no, not at all,' I hastily assured her. 'This was a windfall. You might call it an act of God.'

'You have not been to the races, have you?' she enquired in a tone of mock censure.

'I think you know me better than that, Sister.' I employed her denouncing tone. 'I do not go to the races nor do I indulge in *tien kow*, mah-jong or chess in the park with other aged buffers like myself. You should be ashamed of yourself to think such a thing of an old man. Not to mention, as you will keep on insisting, a Holy Father. As for my regular contribution, that will continue to be paid direct to your bank account from mine as long as I am here.'

'You are a good man, Father,' Sister Joseph said softly and, looking at her, I saw there were tears in her eyes.

'Man yes, Sister, Father no,' I replied.

She stood up, placed my envelope on her desk next to the Virgin Mary and then, to my considerable astonishment, she bent over and kissed me right in the middle of my forehead, as one might a child.

'Man or priest,' she whispered, 'there is much of Our Lord in you.'

I wanted to argue that point strongly but decided against it. Instead, I rose from the chair, discovering that my legs were more firm for the rest.

'One thing before I leave, Sister,' I said.

'You can ask anything of us, Father.'

'What is the girl's name?'

'You know,' Sister Joseph leaned on the edge of her desk, 'I have often wondered how long it would be before you asked me that.'

She was not volunteering the information, but instead looked at me with a half-smile on her lips, her head tilted slightly to one side. I realised that she was not a young woman. It is impossible to judge the age of a nun: she is either very young, very plain or very old. Without looking at a woman's body there is often no way of accurately assessing how long they have lived. In Sister Joseph's case, I studied her eyes and reckoned she was in her early fifties.

'Well?' I demanded as she did not tell me.

'Her name is Julia. Julia Ho.'

'Did you give her this?' I asked.

'Yes. If they do not already possess one, we give all our pupils a European name when they arrive. It makes calling the register so much easier. Besides, most Chinese find themselves a Western name these days. It aids them in business.'

'What was her Chinese name?' I enquired.

'I don't recall. I could look it up in our records.'

She did not wait for me to request this but went behind her desk, opened a drawer and removed a file through the contents of which she thumbed her way, muttering to herself under her breath.

'Here it is,' she announced at last. 'I'm afraid the file is not in alphabetical order. Now,' she put it on the top of her desk, running her finger down a typewritten list, 'Julia Ho.' Here we are. Her Chinese name is Ho Mei-ling.'

From the *hutong* below my window came the characteristic sounds of the honey-cart accompanied by muffled voices. I looked out but only for a moment: if the hunchback was filling one of his barrels I did not want to be overhead as he raised the lid. Gazing down, I could plainly make out the collector of night-soil but I could not ascertain to whom he was speaking for they were standing in a doorway. Their conversation was brief and, at the conclusion of it, the hunchback set off with his cart wheels creaking and the effluent in his barrels slopping around. Just as he reached the end of the alley, I heard a muffled crash. It sounded as if one of his containers of filth had broken open and I made a mental note to assiduously avoid the rear *hutong* for the next few days.

I finished dressing in my cassock for Father Callaghan had declared the night before we should hold Mass very early in the morning as he wanted to take me out of the town and across the river.

'You'll find it quite beautiful,' he had told me. 'We'll go over in a sampan then walk ourselves up the top of Dragon Hill. Where the pagoda is. From there, you'll have a fine panorama of the town.'

'Had we not better take care?' I asked. 'Because of the revolutionaries?'

He had smiled and said, 'I think we should be quite safe up there, out of the town: no radical elements'll bother us in the mountains.' He had rubbed his hands together with glee at the prospect of a day in the country and went on, 'That done, we'll head west for a half hour or so, down through the pine woods. The scent of the bark is unforgettable. There's a flood plain on the far side, opposite *Bak Hok Shan*. All paddy-fields.' He had laughed and continued, 'Has it ever occurred to you, Father Stephen, that China must have been waiting for the likes of us?'

'No,' I had replied. 'Why do you say that?'

'Because it bears our name. Paddy-fields. The fields of Patrick.'
He had laughed. 'Maybe of our blessed saint, even.'

'I think,' I remarked, 'the etymology might prove you wrong.'

'To be sure, that's not the root of the name. What it is, mind
you, I've never discovered.' He had drunk the last few dregs of his
gin and went on, 'You know, Father Stephen, you're sometimes a
very serious fellow.'

'I am?' I answered.

'Yes, you are. And I like that in a young man but you must also
learn to be a little – how shall I put it? – happier. Life is not a sad
train of events. It is a joyous span of years upset only by transient
sorrows. You must be a less phlegmatic and more accepting of the
bounties of Our Lord. He didn't make us in His image to cry and
frown but to laugh and smile.'

He had put his hand on my shoulder then and patted it.

'You're a good man, Father Stephen,' he stated. 'A good man.
I'm glad they sent you to me.'

The first light of dawn was seeping into a sky devoid of
even the merest vestige of cloud. Once more it was going to
be a sweltering day. There was no breeze nor even any early
bird song.

Leaving my room, I descended the staircase and made my
way towards the chapel, tapping my finger on the barometer.
The needle jarred but stayed firmly in the area marked *Fair* in
Gothic script. Even at this hour, the thermometer registered 78°
and the slider in the mercury indicated it had not dropped below
74° during the night.

The mission was very quiet. Not a sound came from the girls'
quarters and I was suddenly afraid I was late, that my clock had
faltered in the night. It had not been keeping good time ever since I
arrived, presumably because the mechanism was not manufactured
to stand up to the extremes of the Oriental climate.

The door to the chapel was open. I entered it and, a few steps
over the lintel, bent my knee to the altar.

Apart from myself, the chapel was quite empty. The candles
on the altar had been lit but there seemed to be no other
preparation made for the celebration of Mass although, on the
side table, I could see the wine and water jugs in place and

the rice bowl in which Father Callaghan carried the wafers was beside them.

I walked down to the altar and, mounting the steps, looked both left and right but there was no one present. Clearly I was not late for Mass but early: my clock, far from being slow must somehow have speeded up although I could not imagine how the spring might have achieved such a trick.

A soft sound drew my attention. It was like a whisper but it formed no words. I looked up at the rafters in case the little devil-lizard had appeared again. As I searched for it a vague, all but indiscernible shadow moved over the beams. I turned and, not ten paces behind me, was a young Chinese man. He was barefoot and wore a black *fu* with a red sash at his waist, another around his brow. His chest was bare and I could see, even in the slight morning light, drops of sweat standing out on his skin like glass beads. In his hands he held a short curved sword.

'What do you want?' I demanded. It did not occur to me he would not understand, any conversation utterly pointless.

He made no reply but remained quite still as if, by my facing round, I had frozen him. It was like a bizarre child's game of statues: if I was to look away, I thought, he would move once more towards me. Yet this was no game. I did not turn my back and he started towards me once more, the sword coming up level to his shoulder. He began to move it sideways in readiness for striking.

'*Ha!*' he suddenly cried and rushed me.

I leapt aside and the sword smashed onto the altar, slicing through the altar cloth into the wood. His first blow made, he stopped and watched me like a predator. I edged my way round the altar to position it between us.

On the floorboards behind the altar lay Father Callaghan. He was on his back, his arms crossed over his breast with his fingers stroking aimlessly at his neck. His throat was cut, his whispering breath bubbling through a pink foam.

'*Ha!*' the Chinese exclaimed again, his sword up and ready.

I waited until he was prepared to run at me, swipe at me with his blade once more. He gathered himself. I could see his muscles grow tight and bunch. Just as he sprang, with the agility and fluid motion of a wild cat, I snatched the cross from the altar and blocked his swing with it. The sword smashed into the crucifix, the force of the impact jerking my arm. The Chinese, not expecting to meet resistance, momentarily lost his balance. His sword, glancing off the cross, was down.

With all the strength I could muster, I swung the cross at his head. One of the bars caught him just behind the ear and he fell to the ground, the sword clattering across the floor and his arms scrabbling. I struck him again on the head, the silver of the figure of Christ flashing in the early light. His skull cracked. It was such a loud sound it might have been the gecko after all, clicking its outlandish noise overhead.

The Chinese tumbled forwards, his legs twitching and hands slapping the floor. Moving quickly to his sword, I picked it up, raised it over my head and brought it down on the back of his neck. I am not sure how many times I struck him: I just continued to hit him, as if I was chopping wood, until his hands ceased their tattoo on the floorboards and my rage was spent. My only thought was to kill him, a cool anger taking over my soul. I was not frenzied but quite composed, deliberate: there was no other motive in my mind but to end this life spread-eagled before me.

Sure the Chinese was dead, I dropped to Father Callaghan's side. Air was no longer frothing at his neck. I took hold of his hand and fancied I felt it tighten on my own.

'*Illumina oculos meos, ne unquam obdormiam in morte, ne quando dicat inimicus meus. Prævalui adversus eum,*' I prayed, but then I stopped.

It was a senseless exercise. There was no god present, no holiness in the chapel. The cross lay on the floor nearby, the left arm cracked, the figure of the tortured Christ smeared with the blood of the dead Chinese. The sword lay next to the cross, soiled by both Father Callaghan's and his enemy's flesh.

There was another sound, of soft footfalls coming down the aisle. I shifted myself as silently as I could and reached for the sword. The handle was carved of bone and damp from its owner's sweat. I grasped it in both hands as I had seen the Chinese do and, with as much power as I could muster, leapt from the side of the altar, the sword raised above my head. What I lacked in sword-fighting skills I hoped to make up with the element of fierce surprise.

In the centre of the aisle was Ah Fong. He stood with his hands hanging at his sides, his face an unearthly white in the grey swelling light of the morning.

'No hit, master! No hit! I Ah Fong,' he said in a wavering voice.

I was not sure whether to trust him so did not relinquish my grip on the sword.

'Where Farfer *Ka Lai Hon*?'

'Father Callaghan is dead.'

I pointed behind the altar. Ah Fong walked hesitantly towards me and peered round the edge of the table. He moaned, just the once.

'He good man,' he said quietly: then he saw the dead Chinese. 'He kill *I Ho Ch'üan*.'

'No. I killed him,' I said, putting the sword down on the floor: it did not seem right to rest it on the altar. Besides, it would mark the altar cloth. 'We must take his body out before the girls come in, and hide the murderer.' I thought for a moment. 'We shall throw the I *Ho Ch'üan* in the river tonight. For the dragons,' I added.

'Oh, Farfer *See Faat Han*,' Ah Fong said: it was the first time he had used my nickname, 'girl gone. All gone.'

'On, no,' I said. A terrible emptiness rushed into my heart. 'Not gone too.'

'Yes, master. All gone. Gone.'

'All dead?' I asked. I could not believe every single one of them had been slaughtered.

'No dead, master. Gone away. Sister gone, too. She one away.'

'Run away?'

For a moment, I found it hard to comprehend what he was saying: then a picture flashed across my mind. It was of Sister Margaret in the temple, waving her incense sticks.

'What about the babies?' I asked. 'What about the infants?'

I did not wait for an answer but snatched at the altar cloth, tugging it free, the candles falling to the ground and extinguishing themselves, the candlesticks separating from them and bouncing down the steps. I covered Father Callaghan with the cloth then, beckoning to Ah Fong, picked up the sword and ran through the courtyard to the nursery. The heavy door was shut. I pushed on it and it opened. All the cribs were empty, Ah Mee's body slouched against the wall at the end of the room: she, too, had had her throat cut. I went to the baby posting box. It was broken into several pieces and there was a hole in the wall to the *hutong*.

'God damn this!' I swore.

It was evident the sound I had heard from my room was not a honey-cart barrel overturning but must have been the baby posting box being wrenched free to allow the assassin entry.

'More man come,' Ah Fong said, his voice emotionless with terror. 'One come now. Do kill. When he kill, he call his f'ends. If he no hear him, he come too by an' by.'

'Ah Fong,' I ordered. 'Get your possessions. Just enough for you to carry. Put them in a bag and we shall go.'

'Go where, master?'

I thought for a moment, for both of us.

'Hong Kong,' I decided. 'We go Hong Kong side.'

He left the nursery and I rushed to my room, quickly thrusting off my cassock and struggling into my Chinese clothing. Into my leather bag I crammed a few essentials – a pocket knife, some candles, my clock, a hip flask containing brandy for emergencies, articles of clothing, some other odds and sods and my diary. For some reason, I added a photograph of myself taken in Dublin upon my ordination: had I been in my right mind, I should have left it.

My hurried packing done, I returned quickly to the chapel. The blood had soaked through the altar cloth from Father Callaghan's wounds. Quickly, I mixed the wine and water in the chalice, muttered what I hoped would pass as a blessing and a consecration then put a drop upon his lips. The remainder I drank in one gulp to prevent it falling into the hands of the *I Ho Ch'üan*. From Father Callaghan's pocket I took the ring of mission keys and, from around his neck, removed his bloodstained stole and, hastily wrapping the chalice and paten in it, placed them in my bag along with the candlesticks, two jugs and the cross, which I hurriedly wiped clean on a corner of the altar cloth.

In Father Callaghan's room, I unlocked the padlock on his sea chest and flung open the lid, removing all the money it contained. This was quite a considerable sum in letters of credit, bank and promissory notes, some silver sycee and coins, the bulk of the latter in trade and Mexican dollars. I placed it all in a canvas satchel hanging in the cupboard. As I passed his bookshelf, I saw sitting upon it a small opium-smoker's lamp and a few dozen small jade carvings, including a translucent white one in the shape of a tortoise's shell. In an impulse and with panic rising in me, I took these, too.

When I returned to the ground floor, Ah Fong was standing by the chapel door, a bamboo basket in his hand.

'We go Master Mowisbee house?' he suggested.

I gave this proposal a quick consideration before abandoning it. If the mission had been attacked it was a certainty Morrisby, the Blairs, Tremletts and Mr Doble would have similarly been dealt with: they were either dead or on their way down-river. I did not intend to discover which.

'No,' I repeated, 'We go Hong Kong side.'

'Hong Kong long way, master.'

'Yes,' I acknowledged, 'it is.'

Yet my mind was set: there was no other option, as I saw it, than to make for the safety of the colony, its garrison and its British government.

'How we go, master?'

'By the river.'

'*Lucky Moon* no here,' Ah Fong said. 'Go Nanning side.'

I had not for one moment given the steam pinnace a thought. Even if she had been in Wuchow she would have been useless: the *I Ho Ch'üan* would be watching her.

'We steal a sampan,' I declared. 'Let us go.'

Cautiously, Ah Fong opened the mission gate. The *hutong* was empty. We slipped out, walked quickly down to the street at the end and set off through the town.

There were few people abroad. In the Street of The Cranes, a man was pushing a handcart laden with charcoal and coal dust slabs past a row of closed eating stalls. From behind the shutters of one of them emanated the grunt of stentorian snoring. A dog sauntered in the middle of the thoroughfare, sniffing at wet patches on the cobbles. The further we went from the mission, the busier the streets became. The town's-folk were readying themselves for the day, with shopkeepers starting to open their premises, vegetable sellers setting up their stalls and arranging produce on the pavements.

As we reached the main square, Ah Fong said quietly, out of the corner of his mouth, 'Where we go, master?'

'Go Si Kiang side,' I replied, not turning my head to look at him. 'Take sampan near jetty.'

It occurred to me on the spur of the moment that if there was a trading vessel in mid-stream, we might row out to her and beg asylum.

Halfway across the main square, at roughly the point where my trousers had started to drop, there came a shout.

'*T'ien chu kiao!*'

The voice almost sang out the words. They sounded like a drawn out chant, a mocking melody, a deadly diapason.

'Do not stop,' I muttered. 'Do not look round, Ah Fong. Do not run. Walk all same.'

'*T'ien chu kiao!*' the sing-song voice reiterated. '*T'ien chu kiao!*'

I glanced over my shoulder. There were three young Chinese men fast approaching us. Each had a red scarf around his head: one carried a cudgel and the other two short swords of the sort that had killed Father Callaghan.

'You go, master!' Ah Fong said. 'Go quick. No stop. I talk man.'

'No!' I replied insistently, *sotto voce*. 'Keep going.'

'Go, Master. Go. No af'aid Ah Fong.'

He stopped and faced around. I heard him say something in Cantonese which was greeted by a torrent of obvious abuse.

Yet I did not stop. I did not put down my bags and join him. I continued to walk, my mind numb. Perhaps together we could have seen off the three thugs but I did not consider it. I made my way towards the Street of Righteous Enlightenment.

The shouting continued behind me. Other people had now joined in. I could not hear Ah Fong in the clamour: then, over the turmoil there came a shrill voice, high-pitched and querulous.

'*G'oria in ex'lsis Deo et in terra pax homi'bus*,' it shouted. There was a brief pause before it continued, '*Yeh so Gei duk*, I come you bankwet table in fear an' t'embling, for I a sinner, an' no much good . . .'

A huge shout rose from the crowd. A scream echoed round the market place and was then cut off.

The sampan I decided upon was about fifteen feet long, tethered to a stake in the mud not far from the point at which I had embarked from the *Lucky Moon*. There were a few fisherman attending to similar craft along the bank, sorting nets or scrubbing down hulls, but otherwise it was devoid of people. I was thankful most fishing was done in the evening and early night, by the light of lamps.

Without any hesitation, I walked straight towards the vessel, placed my bags in the well with a jumble of fishing equipment and cast off, punting the sampan clear of the bank with one of the long oars. None of the other fishermen paid me the least attention and, within minutes, I was a hundred yards out into the river and a quarter of a mile downstream, riding on a swift current.

My idea that I might seek refuge on a foreign trading vessel was thwarted: there was not a single ship anchored in the river. I assumed they had perhaps already set sail with those Europeans who had received a warning in the night, or avoided assassination by chance.

Once past Dragon Island, I set about tidying my craft, preparing it for the journey ahead. The jumble in the sampan consisted of three nets, a wooden bucket, some lengths of rope, a lantern the reservoir of which was at least half-filled with oil and a grappling hook. Two long oars lay against the gunwale. I retained the smallest of the nets for my own use and threw the others over the side along with some dead and mutilated fish swishing about in an inch or two of bilge-water. This done, I opened a hatch under the small rear deck upon which I should have to stand to row. Behind it I discovered, to my blessing, a smaller bucket of rice bowls and chopsticks, several spoons and a cloth bag containing at least two catties of rice and some dried, salt fish. Wedged under the deck planking was a tinder box, a bundle of joss sticks and, at the rear of the compartment, a pointed rattan hat. As the little hold was dry, I shoved my bags into it and slid the hatch shut.

Tying a length of rope around the larger bucket, I lowered it over the side and was amazed at the strength of the current and the speed at which my vessel was travelling. I watched the shore and guessed that I must be going at least six knots if not faster. Hauling the bucket in, I set it in the well and splashed my face with the cold water.

With my chores done, I decided not to try and row but let the current take me. I lay back against the side of the sampan and found myself convulsed by bone-wracking shivering. My first thoughts were that I had contracted a malarial fever but it was a reaction of shock come upon me now that I was free.

With no preparations for my journey left to do, I found my mind fixing itself upon the events of the day: it was not yet eight o'clock and I had seen murder, and done murder.

This was no proxy killing of an ignorant peasant. I had killed a man with my own hands, giving no thought to the sanctity of life, the creed by which I was supposed to abide. Leaning forward, I saw dark smudges on my shoes. They were not wet, not water spilled from the bucket, but stiff blots.

Tearing them off, I rammed them into the bucket and scrubbed the leather with my hands. A faint pinkness seeped gradually into the water. When, at last, I had removed the revolutionary's blood from my footwear, I tipped the bucket over the side.

Yet what, I thought as the water ran out, if that was not *I Ho Ch'üan* heathen blood, but that of Father Callaghan? It was then I saw him as if he was before me in the sampan, lying on his back with his hands to his throat: the hissing of the water pouring away was his last breath fighting to fill his lungs, whilst the banging of the bucket on the side of the vessel as it rocked over some wavelets was the hammering of swords and cudgels upon Ah Fong's skull.

I leaned back against the fishing net and was shaken by a fresh bout of shivering. The sun was up and hot yet my flesh was as cold as death. My hands could not keep still, my teeth chattered and my legs twitched. I sensed the muscles on my face contorting and tried vainly to control them.

An exhausted sleep must have come upon me for the next I remember was waking up with the sun blazing on to my face and my lips cracked. The sampan was drifting at an increased speed in a current quite close to the south bank. I sat up and surveyed the country through which I was travelling. The hills were close to the river, not a hundred yards from the water, and covered in thick sub-tropical forest. The bank was high and I could not see what lay immediately behind it but, every once in a while, I spied a rooftop.

Every muscle in my body aching, I removed my *sam* and undervest and, refilling the bucket, soaked myself. This done, I put the coolie hat on my head: it was a wise move for not only did it afford me some shade from the merciless sun but it also gave me a disguise.

As there was no need to steer my craft, I had nothing to do and this enforced idleness gave my mind the opportunity once more to dwell upon my predicament, my actions and my future.

'I should have buried him,' I said aloud. 'I should have placed his body where they could not get it, could not mutilate it, could not . . .'

I saw Father Callaghan's corpse hanging from a stake on the dais in the main square, his blood dripping to the ground with small, jet-eyed birds drinking from the puddle. Next to him was Ah Fong, but he was headless and would therefore never get to heaven.

'And the girls,' I went on, talking to myself just as Father Callaghan had recommended. 'Where have the girls gone?'

They were dead. I knew it. If not in the flesh, then in every other respect. Just as Mei-ling had swallowed the thin leaves of gold so had they the false gold of religion. They would soon be syphilitic whores waiting to die in flowerboats, slaves or concubines. Not one would reach the safety of European employ on the coast.

I had sold them out, just as they had sold themselves to Christ.

The sun scorched my legs, even through the material of my

fu, and the rattan of my hat became so hot as to make it almost painful to touch.

'This is my penance,' I declared to myself. 'The first penance. No Hail Marys, no mumbo-jumbo. Just heat and discomfort.'

Yet what had I to repent, I asked myself. I had committed no sin. I had not killed Father Callaghan nor had I forced Ah Fong to cover my retreat. I had, it was true, done for the Chinese assassin but, I reasoned, he was a heathen and the history of Roman Catholicism was filled with righteous killings. Knights in the Holy Crusades would not have thought twice about what I had done that early morning. All that had happened was that I was the tool of circumstance. If anyone were to blame, I considered, it was God who had made the world what it was. If he really loved his creations, I said to myself, he would have prevented it.

Late in the afternoon, I began to see more craft on the river. I had from time to time passed by cargo junks or low hulled barges laden with timber or bamboo, but, as the sun lowered, more sampans began to appear. To aid in my camouflage, I pretended to fish, casting the net over the side and trawling with it. Much to my amazement, I actually caught a number of small fish, which I brought in and ate raw with some of the rice.

At the bow of the sampan was the customary little shrine such as I had seen on the old lady's boat as she ferried myself and Father Callaghan across to the Residency party. I moved forward and studied it. A simple affair, the shrine consisted of a skilfully printed woodblock of a goddess which had been touched up with gold leaf and red paint. Before her, nailed to the deck, was a metal cup filled with sand and the red stalks of half a dozen burnt-out joss sticks. A child's rice bowl contained a few grains of rice and a fragment of salt fish.

Going to the hatch, I removed two joss sticks from the bundle and, hunching myself forward against the warm evening breezes, lit them with the tinder box. When they were glowing brightly, I stuck them in the cup where they quickly burned. It was not a religious act. I was already past caring about gods. It was more a totemic reflex such as any man might make in order to try and balance fate in his favour: it was no more than crossing one's fingers or avoiding walking under a ladder. Yet, as I sat back with the late sun casting my shadow forwards over the little shrine, I thought how alike I was to Sister Margaret, hedging my bets on the race towards eternity.

On that voyage down the river, I came to serve a new lord: not some ethereal master riding in a chariot of clouds or fire, dispensing love and demanding homage but a dispassionate leader, one for whom love and hate were not demands but facts. The light of Christ was dimmed by the brilliance of reason. I could not justify my actions or the murder of Father Callaghan, the butchery of Ah Fong – and poor little Ah Mee – and the fleeing of the girls within the context of theology, but I could within the tenets of logic.

As night fell, I decided not to moor up but let the sampan drift on its way. Sleep was out of the question, as I had to watch out for other craft engaged in fishing and, twice, I had to take to the oars and steer my way through little fleets of sampans. Just before ten o'clock that night, the stark white quarter-moon disappeared behind dense banks of cloud and, at midnight, it began to rain.

I have always been one to escape and hide.

When I was a child, wracked by some petty guilt I could not understand, when my father had caught me out lying in the trivial ways children have or culpable of some other misdemeanour, I escaped from his wrath and leather belt and hid.

I would to go to the rick behind the byre and tunnel into it, digging with my hands through the close-packed layers of stalks and hay and, back-filling the passage I had made behind me, would disappear and fancy myself invisible, lost to the world. It was dark in there and musty. The further in I went, the warmer and more secure the world became. It was good to be without the searching light of day, the prying eyes of sun and truth. Sometimes I almost suffocated myself in those airless tunnels which I excavated and, when I dreamed my childish dreams of death, I was always in a small dark place where the walls prickled me gently and the air smelled of summer fields, dry dust and mice.

My whole life has been a process of escape and concealment:

I believe now I joined the priesthood in order to get away and hide.

Of course, I was not alone. There were others bent on escaping with me. The priests who instructed me in the ways of God, who taught me my duties, schooled me in fidelity or directed me towards righteousness, and my fellow initiates were all, like me, resolute on secreting themselves away.

No one entertains a cause without a deep and secret selfishness. There is no such thing as a true zealot: there is only a man determined to serve himself.

Looking back on my comrades-in-God, I wonder now what it was they were fleeing. For some, it was crushing poverty, rain-swept fields, sore backs after sixteen hours of labour, the cloying mud sticking to their boots. The church was their refuge just as it had been for centuries: peasants have always either sought temporal relief through devotion and prayer or physical relief by surrendering themselves to God, living the rest of their days in comparative luxury by courtesy of the unquestioningly pious and blindly penitent. Others were escaping cruel masters or duplicitous lovers, running from a fear of the flesh which they sublimated by telling themselves that tyrannical men, beautiful women or pretty young boys were instruments of the devil. Some took holy orders because it gave them a purpose in their otherwise purposeless lives and yet still others because the purpose suborned another of which they were ashamed or afraid.

Yet there were a few who trod the path of God because they were good men, a rare commodity. I do not think, in retrospect, I ever knew a truly good man before I came to China and shook hands with Father Callaghan or walked the streets and *hutongs* of Wuchow in the company of Ah Fong.

Maybe it was reality I wished to avoid, from which I was desperate to save myself and from which I am still flinching. My mining in the hayrick was no different from taking a pipe with Mr Wu, sitting on a bench by the banyan tree before the temple, or jumping into a sampan and casting it off to drift at the mercy of the river and its dragons.

My life has been one long journey of drifting uncontrolled but free.

There again, perhaps I always hid because I had no faith and this scared me. Just as I concealed myself from my father that he might not find me out so did I hide from God because I could not truly believe in him.

Nor was it only my God in which I had no faith but also in myself.

I drifted into holy orders, arrogantly believing I was called by God to do his bidding but I was wrong: it was a fallacy, a self-delusion to give justification for my running and ducking, weaving and fleeing. For my hiding. God either did not want me or, finding out the sham I was, abandoned me: or it might have been in the scheme of things to give me no faith, to set me up as a whipping-boy to whom others could point and say that is what happens to a man of little faith. Perhaps it was an object lesson not in the love of God or the cruelty of Man but all an exercise to teach me to keep to my place. I should have remained a simple peasant in Ireland with his cow and two pigs: instead, as I have chosen or it was chosen for me by circumstance, I have lived my life as a peasant in China. What could have been a shack on the edge of a bog in Kerry is in reality a tenement on the corner of Nanking Street with Woosung Street.

Had I possessed a true faith, been more assured of my veracity, more convinced of what I suppose I did believe, events would have shaped me otherwise and my life would have been an altogether different series of trials. Or I should, long ago, have been martyred in the town square alongside Ah Fong, bludgeoned to death with clubs or hacked to pieces with swords, forgotten by everyone save those who took part in the butchery, a mere instant, no bigger than the minuscule flash of a dying star, of a flicker of heat lightning over the mountain, of bestial history lost in the brutalities of time.

This morning, I briefly revisited Mr Chan's emporium. It was a fleeting visit for what I wanted, for the first time, was to purchase rather than to sell. The cruise ship he was anticipating when I sold him the silver had arrived and the street was so crowded with garishly dressed tourists there was not a tout in sight save for those who sell colour transparency photographs in plastic wallets and offer, to the likely customer, morally dubious examples of other photographic achievement. I was quite unaccosted as I walked the length of Hankow Road except by one of the photograph vendors and a lone tourist wearing a loose shirt decorated with pink flamingos against a backdrop of verdant forests and trousers which, had they not been cream, would have best been described as Oxford bags. He was clutching a swatch of postcards and wished to know directions to the post office. I feigned ignorance, claiming to be a visitor myself which puzzled him for, just a moment earlier, he had heard me address the photoseller in fluent Cantonese.

Mr Chan was busy. Two less exotically attired tourists were mulling over the purchase of some ivory carvings of cavorting horses whilst another couple were considering jade and gold bangles. Mrs Chan, who seldom appears in the shop save to bring her spouse a midday bowl of rice and vegetables, hovered around acting as a sort of store detective.

My greeting today was nothing more than a raised hand and a smile followed by a nod from Mr Chan to imply he would be with me in a moment, but I did not require serving. I knew exactly what I wanted and went straight to one of the heavy cupboards. At a signal from her husband, Mrs Chan unlocked the door. After holding back a number of other items precariously balancing on the front of the bottom shelf, I removed a carved rosewood box with an ornate brass clasp held shut by a long sprung pin.

This was the item I required. When I opened it, I found it lined with deep red brocade padded with down. Turning it upside down, I saw the price was marked at $100 which was, of course, the tourist price. I could buy it for half that and still not dent Mr Chan's acceptable profit margin.

'Good,' I said in Cantonese to Mrs Chan, 'I will buy this one.' The bangle buyers glanced up in surprise to hear one of their supposed number talking the lingo.

She was about to state the price when Mr Chan said in Cantonese over the top of his customers, 'No charge. Just take it. It is not too expensive. Forty dollars.'

'You must let me pay,' I insisted.

'No. It's not an antique. It was made just last year by a factory in Ma Tau Kok. They make over four thousand a week. Unit price is eight dollars. Take it.'

I began to remonstrate but he cut me short, adding, 'Don't upset our friendship. This is just a small gift from one to another.'

'But it is not for myself,' I replied.

'Never mind, take it anyway. I will find a gift for you when you next visit. See you soon?'

'Soon,' I promised, as I had on my last visit, but I lied. I knew this was my final visit to his shop.

Casting a quick look at the laden cabinets and the glass counters with their rows of rings and strings of pearls, gold chains and pendants, I did not feel at all sad. I am done with sorrow now.

At four o'clock, the boy arrived at my flat and, entering, seated himself at my table, producing his books and arranging them on the table in readiness for work.

'How did your fund-raising go?' I enquired before he opened them.

He grinned in the impish way children have when they are pleased with themselves and replied, 'Eleven thousand two hundred and eight dollars, sir.'

'That's quite a sum. Congratulations,' I said and I truly meant it.

'And they jumped in the harbour,' he went on.

'They?'

'Two of the teachers. Mr Reeves and Mr Cordwell. From the side of the Star Ferry pier. Then they swam across to the Kowloon Pier.'

'The harbour is not exactly a healthy place for a dip,' I commented.

'Mr Reeves is a sport,' he declared and I could tell he was unquestioningly proud of his schoolmaster in the way boys of his age are of someone whom they admire.

He is a good boy: I have decided upon this fact. And he will make an excellent *gweilo*: not one of those who lives in an enclave of European housing on the Peak or the exclusive southern shores of Hong Kong island but in the city, in with the people as I have done.

'Did you like the music, sir?' he asked.

'The music?'

'In the *Black Pussy*. The group's performance.'

'Well,' I began, 'I'm afraid I did not stay. It is not, you understand, exactly my taste in music. The place was very crowded and I had a headache. The smoke got to me. I'm a non-smoker.' I thought to add 'of tobacco' but resisted.

He looked a little crestfallen and I realised he wanted my praise, my approval. I was touched.

'However,' I went on, 'I'm told by Sam you were, in your manner of music, exceedingly good. He was most impressed. How did you father react?'

The boy looked surprised.

'How did you know I told him?'

'I believed you would,' I replied. 'You are a trustworthy and truthful boy for whom deceit is not an acquired art. At least, not yet. You forget I was a priest. A cleric knows much more about the nature of humans than anyone else.'

He grinned a little sheepishly.

'He didn't mind. He said it was good I was doing something on my own initiative and that the racket I made at home practising was translating itself into a worthwhile objective.'

'He did not complain about the venue?'

'No. He just told me . . .' He coloured up slightly.

'To keep your pecker in your pocket?' I suggested.

The boy laughed. It was the magic sound of youth.

'Those were his exact words!' he exclaimed.

'Another of the priest's tricks,' I explained. 'Once learnt they do not die out in a lifetime.'

I sat down at the table opposite him, resting my arms along the edge. I felt tired and suddenly very much older in the presence of this young man but, whereas in the past I had resented or envied him his youthfulness I now felt sorry for him: he has so many years ahead of him to be filled with pain, failure, disappointment and misery.

Some minutes must have passed, one of those lost timespans

which have come to me of late, for I was suddenly jerked out of my reverie by the boy's voice.

'May we start, sir?'

'Yes,' I said quickly, 'yes, of course. I'm sorry. My mind was elsewhere.'

'I quite understand, sir,' he said. 'No problem.'

I smiled inwardly at his expression: he was becoming a *gweilo* just as I had done, unconsciously taking in the little nuances of Chinese life that would set him apart from his own kind half a century hence.

'Before we begin,' I said, leaving the table, 'I should like to show you something.'

Going into my bedroom, I took up the rosewood box from my bed and, sitting down once more, handed it to the boy. He was at a loss as to what to say.

'Open it,' I instructed him.

He pulled the brass pin free and lifted the lid. I could smell the vague scent of the wood as it wafted across the table.

'What is it?' he asked, looking inside the box.

'Take it out. Carefully. It is, I should think, fragile.'

He put both his hands in the box and slowly removed the wooden jug I had taken from the bank. Gently, he put it on his Cantonese textbook.

'What is it?' he asked again.

'A wooden jug.' I said. 'Just a wooden jug.'

He turned it round slowly, the veining in the wood moving like hard brown clouds.

'It is of little monetary value, if any,' I continued, 'but it has a history I think you might appreciate.'

I did not elaborate. I fell silent once more and, although my eyes remained open and fixed on the vessel, my thoughts went blank again.

'Will you tell me its story?' I heard the boy say.

He sounded far away and I did not want to shout back to him. Instead, I watched him as if from a great distance while he twisted the jug in his hands.

'I have wanted to ask you about . . .' he began then paused.

He was looking into my face and I had the sense this was

what it must be like for a corpse to stare upwards at a mourner gazing down into the coffin.

'Would you tell me about it, sir?'

I returned from my distant standpoint.

'No,' I replied, 'I think not.'

I opened the drawer in my table and removed the manila envelope containing my black diary. Already, in my mind, it was halfway out of my life.

'This will tell you all you need to know,' I said.

The boy accepted the envelope with both hands as if receiving a libation.

'It has my name on it,' he remarked with some surprise.

'Yes,' I replied obviously. 'It has.'

'May I open it?'

I nodded. He unwound the string and, tipping the envelope up, slid the diary out.

'You asked me – or you wanted to ask me – some questions. This will give you all the answers you sought.'

'May I borrow it, sir?' he enquired.

'It is for you to keep,' I answered. 'With the jug. You will learn about that from the book. It is – it *was* – my diary. Don't open it now. Wait until you get home, to a quiet place.'

'Thank you, sir,' he said, 'thank you very much. I am ...' He glanced around the room as if looking to see if there were any witnesses. 'May I ask you why you are giving this to me?'

'You will appreciate it. You have done what I did when I was a few years older than you. You are, in many ways, so like me.'

'What?' he exclaimed then, finding his manners, added, 'I don't quite understand.'

Indeed, he did not. He had never had to consider such things, the relationship between the old and the young, the mists of history and the bright, sharp, truthful light of the harsh but wondrous present. He was bemused, unable to comprehend what I was saying. In his own mind he could see no links between himself and an old ex-priest with a failing mind.

'You have committed yourself. To China,' I said quietly.

There was a long silence between us. He looked at the book which he had not yet opened and at the jug whilst I just sat looking at him and seeing, passing before my mind's eye, faces I had not gazed upon for many years.

At last, I broke the silence.

'I'm afraid,' I informed him, 'I am unable to teach you any more. I'm sorry, but I think I have had enough. Of course, this is nothing personal,' I added to allay any insult he might have felt. 'It is just that I find it all a bit beyond me now.'

I got slowly to my feet, left the table and looked out of the window, down into Nanking Street, but it was not a busy Kowloon street any longer but the *hutong* at the rear of the mission: and I could not hear the taxi horns and a blaring radio but the dull beat of a gong and the quiet sobbing of a woman.

When I turned, the boy was still seated at the table, his hands beside the jug and my diary, which I no longer thought of as mine. He was almost crying. His shoulders heaved a little but he made no sound so I could not have mistaken him for the woman. I knew her. She had just decided against posting her baby in case I tore out its eyes and sold them.

It seemed so natural to put my hand upon the boy's shoulder. If I had made the sign of the cross over him, I should not have been surprised. Yet I did not. I let him continue to sit before me in silence. It is better to exorcise pain than let it fester.

'You had best go,' I said after a while which I could not calibrate into seconds or minutes.

I relinquished my hold on his shoulder and he rose to his feet, gingerly placing the jug back in its box and putting his textbooks away in his case. Last of all, he put my diary on top of them. I watched it go as if it was a part of myself disappearing. With the removal of the book I was shedding so much I wanted to be freed from, so much that haunted me.

'If you need me, sir . . .' the boy began to say, tucking the box under his arm and lifting his case off the table, but I held my hand up.

'I need nothing now,' I replied.

Showing him to the door, I once more put my hand upon his shoulder. 'Perhaps we'll meet in *The Black Pussy*,' I assured him. 'Or on the Star Ferry. You know, there used to be a saying that if one travelled daily for the whole of one's life upon the ferry one would eventually meet everyone one had ever known. A mere adage, of course. I am sure the Star Ferry does not carry ghosts.'

The boy stopped just outside my door and turning, remarked, 'I'm sure it does, sir. I'm sure it does.'

Then he was gone. He did not wait for the cumbersome, grinding lift but went round the corner and down the dark stairwell. I heard his footsteps retreating then all that was left was the clicking of typewriter keys in Mr Pao's workshop or in the Pei woman's secretarial college.

It has been a hard climb. The path I took went initially along the edge of the cutting in which the railway line to Canton runs before vanishing into the tunnel under the Kowloon hills. Just by the masonry arch of the tunnel entrance, it veered eastwards, passed through a belt of haphazard boulders and dry scrub noisy with crickets, then began to rise sharply, zig-zagging up the contours of the hillside below the jagged outcrop of Lion Rock. Several times, I had to pause to get my breath or sit down on the hard ground to ease the pain running up my legs.

The grass on the steeper slopes is over a foot high and desiccated by cool winter winds and the lack of rain. It has not been burned for years and carries no signs of any former conflagration although, half a mile or so to the west, the hillside is blackened by the recent fires which I have spied from my tenement roof.

In places, I had to grasp the roots of low bushes to pull myself over a particularly steep part of the path. This way is not frequently used: indeed, I doubt if more than a dozen people a year avail themselves of it. Twenty years ago, it was probably resorted to by guerrillas fighting the Japanese, and fifty years ago by woodcutters heading over the mountain range to collect kindling in the valleys above Sha Tin, but now it is abandoned by all save small animals and old fools.

Like the Chinese, I have an affinity for mountains: there is even a festival when the main idea is to get up to the summit of the nearest hill and make an offering. I share that attraction and a place such as this I have, over the years, visited when I have felt the need to rise above my place on earth and get a little nearer to the sky. Not to heaven, or to the gods – in the singular or plural – but just to be where cool winds blow and I can be alone to think.

My perch is at the foot of a smooth rock, twenty feet high and as many wide, on a narrow ledge about the depth of an old-fashioned *k'ang*. The rock is warm from the sunlight shining upon me since mid-morning, when I arrived at this spot. At my side is this morning's early edition of the *Wah Kiu Yat Po*, weighted down by a stone, and a picnic of sorts – two bottles of San Mig., a flask of tea, a small cardboard box of Chinese almond biscuits with the outline of a cockerel embossed upon the pastry and three oranges – but I have not touched any of it. I am not hungry or thirsty despite my exertions.

Most of my life, I have had these nine hills as a background to my every move. Wherever I have gone, whatever I have done, they have looked down on me like a row of sentinels. From their shoulders, I can see my entire world. Spread out before me is the peninsula of Kowloon, shimmering in the first really hot day of the year. The streets and alleys, markets and temples which I have frequented are all down there, laid out flat like a relief map. If I had a stick, I feel I could lean forward and tap them as a schoolmaster raps his blackboard with a ruler.

Gazing out to the west, the sun full in my face, I think of how, far beyond the islands and mountains, the estuary of the Pearl River and the mud delta, lie the streets of Wuchow, untrodden by my feet for over sixty years yet visited every day since then in fragmentary moments of reluctant nostalgia, sorrow or guilt.

The harbour glistens, the vessels riding at anchor all broadside on to me for the tide is racing, straightening them into uniform ranks. Beyond, the verdant hills of Hong Kong island rise as a hazy curtain against the distant ocean and a sky bleached by the sun. A few years ago, the airport runway was extended a mile out into Kowloon Bay, the finger of its tarmac strip pointing down Lei Yue Mun passage to the open sea. As I watch, an aircraft passes beneath me, soaring over the rooftops of Kowloon Tong, dropping slowly all the while towards earth. I do not hear its engines until it has completed its turn and is on the ground, a miniature silver bird heading away from me: even then, the sound is only just discernible over the drone of the city.

Leaning against the rock, I feel its heat pulsing into my back. I have removed my shoes, for my heels were blistered during the climb and I have, in the true fashion of the Chinese, rolled up my *fu* to above the knee. My legs are exceptionally pale, the veins running like blue threads just below the surface of the skin. They look so fragile I marvel at how they have succeeded in carrying my blood about my body all these years.

The sun is fierce. I close my eyes but it does not help: all I see then is the pink of my own blood suspended before me, so I open them again and cast my gaze downwards.

I am, I suppose, ready now for whatever the future holds for me, whatever fate thinks of throwing in my way.

There is a wind lifting from the city, running up the face of the mountain, riffling the pages of my newspaper. It is soft and warm but quite blustery. It might be rising from the underworld.

Ever since I clambered into the sampan, cast off the mooring rope and swung the little boat out into the current, I have carried little pieces of hell about with me. At first, they were heavy burdens but, as time passed, they eroded like sandstone, like the karst mountains of China that are forever crumbling, preserved intact only in delicate paintings on silk or intricate ivory carvings.

At my feet, on the very rim of the ledge, I have lined up five quartz pebbles which I collected on my way up the mountain and, as the day has progressed, I have considered them one by one. Each of them is a part of myself, a little bit of China that is in me, a fragment of history that is mine and which I share with the earth. And each one is a regret.

The first and smoothest stone represents Father Callaghan, the man I respected and, in retrospect, loved yet whom I did not wait to bury, over whom I failed to speak the last rites: and I let him down in more than this for I took revenge for his death. He would not, I often think, have wanted his enemy killed. He was a man of forgiveness and forbearance whilst I was a man for retribution and retaliation. His credo was love thine enemy. Mine was an eye for an eye.

Next to him I have placed a slightly smaller but just as shiny a stone: this is Ah Fong, whom I abandoned to the mob, who died because I was a coward, because I was not prepared to waste myself, to be a martyr for a faith I no longer possessed. How often I have heard his brief scream echo in the halls of emptiness far down inside myself.

I have, many a time, considered my cowardice, if that is what it was. I am doubtful myself. If one believes in destiny then I must regard my behaviour not as the craven act of a poltroon but one of a man of human wisdom. His death and my behaviour have taught me much, not just about myself but about the world in which I have chosen to live and in which I have, in my own way, done some little good.

The survivor experiences death over and over: the slain only knows the end but once. Besides, all men are cowards at heart, if that must be the name for those who weigh up the odds and know when they are beaten.

The third stone is Sister Margaret, who backed both horses and vanished. I do not blame her for, in the final analysis, I followed her example, although I have often questioned why she did not give a warning to Father Callaghan, Ah Fong and me. Perhaps the Dragon Mother's charging stallion was pipping Christ's lame nag as they came to the final jump.

The fourth stone is for the girls for whom I never searched. Often, as I've walked the streets of Hong Kong, I have wondered if there might have been one of them nearby, watching me. She would not recognise me just as I cannot put a face to the name of teachers under whom I studied, priests under whom I prayed, masters under whom I have served and to whom I've sold myself. Sitting with the city at my feet, I consider what the chances might be of one of them living down there somewhere, an old lady in a tiny tenement room working a sewing machine.

And the fifth stone: that is God, who left me in the lurch.

Another aircraft is approaching from the west, out of the sun that is starting to go down over the far-off hills of Lan Tau. As it glides nearer, it seems to be coming so close I might lean out and swat it. I pick up my copy of the *Wah Kiu Yat Po*, roll it into a cylinder and struggle to my feet. The sound of the engines throbs faintly, reverberating off the hillside. Should it come within reach,

I shall knock it down as one might a pestering fly. Yet it does not. Like its predecessor, it passes beneath me and slides off towards the spit of runway.

Looking along the mountainside, I squint against the sun to see if there is another materialising out of the heavens, stealing in on its final approach, but I cannot spy one. All I see are the hot dusty spirals of late-afternoon thermals lifting from the foothills upon which are riding shite-hawks, their heads crooked down on the lookout for snakes, insects, small rodents and, perhaps, dragons.